Alexandre Dumas (1802–70) was the author of more than ninety plays and many novels including the famous *Three Musketeers* (1844), *The Count of Monte Cristo* (1844–45), and *The Man in the Iron Mask* (1848–50). As a youth, Dumas was a storyteller with a vivid imagination, and after moving to Paris, he eventually turned his talent to writing plays, producing *Henri III et sa cour* (1829) to a triumphant reception. After taking part in the revolution of July 1830, he married his mistress, but left her when he had spent her entire dowry. After the successful publication of *The Count of Monte Cristo*, he built his own lavish Château de Monte Cristo. Soon bankrupt, he was forced to flee to Belgium to escape his creditors. His travels included a trip to Russia, then one to Italy, where he joined the fight for its independence. He died penniless but optimistic, saying of death, "I shall tell her a story, and she will be kind to me."

Roger Celestin is professor of French and comparative literature at the University of Connecticut. He has published on French authors from the Renaissance to the contemporary period and is coeditor of the journal *Contemporary French & Francophone Studies: SITES.*

Jack Zipes is a professor of German at the University of Minnesota. He is the author of several books on fairy tales, including *Breaking the Magic Spell* and *Don't Bet on the Prince.* He is also the editor of several volumes of fairy tales, including *Beauties, Beasts and Enchantment: Classic French Fairy Tales, The Fairy Tales of Oscar Wilde, The Fairy Tales of Frank Stockton,* and *Arabian Nights.*

THE MAN IN THE IRON MASK

Alexandre Dumas

*Revised and Updated Translation
by Jacqueline Rogers*

*With a New Introduction
by Roger Celestin
and an Afterword
by Jack Zipes*

SIGNET CLASSICS

SIGNET CLASSICS
Published by New American Library, a division of
Penguin Group (USA) Inc., 375 Hudson Street,
New York, New York 10014, USA
Penguin Group (Canada), 90 Eglinton Avenue East, Suite 700, Toronto,
Ontario M4P 2Y3, Canada (a division of Pearson Penguin Canada Inc.)
Penguin Books Ltd., 80 Strand, London WC2R 0RL, England
Penguin Ireland, 25 St. Stephen's Green, Dublin 2,
Ireland (a division of Penguin Books Ltd.)
Penguin Group (Australia), 250 Camberwell Road, Camberwell, Victoria
3124, Australia (a division of Pearson Australia Group Pty. Ltd.)
Penguin Books India Pvt. Ltd., 11 Community Centre, Panchsheel Park,
New Delhi - 110 017, India
Penguin Group (NZ), cnr Airborne and Rosedale Roads, Albany,
Auckland 1310, New Zealand (a division of Pearson New Zealand Ltd.)
Penguin Books (South Africa) (Pty.) Ltd., 24 Sturdee Avenue,
Rosebank, Johannesburg 2196, South Africa

Penguin Books Ltd., Registered Offices:
80 Strand, London WC2R 0RL, England

Published by Signet Classics, an imprint of New American Library,
a division of Penguin Group (USA) Inc.

First Signet Classics Printing, September 1992
First Signet Classics Printing (Celestin Introduction), May 2006
10 9 8 7 6 5 4 3 2

Introduction

The *Man in the Iron Mask* is the final installment of *The Vicomte de Bragelonne,* the third and last volume of the *Musketeers* trilogy begun by Alexandre Dumas in the mid-1840s. *The Three Musketeers*, the first and best-known volume of the trilogy, was published in 1844, and followed by *Twenty Years After* (1845) and *The Vicomte de Bragelonne,* serialized in the newspaper *Le Siècle* between 20 October 1847 and 12 January 1850, and published in book form in 1850.

When *The Man in the Iron Mask* begins, in the year 1661, it has been a long time since the Musketeers Athos, Porthos, Aramis, and D'Artagnan met and sealed their encounter in words that would become a paean to friendship, youth, and adventure: "All for one and one for all!" When the four first met, the year was 1635 and Louis XIII sat on the throne of France, even if the real power lay in the hands of Cardinal Richelieu. At that time, the Musketeers were like so many young men from the provinces who had "come up to Paris" to make a name for themselves. A passage from *The Three Musketeers* depicts them in that dual condition common to the vast majority of those who had come to the capital: impetuous youth and meager finances. Early in their friendship, they have been reduced to seek as many invitations as possible in order to fill their starving bellies:

> Our four friends had fallen into embarrassment. For some time, Athos supported the association with his private means. Porthos succeeded him, and thanks to one of those disappearances to which they were accustomed, he was able to provide for the common wants for a fortnight. When it came to the turn of Aramis, he performed his part with good grace, and procured

a few pistoles by selling some theological books. . . .
At last when everything was about to fail, a final effort
was made, and eight pistoles were got together, with
which Porthos gambled. Unfortunately, he was out of
luck, and lost the whole besides incurring a debt of
honor of twenty-five pistoles. The embarrassment became distress; and the starving friends were to be seen
with their valets trying to pick up a dinner wherever
they could find one. For Aramis had always advised
that one should sow dinners in prosperity so as to reap
them in adversity. Athos was invited to dine four
times, and each time took his three friends and their
valets. Porthos had six opportunities of doing the
same, and Aramis had eight. As for D'Artagnan, who
knew no one in the capital, he found only a breakfast
of chocolate at the house of a priest from his province,
and a dinner from a cornet of Guards. He led his
army to the priest's house, where they devoured two
months' provisions; and they also performed wonders
at the cornet's house. D'Artagnan considered himself
as humiliated at being able to offer but one repast
and a half—for the breakfast only counted half—in
exchange for the feasts procured by Athos, Porthos,
and Aramis.

This passage takes us back to a time of potentiality and
energy, of young men on the brink of adventure and
fame, even if reduced to scrounging around Paris for
their next meal. The struggles with the nefarious cardinal
and his assorted henchmen, the saving of the queen's
reputation—the famous affair of the necklace—the wild
gallops to catch up with enemies or to evade pursuers,
the countless duels and brawls, and the honors bestowed
upon them by the very powerful, all still lie in the future.
By comparison, *The Man in the Iron Mask*, although not
lacking in dire situations and heroic deeds, is pervaded
by a crepuscular even if cathartic quality: Time has
passed, and something is ending. As one commentator
put it, "Dumas' Invincibles suddenly become mortal:
they outlive the day when companionship and courage
were enough to solve simple problems. . . . They have
been undermined from within by age and regret and,
from without, are assailed by irresistible forces" (David

Coward, "Introduction to *The Man in the Iron Mask*": New York, Oxford University Press, 1988, p. xiv).

This last installment of the *Muskeeter* cycle, set during the Musketeers waning years and in the years of youth and consolidation of Louis XIV's reign can be considered Alexandre Dumas' *Time Regained* (the title of the last volume of Marcel Proust's *Remembrance of Things Past*). This comparison between the final book of Proust's modernist masterpiece, considered by many to be the closing epiphany to one of the greatest novels ever written, and the last volume of Dumas' mid-nineteenth-century popular swashbuckling romance is justified. True, one belongs to the more rarefied world of "great literature" while, throughout the Musketeer saga, and indeed in his oeuvre in general, Dumas was mainly concerned with swiftly, effectively, and dramatically steering his plot, the crucial component of "popular literature." Many of his novels, the *Musketeers* cycle and *The Count of Monte Cristo* most famously, were in fact commissioned by the new cheap newspapers that appeared in France in the mid-nineteenth century and that published novels in serialized form. The encounter between this new medium and Dumas' storytelling skills was indeed the source of the several fortunes made and spent by the author of what Dumas, comparing his novelistic work to Balzac's own epic cycle, the "Human Comedy," called his "Drama of France," a series of novels that would do no less than cover the history of France itself. As the great French historian Jules Michelet wrote about Dumas, "He taught the people of France more history than all the historians put together." Nonetheless, keeping readers interested in "what happens next," the proverbial cliff-hanger, was Dumas' crucial objective as a serialized novelist and it dictated his style. *The Man in the Iron Mask is* no exception. So that when we think of Marcel Proust's famously long, complex sentences, and his exquisitely layered descriptions of mood and character, comparing his *Time Regained* and *The Man in the Iron Mask* with its terse, rapid dialogues and almost frenzied pace can seem an odd proposition indeed. Ultimately, however, what justifies this comparison is the sense of closure deriving from the position of these two volumes at the end of vast frescoes, and their common concern with the passing of an era, the passing of Time itself. In Proust's *Time Regained*, this concern forms the very thematic core of the novel and is linked to the discovery of a writer's vocation; in Dumas' *The Man in the Iron Mask*, it imposes itself at the end of a saga whose heroes, characters we have met in the flower of youth, have arrived at the end of their turbulent, swashbuckling lives.

Thirty-five years have thus passed since we first met D'Artagnan, Athos, Porthos, and Aramis. Now the starving young blades of *The Three Musketeers* have become men of substance. Aramis is Bishop of Vannes and, more secretly, the superior general of the Jesuits, with his eye on the papacy itself; Porthos, now the wealthy Baron de Vallon, lives on his estate; Athos, the Comte de la Fère, lives on his own estate with his son, Raoul, the Vicomte de Bragelonne. D'Artagnan, the only one who is still in active service, is captain of the King's Musketeers, Louis XIV's personal guards.

The year 1661 is a crucial year in the history of France as it sets the stage for Louis XIV's personal government and his subsequent transformation into the Sun King. There had been constant revolts against the crown throughout his father's reign, most notoriously the Fronde, a rebellious movement of nobles and of the parliament. After Louis XIII's death in 1643, the threat of a takeover by one of the factions that formed the Fronde was real. Nevertheless, Louis' widow, Anne of Austria, and Cardinal Mazarin, who had been appointed prime minister, succeeded in defeating the rebellion over the next decade and in keeping the throne of France for Louis XIV, who was only five years old at the time of his father's death. Until 1661, the real master of France was Cardinal Mazarin, who was also rumored to be the queen's lover and even, secretly, her husband. While there is no documented corroboration of this theory, the queen regent and the cardinal–prime minister certainly wielded the royal power while the future Sun King, often humiliated by their tutelage, was obliged to follow their decisions. Still, Mazarin's policies and strategy—dictated by a cold, calculating vision of power and politics—were directed at making France the dominant kingdom in Europe, and in this respect at least, he became Louis' true mentor. The other powerful figure of the period was Nicolas Fouquet, superintendent of finances. Fouquet amassed a fortune in this position, the only one to rival Mazarin's wealth. By the time Mazarin died in 1661, Louis XIV, then a young man in his early twenties, had been trained by his mentor to deal ruthlessly with opposition and to assume the full power of his position. Already he had gathered the nobility of France around him, keeping it occupied in a ceaseless and meticulously choreographed etiquette: the king's awakening and breakfast, his other meals, his hunts, his costumed balls and fireworks, an entire array of activities centered around pleasure . . . and the king. Keeping up with the court's peregrinations from one château to another and with the demands of court life, the nobles could scarcely organize into another Fronde. The memories of that rebellion and of his own humiliations also explain Louis' first official act after Mazarin's death: He abolished the position of prime minister hitherto occupied by the cardinal and formed a king's council, composed of three men whom he could trust absolutely. Fouquet, the richest man in France, hoped to belong to this new body, but in fact his star was already on the decline as the king, relying on men like Jean-Baptiste Colbert, a rival of Fouquet, was already planning his arrest. Rather than please the future Sun King, the fête offered to Louis by his superintendent of finances at the latter's luxurious château at Vaux early on in the novel, only reminds the king of the poor state of his own wealth compared to Fouquet's seemingly limitless opulence. The stage is set for the arrest, and this historical occurrence is intertwined by Dumas with another plotline that gives the novel its name: the presence in the notorious Bastille of a man in an iron mask. Dumas did not invent his man; he actually existed, as entered in the unofficial register kept by the deputy governor of the Bastille, Etienne du Junca, about his successor:

M. de Saint-Mars, formerly Governor of the prisons of Pignerol in Piedmont, Exiles in the Alps, and the island of Sainte-Marguerite off the coast of Cannes, arrived in Paris to take command of the Bastille. He brought with him, "in his litter" a long-term prisoner "whom he kept masked at all times and whose name is not spoken." On 19 November 1703, the unknown prisoner, after a short illness "still masked with a mask of black velvet . . . died this day at half past ten in the evening; he who had been so long a captive, was buried on Tuesday at four in the afternoon, 20th November, in the cemetery of Saint-Paul in this parish. In the register of deaths was entered a name, also unknown." A marginal note in du Junca's hand adds: "I have since learnt that he was named in the Register as M. de Marchiel and that 40 livres were paid for his funeral." The entry in the burial register for 19 November records the death of "Marchioly, aged forty-five years, or thereabouts, [who] departed this life in the Bastille."   (Coward, xvii)

The dates do not coincide, since Dumas' prisoner has already been in the Bastille for a few years as the novel opens in 1661, whereas, according to the historical register, he arrives with the new governor on "19 November 1703," and, of course, rather than iron, the mask worn by the mysterious prisoner is made of black velvet. As for his "true" identity, Dumas' proposition, which will not be revealed here, the few years' discrepancy do not stop him from placing this prisoner at the heart of the intrigues taking place in the French court in 1661. These intrigues will, of course, involve all four Musketeers once again, even if this time around they are far from being on the same side. D'Artagnan is torn between his allegiance to a certain chivalrous ideal embodied for him by Fouquet and his allegiance to the king, while Aramis has no such scruples.

Mixing fact and fiction, roaming freely through the vast store of French history, "from Caesar's invasion of the Gauls to the invasion of the French Republic in Europe," as Dumas summarizes it, fusing the various strands into an exciting, seamless whole—this is the heart of Dumas' technique as a writer of historical fiction, the genre he borrowed from Walter Scott but which he reinvented as the French historical novel. Not absolute historical accuracy, but the ability to bring history to life even at the cost of some inaccuracy is essential to Dumas' technique, for, as he once famously asked: "What is history? A nail on which I hang my novels."

The "nail" is thus Louis XIV's definitive consolidation of his power and the events surrounding this development. What Dumas "hangs on" these events is, essentially, the involvement of the Musketeers in various capacities, all converging on the mysterious prisoner. As the novel begins, Aramis is conversing with the "man in the iron mask," who has been held for six years now in the notorious Bastille. At the time the novel takes place, the Bastille had not yet fallen to the crowds of the Revolution of 1789, but it had already acquired its reputation as a grim prison fortress from which prisoners sometimes never returned. What makes the mysterious prisoner exceptional is not the duration of his imprisonment, but the very mystery surrounding his identity and the horrible iron mask he has been forced to wear. When Aramis visits him in his cell in the first chapter, we are introduced to the plot that has led to his arrest, one that could involve the highest reaches of power, as the masked man is beginning to understand:

"And I, I—" the young man looked sharply at Aramis, "am compelled to live in the obscurity of a prison?"

"Alas I fear so."

"And that, because my presence in the world would lead to the revelation of a great secret?"

"Certainly, a very great secret."

"My enemy must be powerful, to be able to shut up in the Bastille a child such as I then was."

"He is."

Who is "he?" And did the man in the iron mask ever *really* exist? While the answer to the first question is given by Dumas in *The Man in the Iron Mask*, to the second question, he leaves us to our own devices, commenting on his method as the inventor of the French historical novel and on our propensity as readers to believe in events that thrill us, and in people who move us, even if we are not sure that they ever really existed:

There is something I don't know how to do. A book or a play set in places I have not seen. To write *Chris-*

tine, I went to Fontainebleau; to write *Henri III*, I went to Blois; to write the *Musketeers*, I went to Boulogne and to Béthune; to write *Monte Cristo*, I went back to the Catalans in Marseille and to the Chateâu d'Îf. . . . This gives an air of authenticity and truth to what I do, and the characters in specific places grow in such a way that some people end up believing that they've existed.

Perhaps this belief in characters who have existed only in their author's imagination, but have succeeded in growing in our own, is the sign of great literature, popular or not.

—*Roger Celestin*

Note to the Reader

The Man in the Iron Mask is part three of the historical romance, *Le Vicomte de Bragelonne*, which is the last novel in Alexandre Dumas' Musketeer cycle consisting of *The Three Musketeers* (1844) and *Twenty Years After* (1845). In order to understand the context for Aramis' visit to the prisoner in the Bastille, the opening scene in our present volume, it will be important to summarize some of the preceding events that have a bearing on the action in *The Man in the Iron Mask*.

These events take place largely during 1660–61, when King Louis XIV has begun a flirtation with Madame Henrietta, sister of Charles II of England and wife of the Duc d'Orleans, younger brother of Louis XIV. Henrietta is very much in love with Louis, but he takes a liking to one of her attendants, Louise de la Vallière. This affair infuriates Henrietta, who does all she can to sabotage it. At the same time, this affair is a tragedy for Raoul de Bragelonne, son of Athos, Comte de la Fère, one of the original three Musketeers. Raoul had actually been engaged to Louise, and when he asks the king to consent to their marriage, Louis refuses and sends Raoul to England.

At this point Henrietta undermines Louis' command and orders Raoul to return to Paris because she believes Raoul will marry Louise and she will have the king to herself. In addition, she orders Louise to leave her service. Louise, confused and distressed, decides to enter a convent. But now D'Artagnan intercedes on behalf of Louis XIV and convinces Louise to return to the court, where she takes her quarters with M. de Saint-Aignan, the king's favorite. Since there is a trapdoor in M. de Saint-Aigan's apartments, Louis is able to have many secret rendezvous with Louise, and the two are blissful.

Nevertheless, Raoul cannot believe that Louise has betrayed him, and once he discovers what has occurred, he has a breakdown, causing his father, Athos, to visit Louis XIV and berate him for his undignified conduct.

In the meantime, another former Musketeer, Aramis, who is now general of the Jesuits and has close ties to Spain, is seeking to overthrow Louis by revealing a secret which threatens his monarchy—a secret locked away in the dungeon of the Bastille. Aramis even has his eye on becoming pope and will stop at nothing to fulfill his ambitious dreams, even if it means deceiving his friend Porthos, the gentle giant of a Musketeer. Aramis is convinced that Fouquet, the superintendant of finances, who needs money to keep up his luxurious lifestyle, will help him and has taken sides with him against Colbert, who is being helped by the Duchesse de Chevreuse, the former Marie Michon, and old friend of the Musketeers. She wants to have a reconciliation with Anne of Austria and plans Fouquet's downfall, when he refuses to give her money for some incriminating letters that reveal how corrupt he is.

While all these intrigues are in the process of developing, D'Artagnan, the most noble of the Musketeers and the most loyal servant of Louis XIV, begins to suspect that his good friend Aramis is up to mischief. And this is where our novel begins, for Aramis is indeed about to reveal to the prisoner of the Bastille who he is, and just as all the intrigues at the court resemble deceptive moves in an intricate chess game, each step that the cunning Aramis takes from this point on in the action will be geared to checkmate Louis XIV.

—*Jack Zipes*

THE MAN
IN THE
IRON MASK

Contents

4 CONTENTS

CONTENTS 5

CHAPTER I

SINCE Aramis's singular transformation into a confessor
of the order, Baisemeaux was no longer the same man.
Up to that period, Aramis had been for the worthy governor a prelate whom he respected and a friend to whom
he owed a debt of gratitude; but now he felt himself an
inferior, and that Aramis was his master. He lighted a
lantern, summoned a turnkey, and said, returning to Aramis:

"I am at your orders, monseigneur."

Aramis merely nodded his head, as much as to say,
"Very good," and motioned to him to lead the way.
Baisemeaux started out, and Aramis followed him. It was
a beautiful, starry night; the steps of the three men resounded on the flags of the terraces, and the clinking of
the keys hanging from the jailer's belt was heard up to
the top of the towers, as if to remind the prisoners that
liberty was out of their reach. The change in Baisemeaux
seemed to have spread even to the prisoners. The turnkey, the same who, on Aramis's first arrival, had shown
himself so inquisitive and curious, had now become not
only silent, but even impassible. He held his head down,
and seemed afraid to keep his ears open. Thus they
reached the basement of the Bertaudière, the two first
stories of which were climbed silently and somewhat
slowly; for Baisemeaux, though far from disobeying, was
far from exhibiting any eagerness to obey. On arriving at
the door Baisemeaux moved to enter the prisoner's chamber; but Aramis, stopping him on the threshold, said:

"The rules do not allow the governor to hear the prisoner's confession."

Baisemeaux bowed, and made way for Aramis, who
took the lantern and entered; and then motioned to them
to close the door behind him. For an instant he remained
standing, listening whether Baisemeaux and the turnkey
had retired; but as soon as he was assured by the sound
of their dying footsteps that they had left the tower, he

put the lantern on the table and gazed around. On a bed of green serge, similar in all respects to the other beds in the Bastille save that it was newer, and under curtains half-drawn, rested a young man to whom we have already once before introduced Aramis.* According to custom, the prisoner was without a light. At the hour of curfew he was bound to extinguish his lamp, and we see how much he was favored in being allowed to keep it burning, even until then. Near the bed a large leather armchair, with twisted legs, held his clothes. A little table—without pens, books, paper, or ink—stood sadly neglected near the window; while several plates, still full, showed that the prisoner had scarcely touched his recent meal. Aramis saw that the young man was stretched upon his bed, his face half-concealed by his arms. The arrival of a visitor did not cause any change of position; either he was waiting or was asleep. Aramis lit the candle from the lantern, pushed back the armchair, and approached the bed with an evident mixture of interest and respect. The young man raised his head.

"What is it?" said he.

"Didn't you want a confessor?" replied Aramis.

"Yes."

"Because you are ill?"

"Yes."

"Very ill?"

The young man gave Aramis a piercing glance, and answered:

"I thank you." After a moment's silence, "I have seen you before," he continued.

Aramis bowed.

Doubtless, the scrutiny the prisoner had just made of the cold, crafty, and imperious character stamped upon the features of the bishop of Vannes was not very reassuring to one in his situation, for he added:

"I am better."

"And then?" said Aramis.

"Why, then, being better, I have no longer the same need of a confessor, I think."

"Not even of the haircloth, which the note you found in your bread informed you of?"

* In an earlier part, Aramis has visited the prisoner.

The young man started; but before he had either as-
sented or denied, Aramis continued:

"Not even of the priest from whom you were to hear
an important revelation?"

"If it be so," said the young man, sinking again on
his pillow, "it is different; I am listening."

Aramis then looked at him more closely, and was
struck with the easy majesty of his manner, one which
can never be acquired unless God has implanted it in the
blood or heart.

"Sit down, monsieur," said the prisoner. Aramis
bowed, and obeyed.

"How does the Bastille agree with you?" asked the
bishop.

"Very well."

"You do not suffer?"

"No."

"You have nothing to regret?"

"Nothing."

"Not even your liberty?"

"What do you call liberty, monsieur?" asked the prisoner, with the tone of a man who is preparing for a struggle.

"I call liberty the flowers, the air, the light, the stars,
the happiness of going where the quick legs of a twenty-
year-old may wish to carry you."

The young man smiled, whether in resignation or contempt it was difficult to tell.

"Look," he said, "I have in that Japanese vase two
roses picked yesterday evening in the bud from the governor's garden; this morning they have bloomed and
spread their vermilion chalice beneath my gaze; with
every opening petal they unfold the treasures of their
perfume, filling my room with their fragrance. Look,
now, at these two roses; even among roses these are
beautiful, and the rose is the most beautiful of flowers.
Why, then, do you want me to wish for other flowers
when I possess the loveliest of all?"

Aramis gazed at the young man in surprise.

"If *flowers* constitute liberty," the captive sadly went
on, "I am free, for I possess them."

"But the air!" cried Aramis; "air so necessary to
life!"

"Well, monsieur," returned the prisoner, "come near the window; it is open. Between heaven and earth the wind whirls on its storms of hail and lightning, wafts its warm mists, or breathes in gentle breezes. It caresses my face. When I climb up on the back of this armchair, with my arm around the bars of the window to hold myself up, I imagine I am swimming in the wide expanse before me."

The face of Aramis darkened as the young man continued:

"Light I have; what is better than light? I have the sun, a friend who comes to visit me every day, without the permission of the governor or the jailer's company. He comes in at the window, traces in my room a square the shape of the window which lights up the drapery of my bed down to the border. This luminous square increases from ten o'clock till midday, and decreases from one until three slowly, as if, having hastened to come, it was sorry to leave me. When its last ray disappears I have enjoyed its presence for four hours. Is not that sufficient? I have been told that there are unhappy beings who dig in quarries, and laborers who toil in mines, and who never see it at all."

Aramis wiped the drops from his brow.

"As to the stars, which are so delightful to view," continued the young man, "they all resemble one another, save in size and brilliancy. I am a favored mortal, for if you had not lighted that candle you would have been able to see the beautiful stars which I was gazing at from my bed before your arrival, and whose rays were playing over my eyes."

Aramis lowered his head; he felt himself overwhelmed with the bitter flow of that sinister philosophy which is the religion of the captive.

"So much, then, for the flowers, the air, the daylight, and the stars," tranquilly continued the young man; "there remains but my exercise. Do I not walk all day in the governor's garden if the weather is fine—here if it rains? I am cool if it is warm, warm, thanks to my fireplace, if it is cold. Ah, monsieur, believe me," continued the prisoner, not without bitterness, "men have done everything for me that a man can hope for or desire."

"Men!" said Aramis. "Be it so; but it seems to me you are forgetting God."

"Indeed I have forgotten God," murmured the prisoner, without emotion; "but why do you mention it? Of what use is it to talk to a prisoner of God?"

Aramis looked steadily at this singular youth, who possessed the resignation of a martyr with the smile of an atheist.

"Is not God in everything?" he whispered, in a reproachful tone.

"Say, rather, at the end of everything," answered the prisoner firmly.

"Be it so," said Aramis; "but let us return to our starting point."

"I'll be only too glad," said the young man.

"I am your confessor."

"Yes."

"Well, then, you ought, as a penitent, to tell me the truth."

"I'll be glad to tell it to you."

"Every prisoner has committed some crime for which he has been imprisoned. What crime, then, have *you* committed?"

"You asked me the same question the first time you saw me," answered the prisoner.

"And then, as now, you evaded giving me an answer."

"And why do you think that I shall answer you now?"

"Because this time I am your confessor."

"Then, if you wish me to tell what crime I have committed, explain to me what a crime is. For as my conscience does not accuse me, I say that I am not a criminal."

"We are often criminals in the eyes of the great of the earth, not only for having committed crimes, but because we know that crimes have been committed."

The prisoner was paying the deepest attention.

"Yes, I understand you," he said, after a pause; "yes, you are right, monsieur; it is very possible that in that light I am a criminal in the eyes of the great of the earth."

"Ah! then you know something," said Aramis.

"No, I am not aware of anything," replied the young man; "but sometimes I think, and I say to myself . . ."

"What do you say to yourself?"

"That if I were to think any further I would either go mad or would understand a great deal."

"And then—and then?" said Aramis impatiently.

"Then I stop."

"You stop?"

"Yes; my head becomes confused, and my ideas melancholy; I feel *ennui* overtaking me; I wish . . ."

"What?"

"I don't know; but I do not like to give myself up to longing for things that I do not possess, when I am so happy with what I have."

"Are you afraid of death?" said Aramis, with a slight uneasiness.

"Yes," said the young man, smiling.

Aramis felt the chill of that smile, and shuddered.

"Oh, since you fear death, you know more about matters than you say," he cried.

"And you," returned the prisoner, "who bid me to ask to see you; you, who, when I did ask to see you, came here promising a whole world of revelations; how is it that, nevertheless, it is you who are silent, and it is I who speak? Since, then, we both wear masks, either let us both retain them or put them aside together."

Aramis felt the force and justice of the remark, saying to himself:

"This is no ordinary man; I must be cautious. Are you ambitious?" he said suddenly to the prisoner, aloud, without preparing him for the transition.

"What do you mean by ambition?" replied the youth.

"It is," replied Aramis, "a feeling which prompts a man to desire more than he has."

"I said that I was contented, monsieur; but, perhaps, I am mistaken. I am ignorant of the nature of ambition; but it is not impossible I may have some. Tell me your thoughts; it's all I wish."

"An ambitious man," said Aramis, "is one who covets what is beyond his station."

"I covet nothing beyond my station," said the young man, with an assurance of manner which for the second time made the bishop of Vannes tremble.

He was silent. But, to look at the burning eye, the knitted brow, and the reflective attitude of the captive, it

was evident that he was waiting for something more than
silence—a silence which Aramis now broke.

"You lied the first time I saw you," he said.

"Lied!" cried the young man, starting up on his bed,
with such a tone in his voice, and such a flash in his
eyes, that Aramis recoiled in spite of himself.

"I *should* say," returned Aramis, bowing, "you concealed from me what you knew of your childhood."

"A man's secrets are his own, monsieur," retorted the
prisoner, "and not at the mercy of just anyone."

"True," said Aramis, bowing still lower than before,
"it's true. Pardon me, but today, am I still just anyone?
I beg you to reply, monseigneur."

This title slightly disturbed the prisoner; but nevertheless he did not appear astonished that it was given him.

"I do not know you, monsieur," he said.

"Oh, if I but dared, I would take your hand and would
kiss it!"

The young man seemed as if he were going to give
Aramis his hand; but the light which glowed in his eyes
faded away and he coldly and distrustfully withdrew his
hand again.

"Kiss the hand of a prisoner," he said, shaking his
head; "to what purpose?"

"Why did you tell me," said Aramis, "that you were
happy here? Why, that you aspired to nothing? Why, in
a word, by speaking thus, do you prevent me from being
frank in my turn?"

The same light shone a third time in the young man's
eyes, but died away as before.

"You distrust me," said Aramis.

"And why do you say so, monsieur?"

"Oh, for a very simple reason; if you know what you
ought to know, you ought to mistrust everybody."

"Then be not astonished that I am mistrustful, since
you suspect me of knowing what I know not."

Aramis was struck with admiration at this energetic
resistance.

"Oh, monseigneur, you drive me to despair!" he said,
striking the armchair with his fist.

"And, on my part, I do not understand you, monsieur."

"Well, then, try to understand me."

The prisoner looked fixedly at Aramis.

"Sometimes it seems to me," said the latter, "that I have before me the man whom I am looking for, and then . . ."

"And then your man disappears, is it not so?" said the prisoner, smiling. "So much the better."

Aramis rose.

"Certainly," he said; "I have nothing further to say to a man who mistrusts me as you do."

"And I, monsieur," said the prisoner, in the same tone, "have nothing to say to a man who will not understand that a prisoner ought to be mistrustful of everybody."

"Even of his old friends?" said Aramis. "Oh, monseigneur, you are *too* prudent!"

"Of my old friends? Are you one of my old friends?"

"Don't you remember," said Aramis, "that you once saw, in the village where your early years were spent—"

"Do you know the name of the village?" asked the prisoner.

"Noisy-le-Sec, monseigneur," answered Aramis firmly.

"Go on," said the young man, with an immovable expression.

"Stay, monseigneur," said Aramis; "if you are positively resolved to carry on this game, let us break off. I am here to tell you many things, it's true; but you must allow me to see that, on your side, you have a desire to know them. Before revealing the important matters I conceal, be assured I am in need of some encouragement, if not candor; a little sympathy, if not confidence. But you keep yourself entrenched in a supposed ignorance which paralyzes me. Oh, not for the reason you think; for, ignorant as you may be, or indifferent as you pretend to be, you are nonetheless what you are, monseigneur, and there is nothing—nothing, mark me—which can cause you not to be so."

"I promise you," replied the prisoner, "to hear you without impatience. Only it appears to me that I have a right to repeat the question I have already asked—'Who *are* you?' "

"Do you remember, fifteen or eighteen years ago, seeing at Noisy-le-Sec a gentleman, accompanied by a lady in black silk, with flame-colored ribbons in her hair?"

"Yes," said the young man; "I once asked the name of this gentleman, and they told me that he called himself the Abbé d'Herblay. I was astonished that the abbé had so warlike an air, and they replied that there was nothing singular in that, seeing that he was one of Louis XIII's musketeers."

"Well," said Aramis, "that musketeer and abbé, afterward bishop of Vannes, is your confessor now."

"I know it; I recognized you."

"Then, monseigneur, if you know that, I must further add a fact of which you are ignorant—that if the king were to know this evening of the presence of this musketeer, this abbé, this bishop, this confessor, *here*—he, who has risked everything to visit you, would tomorrow see the executioner's ax glitter at the bottom of a dungeon more gloomy and more obscure than yours."

While hearing these words, delivered emphatically, the young man had raised himself on his bed, and gazed more and more eagerly at Aramis.

The result of his scrutiny was that he appeared to derive some confidence from it.

"Yes," he murmured, "I remember perfectly. The woman of whom you speak came once with you, and twice afterward with another."

He hesitated.

"With another woman, who came to see you every month—is it not so, monseigneur?"

"Yes."

"Do you know who this lady was?"

A light seemed ready to flash from the prisoner's eyes.

"I am aware that she was one of the ladies of the court," he said.

"You remember that lady well, do you not?"

"Oh, my recollection can hardly be very confused on this matter," said the young prisoner. "I saw that lady once with a gentleman about forty-five years old. I saw her once with you, and with the lady dressed in black. I have seen her twice since with the same person. These four people, with my master, and old Perronnette, my jailer, and the governor of the prison, are the only persons with whom I have ever spoken, and, indeed, almost the only persons I have ever seen.''

''Then, you were in prison?''

''If I am a prisoner here, there I was comparatively free, although in a very narrow sense—a house which I never left, a garden surrounded with walls I could not leap over, these were my home; but you know it, as you have been there. In a word, being accustomed to live within these bounds, I never cared to leave them. And so you will understand, monsieur, that, not having seen anything of the world, I have nothing left to care for; and, therefore, if you relate anything to me, you will be obliged to explain everything to me.''

''And I will do so,'' said Aramis, bowing, ''for it is my duty, monseigneur.''

''Well, then, begin by telling me who was my tutor.''

''A worthy and, above all, an honorable gentleman, monseigneur; fit guide both for body and soul. Had you ever any reason to complain of him?''

''Oh, no; quite the contrary. But this gentleman of yours often used to tell me that my father and mother were dead. Did he deceive me, or did he speak the truth?''

''He was compelled to comply with the orders given him.''

''Then he lied?''

''In one respect. Your father is dead.''

''And my mother?''

''She is dead for you.''

''But, then, she lives for others, does she not?''

''Yes.''

''And I, I—'' the young man looked sharply at Aramis, ''am compelled to live in the obscurity of a prison?''

''Alas! I fear so.''

''And that, because my presence in the world would lead to the revelation of a great secret?''

''Certainly, a very great secret.''

''My enemy must indeed be powerful, to be able to shut up in the Bastille a child such as I then was.''

''He is.''

''More powerful than my mother, then?''

"And why do you ask that?"

"Because my mother would have protected me."

Aramis hesitated.

"Yes, monseigneur; more powerful than your mother."

"Seeing, then, that my nurse and preceptor were carried off, and that I, also, was separated from them—either they were, or I was, a great danger to my enemy?"

"Yes; a danger from which he freed himself by having the nurse and preceptor disappear," answered Aramis quietly.

"Disappear!" cried the prisoner. "But how did they disappear?"

"In the surest possible way," answered Aramis. "They are dead."

The young man turned visibly pale, and passed his trembling hand over his face.

"From poison?" he asked.

"From poison."

The prisoner thought a moment.

"My enemy must, indeed, have been very cruel, or pushed by necessity, to assassinate those two innocent people, my sole support; for the worthy gentleman and the poor nurse had never harmed a living being."

"In your family, monseigneur, necessity is stern. And so it is necessity which compels me, to my great regret, to tell you that this gentleman and the unhappy lady have been assassinated."

"Oh, you tell me nothing I am not aware of," said the prisoner, knitting his brows.

"How?"

"I suspected it."

"Why?"

"I will tell you."

At this moment the young man, supporting himself on his two elbows, drew close to Aramis's face, with such an expression of dignity, of self-command, and of defiance even, that the bishop felt the electricity of enthusiasm move in devouring flashes from that dried-up heart of his into his brain of steel.

"Speak, monseigneur. I have already told you that by talking with you I am endangering my life. Little value as it has, I implore you to accept it as the ransom of your own.''

"Well," went on the young man, "this is why I suspected that they killed my nurse and my preceptor."

"Whom you used to call your father?"

"Yes; whom I called my father, but I knew I was not his son."

"Who made you to suppose so?"

"For the same reason that you, monsieur, are too respectful for a friend, he was also too respectful for a father."

"I, however," said Aramis, "have no intention to disguise myself."

The young man nodded, and continued:

"Undoubtedly, I was not destined to perpetual seclusion," said the prisoner; "and what makes me believe so, above all, now, is the care that was taken to make me as accomplished a gentleman as possible. The gentleman assigned to be with me taught me everything he knew himself—mathematics, a little geometry, astronomy, fencing, and riding. Every morning I went through military exercises, and practiced on horseback. Well, one morning, during summer, it being very hot, I went to sleep in the hall. Nothing up to that period, except the respect paid me, had enlightened me, or even roused my suspicions. I lived as children, as birds, as plants do, on air and on sun. I had just turned fifteen—"

"This, then, is eight years ago?"

"Yes, nearly; but I have lost track of time."

"Excuse me; but what did your tutor tell you to encourage you to work?"

"He used to say that a man was bound to make for himself, in the world, that fortune which God had refused him at his birth. He added, that, being a poor, obscure orphan, I had no one but myself to look to; and that nobody either did, or ever would, take any interest in me. I was then in the hall I have spoken of, asleep, tired from fencing. My preceptor was in his room on the first floor, just above me. Suddenly I heard him exclaim, and then he called: 'Perronnette! Perronnette!' It was my nurse whom he called."

"Yes, I know it," said Aramis. "Go on, monseigneur."

"Very likely she was in the garden, for my preceptor came hastily downstairs. I rose, anxious at seeing him anxious. He opened the garden door, still crying out, 'Perronnette! Perronnette!' The windows of the hall looked into the court; the shutters were closed; but through a chink in them I saw my tutor draw near a large well, which was almost directly under the windows of his study. He stooped over the edge, looked into the well, again cried out, and made wild and frightened gestures. From where I was, I could not only see, but hear—and see and hear I did."

"Go on, I pray you," said Aramis.

"Dame Perronnette came running up, hearing the governor's cries. He went to meet her, took her by the arm, and drew her quickly toward the edge; after which as they both bent over it together, 'Look, look,' he cried, 'what a misfortune!'

" 'Calm down, calm down,' said Perronnette; 'what is the matter?'

" 'The letter!' he exclaimed; 'do you see that letter?' pointing to the bottom of the well.

" 'What letter?' she cried.

" 'The letter you see down there; the last letter from the queen.'

"At this word I trembled. My tutor—he who passed for my father, he who was continually recommending me modesty and humility—in correspondence with the queen.

" 'The queen's last letter!' cried Perronnette, without showing more astonishment than at seeing this letter at the bottom of the well; 'but how did it get there?'

" 'A chance, Dame Perronnette—a singular chance. I was entering my room, and on opening the door, the window, too, being open, a puff of air came suddenly and carried off this paper—this letter of her majesty's; I darted after it, and ran to the window just in time to see it flutter a moment in the breeze and disappear down the well.'

" 'Well,' said Dame Perronnette; 'and if the letter has fallen into the well it's all the same as if it was burned; as the queen burns all her letters every time she comes.'

"And so, was this lady who came every month the queen?" said the prisoner.

"Yes," replied Aramis, nodding.

" 'Of course, of course,' the old gentleman went on; 'but this letter contained instructions—how can I follow them?'

" 'Write to her immediately; give her a plain account of the accident, and the queen will no doubt write you another letter in place of this.'

" 'Oh! the queen would never believe this story,' said the good gentleman, shaking his head; 'she will imagine that I want to keep this letter instead of giving it up like the rest, so as to have a hold over her. She is so distrustful, and Monsieur de Mazarin so— This devil of an Italian is capable of having us poisoned at the first breath of suspicion.' "

Aramis almost imperceptibly smiled.

" 'You know, Dame Perronnette, they are both so suspicious in all that concerns Philippe.'

" 'Philippe' was the name they gave me," said the prisoner.

" 'Well, it's no use hesitating,' said Dame Perronnette, 'somebody must go down the well.'

" 'Of course; so that the person who goes down may read the paper as he is coming up.'

" 'But let us choose some villager who cannot read, and then you will be at ease.'

" 'Granted; but will not anyone who goes down the well guess that a paper must be important for which we risk a man's life? However, you have given me an idea, Dame Perronnette; somebody shall go down the well, but that somebody will be me.'

"But at this notion Dame Perronnette wept and cried out in such a manner, and so implored the old nobleman, with tears in her eyes, that he promised her to get a ladder long enough to reach down, while she went in search of some stout-hearted youth, whom she was to persuade that a jewel had fallen into the well, and that this jewel was wrapped in a paper. 'And as paper,' remarked my preceptor, 'naturally unfolds in water, the young man would not be surprised at finding nothing, after all, but the letter wide open.'

" 'But perhaps the writing will be already washed out by that time,' said Dame Perronnette.

" 'No matter, provided we have the letter. On returning it to the queen she will see at once that we have not betrayed her; and, consequently, as we shall not rouse the distrust of Mazarin, we shall have nothing to fear from him.'

"Having come to this resolution, they parted. I pushed back the shutter, and, seeing that my tutor was about to reenter, I threw myself on my bed, confused by all I had just heard. My governor opened the door a few moments after, and thinking I was asleep, gently closed it again. As soon as it was shut I rose, and listening, heard the sound of retiring footsteps. Then I returned to the shutter, and saw my tutor and Dame Perronnette go out together. I was alone in the house. They had hardly closed the gate before I sprang from the window and ran to the well. Then, just as my governor had, I leaned over. Something white and luminous glistened in the green and quivering ripples of the water. The brilliant disk was fascinating and attracting me; my eyes became fixed, and I could hardly breathe. The well seemed to draw me in with its large mouth and icy breath; and I thought I read, at the bottom of the water, characters of fire traced upon the letter the queen had touched.

"Then, scarcely knowing what I was about, and urged on by one of those instinctive impulses which drive men upon their destruction, I lowered the cord from the windlass of the well to within about three feet of the water, leaving the bucket dangling, and at the same time taking infinite pains not to disturb that coveted letter, which was beginning to change its white tint for a greenish hue—proof enough that it was sinking—and then, I slid down into the abyss. When I saw myself hanging over the dark pool, when I saw the sky lessening above my head, a cold shudder came over me, a chill fear got the better of me, I was seized with giddiness, and the hair rose on my head; but my strong will still reigned supreme over all the terror and discomfort. I reached the water, and at once plunged into it, holding on by one hand while I immersed the other and seized the dear letter, which alas! came in two in my grasp. I concealed the two fragments in my coat, and, helping myself with my feet against the sides of the pit, and clinging on with my hands, agile and vigorous as I was, and, above all, pressed for time, I regained the edge, drenching it as I touched it with the water that streamed off me. I was no sooner out of the well with my prize than I rushed into the sunlight and took refuge in a kind of shrubbery at the bottom of the garden. As I entered my hiding place, the bell that resounded when the great gate was opened, rang. It was my preceptor come back again. I had just enough time. I calculated that it would take ten minutes before he would reach me, even if, guessing where I was, he came straight to it; and twenty if he were obliged to look for me. But this was time enough to allow me to read the cherished letter, whose fragments I quickly pieced together. The writing was already fading, but I managed to decipher it all.''

"And what did you read there, monseigneur?" asked Aramis, deeply interested.

"Quite enough, monsieur, to see that my tutor was a man of noble rank, and that Perronnette, without being a lady of quality, was far better than a servant; and also to realize that I must myself be high-born, since the queen, Anne of Austria, and Mazarin, the prime minister, commended me so earnestly to their care."

Here the young man paused, quite overcome.

"And what happened?" asked Aramis.

"It happened, monsieur," he answered, "that the workmen they had summoned found nothing in the well, after the closest search; that my governor noticed that the edge was all watery; that I was not so dried by the sun as to escape Dame Perronnette's observing that my garments were moist; and, lastly, that I was seized with a violent fever, owing to the chill and the excitement of my discovery, followed by an attack of delirium, during which I related the whole adventure; so that, guided by my confession, my governor found under my pillow the two pieces of the queen's letter."

"Ah!" said Aramis, "now I understand."

"Beyond this, all is conjecture. Doubtless the unfortunate lady and gentleman, not daring to keep the occurrence secret, wrote to the queen, and sent back to her the torn letter."

"After which," said Aramis, "you were arrested and removed to the Bastille."

"As you see."

"Then your two attendants disappeared?"

"Alas!"

"Let us not take up our time with the dead, but see what can be done with the living. You told me you were resigned."

"I repeat it."

"Without any desire for freedom?"

"As I told you."

"Without ambition, sorrow, or thought?"

The young man made no answer.

"Well," asked Aramis, "why are you silent?"

"I think I have spoken enough," answered the prisoner, "and that now it is your turn. I am weary."

Aramis gathered himself up, and a shade of deep solemnity spread over his face. It was evident that he had reached the important part in the role he had come to the prison to play.

"One question," said Aramis.

"What is it? Speak."

"In the house where you lived there were neither looking glasses nor mirrors?"

"What are those two words, and what is their meaning?" asked the young man. "I have no sort of knowledge of them."

"They designate two pieces of furniture which reflect objects; so that, for instance, you may see in them your own features, as you see mine now, with the naked eye."

"No; then there was neither a glass nor a mirror in the house," answered the young man.

Aramis looked around him.

"Nor is there any here," he said; "they have again taken the same precaution."

"To what end?"

"You will know soon. Now, you have told me that you were instructed in mathematics, astronomy, fencing, and riding; but you have not said a word about history."

"My tutor sometimes told me the great deeds of the King, St. Louis, King Francis I, and King Henry IV."

"Is that all?"

"Very nearly."

"This also was done by design, then; just as they deprived you of mirrors, which reflect the present, so they left you in ignorance of history, which reflects the past. Since your imprisonment, books have been forbidden you; so that you are unacquainted with a number of facts, by means of which you would be able to reconstruct the shattered edifice of your recollections and your hopes."

"It is true," said the young man.

"Listen, then; I will in a few words tell you what took place in France during the last twenty-three or twenty-four years; that is, from the probable date of your birth; in a word, from the time that interests you."

"Go on."

And the young man resumed his serious and attentive attitude.

"Do you know who was the son of Henry IV?"

"At least, I know who his successor was."

"How?"

"By means of a coin dated 1610, which bears the effigy of Henry IV; and another of 1612, bearing that of Louis XIII. So I presumed that, there being only two years between the two dates, Louis was Henry's successor."

"Then," said Aramis, "you know that the last reigning monarch was Louis XIII?"

"I do," answered the youth, slightly reddening.

"Well, he was a prince full of noble ideas and great projects, always, deferred by the troubles of the times and the wars that his minister, Richelieu, fought against the great nobles of France. The king himself was of a weak character, and died young and unhappy."

"I know it."

"He had been long anxious about having an heir; a care which weighs heavily on princes, who want to leave behind them more than a memory, so that their thoughts and their works will live on."

"Did the king, then, die childless?" asked the prisoner, smiling.

"No, but he was without one for a long time, and for a long while thought he should be the last of his race. This idea had reduced him to the depths of despair, when suddenly his wife, Anne of Austria—"

The prisoner trembled.

"Did you know," said Aramis, "that Louis XIII's wife was called Anne of Austria?"

"Go on," said the young man, without replying to the question.

"When suddenly," Aramis went on, "the queen announced an interesting event. There was great joy at the news, and all prayed for her happy delivery. On the 5th of September, 1638, she gave birth to a son."

Here Aramis looked at his companion, and thought he observed him turning pale.

"You are about to hear," said Aramis, "an account which few could now give; for it refers to a secret which they think buried with the dead, or buried in the abyss of the confessional."

"And you will tell me this secret," broke in the youth.

"Oh!" said Aramis, with unmistakable emphasis, "I do not know that I ought to risk this secret by entrusting it to one who has no desire to leave the Bastille."

"I hear you, monsieur."

"The queen, then, gave birth to a son. But while the court was rejoicing over the event, when the king had shown the newborn child to his nobles and his people, and was sitting happily down to table, to celebrate the event, the queen, who was alone in her room, was again in pain and gave birth to a second son."

"Oh!" said the prisoner, betraying a better acquaintance with affairs than he had owned to, "I thought that Monsieur was only born a—"

Aramis raised his finger.

"Let me continue," he said.

The prisoner sighed impatiently, and paused.

"Yes," said Aramis, "the queen had a second son, whom Dame Perronnette, the midwife, received in her arms."

"Dame Perronnette!" murmured the young man.

"They ran at once to the banqueting room, and whispered to the king what had happened; he rose and left the table. But this time it was no longer happiness that his face expressed, but something akin to terror. The birth of twins changed into bitterness the joy which the birth of an only son had caused him, seeing that in France (a fact you are assuredly ignorant of), it is the oldest of the king's sons who succeeds his father."

"I know it."

"And that the doctors and jurists assert that there is ground for doubting whether he who first makes his appearance is the elder by the law of God and of nature."

The prisoner uttered a smothered cry, and became whiter than the sheet under which he hid himself.

"Now you understand," pursued Aramis, "that the king, who with so much pleasure saw himself repeated in one, was in despair about two; fearing that the second might dispute the first's claim to seniority, which had been recognized only two hours before; and thus this second son, relying on party interests and caprices, might one day sow discord and engender civil war in the kingdom, destroying the very dynasty he should have strengthened."

"Oh, I understand! I understand!" murmured the young man.

"Well," continued Aramis, "this is what is told; this is why one of the queen's two sons, shamefully parted from his brother, shamefully sequestered, is buried in the deepest obscurity; this is why that second son has disappeared, and so completely that not a soul in France, save his mother, is aware of his existence."

"Yes, his mother, who has cast him off," cried the prisoner, in a tone of despair.

"Except, also," Aramis went on, "the lady in the black dress; and finally, except—"

"Except yourself. Is it not? You who come and tell all this; you, who rouse in my soul curiosity, hatred, ambition, and, perhaps, even the thirst of vengeance; except you, monsieur, who, if you are the man whom I expect, whom the note I have received applies to; whom, in short, God ought to send me, must possess about you—"

"What?" asked Aramis.

"A portrait of the king, Louis XIV, who at this moment reigns upon the throne of France."

"Here is the portrait," replied the bishop, handing the prisoner a miniature in enamel, on which Louis was depicted lifelike, with a handsome, lofty mien. The prisoner eagerly seized the portrait, and gazed at it with devouring eyes.

"And now, monseigneur," said Aramis, "here is a mirror."

Aramis left the prisoner time to recover his thoughts.

"So high! so high!" murmured the young man, eagerly comparing the likeness of Louis with his own image reflected in the mirror.

"What do you think of it?" Aramis then said.

"I think that I am lost," replied the captive; "the king will never set me free."

"And I—I wonder," added the bishop, glaring piercingly at the prisoner, "I wonder which of the two is the king; the one whom this miniature portrays, or whom the mirror reflects?"

"The king, monsieur," sadly replied the young man, "is he who is on the throne, who is not in prison; and who, on the other hand, has others jailed there. Royalty is power; and you see well how powerless I am."

"Monseigneur," answered Aramis, with a respect he had not yet shown, "do realize that the king, will, if you desire it, be he who, leaving his dungeon, shall sit upon the throne on which his friends will place him."

"Tempt me not, monsieur," broke in the prisoner bitterly.

"Do not be weak, monseigneur," persisted Aramis; "I have brought all the proofs of your birth; consult them; prove to yourself that you are a king's son; and then let us act."

"No, no; it is impossible."

"Unless, indeed," the bishop went on ironically, "it be the destiny of your race that the brothers excluded from the throne should be always princes void of courage and honesty, as was your uncle, Monsieur Gaston d'Orleans, who ten times conspired against his brother, Louis XIII."

"What!" cried the prince, astonished, "my uncle Gaston 'conspired against his brother'; conspired to dethrone him?"

"Exactly, monseigneur; for no other reason. I tell you the truth."

"And he had friends—devoted ones?"

"As much so as I am to you."

"And, what did he do? Failed!"

"He failed, I admit; but always through his own fault; and for the sake of redeeming—not his life—for the life of the king's brother is sacred and inviolable—but his liberty, he sacrificed the lives of all his friends, one after another. And so, to this day, he is the very shame of history, and the detestation of a hundred noble families in this kingdom.''

''I understand, monsieur; was it by weakness or treachery, that my uncle slew his friends?''

''By weakness; which, in princes, is always treachery.''

''Cannot a man fail from incompetence and ignorance? Do you really believe it possible that a poor captive such as I, brought up not only at a distance from the court but even from the world—do you believe it possible that he could help those of his friends who should attempt to serve him?''

And, as Aramis was about to reply, the young man suddenly cried out, with a violence which showed the temper of his blood:

''We are speaking of friends; but how can I have any friends—I, whom no one knows, and have neither liberty, money, nor influence, to gain any?''

''It seems I have the honor to offer myself to your royal highness.''

''Oh, do not call me so, monsieur; it's either treachery or cruelty. Let me think only of these prison walls, which confine me; let me again love, or, at least, submit to my slavery and my obscurity.''

''Monseigneur, monseigneur, if you again utter these desperate words—if, after having received proof of your high birth, you still remain weak in body and soul, I will comply with your desire, I will leave, and renounce forever the service of a master to whom so eagerly I came to devote my assistance and my life!''

''Monsieur,'' cried the prince, ''would it not have been better for you to have considered, before telling me all that you have done, that you have broken my heart forever!''

''And so I wished to do, monseigneur.''

''To talk to me about power, grandeur, and even royalty, is a prison the fitting place? You want to make me believe in splendor, and we are lying hidden in the night; you boast of glory, and we are hushing up our words in the curtains of this miserable bed; you give me glimpses of absolute power, and I hear the step of the jailer in the corridor, that step which makes you tremble more than it does me. To make me believe more, free me from the Bastille; let me breathe the fresh air; give me spurs and a sword, then we shall begin to understand each other.''

''It is precisely my intention to give you all this, monseigneur, and more; only, do you wish it?''

''A word more,'' said the prince. ''I know there are guards in every gallery, bolts to every door, cannon and soldiery at every barrier. How will you overcome the sentries—spike the guns? How will you break through the bolts and bars?''

''Monseigneur—how did you get the note which announced my arrival?''

''You can bribe a jailer for such a thing as a note.''

''If we can corrupt one turnkey, we can corrupt ten.''

''Well, I admit that it may be possible to release a poor captive from the Bastille; possible to conceal him so that the king's people shall not again capture him; possible, in some unknown retreat, to sustain the unhappy wretch in some suitable manner.''

''Monseigneur!'' said Aramis, smiling.

''I admit that, whoever would do this for me, would seem more than mortal in my eyes; but as you tell me I am a prince, brother of a king, how can you restore me to the rank and power which my mother and my brother have deprived me of? And since I must lead a life of conflict and hatred, how will you make me prevail in those conflicts—render me invulnerable to my enemies? Ah! monsieur, reflect upon this; place me, tomorrow, in some dark cavern in a mountain; give me the pleasure of hearing in freedom the sounds of river and plain, of seeing in freedom the sun or the stormy sky, and it is enough. Promise me no more than this, for, indeed, more you cannot give, and it would be a crime to deceive me, since you call yourself my friend.''

Aramis waited in silence.

''Monseigneur,'' he went on, after a moment's reflection, ''I admire the firm, sound sense which dictates your words; I am happy to have discovered my monarch's mind.''

''Again, again! oh! for mercy's sake,'' cried the prince, pressing his icy hands upon his clammy brow, ''do not

play with me! I have no need to be a king to be the
happiest of men."

"But I, monseigneur, wish you to be a king for the
happiness of humanity."

"Ah!" said the prince, with fresh distrust inspired by
the word, "ah! what, then, does humanity hold against
my brother?"

"I forgot to say, monseigneur, that if you would allow
me to guide you, and if you consent to become the most
powerful monarch on earth, you will have promoted the
interests of all the friends whom I devote to the success
of your cause, and these friends are numerous."

"Numerous?"

"More powerful than numerous, monseigneur."

"Explain yourself."

"It is impossible; I will explain, I swear before God,
on that day that I see you sitting on the throne of France."

"But my brother?"

"You shall decree his fate. Do you pity him?"

"Him, who leaves me to perish in a dungeon? No, I
pity him not."

"So much the better."

"He could have come to this prison, have taken me by
the hand and said, 'My brother, God created us to love,
not to fight with one another. I come to you. A wicked
prejudice has condemned you to pass your days in obscurity, far from all men, and deprived of every joy. I will
make you sit down beside me; I will buckle around your
waist our father's sword. Will you take advantage of this
reconciliation to suppress me? Will you use that sword
to spill my blood?' 'Oh! never!' I would have replied to
him. 'I look on you as my savior, and will respect you
as my master. You give me far more than God has given
me; for through you I possess liberty and the privilege
of loving and being loved in this world.' "

"And you would have kept your word, monseigneur?"

"On my life! But now—now I have culprits to punish."

"In what manner, monseigneur?"

"What do you think of the resemblance that God has
given me to my brother?"

"I say that there was in that likeness a providential
instruction which the king should not have disregarded;

I say that your mother committed a crime in making those different in happiness and fortune whom nature created so similar in her womb; and I conclude that the goal of punishment should be only to restore the balance.''

"By which you mean—"

"That if I restore you to your place on your brother's throne, he shall take yours in prison."

"Alas! there is so much suffering in prison, especially for a man who has drunk so deeply of the cup of life."

"Your royal highness will always be free to act as you may desire; and if it seems right to you, after punishment, may pardon him."

"Good. And now, are you aware of one thing, monsieur?"

"Tell me, my prince."

"It is that I will hear nothing further from you until I am out of the Bastille."

"I was going to say to your highness that I should only have the pleasure of seeing you once again."

"When?"

"The day my prince leaves these gloomy walls."

"Heavens! how will you give me notice of it?"

"By coming to get you."

"Yourself?"

"My prince, leave this room only with me, or if in my absence you are compelled to do so, remember that I am not involved."

"And so I am not to speak a word of this to anyone except you?"

"Only me."

Aramis bowed very low; the prince offered his hand.

"Monsieur," he said, in a tone that came from his heart, "one last word. If you have sought me for my destruction, if you are only a tool in the hands of my enemies, if from our meeting, in which you have sounded the depths of my mind, anything worse than captivity result, that is to say, if death befalls me, still receive my blessing, for you will have ended my troubles and given me rest from the torment that has preyed upon me these eight years."

"Monseigneur, wait before you judge me," said Aramis.

"I say that, in such a case, I bless and forgive you. If,

on the other hand, you have come to restore me to that position in the sunshine of fortune and glory to which I was destined by God; if by your means I can live in the memory of man, and do credit to my race by deeds of valor, or by services to my people; if, from my present depths of sorrow, helped by your generous hand, I raise myself to the very height of honor, then to you, whom I thank and whom I bless, to you will I offer half my power and my glory; you will still be but partly rewarded, since I shall not be able to share with you the happiness received at your hands.''

''Monseigneur,'' replied Aramis, moved by the pallor and excitement of the young man, ''the nobility of your heart fills me with joy and admiration. It is not you who will have to thank me, but rather the nation whom you will render happy, your descendants whose name you will make glorious. Yes; I shall indeed have given you more than life, as I shall have given you immortality.''

The prince offered his hand to Aramis, who bent down upon his knee and kissed it.

''It is the first act of homage paid to our future king,'' he said. ''When I see you again, I shall say, 'Good day, sire.' ''

''Until then,'' said the young man, pressing his pale and thin fingers over his heart, ''until then, no more dreams, no more strain upon my life; it would break. Oh, monsieur, how small is my prison, how low the window, how narrow are the doors! To think that so much pride, splendor, and happiness should be able to enter in and remain here!''

''Your royal highness makes me proud,'' said Aramis, ''since you claim it is I who brought all this.''

And he rapped immediately on the door. The jailer came to open it with Baisemeaux, who, devoured by fear and anxiety, was beginning, in spite of himself, to listen at the door. Happily, neither of the speakers had forgotten to hush his voice, even in the most passionate outbreaks.

''What a confession!'' said the governor, forcing a laugh. ''Who would believe that a mere recluse, a man almost dead, could have committed sins so numerous and so long in the telling?''

Aramis made no reply. He was eager to leave the Bastille, where the secret which overwhelmed him seemed to double the weight of the walls. As soon as they reached Baisemeaux's quarters:

"Let us proceed to business, my dear governor," said Aramis.

"Alas!" replied Baisemeaux.

"You have asked me for my receipt for one hundred and fifty thousand livres," said the bishop.

"And to pay over the first third of the sum," added the poor governor with a sigh, taking three steps toward his iron strongbox.

"Here is the receipt," said Aramis.

"And here is the money," returned Baisemeaux, with a triple sigh.

"The order instructed me only to give a receipt; it said nothing about receiving the money," said Aramis. "Adieu, Monsieur le Gouverneur."

And he left, leaving Baisemeaux almost choking with joy and surprise at this regal present so liberally given by the confessor-extraordinary to the Bastille.

CHAPTER II

HOW MOUSTON HAD BECOME FATTER WITHOUT INFORMING PORTHOS, AND THE TROUBLES WHICH CONSEQUENTLY BEFELL THAT WORTHY GENTLEMAN

SINCE the departure of Athos for Blois, Porthos and D'Artagnan were seldom together. One was occupied with tiring duties for the king, the other had been making many purchases of furniture which he intended to take to his estate, and thanks to which he hoped to establish in his various residences something of that court luxury which he had witnessed in all its dazzling brightness in his majesty's society. D'Artagnan, ever faithful, one morning, during an interval of service, thought about Porthos, and being uneasy at not having heard anything

of him for a fortnight, directed his steps toward his hotel,
and found him just as he was getting up. The worthy
baron had a pensive—nay, more than pensive—a melancholy air. He was sitting on his bed only half-dressed,
and with legs dangling over the edge, contemplating a
host of garments, which, with their fringes, lace, embroidery and slashes of ill-assorted hues, were strewn
all over the floor. Porthos, sad and reflective as La Fontaine's hare, did not observe D'Artagnan's entrance, which
was, moreover, screened at this moment by M. Mouston, whose personal corpulence, quite enough at any
time to hide one man from another, was for the time
being doubled by a scarlet coat which the attendant was
holding up by the sleeves for his master's inspection so
that he might see it better. D'Artagnan stopped at the
threshold and looked at the pensive Porthos, and then,
as the sight of the innumerable garments strewing the
floor caused mighty sighs to heave from the bosom of
that excellent gentleman, D'Artagnan thought it time to
put an end to these dismal reflections, and coughed to
announce himself.

"Ah!" exclaimed Porthos, whose face brightened with
joy. "Here is D'Artagnan. I shall then get hold of an
idea!"

At these words, Mouston, suspecting what was going
on behind him, got out of the way, smiling kindly at the
friend of his master, who thus found himself freed from
the material obstacle which had prevented his reaching
D'Artagnan. Porthos made his sturdy knees crack as he
rose, and crossing the room in two strides, found himself
face to face with his friend, whom he folded to his chest
with a force of affection that seemed to increase every
day.

"Ah!" he repeated, "you are always welcome, dear
friend; but just now you are more welcome than ever."

"But you seem in the dumps here?" exclaimed D'Artagnan.

Porthos replied by a dejected look.

"Well, then, tell me all about it, Porthos, my friend,
unless it is a secret."

"In the first place," said Porthos, "you know I have
no secrets from you. This is what saddens me."

"Wait a minute, Porthos; let me first get rid of all this litter of satin and velvet."

"Oh, never mind," said Porthos contemptuously; "it is all trash."

"Trash, Porthos! Cloth at twenty livres an ell! Gorgeous satin! regal velvet!"

"Then you think these clothes are—"

"Splendid, Porthos, splendid! I'll bet that you alone in France have so many; and suppose you never had any more made, and were to live a hundred years, which wouldn't astonish me, you could still wear new clothes the day of your death, without being obliged to see the nose of a single tailor from now until then."

Porthos shook his head.

"Come, my friend," said D'Artagnan, "this unnatural melancholy in you frightens me. My dear Porthos, pray get out of it. And the sooner the better."

"Yes, my friend, so I will; if, indeed, it is possible."

"Perhaps you have received bad news from Bracieux?"

"No; they have felled the woods, and it has yielded a third more than the estimate."

"Then has there been a falling off in the pools of Pierrefonds?"

"No, my friend; they have been fished, and there is enough left to stock all the pools in the neighborhood."

"Perhaps your estate at Vallon has been destroyed by an earthquake?"

"No, my friend; on the contrary, the ground was struck by lightning a hundred paces from the chateau, and a spring appeared in a place entirely destitute of water."

"What in the world *is* the matter, then?"

"The fact is, I have received an invitation for the *fête* at Vaux," said Porthos, with a lugubrious expression.

"And, you complain? The king has broken a hundred hearts among the courtiers by refusing invitations. And so, my dear friend, you are really going to Vaux?"

"Indeed I am."

"You will see a magnificent sight."

"Alas! I think so."

"Everything that is grand in France will be brought together there."

"Ah!" cried Porthos, tearing out a lock of his hair in despair.

"Good heavens, are you ill?" cried D'Artagnan.

"I am as well as the Pont-Neuf. It isn't that."

"But what is it, then?"

"It's that I have no clothes."

D'Artagnan stood petrified.

"No clothes! Porthos, no clothes!" he cried, "when I see at least fifty suits on the floor."

"Fifty, truly; but not one which fits me."

"What, not one that fits you? But are you not measured, then, when you give an order?"

"To be sure he is," answered Mouston; "but, unfortunately, *I* have grown bigger!"

"What, *you* bigger?"

"So much so that I am now bigger than the baron. Would you believe it, monsieur?"

"*Parbleu!* it seems to me that is quite obvious."

"Do you see, stupid?" said Porthos, "that is quite obvious."

"Really, my dear Porthos," D'Artagnan went on, becoming slightly impatient. "I don't understand why your clothes should not fit you because Mouston has grown stouter."

"I am going to explain," said Porthos. "You remember telling me the story of the Roman general, Antony, who always had seven wild boars kept roasting, each cooked up to a different tenderness, so that he might be able to have his dinner at any time of the day he chose to ask for it. Well, I decided that, since at any time I might be invited to court to spend a week, I should have always seven suits ready for the occasion."

"Beautiful reasoning, Porthos—only a man must have a fortune like yours to gratify such whims. Without counting the time lost in being measured, the fashions are always changing."

"That is exactly the point," said Porthos. "I flatter myself that I had hit on a very ingenious device to deal with it."

"Tell me what it is; for I don't doubt your genius."

"You remember what Mouston* once was, then?"

"Yes; his name was Mousqueton."

"And you remember too, the period when he began to grow fatter?"

"No, not exactly. I beg your pardon, my good Mouston."

"You are not at fault, monsieur," said Mouston graciously. "You were in Paris, and as for us, we were in Pierrefonds."

"Anyway, my dear Porthos, there was a time when Mouston began to grow fat. Is that what you meant?"

"Yes, my friend; and I greatly rejoiced at that time."

"Indeed, I believe you did!" exclaimed D'Artagnan.

"You understand," continued Porthos, "what a world of trouble it spared me."

"No, I do not, though."

"I'll tell you, my friend. In the first place, as you have said, to be measured is a loss of time, even though it occurs only once a fortnight. And then, one may be traveling; and then you wish to have seven suits always with you. In short, I hate letting anyone measure me. Confound it! either one is a nobleman or not. To be scrutinized and scanned by a fellow who completely analyzes you, by inch and line—it's degrading! Here, they find you too hollow; there, too prominent. They see your strong and weak points. When you leave the measurer's hands, you are like those strongholds whose angles and different thicknesses have been ascertained by a spy."

"Really, my dear Porthos, you have ideas that are entirely your own."

"Ah! you see when a man is an engineer—"

"And has fortified Belle-Isle—it's natural, my friend."

"Well, I had an idea, which would doubtless have proved a good one, but for Mouston's carelessness."

D'Artagnan glanced at Mouston, who replied by a slight movement of his body, as if to say, "You will see whether I am at all to blame in all this."

"I congratulated myself, then," went on Porthos, "at seeing Mouston get fat; and I did all I could, by means

* Mousqueton (which means carabine) has changed his name to Mouston. Dumas forgets this later in the book.

of substantial feeding, to make him stout—always in the hope that he would come to equal me in girth, and could then be measured in my place."

"I see!" cried D'Artagnan. "That spared you both time and humiliation."

"Consider my joy when, after a year and a half's judicious feeding—for I used to feed him up myself—the fellow—"

"Oh! I lent a good hand myself, monsieur," said Mouston humbly.

"That's true. Consider my joy when, one morning, I noticed that Mouston was obliged to squeeze in, as I once did myself, to get through the little secret door that those architects had made in the chamber of the late Madame du Vallon, in the Château de Pierrefonds. And, by the way, about that door, my friend, I would like to ask you, who know everything, why these wretches of architects, who ought by rights to have a sure eye, came to make doorways through which nobody but thin people could pass?"

"Oh, those doors," answered D'Artagnan, "were meant for lovers, and they have generally slight and slender figures."

"Madame du Vallon had no lover!" answered Porthos majestically.

"Perfectly true, my friend," replied D'Artagnan; "but the architects were imagining the possibility of your marrying again."

"Ah! that is possible," said Porthos. "And now I have received an explanation how it is that doorways are made too narrow, let us return to the subject of Mouston's fatness. But see how the two things apply to each other. I have always noticed that ideas run parallel. And so, observe this phenomenon, D'Artagnan. I was talking to you of Mouston, who is fat, and it led us on to Madame du Vallon—"

"Who was thin?"

"Isn't it marvelous?"

"My dear friend, a scholar of my acquaintance, Monsieur Costar, has made the same observation as you have, and he calls the process by some Greek name which I forget."

"My remark is not original?" cried Porthos, astounded. "I thought I invented it."

"My friend, the fact was known before Aristotle's days—that is to say, nearly two thousand years ago."

"Well, well, it's no less true," said Porthos, delighted at the idea of having concurred with the sages of antiquity.

"Wonderful! But suppose we return to Mouston. It seems to me we have left him fattening under our very eyes."

"Yes, monsieur," said Mouston.

"Well," said Porthos, "Mouston fattened so well that he gratified all my hopes by reaching my size; a fact which I was able to convince myself of by seeing the rascal one day in a waistcoat of mine, which he had turned into a coat—a waistcoat, the mere embroidery of which was worth a hundred pistoles."

"It was only to try it on, monsieur," said Mouston.

"From that moment I decided to put Mouston in touch with my tailors, and to have him measured instead of myself."

"A splendid idea, Porthos; but Mouston is a foot and a half shorter than you."

"Exactly! They measured him down to the ground, and the tip of the suit came just below my knee."

"What a wonder you are, Porthos! Such a thing could happen only to you."

"Yes, congratulate me, and rightly so. It was exactly at that time—that is to say, nearly two and a half years ago—that I set out for Belle-Isle, instructing Mouston, in order to have at all times a sample of every fashion, to have a suit made for himself every month."

"And did Mouston neglect complying with your instructions? That would not be right, Mouston."

"No, monsieur; quite the contrary, quite the contrary!"

"No, he never forgot to have his suits made; but he forgot to inform me that he had gotten stouter!"

"But it was not my fault, monsieur. Your tailor never told me."

"And he grew to such an extent, monsieur," continued Porthos, "that in two years he has gained eighteen inches in girth, and so my last dozen suits are all too large, from a foot to a foot and a half!''

''But the rest; those which were made when you were of the same size?''

''They are no longer in fashion, my dear friend. If I put them on, I would look like a fresh arrival, from Siam, and as though I had been two years away from court.''

''I understand your difficulty. You have how many new suits—nine? thirty-six? and yet not one to wear. Well, you must have a thirty-seventh made, and give the thirty-six to Mouston.''

''Monsieur!'' said Mouston, with a gratified air. ''The truth is that monsieur has always been very generous to me.''

''Do you think that I hadn't that idea, or that I was deterred by the expense? But the *fête* is only two days away; I received the invitation yesterday, sent Mouston here with my wardrobe, and only this morning discovered my misfortune; and from now until the day after tomorrow, there isn't a single fashionable tailor who will undertake to make me a suit.''

''That is to say, one covered all over with gold, isn't it?''

''Yes, all over.''

''We shall manage it. You won't leave for three days. The invitations are for Wednesday, and this is only Sunday morning.''

''It's true; but Aramis has strongly advised me to be at Vaux twenty-four hours beforehand.''

''What, Aramis?''

''Yes, it was Aramis who brought me the invitation.''

''Good, I understand. You are invited by Monsieur Fouquet?''

''No; by the king, dear friend. The letter bears the following, as large as life: 'Monsieur le Baron du Vallon is informed that the king has deigned to place him on the invitation list . . .' ''

''Very good; but you leave with Monsieur Fouquet?''

''And when I think,'' cried Porthos, stamping on the floor, ''when I think I shall have no clothes, I am ready to burst with rage. I should like to strangle somebody or destroy something!''

''Neither strangle anybody nor destroy anything, Porthos; I will manage it all; put on one of your thirty-six suits, and come with me to a tailor."

"My agent has seen them all this morning."

"Even Monsieur Percerin?"

"Who is Monsieur Percerin?"

"Only the king's tailor."

"Oh! yes," said Porthos, who wanted to appear to know the king's tailor, but was hearing his name mentioned for the first time; "to Monsieur Percerin's. I thought he would be too busy."

"Doubtless he will be; but don't worry, Porthos; he will do for me what he won't do for another. Only you must allow yourself to be measured."

"Ah!" said Porthos, with a sigh, "it's unfortunate, but what would you have me do?"

"Do? as others do; as the king does."

"What! do they measure the king, too? Does *he* put up with it?"

"The king likes clothes, my good friend, and so do you, too, whatever you may say about it."

Porthos smiled triumphantly.

"Let us go to the king's tailor," he said; "and, since he measures the king, I think, indeed! I may well allow him to measure me."

CHAPTER III

WHO M. JEAN PERCERIN WAS

THE king's tailor, M. Jean Percerin, lived in a rather large house in the Rue St. Honoré, near the Rue de l'Arbre Sec. He was a man of great taste in elegant fabrics, embroideries, and velvet, being hereditary tailor to the king. The history of his house reached as far back as the time of Charles IX; from whose reign dated, as we know, deeds of *bravery* difficult enough to gratify. The Percerin of that period was a Huguenot, like Ambroise Paré, and had been spared by the Queen of Navarre, the beautiful Margot, as they used to write and say, too, in those days; because he was the only one who could make for her those wonderful riding habits which she loved to wear, seeing that they were marvelously well suited to hide certain anatomical defects which the Queen of Navarre used to conceal very carefully. Percerin being saved, made, out of gratitude, some beautiful black bodices, very inexpensive indeed, for Queen Catherine, who ended by being pleased at the preservation of a Huguenot, on whom she had long looked with aversion. But Percerin was a very prudent man; and having heard it said that there was no more dangerous sign for a Protestant than to be smiled upon by Catherine; and having observed that her smiles were more frequent than usual, he speedily turned Catholic with all his family; and having thus become irreproachable, attained the lofty position of master tailor to the crown of France. Under Henry III, vain king as he was, this position reached the height of one of the loftiest peaks of the Cordilleras. Now Percerin had been a clever man all his life, and by way of keeping up his reputation beyond the grave, took very good care not to make a bad death of it, and so died very skillfully, and that at the very moment he felt his powers of invention declining. He left a son and daughter, both worthy of the name they were called upon to bear; the son, a cutter as unerring and exact as the square rule; the daughter, apt at embroidery and at designing ornaments. The marriage of Henry IV and Marie de Medici, and the exquisite court mourning for the aforementioned queen, together with a few words dropped by M. de Bassompierre, king of the beaus of the period, made the fortune of the second generation of Percerins. M. Concino Concini, and his wife, Galligai, who subsequently shone at the French court, sought to Italianize the fashion, and introduced some Florentine tailors; but Percerin, touched to the quick in his patriotism and self-esteem, entirely defeated these foreigners, and that so well that Concino was the first to give up his compatriots, and held the French tailor in such esteem that he would never employ any other, and thus wore a doublet of his on the very day that Vitry blew out his brains with his pistol at the Pont du Louvre.

And this is the doublet, issuing from M. Percerin's workshop, which the Parisians rejoiced in hacking into so many pieces with the human flesh it covered. Despite

the favor Concino Concini had shown Percerin, King
Louis XIII had the generosity to bear no malice to his
tailor, and to retain him in his service. At the time that
Louis the Just was showing this great example of fair-
ness, Percerin had brought up two sons, one of whom
made his *début* at the marriage of Anne of Austria, invented that admirable Spanish costume in which Richelieu danced a saraband, made the costumes for the
tragedy of "Mirame," and stitched onto Buckingham's
mantle those famous pearls which were destined to be
scattered about the pavement of the Louvre. A man becomes easily notable who has made the clothes of M. de
Buckingham, M. de Cinq-Mars, Mlle. Ninon, M. de
Beaufort, and Marion de Lorme. And thus Percerin III
had attained the summit of his glory when his father died.
This same Percerin III, old, famous, and wealthy, yet
further dressed Louis XIV; and having no son, which
was a great cause of sorrow to him, seeing that with
himself his dynasty would end, he had brought up several
hopeful pupils. He possessed a carriage, a country house,
menservants the tallest in Paris, and, by special authority
from Louis XIV, a pack of hounds. He worked for MM.
de Lyonne and Letellier, under a sort of patronage; but
political man as he was, and versed in state secrets, he
never succeeded in fitting M. Colbert. This is beyond
explanation; it is matter for intuition.

Great geniuses of every kind live upon unseen, intan-
gible ideas; they act without themselves knowing why.
The great Percerin (for, contrary to the rule of dynasties,
it was, above all, the last of the Percerins who deserved
the name of Great), the great Percerin was inspired when
he cut a skirt for the queen, or a coat for the king; he
could invent a coat for Monsieur, the clock of a stocking
for Madame*; but in spite of his supreme talent, he could
never hit the measure of M. Colbert.

"That man," he used often to say, "is beyond my art;
my needle never can hit him off."

We need scarcely say that Percerin was M. Fouquet's
tailor, and that the surintendant held him in high esteem.
M. Percerin was nearly eighty years old, nevertheless

* Monsieur, the duke of Orléans, the king's brother. Madame, Monsieur's
wife.

still vigorous, and at the same time so dry, the courtiers used to say, that he was positively brittle. His renown and his fortune were great enough for M. le Prince, that king of fops, to take his arm when talking over the fashions; and for those least eager to pay never to dare to leave their accounts in arrears with him; for Master Percerin would make clothes upon credit once, but never a second time, unless he had been paid for the first order.

It is easy to see at once that a tailor of such standing, instead of running after customers, had difficulties about obliging any new ones. And so Percerin declined to fit *bourgeois,* or those who had but recently obtained patents of nobility. A story used to circulate that even M. de Mazarin, in exchange for Percerin supplying him with a full suit of ceremonial vestments as cardinal, one fine day slipped letters of nobility into his pocket.

It was to the house of this great lord of tailors that D'Artagnan took the despairing Porthos; who, as they were going along, said to his friend:

"Take care, my good D'Artagnan, not to compromise the dignity of a man such as I am with the arrogance of this Percerin, who will, I expect, be very impertinent; for I give you notice, my friend, that if he is not respectful I will punish him."

"Introduced by me," replied D'Artagnan, "you have nothing to fear, even if you were what you are not."

"Ah! it is because—"

"What? Do you have something against Percerin, Porthos?"

"I think that I once sent Mouston to a fellow of that name."

"And then?"

"The fellow refused to supply me."

"Oh, a misunderstanding, no doubt, which it's pressing to set right. Mouston must have made a mistake."

"Perhaps."

"He has confused the names."

"Possibly. That rascal Mouston never can remember names."

"I will take care of it."

"Very good."

"Stop the carriage, Porthos; here we are."

"Here! how here? We are at the Halles; and you told

me the house was at the corner of the Rue de l'Arbre
Sec.''

"It's true; but look."

"Well, I do look, and I see—"

"What?"

"*Pardieu!* that we are at the Halles."

"You do not, I suppose, want our horses to climb up
on the top of the carriage in front of us."

"No."

"Nor the carriage in front of us to climb on the one
in front of it. Nor that the second should be driven over
the roofs of the thirty or forty others which have arrived
before us?"

"No, you are right, indeed. So many people! And what
are they all doing?"

"It's very simple. They are waiting their turn."

"Have the actors of the Hotel de Bourgogne shifted
their quarters?"

"No; their turn to obtain an entrance to Monsieur Percerin's house."

"And we are going to wait, too?"

"Oh, we shall be more clever and less proud than
they."

"What are we to do, then?"

"Get down, go through the footmen and lackeys, and
enter the tailor's house, which I will answer for our doing, if you go first."

"Come, then," said Porthos.

They both climbed down and made their way on foot
toward the establishment. The cause of the confusion was
that M. Percerin's doors were closed, while a servant
standing before them was explaining to the illustrious
customers of the illustrious tailor that just then M. Percerin could not receive anybody. The great lackey told
some great noble whom he favored, in confidence, that
M. Percerin was working on five suits for the king, and
that, owing to the urgency of the case, he was meditating
in his office on the ornaments, colors, and cut of these
five suits. Some, contented with this reason, went away,
happy to repeat it to others; but others, more tenacious,
insisted on having the doors opened, and among these
were the last three Blue Ribbons, who intended to take
part in a ballet, which should inevitably fail unless they

had their costumes cut by the hand of the great Percerin himself. D'Artagnan, pushing on Porthos, who scattered the groups of people right and left, succeeded in reaching the counter, behind which the apprentice tailors were doing their best to answer queries. At the door they wanted to put off Porthos like the rest, but D'Artagnan showed himself, and pronounced merely these words, "The king's order," and was let in with his friend. The poor fellows had much to do, and did their best to reply to the demands of the customers in the absence of their master, leaving off drawing a stitch to turn a sentence; and when wounded pride, or disappointed expectation, brought down upon them too cutting rebukes, he who was attacked made a dive and disappeared under the counter. The line of discontented lords formed a very remarkable picture. Our captain of musketeers, a man of sure and rapid observation, took it all in at a glance; but having examined the group, his eye rested on a man in front of him. This man, seated upon a stool, scarcely showed his head above the counter which sheltered him. He was about forty years old, with a melancholy aspect, pale face, and soft, luminous eyes. He was looking at D'Artagnan and the rest, with his chin resting upon his hand, like a calm and inquiring amateur. Only on seeing, and doubtless recognizing, our captain, he pulled his hat down over his eyes. It was this action, perhaps, that attracted D'Artagnan's attention. If so, the gentleman who had pulled down his hat produced an effect entirely different from what he had desired. In other respects his clothes were plain, and his hair evenly cut enough for customers, who were not careful observers, to take him for a mere tailor's apprentice, perched behind the board, and carefully stitching cloth or velvet. Nevertheless, this man held up his head too often to be very productively employed with his fingers. D'Artagnan was not deceived—not he; and he saw at once that if this man was working at anything, it certainly was not at velvet.

"Eh!" he said, addressing this man, "and so you have become a tailor's boy, Monsieur Molière?"

"Hush, Monsieur d'Artagnan!" replied the man softly, "you will make them recognize me."

"Well, and what harm?"

"The fact is, there is no harm, but—"

"You mean there is no good in doing it either, is it not so?"

"No; for I was busy looking at some interesting faces."

"Go on, go on, Monsieur Molière. I quite understand the interest you take in it. I will not disturb your study."

"Thank you."

"But on one condition: that you tell me where Monsieur Percerin really is."

"Willingly; in his own room. Only . . ."

"Only one can't enter it?"

"Unapproachable."

"For everybody?"

"For everybody. He brought me here so that I might be at my ease to make my observations, and then he went away."

"Well, my dear Monsieur Molière, you will go and tell him I am here."

"Me!" exclaimed Molière, in the tone of a courageous dog from which you snatch the bone it has legitimately won; "I should disturb myself! Monsieur d'Artagnan, how hard you are on me . . ."

"If you don't go directly and tell Monsieur Percerin that I am here, my dear Molière," said D'Artagnan in a low tone, "I warn you of one thing; that I won't show you the friend I have brought with me."

Molière indicated Porthos by an imperceptible gesture:

"This gentleman, isn't it?"

"Yes."

Molière gave Porthos one of those looks which penetrate the minds and hearts of men. The subject doubtless appeared very promising to him, for he immediately rose and led the way into the adjoining room.

CHAPTER IV

THE SAMPLES

DURING all this time the crowd was slowly moving away, leaving at every angle of the counter either a mur-

mur or a curse, as the waves leave foam or scatter sea-
weed on the sands when they retire with the ebbing tide.
In about ten minutes Molière reappeared, making another sign to D'Artagnan from under the drapery. The
latter hurried after him, with Porthos in the rear, and
after threading a labyrinth of corridors, Molière led him
to M. Percerin's room. The old man, with his sleeves
rolled up, was gathering up in folds a piece of gold-
flowered brocade, so as to exhibit better its luster. Seeing
D'Artagnan, he put the silk aside and came to meet him,
by no means radiant with joy, and by no means courteous, but, on the whole, in a tolerably civil manner.

"The captain of the musketeers will excuse me, I am
sure, for I am busy."

"Yes, on the king's costumes; I know that, my dear
Monsieur Percerin. You are making three, they tell me."

"Five, my dear monsieur, five."

"Three or five, it's all the same to me, my dear monsieur; and I know that you will make them most exquisitely."

"Yes, I know. Once made, they will be the most
beautiful in the world, I do not deny it; but that they may
be the most beautiful in the world, they must first be
made; and to do this, captain, I need time."

"There are two days yet; it's much more than you need,
Monsieur Percerin," said D'Artagnan in the coolest possible manner.

Percerin raised his head with the air of a man little
accustomed to being contradicted, even in his whims; but
D'Artagnan did not pay the least attention to the airs
which the illustrious tailor began to assume.

"My dear Monsieur Percerin," he continued, "I am
bringing you a customer."

"Ah!" exclaimed Percerin crossly.

"Monsieur le Baron du Vallon de Bracieux de Pierrefonds," continued D'Artagnan.

Percerin attempted to bow, which found no favor in
the eyes of the terrible Porthos, who, from his first entry
into the room, had been looking at the tailor crossly.

"A very good friend of mine," concluded D'Artagnan.

"I will take care of monsieur," said Percerin, "but
later."

"Later? But when?"

"When I have time."

"You have already told my valet as much," broke in Porthos discontentedly.

"Very likely," said Percerin; "I am nearly always pressed for time."

"My friend," returned Porthos sententiously, "there is always time when one chooses to find it."

Percerin turned crimson; a very ominous sign indeed in old men white with age.

"Monsieur is very free to shop elsewhere."

"Come, come, Percerin," interposed D'Artagnan, "you are not in a good mood today. I will say one more word to you and it will bring you on your knees; monsieur is not only a friend of mine, but more, a friend of Monsieur Fouquet."

"Ah!" exclaimed the tailor, "that is another thing."

Then, turning to Porthos, "Is Monsieur le Baron attached to the surintendant?" he inquired.

"I am attached to myself," shouted Porthos, at the very moment that the curtain was raised to introduce a new speaker in the dialogue. Molière was all observation, D'Artagnan laughed, Porthos swore.

"My dear Percerin," said D'Artagnan, "you will make a suit for the baron. It is I who ask you."

"To you I will not say no, captain."

"But that is not all; you will make it for him at once."

"It's impossible before eight days."

"That, then, is as much as to refuse, because the dress is wanted for the *fête* at Vaux."

"I repeat that it is impossible," said the obstinate old man.

"By no means, dear Monsieur Percerin; above all, if *I* ask you," said a mild voice at the door, a silvery voice which made D'Artagnan prick up his ears. It was the voice of Aramis.

"Monsieur d'Herblay!" cried the tailor.

"Aramis!" whispered D'Artagnan.

"Ah, poor bishop!" said Porthos.

"Good morning, D'Artagnan; good morning, Porthos; good morning, my dear friends," said Aramis. "Come, come, Monsieur Percerin, make the baron's suit; and I will answer for it you will gratify Monsieur Fouquet.'' And he accompanied the words with a sign, which seemed to say, ''Agree, and dismiss them.''

It appeared that Aramis had an influence over Master Percerin that was superior even to D'Artagnan's, for the tailor bowed in assent, and turned to Porthos:

''Go and get measured on the other side,'' he said rudely.

Porthos colored in a formidable manner. D'Artagnan saw the storm coming, and, addressing Molière, said to him, in an undertone:

''You see before you, my dear monsieur, a man who considers himself disgraced if you measure the flesh and bones that Heaven has given him; study his type for me, Master Aristophanes, and profit by it.''

Molière had no need of encouragement, and his gaze dwelt upon the Baron Porthos.

''Monsieur,'' he said, ''if you will come with me, I will make them take your measure without the measure touching you.''

''How do you make that out, my friend?'' said Porthos.

''I say that they will apply neither line nor rule to the seams of your suit. It is a new method we have invented for measuring people of quality, who are too sensitive to allow low-born fellows to touch them. We know some susceptible persons who will not put up with being measured, a process which, in my opinion, wounds the natural dignity of man; and if by chance monsieur should be one of these . . .''

''*Corbœuf!* I believe I am, too.''

''Well, that is a wonderful coincidence, and you will have the benefit of our invention.''

''But how in the world can it be done?'' asked Porthos, delighted.

''Monsieur,'' said Molière, bowing, ''if you will deign to follow me, you will see.''

Aramis observed this scene with all his eyes. Perhaps he imagined, from D'Artagnan's liveliness, that he would leave with Porthos, so as not to lose the conclusion of a scene so well begun. But, clear-sighted as he was, Aramis was mistaken. Porthos and Molière left together, alone. D'Artagnan remained with Percerin. Why? From curiosity, doubtless; probably to enjoy a little longer the society of his good friend, Aramis. As Molière and Porthos disappeared, D'Artagnan drew near the bishop of Vannes, a proceeding which appeared to annoy this one particularly.

"A suit for you, also, is it not, my friend?"

Aramis smiled.

"No," he said.

"You will go to Vaux, however?"

"I shall go, but without a new suit. You forget, dear D'Artagnan, that a poor bishop of Vannes is not rich enough to have new outfits for every *fête.*"

"Bah!" said the musketeer, laughing, "and do we no longer write poems now, either?"

"Oh, D'Artagnan!" exclaimed Aramis, "I have long given over all these follies."

"True," repeated D'Artagnan, only half-convinced.

As for Percerin, he had relapsed into his contemplation of the brocades.

"Don't you notice," said Aramis, smiling, "that we are greatly boring this good gentleman, my dear D'Artagnan?"

"Ah!" whispered the musketeer; "that is, I am boring you, my friend." Then, aloud, "Well, then, let us leave; I have no further business here, and if you are as free as I, Aramis—"

"No, not I—I wanted—"

"Ah! you had something particular to say to Monsieur Percerin? Why did you not tell me so at once?"

"Something particular, certainly," repeated Aramis; "but not for you, D'Artagnan. But, at the same time, I hope you will believe that I can never have anything so particular to say that a friend like you may not hear it."

"Oh, no, no! I am going," said D'Artagnan, imparting to his voice an evident tone of curiosity; for Aramis's annoyance, well concealed as it was, had not at all escaped him; and he knew that, in that impenetrable mind, everything, even the most apparently trivial, was designed to some end; an unknown one, but one which, from the knowledge he had of his friend's character, the musketeer felt must be important.

As for Aramis, he saw that D'Artagnan was not without suspicion, and pressed him.

"Stay, by all means," he said; "this is what it is." Then,

turning toward the tailor: "My dear Percerin," he said; "I am even very happy that you are here, D'Artagnan."

"Oh, indeed!" exclaimed the Gascon, for the third time, even less deceived this time than before.

Percerin never moved. Aramis roused him violently by snatching from his hands the fabric upon which he was engaged.

"My dear Percerin," he said, "I have, near at hand, Monsieur Le Brun, one of Monsieur Fouquet's painters."

"Ah, very good," thought D'Artagnan; "but why Le Brun?"

Aramis looked at D'Artagnan, who seemed to be occupied with an engraving of Mark Antony.

"And you wish to have a suit similar to those of the Epicureans made for him?" answered Percerin.

And while saying this, in an absent manner, the worthy tailor was trying to recapture his piece of brocade.

"An Epicurean's suit?" asked D'Artagnan, in a tone of inquiry.

"I see," said Aramis, with a most engaging smile; "it is written that our dear D'Artagnan shall know all our secrets this evening. Yes, friend, you have surely heard of Monsieur Fouquet's Epicureans, have you not?"

"Undoubtedly. Is it not a kind of poets society, of which La Fontaine, Loret, Pélisson, and Molière are members, and which holds its meetings at St. Mandé?"

"Exactly so. Well, we are going to put our poets in uniform, and enroll them in a regiment for the king."

"Oh, very well; I understand. A surprise of Monsieur Fouquet for the king. Do not worry; if that is the secret about Monsieur Le Brun, I will not mention it."

"Always agreeable, my friend. No, Monsieur Le Brun has nothing to do with this part of it; the secret which concerns him is far more important than the other."

"Then, if it is so important as all that, I prefer not to know it," said D'Artagnan, making a move to leave.

"Come in, Monsieur Le Brun, come in," said Aramis, opening a side door with his right hand, and holding back D'Artagnan with his left.

"Really, I, too, am quite in the dark," said Percerin.

"My dear Monsieur Percerin," Aramis continued, "you are making five suits for the king, are you not? One in brocade, one in hunting cloth, one in velvet, one in satin, and one in Florentine stuffs?"

"Yes; but how do you know all that, monseigneur?" said Percerin, astounded.

"It is all very simple, my dear monsieur. There will be a hunt, a banquet, a concert, a walk, and a reception; these five kinds of dress are required by etiquette."

"You know everything, monseigneur."

"And a great many more things, too," murmured D'Artagnan.

"But," cried the tailor, in triumph, "what you do not know, monseigneur—prince of the church though you are—what nobody will know—what only the king, Mademoiselle de la Vallière, and myself do know, is the color of the materials and nature of the ornaments, and the cut, the *ensemble,* the finish of it all."

"Well," said Aramis, "that is precisely what I have come to ask you, dear Percerin."

"Ah, bah!" exclaimed the tailor, terrified, though Aramis had pronounced these words in his sweetest and most honeyed voice. The request appeared, on reflection, so exaggerated, so ridiculous, so monstrous to M. Percerin that first he laughed to himself, then aloud, and finished with a shout. D'Artagnan followed his example, not because he found the matter so very funny, but in order not to allow Aramis to cool.

"At the outset I appear to be asking an absurd question, do I not?" said Aramis. "But D'Artagnan, who is incarnate wisdom itself, will tell you that I could not do otherwise than ask you this."

"Let us see," said the attentive musketeer, perceiving, with his wonderful instinct, that they had only been skirmishing till now, and that the hour of battle was approaching.

"Let us see," said Percerin incredulously.

"Why," continued Aramis, "is Monsieur Fouquet giving the king a *fête?* Is it not to please him?"

"Surely," said Percerin.

D'Artagnan nodded assent.

"By delicate attentions? by some happy device? by a succession of surprises, like the one we were talking about—the enrollment of our Epicureans."

"Admirable."

"Well, then, this is the surprise we intend. Monsieur Le Brun here is a man who draws most precisely."

"Yes," said Percerin; "I have seen his pictures, and observed that the suits were very carefully made. That is why I at once agreed to make him an outfit—whether to match with those of the Epicureans, or an original one."

"My dear monsieur, we accept your offer, and shall presently avail ourselves of it; but just now, Monsieur Le Brun doesn't need the clothes you will make for him, but those you are making for the king."

Percerin jumped backward, which D'Artagnan—calmest and most appreciative of men—did not consider overdone; the proposal which Aramis had just put forth contained so many strange and startling aspects.

"The king's clothes! Give the king's clothes to any mortal whatever! Oh! for once, monseigneur, your grace is mad!" cried the poor tailor, exasperated.

"Help me now, D'Artagnan," said Aramis, more and more calm and smiling. "Help me now to persuade monsieur, for *you* understand, do you not?"

"Eh, er! not exactly, I declare."

"What! you do not understand that Monsieur Fouquet wishes to give the king the surprise of finding his portrait on his arrival at Vaux; and that the portrait, which will be a striking resemblance, ought to be dressed exactly as the king will be on the day it is shown?"

"Oh! yes, yes," said the musketeer, nearly convinced, so plausible was this reasoning. "Yes, my dear Aramis, you are right; it is a happy idea. I will bet it is one of your own, Aramis."

"Well, I don't know," replied the bishop; "either mine or Monsieur Fouquet's." Then, searching Percerin's face after noticing D'Artagnan's hesitation, "Well, Monsieur Percerin," he asked, "what do you say to this?"

"I say that—"

"That you are, of course, free to refuse. I know it well, and I by no means count upon forcing you, my dear monsieur. I will say more, I even understand all the delicacy you feel in taking up with Monsieur Fouquet's idea; you dread appearing to flatter the king. A noble spirit, Monsieur Percerin, a noble spirit."

The tailor stammered.

"It would, indeed, be a very pretty compliment to pay

the young prince," continued Aramis; "but as the surintendant told me, 'If Percerin refuses, tell him that it will not at all lower him in my opinion, and I shall always esteem him, only . . .' "

" 'Only'?" repeated Percerin, rather troubled.

" 'Only,' " continued Aramis, "I shall be compelled to say to the king'—you understand, my dear Monsieur Percerin, that these are Monsieur Fouquet's words—'I shall be constrained to say to the king, Sire, I had intended to present your majesty with your portrait, but owing to a feeling of delicacy, slightly exaggerated perhaps, although creditable, Monsieur Percerin opposed the project.' "

"Opposed!" cried the tailor, terrified at the responsibility which would weigh upon him; "I oppose the desire, the will of Monsieur Fouquet when he is seeking to please the king! Oh, what a hateful word you have uttered, monseigneur. Oppose! Oh, it's not I who said it, Heaven have mercy on me. I call the captain of the musketeers to witness it. Is it not true, Monsieur d'Artagnan, that I have opposed nothing?"

D'Artagnan nodded, indicating that he wished to remain neutral. He felt that there was an intrigue at the bottom of it, whether comedy or tragedy; he was at his wits' end at not being able to guess it, but in the meanwhile wished to keep clear.

But already Percerin, goaded by the idea that the king would be told he stood in the way of a pleasant surprise, had offered Le Brun a chair, and proceeded to bring from a wardrobe four magnificent suits, the fifth being still in the workmen's hands; and these masterpieces he successively fitted upon four dummies, which, imported into France in the time of Concini, had been given to Percerin II by Marshal d'Onoro, after the discomfiture of the Italian tailors, ruined in their competition. The painter set to work to draw and then to paint the suits. But Aramis, who was closely watching all the phases of his toil, suddenly stopped him.

"I think you have not quite got it, my dear Le Brun," he said; "your colors will deceive you, and on canvas we shall lack that exact resemblance which is absolutely requisite. Time is necessary for attentively observing the finer shades."

"Quite true," said Percerin, "but time is wanting, and about it, you will agree with me, monseigneur, I can do nothing."

"Then the affair will fail," said Aramis quietly, "and that because of a lack of precision in the colors."

Nevertheless, Le Brun went on copying the materials and ornaments with the closest fidelity, a process which Aramis watched with ill-concealed impatience.

"What in the world, now, is the meaning of this imbroglio?" the musketeer kept saying to himself.

"That will certainly never do," said Aramis. "Monsieur Le Brun, close your box, and roll up your canvas."

"But, monsieur," cried the vexed painter, "the light is abominable here."

"An idea, Monsieur Le Brun, an idea! If we had a sample of the materials, for example, and with time, and better light . . ."

"Oh, then," cried Le Brun, "I would answer for the effect."

"Good," said D'Artagnan, "this ought to be the knotty point of the whole thing; they want a pattern of each of the materials. *Mordioux!* will this Percerin give us some?"

Percerin, beaten in his last retreat, and duped, moreover, by the feigned good nature of Aramis, cut out five samples and handed them to the bishop of Vannes.

"I like this better. That is your opinion, isn't it?" said Aramis to D'Artagnan.

"My dear Aramis," said D'Artagnan, "my opinion is that you are always the same."

"And, consequently, always your friend," said the bishop, in a charming tone.

"Yes," said D'Artagnan aloud; then, in a low voice, "If I am your dupe, double Jesuit that you are, I will not be your accomplice; and to prevent it, it's time I left this place."

"Adieu, Aramis," he added aloud, "adieu; I am going to join Porthos."

"Then wait for me," said Aramis, pocketing the samples, "for I am done, and shall not be sorry to say a parting word to our friend."

Le Brun packed up, Percerin put the suits back into the closet, Aramis put his hand on his pocket to make sure the samples were secure—and they all left the study.

CHAPTER V

WHERE, PROBABLY, MOLIÈRE FORMED HIS
FIRST IDEA OF THE BOURGEOIS GENTILHOMME

D'ARTAGNAN found Porthos in the adjoining room;
but no longer an irritated Porthos, or a disappointed Porthos, but Porthos radiant, blooming, fascinating, and
chatting with Molière, who was looking at him adoringly
and as a man would who had not only never seen anything better, but had never seen anything as good. Aramis went straight up to Porthos and offered him his
delicate white hand, which lost itself in the gigantic hand
of his old friend—a gesture which Aramis never attempted without a certain uneasiness. But the friendly
pressure having been performed not too painfully for him,
the bishop of Vannes turned to Molière.

"Well, monsieur," he said, "will you come with me
to St. Mandé?"

"I will go anywhere you like, monseigneur," answered Molière.

"To St. Mandé!" cried Porthos, surprised at seeing
the proud bishop of Vannes fraternizing with an apprentice tailor. "What, Aramis, are you going to take this
gentleman to St. Mandé?"

"Yes," said Aramis, smiling, "our work is pressing."

"And, besides, my dear Porthos," continued D'Artagnan, "Monsieur Molière is not altogether what he
seems."

"In what way?" asked Porthos.

"Why, this gentleman is one of Monsieur Percerin's
chief clerks, and is expected at St. Mandé to try on the
clothes which Monsieur Fouquet has ordered for the
Epicureans."

"It's precisely so," said Molière.

"Yes, monsieur."

"Come, then, my dear Monsieur Molière," said Aramis, "that is, if you are done with Monsieur du Vallon?"

"We are done," replied Porthos.

"And are you satisfied?" asked D'Artagnan.

"Completely so," replied Porthos.

Molière took his leave of Porthos with much ceremony, and grasped the hand which the captain of the musketeers furtively offered him.

"Pray, monsieur," concluded Porthos mincingly, "above all, be punctual."

"You will have your suit after tomorrow, Monsieur le Baron," answered Molière.

And he left with Aramis.

Then D'Artagnan took Porthos's arm:

"What has this tailor done for you, my dear Porthos," he asked, "that you are so pleased with him?"

"What has he done for me, my friend—done for me?" cried Porthos enthusiastically.

"Yes, I ask you, what has he done for you?"

"My friend, he has done what no tailor ever yet accomplished; he has taken my measure without touching me."

"Tell me how he did it."

"First, then, they went, I don't know where, for a number of dummies, of all heights and sizes, hoping there would be one to suit mine, but the largest—that of the drum major of the Swiss Guard—was two inches too short, and half a foot too slender."

"Indeed!"

"It is exactly as I tell you, D'Artagnan; but he is a great man, or at the very least, a great tailor, is this Monsieur Molière. He was not at all puzzled by the circumstance."

"What did he do, then?"

"It is a very simple matter. Indeed, how can people be so stupid as not to have discovered this method from the start. What annoyance and humiliation they would have spared me."

"Not to speak of the suits, my dear Porthos."

"Yes, thirty suits."

"Well, my dear Porthos, come, tell me Monsieur Molière's plan."

"Molière? You call him so, do you? I shall make a point of remembering his name."

"Yes; or Poquelin, if you prefer that."

"No; I like Molière best. When I want to remember his name I shall think of Volière (an aviary); and as I have one at Pierrefonds—"

"Splendid," returned D'Artagnan. "And Monsieur Molière's plan?"

"This is it: Instead of pulling me to pieces, as all these rascals do—of making me bend in my back, and double my joints—all of them low and dishonorable practices . . ."

D'Artagnan nodded approvingly.

" 'Monsieur,' he said to me," continued Porthos, " 'a gentleman ought to measure himself. Do me the pleasure to come near this mirror,' and I came near the mirror. I must say, I did not exactly understand what this good Monsieur Volière wanted with me."

"Molière."

"Ah, yes, Molière—Molière. And as the fear of being measured still possessed me, 'Take care,' I said to him, 'what you are going to do with me; I am very ticklish, I warn you.' But he, with his soft voice (for he is a courteous fellow, we must admit, my friend), he, with his soft voice, 'Monsieur,' he said, 'that your suit may fit you well, it must be made according to your figure. Your figure is exactly reflected in this mirror. We shall take the measure of this reflection.' "

"In fact," said D'Artagnan, "you saw yourself in the mirror. But where did they find one in which you could see your whole figure?"

"My good friend, it is the very mirror in which the king sees himself."

"Yes; but the king is a foot and a half shorter than you are."

"Well, I don't know how that may be; it would no doubt be a way of flattering the king; but the mirror was too large for me. It's true that its height was made up of three Venetian plates of glass, placed one above another, and its breadth of three similar pieces in juxtaposition."

"Porthos, what an excellent vocabulary you have. Where in the world did you learn it?"

"At Belle-Isle. Aramis explained these things to the architect."

"Very good. Let us return to the mirror, my friend."

"Then, this good Monsieur Volière—"

"Molière."

"Yes, Molière—you are right. You will see, now, my dear friend, that I shall remember his name too well. This excellent Monsieur Molière set to work tracing out lines on the mirror, with a piece of Spanish chalk, following in all the make of my arms and my shoulders, all the while expounding this maxim, which I thought admirable: 'A suit must not constrain its wearer.'"

"In fact," said D'Artagnan, "that is an excellent maxim, which is, unfortunately, seldom carried out in practice."

"That is why I found it all the more astonishing, when he elaborated on it."

"Did he elaborate?"

"Parbleu!"

"Let me hear his theory."

"'Seeing that,' he continued, 'one may, in awkward circumstances, or in a troublesome position, have one's coat on one's shoulder, and not desire to take one's coat off—'"

"True," said D'Artagnan.

"'And so,' continued Monsieur Volière—"

"Molière."

"Molière, yes. 'And so,' went on Monsieur Molière, 'you want to draw your sword, monsieur, and you have your coat on your back. What do you do?'

"'I take it off,' I answered.

"'Well, no,' he replied.

"'How, no?'

"'I say that the suit should be so well made that it can in no way constrain you, even in drawing your sword.'

"'Ah! ah!'

"'Throw yourself on guard,' he pursued.

"I did it with such wondrous firmness that two panes of glass burst out of the window.

"'It's nothing, nothing,' he said. 'Keep your position.'

"I raised my left arm in the air, the forearm gracefully bent, the ruffle drooping, and my wrist curved, while my right arm, half-extended, securely covered my waist with the elbow and my chest with the wrist."

"Yes," said D'Artagnan; "it's the true guard—the academic guard."

"You have said the very word, dear friend. Meanwhile, Volière—"

"Molière."

"Hold! I should certainly, after all, prefer to call him—what did you say his other name was?"

"Poquelin."

"I prefer to call him Poquelin."

"And how will you remember this name better than the other?"

"You understand, he calls himself Poquelin, doesn't he?"

"Yes."

"I shall remember Madame Coquenard."*

"Good."

"I shall change *Coc* into *Poc, nard* into *lin;* and instead of Coquenard I shall have Poquelin."

"It's wonderful!" cried D'Artagnan, astounded. "Go on, my friend; I am listening to you with admiration."

"This Coquelin sketched my arm on the mirror."

"I beg your pardon—Poquelin."

"What did I say, then?"

"You said Coquelin."

"Ah! true. This Poquelin, then, sketched my arm on the mirror; but he took his time over it; he kept looking at me a good deal. The fact is, that I was very handsome.

" 'Is it tiring?' he asked.

" 'A little,' I replied, bending my knees, 'but I could yet hold out an hour.'

" 'No, I will not allow it; we have here willing young men who will support your arms, as of old, when men used to support those of the prophet.'

" 'Very good,' I answered.

" 'That will not be humiliating to you?'

" 'My friend,' I said, 'there is, I think, a great difference between being supported and being measured.' "

"The distinction is clear," interrupted D'Artagnan.

"Then," continued Porthos, "he nodded; two lads approached; one supported my left arm, while the other, with infinite skill, supported my right."

* The late wife of Porthos.

" 'Another, my man,' he cried. A third approached. 'Support monsieur by the waist,' he said. The *garçon* complied."

"So that you were at rest?" asked D'Artagnan.

"Perfectly; and Pocquenard drew me on the mirror."

"Poquelin, my friend."

"Poquelin—you are right. Well, I definitely prefer calling him Volière."

"Yes; and then it was over, wasn't it?"

"During that time Volière drew me on the mirror."

"It was very discreet."

"I much like the plan; it is respectful, and keeps everyone in his place."

"And there it ended?"

"Without a soul having touched me, my friend."

"Except the three *garçons* who supported you."

"Yes, but I have, I think, already explained to you the difference there is between supporting and measuring."

"It's true," answered D'Artagnan, who said afterward, to himself, "If I am not mistaken, I have been the means of a windfall to that rascal Molière, and surely we shall see the scene come to life in some comedy or other."

Porthos smiled.

"What are you laughing at?" asked D'Artagnan.

"Must I tell? Well, I was laughing over my good fortune."

"Oh, that is true; I don't know a happier man than you. But what is this last piece of luck that has befallen you?"

"Well, my dear fellow, congratulate me."

"Gladly."

"It seems that I am the first who has had his measurements taken in this manner."

"Are you sure of it?"

"Nearly so. Certain signs of intelligence which passed between Volière and the other boys let me know the fact."

"Well, my friend, that does not surprise me from Molière," said D'Artagnan.

"Volière, my friend."

"Oh, no, no, indeed! I am very willing to let you say Volière; but myself, I shall continue to say Molière. As

I was saying, this does not surprise me, coming from
Molière, who is a very ingenious fellow, and who you
inspired with this grand idea.''

"It will be of great use to him later on, I am sure.''

"It will be of use to him, indeed! I believe it will, and
not just a little; for, you see, my friend Molière is of all
known tailors the man who best clothes our barons,
counts, and marquesses—according to their measure.''

On this observation, neither the application nor depth
of which shall we discuss, D'Artagnan and Porthos left
M. Percerin's house and went back to their carriage,
where we will leave them, in order to look after Molière
and Aramis at St. Mandé.

CHAPTER VI

THE BEEHIVE, THE BEES, AND THE HONEY

THE bishop of Vannes, much annoyed at having met
D'Artagnan at M. Percerin's, returned to St. Mandé in a
very bad humor. Molière, on the other hand, quite delighted at having made such a wonderful rough sketch,
and at knowing where to find the original again, whenever he should desire to convert his sketch into a picture,
arrived in the merriest of moods. All the first floor of the
left wing was occupied by the most celebrated Epicureans
in Paris, and those on the freest footing in the house—
everyone in his compartment, like the bees in their cells,
employed in producing the honey intended for that royal
cake which M. Fouquet proposed to offer His Majesty
Louis XIV during the *fête* at Vaux. Pélisson, his head
leaning on his hand, was engaged in drawing out the plan
of the prologue to the ''Fâcheux,''* a comedy in three
acts which was to be put on the stage by Poquelin de
Molière, as D'Artagnan called him, or Coquelin de Volière, as Porthos called him. Loret, with all the charming
innocence of a journalist—the journalists of all ages have
always been so artless!—Loret was composing an ac-

* "Les Fâcheux," play ballet of Molière, commissioned for the fête of Vaux.

count of the *fêtes* of Vaux, before those *fêtes* had taken place. La Fontaine was wandering about from one to the other, a wandering, absent, boring, unbearable shade, who kept buzzing and humming at everybody's shoulder a thousand poetic abstractions. He disturbed Pélisson so often that the latter, raising his head crossly, said:

"At least, La Fontaine, give me a rhyme, since you have the run of the gardens at Parnassus."

"What rhyme do you want?" asked the *Fablier,* as Mme. de Sévigné used to call him.

"I want a rhyme to *lumière.*"

"*Ornière,*" answered La Fontaine.

"Ah! but, my good friend, one cannot talk of *ruts* when celebrating the delights of Vaux," said Loret.

"Besides, it doesn't rhyme," answered Pélisson.

"How! doesn't rhyme?" cried La Fontaine, in surprise.

"Yes; you have an abominable habit, my friend, a habit which will ever prevent your becoming a poet of the first order. You rhyme in a slovenly manner."

"You think so, do you, Pélisson?"

"Yes, I do, indeed. Remember that a rhyme is never good so long as one can find a better."

"Then I will never write anything again but in prose," said La Fontaine, who had taken up Pélisson's reproach in earnest. "I often suspected I was nothing but a rascally poet. Yes, it is the very truth."

"Do not say so; your remark is too sweeping, and there is much that is good in your 'Fables.' "

"And to begin," continued La Fontaine, following up his idea, "I will go and burn a hundred lines I have just written."

"Where are your lines?"

"In my head."

"Well, if they are in your head you cannot burn them."

"True," said La Fontaine; "but if I do not burn them—"

"Well, what will happen if you do not burn them?"

"They will remain in my mind, and I shall never forget them."

"Darn!" cried Loret; "that's dangerous. One would go mad with it!"

"Darn!" repeated La Fontaine; "what can I do?"

"I have discovered the way," said Molière, who had entered just at this stage of the conversation.

"What way?"

"Write them first, and burn them afterward."

"How simple it is! Well, I should never have discovered that. What a mind that devil Molière has!" said La Fontaine. Then, striking his forehead, "You will never be but an ass, Jean de La Fontaine!" he added.

"*What* are you saying, my friend?" broke in Molière, approaching the poet.

"I say I shall never be but an ass," answered La Fontaine, with a heavy sigh and swimming eyes. "Yes, my friend," he added, with increasing grief, "it seems that I rhyme in a slovenly manner."

"Oh, it's wrong to say so."

"No, I am a poor creature!"

"Who said so?"

"*Parbleu!* it was Pélisson; right, Pélisson?"

Pélisson, again lost in his work, took good care not to answer.

"But if Pélisson said you were so," cried Molière, "Pélisson has seriously offended you."

"Do you think so?"

"I advise you, as you are a gentleman, not to leave an insult like that unpunished."

"How?" exclaimed La Fontaine.

"Did you ever fight?"

"Only once, with a lieutenant in the light horses."

"What wrong had he done you?"

"It seems he had seduced my wife."

"Ah!" said Molière, becoming slightly pale; but, as at La Fontaine's declaration the others had turned around, Molière kept upon his lips the mocking smile which had so nearly died away, and continuing to make La Fontaine speak, "and what was the result of the duel?"

"The result was, that on the ground my opponent disarmed me, and then made an apology, promising never again to set foot in my house."

"And you were satisfied?" said Molière.

"Not at all; on the contrary, I picked up my sword. 'I beg your pardon, monsieur,' I said. 'I have not fought you because you were my wife's lover, but because I was told I ought to fight. So, as I have never known any peace except since you made her acquaintance, do me the pleasure to continue your visits as before, or, *morbleu!* let us set to again.' And so," continued La Fontaine, "he was compelled to remain my wife's lover, and I continue to be the happiest of husbands."

All burst out laughing. Molière alone passed his hand across his eyes. Why? Perhaps to wipe away a tear, perhaps to smother a sigh. We know that Molière was a moralist, but he was not a philosopher.

"It's all the same," he said, returning to the topic of the conversation, "Pélisson has insulted you."

"Ah, truly; I had already forgotten it."

"And I am going to challenge him on your behalf."

"Well, you can do so, if you think it indispensable."

"I do think it indispensable, and I am going to—"

"Wait!" exclaimed La Fontaine. "I want your advice."

"Upon what? this insult?"

"No; tell me really, now, whether *lumière* does not rhyme with *ornière.*"

"I would make them rhyme! I knew you would—and I have made a hundred thousand such rhymes in my time."

"A hundred thousand!" cried La Fontaine, "four times as many as La Pucelle, which Monsieur Chaplain is meditating. Is it also on this subject that you have composed a hundred thousand lines?"

"Listen to me, you eternally absent-minded creature," said Molière.

"It is certain," continued La Fontaine, "that *légume*, for instance, rhymes with *posthume.*"

"In the plural, above all."

"Yes, above all, in the plural, seeing that then it rhymes not with three letters, but with four, as *ornière* does with *lumière.*"

"Put *ornières* and *lumières* in the plural, my dear Pélisson," said La Fontaine, clapping his hand on the shoulder of his friend, whose insult he had quite forgotten, "and they will rhyme."

"Hem!" cried Pélisson.

"Molière says so, and Molière is a judge of it; he declares he has himself made a hundred thousand lines."

"Come," said Molière, laughing, "he is off now."

"It is like *rivage*, which rhymes admirably with *herbage*, I would swear on it."

"But—" said Molière. . . .

"I tell you all this," continued La Fontaine, "because you are preparing a *divertissement* for Vaux, aren't you?"

"Yes, the 'Fâcheux.' "

"Ah, yes, the 'Fâcheux'; yes, I remember. Well, I was thinking a prologue would admirably suit your *divertissement*."

"Doubtless it would suit perfectly."

"Do you agree with me?"

"So much so that I have asked you to write this prologue."

"You asked *me* to write it?"

"Yes, you, and on your refusal begged you to ask Pélisson, who is working on it at this moment."

"That is what Pélisson is doing, then? My dear Molière, you might indeed often be right."

"When?"

"When you call me absent-minded. It is a wretched defect; I will cure myself of it, and do your prologue for you."

"But seeing that Pélisson is writing it . . . "

"True, double rascal that I am! Loret was indeed right in saying I was a poor creature."

"It was not Loret who said so, my friend."

"Well, then, whoever said so, it's the same to me. And so your *divertissement* is called the 'Fâcheux'? Well, can you not make *heureux* rhyme with *fâcheux?*"

"If obliged, yes."

"And even with *capricieux.*"

"Oh, no, no!"

"It would be risky, and yet why so?"

"There is too great a difference in the cadences."

"I was fancying," said La Fontaine, leaving Molière for Loret, "I was fancying. . ."

"What were you fancying?" said Loret, in the middle of a sentence. "Hurry."

"You are writing the prologue to the 'Fâcheux,' are you not?"

"No! *mordieu!* it is Pélisson."

"Ah, Pélisson," cried La Fontaine, going over to him.

"I was fancying," he continued, "that the nymph of Vaux—"

"Beautiful!" cried Loret. "The nymph of Vaux! thank you, La Fontaine; you have just given me the two concluding lines of my paper."

"Well, if you can rhyme so well, La Fontaine," said Pélisson, "tell me now in what way you would begin my prologue?"

"I should say, for instance, 'Oh! nymph, who . . .' After 'who' I should place a verb in the second person singular of the present indicative; and should go on thus: 'this grot profound.' "

"But the verb, the verb," asked Pélisson.

"To admire the greatest king of all kings around," continued La Fontaine.

"But the verb, the verb," obstinately insisted Pélisson. "This second person singular of the present indicative?"

"Well, then, 'quittest':

"O, nymph, who quittest now this grot profound,
To admire the greatest king of all kings around"

"You would put 'who quittest,' would you?"

"Why not?"

" 'Gentlest,' after 'you who'?"

"My dear fellow," exclaimed La Fontaine, "you are a shocking pedant!"

"Without counting," said Molière, "that the second line, 'king of all kings around,' is very weak, my dear La Fontaine."

"Then you see clearly I am nothing but a poor creature—a shuffler, as you said."

"I never said so."

"Then, as Loret said."

"And it was not Loret, either; it was Pélisson."

"Well, Pélisson was right a hundred times over. But what annoys me more than anything, my dear Molière, is that I fear we shall not have our Epicurean suits."

"You expected yours, then, for the *fête?*"

"Yes, for the *fête,* and then for after the *fête.* My housekeeper told me that my own is rather faded."

"Diable! your housekeeper is right; rather more than faded."

"You see," La Fontaine went on, "the fact is, I left it on the floor in my room, and my cat—"

"Well, your cat—"

"My cat had her kittens on it, which has rather altered its color."

Molière burst out laughing; Pélisson and Loret followed his example. At this point the bishop of Vannes appeared, with a roll of plans and parchments under his arm. As if the angel of death had chilled all happy and sprightly fancies—as if that wan form had scared away the Graces to whom Xenocrates sacrificed—silence immediately reigned through the study, and everyone resumed his self-possession and his pen. Aramis distributed the invitations, and thanked them in the name of M. Fouquet.

"The surintendant," he said, "being kept to his room by business, could not come and see them, but begged them to send him some of the fruits of their day's work, to enable him to forget the fatigue of his labor in the night."

At these words all settled to work. La Fontaine placed himself at a table, and set his rapid pen running over the vellum; Pélisson made a fair copy of his prologue; Molière gave fifty fresh lines, with which his visit to Percerin had inspired him; Loret, his article on the marvelous *fêtes* he predicted; and Aramis, laden with his booty like the king of the bees, that great black drone, decked with purple and gold, reentered his apartment, silent and busy. "Remember gentlemen," he said before departing, "we all leave tomorrow evening."

"In that case I must give notice at home," said Molière.

"Yes; poor Molière!" said Loret, smiling, "he loves his home."

" *'He* loves,' yes," replied Molière, with his sad, sweet smile. " 'He loves,' that does not mean they love *him."*

"As for me," said La Fontaine, "they love me at Château Thierry, I am very sure."

Aramis reentered the room, after a brief disappearance.

"Will anyone go with me?" he asked. "I am going to Paris, after having spent a quarter of an hour with Monsieur Fouquet. I offer my carriage."

"Good," said Molière. "I accept it. I am in a hurry."

"I shall dine here," said Loret. "Monsieur de Gourville has promised me some crawfish."

"He has promised me some whitings. Find a rhyme for that, La Fontaine."

Aramis went out laughing, as only he could laugh, and Molière followed him. They were at the bottom of the stairs when La Fontaine opened the door and shouted out:

> "He has promised us some whitings,
> In return for all our writings."

The shouts of laughter reached the ears of Fouquet at the moment Aramis opened the door of the study. As to Molière, he had undertaken to order the horses, while Aramis went to exchange a parting word with the surintendant.

"Oh, how they are laughing up there," said Fouquet, with a sigh.

"Don't you laugh, monseigneur?"

"I laugh no longer now, Monsieur d'Herblay."

"The *fête* is approaching. Money is departing."

"Have I not told you that was my business?"

"Yes; you promised me millions."

"You shall have them the day after the king's *entrée* into Vaux."

Fouquet looked closely at Aramis, and passed his icy hand across his moistened brow. Aramis perceived that the surintendant either doubted him or felt he was powerless to obtain the money. How could Fouquet suppose that a poor bishop, ex-abbé, ex-musketeer, could find any?

"Why doubt me?" said Aramis.

Fouquet smiled, and shook his head.

"Man of little faith!" added the bishop.

"My dear Monsieur d'Herblay," answered Fouquet, "if I fall . . ."

"Well, if you 'fall'?"

"I shall, at least, fall from such a height that I shall

shatter myself in falling." Then, shaking his head as
though to escape from himself, "Where do you come
from," said he, "my friend?"

"From Paris—from Percerin."

"And what have you been doing at Percerin's, for I
suppose you attach no great importance to our poets'
clothes?"

"No; I went to prepare a surprise."

"Surprise?"

"Yes; which you are to give to the king."

"And will it cost much?"

"A hundred pistoles you will give Le Brun."

"A painting? Fine! And what is this painting to represent?"

"I will tell you; then, at the same time, whatever you
may say of it, I went to see the clothes for our poets."

"And they will be rich and elegant?"

"Splendid! Few lords will wear such clothes. People
will see the difference there is between the courtiers of
wealth and those of friendship."

"Ever generous and witty, dear prelate."

"In your school."

Fouquet grasped his hand.

"And where are you going?" he said.

"I am off to Paris, after you have given me a certain
letter."

"For whom?"

"Monsieur de Lyonne."

"And what do you want with Lyonne?"

"I want to make him sign a *lettre de cachet.*"

"*Lettre de cachet!* Do you want to put somebody in
the Bastille?"

"On the contrary—to let somebody out."

"And who?"

"A poor devil, a youth, a lad who has been Bastilled
these ten years for two Latin lines he wrote against the
Jesuits."

" 'Two Latin lines!' And for 'two Latin lines' the miserable being has been in prison for ten years?"

"Yes."

"And has committed no other crime?"

"Beyond this, he is as innocent as you or I."

"On your word?"

"On my honor!"

"And his name is?"

"Seldon."

"This is too much! You knew this, and you never told me."

"It was only yesterday his mother spoke to me, monseigneur."

"And the woman is poor?"

"In the deepest poverty."

"Oh, Heaven!" said Fouquet, "we sometimes allow such injustice on earth that I understand why there are wretches who don't trust us. Stay, Monsieur d'Herblay."

And Fouquet, taking a pen, wrote a few rapid lines to his colleague, Lyonne. Aramis took the letter and got ready to go.

"Wait," said Fouquet. He opened his drawer, and took ten government notes which were there, each for a thousand pounds. "Wait," he said; "set the son at liberty, and give this to the mother; but, above all, do not tell her . . ."

"What, monseigneur?"

"That she is ten thousand pounds richer than I. She would say I am a poor surintendant. Go, and I hope that God will bless those who are mindful of His poor!"

"That's what I hope too," replied Aramis, kissing Fouquet's hand. And he went out quickly, carrying the letter for Lyonne and the notes for Seldon's mother, and taking along Molière, who was beginning to lose patience.

CHAPTER VII

ANOTHER SUPPER AT THE BASTILLE

SEVEN o'clock was striking from the great clock of the Bastille, that famous clock, which, like all the accessories of the state prison, the very use of which is a torture, recalled to the prisoners' minds the destination of every hour of their punishment. The timepiece of the Bastille, adorned with figures, like most of the clocks of the pe-

riod, represented St. Peter in bonds. It was the supper
hour of the unfortunate captives. The doors, grating on
their enormous hinges, were opening for the passage of
the baskets and trays of provisions, the delicacy of which,
as M. de Baisemeaux has himself taught us, was regulated by the condition in life of the prisoner. We understand, on this matter, the theories of M. de Baisemeaux,
sovereign dispenser of gastronomic delicacies, head cook
of the royal fortress, whose trays, fully laden, were ascending the steep staircases, carrying some consolation
to the prisoners in the bottom of honestly filled bottles.
This same hour was that of M. le Gouverneur's supper
as well. He had a guest today, and the spit turned more
heavily than usual. Roast partridges flanked with quails
and flanking a larded hare; boiled fowls, ham, fried and
sprinkled with white wine, cardons of Guipuzcoa and a
crayfish *bisque*—these, together with the soups and *hors
d'œuvre,* constituted the governor's bill of fare. Baisemeaux, seated at the table, was rubbing his hands and
looking at the bishop of Vannes, who, booted like a horseman, dressed in gray and sword at side, kept talking of
his hunger and showing the liveliest impatience. M. de
Baisemeaux de Montlezun was not accustomed to the un-
bending movements of his greatness, my lord of Vannes,
and this evening Aramis, becoming quite sprightly, vol-
unteered confidence on confidence. The prelate had again
a little touch of the musketeer about him. The bishop's
talk was bordering on bawdy. As for M. de Baisemeaux,
with the ease of vulgar people, he let himself go entirely.

"Monsieur," he said, "for indeed tonight I dare not
call you monseigneur."

"By no means," said Aramis; "call me monsieur; I
am booted."

"Do you know, monsieur, whom you remind me of
this evening?"

"No, indeed!" said Aramis, taking up his glass; "but
I hope I remind you of a wonderful guest."

"You remind me of two, monsieur. François, shut the
window; the wind may annoy his greatness."

"And let him go," added Aramis. "The supper is
served, and we shall eat it very well without waiters. I
very much like to be alone with a friend."

Baisemeaux bowed respectfully.

"I like very much," continued Aramis, "to help myself."

"Retire, François," cried Baisemeaux. "I was saying that your greatness reminds me of two persons: one very illustrious, the late cardinal, the great Cardinal de la Rochelle, who wore boots like you."

"Indeed," said Aramis; "and the other?"

"The other was a certain musketeer, very handsome, very brave, very adventurous, very fortunate, who, from being abbé, turned musketeer, and from musketeer turned abbé." Aramis condescended to smile. "From abbé," continued Baisemeaux, encouraged by Aramis's smile, "from abbé, bishop—and from bishop—"

"Stop there, I beg!" exclaimed Aramis.

"I say, monsieur, that you look to me like a cardinal."

"Enough, dear Monsieur Baisemeaux. As you said, I have on the boots of a horseman, but I do not intend, for all that, to get in trouble with the church this evening."

"But you have wicked intentions, however, monseigneur."

"Oh, yes, wicked, I must admit, as everything mundane is."

"You cross the town and the streets in disguise?"

"In disguise, as you say."

"And do you still use your sword?"

"Yes, I should think so; but only when I am compelled. Do me the pleasure to summon François."

"You have wine there."

"It is not for wine, but because it is hot here, and the window is shut."

"I shut the windows at suppertime, so as not to hear the sounds of the arrival of couriers."

"Do you hear them when the window is open?"

"Only too well, and that disturbs me. You understand."

"Nevertheless, I am suffocating. François!" François entered. "Open the window, I pray you, Master François," said Aramis. "You will allow him, dear Monsieur Baisemeaux."

"You are at home here," answered the governor. The window was opened. "Do you know," said M. de Baisemeaux, "that you will find yourself very lonely, now

Monsieur de la Fère has returned to his home in Blois? He is a very old friend, is he not?''

''You know it as I do, Baisemeaux, seeing that you were in the musketeers with us.''

''With my friends I count neither bottles of wine nor years.''

''And you are right. But I do more than love Monsieur de la Fère, dear Baisemeaux; I venerate him.''

''Well, for my part, though it's odd,'' said the governor, ''I prefer Monsieur d'Artagnan to him. There is a man who drinks long and well. That kind of person allows you, at least, to penetrate their thoughts.''

''Baisemeaux, make me tipsy tonight; let us live it up as of old, and if I have a sorrow at the bottom of my heart, I promise you, you shall see it as you would a diamond at the bottom of your glass.''

''Bravo!'' said Baisemeaux, and he poured out a glass of wine and drank it, trembling with joy at the idea of being, by hook or by crook, in the secret of some high archiepiscopal misdemeanor. While he was drinking he did not notice that Aramis was listening attentively to the sounds in the great court. A courier came in about eight o'clock, as François brought in the fifth bottle, and, although the courier made much noise, Baisemeaux heard nothing.

''The devil take him!'' said Aramis.

''What! who?'' asked Baisemeaux. ''I hope it's neither the wine you drink nor your host.''

''No; it is a horse, who is making enough noise in the court for a whole squadron.''

''Some courier or other,'' replied the governor, drinking again. ''Yes; and may the devil take him, and so quickly that we shall never hear him speak more. Hurrah! hurrah!''

''You are forgetting me, Baisemeaux; my glass is empty,'' said Aramis, showing his dazzling goblet.

''You delight me. François, wine!''

François entered.

''Wine, fellow! and better.''

''Yes, monsieur, yes; but a courier has just arrived.''

''Let him go to the devil, I say.''

''Yes, monsieur, but . . .''

"Let him leave his news at the office; we will see it tomorrow. Tomorrow, there will be time tomorrow; there will be daylight," said Baisemeaux, chanting the words.

"Ah, monsieur!" grumbled the soldier François, in spite of himself, "monsieur!"

"Take care," said Aramis, "take care."

"Of what, dear Monsieur d'Herblay?" said Baisemeaux, half-intoxicated.

"The letter which the courier brings to the governor of a fortress is sometimes an order."

"Nearly always."

"Do not orders come from the ministers?"

"Yes, undoubtedly; but . . ."

"And what do these ministers do but countersign the signature of the king?"

"Perhaps you are right. Nevertheless, it's very tiresome when you are sitting before a good table, alone with a friend—Ah! I beg your pardon, monsieur; I forgot that I am your host, and that I am speaking to a future cardinal."

"Let us pass over that, dear Baisemeaux, and return to our soldier, to François."

"Well, what has François done?"

"He has grumbled."

"He was wrong, then."

"However, he *has* grumbled, you see; it's because there is something extraordinary in this matter. It is very possible that it was not François who was wrong in grumbling, but you, who will be wrong in not listening to him."

"Wrong? I wrong before François? That seems rather hard."

"Excuse me, merely an irregularity. But I thought it my duty to make an observation which I consider important."

"Perhaps you are right," stammered Baisemeaux. "The king's order is sacred; but as to orders that arrive when one is at supper, I repeat that the devil—"

"If you had said as much to the great cardinal, my dear Baisemeaux, and if his order had any importance."

"I do it that I may not disturb a bishop. *Mordioux!* am I not, then, excusable?"

"Do not forget, Baisemeaux, that I have worn the sol-

dier's coat, and I am accustomed to seeing obedience
everywhere.''

"You wish, then . . .''

"I wish that you should do your duty, my friend; yes,
at least, before this soldier.''

"It's absolutely correct,'' exclaimed Baisemeaux.
François was still waiting. "Let them send this order of
the king's up to me,'' he repeated, recovering himself.
And he added, in a low tone, "Do you know what it is?
I will tell you, something about as interesting as this:
'Beware of fire near the powder magazine'; or, 'Watch
so and so, who is clever at escaping.' Ah! if you only
knew, monseigneur, how many times I have been suddenly awakened from the very sweetest and deepest
slumber by messengers arriving at full gallop to tell me,
or, rather, bring me a slip of paper containing these
words: 'Monsieur de Baisemeaux, what news?' It's clear
enough that those who waste their time writing such orders have never slept in the Bastille. They would know
better; the thickness of my walls, the vigilance of my
officers, the number of rounds we go. But, indeed, what
can you expect, monseigneur? It is their business to write
and torment me when I am at rest, and to trouble me
when I am happy,'' added Baisemeaux, bowing to Aramis. "Then let them do their business.''

"And do you do yours,'' added the bishop, smiling.

François reentered; Baisemeaux took the minister's order. He slowly undid it, and slowly read it.

Aramis pretended to be drinking, so as to be able to
watch his host through the glass. Then, Baisemeaux having read it:

"What was I just saying?'' he exclaimed.

"What is it?'' asked the bishop.

"An order of release! There, now; excellent news, indeed, to disturb us.''

"Excellent news for him whom it concerns, you will,
at least, agree, my dear governor.''

"And at eight o'clock in the evening!''

"It is charitable.''

"Charity is all very well, but it is for that fellow who
says he is bored, not for me who am enjoying myself,''
said Baisemeaux, exasperated.

"Will you lose by him, then? And is the prisoner who is to be set free a high payer?"

"Oh, yes, indeed; a miserable, five-franc rat."

"Let me see it," asked M. d'Herblay. "It is indiscreet?"

"By no means; read it."

"There is 'Urgent' on the paper; you have seen that, I suppose?"

"Oh, admirable. 'Urgent!'—a man who has been here ten years. It is *urgent* to set him free today, this very evening, at eight o'clock!—*urgent!*" And Baisemeaux, shrugging his shoulders with an air of supreme disdain, flung the order on the table, and began eating again. "They have those impulses!" he said, with his mouth full; "they seize a man some fine day, maintain him for ten years, and write to you, 'Watch this fellow well,' or, 'Keep him free.' And then, as soon as you are accustomed to seeing the prisoner as a dangerous man, all of a sudden, without cause or precedent, they write, 'Set him at liberty'; and actually add to their missive, 'urgent.' You will admit, my lord, it's enough to make anyone shrug his shoulders."

"What do you expect? It is they who write," said Aramis, "and it is for you to carry out the order."

"Good! good! I carry it out! Oh, patience! You must not think that I am a slave."

"Gracious Heaven! my very good Monsieur Baisemeaux, whoever said so? Your independence is known."

"Thank Heaven!"

"But your good heart also is known."

"Don't speak of it!"

"And your obedience to your superiors. Once a soldier, you see, Baisemeaux, always a soldier."

"And so I shall strictly obey; and tomorrow morning, at daybreak, the prisoner referred to shall be set free."

"Tomorrow?"

"At dawn."

"Why not this evening, seeing that the *lettre de cachet* bears, both on the direction and inside, *'urgent'?*"

"Because this evening we are at supper, and our affairs are urgent, too."

"Dear Baisemeaux, booted though I be, I feel myself a priest, and charity has higher claims upon me than hunger and thirst. This unfortunate man has suffered long enough, since you have just told me that he has been your prisoner these ten years. Shorten his suffering. His good time has come; give it to him quickly. God will repay you in paradise with years of felicity."

"You wish it?"

"I beg you."

"What! in the very middle of our meal?"

"I implore you; such an action is worth ten Benedicites."

"It shall be as you desire, only our supper will get cold."

"Never mind that."

Baisemeaux leaned back to ring for François, and, by a very natural motion, turned around toward the door. The order had remained on the table; Aramis seized the opportunity, when Baisemeaux was not looking, to exchange the paper for another, folded in the same manner, and which he took from his pocket.

"François," said the governor, "let the major come up here with the turnkeys of the Bertaudière."

François bowed and left the room, leaving the two companions alone.

CHAPTER VIII

THE GENERAL OF THE ORDER

THERE was now a brief silence, during which Aramis did not remove his eyes from Baisemeaux for a moment. The latter seemed only half decided to be disturbed in such a manner in the middle of supper, and it was clear he was seeking some pretext, whether good or bad, for delay, at any rate until after dessert. It appeared also that he had hit upon a pretext at last.

"But it is impossible!" he cried.

"How, impossible?" said Aramis. "Give me a glimpse of this impossibility."

"It's impossible to set a prisoner free at such an hour. Where can he go, he, who is unacquainted with Paris?"

"He will go wherever he can."

"You see, now, one might as well set a blind man free."

"I have a carriage, and will take him wherever he wishes."

"You have an answer for everything. François, tell Monsieur le Major to go and open the cell of Monsieur Seldon, No. 3, Bertaudière."

"Seldon!" exclaimed Aramis very naturally. "You said Seldon, I think?"

"I said Seldon, of course. It's the name of the man they set free."

"You mean to say Marchiali?" said Aramis.

"Marchiali? Yes, indeed. No, no; Seldon."

"I think you are making a mistake, Monsieur Baisemeaux."

"I have read the order."

"And I as well."

"And I saw 'Seldon' in letters as large as that," and Baisemeaux held up his finger.

"And I read 'Marchiali,' in characters as large as this," said Aramis, also holding up two fingers.

"To the proof; let us throw a light on the matter," said Baisemeaux, confident he was right. "There is the paper, you have only to read it."

"I read 'Marchiali,' " returned Aramis, spreading out the paper. "Look."

Baisemeaux looked, and his arm dropped suddenly.

"Yes, yes," he said, quite overwhelmed; "yes, Marchiali. It's plainly written Marchiali. Quite true!"

"Ah!"

"What! the man of whom we have talked so much? The man whom they are every day telling me to take such care of?"

"There is 'Marchiali,' " repeated the inflexible Aramis.

"I must admit it, monseigneur. But I understand nothing about it."

"You believe your eyes, at any rate."

"To tell me very plainly there is 'Marchiali.' "

"And in a good handwriting, too."

"It's a wonder! I still see this order and the name of

Seldon, Irishman. I see it. I even remember that under his name there was a blot of ink.''

"No, there is no ink; no, there is no blot.''

"But there was, though; I know it, because I rubbed the powder that was over the blot.''

"In a word, be it how it may, dear Monsieur Baisemeaux,'' said Aramis, "and whatever you may have seen, the order is signed to release Marchiali, blot or no blot.''

"The order is signed to release Marchiali,'' replied Baisemeaux mechanically, endeavoring to regain his courage.

"And you are going to release this prisoner. If your heart tells you to free Seldon as well, I tell you I will not oppose it the least in the world.''

Aramis accompanied this remark with a smile, the irony of which dispelled Baisemeaux's confusion of mind, and restored his courage.

"Monseigneur,'' he said, "this Marchiali is the very same prisoner whom the other day a priest, confessor of *our order,* came to visit in so imperious and so secret a manner.''

"I don't know that, monsieur,'' replied the bishop.

"It's not such a long time ago, dear Monsieur d'Herblay.''

"It is true. But *with us,* monsieur, it is good that the man of today should no longer know what the man of yesterday did.''

"In any case,'' said Baisemeaux, "the visit of the Jesuit confessor must have brought good luck to this man.''

Aramis made no reply, but started eating and drinking again. As for Baisemeaux, no longer interested in anything that was on the table, he again took up the order and examined it in every way. This investigation, under ordinary circumstances, would have made the ears of the impatient Aramis burn with anger; but the bishop of Vannes did not become incensed for so little, above all, since he had told himself that to do so was dangerous.

"Are you going to release Marchiali?'' he said. "What mellow and fragrant sherry this is, my dear governor.''

"Monseigneur,'' replied Baisemeaux, "I shall release the prisoner Marchiali when I have summoned the courier who brought the order, and, above all, when by questioning him, I have made sure—''

''The order is sealed, and the courier is ignorant of
the contents. What do you want to make sure of?''

''So be it, monseigneur; but I shall send to the ministry, and Monsieur de Lyonne will either confirm or
withdraw the order.''

''What is the good of all that?'' asked Aramis coldly.

''What good?''

''Yes; what is your point, I ask?''

''The point is never to make a mistake, monseigneur;
never to lack in the respect which a subaltern owes to his
superior officers, never to break the laws of that service
which one has voluntarily accepted.''

''Very good; you have just spoken so eloquently that
I cannot but admire you. It is true that a subaltern owes
respect to his superiors; he is guilty when he makes a
mistake, and he should be punished if he transgresses
either the duties or laws of his office.''

Baisemeaux looked at the bishop with astonishment.

''It follows,'' pursued Aramis, ''that you are going to
ask advice, to put your conscience at ease in the matter?''

''Yes, monseigneur.''

''And if a superior officer gives you orders, you will
obey?''

''Never doubt it, monseigneur.''

''You know the king's signature well, Monsieur de
Baisemeaux?''

''Yes, monseigneur.''

''Is it not on this order of release?''

''It is true, but it may—''

''Be forged, you mean?''

''That is obvious, monseigneur.''

''You are right. And that of Monsieur de Lyonne?''

''I see it plain enough on the order; but for the same
reason that the king's signature may have been forged,
so also, even more likely, may Monsieur de Lyonne's.''

''Your logic has the stride of a giant, Monsieur de
Baisemeaux,'' said Aramis; ''and your reasoning is irresistible. But on what special grounds do you base your
idea that these signatures are false?''

''On this: the absence of countersignatures. Nothing
checks his majesty's signature; and Monsieur de Lyonne
is not there to tell me he has signed.''

"Well, Monsieur de Baisemeaux," said Aramis, giving the eagle eye to the governor, "I adopt so frankly your doubts, and your mode of clearing them up, that I will take a pen if you will give me one."

Baisemeaux gave him a pen.

"And a sheet of white paper."

"Now, I—I, also—I, here present—incontestably, I—am going to write an order to which I am certain you will give credence, incredulous as you are."

Baisemeaux turned pale at this icy assurance of manner. It seemed to him that that voice of the bishop, who was just now so smiling and cheerful, had become funereal and sad; that the wax lights changed into the candles of a mortuary chapel, and the glasses of wine into chalices of blood.

Aramis took a pen, and wrote. Baisemeaux, in terror, read over his shoulder.

"A. M. D. G.," wrote the bishop; and he drew a cross under these four letters, which signify *ad majorem Dei gloriam*, "to the greater glory of God"; and thus he continued, "It is our pleasure that the order brought to Monsieur de Baisemeaux de Montlezun, governor for the king of the castle of the Bastille, be held by him good and effectual, and be immediately carried into operation.

"(Signed)   D'Herblay,

"General of the Order, by the grace of God."

Baisemeaux was so profoundly astonished that his features remained tense, his lips parted, and his eyes fixed. He did not move an inch, nor articulate a sound. Nothing could be heard in that large room but the buzzing of a little moth, which was fluttering about the candles. Aramis, without even deigning to look at the man whom he had reduced to so miserable a condition, drew from his pocket a small case of black wax; he sealed the letter, and stamped it with a seal suspended at his chest, beneath his coat, and when the operation was concluded, presented—still in silence—the missive to M. de Baisemeaux. The latter, whose hands were trembling in a manner to excite pity, turned a dull and meaningless gaze upon the letter. A last gleam of feeling played over his features, and he fell, as if thunderstruck, on a chair.

"Come, come," said Aramis, after a long silence, during which the governor of the Bastille had slowly recovered his senses, "do not lead me to believe, dear Baisemeaux, that the presence of the general of the order is as terrible as God, and that men die merely from having seen Him. Take courage, rouse yourself; give me your hand, and obey."

Baisemeaux, reassured if not satisfied, obeyed, kissed Aramis's hand, and rose.

"Immediately?" he murmured.

"There is no reason to make haste, my host; take your place again, and do honors to this beautiful dessert."

"Monseigneur, I shall never recover such a shock as this; I, who have laughed, who have jested with you! I, who have dared to treat you on a footing of equality!"

"Say nothing about it, old comrade," replied the bishop, who perceived how strained the cord was, and how dangerous it would have been to break it; "say nothing about it. Let us each live in our own way; to you, my protection and my friendship; to me, your obedience. Having exactly fulfilled these two requirements, let us live happily."

Baisemeaux thought; he perceived, at a glance, the consequence of this withdrawal of a prisoner by means of a forged order; and, comparing with the guarantee offered him by the official order of the general, did not consider this one of much consequence.

Aramis guessed his thoughts.

"My dear Baisemeaux," he said, "you are a simpleton. Lose this habit of reflection when I trouble myself to think for you."

And at another gesture he made, Baisemeaux bowed again.

"How shall I set about it?" he said.

"What is the process for releasing a prisoner?"

"I have the regulations."

"Well, then, follow the regulations, my friend."

"I go with my major to the prisoner's room, and escort him, if he is an important person."

"But this Marchiali is not an important person," said Aramis carelessly.

"I don't know," answered the governor; as if he would have said, "It is for you to instruct me."

"Then, if you don't know it, I am right; so act toward Marchiali as you act toward one of obscure station."

"Good; the regulations so provide. They are to the effect that the turnkey, or one of the lower officials, shall bring the prisoner before the governor, in the office."

"Well, it's very wise, that; and then?"

"Then we return to the prisoner the valuables he wore at the time of his imprisonment, his clothes and papers, if the minister's orders have not otherwise directed."

"What was the minister's order as to this Marchiali?"

"Nothing; for the unhappy man arrived here without jewels, without papers, and almost without clothes."

"See how simple it all is. Indeed, Baisemeaux, you make a mountain of everything. Stay here, and make them bring the prisoner to the governor's house."

Baisemeaux obeyed. He summoned his lieutenant, and gave him an order, which the latter passed on calmly to the next whom it concerned.

Half an hour afterward they heard a gate shut in the court; it was the door to the dungeon, which had just restored its prey to the free air. Aramis blew out all the candles but one, which he left burning behind the door. This flickering glare prevented the eyes from resting steadily on any object. It multiplied their changing forms and shadows by its wavering uncertainty. Steps drew near.

"Go and meet your men," said Aramis to Baisemeaux.

The governor obeyed. The sergeant and turnkeys disappeared. Baisemeaux reentered, followed by a prisoner. Aramis had placed himself in the shade; he saw without being seen. Baisemeaux, in an agitated tone of voice, made the young man acquainted with the order which set him free. The prisoner listened, without making a single gesture or saying a word.

"You will swear as the regulation requires," added the governor, "never to reveal anything that you have seen or heard in the Bastille?"

The prisoner saw a crucifix; he stretched out his hands, and swore with his lips.

"And now, monsieur, you are free; where do you intend to go?"

The prisoner turned his head, as if looking behind him

for some protection, on which he ought to rely. Then
Aramis came out of the shade.

"I am here," he said, "to offer the gentleman whatever service he may want."

The prisoner slightly reddened, and, without hesitation, passed his arm through that of Aramis.

"God have you in His holy keeping," he said, in a
voice the firmness of which made the governor tremble
as much as the form of the blessing astonished him.

Aramis, on shaking hands with Baisemeaux, said to
him:

"Does my order trouble you? Do you fear their finding
it here, if they came to search?"

"I want to keep it, monseigneur," said Baisemeaux.
"If they found it here, it would be a certain indication I
would be lost, and, in that case, you would be a powerful
and a last auxiliary to me."

"Being your accomplice, you mean?" answered Aramis, shrugging his shoulders. "Adieu, Baisemeaux,"
he said.

The horses were waiting, shaking the carriage with
their impatience. Baisemeaux accompanied the bishop to
the bottom of the steps. Aramis had his companion go in
before him, then followed, and without giving the driver
any further order, "Go on," he said. The carriage rattled
over the pavement of the courtyard. An officer with a
torch went before the horses, and gave orders at every
post to let them pass. During the time taken in opening
all the barriers, Aramis barely breathed and you might
have heard his heart knock against his ribs. The prisoner,
buried in a corner of the carriage, made no more sign of
life than his companion. At length, a jolt more severe
than the others indicated to them that they had crossed
the last stream. Behind the carriage closed the last gate,
that in the Rue St. Antoine. No more walls either on the
right or left; heaven everywhere, liberty everywhere, and
life everywhere. The horses, kept in check by a strong
hand, went quietly as far as the middle of the faubourg.
There they began to trot. Little by little, whether they
warmed over it, or whether they were urged, they gained
speed, and, once past Bercy, the carriage seemed to fly,
so great was their energy. These horses ran as far as
Villeneuve St. George's, where relays were waiting.

Then, four instead of two whirled the carriage away in the direction of Melun, and pulled up for a moment in the middle of the forest of Sénart. No doubt the order had been given to the postilion beforehand, for Aramis did not even have an occasion to make a sign.

"What is the matter?" asked the prisoner, as if waking from a long dream.

"The matter is, monseigneur," said Aramis, "that before going further it is necessary that your royal highness and I talk."

"I will wait for an opportunity, monsieur," answered the young prince.

"We could not have a better, monseigneur; we are in the middle of a forest, and no one can hear us."

"The postilion?"

"The postilion of this relay is deaf and dumb, monseigneur."

"I am at your service, Monsieur d'Herblay."

"Do you care to stay in the carriage?"

"Yes; we are comfortably seated, and I like this carriage, for it has restored me to liberty."

"Wait, monseigneur; there is yet a precaution to be taken."

"What?"

"We are here on the highway; horsemen or carriages traveling like ourselves might pass, and, seeing us stopped, might think we are in some difficulty. Let us avoid offers of assistance which would embarrass us."

"Give the postilion orders to conceal the carriage in one of the side avenues."

"It's exactly what I wanted to do, monseigneur."

Aramis made a sign to the deaf and dumb driver of the carriage, whom he touched on the arm. The latter dismounted, took the horses by the bridle, and led them over the velvet heather and the mossy grass of a winding alley, at the end of which, on this moonless night, the deep shades formed a curtain blacker than ink. This done, the man lay down on a slope near his horses, who, on either side, kept nibbling the young oak shoots.

"I am listening," said the young prince to Aramis; "but what are you doing there?"

"I am disarming myself of my pistols, of which we have no further need, monseigneur."

CHAPTER IX

THE TEMPTER

"My prince," said Aramis, turning in the carriage toward his companion, "weak creature as I am, so unpretending in genius, so low in the scale of intelligent beings, it has never happened to me to talk with a man without penetrating his thoughts through that living mask which has been thrown over our mind, in order to retain its expression. But tonight, in this darkness, in the reserve which you maintain, I can read nothing on your features, and something tells me that I shall have great difficulty in wresting from you a sincere declaration. I beg you, then, not for love of me, for subjects should weigh nothing in the balance which princes hold, but for love of yourself, to remember every one of my syllables, every one of my inflections which, under our present grave circumstances will all have a sense and value as important as any ever uttered in the world."

"I am listening," repeated the young prince, "without fearing anything you are about to say to me."

And he buried himself still deeper in the thick cushions of the carriage, trying to deprive his companion not only of the sight of him, but even of the very idea of his presence.

Black was the darkness which fell wide and dense from the tops of the intertwining trees. The carriage, covered by this vast roof, would not have received a particle of light, not even if a ray could have struggled through the wreaths of mist which were rising in the avenue of the wood.

"Monseigneur," Aramis went on, "you know the history of the government which today controls France. The king came from a childhood imprisoned like yours, obscure as yours, and confined as yours. Only, instead of ending, like yourself, this slavery in a prison—this obscurity in solitude, these straitened circumstances in concealment—he had to bear all these miseries, humili-

ations, and distresses in full daylight, under the pitiless
sun of royalty, on an elevation so flooded with light,
where every stain seems a miserable blemish, and every
glory a stain. The king has suffered; it rankles in his
mind; and he will avenge himself. He will be a bad
king. I say not that he will shed blood, like Louis XI
or Charles IX, for he has no mortal injuries to avenge;
but he will devour the means and subsistence of his
people; for he has himself undergone wrongs in his own
interest and money. In the first place, then, I have no
qualms, when I consider openly the merits and faults
of this prince; and if I condemn him, my conscience
absolves me.''

Aramis paused. It was not to listen if the silence of the
forest remained undisturbed, but it was to gather his
thoughts from the very bottom of his soul—to leave the
thoughts he had uttered sufficient time to eat deeply into
the mind of his companion.

''All that God does, God does well,'' continued the
bishop of Vannes; ''and I am so convinced of it that I
have long been thankful to have been chosen depository
of the secret which I have helped you to discover. To a
just God was necessary an instrument, at once penetrating, persevering, and convincing, to accomplish a great
work. I am this instrument. I possess penetration, perseverance, conviction; I govern a mysterious people, who
has taken for its motto the motto of God, *Patiens quia
æternus.*''* The prince moved. ''I guess, monseigneur,
why you are raising your head, and are surprised at the
people I have under my command. You did not know you
were dealing with a king—oh! monseigneur, king of a
people very humble, much disinherited; humble, because they have no force except when creeping; disinherited, because never, almost never in this world, do
my people reap the harvest they sow, nor eat the fruit
they cultivate. They labor for an abstract idea; they heap
together all the atoms of their power, to form one man;
and around this man, with the sweat of their labor, they
create a cloud, which his genius shall, in turn, turn into
a halo gilded with the rays of all the crowns in Christen-

* ''He is patient, because he is eternal.'' It's not, however, the motto of the
Jesuits but ''Ad majorem Dei gloriam.''

dom. Such is the man you have beside you, monseigneur. It is to tell you that he has drawn you from the abyss for a great purpose, and that he wishes, for this sublime purpose, to raise you above the powers of the earth— above himself.''

The prince lightly touched Aramis's arm.

"You speak to me," he said, "of that religious order whose leader you are. For me, the result of your words is, that the day you wish to hurl down the man you shall have raised, it will be done; and that you will keep under your hand your creature of yesterday."

"Do not believe this, monseigneur," replied the bishop. "I should not take the trouble to play this terrible game with your royal highness if I had not a double interest in winning it. The day you are elevated, you are elevated forever; you will overturn the footstool, as you rise, and will send it rolling so far that not even the sight of it will ever again remind you of its right to gratitude."

"Oh, monsieur!"

"Your reaction, monseigneur, arises from an excellent disposition. I thank you. Be well assured, I aspire to more than gratitude. I am convinced that, when you arrive at the summit, you will judge me still more worthy to be your friend; and then, monseigneur, we two will do such great deeds that ages hereafter shall long speak of them."

"Tell me plainly, monsieur—tell me without disguise—what I am today, and what you aim at my being tomorrow."

"You are the son of King Louis XIII, brother of Louis XIV, natural and legitimate heir to the throne of France. In keeping you near him, as Monsieur has been kept— Monsieur, your younger brother—the king reserved for himself the right of being legitimate sovereign. Only the doctors could dispute his legitimacy. But the doctors always prefer the king who is to the king who is not. God has willed that you should be persecuted; and this persecution today consecrates you King of France. You had, then, a right to reign, seeing that it is disputed; you had a right to be proclaimed, seeing that you have been jailed; and you possess royal blood, since no one has dared to shed yours, as your servants' has been shed. Now, see, then, what this God, which you have so often accused of having in every way thwarted you, has done for you. He has given you the features, figure, age, and voice of your brother; and the very causes of your persecution are about to become those of your triumphant restoration. Tomorrow, after tomorrow—at the first occasion, regal phantom, living shade of Louis XIV, you will sit upon his throne, from where the will of God, entrusted to the arm of a man, will have hurled him, without hope of return.''

''I understand,'' said the prince; ''my brother's blood will not be shed, then?''

''You will be sole arbiter of his fate.''

''The secret of which they made an evil use against me?''

''You will use it against him. What did he do to conceal it? He concealed you. Living image of himself, you will defeat the conspiracy of Mazarin and Anne of Austria. You, my prince, will have the same interest in concealing him, who will, as a prisoner, resemble you, as you will resemble him as king.''

''I fall back on what I was saying to you. Who will guard him?''

''Those who guarded you.''

''You know this secret—you have used it in my favor. Who else knows it?''

''The queen mother and Madame de Chevreuse.''

''What will they do?''

''Nothing, if you choose.''

''How is that?''

''How can they recognize you, if you act in a manner that no one can recognize you?''

''It's true; but there are great difficulties.''

''State them, prince.''

''My brother is married; I cannot take my brother's wife.''

''I will have Spain consent to a divorce; it is in the interest of your new policy; it is human morality. All that is really noble and really useful in this world will be satisfied.''

''The imprisoned king will speak.''

''To whom do you think he will speak—to the walls?''

''You mean, by walls, the men you have entrusted.''

''If need be, yes. And, besides, your royal highness—''

"Besides?"

"I was going to say that the designs of God do not stop on such a fair road. Every scheme of this caliber is completed by its results, like a geometrical calculation. The king, in prison, will not be for you the cause of embarrassment that you have been for the king enthroned. His soul is naturally proud and impatient; it is, moreover, disarmed and enfeebled, by being accustomed to honors, and by the license of supreme power. The same God who has willed that the concluding step in the geometrical calculation I have had the honor of describing to your royal highness should be your accession to the throne, and the destruction of him who is hurtful to you, has also determined that the conquered one shall end soon both his own and your sufferings. Therefore, his soul and body have been prepared for a brief agony. Put into prison as a private individual, left alone with your doubts, deprived of everything, with the habit of a tough life, you have resisted. But your brother, a captive, forgotten, and in bonds, will not long endure his misfortune; and God will recover his soul at the appointed time—that is to say, *soon*."

At this point in Aramis's gloomy analysis, a bird of night uttered from the depths of the forest that prolonged and plaintive cry which makes every creature tremble.

"I will exile the deposed king," said Philippe, shuddering; "it will be more human."

"The king will decide on this at his pleasure," said Aramis. "But has the problem been well put? Have I brought out the solution according to the wishes or the expectations of your royal highness?"

"Yes, monsieur, yes; you have forgotten nothing—except, indeed, two things."

"The first?"

"Let us speak of it at once, with the same frankness we have already been conversing in. Let us speak of the causes which may bring about the ruin of all the hopes we have conceived. Let us speak of the risks we are running."

"They would be immense, infinite, terrific, insurmountable, if, as I have said, all things did not concur in rendering them of absolutely no account. There is no danger either for you or for me, if the constancy and

intrepidity of your royal highness are equal to that per-
fection of resemblance to your brother which nature has
bestowed upon you. I repeat it, there are no dangers,
only obstacles; this word, indeed, which I find in all languages, but have never understood, and, were I king,
would have obliterated as useless and absurd.''

''But of course, monsieur, there is a very serious obstacle, an insurmountable danger, which you are forgetting.''

''Ah!'' said Aramis.

''There is conscience, which cries loud; remorse,
which never dies.''

''True, true,'' said the bishop; ''there is a weakness
of heart of which you remind me. You are right, too, for
that indeed is an immense obstacle. The horse afraid of
the ditch leaps into the middle of it, and is killed. The
man who tremblingly crosses his sword with that of another leaves loopholes whereby his enemy has him in his
power.''

''Do you have a brother?'' the young man asked Aramis.

''I am alone in the world,'' said the latter, with a hard,
dry voice.

''But, surely, there is someone in the world whom you
love?'' asked Philippe.

''No one—yes, I love you.''

The young man sank into so profound a silence that
the mere sound of his breathing seemed like a roaring
tumult for Aramis.

''Monseigneur,'' he went on, ''I have not said all I
had to say to your royal highness; I have not offered you
all the helpful counsels and useful resources which I have
at my disposal. It is useless to flash bright visions before
the eyes of one who seeks and loves darkness; useless,
too, is it to let the magnificence of the cannon's roar be
heard in the ears of one who loves repose and the quiet
of the country. Monseigneur, I have your happiness
spread out before me in my thoughts; listen to my words:
precious they are indeed, in their import and their sense,
for you who look with such tender regard upon the bright
heavens, the green meadows, the pure air. I know a
country of delights of every kind, an unknown paradise,
a secluded corner of the world—where alone, free, and

unknown, in the woods, amid flowers and streams of rip-
pling water, you will forget all the misery that human
folly has so recently allotted you. Oh! listen to me, my
prince. I do not jest. I have a heart, and mind, and soul,
and can read to the depths of your own. I will not take
you, incomplete for your task, in order to cast you into
the crucible of my own desires, or my whim, or my ambition. All or nothing. You are hurt and sick at heart,
almost overcome by the excess of emotion which but one
hour's liberty has produced in you. For me, that is a
certain and unmistakable sign that you do not wish to
continue at liberty. Would you prefer a more humble life,
a life more suited to your strength? God is my witness
that I wish your happiness to be the result of the trial to
which I have exposed you.''

''Speak, speak!'' said the prince, with an alertness
which did not escape Aramis.

''I know,'' the prelate went on, ''in the Bas-Poitou, a
canton, of which no one in France suspects the existence.
Twenty leagues of country is immense, is it not? Twenty
leagues, monseigneur, all covered with water and herbage, and reeds of the most luxuriant nature; the whole
studded with islands covered with woods of the densest
foliage. These large marshes, covered with reeds as with
a thick mantle, sleep silently and calmly beneath the sun's
soft and genial rays. A few fishermen with their families
indolently live their lives there, with their large rafts of
poplars and alders, the floor made of reeds, and the roof
woven out of thick rushes. These boats, these floating
houses, are wafted to and fro by the changing winds.
Whenever they touch a bank, it is by chance; and so
gently, too, that the sleeping fisherman is not awakened
by the shock. Should he wish to land, it is merely because he has seen a large flight of landrails or plovers,
of wild ducks, teals, widgeons, or woodcocks, which fall
easy prey to his nets or his gun. Silver shad, eels, greedy
pike, red and gray mullet, fall in masses into his nets;
he has but to choose the finest and largest, and return the
others to the waters. Never yet has the foot of man, be
he soldier or simple citizen, never has anyone, indeed,
entered into that district. The sun's rays there are soft
and tempered, in plots of solid earth, whose soil is rich
and fertile, grows the vine, which nourishes with its gen-

erous juice its black and white grapes. Once a week a boat is sent to fetch the bread which has been baked at an oven—the common property of all. There—like the noblemen of early days—powerful because of your dogs, your fishing lines, your guns, and your beautiful reed-built house, you will live, rich in the produce of the hunt, in the plenitude of perfect security. There, years of your life will roll away, at the end of which, no longer recognizable, for you will have been perfectly transformed, you will have forced God to reshape your destiny. There are a thousand pistoles in this bag, monseigneur—more, far more, than sufficient to purchase the whole marsh of which I have spoken; more than enough to live there as many years as you have days to live; more than enough to make you the richest, the freest, and the happiest man in the country. Accept it, as I offer it to you—sincerely, cheerfully. Right away, without a moment's pause, I will unharness two of my horses, which are attached to the carriage over there, and they, accompanied by my servant, my deaf and dumb attendant, shall conduct you—traveling throughout the night, sleeping during the day—to the place I have mentioned; and I shall, at least, have the satisfaction of knowing that I have rendered to my prince the service that he himself most preferred. I shall have made one man happy; and God for that will hold me in better account than if I had made one man powerful; for that is far more difficult. And now, monseigneur, your answer to this proposition? Here is the money. Do not hesitate. In Poitou you risk nothing, except the chance of catching the fevers prevalent there; and even of them the so-called wizards of the country may cure you, in exchange for your pistoles. If you play the other game, you run the chance of being assassinated on a throne, or of being strangled in a prison. Upon my soul, I assure you, now that I compare them, I should hesitate which of the two I should accept.''

''Monsieur,'' replied the young prince, ''before I decide, let me get out of this carriage, walk on the ground, and consult that still voice which God speaks through nature. Ten minutes is all I ask, and then you shall have your answer.''

''As you please, monseigneur,'' said Aramis, bowing

before him with respect, so solemn and majestic had been the voice which had just spoken.

CHAPTER X

CROWN AND TIARA

ARAMIS was the first to get out of the carriage; he held the door open for the young man. He saw him place his foot on the mossy ground with a trembling of his whole body, and walk around the carriage with an unsteady and almost tottering step. It seemed as if the poor prisoner was unaccustomed to walk on God's earth. It was the 15th of August, about eleven o'clock at night; thick clouds, portending a tempest, overspread the sky, and shrouded all light and prospect beneath their heavy folds. The extremities of the avenues were imperceptibly detached from the copse by a lighter shadow of opaque gray, which, upon closer examination, became visible in the midst of the obscurity. But the smell which ascended from the grass, fresher and more penetrating than that which exhaled from the trees around him; the warm and balmy air which enveloped him for the first time for many years past; the ineffable enjoyment of liberty in an open country, spoke to the prince in so appealing a language, that, in spite of the great caution, we would almost say the dissimulation of his character, of which we have tried to give an idea, he could not restrain his emotion, and breathed a sigh of joy. Then, by degrees, he raised his aching head and inhaled the perfumed air, as it was wafted in gentle gusts across his uplifted face. Crossing his arms on his chest, as if to control this new sensation of delight, he drank in delicious draughts of that mysterious air which penetrates at nighttime through lofty forests. The sky he was contemplating, the murmuring waters, the moving creatures; was not this reality? Was not Aramis a madman to suppose that there was something else to dream of in this world? Those exciting pictures of country life, so free from cares, from fears, and troubles, that ocean of happy days which glitters incessantly before all youthful imaginations, are real allurements wherewith to fascinate a poor, unhappy prisoner, worn out by prison life, and emaciated by the close air of the Bastille. It was the picture, it will be remembered, drawn by Aramis, when he offered the thousand pistoles which he had with him in the carriage to the prince, and the enchanted Eden which the deserts of Bas-Poitou hid from the eyes of the world.

Such were the reflections of Aramis as he watched, with an anxiety impossible to describe, the silent progress of the emotions of Philippe, whom he saw gradually becoming more and more absorbed in his meditations. The young prince was offering up an inward prayer to God, to be divinely guided in this trying moment upon which his life or death depended. It was a terrible time for the bishop of Vannes, who had never before been so perplexed. His iron will, accustomed to overcoming all obstacles, never finding itself inferior or vanquished on any occasion, was it going to fail in so vast a project from not having foreseen the influence which a few leaves and a few liters of air would have on the human mind? Aramis, overwhelmed by anxiety, contemplated with emotion the painful struggle which was taking place in Philippe's mind. This suspense lasted the whole ten minutes which the young man had requested. During this eternity, Philippe continued gazing with an imploring and sorrowful look toward the sky; Aramis did not remove the piercing glance he had fixed on Philippe.

Suddenly the young man bowed his head. His thoughts returned to the earth, his looks perceptibly hardened, his brow contracted, his mouth assumed an expression of fierce courage; and then again his look became fixed, but this time it wore a worldly expression, hardened by covetousness, pride, and strong desire. Aramis's look then became as soft as it had before been gloomy. Philippe, seizing his hand in a quick, agitated manner, exclaimed:

"Let us go where the crown of France is to be found."

"Is this your decision, monseigneur?" asked Aramis.

"It is."

"Irrevocably so?"

Philippe did not even deign to reply. He gazed earnestly at the bishop, as if to ask him if it were possible for a man to waver after having once made up his mind.

"Those looks are flashes of fire which portray character," said Aramis, bowing over Philippe's hand; "you will be great, monseigneur, I will answer for that."

"Let us resume our conversation. I wish to discuss two points with you; in the first place, the dangers or the obstacles we may meet with. That point is decided. The other is the conditions you intend to impose on me. It is your turn to speak, Monsieur d'Herblay."

"The conditions, monseigneur?"

"Of course. You will not allow so mere a trifle to stop me, and you will not do me the injustice to suppose that I think you have no interest in this affair. Therefore, without subterfuge or hesitation, tell me the truth."

"I will do so, monseigneur. Once king—"

"When will that be?"

"Tomorrow evening. I mean in the night."

"Explain to me now."

"When I have asked your highness a question."

"Do so."

"I sent to your highness a man in my confidence, with instructions to deliver some closely written notes, carefully drawn up, which thoroughly acquaint your highness with the different people who make up and will make up your court."

"I read all the notes."

"Attentively?"

"I know them by heart."

"And understand them? Pardon me, but I may ask that question of the poor captive of the Bastille. Obviously, in a week I will no more question a mind like yours, when you will then be in full possession of your freedom."

"Interrogate me, then, and I will be the pupil repeating his lesson to his master."

"We will begin with your family, monseigneur."

"My mother, Anne of Austria, all her sorrows, her painful illness. I know her—I know her!"

"Your second brother?" asked Aramis, bowing.

"To these notes," replied the prince, "you have added portraits so faithfully painted that I am able to recognize the people whose characters, manners, and history you have so carefully portrayed. Monsieur, my brother, is a fine, dark young man, with a pale face; he does not love his wife, Henriette, whom I, Louis XIV, loved a little, and still flirt with, even though she made me weep on the day she wished to dismiss Mademoiselle de la Vallière.''

"You will have to be careful with regard to the latter," said Aramis; "she is sincerely attached to the actual king. The eyes of a woman who loves are not easily deceived."

"She is fair, has blue eyes, whose affectionate gaze will reveal her identity. She limps slightly; she writes a letter every day, to which I have to send an answer by Monsieur de St. Aignan."

"Do you know the latter?"

"As if I saw him, and I know the last verses he composed for me, as well as those I composed in answer to his."

"Very good. Do you know your ministers?"

"Colbert, an ugly, dark-browed man, but intelligent enough; his hair covering his forehead, a large, heavy, full head; the mortal enemy of Monsieur Fouquet."

"As for the latter, let us not worry about him."

"No; because, necessarily, you will require me to exile him, I suppose?"

Aramis, struck with admiration at the remark, said:

"You will become very great, monseigneur."

"You see," added the prince, "that I know my lesson by heart, and with God's assistance, and yours afterward, I shall seldom go wrong."

"You have still an awkward pair of eyes to deal with, monseigneur."

"Yes, the captain of the musketeers, Monsieur D'Artagnan, your friend."

"Yes; I can well say 'my friend.' "

"He who escorted La Vallière to Chaillot; he who delivered up Monk, fastened in an iron box, to Charles II; he who so faithfully served my mother; he to whom the crown of France owes so much that it owes everything. Do you intend to ask me to exile him also?"

"Never, sire. D'Artagnan is a man to whom, at a certain given time, I will undertake to reveal everything; but be on your guard with him; for if he discovers our plot before it is revealed to him, you or I will certainly be killed or captured. He is a man of action."

"I will think it over. Now tell me about Monsieur Fouquet. What do you wish to be done with him?"

"One moment more, I entreat you, monseigneur; and forgive me if I seem to lack respect in questioning you further."

"It is your duty to do so, and, more than that, your right also."

"Before we go on to Monsieur Fouquet, I should very much regret forgetting another friend of mine."

"Monsieur du Vallon, the Hercules of France, you mean; oh! as far as he is concerned, his fortune is safe."

"No; I didn't mean him."

"The Comte de la Fère, then?"

"And his son, the son of all four of us."

"That poor boy who is dying of love for La Vallière, whom my brother so disloyally deprived him of? Don't worry, I shall know how to get her back to him. Tell me only one thing, Monsieur d'Herblay; do men, when they love, forget the treachery that has been shown them? Can a man ever forgive the woman who has betrayed him? Is that a French custom, or is it one of the laws of the human heart?"

"A man who loves deeply, as deeply as Raoul loves Mademoiselle de la Vallière, ends up forgetting the fault or crime of the woman he loves; but I do not know if Raoul will be able to forget."

"I will see to that. Do you have anything further to say about your friend?"

"No; that is all."

"Now for Monsieur Fouquet. What do you wish me to do for him?"

"I beg you to continue him as surintendant."

"Be it so; but he is the prime minister today."

"Not quite so."

"A king, ignorant and embarrassed as I shall be, will, as a matter of course, require a prime minister."

"Your majesty will require a friend."

"I have only one, and that is you."

"You will have many others later, but none so devoted, none so zealous for your glory."

"You will be my prime minister."

"Not immediately, monseigneur, for that would create too much suspicion and astonishment."

"Monsieur de Richelieu, the prime minister of my

grandmother, Marie de Medici, was simply bishop of Luçon, as you are bishop of Vannes.''

''I see that your royal highness has studied my notes well; your amazing insight overpowers me with delight.''

''I am perfectly aware that Monsieur de Richelieu, by means of the queen's protection, soon became cardinal.''

''It would be better,'' said Aramis, bowing, ''that I should not be appointed prime minister until your royal highness has named me cardinal.''

''You shall be named before two months are past, Monsieur d'Herblay. But that is very little; you would not offend me if you were to ask more than that, and you would cause me serious regret if you were to limit yourself to that.''

''In that case, I have something still further to hope for, monseigneur.''

''Speak, speak!''

''Monsieur Fouquet will not stay at the head of affairs for long, he will soon get old. He is fond of pleasure, thanks to the youthfulness he still retains; but this youthfulness will disappear with the first serious grief or with the first illness he experiences. We will spare him the griefs, because he is an agreeable and noble-hearted man; but we cannot save him from ill health. So it is determined. When you have paid all Monsieur Fouquet's debts, and restored the finances to a sound condition, Monsieur Fouquet will be able to remain the sovereign ruler in his little court of poets and painters, but we shall have made him rich. When that has been done, and I shall have become your royal highness's prime minister, I shall be able to think of my own interests and yours.''

The young man looked at his interrogator.

''Monsieur de Richelieu, of whom we were speaking just now, was very wrong in devoting himself to govern only France. He allowed two kings, King Louis XIII and himself, to be seated upon the same throne, while he might have installed them more conveniently upon two separate and distinct thrones.''

''Upon two thrones?'' said the young man thoughtfully.

''In fact,'' pursued Aramis quietly, ''a cardinal, prime minister of France, with the favor and the support of His Most Christian Majesty the King of France, a cardinal to whom the king, his master, lends the treasures of the state, his army, his counsel, such a man would be acting with twofold injustice in applying these mighty resources to France alone. Besides,'' added Aramis, ''you will not be a king such as your father was, delicate in health, slow in judgment, whom all things wearied; you will be a king governing by your brain and by your sword; you will have in the government of the state no more than you could manage unaided; I should only interfere with you. Besides, our friendship ought never to be, I do not say impaired, but in any way affected by a secret thought. I shall have given you the throne of France, you will confer on me the throne of St. Peter. When your loyal, firm, and armed hand has joined the hand of a pope such as I shall be, neither Charles V, who owned two-thirds of the globe, nor Charlemagne, who possessed it entirely, will be able to stand up to your height. I have no alliances, I have no prejudices; I will not throw you into persecutions of heretics, nor will I cast you into the troubled waters of family dissension; I will simply say to you: 'The whole universe is our own; for me the souls of men, for you their bodies.' And as I shall be the first to die, you will have my inheritance. What do you say of my plan, monseigneur?''

''I say that you make me happy and proud, just from having understood you thoroughly. Monsieur d'Herblay, you shall be cardinal, and when cardinal, my prime minister; and then you will point out to me the necessary steps to be taken to secure your election as pope, and I will take them. You can ask what guarantees from me you please.''

''It is useless. I shall never act except in such a manner that you are the gainer; I shall never climb the ladder of fortune, fame, or position, until I shall have first seen you placed upon the step of the ladder immediately above me; I shall always hold myself sufficiently aloof from you to escape incurring your jealousy, sufficiently near to sustain your personal advantage and to watch over your friendship. All the contracts in the world are easily broken, because the interest included in them leans more to one side than to another. With us, however, it will never be the case; I have no need of any guarantees.''

''And so . . . my dear brother . . . will disappear?''

"Simply. We will remove him from his bed by means of a plank which yields to the pressure of the finger. Having retired to rest as a crowned sovereign, he will awaken in captivity. Alone, you will rule from that moment, and you will have no interest dearer and better than that of keeping me near you."

"I believe it. There is my hand on it, Monsieur d'Herblay."

"Allow me to kneel before you, sire, most respectfully. We will embrace each other on the day we shall both have on our foreheads, you the crown, and I the tiara."

"Embrace me this very day as well, and be, for and toward me, more than great, more than skillful, more than sublime in genius; be kind and indulgent—be my father."

Aramis was almost overcome as he listened to his voice; he thought he detected in his own heart an emotion until then unknown to him; but this impression was quickly removed.

"His father," he thought; "yes, his holy father."

And they resumed their seats in the carriage, which sped rapidly along the road leading to Vaux-le-Vicomte.

CHAPTER XI

THE CHÂTEAU DE VAUX-LE-VICOMTE

THE Château de Vaux-le-Vicomte, situated about a league from Melun, had been built by Fouquet in 1655, at a time when there was a scarcity of money in France; Mazarin had taken all that there was, and Fouquet was spending the remainder. However, as certain men have fertile defects and useful vices, Fouquet, in scattering millions in the construction of this palace, had found means of gathering three illustrious men together: Levau, the architect of the building; Le Nôtre, the designer of the gardens; and Le Brun, the decorator of the apartments.

If the Château de Vaux possessed a single fault with

which it could be reproached, it was its grand, pretentious character. It is even at the present day proverbial to calculate the number of acres of roofing, the reparation of which would, in our age, be the ruin of fortunes shrunk as everything also. Vaux-le-Vicomte, when its magnificent gates, supported by Caryatides, have been passed through, has the main building, opening upon a vast court of honor, enclosed by deep ditches, bordered by a magnificent stone balustrade. Nothing could be more noble than the forecourt of the middle, raised upon a flight of steps like a king upon his throne, having around it four pavilions forming the angles, the immense Ionic columns of which rise majestically to the whole height of the building. The friezes ornamented with arabesques, and the pediments which crown the pilasters, confer richness and grace upon every part of the building, while the domes which surmount the whole add proportion and majesty. This mansion, built by a subject, bore a far greater resemblance to those royal residences which Wolsey felt obliged to give to his master for the fear of making him jealous. But if magnificence and splendor were displayed in any particular part of this palace more than in another—if anything could be preferred to the wonderful arrangement of the interior, to the profusion of the paintings and statues—it would be the park and gardens of Vaux. The *jets d'eau,* viewed as wonderful in 1653, are still so, even at the present time; the waterfalls awakened the admiration of kings and princes; and as for the famous grotto, the theme of so many famous poems, the residence of that illustrious nymph of Vaux, of whom Pélisson and La Fontaine had spoken, we must be spared the description of all its beauties. We will do as Despréaux did—we will enter the park, the trees of which are eight years old, and whose tops even yet, as they proudly tower aloft, blushingly unfold their leaves to the first rays of the sun. Le Nôtre had sped up the pleasure of the Maecenas of his period; all the nursery grounds had furnished trees whose growth had been accelerated by careful culture and rich manure. Every tree in the neighborhood which showed a healthy growth had been taken up by its roots and transplanted to the park. Fouquet could well afford to purchase trees to ornament his park, since he had bought up three villages and their contents to increase the extent of his garden. M. de Scudéry said of this palace that, for the purpose of keeping the grounds and gardens well watered, M. Fouquet had divided a river into a thousand fountains, and gathered the waters of a thousand fountains into torrents. This same M. de Scudéry said a great many other things, in his "Clélie," about this palace of Valterre, the charms of which he describes in minute detail. We will be far wiser to send our curious readers to Vaux to judge for themselves than to refer them to "Clélie"; and yet there are as many leagues from Paris to Vaux as there are volumes of the "Clélie."

This magnificent palace was ready for the reception of the greatest king of the time. M. Fouquet's friends had brought along, some their actors and their sets, others their troops of sculptors and artists; not forgetting others with their sharpened pens. Floods of impromptus were contemplated. The cascades poured forth their waters brighter than crystal; they scattered over the bronze tritons and nymphs their waves of foam, which glistened in the rays of the sun. An army of servants was hurrying to and fro in the courtyard and corridors; while Fouquet, who had arrived only that morning, was walking all through the palace with a calm, observant glance, in order to give his last orders, after his intendants had inspected everything.

Assured that Aramis had made arrangements to distribute fairly the vast number of guests throughout the palace, and that he had not omitted to attend to any of the internal regulations for their comfort, Fouquet devoted his entire attention to the *ensemble* alone. Here De Gourville showed him the preparations which had been made for the fireworks; there Molière led him to the theater; at last, after he had visited the chapel, the salons, and the galleries, and was again going downstairs, exhausted with fatigue, Fouquet saw Aramis on the staircase. The prelate was waving to him. The surintendant joined his friend and with him paused before a large picture that was not yet finished. Applying himself, heart and soul, to his work, the painter, Le Brun, covered with perspiration, stained with paint, pale from fatigue and inspiration, was putting the last finishing touches with his rapid brush. It was the portrait of the king, whom

they were expecting, dressed in the court suit which Percerin had deigned to show beforehand to the bishop of
Vannes. Fouquet stood before this portrait, which seemed
to live, as one might say, in the freshness of its flesh and
in its warmth of color. He gazed upon it long and fixedly,
estimated the enormous amount of time and work spent
upon it, and, not being able to find any form of payment
great enough for this Herculean effort, he passed his arms
around the painter's neck, and kissed him. The surintendant, by this action, had utterly ruined a suit of clothes
worth a thousand pistoles, but he had satisfied Le Brun.
It was a happy moment for the artist; it was an unhappy
one for M. Percerin, who was walking behind Fouquet,
and was engaged in admiring in Le Brun's painting the
suit that he had made for his majesty, a perfect *objet
d'art,* as he called it, which was not to be matched except
in the wardrobe of the surintendant. His distress and his
exclamations were interrupted by a signal which had been
given from the top of the mansion. In the direction of
Melun, in the still empty, open plain, the sentinels of
Vaux had seen the advancing procession of the king and
the queens. His majesty was entering into Melun with
his long train of carriages and horsemen.

"In an hour," said Aramis to Fouquet.

"In an hour," replied the latter, sighing.

"And the people wonder what is the good of these
royal *fêtes!*" continued the bishop of Vannes, laughing,
with his false smile.

"Alas! I, too, who am not the people, ask the same
thing."

"I will answer you in twenty-four hours, monseigneur.
Look cheerful, for it should be a day of true rejoicing."

"Well, believe me or not, as you like, D'Herblay,"
said the surintendant, with a swelling heart, pointing at
the *cortège* of Louis, visible in the horizon, "he certainly
doesn't love me much, nor do I care much for him; but
I cannot tell you how, since he has been approaching
toward my house . . ."

"Well, what?"

"Well, since I know he is on his way here, as my
guest, he is more sacred than ever for me; he is my king,
and as such he is almost dear to me."

"Dear? yes," said Aramis, playing upon the word, as the Abbé Tenay did, at a later period, with Louis XV.

"Do not laugh, D'Herblay; I feel that if he were willing, I could love that young man."

"You should not say that to me," Aramis returned, "but rather to Monsieur Colbert."

"To Monsieur Colbert!" exclaimed Fouquet. "Why so?"

"Because he will allow you a pension out of the king's privy purse, as soon as he becomes surintendant," said Aramis, preparing to leave as soon as he had dealt this last blow.

"Where are you going?" returned Fouquet, with a gloomy look.

"To my own apartment, in order to change clothes, monseigneur."

"Where are you lodging, D'Herblay?"

"In the blue room, on the second story."

"The room immediately over the king's room?"

"Precisely."

"You will be subject to very great restraint there. What an idea, to condemn yourself to a room where you cannot move about!"

"During the night, monseigneur, I sleep or read in my bed."

"And your servants?"

"I have only one person with me. I find my reader quite sufficient. Adieu, monseigneur; do not tire yourself; keep yourself fresh for the arrival of the king."

"Shall we see you? And shall we see your friend Du Vallon also?"

"He is lodging next to me, and is at this moment dressing."

And Fouquet, bowing, with a smile, passed on like a commander-in-chief who pays the different outposts a visit after the enemy has been signaled in sight.

CHAPTER XII

THE WINE OF MELUN

THE king had, in fact, entered Melun with the intention of merely passing through the city. The youthful monarch was anxious for pleasures. Only twice during the journey had he been able to catch a glimpse of La Vallière, and, suspecting that his only opportunity of speaking to her would be after nightfall, in the gardens, after the ceremony, he had been very anxious to arrive at Vaux as early as possible. But he reckoned without his captain of the musketeers, and without M. Colbert. Like Calypso, who could not be consoled at the departure of Ulysses, our Gascon could not console himself for not having guessed why Aramis had asked Percerin to show him the king's new costumes. "There is not a doubt," he said to himself, "that my friend, the bishop of Vannes, had some motive in that"; and then he began to rack his brains most uselessly. D'Artagnan, so intimately acquainted with all the court intrigues, who knew the position of Fouquet better even than Fouquet himself did, had conceived the strangest suspicions at the announcement of the *fête*, which would have ruined a wealthy man, and which became utter madness for a man as destitute as he was. And then, the presence of Aramis, who had returned from Belle-Isle and been named by M. Fouquet inspector-general of all the arrangements; his involvement in all the surintendant's affairs; his visits to Baisemeaux—all this suspicious conduct had deeply troubled D'Artagnan during the last several weeks.

"With men of Aramis's stamp," he said, "one is never the stronger except sword in hand. So long as Aramis was a soldier, there was hope of getting the better of him; but since he has covered his breast plate with a stole, we are lost. But what can Aramis's intention possibly be?" And D'Artagnan plunged again into deep thought. 'What does it matter to me, after all," he continued, "if his only object is to overthrow Monsieur Colbert? And what

else can he be after?'' And D'Artagnan rubbed his forehead—that fertile land where the plowshare of his nails
had turned up so many and such admirable ideas in his
time. He thought at first of talking the matter over with
Colbert, but his friendship with Aramis, and the oath*
of earlier days, were binding him too strictly. He decided
against it. Besides, he hated the financier.

Then, he wished to unburden his mind to the king; but
the king would not be able to understand the suspicions
which had not even a shadow of reality at their base.

He resolved to talk to Aramis, directly, the first time
he met him. ''I will catch him,'' said the musketeer,
''between a couple of candles, suddenly, and when he
least expects it, I will place my hand upon his heart, and
he will tell me . . . What will he tell me? Yes, he will
tell me something, for *mordioux!* there is something in
it, I know.''

Somewhat calmer, D'Artagnan made every preparation for the journey, and took the greatest care that the
military household of the king, as yet not very large,
should be well staffed and well disciplined in its limited
proportions. The result was that, through the captain's
arrangements, the king, on arriving at Melun, was put at
the head of the musketeers, his Swiss guards, as well as
a picket of the French guards. It seemed like a small
army. M. Colbert looked at the troops with great delight;
he even wished there had been a third more in number.

''But why?'' said the king.

''In order to show greater honor to Monsieur Fouquet,'' replied Colbert.

''In order to ruin him sooner,'' thought D'Artagnan.

When this little army appeared before Melun, the chief
magistrates presented the king with the keys of the city,
and invited him to enter the Hôtel de Ville, in order to
share in the wine of honor. The king, who had expected
to pass through the city and to proceed to Vaux without
delay, became quite vexed.

''Who is the fool who caused this delay?'' muttered
the king, between his teeth, as the chief magistrate was
in the middle of a long speech.

* ''All for one and one for all.''

"Not I, certainly," replied D'Artagnan, "but I believe it was Monsieur Colbert."

Colbert, having heard his name pronounced, said:

"What would Monsieur d'Artagnan like to know?"

"I'd like to know whether it was you who stopped the king's progress, so that he might taste the wine of Brie. Was I right?"

"Quite so, monsieur."

"In that case, then, it was you whom the king called some name or other."

"What name?"

"I hardly know; but wait a moment—idiot, I think it was—no, no; it was fool or stupid. Yes; his majesty said that the man who had thought of the wine of Melun was something of the sort."

D'Artagnan, after this attack, quietly caressed his mustache; M. Colbert's large head seemed to become larger than ever. D'Artagnan, seeing how ugly anger made him, did not stop halfway. The orator went on with his speech, while the king's color was visibly increasing.

"Mordioux!" said the musketeer coolly, "the king is going to have a stroke. Where the deuce did you get that idea, Monsieur Colbert? You have no luck."

"Monsieur," said the financier, drawing himself up, "my zeal for the king's service inspired me with the idea."

"Bah!"

"Monsieur, Melun is a city, an excellent city, which pays well, and which it would be useless to displease."

"I, who do not pretend to be a financier, saw only one idea in your idea."

"What was that, monsieur?"

"That of causing a little annoyance to Monsieur Fouquet, who is working himself into a state waiting for us."

The blow was just, and hard. Colbert was completely thrown out of his saddle by it, and retired, crestfallen. Fortunately, the speech was now at an end; the king drank the wine and then everyone resumed the progress through the city. The king was biting his lips in anger, for the evening was closing in, and all hope of a walk with La Vallière was at an end.

In order for the king's household to enter Vaux, four hours were necessary, owing to the different arrangements. The king, therefore, who was boiling with impatience, hurried forward as much as possible, in order to reach it before nightfall. But, at the moment he was setting off again, other and fresh difficulties arose.

"Is not the king going to sleep at Melun?" said Colbert, in a soft tone, to D'Artagnan.

M. Colbert must have been badly inspired that day, to speak in that manner to the chief of the musketeers; for the latter guessed that the king was anxious to leave. D'Artagnan wanted him to enter Vaux well accompanied: therefore, he wanted his majesty to enter only with his whole escort. On the other hand, he felt that delays would irritate that impatient character. In what way could he possibly reconcile these two difficulties? D'Artagnan took up Colbert's remark, and decided to repeat it to the king.

"Sire," he said, "Monsieur Colbert has been asking me if your majesty dos not intend to sleep in Melun."

"Sleep in Melun! What for?" exclaimed Louis XIV. "Sleep in Melun! Who, in Heaven's name, can have thought of such a thing, when Monsieur Fouquet is expecting us this evening?"

"It was simply," replied Colbert quickly, "the fear of causing your majesty any delay; for according to established etiquette, you can not enter any place, with the exception of your own royal residences, until the soldiers' quarters have been marked out by the quartermaster, and the garrison properly distributed."

D'Artagnan listened with the greatest attention, biting his mustache; and the queens listened attentively as well. They were tired, and would have liked to sleep without proceeding any further; and especially, in order to prevent the king walking about in the evening with M. de St. Aignan and the ladies of the court; for, if etiquette required the princesses to remain within their own rooms, the ladies of honor, as soon as they had performed the services required of them, were at liberty to walk about as they pleased. One can see that all these rival interests, gathering together in vapors, must necessarily produce clouds, and that the clouds would be followed by a tempest. The king had no mustache to gnaw, and therefore kept biting the handle of his whip instead, with ill-concealed impatience. How could he get out of it? D'Artagnan looked as agreeable as possible, and Colbert as sulky as he could. Whom would he bite?

"We will consult the queen," said Louis XIV, bowing to the royal ladies. And this kindness of consideration softened Maria Theresa's heart, for she was of a kind and generous disposition, and she replied:

"I shall be delighted to do whatever your majesty wishes."

"How long will it take us to get to Vaux?" inquired Anne of Austria, in slow and measured accents, and placing her hand upon her bosom, where lay the center of her pain.

"An hour for your majesties' carriages," said D'Artagnan; "the roads are tolerably good."

The king looked at him.

"And a quarter of an hour for the king," he hastened to add.

"We should arrive by daylight?" said Louis XIV.

"But the billeting of the king's military escort," objected Colbert softly, "will make his majesty lose all the advantage of his speed, however quick he may be."

"Double ass that you are!" thought D'Artagnan; "if I had any interest or motive in demolishing your credit, I could do it in ten minutes. If I were in the king's place," he added, aloud, "I would, when I go to Monsieur Fouquet, who is a man of honor, leave my escort behind me; I would go to him as a friend; I would enter accompanied only by my captain of the guards; I would be greater and nobler by doing so."

Delight sparkled in the king's eyes.

"That is indeed a very good suggestion. We will go to see a friend as friends; those gentlemen who are with the carriages can go slowly; but we who are mounted will ride on."

And he rode off, accompanied by all those who were mounted. Colbert hid his big surly head behind his horse's neck.

"I shall be free," said D'Artagnan, as he galloped along, "to have a little talk with Aramis this evening. And then, Monsieur Fouquet is a man of honor. *Mordioux!* I have said so, and it must be so."

And this was the way how, toward seven o'clock in the evening, without announcing his arrival by the din of trumpets, and without even his advanced guard, without outriders or musketeers, the king appeared before the gate of Vaux where Fouquet, who had been informed of his royal guest's approach, had been waiting for the last half hour, with his head uncovered, surrounded by his household and his friends.

CHAPTER XIII

NECTAR AND AMBROSIA

M. FOUQUET held the stirrup of the king, who, having dismounted, bowed most graciously, and more graciously still held out his hand to him, which Fouquet, in spite of a slight resistance on the king's part, carried respectfully to his lips. The king wished to wait in the first courtyard for the arrival of the carriages, nor had he long to wait, for the roads had been put into excellent order by the surintendant, and a stone the size of an egg would hardly have been found the whole way from Melun to Vaux. Thus the carriages, rolling along as though on a carpet, brought the ladies to Vaux, without jolting or fatigue, by eight o'clock. They were received by Mme. Fouquet, and at the moment they made their appearance, a light as bright as day burst forth from all the trees and vases and marble statues. This enchantment lasted until their majesties had retired into the palace. All these wonders and magical effects which the chronicler has heaped up, or, rather, preserved, in his report, at the risk of rivaling the creations of a novelist; these splendors whereby night seemed conquered and nature corrected, together with every delight and luxury combined for the satisfaction of all the senses, as well as of the mind, Fouquet did, in real truth, offer then to his sovereign in that enchanting retreat of which no monarch could, at that time, boast of possessing an equal.

We do not intend to describe the grand banquet, at which all the royal guests were present, nor the concerts, nor the fairylike and magical transformations and metamorphoses. It will be sufficient to depict the face of the king, which, from being cheerful, soon wore a gloomy, strained, and irritated expression. He remembered his own residence, royal though it was, and the mediocre luxury which prevailed there, and which was merely useful for the royal wants, without being his own personal property. The large vases of the Louvre, the old furniture and plate of Henry II, of Francis I, of Louis XI, were merely historical monuments of earlier days; they were nothing but specimens of art, the relics of his predecessors; while with Fouquet the value of the article was as much in the workmanship as in the article itself. Fouquet ate from a gold service, which his artists had modeled and cast for himself alone. Fouquet drank wines of which the King of France did not even know the name, and drank them out of goblets each more precious than the whole royal cellar.

What, too, can be said of the apartments, the draperies, the pictures, the servants and officers, of every description, of his household? What can be said of the mode of service in which etiquette was replaced by order; stiff formality by comfort; the happiness and contentment of the guest became the supreme law of all who obeyed the host. The perfect swarm of busily engaged persons moving about noiselessly; the multitude of guests—who were, however, even less numerous than the servants who waited on them—the myriad of exquisitely prepared dishes, of gold and silver vases; the floods of dazzling light, the masses of unknown flowers of which the hothouses had been stripped, and which overwhelmed with their beauty; the perfect harmony of everything which surrounded them, and which, indeed, was no more than the prelude of the promised *fête*, more than charmed all who were there, and who showed their admiration over and over again, not by voice or gesture, but by deep silence and rapt attention, those two languages of the courtier which acknowledge the hand of no master powerful enough to restrain them.

As for the king, his eyes filled with tears; he dared not look at the queen. Anne of Austria, whose pride, as it ever had been, was superior to that of any creature, crushed her host by the contempt with which she treated everything handed to her. The young queen, kind-hearted by nature and curious by disposition, praised Fouquet, ate with an exceedingly good appetite, and asked the names of the different fruits which were placed upon the table. Fouquet replied that he was not aware of their names. The fruits came from his own stores; he had often cultivated them himself, having an intimate acquaintance with the cultivation of exotic fruits and plants. The king felt and appreciated the delicacy of the reply, but was only the more humiliated at it; he thought that the queen was a little too familiar in her manners, and that Anne of Austria resembled Juno a little too much; his chief care, however, was that he remain distant in his behavior, bordering slightly on the limits of extreme disdain or of simple admiration.

But Fouquet had foreseen all that; he was, in fact, one of those men who foresees everything. The king had expressly declared that so long as he remained under M. Fouquet's roof he did not wish his own different meals to be served in accordance with the usual etiquette, and that he would, consequently, dine with the rest of the society; but by the thoughtful attention of the surintendant, the king's dinner was served up separately, if one may so express it, in the middle of the general table. The dinner, wonderful in every respect, included everything the king liked, and which he generally preferred to anything else. Louis had no excuse—he, indeed, who had the keenest appetite in his kingdom—for saying that he was not hungry. M. Fouquet even did better still; he certainly, in obedience to the king's expressed desire, seated himself at the table, but as soon as the soups were served, he rose and personally waited on the king, while Mme. Fouquet stood behind the queen mother's armchair. The disdain of Juno and the sulky fits of temper of Jupiter could not resist this excess of kindly feeling and polite attention. The queen ate a biscuit dipped in a glass of San Lucar wine; and the king ate of everything, saying to M. Fouquet:

"It is impossible, Monsieur le Surintendant, to dine better anywhere."

Whereupon, the whole court began, on all sides, to devour the dishes spread before them, with such enthusiasm that it looked like a cloud of Egyptian locusts settling down upon the uncut crops.

As soon, however, as his hunger was appeased, the

king became dull and gloomy again; the more so in proportion to the satisfaction he had felt he should show, and particularly on account of the deferential manner which his courtiers had shown toward Fouquet. D'Artagnan, who ate a good deal and drank hard, without allowing it to be noticed, did not lose a single opportunity, but made a great number of observations which he used to his benefit.

When the supper was finished the king expressed a wish not to miss the evening walk. The park was illuminated; the moon, too, as if she had placed herself at the orders of the lord of Vaux, silvered the trees and lake with her bright, phosphoric light. The air was soft and balmy; the graveled walks through the thickly set avenues yielded luxuriously to the feet. The *fête* was complete in every respect, for the king, having met La Vallière in one of the winding paths of the wood, was able to take her by the hand and say, "I love you," without anyone overhearing him except M. D'Artagnan who was following, and M. Fouquet, who was preceding him.

The night of magical enchantments went on. The king requested to be shown his room, and there was immediately movement in every direction. The queens went to their own apartments, accompanied by the music of theorbos and lutes; the king found his musketeers awaiting him on the grand flight of steps, for M. Fouquet had brought them on from Melun, and had invited them to supper. D'Artagnan's suspicions at once disappeared. He was weary, he had supped well, and wished, for once in his life, thoroughly to enjoy a *fête* given by a man who was in every sense of the word a king.

"Monsieur Fouquet," he said, "is my man."

The king was led with the greatest ceremony to the chamber of Morpheus, of which we owe some slight description to our readers. It was the handsomest and the largest in the palace. Le Brun had painted on the vaulted ceiling the happy and the sad dreams which Morpheus sends to kings as well as other men. With everything that sleep gives birth to that is lovely—its perfumes, its flowers and nectar, the wild voluptuousness or the deep rest of the senses—had the painter enriched with his frescoes. It was a composition as soft and pleasing in one part as dark and gloomy and terrible in another. The poisoned chalice, the glittering dagger suspended over the head of the sleeper; wizards and phantoms with hideous masks, those half-dim shadows more terrifying than the brightness of flame or the blackness of night; these, he had made then the counterpoint of his more pleasing pictures. No sooner had the king entered the room than a cold shiver seemed to pass through him, and on Fouquet's asking him the cause of it, the king replied, as pale as death:

"I am sleepy, that is all."

"Does your majesty wish for your attendants at once?"

"No; I have to talk with a few persons first," said the king. "Will you have the goodness to tell Monsieur Colbert I wish to see him?"

Fouquet bowed, and left the room.

CHAPTER XIV

A GASCON AND A GASCON AND A HALF

D'ARTAGNAN had decided to waste no time, and, in fact, he never was in the habit of doing so. After having asked for Aramis, he had looked for him in every direction, until he succeeded in finding him. Besides, no sooner had the king entered into Vaux than Aramis had retired to his own room, meditating, doubtlessly, some new piece of gallant attention for his majesty's amusement. D'Artagnan asked the servants to announce him, and found on the second floor, in a beautiful room called the blue room, on account of the color of its drapery, the bishop of Vannes in company with Porthos and several of the modern Epicureans. Aramis came forward to embrace his friend, and offered him the best seat. As it was clear among those present that the musketeer wished to talk secretly with Aramis, the Epicureans took their leave. Porthos, however, did not stir; for true it is, that, having dined exceedingly well, he was fast asleep in his armchair; and the freedom of conversation therefore was not interrupted by a third person. Porthos had a deep, harmonious snore, and people might talk in the midst of its

loud bass without fear of disturbing him. D'Artagnan felt
that he was called upon to open the conversation.

"Well, and so we have come to Vaux," he said.

"Why, yes, D'Artagnan. And how do you like the
place?"

"Very much, and I like Monsieur Fouquet also."

"Is he not a charming host?"

"No one could be more so."

"I am told that the king began by being distant toward
Monsieur Fouquet, but that his majesty became much
more cordial afterward."

"You did not notice it, then, since you say you have
been told so?"

"No; I was engaged with those gentlemen who have
just left the room about the theatrical performances and
the tournaments which are to take place tomorrow."

"Ah, indeed! you are the comptroller-general of the
fêtes here, then?"

"You know I am fond of amusement where the exercise of the imagination is required; I have always been a
poet in one way or another."

"Yes, I remember the poems you used to write; they
were charming."

"I have forgotten them, but I am delighted to read the
poems of others, when those others are known by the
names of Molière, Pélisson, La Fontaine, and so on."

"Do you know what idea occurred to me this evening,
Aramis?"

"No; tell me what it was, for I should never be able
to guess it, you have so many."

"Well, the idea occurred to me that the true King of
France is not Louis XIV."

"What!" said Aramis involuntarily, looking the musketeer full in the eyes.

"No; it is Monsieur Fouquet."

Aramis breathed again, and smiled.

"You are like all the rest: jealous," he said. "I would
bet that it was Monsieur Colbert who came up with that
pretty phrase."

D'Artagnan, in order to throw Aramis off his guard,
told of Colbert's misadventure with regard to the wine of
Melun.

"He comes of a mean race, does Colbert," said Aramis.

"Quite true."

"When I think," added the bishop, "that that fellow will be your minister within four months, and that you will serve him as blindly as you did Richelieu or Mazarin."

"And as you serve Monsieur Fouquet," said D'Artagnan.

"With the difference, though, that Monsieur Fouquet is not Monsieur Colbert."

"True, true," said D'Artagnan, as he pretended to become sad and full of reflection; and then, a moment after, he added, "Why do you tell me that Monsieur Colbert will be minister in four months?"

"Because Monsieur Fouquet will have ceased to be so," replied Aramis.

"He will be ruined, you mean?" said D'Artagnan.

"Completely so."

"Why does he give these *fêtes,* then?" said the musketeer, in a tone so full of thoughtful consideration, and so genuine, that the bishop was for the moment deceived by it. "Why did you not dissuade him from it?"

The latter part of the phrase was just a little too much, and Aramis's former suspicions were again aroused.

"It is done with the intent of humoring the king."

"By ruining himself?"

"Yes, by ruining himself for the king."

"A singular calculation, that."

"Necessity."

"I don't see that, dear Aramis."

"Do you not? Have you not noticed Monsieur Colbert's daily increasing antagonism, and that he is doing his utmost to drive the king to get rid of the surintendant?"

"One must be blind not to see it."

"And that a cabal is formed against Monsieur Fouquet?"

"That is well known."

"What likelihood is there that the king would join a party formed against a man who will have spent everything he had to please him?"

"True, true," said D'Artagnan slowly, hardly convinced,

yet curious to broach another phase of the conversation.
"There are follies and follies," he went on, "and I do
not like those you are committing."

"What do you allude to?"

"As for the banquet, the ball, the concert, the theat-
ricals, the tournaments, the cascades, the fireworks, the
illuminations, and the presents, these are well and good,
I grant you that; but why were not these expenses sufficient? Was it necessary to have new liveries and outfits
for your whole household?"

"You are quite right. I told Monsieur Fouquet that myself; he replied that if he were rich enough, he would
offer the king a newly erected chateau, from the vanes at
the top of the house to the very cellar; completely new
inside and out; and that, as soon as the king had left, he
would burn the whole building and its contents, in order
that it might not be made use of by anyone else."

"How completely Spanish!"

"I told him so, and he then added this: 'Whoever ad-
vises me to spare expense I shall look upon as my enemy.' "

"It is positive madness; and that portrait, too!"

"What portrait?" said Aramis.

"That of the king; and the surprise as well."

"What surprise?"

"The surprise you seem to have in view, and on account of which you took some samples, when I met you
at Percerin's."

D'Artagnan paused. The spear had hit its mark, and
all he had to do was to wait and watch its effect.

"That is merely an act of courtesy," replied Aramis.

D'Artagnan went up to his friend, took hold of both
his hands, and looking him full in the eyes, said:

"Aramis, do you still care for me a little?"

"What a question to ask!"

"Very good. One favor, then. Why did you take some
samples of the king's outfits at Percerin's?"

"Come with me and ask poor Le Brun, who has been
working with them for the last two days and two nights."

"Aramis, that may be the truth for everybody else,
but for me . . ."

"Upon my word, D'Artagnan, you astonish me!"

"Be a little considerate of me. Tell me the exact truth;

you would not like anything disagreeable to happen to me, would you?''

"My dear friend, you are becoming quite incomprehensible. What suspicion can you possibly have got hold of?''

"Do you believe in my instinctive feelings? Formerly you used to have faith in them. Well, then, an instinct tells me that you have some concealed project on foot.''

"I, a project?''

"I am convinced of it.''

"What nonsense!''

"I am not only sure of it, but I would even swear to it.''

"Indeed, D'Artagnan, you cause me the greatest pain. Is it likely, if I have any project in hand that I ought to keep secret from you, I should tell you about it? If I had one that I ought to reveal, should I not have already told it to you?''

"No, Aramis, no. There are certain projects which are never revealed until the favorable opportunity arrives.''

"In that case, my dear fellow,'' returned the bishop, laughing, "the only thing now is that the opportunity has not yet arrived.''

D'Artagnan shook his head with a sorrowful expression.

"Oh, friendship, friendship!'' he said, "what an idle word you are. Here is a man, who, if I were to ask him, would allow himself to be cut in pieces for my sake.''

"You are right,'' said Aramis nobly.

"And this man, who would shed every drop of blood in his veins for me, will not open the smallest corner in his heart. Friendship, I repeat, is nothing but a mere unsubstantial shadow and a lure, like everything else which shines in this world.''

"Do not speak of *our* friendship in that way,'' replied the bishop, in a firm, assured voice; "for ours is not of the same nature as those you have been speaking of.''

"Look at us, Aramis; three out of the old 'four.' You are deceiving me; I suspect you; and Porthos is fast asleep. An admirable trio of friends, don't you think so? A beautiful relic of former times.''

"I can only tell you one thing, D'Artagnan, and I swear it on the Bible; I love you just as I used to do. If

I ever suspect you, it is on account of others, and not on account of either of us. In everything I may do, and should happen to succeed in, you will find your share. Will you promise me the same favor?''

"If I am not mistaken, Aramis, your words, at the moment you pronounce them, are full of generous feeling.''

"That is possible.''

"You are conspiring against Monsieur Colbert. If that be all, *mordioux!* tell me so at once. I have the instrument in my own hand, and will pull out the tooth easily enough.''

Aramis could not restrain the smile of disdain which passed across his noble features.

"And supposing that I were conspiring against Colbert, what harm would there be in that?''

"No, no; that would be too trifling a matter for you to take in hand, and it was not on that account you asked Percerin for those samples of the king's outfits. Oh! Aramis, we are not enemies, remember, but brothers. Tell me what you wish to undertake, and, upon the word of a D'Artagnan, if I cannot help you, I will swear to remain neutral.''

"I am undertaking nothing,'' said Aramis.

"Aramis, a voice speaks within me, and seems to enlighten my darkness; it is a voice which has never yet deceived me. It is the king you are conspiring against.''

"The king?'' exclaimed the bishop, pretending to be annoyed.

"Your face will not convince me; the king, I repeat.''

"Will you help me?'' said Aramis, smiling ironically.

"Aramis, I will do more than help you—I will do more than remain neutral—I will save you.''

"You are mad, D'Artagnan.''

"I am the wiser of the two, in this matter.''

"You to suspect me of wishing to assassinate the king!''

"Who spoke of that at all?'' said the musketeer.

"Well, let us understand each other. I do not see what anyone can do to a legitimate king, as ours is, if he does not assassinate him.''

D'Artagnan did not say a word.

"Besides, you have your guards and your musketeers here," said the bishop.

"True."

"You are not in Monsieur Fouquet's house, but in your own."

"True; but in spite of that, Aramis, grant me, for pity's sake, but one single word of a true friend."

"A friend's word is the truth itself. If I think of touching, even with my finger, the son of Anne of Austria, the true king of this realm of France; if I have not the firm intention of prostrating myself before his throne; if in every idea I may entertain tomorrow, here at Vaux, will not be the most glorious day my king ever enjoyed—may Heaven's lightning blast me where I stand!"

Aramis had pronounced these words with his face turned toward the alcove of his own bedroom, where D'Artagnan, seated with his back toward the alcove, could not suspect that anyone was lying concealed. The earnestness of his words, the studied slowness with which he pronounced them, the solemnity of his oath, gave the musketeer the most complete satisfaction. He took hold of both Aramis's hands, and shook them cordially. Aramis had endured the reproaches without turning pale, and had blushed as he listened to the words of praise. D'Artagnan, deceived, did him honor; but D'Artagnan, trustful and reliant, made him feel ashamed.

"Are you going away?" he said, as he embraced him, in order to conceal the flush on his face.

"Yes; my duty summons me. I have to get the watchword. It seems I am to be lodged in the king's anteroom. Where does Porthos sleep?"

"Take him away with you, if you like, for he snores like a cannon."

"Ah! Isn't he staying with you?" said D'Artagnan.

"Not a chance in the world. He has his room to himself, but I don't know where."

"Very good," said the musketeer, from whom this separation of the two associates removed his last suspicion; and he touched Porthos lightly on the shoulder. The latter replied with a terrible yawn.

"Come," said D'Artagnan.

"What, D'Artagnan, my dear fellow, is that you? What

a lucky chance! Oh, yes, true, I had forgotten; I am at the *fêtes* at Vaux.''

''Yes; and your beautiful suit, too.''

''Yes, it was very kind of Monsieur Coquelin de Volière, was it not?''

''Hush!'' said Aramis. ''You are walking so heavily you will make the floor give way.''

''True,'' said the musketeer; ''this room is above the dome, I think.''

''And I did not choose it for a fencing room, I assure you,'' added the bishop. ''The ceiling of the king's room has all the sweetness and calm delights of sleep. Do not forget, therefore, that my floor is merely the covering of his ceiling. Good night, my friends, and in ten minutes I shall be fast asleep.''

And Aramis accompanied them to the door, laughing quietly all the while. As soon as they were outside he bolted the door hurriedly, closed up the chinks of the windows, and then called out:

''Monseigneur! monseigneur!''

Philippe made his appearance from the alcove, as he pushed aside a sliding panel placed behind the bed.

''Monsieur D'Artagnan has a great many suspicions, it seems,'' he said.

''You recognized Monsieur D'Artagnan, then?''

''Before you called him by his name, even.''

''He is your captain of musketeers.''

''He is very devoted to *me*,'' replied Philippe, laying a stress upon the personal pronoun.

''As faithful as a dog; but he bites sometimes. If D'Artagnan does not recognize you before *the other* has disappeared, rely upon D'Artagnan to the end of the world; for, in that case, if he has seen nothing, he will keep his fidelity. If he sees, when it is too late, he is a Gascon, and will never admit that he has been deceived.''

''I thought so. What are we to do now?''

''You will go to the observation post, and watch the moment of the king's retiring to rest, so as to learn how that ceremony is performed.''

''Very good. Where shall I place myself?''

''Sit down on this folding chair. I am going to push aside a portion of the floor; you will look through the opening, which corresponds to one of the false windows made in the dome of the king's apartment. Can you see?''

"Yes," said Philippe, quivering at the sight of an enemy; "I see the king."

"What is he doing?''

"He wants some man to sit down close to him.''

"Monsieur Fouquet?''

"No, no; wait a moment . . ."

"Look at the notes and portraits, my prince.''

"The man whom the king wishes to sit down in his presence is Monsieur Colbert.''

"Colbert sit down in the king's presence!'' exclaimed Aramis; "it is impossible.''

"Look!''

Aramis looked through the opening in the floor.

"Yes," he said. "Colbert himself. Oh, monseigneur! what are we going to hear, and what can result from this intimacy?''

"Nothing good for Monsieur Fouquet, in all events.''

The prince was not mistaken.

We have seen that Louis XIV had sent for Colbert, and that Colbert had arrived. The conversation began between them by the king, according to him one of the highest favors that he had ever done; it was true, the king was alone with his subject.

"Colbert," he said, "sit down.''

The intendant, overcome with delight—for he feared he should be dismissed—refused this unprecedented honor.

"Does he accept?'' said Aramis.

"No; he remains standing.''

"Let us listen, then.''

And the future king and the future pope listened eagerly to the simple mortals whom they held under their feet, ready to crush them if they had liked.

"Colbert," said the king, "you have annoyed me exceedingly today.''

"I know it, sire.''

"Very good; I like that answer. Yes, you knew it, and there was courage in having done it.''

"I ran the risk of displeasing your majesty, but I risked also concealing what were your true interests from you.''

"What! you were afraid of something on my account?"

"I was, sire, even if it were nothing more than an indigestion," said Colbert; "for people do not give their sovereigns such banquets as the one of today, except to stifle them under the weight of good food."

Colbert waited for the effect which this coarse joke would produce upon the king, and Louis XIV, who was the vainest and the most fastidiously delicate man in his kingdom, forgave Colbert the joke.

"The truth is," he said, "that Monsieur Fouquet has given me too good a meal. Tell me, Colbert, where does he get all the money needed for this enormous expenditure. Can you tell?"

"Yes, I do know, sire."

"Will you be able to prove it with tolerable certainty?"

"Easily; to the very farthing."

"I know you are very exact."

"It is the principal qualification required in an intendant of finances."

"But all are not so."

"I thank your majesty for so flattering a compliment from your own lips."

"Monsieur Fouquet, therefore, is rich, very rich, and I suppose every man knows he is so."

"Everyone, sire; the living as well as the dead."

"What does that mean, Monsieur Colbert?"

"The living are witnesses of Monsieur Fouquet's wealth—they admire and applaud the result produced; but the dead, wiser and better informed than we are, know how that wealth was obtained, and they rise up in accusation."

"So that Monsieur Fouquet owes his wealth to some cause or other."

"The occupation of an intendant very often favors those who practice it."

"You have something to say to me more confidentially, I perceive; do not be afraid, we are quite alone."

"I am never afraid of anything under the shelter of my own conscience, and under the protection of your majesty," said Colbert, bowing.

"If the dead, therefore, were to speak . . ."

"They do speak sometimes, sire; read."

"Ah!" murmured Aramis in the prince's ear, who, close beside him, was listening without losing a syllable, "since you are placed here, monseigneur, in order to learn your vocation of a king, listen to a truly royal piece of infamy. You are about to be a witness to one of those scenes which the Devil alone can conceive and execute. Listen attentively—you will find your advantage in it."

The prince was doubly attentive, and saw Louis XIV take from Colbert's hands a letter which the latter held out to him.

"The late cardinal's handwriting," said the king.

"Your majesty has an excellent memory," replied Colbert, bowing; "it is an immense advantage for a king who is destined for hard work to recognize handwritings at first glance."

The king read Mazarin's letter.

"I do not quite understand," he said, greatly interested.

"Your majesty has not yet acquired the habit of going through the public accounts."

"I see that it refers to money which had been given to Monsieur Fouquet."

"Thirteen million. Quite a good sum."

"Yes. Well, and these thirteen million are wanting to balance the total of the accounts. That is what I do not understand very well. How was this deficit possible?"

"Possible, I do not say; but there is no doubt about the fact that it really is so."

"You say that these thirteen million are found to be wanting in the accounts?"

"I do not say so, but the books do."

"And this letter of Monsieur Mazarin indicates the use of that sum, and the name of the person with whom it was deposited?"

"As your majesty can judge for yourself."

"Yes; and the result is, then, that Monsieur Fouquet has not yet repaid the thirteen million."

"That results from the accounts, certainly, sire."

"Well, then?"

"Well, sire, in that case, inasmuch as Monsieur Fouquet has not yet given back the thirteen million, he must have appropriated them for his own purposes; and with those thirteen million one could incur four times and a little more as much expense, and make four times as great a display as your majesty was able to do at Fontainebleau, where we only spent three million altogether, if you remember.''

This allusion to the *fête*, where the king had become aware for the first time of his inferiority, was a clever piece of treachery. Colbert was paying back at Vaux what Fouquet had done to him at Fontainebleau, and, as a good financier, he was doing it with the best interests. Having once disposed the king's mind in that way, Colbert had nothing of much importance to detain him. He felt that such was the case, for the king had sunk into a gloomy state. Colbert awaited the first words from the king's lips with as much impatience as Philippe and Aramis did from their observation post.

''Are you aware what is the consequence of all this, Monsieur Colbert?'' said the king, after a few moments' reflection.

''No, sire, I do not know.''

''Well, then, the fact of the appropriation of the thirteen million, if it can be proved . . .''

''But it is so already.''

''I mean if it were to be declared and certified, Monsieur Colbert.''

''I think it will be tomorrow, if your majesty . . .''

''Were we not under Monsieur Fouquet's roof, you were going to say, perhaps?'' replied the king with dignity.

''The king is in his own palace, wherever he may be, and especially in houses which his own money has paid for.''

''I think,'' said Philippe, in a low tone, to Aramis, ''that the architect who constructed this dome ought, anticipating what use could be made of it, to have contrived that it might easily fall on the heads of scoundrels such as that Monsieur Colbert.''

''I thought so, too,'' replied Aramis; ''but Monsieur Colbert is so very near the king at this moment.''

''That is true, and that would open the succession.''

''Of which your younger brother would reap all the advantage, monseigneur. But wait, let us keep quiet, and go on listening.''

"We shall not have long to listen," said the young prince.

"Why not, monseigneur?"

"Because, if I were the king, I should not reply any longer."

"And what would you do?"

"I should wait until tomorrow morning to give myself time for reflection."

Louis XIV at last raised his eyes, and finding Colbert attentively waiting for his next remarks, said, hastily changing the conversation:

"Monsieur Colbert, I see it is getting very late, and I shall now retire to bed. By tomorrow morning I shall have made up my mind."

"Very good, sire," returned Colbert, greatly incensed, although he restrained himself in the presence of the king.

The king made a gesture of adieu, and Colbert withdrew with a respectful bow.

"My attendants," cried the king; and, as they entered the apartment, Philippe was about to leave his post of observation.

"A moment longer," said Aramis to him, with his accustomed gentleness of manner. "What has just now taken place is only a detail, and tomorrow we will not even think about it; but the ceremony of the king's retiring to rest, the etiquette observed in addressing the king, that indeed is of the greatest importance. Learn, sire, and study well how you ought to go to bed. Look! look!"

CHAPTER XV

COLBERT

HISTORY will tell us, or, rather, history has told us, of the various events of the following day, of the splendid *fêtes* given by the surintendant to his sovereign. There was nothing but amusement and delight allowed to prevail throughout the whole of the following day; there was a walk, a banquet, a comedy to be acted; and a comedy, too, in which, to his great amazement, Porthos recognized M. Coquelin de Volière as one of the actors, in the play called "Les Fâcheux." Full of preoccupation, however, from the scene of the previous evening, and hardly recovered from the effects of the poison which Colbert had then administered to him, the king, during the whole day, so brilliant in its effects, so full of unexpected and startling novelties, in which all the wonders of the "Arabian Nights" seemed to be reproduced for his especial amusement—the king, we say, showed himself cold, reserved, and taciturn. Nothing could smooth the frown upon his face; everyone who observed him noticed that a deep resentment of remote origin, increased by slow degrees, as the source becomes a river, thanks to the thousand threads of water which increase its body, was keenly alive in the depths of the king's heart. Toward the middle of the day only did he begin to recover a little serenity, and by that time he had, in all probability, made up his mind. Aramis, who was following him, step by step, in his thoughts, as in his walk, concluded that the event that he was expecting would not be long before it was announced. This time Colbert seemed to walk in concert with the bishop of Vannes, and had he received for every annoyance which he inflicted on the king a word of direction from Aramis, he could not have done better. During the whole day the king, who, in all probability, wished to free himself from some of the thoughts which disturbed his mind, seemed to seek La Vallière's society as actively as he seemed to show his anxiety to flee that of M. Colbert or M. Fouquet. The evening came. The king had expressed a wish not to walk in the park until after cards in the evening. In the interval between supper and the walk, cards and dice were introduced. The king won a thousand pistoles, and, having won them, put them in his pocket, and then rose, saying:

"And now, gentlemen, to the park."

He found the ladies of the court already there. The king, we have before observed, had won a thousand pistoles, and had put them in his pocket; but M. Fouquet had somehow contrived to lose ten thousand, so that among the courtiers there was still left a hundred and ninety thousand francs' profit to divide, a circumstance which made the faces of the courtiers and the officers of

the king's household the most joyous faces in the world.
It was not the same, however, with the king's face; for,
in spite of his success at play, to which he was by no
means insensitive, there still remained a slight shade of
dissatisfaction. Colbert was waiting for him at the corner
of one of the avenues. He probably had a rendezvous
with the king, since Louis XIV, who had avoided him,
gestured to him and went far into the park with him. But
La Vallière too had seen the king's gloomy face, and
since her love knew everything that lay hidden in his
heart, she understood that this repressed wrath was
threatening someone. She stood on the path of his revenge like an angel of mercy. Sad, confused, deeply distressed at having been separated so long from her lover,
disturbed at the sight of that emotion which she had
guessed, she presented herself to the king with an embarrassed look which in his current position of mind the
king interpreted unfavorably. Then, as they were alone,
nearly alone, inasmuch as Colbert, as soon as he perceived the young girl approaching, had stopped and
drawn back a dozen paces, the king advanced toward La
Vallière and took her by the hand.

"Mademoiselle," he said to her, "shall I be guilty of
an indiscretion if I ask what is the matter? You seem
oppressed, and your eyes are filled with tears."

"Oh! sire, if I be indeed so, and if my eyes are indeed
full of tears, I am sad only at the sadness which seems
to oppress your majesty."

"My sadness? You are mistaken, mademoiselle; no, it
is not sadness I experience."

"What is it, then, sire?"

"Humiliation."

"Humiliation? Oh, sire, what a word for you to use!"

"I mean, mademoiselle, that wherever I may happen
to be, no one else ought to be the master. Well, then,
look, and judge whether I am not eclipsed, I, the King
of France, before the king of this domain. Oh!" he continued, clenching his hands and teeth, "when I think that
this king . . ."

"Well, sire?" said Louise, terrified.

"That this king is a faithless, unworthy servant, who
becomes arrogant with stolen property! And, therefore,
am I about to change this impudent minister's *fête* into a

scene of mourning, which the nymph of Vaux, as the poets say, shall not soon forget.''

"Oh! your majesty . . .''

"Well, mademoiselle, are you about to take Monsieur Fouquet's side?'' said Louis impatiently.

"No, sire; I will only ask whether you are well informed. Your majesty has more than once learned the value of accusations made at court.''

Louis XIV gestured for Colbert to approach.

"Speak, Monsieur Colbert,'' said the young prince, "for I almost believe that Mademoiselle de la Vallière has need of your assurance before she can put any faith in the king's word. Tell mademoiselle what Monsieur Fouquet has done; and you, mademoiselle, will perhaps have the kindness to listen. It will not be long.''

Why did Louis XIV insist upon it in such a manner? A very simple reason: his heart was not at rest; his mind was not thoroughly convinced; he imagined there was some dark, hidden, tortuous intrigue concealed beneath these thirteen million francs; and he wished that the pure heart of La Vallière, revolted at the idea of a theft, should approve, even were it only by a single word, the resolution he had taken, and which, nevertheless, he hesitated about carrying into execution.

"Speak, monsieur,'' said La Vallière to Colbert, who stepped forward; "speak, since the king wishes me to listen to you. Tell me, what is the crime with which Monsieur Fouquet is charged?''

"Not very serious, mademoiselle,'' he said; "a simple breach of trust.''

"Speak, speak, Colbert; and when you shall have told her, leave us, and go and inform Monsieur d'Artagnan that I have certain orders to give him.''

"Monsieur D'Artagnan, sire!'' exclaimed La Vallière: "but why send for Monsieur D'Artagnan? I beg you to tell me.''

"Pardieu! in order to arrest this arrogant Titan, who, true to his menace, threatens to scale my heaven.''

"Arrest Monsieur Fouquet, do you say?''

"Does that surprise you?''

"In his own house?''

"Why not? If he be guilty, he is guilty in his own house as anywhere else.''

"Monsieur Fouquet, who at this moment is ruining himself for his sovereign."

"In plain truth, mademoiselle, it seems as if you were defending this traitor."

Colbert began to chuckle silently. The king turned around at the sound of this suppressed mirth.

"Sire," said La Vallière, "it is not Monsieur Fouquet I am defending; it is yourself."

"Me! you defend me?"

"Sire, you would be dishonoring yourself if you were to give such an order."

"Dishonor myself!" murmured the king, turning pale with anger. "In plain truth, mademoiselle, you show a strange emotion in what you say."

"If I do so, sire, my only motive is that of serving your majesty," replied the noble-hearted girl; "for that I would risk, I would sacrifice my very life, without the slightest reserve."

Colbert seemed inclined to grumble and complain. La Vallière, that gentle lamb, turned around upon him, and with a glance like lightning imposed silence upon him.

"Monsieur," she said, "when the king acts well, whether, in doing so, he does either myself or those who belong to me an injury, I have nothing to say; but were the king to help me or mine, if he acted badly, I should tell him so."

"But it appears to me, mademoiselle," Colbert ventured to say, "that I, too, love the king."

"Yes, monseigneur, we both love him, but each in a different manner," replied La Vallière, with such an accent that the heart of the young king was powerfully affected by it. "I love him so deeply that the whole world is aware of it; so purely that the king himself does not doubt my affection. He is my king and my master; I am the humblest of his servants. But he who touches his honor touches my life. Therefore, I repeat, that they dishonor the king who advise him to arrest Monsieur Fouquet under his own roof."

Colbert hung down his head, for he felt that the king had abandoned him. However, as he bent his head he whispered:

"Mademoiselle, I have only one word to say."

"Do not say it, then, monsieur; for I would not listen

to it. Besides, what could you have to tell me? That Monsieur Fouquet has been guilty of certain crimes? I know he has, because the king has said so; and from the moment the king said, 'I think so,' I have no need for other lips to say, 'I affirm it.' But, were Monsieur Fouquet the vilest of men, I should say aloud, 'Monsieur Fouquet's person is sacred to the king, because he is the king's host.' Were his house a den of thieves, were Vaux a cave of counterfeiters or robbers, his home is sacred, his palace is inviolable, since his wife is living in it, and that is an asylum which even executioners would not dare to violate.''

La Vallière paused, and was silent. In spite of himself, the king could not but admire her; he was overpowered by the passionate energy of her voice, by the nobility of the cause she advocated. Colbert yielded, overcome by the inequality of the struggle. At last the king breathed again more freely, shook his head, and held out his hand to La Vallière.

''Mademoiselle,'' he said gently, ''why do you decide against me? Do you know what this wretched fellow will do, if I give him time to breathe?''

''Is he not a prey which will always be within your grasp?''

''And if he escapes, and flees?'' exclaimed Colbert.

''Well, monsieur, it will always remain on record, to the king's eternal honor, that he allowed Monsieur Fouquet to flee; and the more guilty he may have been, the greater will the king's honor and glory appear, when once compared with such misery and such shame.''

Louis kissed La Vallière's hand as he knelt before her.

''I am lost,'' thought Colbert; then suddenly his face brightened up again. ''No, no, not yet,'' he said to himself.

And while the king, protected by the thick covert of an enormous linden tree, was embracing La Vallière with all the ardor of ineffable love, Colbert calmly looked among the papers in his pocketbook, and drew out of it a paper folded in the form of a letter, slightly yellow, perhaps, but which must have been very precious, since the intendant smiled as he looked at it; he then cast a look, full of hatred, upon the charming pair which the young girl and the king made—a pair which was revealed for a moment, as the light of the approaching torches shone upon them. Louis noticed the light reflected upon La Vallière's white dress.

"Leave me, Louise," he said, "for someone is coming."

"Mademoiselle, mademoiselle, someone is coming!" cried Colbert, to hurry the young girl's departure.

Louise disappeared rapidly among the trees; and then, as the king, who had been on his knees before the young girl, was rising from his humble posture, Colbert exclaimed:

"Ah! Mademoiselle de La Vallière has dropped something."

"What is it?" inquired the king.

"A paper, a letter, something white; look there, sire."

The king stooped down immediately and picked up the letter, crumbling it in his hand as he did so; and at the same moment the torches arrived, flooding with light this obscure scene.

CHAPTER XVI

JEALOUSY

THE torches we have just referred to, the eager attention which everyone displayed, and the new ovation paid to the king by Fouquet, arrived in time to suspend the effect of a resolution which La Vallière had already considerably shaken in Louis XIV's heart. He looked at Fouquet with a feeling almost of gratitude for having given La Vallière an opportunity of showing herself so generously disposed, so powerful in the influence she exercised over his heart. The moment of the last and greatest display had arrived. Hardly had Fouquet led the king toward the chateau, than a mass of fire burst from the dome of Vaux, with a prodigious uproar, pouring a flood of dazzling light on every side, and illuminating the farthest corners of the gardens. The fireworks began. Colbert, at twenty paces from the king, who was surrounded and feted by

the owner of Vaux, seemed, by the obstinate persistence
of his gloomy thoughts, to do his utmost to recall Louis's
attention, which the magnificence of the spectacle was
already, in his opinion, too easily diverting. Suddenly,
just as Louis was about to hold it out to Fouquet, he
perceived in his hand the paper which, as he believed,
La Vallière had dropped at his feet as she hurried away.
The still stronger magnet of love drew the young prince's
attention toward his mistress; and, by the brilliant light,
which increased momentarily in beauty, and drew forth
from the neighboring villages loud exclamations of admiration, the king read the letter, which he supposed was
a love letter which La Vallière had intended for him. As
he read it, a deathlike pallor stole over his face, and his
silent anger, lighted by the many-colored fires, was a
terrifying sight, which everyone would have shuddered
at, if they could have read into his heart, torn by the most
sinister passions. There was no truce for him now, influenced as he was by jealousy and mad passion. From the
very moment when the dark truth was revealed to him,
it all disappeared: pity, kindness, the religion of hospitality. In the bitter pang which wrung his heart, still too
weak to hide his sufferings, he was almost about to utter
a cry of alarm, and to call to his guards to gather around
him.

This letter which Colbert had thrown down at the king's
feet, the reader has doubtless guessed, was the same that
had disappeared with the porter, Toby, at Fontainebleau,
after the attempt which Fouquet had made upon La Vallière's heart. Fouquet saw the king's pallor, and was far
from guessing the evil; Colbert saw the king's anger, and
rejoiced inwardly at the approach of the storm. Fouquet's
voice drew the young prince from his wrathful reverie.

"What is the matter, sire?" inquired the surintendant,
with an expression of graceful interest.

Louis made a violent effort to control himself, as he
replied:

"Nothing."

"I am afraid your majesty is suffering."

"I am suffering, and have already told you so, monsieur; but it is nothing."

And the king, without waiting for the end of the

fireworks, turned toward the chateau. Fouquet accompanied him, and the whole court followed after them, leaving the remains of the fireworks burning for their own amusement. The surintendant tried again to question Louis XIV, but could not succeed in obtaining a reply. He imagined there had been some misunderstanding between Louis and La Vallière in the park, which had resulted in a slight quarrel; and that the king, who was not ordinarily sulky by disposition, but completely absorbed by his passion for La Vallière, had taken a dislike to everyone because his mistress had shown herself offended with him. This idea was sufficient to console him; he had even a friendly and kindly smile for the young king when the latter wished him good night. This, however, was not all the king had to submit to; he was obliged to undergo the usual ceremony, which on that evening was marked by the closest adherence to etiquette. The next day was the one set for the departure; it was but proper that the guests should thank their host, and should show him a little attention in return for his twelve million. The only remarks approaching amiability which the king could find to say to M. Fouquet, as he took leave of him, were these words:

"Monsieur Fouquet, you shall hear from me. Be good enough to send for Monsieur d'Artagnan."

And the blood of Louis XIII, who had concealed so much, was boiling in his veins; and he was perfectly ready to have M. Fouquet's throat cut, with the same readiness, indeed, as his predecessor had le Maréchal d'Ancre assassinated; and so he disguised the terrible resolution he had formed beneath one of those royal smiles which are the lightning flashes indicating *coups d'état*. Fouquet took the king's hand and kissed it; Louis shuddered throughout his whole frame, but let M. Fouquet touch his hand with his lips. Five minutes afterward D'Artagnan, to whom the royal order had been communicated, entered Louis XIV's bedroom. Aramis and Philippe were in theirs, still eagerly attentive, and still listening intently. The king did not even give the captain of the musketeers time to approach his armchair, but ran forward to meet him.

"Take care," he exclaimed, "that no one enters here."

"Very good, sire," replied the captain, who had been

studying for a long time the ravages on the king's face.
He gave the necessary order at the door; but, returning
to the king, he said:

"Is there something new that is wrong, your majesty?"

"How many men have you here?" inquired the king,
without answering the question asked of him.

"What for, sire?"

"How many men have you, I say?" repeated the king,
stamping the ground with his foot.

"I have the musketeers."

"Well, and what others?"

"Twenty guards and thirteen Swiss."

"How many men will be required to . . ."

"To do what, sire?" replied the musketeer, opening
his large, calm eyes.

"To arrest Monsieur Fouquet."

D'Artagnan fell back a step.

"To arrest Monsieur Fouquet!" he burst forth.

"Are you going to tell me that it is impossible?" exclaimed the king, with cold and vindictive passion.

"I never say that anything is impossible," replied
D'Artagnan, wounded to the quick.

"Very well; do it, then."

D'Artagnan turned on his heel, and made his way toward the door; it was a short distance, and he cleared it
in half a dozen steps; when he reached it he suddenly
paused, and said:

"Your majesty will forgive me, but, in order to carry
out this arrest, I would like a written order."

"For what purpose—and since when has the king's
word not been enough for you?"

"Because the word of a king, when it springs from a
feeling of anger, may possibly change when the feeling
changes."

"Enough talk, monsieur; you have another thought besides that."

"Oh! I, at least, have certain thoughts and ideas,
which, unfortunately, others have not," D'Artagnan replied impertinently.

The king, in his moment of anger, hesitated, and gave
way in the face of D'Artagnan's frank courage.

"What is your thought?" he exclaimed.

"This, sire," replied D'Artagnan: "You have a man arrested when you are still under his roof, and anger alone is the cause of that. When your anger passes away you will regret what you have done; and then I want to be able to show you your signature. If that, however, doesn't mend anything, it will, at least, show us that the king is wrong to lose his temper."

"Wrong to lose his temper!" cried the king, in a loud, passionate voice. "Did not my father, as well as my grandfather before me, lose their temper at times, in Heaven's name?"

"The king, your father, and the king, your grandfather, only lost their temper in their own palace."

"The king is master, wherever he may be."

"That is a flatterer's remark, which must come from Monsieur Colbert; but it happens not to be true. The king is at home in any house when he has driven its owner out of it."

The king bit his lip, but said nothing.

"Can it be possible?" said D'Artagnan; "here is a man who is positively ruining himself in order to please you, and you wish to have him arrested? *Mordioux!* Sire, if my name was Fouquet, and people treated me in this way I would swallow, in a single gulp, ten fireworks, set fire to them, and blow myself and everybody else up to the sky. But of course, it is your wish, and it shall be done."

"Go," said the king; "but do you have enough men?"

"Do you think I am going to take a whole army to help me? Arrest Monsieur Fouquet! why, that is so easy that a child could do it. It is like drinking a glass of bitters; you make an ugly face, and that is all."

"What if he defends himself?"

"That is not at all likely. Defend himself when such extreme harshness as you are going to enforce makes him king and martyr! No, I am sure that if he had a million francs left, which I doubt, he would give it in order to have such an end as this. But what does that matter? It shall be done at once."

"Wait," said the king; "do not make his arrest a public affair."

"That will be more difficult."

"Why so?"

"Because nothing is easier than to go up to Monsieur Fouquet in the midst of a thousand enthusiastic guests and say, 'In the king's name, I arrest you.' But to go up to him, to turn him first one way and then another, to drive him into one of the corners of the chessboard, so that he cannot escape; to take him away from his guests, and keep him a prisoner for you, without any of his *alas* being heard—that indeed is a real difficulty, the greatest of all, in fact; and I hardly see how it can be done."

"You had better say it is impossible, and you will have finished much sooner. Heaven help me, but I seem to be surrounded by people who prevent me from doing what I wish."

"I do not prevent you from doing anything. Are you decided?"

"Take care of Monsieur Fouquet, until I make up my mind tomorrow morning."

"That shall be done, sire."

"And return when I rise in the morning for further orders; and now leave me to myself."

"You do not even want Monsieur Colbert?" asked the musketeer, firing this last shot as he was leaving the room. The king trembled. With his whole mind fixed on the thought of revenge, he had forgotten the cause and substance of the offense.

"No, no one," he said; "no one. Leave me."

D'Artagnan left the room. The king closed the door with his own hands, and began to pace his apartment furiously, like a wounded bull in an arena, dragging after him the colored streamers and iron darts. At last he began to take comfort in the expression of his violent feelings.

"Miserable wretch that he is! not only does he squander my finances, but with his ill-gotten plunder he corrupts secretaries, friends, generals, artists, and all, and tries to rob me of my mistress. And that is the reason why that treacherous girl defended him! Gratitude! and who knows? . . . maybe even love."

He allowed himself to dwell on those bitter reflections for a moment.

"A satyr!" he thought, with that deep hatred with which young men regard those more advanced in life who still think of love. "A man who has never found opposition or resistance in anyone, who lavishes his gold and jewels in every direction, and who keeps his staff of painters in order to have the portraits of his mistresses in costumes of goddesses.''

The king trembled with passion, as he continued:

''He defiles everything. He destroys everything. He will be my death at last, I know. That man is too much for me; he is my mortal enemy. He shall fall! I hate him . . . I hate him . . . I hate him!'' And as he spoke these words he violently struck the arm of the chair in which he was sitting, over and over again, and then rose like one in an epileptic fit. ''Tomorrow! tomorrow! oh, happy day!'' he murmured. ''When the sun rises, having no rival but me, that man shall fall so low that when people look at the utter ruin which my anger will have caused, they will be forced to admit at last that I am indeed greater than he.''

The king, incapable of mastering his emotions any longer, with a blow of his fist knocked over a small table placed close to his bedside, and in the bitterness of feeling from which he was suffering, almost weeping, and half-suffocated by his passion, he threw himself on his bed, dressed as he was, to bite the sheets and to find there some rest. The bed creaked beneath his weight, and, except for a few sighs which escaped from his panting chest, complete silence soon reigned in the chamber of Morpheus.

CHAPTER XVII

HIGH TREASON

THE uncontrollable anger which took hold of the king at the sight of Fouquet's letter to La Vallière slowly subsided into a feeling of pain and extreme weariness. Youth, invigorated by health and lightness of spirit, and requiring that what it loses should be immediately restored—youth knows not those endless, sleepless nights which enable us to realize the fable of the vulture feeding on Prometheus's liver. In instances where the man in middle life, in his strength, and the older man, in his exhaustion,

find an incessant increase of their bitter sorrow, a young
man, surprised by the sudden appearance of a misfortune, weakens himself in sighs, groans, tears, in direct
struggles with it, and is thereby sooner overthrown by
the inflexible enemy with whom he is engaged. Once
overthrown, his struggles cease.

Louis could not hold out more than a few minutes;
then he stopped clenching his hands, and burning up with
his eyes the invincible objects of his hatred; he soon
stopped attacking with his violent imprecations not only
M. Fouquet, but even La Vallière; from fury he subsided
into despair, and from despair to prostration. After he
had thrown himself to and fro for a few minutes on his
bed, his nerveless arms fell quietly at his side; his head
lay languidly on his pillow; his limbs, exhausted from
his excessive emotions, still trembled occasionally, agitated by slight muscular contractions; and from his breast
came only rare sighs. Morpheus, the god of the apartment, toward whom Louis raised his eyes, wearied by
anger and reddened by tears, showered upon him the
poppies with which his hands were filled; so that the king
gently closed his eyes and fell asleep.

Then it seemed to him, as it often happens in that first
sleep, so light and gentle, which raises the body above
the bed, the soul above the earth—it seemed to him, we
say, as if the god Morpheus, painted on the ceiling, was
looking at him with human eyes; that something was
shining brightly, and moving to and fro in the dome above
the sleeper; that the crowd of terrible dreams which
thronged together in his brain, and which were interrupted for a moment, half-revealed a human face, with a
hand resting against the mouth, in an attitude of deep
and absorbed meditation. And, strange enough, too, this
man bore so wonderful a resemblance to the king himself
that Louis thought he was looking at his own face reflected in a mirror; with the exception, however, that the
face was saddened by a feeling of deep pity. Then it
seemed to him as if the dome gradually receded, disappearing from his gaze, and that the figures and attributes
painted by Le Brun became darker and darker as the distance became more and more remote. A gentle, easy
movement, as regular as that by which a ship dips with
the waves, followed the immobility of the bed. Doubtless

the king was dreaming, and in this dream the crown of
gold, which fastened the curtains together, seemed to re-
cede from his vision, just as the dome, to which it remained suspended, had done, so that the winged genius
which, with both its hands, was holding the crown,
seemed to call the king in vain, who was fast disappearing from it.

The bed was still sinking. Louis, with his eyes open,
was misled by this cruel hallucination. At last, as the
light of the royal chamber faded away into darkness,
something cold, gloomy, and inexplicable in its nature
seemed to infect the air. No paintings, nor gold, nor velvet draperies were visible any longer; nothing but walls
of a dull-gray color, which the increasing gloom made
darker every moment. And yet the bed still continued to
descend, and after a minute, which seemed an age to the
king, it reached a layer of air black and icy-cold, and
then it stopped. The king could no longer see the light
in his room, except as from the bottom of a well we can
see light of day.

"I am having a terrible dream," he thought. "It is
time to wake up. Come! let me wake up."

Everyone has experienced what the above remark con-
veys; there is hardly a person who, in the midst of a
suffocating nightmare, has not said to himself, with the
help of that light which still burns in the brain when every
human light is extinguished, "It is nothing but a dream."
This was precisely what Louis XIV said to himself; but
when he said, "Come, come! wake up!" he noticed that
not only was he already awake, but even more, that he
had his eyes open as well; he then looked around him.
On his right and on his left two armed men stood silently,
each wrapped in a huge cloak, their faces covered with
a mask; one of them held a small lamp in his hand, whose
glimmering light revealed the saddest picture a king could
see. Louis could not help saying to himself that his dream
was still going on and that all he had to do to make it
disappear was to move his arms or to say something
aloud. He darted from his bed, and found himself upon
the damp, moist ground. Then, speaking to the man who
was holding the lamp in his hand, he said:

"What is this, monsieur, and what is the meaning of
this jest?"

"It is no jest," replied, in a deep voice, the masked figure that held the lantern.

"Do you belong to Monsieur Fouquet?" inquired the king, greatly astonished at his situation.

"It matters very little to whom we belong," said the phantoms; "we are your masters now; that is enough."

The king, more impatient than intimidated, turned to the other masked figure.

"If this is a comedy," he said, "you will tell Monsieur Fouquet that I find it improper, and that I demand it should cease."

The second masked person to whom the king had spoken was a tall and large man. He held himself erect and motionless as a block of marble.

"Well," added the king, stamping his foot, "aren't you answering?"

"We are not answering you, my good monsieur," said the giant, in a stentorian voice, "because there is nothing to answer."

"At least, tell me what you want," exclaimed Louis, folding his arms with a passionate gesture.

"You will know later," replied the man who held the lamp.

"In the meantime, tell me where I am?"

"Look."

Louis looked around him; but by the light of the lamp which the masked figure raised for the purpose, he could perceive nothing but the damp walls, which glistened here and there with the slimy traces of snails.

"Oh, a dungeon!" said the king.

"No, a tunnel."

"Which leads . . ."

"Will you be good enough to follow us?"

"I shall not move from here!" cried the king.

"If you are obstinate, my dear young friend," replied the taller and stouter of the two, "I will lift you up in my arms, roll you up in a cloak, and if you are suffocated there, why, so much the worse for you."

And as he said this, he disengaged from beneath his cloak a hand which Milo of Cortona would have envied, on the day when he had that unhappy idea of cutting down his last oak. The king dreaded violence, for he understood that the two men into whose power he had fallen had not gone so far with any idea of drawing back, and that they would consequently be ready to proceed to extremities, if necessary. He shook his head, and said:

"It seems I have fallen into the hands of a couple of assassins. Move on, then."

Neither of the men answered this remark. The one who was holding the lantern walked first, the king followed him, while the second masked figure closed the procession. In this manner they moved along a winding gallery of some length, with as many staircases leading out of it as are to be found in the mysterious and gloomy palaces of Ann Radcliff's creation. All these windings and turnings, during which the king heard the sound of falling water over his head, ended at last in a long corridor closed by an iron door. The figure with the lamp opened the door with one of the keys he wore suspended at his belt, where, during the whole time, the king had heard them rattle. As soon as the door was opened and let in the air, Louis recognized the balmy odors exhaled by the trees after a hot summer's day. He paused for a moment or two; but his huge companion who was following him thrust him out of the underground passage.

"Once more," said the king, turning toward the one who had just had the audacity to touch his sovereign. "What do you intend to do with the King of France?"

"Try and forget that word," replied the man with the lamp, in a tone to which one could not say no any more than to one of the famous decrees of Minos.

"You deserve to be broken on the wheel for the word you have just used," said the giant, as he extinguished the lamp his companion handed him; "but the king is too kind-hearted."

Louis, at that threat, made so sudden a movement that it seemed as if he wanted to escape; but the giant's hand was in a moment placed on his shoulder, and fixed him motionless where he stood.

"But tell me, at least, where we are going," said the king.

"Come," replied the former of the two men, with a kind of respect in his manner, and leading his prisoner toward a carriage which seemed to be waiting.

The carriage was completely concealed amid the trees.

Two horses, with their feet fettered, were fastened by a halter to the lower branches of a large oak.

"Get in," said the same man, opening the carriage door and letting down the step. The king obeyed, sat at the back of the carriage, the padded door of which was shut and locked immediately. As for the giant, he cut the fastenings by which the horses were bound, harnessed them himself, and mounted to the box, which was unoccupied. The carriage set off immediately at a quick trot, turned into the road to Paris, and in the forest of Sénart found a relay of horses fastened to the trees in the same manner the first horses had been, and without a postilion. The man on the box changed the horses, and continued to follow quickly the road toward Paris, and entered the city about three o'clock in the morning. The carriage proceeded along the Faubourg St. Antoine, and after having called out to the sentinel, "By the king's order," the driver conducted the horses into the circular enclosure of the Bastille, looking out upon the courtyard, called La Cour du Gouvernement. There the horses drew up, reeking with sweat, at the flight of steps, and a sergeant of the guard ran forward.

"Go and wake the governor," said the coachman, in a voice of thunder.

With the exception of this voice, which might have been heard at the entrance of the Faubourg St. Antoine, everything remained as calm in the carriage as in the prison. Ten minutes afterward M. de Baisemeaux appeared in his dressing gown on the threshold of the door.

"What is the matter now?" he asked, "and whom have you brought me there?"

The man with the lantern opened the carriage door, and said two or three words to the one who acted as driver, who immediately got down from his seat, took up a short musket which he kept under his feet, and placed its muzzle on the prisoner's chest.

"And fire at once if he speaks!" added aloud the man who got out of the carriage.

"Very good," replied his companion, without any other remark.

With this recommendation, the person who had accompanied the king in the carriage climbed the steps, at the top of which the governor was awaiting him.

"Monsieur d'Herblay!" said the latter.

"Hush!" said Aramis. "Let us go into your room."

"Good heavens! what brings you here at this hour?"

"A mistake, my dear Monsieur de Baisemeaux," Aramis replied quietly. "It appears that you were quite right the other day."

"What about?" inquired the governor.

"About the order of release, my dear friend."

"Tell me what you mean, monsieur—no, monseigneur," said the governor, almost suffocated by surprise and terror.

"It is a very simple affair. You remember, dear Monsieur Baisemeaux, that an order of release was sent to you."

"Yes, for Marchiali."

"Very good; we both thought that it was for Marchiali."

"Certainly; you will recollect, however, that I would not believe it, but that you compelled me."

"Oh! Baisemeaux, my good fellow, what a word to use—strongly recommended, that was all."

"Strongly recommended, yes; strongly recommended to give him up to you; and that you carried him off with you in your carriage."

"Well, my dear Monsieur de Baisemeaux, it was a mistake; it was discovered at the ministry, so that I now bring you an order from the king to free Seldon, that poor Scotch fellow, you know."

"Seldon! Are you sure this time?"

"Well, read it yourself," added Aramis, handing him the order.

"Why," said Baisemeaux, "this order is the very same that has already passed through my hands."

"Indeed?"

"It is the very one I assured you I saw the other evening. *Parbleu!* I recognize it by the blot of ink."

"I do not know whether it is that; but all I know is, that I am bringing it to you."

"But, then, what about the other?"

"What other?"

"Marchiali."

"I have got him here with me."

"But that is not enough for me. I require a new order to take him back again."

"Don't talk such nonsense, my dear Baisemeaux; you are speaking like a child! Where is the order you received respecting Marchiali?"

Baisemeaux ran to his iron chest and took it out. Aramis seized it, coolly tore it into four pieces, held them to the lamp, and burned them.

"Good heavens! what are you doing?" exclaimed Baisemeaux, in an extremity of terror.

"Look at your position a little quietly, my dear governor," said Aramis, with his imperturbable self-possession, "and you will see how very simple the whole affair is. You no longer possess any order justifying Marchiali's release."

"I am a lost man!"

"Far from it, my good fellow, since I have brought Marchiali back to you, and it is just the same as if he had never left."

"Ah!" said the governor, completely overcome by terror.

"Plain enough, you see; and you will go and shut him up immediately."

"I should think so, indeed."

"And you will hand over this Seldon to me, whose liberation is authorized by this order. Do you understand?"

"I . . . I . . ."

"You do understand, I see," said Aramis. "Very good."

Baisemeaux clasped his hands together.

"But why, after having taken Marchiali away from me, do you bring him back again?" cried the unhappy governor in a spasm of terror and emotion.

"For a friend such as you," said Aramis, "for so devoted a servant, I have no secrets"; and he put his mouth close to Baisemeaux's ear, as he said, in a low tone of voice, "You know the resemblance between that unfortunate fellow and . . ."

"And the king? Yes."

"Very good; the very first use that Marchiali made of his liberty was to claim . . . Can you guess what?"

"How do you want me to guess?"

"To claim that he was the King of France; to dress himself up in clothes like those of the king; and then to pretend that he was the king himself."

"Gracious heavens!"

"That is the reason why I have brought him back again, my dear friend. He is crazy, and lets everyone see how crazy he is."

"What is to be done, then?"

"That is very simple; let no one talk with him. You understand that when his peculiar style of madness reached the king's ears, the king, who had pitied his terrible affliction, and saw how his kindness had been repaid by such black ingratitude, became perfectly furious; so that, now—and remember this very distinctly, dear Monsieur de Baisemeaux, for it concerns you most closely—so that there is now, I repeat, sentence of death pronounced against all those who may allow him to communicate with anyone else but me or the king himself. You understand, Baisemeaux, a sentence of death!"

"You do not need to ask me whether I understand."

"And now, let us go down and lead this poor devil back to his dungeon, unless you prefer he come up here."

"What would be the good of that?"

"It would be better, perhaps, to register his name in the prison book immediately."

"Of course."

"In that case, let's go."

Baisemeaux ordered the drums to be beaten, and the bell rung, as a warning to everyone to retire, in order to avoid meeting a mysterious prisoner. Then, when the passages were free, he went to take the prisoner from the carriage, at whose chest Porthos, faithful to the directions which had been given him, still kept his rifle leveled.

"Ah! is that you, miserable wretch?" cried the governor as soon as he saw the king. "Very good, very good!"

And immediately, making the king get out of the carriage, he led him, still accompanied by Porthos, who had not taken off his mask, and Aramis, who put his back on, up the stairs to the second Bertaudière and opened the door of the room in which Philippe for eight long years had bemoaned his existence. The king entered into the cell without pronouncing a single word; he was pale and haggard. Baisemeaux shut the door after him, turned the key twice in the lock, and then returned to Aramis.

"It is quite true," he said, in a low tone, "that he has a rather strong resemblance to the king; but still less so than you said."

"So that," said Aramis, "you would not have been deceived by the substitution of the one for the other?"

"What a question!"

"You are a most valuable fellow, Baisemeaux," said Aramis; "and now set Seldon free."

"Oh, yes! I was about to forget that. I will go and give orders at once."

"Tomorrow will be time enough."

"Tomorrow! Oh, no! This very minute."

"Well, go off to your affairs, I shall go away to mine. But it is quite understood, is it not?"

"What 'is quite understood'?"

"That no one is to enter the prisoner's cell, except with an order from the king—an order which I will myself bring."

"Quite so. Adieu, monseigneur."

Aramis returned to his companion.

"Now, Porthos, my good fellow, back again to Vaux, and as fast as possible."

"A man is light and easy enough when he has faithfully served his king, and, in serving him, saved his country," said Porthos. "The horses will have nothing to pull. So let us be off."

And the carriage, lightened of a prisoner, who might well be, as he in fact was, very heavy for Aramis, passed across the drawbridge of the Bastille, which was raised again immediately after them.

CHAPTER XVIII

A NIGHT AT THE BASTILLE

WHEN the young king, stupefied and crushed, found himself led to a cell in the Bastille, he imagined that

death itself is like sleep; that it, too, has its dreams; that
the bed had broken through the floor of his room at Vaux;
that death had resulted; and that, still carrying out his
dream, as the king, Louis XIV, now no longer living,
was dreaming one of those horrors, impossible to realize
in life, which is termed dethronement, imprisonment,
and insult toward a sovereign who formerly wielded un-
limited power. To be present at—an actual witness, as
well—his painful death; to float, in an incomprehensible
mystery, between fantasy and reality; to hear everything,
to see everything, without missing a single detail of his
agony, was—so the king thought—a torture far more terrible, since it might last forever.

"Is this what is called eternity, hell?" he whispered,
at the moment the door closed behind him, pushed by
Baisemeaux.

He did not even look around him; and in the room,
leaning against the wall, he allowed himself to be carried
away by the terrible supposition that he was already dead,
as he closed his eyes, in order to avoid looking upon
something even worse still.

"How can I have died?" he said to himself, sick with
terror. "Could that bed have been let down by some ar-
tificial means? But no! I do not remember having received any contusion, nor any shock either. Could they
have poisoned me at one of my meals, or with the fumes
of wax, as they did my ancestress, Jeanne d'Albret?"

Suddenly, the chill of the dungeon seemed to fall like
a cloak upon Louis's shoulders.

"I saw," he said, "my father lying dead upon his funeral bed, in his regal robes. That pale face, so calm and
worn; those hands, once so skillful, lying nerveless by
his side; those limbs stiffened by the icy grasp of death;
nothing there intimated a sleep peopled with dreams. And
yet how numerous were the dreams which God might
have sent that corpse—him, whom so many others had
preceded, hurried away by him into eternal death! No,
that king was still the king; he was still enthroned upon
that funeral bed, as upon a velvet armchair; he had ab-
dicated nothing of his majesty. God, who did not punish
him, cannot, will not punish me, who have done nothing."

A strange sound attracted the young man's attention.

He looked around him, and saw on the mantelpiece, just below an enormous crucifix, coarsely painted in fresco on the wall, an enormous rat nibbling a piece of dry bread, while focusing all the time an intelligent and inquiring eye upon the new occupant of the cell. The king could not resist a sudden impulse of fear and disgust; he moved back toward the door, uttering a loud cry; it was as if he needed this cry, which escaped from his breast almost unconsciously, to recognize himself. Louis knew that he was alive and in full possession of his natural senses.

"A prisoner!" he cried. "I, I am a prisoner!"

He looked for a bell to summon someone to him.

"There are no bells at the Bastille," he said, "and it is in the Bastille I am imprisoned. In what way can I have been made a prisoner? It must have been a conspiracy of Monsieur Fouquet. I have been drawn to Vaux, as into a snare. Monsieur Fouquet cannot be acting alone in this affair. His agent . . . That voice that I just now heard was Monsieur d'Herblay's; I recognized it. Colbert was right, then. But what is Fouquet's goal? To reign in my place? Impossible! Yet, who knows?" thought the king, relapsing into gloom. "Perhaps my brother, the Duc d'Orleans, is doing what my uncle wanted to do during all his life against my father. But the queen? My mother, too? And La Vallière? Oh, La Vallière, she will have been handed over to Madame. Dear, dear girl! Yes, it is—it must be so. They must have shut her up as they have me. We are separated forever!"

And at this idea of separation the lover burst into tears, sobs, and groans.

"There is a governor in this place," the king continued, in a fury of passion. "I will speak to him, I will summon him to me."

He called, but no voice replied. He seized hold of his chair, and hurled it against the massive oak door. The wood resounded against the door, and awakened a mournful echo in the depths of the staircase; but from a human creature, there was not one sound.

This was a new proof for the king of the slight regard in which he was held at the Bastille. Therefore, when his first fit of anger passed away, he noticed a sliver of light through a barred window, which must be dawn, and he began to call out, at first gently enough, then louder and louder still; but no one answered him. Twenty other attempts which he made, one after another, obtained no other or better success. His blood began to boil, and rise to his head. His nature was such that, accustomed to command, he trembled at the idea of disobedience. By degrees his anger increased. The prisoner broke the chair, which was too heavy for him to lift, and used it as a battering ram to strike against the door. He struck so loudly, and so repeatedly, that sweat soon began to pour down his face. The sound became tremendous and continuous; some stifled, smothered cries replied from various directions. This sound produced a strange effect upon the king. He paused to listen; it was the voices of the prisoners, formerly his victims, now his companions. The voices rose like vapors through the thick ceilings and the massive walls, and accused the author of this noise, as doubtless their sighs and tears accused, in whispered tones, the author of their captivity. After having deprived so many people of their liberty, the king came among them to rob them of their rest. This idea almost drove him mad; it redoubled his strength, or, rather his will, bent upon obtaining some information, or a conclusion to the affair. With a portion of the broken chair he recommenced the noise. At the end of an hour Louis heard something in the corridor, behind the door of his cell, and a violent blow, which was returned upon the door itself, made him cease his own.

"Are you mad," said a rude, brutal voice. "What is the matter with you this morning?"

"This morning!" thought the king; but he said aloud politely, "Monsieur, are you the governor of the Bastille?"

"My good fellow, you are deranged," replied the voice; "but that is no reason why you should make such a terrible disturbance. Be quiet, *mordioux!*"

"Are you the governor?" the king inquired again.

He heard a door on the corridor close; the jailer had just left, not even condescending to reply a single word. When the king had assured himself of his departure, his fury no longer knew any bounds. As agile as a tiger, he leaped from the table to the window, and struck the iron bars with all his might. He broke a pane of glass, the pieces of which fell clanking into the courtyard below. He shouted with increasing hoarseness, ''The governor! the governor!'' This outburst lasted fully an hour, during which time he was in a burning fever. With his hair in disorder and matted on his forehead, his dress torn and whitened, his linen in shreds, the king did not rest until his strength was utterly exhausted, and it was not until then that he clearly understood the pitiless thickness of the walls, the impenetrable nature of the cement, invincible to all other influence but that of time, and possessed of no other weapon but despair. He leaned his forehead against the door and let his heart calm down by degrees; it had seemed as if one single additional beat would have made it burst.

''A moment will come when the food that is given to the prisoners will be brought to me. I shall then see someone; I shall speak to him, and get an answer.''

And the king tried to remember at what time the first meal was served at the Bastille; he was ignorant even of this detail. The feeling of remorse at this memory struck him like the keen thrust of a dagger, that he should have lived for twenty-five years a king, and enjoying every happiness, without bestowing a moment's thought on the misery of those who had been unjustly deprived of their liberty. The king blushed out of shame. He felt that God, in permitting this fearful humiliation, did no more than render on him the same torture as had been inflicted by him upon so many others. This soul, overwhelmed by the suffering of others, might have returned to religion. But Louis dared not even kneel in prayer to God to entreat Him to terminate his bitter trial.

''God is right,'' he said; ''God acts wisely. It would be cowardly to ask God what I have so often refused my own fellow creatures.''

He had reached this stage of his reflections, that is, of his agony of mind, when a similar noise was again heard behind his door, followed this time by the sound of the key in the lock, and of the bolts being withdrawn from their staples. The king bounded forward to be nearer to the person who was about to enter, but, suddenly reflecting that it was a movement unworthy of a sovereign, he paused, assumed a noble and calm expression, which for him was easy enough, and waited with his back turned toward the window, in order, to some extent, to conceal his agitation from the person who was about to enter. It was only a jailer with a basket of food. The king looked at the man with restless anxiety, and waited until he spoke.

"Ah!" said the latter, "you have broken your chair. That's what I was saying. Why, you must have become quite mad."

"Monsieur," said the king, "be careful what you say; it will be a very serious affair for you."

The jailer placed the basket on the table, and looked at his prisoner steadily.

"Eh?" he said.

"Have the governor come to me," added the king, in accents full of calm dignity.

"Come, my boy," said the turnkey, "you have always been very good, but you are getting vicious, it seems, and I want to warn you: you have broken your chair, and made a great disturbance; that is an offense punishable by imprisonment in one of the lower dungeons. Promise me not to do it again, and I will not say a word about it to the governor."

"I wish to see the governor," replied the king, still controlling his passion.

"He will send you off to one of the dungeons, I tell you; so take care."

"I insist upon it, do you hear?"

"Ah, ah! your eyes are becoming wild again. Very good! I shall take away your knife."

And the jailer did what he said, left the prisoner, and closed the door, leaving the king more astounded, more wretched, and more isolated than ever. It was useless, though he tried, to make the same noise again on his door, and equally useless that he threw the plates and dishes out of the window; not a single sound was heard in response. Two hours afterward he could not be recognized as a king, a gentleman, a man, a human being; he might rather be called a madman, tearing the door with his nails, trying to tear up the flooring of his cell, and uttering such wild and fearful cries that the old Bastille seemed to tremble to its very foundations for having revolted against its master. As for the governor, he had not even moved; the turnkeys and the sentinels had reported the occurrence to him, but what was the good of it? were not these madmen common enough in the fortress? and were not the walls still stronger than they? M. de Baisemeaux, thoroughly impressed with what Aramis had told him, and in perfect conformity with the king's order, hoped only that one thing might happen; namely, that the madman Marchiali might be mad enough to hang himself on the canopy of his bed, or from one of the bars of the window. In fact, the prisoner was anything but a profitable investment for M. Baisemeaux, and became more annoying than agreeable to him. These complications of Seldon and Marchiali—the complications, first of setting at liberty and then imprisoning again, the complications arising from the strong likeness in question— might have a very practical ending. Baisemeaux even thought he had noticed that D'Herblay himself was not altogether dissatisfied with it.

"And then, really," said Baisemeaux to his next in command, "an ordinary prisoner is already unhappy enough in being a prisoner; he suffers quite enough indeed to induce one to hope charitably enough that his death may not be far distant. With still greater reason, then, when the prisoner has gone mad, and might bite and make a terrible disturbance in the Bastille; why, in that case, it is not simply an act of mere charity to wish him dead; it would be almost a good, and even commendable action, to quietly put him out of his misery."

And the good-natured governor thereupon sat down to his late breakfast.

CHAPTER XIX

THE SHADOW OF M. FOUQUET

D'ARTAGNAN, still confused and oppressed by the conversation he had just had with the king, was wondering if he were really in possession of his senses, if he were really and truly at Vaux, if he, D'Artagnan, were really the captain of the musketeers and M. Fouquet the owner of the chateau in which Louis XIV was at that

moment partaking of his hospitality. These reflections
were not those of a drunken man, although everything
was in prodigal profusion at Vaux, and the surintendant's
wines had met with a distinguished reception at the *fête*.
The Gascon, however, was a man of calm self-
possession; and no sooner did he touch his bright steel
blade than he knew how to adopt morally the cold, keen
weapon as his guide of action.

"Well," he said, as he left the royal apartment, "I
seem now to be mixed up historically with the destinies
of the king and the minister; it will be written that Monsieur D'Artagnan, a younger son of a Gascon family,
placed his hand on the shoulder of Monsieur Nicolas
Fouquet, the surintendant of finances of France. My descendants, if I have any, will flatter themselves with the
distinction which this arrest will confer, just as the members of the De Luynes family have done with regard to
the estates of the poor Maréchal d'Ancre. But the question is, how to execute the king's order in a proper manner. Any man would know how to say to Monsieur
Fouquet, 'Your sword, monsieur.' But it is not everyone
who would be able to take care of Monsieur Fouquet
without others knowing anything about it. How am I to
manage, then, that Monsieur le Surintendant pass from
the height of favor to the direst disgrace; that Vaux be
turned into a dungeon for him; that after having been
steeped to his lips, as it were, in all the perfumes and
incense of Assuerus, he is transferred to the gallows of
Haman—in other words, of Enguerraud de Marigny?"

And at this reflection D'Artagnan's brow became
clouded with perplexity. The musketeer had certain scruples on the matter, it must be admitted. To deliver up to
death (for not a doubt existed that Louis hated Fouquet
mortally) the man who had just shown himself so delightful and charming a host in every way, was a real case of
conscience.

"It almost seems," said D'Artagnan to himself, "that
if I am not a poor, mean, miserable fellow, I should let
Monsieur Fouquet know the opinion the king has of him.
Yet, if I betray my master's secret, I shall be a false-
hearted, treacherous knave, a traitor, too—a crime provided for and punishable by military laws—so much so,
indeed, that twenty times, in former days when wars were

rife, I have seen many a miserable fellow strung up to a tree for doing, in a small degree, what my scruples counsel me to do to a greater extent now. No, I think that a man of true quickness of mind ought to get out of this difficulty with more skill than that. And now, let us admit that I do possess a little quickness of mind—it is not at all certain, though, for, after having used so large a quantity for forty years, I shall be lucky if there were to be a pistole's worth left.''

D'Artagnan buried his head in his hands, tore his mustache in sheer vexation, and added:

''What can be the reason for Monsieur Fouquet's disgrace? There seem to be three good ones: the first, because Monsieur Colbert doesn't like him; the second, because he wished to fall in love with Mademoiselle de la Vallière, and, lastly, because the king likes Monsieur Colbert and loves Mademoiselle de la Vallière. Oh, he is a lost man! But shall I put my foot on his neck, I of all men, when he is falling prey to the intrigues of a set of women and clerks? For shame! If he is dangerous, I will lay him low enough; if, however, he is only persecuted, I will look on. I have reached a stage where neither king nor living man shall change my opinion. If Athos were here, he would do as I have done. Therefore, instead of going cold-bloodedly up to Monsieur Fouquet, and arresting him and shutting him up, I will try to conduct myself like a man who understands what good manners are. People will talk about it, of course; but they shall talk well of it.''

And D'Artagnan, in a gesture peculiar to himself, drew his shoulder belt over his shoulder and went straight off to M. Fouquet, who, after he had taken leave of his guests, was preparing to retire for the night and to sleep peacefully after the triumphs of the day. The air was still perfumed, or infected, whichever way it may be viewed, with the smell of the fireworks. The wax lights were dying away in their sockets, the flowers fell unfastened from the garlands, the groups of dancers and courtiers were separating in the sitting rooms. Surrounded by his friends, who complimented him and received his flattering remarks in return, the surintendant half-closed his weary eyes. He longed for rest; he sank upon the bed of laurels, which had been heaped up for him for so many days past; it might almost have been said that he seemed bowed beneath the weight of the new debts which he had incurred for the purpose of giving the greatest possible honor to this *fête*. Fouquet had just retired to his room, still smiling, but more than half-dead. He could listen to nothing more, he could hardly keep his eyes open; his bed seemed to possess a fascinating and irresistible attraction for him. The god Morpheus, the presiding deity of the dome painted by Le Brun, had extended his influence over the adjoining rooms, and showered down his most sleep-inducing poppies upon the master of the house. Fouquet, almost entirely alone, was being assisted by his servant to undress, when M. D'Artagnan appeared at the entrance of the room. D'Artagnan had never been able to succeed in making himself common at court; and notwithstanding he was seen everywhere and on all occasions, he never failed to produce an effect wherever and whenever he made his appearance. Such is the happy privilege of certain natures, which in that respect resemble either thunder or lightning; everyone recognizes them; but their appearance never fails to arouse surprise, and whenever they occur, the impression is always left that the last was the most violent.

"What! Monsieur D'Artagnan?" said Fouquet, who had already taken his right arm out of the sleeve of his doublet.

"At your service," replied the musketeer.

"Come in, my dear Monsieur D'Artagnan."

"Thank you."

"Have you come to criticize the *fête?* You are clever enough in your criticisms, I know."

"By no means."

"Are your men looked after properly?"

"In every way."

"You are not comfortably lodged, perhaps?"

"Nothing could be better."

"In that case, I have to thank you for being so amiably disposed, and I am grateful to you for all your flattering kindness."

These words were as much as to say, "My dear D'Artagnan, pray go to bed, since you have a bed to lie down on, and let me do the same."

D'Artagnan did not seem to understand it.

"Are you going to bed already?" he said to the surintendant.

"Yes; have you anything to say to me?"

"Nothing, monsieur, nothing at all. You sleep in this room, then?"

"Yes, as you see."

"You have given a most charming *fête* to the king."

"Do you think so?"

"Oh, beautiful!"

"Is the king pleased?"

"Enchanted."

"Did he desire you to say as much to me?"

"He would not choose so unworthy a messenger, monsieur."

"You do not do yourself justice, Monsieur D'Artagnan."

"Is that your bed there?"

"Yes; but why do you ask? Are you not satisfied with your own?"

"May I speak frankly to you?"

"Surely."

"Well, then, I am not."

Fouquet started, and then replied:

"Will you take my room, Monsieur D'Artagnan?"

"What! deprive you of it, monseigneur? Never!"

"What am I to do, then?"

"Allow me to share yours with you."

Fouquet looked at the musketeer fixedly.

"Ah! ah!" he said, "you have just left the king."

"I have, monseigneur."

"And the king wants you to spend the night in my room?"

"Monseigneur . . ."

"Very well, Monsieur D'Artagnan, very well. You are master here."

"I assure you, monseigneur, that I do not want to intrude . . ."

Fouquet turned to his valet, and said:

"Leave us."

When the man had left he said to D'Artagnan:

"You have something to say to me?"

"I?"

"A man of your superior intelligence cannot have come to talk with a man like myself, at such an hour as the present without grave motives."

"Do not interrogate me."

"On the contrary. What do you want with me?"

"Nothing more than the pleasure of your society."

"Come into the garden, then," said the surintendant suddenly, "or into the park."

"No," replied the musketeer hastily, "no!"

"Why?"

"The fresh air . . ."

"Come, admit at once that you are arresting me," said the surintendant to the captain.

"Never!" said the latter.

"You intend to look after me, then?"

"Yes, monseigneur; I do, upon my honor."

"Upon your honor? Ah! that is quite another thing. So I am to be arrested in my own house!"

"Do not say such a thing."

"On the contrary, I will proclaim it aloud."

"If you do so, I shall be compelled to request you to be silent."

"Very good! Violence toward me, and in my own house, too!"

"We do not seem to understand each other at all. Stay a moment; there is a chessboard there; let us play, please, monseigneur."

"Monsieur D'Artagnan, I am in disgrace, then?"

"Not at all; but . . ."

"Am I forbidden from withdrawing from your sight?"

"I do not understand a word you are saying, monseigneur; and if you want me to withdraw, tell me so."

"My dear Monsieur D'Artagnan, your ways will drive me mad; I was almost falling asleep, but you have completely awakened me."

"I shall never forgive myself, I am sure; and if you wish to reconcile me with myself, why, go to sleep in your bed in my presence; I shall be delighted."

"I am under surveillance, I see."

"I will leave the room if you say such a thing as that."

"I don't understand you."

"Good night, monseigneur," said D'Artagnan, as he pretended to leave.

Fouquet ran after him.

"I will not lie down," he said. "Seriously, and since you refuse to treat me as a man, and since you are playing with me, I will try and set you at bay, as a hunter does a wild boar."

"Bah!" cried D'Artagnan, pretending to smile.

"I shall order my horses, and set off for Paris," said Fouquet, jarring the captain of the musketeers.

"If that be the case, monseigneur, it is very different."

"You will arrest me, then?"

"No; but I shall go with you."

"That is quite sufficient, Monsieur D'Artagnan," returned Fouquet in a cold tone of voice. "It is not idly that you have acquired your reputation as a man of intelligence and full of resources; but with me that is quite superfluous. Let us two come to the point. Grant me a request. Why do you arrest me? What have I done?"

"I know nothing about what you have done; but I do not arrest you—this evening, at least."

"This evening!" exclaimed Fouquet, turning pale, "but tomorrow?"

"It is not tomorrow just yet, monseigneur. Who can ever answer for the morrow?"

"Quick, quick, captain! Let me speak to Monsieur d'Herblay."

"Alas! that is quite impossible, monseigneur. I have strict orders to see that you hold no communication with anyone."

"With Monsieur d'Herblay, captain—with your friend."

"Monseigneur, isn't Monsieur d'Herblay the only person with whom you ought to be prevented holding any communication?"

Fouquet colored, and then, assuming an air of resignation, he said:

"You are right, monsieur; you have taught me a lesson that I ought not to have provoked. A fallen man cannot assert his right to anything, even from those whose fortunes he has made; all the more from those to whom he never had the happiness of doing a service."

"Monseigneur!"

"It is perfectly true, Monsieur D'Artagnan; you have

always acted in the most admirable manner toward me—
in such a manner, indeed, as most becomes the man who
is destined to arrest me. You, at least, have never asked
me anything.''

"Monseigneur," replied the Gascon, touched by his
eloquent and noble tone of grief, "will you—I ask it as
a favor—pledge me your word as a man of honor that you
will not leave this room?"

"What is the use of it, dear Monsieur d'Artagnan,
since you keep watch over me? Do you suppose that I
should struggle against the most valiant sword in the
kingdom?"

"It is not that at all, monseigneur; but that I am going
to look for Monsieur d'Herblay, and, consequently, to
leave you alone."

Fouquet uttered a cry of delight and surprise.

"To look for Monsieur d'Herblay! to leave me alone!"
he exclaimed, clasping his hands together.

"Which is Monsieur d'Herblay's room? The blue
room, is it not?"

"Yes, my friend, yes."

"Your friend! thank you for that word, monseigneur;
you confer it upon me today, at least, if you have never
done so before."

"Ah! you have saved me."

"It will take me a good ten minutes to go from here
to the blue room, and to return?" said D'Artagnan.

"Nearly so."

"And then to wake Aramis, who sleeps very soundly
when he is asleep, I put that down at another five minutes; making a total of fifteen minutes' absence. And
now, monseigneur, give me your word that you will not
in any way attempt to make your escape, and that when
I return I shall find you here again."

"I give it to you, monsieur," replied Fouquet, with an
expression of the warmest gratitude.

D'Artagnan disappeared. Fouquet looked at him as he
left the room, waited with a feverish impatience until the
door was closed behind him, and, as soon as it was shut
flew to his keys, opened two or three secret doors concealed in various pieces of furniture in the room, looked
vainly for certain papers, which doubtless he had left at
St. Mandé, and which he seemed to regret not having

found; then, hurriedly seizing letters, contracts, and various writings, he heaped them into a pile, which he burned hastily on the marble hearth of the fireplace, not even taking time to take out the vases and pots of flowers with which it was filled. As soon as he had finished, like a man who has just escaped imminent danger, and who loses his strength as soon as the danger is past, he sank down, completely overcome, on an armchair. When D'Artagnan returned he found Fouquet in the same position; the worthy musketeer had not the slightest doubt that Fouquet, having given his word, would not even think of failing to keep it, but he thought it most likely that Fouquet would make use of his absence to the best advantage to get rid of all papers, memorandums, and contracts which might make his position, which was now serious enough, more dangerous than ever. And so, raising his head like a dog who catches the scent, he detected a smell of smoke which he had expected to find, and having found it, he nodded with satisfaction. When D'Artagnan had entered Fouquet had raised his head, and not one of D'Artagnan's movements had escaped him. And then the eyes of the two men met, and they both saw that they had understood each other without exchanging a syllable.

"Well!" asked Fouquet, "and Monsieur d'Herblay?"

"Upon my word, monseigneur," replied D'Artagnan, "Monsieur d'Herblay must be fond of walks by night, and composing poetry by moonlight in the park of Vaux with some of your poets, for he is not in his room."

"What! not in his room?" cried Fouquet, whose last hope had thus escaped him; for, without knowing in what way the bishop of Vannes could help him, he knew that in fact he could not expect assistance from anyone but him.

"Or, indeed," continued D'Artagnan, "if he is in his room, he has very good reasons for not answering."

"But surely you did not call him in such a manner that he could have heard you?"

"You can hardly suppose, monseigneur, that having already exceeded my orders, which forbid me from leaving you a single moment—you can hardly suppose, I say, that I should have been mad enough to rouse the whole house and allow myself to be seen in the corridor of the bishop of Vannes, in order that Monsieur Colbert might find out that I gave you time to burn your papers.''

"My papers?''

"Of course; at least, that is what I would have done in your place; when anyone opens a door for me, I always take advantage of it.''

"Yes, yes, and I thank you, for I have taken advantage of it.''

"And what you have done is perfectly right. Every man has his own peculiar secrets which others have nothing to do with. But let us return to Aramis, monseigneur.''

"Well, then, I tell you, you could not have called loud enough, or Aramis would have heard you.''

"However softly anyone may call Aramis, monseigneur, Aramis always hears when he has an interest in hearing. I repeat what I said before—Aramis was not in his room, or Aramis had certain reasons for not recognizing my voice, of which I am ignorant, and of which you even may be ignorant yourself, no matter how devoted to you his greatness the Lord Bishop of Vannes is.''

Fouquet let out a sigh, rose from his seat, paced his room three or four times, and finally, with an expression of extreme dejection, sat on his magnificent velvet bed, trimmed with splendid lace. D'Artagnan looked at Fouquet with deepest pity.

"I have seen a good many men arrested in my life,'' said the musketeer sadly; "I have seen both Monsieur de Cinq-Mars and Monsieur de Chalais arrested, though I was very young then. I have seen Monsieur de Condé arrested with the prince; I have seen Monsieur de Retz arrested; I have seen Monsieur Broussel arrested. Wait a moment, monseigneur, it is unpleasant to have to say it, but the one whom you most resemble at this moment is that poor fellow, Broussel. You were very near doing as he did, putting your dinner napkin in your portfolio, and wiping your mouth with your papers. *Mordioux!* Monseigneur Fouquet, a man like you ought not to be dejected in this manner. Suppose your friends saw you?''

"Monsieur d'Artagnan,'' replied the surintendant, with a smile full of gentleness, "you do not understand me; it is precisely because my friends do not see me that

I am as you see me now. I do not live, exist even, isolated from others; I am nothing when left to myself. Understand that throughout my whole life I have spent every moment of my time making friends, whom I hoped would support me. In times of prosperity, all these happy voices created in my honor a concert of praises and thanks. In the least disfavor, these humbler voices accompanied in harmonious accents the murmur of my own heart. Isolation I have never yet known. Poverty (a phantom I have sometimes beheld, clad in rags, awaiting me at the end of my journey through life)—this poverty has been the specter with which many of my own friends have trifled for years past, which they poetize and caress, and which has attracted me to them. Poverty! I accept it, acknowledge it, receive it, as a disinherited sister; for poverty is not solitude, nor exile, nor imprisonment. Is it likely I shall ever be poor, with such friends as Pélisson, as La Fontaine, as Molière? with such a mistress as . . . Oh! if you knew how utterly lonely and desolate I feel at this moment, and how you, who separate me from all I love, seem to be the image of solitude, of annihilation, and of death itself!''

"But I have already told you, Monsieur Fouquet," replied D'Artagnan, moved to the depths of his soul, "that you exaggerate matters. The king likes you."

"No, no!" said Fouquet, shaking his head.

"Monsieur de Colbert hates you."

"Monsieur de Colbert! What does that matter to me?"

"He will ruin you."

"Oh! I defy him to do that, for I am ruined already."

At this confession of the surintendant, D'Artagnan looked around the room; and although he did not open his lips, Fouquet understood him so thoroughly that he added:

"What can we do with those splendors when we are no more splendid? What's the use of our possessions? They will merely disgust us, by their very splendor, with everything which does not equal this splendor. Vaux! you will say, and the wonders of Vaux! Well, what? What shall I do with this marvel? If I am ruined, how shall I fill the urns which my Naiads bear in their arms, or force the air into the lungs of my Tritons? To be rich enough, Monsieur d'Artagnan, a man must be too rich."

D'Artagnan shook his head.

"Oh! I know very well what you think," replied Fouquet quickly. "If Vaux were yours, you would sell it, and would purchase an estate in the country; an estate which would have woods, orchards, and land, and that this estate would support its master. With forty million you might—"

"Ten million," interrupted D'Artagnan.

"Not a million, my dear captain. No one in France is rich enough to give two million for Vaux, and to continue to maintain it as I have done; no one could do it, no one would know how."

"Well," said D'Artagnan, "in any case, a million is not abject misery."

"It is not far from it, my dear monsieur. But you do not understand me. No; I will not sell my residence at Vaux; I will give it to you, if you like"; and Fouquet accompanied these words with a movement of his shoulders to which it would be impossible to do justice.

"Give it to the king; you will make a better bargain."

"The king does not need that I give it to him," said Fouquet; "he will take it away from me with the most perfect ease and grace, if he wants to do so; and that is the reason why I would prefer to see it perish. Do you know, Monsieur D'Artagnan, that if the king did not happen to be under my roof, I would take this candle, go straight to the dome, and set fire to a couple of huge chests of fuses and fireworks which are in reserve there, and would reduce my palace to ashes?"

"Bah!" said the musketeer negligently. "In all events, you would not be able to burn the gardens, and that is the best part about the place."

"And yet," resumed Fouquet thoughtfully, "what was I saying? Great heavens! burn Vaux! destroy my palace! But Vaux is not mine; it is true, these wonderful creations are the property, as far as sense of enjoyment goes, of the man who has paid for them; but as far as duration is concerned, they belong to those who created them. Vaux belongs to Le Brun, to Le Nôtre, to Pélisson, to Levau, to La Fontaine, to Molière; Vaux belongs to posterity, in fact. You see, Monsieur D'Artagnan, that my very house ceases to be my own."

"Good," said D'Artagnan; "here is an idea I like, and

I recognize Monsieur Fouquet himself in it. That idea, indeed, makes me forget that fellow Broussel altogether; and I now fail to recognize in you the whining complaints of that old frondeur. If you are ruined, monsieur, look at the affair manfully, for you too, *mordioux!* belong to posterity, and have no right to lessen yourself in any way. Wait a moment; look at me, I who seem to hold a kind of superiority over you, because I am arresting you; fate, who distributes their different parts to the comedians of this world, gave me a less agreeable and less advantageous part to fill than yours has been; I am one of those who think that the parts which kings and powerful nobles are called upon to act are of more worth than the parts of beggars or lackeys. It is far better even on the stage— on the stage, I mean, of another theater than the theater of this world—it is far better to wear a fine coat and to talk fine language than to walk the boards shod with a pair of old shoes, or to get one's backbone gently caressed by a sound thrashing with a stick. In one word, you have been a prodigal with money, you have ordered and been obeyed—have been steeped to the lips in enjoyment; while I have dragged my tether after me, have been commanded and have obeyed, and have drudged my life away. Well, although I may seem of such trifling importance beside you, monseigneur, I do declare to you that the memory of what I have done serves as a spur, and prevents me from bowing my old head too soon. I shall remain until the very end a good trooper; and when my turn comes I shall fall perfectly straight, all in a heap, still alive, after having selected my place beforehand. Do as I do, Monsieur Fouquet; you will not find yourself the worse for it; that happens only once in a lifetime to men like yourself, and the main thing is to do it well when the chance presents itself. There is a Latin proverb—the words have escaped me, but I remember the sense of it very well, for I have thought over it more than once, which says, 'The end crowns the work!' ''

Fouquet rose from his seat, put his arm around D'Artagnan's neck, and clasped him in a close embrace, while with the other hand he pressed his hand.

"An excellent sermon," he said, after a moment's pause.

"A soldier's, monseigneur."

"I can see that you like me, you who tell me all that."

"Perhaps."

Fouquet resumed his pensive attitude once again, and then, a moment later, he said:

"Where can Monsieur d'Herblay be? I dare not ask you to send for him."

"You would not ask me, because I would not do it, Monsieur Fouquet. People would hear about it, and Aramis, who is not mixed up with the affair, might be compromised and included in your disgrace."

"I will wait here until daylight," said Fouquet.

"Yes; that is best."

"What shall we do when daylight comes?"

"I know nothing at all about it, monseigneur."

"Monsieur D'Artagnan, will you do me a favor?"

"Most willingly."

"You watch me, I stay, you are acting in the full discharge of your duty, I suppose?"

"Certainly."

"Very good, then; stay as close to me as my shadow, if you like; and I infinitely prefer such a shadow to anyone else."

D'Artagnan bowed to this compliment.

"But, forget that you are Monsieur D'Artagnan, captain of the musketeers; forget that I am Monsieur Fouquet, surintendant of finances, and let us talk about my affairs."

"That is rather a delicate subject."

"Indeed?"

"Yes; but, for your sake, Monsieur Fouquet, I will do the impossible."

"Thank you. What did the king say to you?"

"Nothing."

"Ah! is that the way you talk?"

"Of course!"

"What do you think of my situation?"

"Nothing."

"However, unless you have some ill feeling against me . . ."

"Your position is a difficult one."

"In what respect?"

"Because you are under your own roof."

"However difficult it may be, yet I understand it very well."

"Do you suppose that with anyone else but yourself I should have shown so much frankness?"

"What! so much frankness, do you say? you, who refuse to tell me the slightest thing?"

"In all events, then, so much ceremony and consideration."

"Ah! I have nothing to say in that respect."

"One moment, monseigneur; let me tell you how I would have behaved toward anyone else but yourself. It might be that I happened to arrive at your door just as your guests or your friends had left you, or, if they had not yet gone, I would wait until they were leaving, and would then catch them one after the other, like rabbits; I would lock them up quietly enough; I would steal softly along the carpet of your corridor, and with one hand upon you, before you suspected the slightest thing, I would keep you safely until my master's breakfast in the morning. In this way, I would just the same have avoided all publicity, all disturbance, all opposition; but there would also have been no warning for Monsieur Fouquet, no consideration for his feelings, none of those delicate concessions which are shown by courteous people in decisive moments. Are you satisfied with that plan?"

"It makes me shudder."

"I thought you would not like it. It would have been sad to have appeared tomorrow, without any preparation, and to have asked you to hand over your sword."

"Oh, monsieur, I would have died from sheer shame and anger!"

"Your gratitude is too eloquently expressed. I have not done enough to deserve it, I assure you."

"Most certainly, monsieur, you will never get me to believe that."

"Well, then, monseigneur, if you are satisfied with what I have done, and have somewhat recovered from the shock which I prepared you for as much as I possibly could, let us allow the few hours that remain to pass away undisturbed. You are tired out, and need to order your thoughts; I beg you, therefore, to go to sleep, or pretend to go to sleep, either on your bed or in your bed; I shall sleep in this armchair; and when I fall asleep, my rest is so sound that a cannon would not wake me.''

Fouquet smiled.

''I except, however,'' continued the musketeer, ''the case of a door being opened, whether a secret door or any other, or the case of anyone going out of or coming into the room. For anything like that my ear is as sensitive as possible. Any creaking noise makes me jump. It arises, I suppose, from a natural antipathy to anything of the kind. Move about as much as you like; walk up and down in my part of the room; write, erase, destroy, burn—nothing like that will prevent me from going to sleep, or even prevent me from snoring; but do not touch either the key or the handle of the door! for I would wake up with a start, and that would rattle my nerves terribly.''

''Monsieur D'Artagnan,'' said Fouquet, ''you are certainly the most witty and the most courteous man I ever met; and you will leave me with only one regret, that of having made your acquaintance so late.''

D'Artagnan drew a deep sigh, which seemed to say, ''Alas! you have, perhaps, made it too soon.'' He then settled himself in his armchair, while Fouquet, half-lying on his bed and leaning on his arm, meditated upon his adventure. In this way, both of them, leaving the candles burning, waited for dawn; and when Fouquet happened to sigh too loudly, D'Artagnan only snored the louder. Not a single visit, not even from Aramis, disturbed them; not a sound was heard throughout the vast palace. Outside, however, the guards of honor, and the patrols of the musketeers, paced up and down; and the sound of their feet could be heard on the gravel walks. It seemed to act as an additional soporific for the sleepers; while the murmuring of the wind through the trees, and the unceasing music of the fountains, whose waters fell tumbling into the basins, still went on uninterrupted, undisturbed by the small noises and small matters which make up the life and death of man.

CHAPTER XX

THE MORNING

In contrast to the sad destiny of the king imprisoned in the Bastille, tearing in sheer despair the bolts and bars of his dungeon, the tales of the old chroniclers would not fail to present, as a complete antithesis, the picture of Philippe lying asleep beneath the royal canopy.

The young prince had descended from Aramis's room, in the same way the king had descended from the apartment dedicated to Morpheus. The dome gradually and slowly sank down under Aramis's pressure, and Philippe stood beside the royal bed, which had ascended again after having deposited its prisoner in the secret depths of the underground passage. Alone, in the presence of all the luxury which surrounded him; alone, in the presence of his power; alone, with the part he was about to be forced to act, Philippe for the first time felt his heart, and mind, and soul expand to the thousand varied emotions which are the vital throbs of a king's heart. But he turned pale when he looked at the empty bed, still tumbled by his brother's body. This mute accomplice had returned, after having completed the work it had been destined to perform; it returned with the traces of the crime; it spoke to the guilty author of that crime, with the frank and unreserved language which an accomplice never fears using toward his companion in guilt; for it spoke the truth. Philippe bent over the bed, and perceived a pocket handkerchief lying on it, which was still damp from the cold sweat which had poured from Louis XIV's face. This sweat terrified Philippe, as the blood of Abel had terrified Cain.

"I am now face to face with my destiny," said Philippe, with his eyes on fire and his face livid. "Is it likely to be more terrifying than my captivity has been painful? When I am compelled to follow out, at every moment, the sovereign power I have usurped, shall I never cease to listen to the scruples of my heart? Yes; the king has lain on this bed; it is indeed his head that has left its impression on this pillow; his bitter tears which have stained this handkerchief; and yet I hesitate to throw myself on the bed, or to press in my hand the handkerchief which is embroidered with my brother's arms. Away with this weakness! let me imitate Monsieur d'Herblay, whose thoughts are of and for himself alone, who regards himself as a man of honor, so long as he injures or betrays only his enemies. I—I alone should have occupied this bed, if Louis XIV had not, owing to my mother's criminal abandonment of me, stood in my way; and this handkerchief, embroidered with the arms of France, would, in right and justice, belong to me alone, if, as Monsieur d'Herblay observes, I had been left in my place in the royal cradle. Philippe, son of France, take your place in that bed! Philippe, sole King of France, take back your coat of arms! Philippe, sole heir presumptive to Louis XIII, your father, show yourself without pity for the usurper who, at this moment, has no remorse for all you have suffered!''

With these words, Philippe, in spite of an instinctive repugnance, and in spite of the shudder of terror which his will mastered, threw himself on the royal bed, and forced his muscles to press the still warm place where Louis XIV had lain, while he buried his face in the handkerchief still moistened by his brother's sweat. With his head thrown back and buried in the soft down of his pillow, Philippe saw above him the crown of France, held, as we have stated, by angels with golden wings.

A man may be eager to lie in the lion's bed, but can hardly hope to sleep there quietly. Philippe listened attentively to every sound; his heart throbbed at the very suspicion of approaching terror; but confident in his own strength, he waited until some decisive circumstance should permit him to judge himself. He hoped that some imminent danger would be revealed for him, like those phosphoric lights of the tempest which show the sailors the height of the waves against which they have to struggle.

But nothing came. Silence, the mortal enemy of restless hearts, the mortal enemy of ambitious minds, all night covered in its heavy mist the future King of France, sheltered beneath his stolen crown. Toward morning a shadow, rather than a body, glided into the royal chamber; Philippe was expecting it and was not surprised.

"Well, Monsieur d'Herblay?" he said.

"Well, sire, all is done."

"How?"

"Exactly as we expected."

"Did he resist?"

"Terribly; tears and cries."

"And then?"

"A perfect stupor."

"But at last?"

"Oh, at last, a complete victory, and absolute silence."

"Did the governor of the Bastille suspect anything?"

"Nothing."

"The resemblance, however . . ."

"That was the reason of the success."

"But the prisoner will certainly explain himself. Think of that. I have, myself, been able to do that, on a former occasion."

"I have already provided for everything. In a few days, sooner if necessary, we will take the captive out of his prison and will send him out of the country, to a place of exile so remote . . ."

"People can return from their exile, Monsieur d'Herblay."

"To a place of exile so distant, I was going to say, that human strength and the duration of human life would not be enough for his return."

And once more a cold look of intelligence passed between Aramis and the young king.

"And Monsieur du Vallon?" asked Philippe, in order to change the conversation.

"He will be introduced to you today, and confidentially will congratulate you on the danger which that conspirator has made you run."

"What is to be done with him?"

"With Monsieur du Vallon?"

"Yes; confer a dukedom on him, I suppose?"

"A dukedom," replied Aramis, smiling oddly.

"Why do you laugh, Monsieur d'Herblay?"

"I laugh at the extreme caution of your idea."

"Cautious? Why so?"

"Your majesty is doubtless afraid that poor Porthos will probably become a troublesome witness, and you wish to get rid of him."

"What! in making him a duke?"

"Certainly; you would surely kill him, for he would die from joy, and the secret would die with him."

"Good heavens!"

"Yes," said Aramis phlegmatically; "I should lose a very good friend."

At this moment, and in the middle of this light conversation, under which the two conspirators were concealing their joy and pride at their mutual success, Aramis heard something which made him prick up his ears.

"What is that?" said Philippe.

"Dawn, sire."

"Well?"

"Well, before you retired to bed last night, you probably decided to do something this morning?"

"Yes, I told my captain of the musketeers," replied the young man hurriedly, "that I should expect him."

"If you told him that, he will certainly be here, for he is a most punctual man."

"I hear a step in the vestibule."

"It must be he."

"Come, let us begin the attack," said the young king resolutely.

"Be careful, for Heaven's sake; to begin the attack, and with D'Artagnan, would be madness. D'Artagnan knows nothing, he has seen nothing; he is far from suspecting our mystery in the slightest degree, but if he is the first to come into this room this morning, he will be sure to detect that something has taken place, and he would think it his business to occupy himself with it. Before we allow D'Artagnan to enter into this room, we must air the room thoroughly, or introduce so many people into it that the keenest scent in the whole kingdom may be deceived by the traces of twenty different persons."

"But how can I send him away, since I have given him a rendezvous?" observed the prince, impatient to measure swords with so formidable an opponent.

"I will take care of that," replied the bishop; "and in

order to begin, I am going to strike a blow that will completely stupefy our man.''

"He, too, is striking a blow, for I hear him at the door," added the prince hurriedly.

And, in fact, a knock at the door was heard at that moment. Aramis was not mistaken; for it was indeed D'Artagnan who adopted that mode of announcing himself.

We have seen how he spent the night in philosophizing with M. Fouquet; but the musketeer was very tired even of pretending to fall asleep, and as soon as the dawn lit with its pale-blue light the sumptuous cornices of the surintendant's room, D'Artagnan rose from his armchair, arranged his sword, brushed his coat and hat with his sleeve, like a private soldier getting ready for inspection.

"Are you going out?" said Fouquet.

"Yes, monseigneur. And you?"

"No; I am staying."

"You give me your word?"

"Certainly."

"Very good. Besides, my only reason for going out is to try and get that reply—you know what I mean?"

"That sentence, you mean . . .''

"You see, I have something of the old Roman in me. This morning, when I got up, I noticed that my sword had not caught in one of the *aiguillettes,* and that my shoulder belt had slipped quite off. That is an infallible sign.''

"Of prosperity?"

"Yes, be sure of it; for every time that that confounded belt of mine stuck fast to my back, it meant a punishment from Monsieur de Tréville, or a refusal of money by Monsieur de Mazarin. Every time my sword hung fast to my shoulder belt, it always predicted some disagreeable duty, and I have had showers of them all my life. Every time, too, my sword danced about in its sheath, a duel, fortunate in its result, was sure to follow; whenever it dangled about the calves of my legs, it was a slight wound; every time it fell completely out of the scabbard, I knew I would have to remain on the field of battle, with two or three months under the surgeon's care into the bargain.''

"I never knew your sword kept you so well in-

formed,'' said Fouquet, with a faint smile, which showed
how he was struggling against his own weakness. ''Is
your sword bewitched, or under the influence of some
charm?''

''Why, you must know that my sword may almost be
seen as part of my own body. I have heard that certain
men seem to have warnings given them by feeling something the matter with their legs, or by a throbbing of their
temples. With me it is my sword that warns me. Well, it
told me of nothing this morning. Ah! Yes, it has just
fallen of its own accord into the last hole of the belt. Do
you know what that is a warning of?''

''No.''

''Well, that tells me of an arrest that will have to be
made this very day.''

''Well,'' said the surintendant, more astonished than
annoyed by this frankness, ''if there is nothing disagreeable predicted to you by your sword, I am to conclude
that it is not disagreeable for you to arrest me.''

''You? Arrest you?''

''Of course. The warning—''

''Does not concern you, since you have been arrested
ever since yesterday. It is not you I shall have to arrest,
be assured of that. That is the reason why I am delighted,
and also the reason why I said that my day will be a
happy one.''

And with these words, pronounced with the most affectionate graciousness of manner, the captain took leave
of Fouquet in order to wait upon the king. He was about
to leave the room, when Fouquet said to him:

''One last mark of your kindness.''

''What is it, monseigneur?''

''Monsieur d'Herblay; let me see Monsieur d'Herblay.''

''I am going to try and get him to come to you.''

D'Artagnan did not think himself so good a prophet.
It was written that the day would pass away and all the
predictions that had been made in the morning would
come true.

He had knocked, as we have seen, at the king's door.
The door opened. The captain thought that it was the
king who had just opened it himself, and he might have
been right, considering the state of agitation in which he

had left Louis XIV the previous evening; but instead of
his royal master, whom he was about to salute with the
greatest respect, he saw the long, calm features of Aramis. So extreme was his surprise that he could hardly
refrain from uttering a loud exclamation.

"Aramis!" he said.

"Good morning, dear D'Artagnan," replied the prelate coldly.

"You here!" stammered the musketeer.

"His majesty wants you to report that he is still sleeping after having been very tired during the whole night."

"Ah!" said D'Artagnan, who could not understand
how the bishop of Vannes, who had been so indifferent
a favorite the previous evening, had become, in half a
dozen hours, the largest mushroom of fortune which had
ever sprung up in a sovereign's bedroom. In fact, to
transmit the orders of the king at the threshold of that
monarch's room, to serve as an intermediary of Louis
XIV, to order in his name a couple of paces from him,
he must be greater than Richelieu had ever been to Louis
XIII. D'Artagnan's expressive eye, half-opened lips, his
curling mustache, said as much indeed in the plainest
language to the chief favorite, who remained calm.

"Moreover," continued the bishop, "you will be good
enough, Monsieur le Capitaine des Mousquetaires, to allow only those who have special permission to pass into
the king's room this morning. His majesty does not wish
to be disturbed just yet."

"But," objected D'Artagnan, ready to rebel, and particularly to explode with the suspicions which the king's
silence had aroused; "but, Monsieur l'Evêque, his majesty gave me a rendezvous for this morning."

"Later, later," said the king's voice from the back of
the alcove, a voice which made the musketeer shudder.
He bowed, amazed, confused, and stupefied by the smile
with which Aramis crushed him, as soon as those words
had been pronounced.

"And then," continued the bishop, "as an answer to
what you were coming to ask the king, my dear D'Artagnan, here is an order of his majesty, which you will
be good enough to attend to right away, for it concerns
Monsieur Fouquet."

D'Artagnan took the order which was held out to him.

"Free!" he murmured. "Ah!" and he uttered a second "Ah!" still more full of intelligence than the former; for this order explained Aramis's presence with the king, and Aramis, in order to have obtained Fouquet's pardon, must have made considerable progress in the royal favor, and this favor explained in turn the incredible assurance with which M. d'Herblay was giving orders in the king's name. For D'Artagnan it was quite sufficient to have understood something in order to understand everything. He bowed and took a couple of steps, as if he were about to leave.

"I am going with you," said the bishop.

"Where to?"

"To Monsieur Fouquet; I wish to be a witness of his delight."

"Ah! Aramis, how you puzzled me just now!" said D'Artagnan again.

"But you understand now, I suppose?"

"Of course I understand," he said aloud; but then added, in a low tone, to himself, almost hissing the words between his teeth, "No, no, I do not understand yet. But it is all the same, for here is the order for it." And then he added, "I will lead the way, monseigneur"; and he led Aramis to Fouquet's apartment.

CHAPTER XXI

THE KING'S FRIEND

FOUQUET was waiting with anxiety; he had already sent away many of his servants and his friends, who, anticipating the hour of his daily receptions, had called at his door to inquire after him. Saying nothing of the danger which hung over his head, he only asked them where Aramis was. When he saw D'Artagnan return, and when he saw the bishop of Vannes behind him, he could hardly restrain his delight; it was equal to his previous uneasiness. The mere sight of Aramis made up for the unhappiness he had undergone in being arrested. The prelate was silent and grave; D'Artagnan was completely bewildered by such an accumulation of events.

"Well, captain, so you have brought Monsieur d'Herblay to me?"

"And something better still, monseigneur."

"What is that?"

"Freedom."

"I am free?"

"Yes, by the king's order."

Fouquet resumed his usual serenity, to question Aramis with a look.

"Oh, yes, you can thank Monsieur l'Evêque de Vannes," pursued D'Artagnan, "for you owe him the change that has taken place in the king."

"Oh!" said Fouquet, more humiliated at the service than grateful at its success.

"But you," continued D'Artagnan, speaking to Aramis, "you, who have become Monsieur Fouquet's protector and patron, can you not do something for me?"

"Anything you like, my friend," replied the bishop, in a calm voice.

"One thing only, then, and I shall be perfectly satisfied. How have you managed to become the favorite of the king, you, who have never spoken to him more than twice in your life?"

"From a friend such as you are," said Aramis, "I cannot conceal anything."

"Ah! very good; tell me, then."

"Very well. You think that I have seen the king only twice, while the fact is I have seen him more than a hundred times; only we have kept it very secret, that is all."

And without trying to remove the color which at this revelation made D'Artagnan's face flush scarlet, Aramis turned toward M. Fouquet, who was as surprised as the musketeer.

"Monseigneur," he went on, "the king wants me to inform you that he is more than ever your friend, and that your beautiful *fête*, so generously offered by you on his behalf, has touched him to the very heart."

And he saluted M. Fouquet so respectfully that the latter, incapable of understanding such diplomacy, remained speechless and motionless. D'Artagnan could tell that these two men had something to say to each other, and he was about to yield to that feeling of instinctive politeness which in such a case hurries a man toward the door, when he feels his presence is an inconvenience for others; but his eager curiosity, spurred on by so many mysteries, advised him to remain.

Aramis then turned toward him and said, in a quiet tone:

"You will not forget, my friend, the king's order respecting those whom he intends to receive this morning on rising."

These words were clear enough, and the musketeer understood them; he therefore bowed to Fouquet, and then to Aramis—to the latter with a mix of irony and respect—and disappeared.

No sooner had he left than Fouquet, whose impatience had hardly been able to wait for that moment, darted toward the door to close it, and then, returning to the bishop, he said:

"My dear D'Herblay, I think it now high time you explain to me what is happening, for, in plain and honest truth, I do not understand anything."

"We will explain all that to you," said Aramis, sitting down, and making Fouquet sit down also. "Where shall I begin?"

"With this, first of all. Why does the king set me free?"

"You ought rather to ask me what was his reason for having you arrested."

"Since my arrest I have had time to think it over, and my idea is that it arises out of some slight feeling of jealousy. My *fête* put Monsieur Colbert out of temper, and Monsieur Colbert discovered some cause of complaint against me; Belle-Isle, for instance."

"No; there is no question at all just now of Belle-Isle."

"What is it, then?"

"Do you remember those receipts for thirteen million which Monsieur de Mazarin contrived to get stolen from you?"

"Yes, of course."

"Well, you are pronounced to be a public robber."

"Good heavens!"

"Oh, that is not all. Do you also remember that letter you wrote to La Vallière?"

"Alas! yes."

"That proclaims you a traitor and suborner."

"Why should he have forgiven me, then?"

"We have not yet arrived at that part of our argument. I wish you to be quite convinced of the fact itself. Observe this well: the king knows you to be guilty of an appropriation of public funds. Oh, of course *I* know that you have done nothing of the kind; but, at all events, the king has not seen the receipts, and he cannot do otherwise than believe you criminal."

"I beg your pardon, I do not see . . ."

"You will see presently, though. The king, moreover, having read your love letter to La Vallière, and the offers you made her, cannot retain any doubt of your intentions with regard to that young lady; you will admit that, I suppose?"

"Certainly. But conclude."

"In a few words. The king is, therefore, a powerful, implacable, and eternal enemy for you."

"Agreed. But am I, then, so powerful that he has not dared to sacrifice me, in spite of his hatred, with all the means which my weakness, or my misfortunes, may have given him as a hold upon me?"

"It is clear, beyond all doubt," pursued Aramis cooly, "that the king has quarreled irreconcilably with you."

"But since he absolves me . . ."

"Do you believe that likely?" asked the bishop, with a searching look.

"Without believing in his sincerity of heart, I believe in the truth of the fact."

Aramis slightly shrugged his shoulders.

"But why, then, should Louis XIV have asked you to tell me what you have just stated?"

"The king has not asked me to tell you anything."

"He hasn't?" said the surintendant, stupefied. "But that order, then . . ."

"Oh, yes! You are quite right. There is an order, certainly"; and these words were pronounced by Aramis in so strange a tone that Fouquet could not resist trembli

"You are concealing something from me, I see. Wh is it?"

Aramis softly rubbed his white fingers over his chin, but said nothing.

"Is the king sending me into exile?"

"Do not act as if you were playing the game children play when they have to try and guess where a thing has been hidden, and are informed by a bell being rung when they are getting close or far."

"Speak, then."

"Guess."

"You alarm me!"

"Bah! that is because you have not guessed, then."

"What did the king say to you? In the name of our friendship, do not deceive me."

"The king has not said a word to me."

"You are killing me with impatience, D'Herblay. Am I still surintendant?"

"As long as you like."

"But what extraordinary empire have you so suddenly acquired over his majesty's mind?"

"Ah! that is it."

"You make him do as you like."

"I believe so."

"It is hardly credible."

"So anyone would say."

"D'Herblay, by our alliance, by our friendship, by everything you hold dearest in the world, speak openly, I implore you. By what means have you succeeded in overcoming Louis XIV's prejudices, for he did not like you, I know?"

"The king will like me *now*," said Aramis, laying stress upon the last word.

"You have something particular, then, between you?"

"Yes."

"A secret, perhaps?"

"Yes, a secret."

"A secret of such a nature as to change his majesty's interests?"

"You are indeed a man of superior intelligence, monseigneur, and have made a very accurate guess. I have, in fact, discovered a secret of a nature to change the interests of the King of France."

"Ah!" said Fouquet, with the reserve of a man who does not wish to ask any questions.

"And you shall judge of it yourself," pursued Aramis; "and you shall tell me if I am mistaken with regard to the importance of this secret."

"I am listening, since you are good enough to be open with me; only do not forget that I have asked you nothing which may be indiscreet."

Aramis seemed, for a moment, as if he were collecting himself.

"Do not speak," said Fouquet; "there is still time enough."

"Do you remember," said the bishop, casting down his eyes, "the birth of Louis XIV?"

"As if it were yesterday."

"Have you ever heard anything particular about his birth?"

"Nothing, except that the king was not really the son of Louis XIII."

"That does not matter to us, or the kingdom either; he is the son of his father, says the French law, whose father is recognized by the law."

"True; but it is a grave matter, when the quality of races is called into question."

"A mere secondary question, after all. So that, in fact, you have never learned or heard anything in particular?"

"Nothing."

"That is where my secret begins. The queen, you must know, instead of delivering one son, delivered two children."

Fouquet looked up suddenly, as he replied:

"And the second is dead?"

"You will see. These twins seemed likely to be the pride of their mother and the hope of France; but the weak nature of the king, his superstitious feelings, made him fear a series of conflicts between two children whose rights were equal; so he suppressed one of the twins."

"Suppressed, do you say?"

"Be patient. Both the children grew up; the one on the throne, whose minister you are; the other, who is my friend, in gloom and isolation."

"Good heavens! What are you saying, Monsieur d'Herblay? And what is this poor prince doing?"

"Ask me, rather, what he has done."

"Yes, yes."

"He was brought up in the country, and then thrown into a fortress which goes by the name of the Bastille."

"Is it possible?" cried the surintendant, clasping his hands.

"The one was the most fortunate of men; the other the most unhappy and most miserable of all living beings."

"Does his mother not know this?"

"Anne of Austria knows it all."

"And the king?"

"Knows absolutely nothing."

"So much the better," said Fouquet.

This remark seemed to make a great impression on Aramis; he looked at Fouquet with the most anxious expression.

"I beg your pardon; I interrupted you," said Fouquet.

"I was saying," resumed Aramis, "that this poor prince was the unhappiest of human beings, when God, whose thoughts are over all His creatures, undertook to come to his help."

"Oh! in what way? Tell me."

"You will see. The reigning king—I say the reigning king, you can guess very well why?"

"No. Why?"

"Because both of them, being legitimately entitled from their birth, ought both to have been kings. Isn't it your opinion?"

"It is, certainly."

"Unreservedly so?"

"Most unreservedly; twins are one person in two bodies."

"I am pleased that a legist of your learning and authority should have pronounced such an opinion. It is agreed, then, that both of them possessed the same rights, is it not?"

"Incontestably so; but, heavens! what an extraordinary circumstance."

"We are not at the end of it yet. Patience."

"Oh! I shall find patience enough."

"God wished to raise up for that oppressed child an avenger, or a supporter, if you prefer it. It happened that the reigning king, the usurper—you are quite of my opinion, I believe, that it is an act of usurpation to enjoy quietly and selfishly an inheritance to which one has only the right of one half?''

"Yes, usurpation is the word.''

"In that case, I continue. It was God's will that the usurper should possess, in the person of his first minister, a man of great talent, of large and generous nature.''

"Good, good,'' cried Fouquet, "I understand you; you have relied upon me to repair the wrong which has been done to this unhappy brother of Louis XIV. You have thought well; I will help you. I thank you, D'Herblay, I thank you.''

"Oh, no, it is not that at all; you are not letting me finish,'' said Aramis, perfectly unmoved.

"I will not say another word, then.''

"Monsieur Fouquet, I was saying, the minister of the reigning sovereign was suddenly taken into the greatest aversion, and threatened in his fortune, in his liberty, in his life even, by intrigue and personal hatred, to which the king gave too readily an attentive ear. But God granted (still, however, out of consideration for the unhappy prince who had been sacrificed) that Monsieur Fouquet should in his turn have a devoted friend who knew this state secret, and felt that he possessed strength enough to divulge this secret, after having had the strength to carry it locked up in his own heart for twenty years.''

"Do not go on any further,'' said Fouquet, full of generous feelings. "I understand you, and can guess everything now. You went to see the king when the news of my arrest reached you; you begged him; he refused to listen to you; then you threatened him with that secret, threatened to reveal it, and Louis XIV, alarmed, had to grant to the terror of your indiscretion what he refused to your generous intercession. I understand, I understand; you have the king in your power; I understand.''

"You understand nothing as yet,'' replied Aramis, "and again you have interrupted me. And then, too, allow me to observe that you pay no attention to logic, and seem to forget what you ought most to remember.''

"What do you mean?''

"Do you know what I stressed at the beginning of our conversation?''

"Yes; his majesty's hatred, invincible hatred for me;

yes, but what hatred could resist the threat of such a revelation?"

"Such a revelation, do you say? that is the very point where your logic fails you. What! do you suppose that if I had made such a revelation to the king, I would be alive now?"

"You were with the king less than ten minutes ago."

"That may be. He might not have had the time to get me killed, but he would have had the time to get me gagged and thrown into a dungeon. Come, come, show a little consistency in your reasoning, *mordioux!*"

And by the mere use of this word, which was so thoroughly his old musketeer's expression, a slip by him who never made a slip, Fouquet had to understand to what a pitch of exaltation the calm, impenetrable bishop of Vannes had wrought himself. He shuddered at it.

"And then," replied the latter, after having mastered his feelings, "should I be the man I really am, should I be the true friend you see me as, if I were to expose you, you whom the king hates already, to a feeling even more threatening in that young king? To have robbed him is nothing; to have courted the woman he loves is not much; but to hold in your hand both his crown and his honor, why, he would rather pluck out your heart with his own hands."

"You have not let him penetrate your secret, then?"

"I would sooner have swallowed all the poisons that Mithridates drank in twenty years in order to try and avoid death."

"What have you done, then?"

"Ah! now we are coming to the point, monseigneur. I don't think I shall fail to arouse a little interest. You are listening, I hope."

"How can you ask me if I am listening? Go on."

Aramis walked softly around the room, satisfied himself that they were alone, and that all was silent, and then returned and placed himself close to the armchair in which Fouquet was seated, awaiting with the deepest anxiety the revelations he had to make.

"I forgot to tell you," Aramis went on, addressing himself to Fouquet, who was listening to him with the most absorbed attention, "I forgot to mention a most remarkable circumstance respecting these twins, namely,

that God had formed them so startlingly, so miracu-
lously, like each other that it would be utterly impossible
to distinguish one from the other. Their own mother
would not be able to distinguish them.''

''Is it possible?'' exclaimed Fouquet.

''The same noble character in their features, the same
carriage, the same stature, the same voice.''

''But their thoughts, degree of intelligence, their
knowledge of human life?''

''There is inequality there, I admit, monseigneur. Yes;
for the prisoner of the Bastille is, most incontestably,
superior in every way to his brother; and if, from his
prison, this unhappy victim were to pass to the throne,
France would not, from the earliest period of its history,
perhaps, have had a master more powerful by his genius
and nobility of character.''

Fouquet buried his face in his hands, as if he were
overwhelmed by the weight of this immense secret. Aramis came near him.

''There is a further inequality,'' he said, continuing
his work of temptation, ''an inequality which concerns
yourself, monseigneur, between the twins, both sons of
Louis XIII, namely, the last one does not know Monsieur
Colbert.''

Fouquet raised his head immediately, his features pale
and distorted. The arrow had hit its target—not his heart,
but his mind and comprehension.

''I understand you,'' he said to Aramis; ''you are pro-
posing a conspiracy?''

''Something like it.''

''One of those attempts which, as you said at the beginning of this conversation, alters the fate of empires?''

''And of the surintendant, too; yes, monseigneur.''

''In a word, you propose that I should agree to the
substitution of the son of Louis XIII who is now a prisoner in the Bastille, for the son of Louis XIII who is now
at this moment asleep in the chamber of Morpheus?''

Aramis smiled with the sinister expression of his sinister thought.

''Exactly,'' he said.

''Have you thought,'' continued Fouquet, ''that we
must assemble the nobility, the clergy, and the third estate of the realm; that we shall have to depose the reign-

ing sovereign, to disturb by so frightful a scandal the
tomb of their dead father, to sacrifice the life, the honor
of a woman, Anne of Austria, the life and peace of mind
and heart of another woman, Maria Theresa; and suppose that all were done, if we were to succeed in doing
it—"

"I do not understand you," said Aramis coldly.
"There is not one useful word in what you have just
said."

"What!" said the surintendant, surprised, "a man like
you refuse to view the practical side of the case! You are
confining yourself to the childish delight of a political
illusion, and neglecting the possibilities of its being carried into execution—in other words, reality itself—is it
possible?"

"My friend," said Aramis, emphasizing the word with
a kind of disdainful familiarity, "what does God do in
order to substitute one king for another?"

"God!" exclaimed Fouquet. "God gives directions to
His agent, who seizes upon the doomed victim, hurries
him away, and seats the triumphant rival on the empty
throne. But you forget that this agent is called death. Oh!
Monsieur d'Herblay, in Heaven's name, tell me if you
have had the idea—"

"There is no question of that, monseigneur; you are
going beyond the object in view. Who is speaking of
Louis XIV's death? Who is speaking of adopting the example that God sets in following out the strict execution
of his decrees? No, I meant that God acts without confusion, without scandal, without efforts; and that men
inspired by God succeed like him in all their undertak-
ings, in all they attempt, in all they do."

"What do you mean?"

"I mean, my *friend*," returned Aramis, with the same
intonation on the word "friend" that he had used the
first time, "I mean that if there has been any confusion,
scandal, and even effort in the substitution of the prisoner
for the king, I defy you to prove it."

"What!" cried Fouquet, whiter than the handkerchief
with which he wiped his temples, "what are you saying?"

"Go to the king's apartment," continued Aramis tranquilly, "and you who know the mystery, I defy even you

to notice that the prisoner of the Bastille is lying in his brother's bed.''

"But the king?" stammered Fouquet, seized with horror at this news.

"What king?" said Aramis, in his gentlest tone, "the one who hates you, or the one who likes you?"

"The king—of yesterday."

"The king of yesterday! Rest easy on that score; he has taken the place in the Bastille which his victim has occupied for too long."

"Great God! And who took him there?"

"I."

"You?"

"Yes; and in the simplest way. I carried him away last night; and while he was descending into darkness, the other was ascending into light. I do not think there has been any disturbance created in any way. A flash of lightning without thunder never awakens anyone."

Fouquet uttered a faint cry, as if he had been struck by some invisible blow, and clasping his head between his hands, he whispered:

"You did that?"

"Cleverly enough, too. What do you think of it?"

"You dethroned the king? imprisoned him, too?"

"Yes, that has been done."

"And such an act has been committed here, at Vaux?"

"Yes, here, at Vaux, in the chamber of Morpheus. It would almost seem that it had been built in anticipation of such an act."

"And at what time did it occur?"

"Last night, between twelve and one o'clock."

Fouquet gestured as if he were about to spring on Aramis, but he restrained himself.

"At Vaux, under my roof!" he said, in a half-strangled voice.

"I believe so; for it is still your house, and is likely to continue to be so, since Monsieur Colbert cannot rob you of it now."

"It was under my roof, then, monsieur, that you committed this crime?"

"This crime?" said Aramis, stupefied.

"This abominable crime!" pursued Fouquet, becoming more and more excited, "this crime more execrable

than an assassination! this crime which dishonors my
name forever, and condemns me to the horror of posterity!''

"You are raving, monsieur," replied Aramis, in an
irresolute tone of voice; "you are speaking too loudly;
be careful!''

"I will call out so loudly that the whole world shall
hear me."

"Monsieur Fouquet, be careful!''

Fouquet turned toward the prelate, whom he looked at
full in the face.

"You have dishonored me," he said, "in committing
so foul an act of treason, so heinous a crime upon my
guest, upon he who was peacefully resting beneath my
roof. Oh! woe, woe is me!''

"Woe to the man, rather, who, beneath your roof,
meditated the ruin of your fortune, your life! Do you
forget that?''

"He was my guest, my sovereign."

Aramis rose, his eyes bloodshot, his mouth trembling
convulsively.

"Am I dealing with a man out of his mind?''

"You are dealing with an honorable man."

"You are mad.''

"A man who will prevent you from carrying out your
crime."

"You are mad, I say."

"A man who would rather die; who would kill you
even, rather than allow you to complete his dishonor.''

And Fouquet snatched up his sword, which D'Artagnan had placed at the head of his bed, and clinched it
resolutely in his hand. Aramis frowned, and thrust his
hand into his chest as if in search of a weapon. This
movement did not escape Fouquet, who, noble and superb in his magnanimity, threw his sword away, and approached Aramis so close as to touch his shoulder with
his disarmed hand.

"Monsieur," he said, "I would sooner die here on the
spot than survive this terrible disgrace; and if you have
any pity left for me, I beg you to take my life.''

Aramis remained silent and motionless.

"Aren't you replying?" said Fouquet.

Aramis raised his head gently, and a glimmer of hope again began to animate his eyes.

"Think, monseigneur," he said, "of everything we have to expect. As the matter now stands, the king is still alive, and his imprisonment saves your life."

"Yes," replied Fouquet; "you may have been acting on my behalf, but I will not, do not accept your services. But, first of all, I do not wish your ruin. You will leave this house."

Aramis stifled the exclamation which almost escaped his broken heart.

"I am hospitable toward all my guests," continued Fouquet, with an air of inexpressible majesty; "you will not be sacrificed any more than the man you plotted against."

"You will be," said Aramis, in a hoarse, prophetic voice, "you will be, believe me."

"I accept the omen, Monsieur d'Herblay; but nothing shall prevent me, nothing shall stop me. You will leave Vaux—you must leave France; I give you four hours to place yourself out of the king's reach."

"Four hours?" said Aramis scornfully and incredulously.

"Upon the word of Fouquet, no one shall follow you before the expiration of that time. You will, therefore, be four hours ahead of those whom the king may wish to send after you."

"Four hours!" roared Aramis.

"It is more than you will need to get on board a vessel and flee to Belle-Isle, which I give you as a place of refuge."

"Ah!" murmured Aramis.

"Belle-Isle is as much mine for you as Vaux is mine for the king. Go, D'Herblay, go! as long as I live, not a hair of your head shall be harmed."

"Thank you," said Aramis, with cold irony.

"Go at once, then, and give me your hand, before we both hasten away, you to save your life, I to save my honor."

Aramis withdrew from his chest the hand he had concealed there; it was stained with his blood. He had dug his nails into his flesh, as if in punishment for having nursed so many plans, more vain, crazy, and fleeting than

the life of man himself. Fouquet was horror-stricken, and
then his heart filled with pity. He threw open his arms to
Aramis.

"I had no weapons," murmured Aramis, as wild and
terrible as the shade of Dido.

And then, without touching Fouquet's hand, he turned
his head aside, and stepped back a pace or two. His last
word was an imprecation, as his blood-stained hand
sprinkled on Fouquet's face a few drops of his blood.
And both of them darted out of the room by the secret
staircase which led down to the inner courtyard. Fouquet
ordered his best horses, while Aramis paused at the foot
of the staircase which led to Porthos's apartment. He
thought for some time, while Fouquet's carriage was
leaving the stone-paved courtyard at full gallop.

"Shall I go alone?" said Aramis to himself, "or warn
the prince? Oh, curses! Warn the prince, and then . . .
do what? Take him with me? To carry this accusing witness about with me everywhere? War, too, would follow,
civil war implacable in its nature! And without any resource, it is impossible! What will he do without me?
Oh! without me he will be utterly destroyed. Yet who
knows . . . let destiny be fulfilled . . . condemned he
was, let him remain so, then. Good or evil Spirit, gloomy
and scornful Power, whom men call the Genius of man,
you are a power more restlessly uncertain, more base-
lessly useless, than the wild wind in the mountains;
Chance you call yourself, but you are nothing; you in-
flame everything with your breath, crumble mountains at
your approach, and suddenly are yourself destroyed at
the presence of the cross of dead wood, behind which
stands another power invisible like yourself—whom you
deny, perhaps, but whose avenging hand is on you, and
hurls you in the dust, dishonored and unnamed! Lost! I
am lost! What can be done? Flee to Belle-Isle! Yes, and
leave Porthos behind to talk and tell the whole affair to
everyone! Porthos, too, who will suffer. I will not let
poor Porthos suffer. He is one of my limbs; and his grief
is mine. Porthos will leave with me, and will follow my
destiny. It must be so."

And Aramis, afraid of meeting anyone to whom his
hurry might appear suspicious, went up the staircase
without being noticed. Porthos, so recently back from

Paris, was already in a deep sleep; his huge body forgot
its fatigue, as his mind forgot its thoughts. Aramis entered, light as a shadow, and placed his nervous grasp
on the giant's shoulder.

"Come, Porthos," he cried, "come!"

Porthos obeyed, rose from his bed, opened his eyes,
even before his mind seemed to be awake.

"We are going off," said Aramis.

"Ah!" said Porthos.

"We shall go on horseback, and faster than we have
ever gone in our lives!"

"Ah!" repeated Porthos.

"Get dressed, my friend."

And he helped the giant to get dressed, and thrust his
gold and diamonds into his pocket. While he was thus
engaged, a slight noise attracted his attention, and on
looking up, he saw D'Artagnan watching them through
the half-open door. Aramis gave a start.

"What the devil are you doing there in such an agitated manner?" said the musketeer.

"Hush!" said Porthos.

"We are going off on a mission," added the bishop.

"You are very fortunate," said the musketeer.

"Oh, dear me!" said Porthos; "I feel so weary; I
would rather sleep. But the service of the king . . ."

"Have you seen Monsieur Fouquet?" said Aramis to
D'Artagnan.

"Yes, this very minute, in a carriage."

"What did he say to you?"

" 'Adieu,' nothing more."

"Was that all?"

"What else do you think he could say? Am I worth
anything now, since you all are in such high favor?"

"Listen," said Aramis, embracing the musketeer.
"Your good times are back. You will have no occasion
to be jealous of anyone."

"Ah, bah!"

"I predict that something will happen to you today
which will increase your importance more than ever."

"Really?"

"You know that I know all the news?"

"Oh, yes!"

"Come, Porthos, are you ready? Let us go."

"I am quite ready, Aramis."

"Let us embrace D'Artagnan first."

"Most certainly."

"But the horses?"

"Oh! there are plenty of them here. Will you have mine?"

"No; Porthos has his own stable. So, adieu, adieu!"

The two fugitives mounted their horses beneath the captain of the musketeers' eyes, who held Porthos's stirrup for him, and stared at them until they were out of sight.

"On any other occasion," thought the Gascon, "I would say that those gentlemen were escaping; but in these days politics seem so changed that it is called going on a mission. I have no objection; let me attend to my own affairs, that is quite enough"; and he philosophically entered his apartments.

CHAPTER XXII

SHOWING HOW ORDERS WERE RESPECTED
AT THE BASTILLE

FOUQUET raced along as fast as his horses could drag him. On his way he trembled with horror at the idea of what had just been revealed to him.

"What must have been," he thought, "the youth of those extraordinary men, who, as they age are still able to think up such plans, and can carry them out without hesitating?"

At times he wondered whether what Aramis had just been telling him was nothing more than a dream, and whether the story was not a trap; and whether when he arrived at the Bastille, he might possibly find an order of arrest, which would send him to join the dethroned king. Strongly impressed with this idea, he gave certain sealed orders on his route, while fresh horses were being harnessed to his carriage. These orders were addressed to M. D'Artagnan and to certain others whose fidelity to the king was far above suspicion.

"In this way," said Fouquet to himself, "prisoner or not, I shall have performed the duty which I owe to my honor. The orders will not reach them until after my return, if I should return free, and, consequently, they will not have been unsealed. I shall take them back. If I am delayed, it will be because some misfortune will have befallen me; and in that case assistance will be sent for me as well as for the king."

Prepared in this manner, the surintendant arrived at the Bastille; he had traveled at the speed of five leagues and a half an hour. Every delay which Aramis had escaped in his visit to the Bastille befell Fouquet. It was useless giving his name, equally useless his being recognized; he could not succeed in gaining entrance. By using entreaties, threats, commands, he succeeded in inducing a sentinel to speak to one of the subalterns, who went and told the major. As for the governor, they did not dare to disturb him. Fouquet sat in his carriage, at the outer gate of the fortress, fuming with rage and impatience, awaiting the return of the officers, who reappeared at last with a rather sulky air.

"Well," said Fouquet impatiently, "what did the major say?"

"Well, monsieur," replied the soldier, "the major laughed in my face. He told me that Monsieur Fouquet was at Vaux, and that even were he in Paris, Monsieur Fouquet would not get up at so early an hour."

"Mordieux! you are a perfect set of fools," cried the minister, darting out of the carriage; and before the subaltern had had time to shut the gate, Fouquet sprang through it and ran forward in spite of the soldier, who cried out for assistance. Fouquet gained ground, regardless of the cries of the man, who, however, having at last caught up with Fouquet, called out to the sentinel of the second gate:

"Look out! look out, sentinel!"

The man crossed his pike before the minister; but the latter, robust and agile, and energized by his anger, grabbed the pike from the soldier and struck him a violent blow on the shoulder with it. The subaltern, who approached too closely, was hit as well. Both of them uttered loud and furious cries, at the sound of which the whole bodyguard poured out of the guardhouse. Among

them there was one, however, who recognized the surintendant, and who called out:

"Monseigneur! ah, monseigneur! Stop, stop, you fellows!"

And he indeed stopped the soldiers, who were about
to revenge their companions. Fouquet ordered them to
open the gate, but they refused to do so without orders;
he ordered them to inform the governor of his presence,
but the latter had already heard the disturbance at the
gate. He ran forward, followed by his major, and accompanied by a picket of twenty men, persuaded that an attack was being made on the Bastille. Baisemeaux also
recognized Fouquet immediately, and dropped his sword,
which he had been brandishing about.

"Ah, monseigneur!" he stammered, "how can I apol-
ogize—"

"Monsieur," said the surintendant, red and sweating,
"I congratulate you. You are admirably protected."

Baisemeaux turned pale, thinking that this remark was
said ironically, announcing a furious anger. But Fouquet
had recovered his breath, and, calling the sentinel and
the subaltern, who were rubbing their shoulders, toward
him, he said:

"Here are twenty pistoles for the sentinel, and fifty for
the officer. Please receive my compliments, gentlemen.
I will not fail to speak to his majesty about you. And
now, Monsieur Baisemeaux, a word with you."

And he followed the governor to his official residence,
accompanied by a murmur of general satisfaction. Baisemeaux was already trembling with shame and uneasiness.
Aramis's early visit seemed to already have terrifying con-
sequences. It was quite another thing, however, when Fouquet, in a sharp tone of voice, and with an imperious look,
said:

"Have you seen Monsieur d'Herblay this morning?"

"Yes, monseigneur."

"And are you not horrified at the crime of which you
have made yourself an accomplice?"

"Well," thought Baisemeaux, "good so far," and then
he added, aloud: "But what crime, monseigneur, do you
allude to?"

"That for which you can be quartered alive, monsieur,

do not forget that! But this is not a time to show anger. Take me immediately to the prisoner.''

''To what prisoner?'' said Baisemeaux tremblingly.

''You pretend to be ignorant? Very good—it is the best thing for you to do, perhaps; for if, in fact, you were to admit your participation in it, it would be all over with you. I am willing, therefore, to pretend to believe in your ignorance.''

''I entreat you, monseigneur—''

''That will do. Take me to the prisoner.''

''To Marchiali?''

''Who is Marchiali?''

''The prisoner who was brought back this morning by Monsieur d'Herblay.''

''He is called Marchiali?'' said the surintendant, his conviction somewhat shaken by Baisemeaux's cool manner.

''Yes, monseigneur; that is the name under which he was registered here.''

Fouquet looked steadily at Baisemeaux, as if he would read his heart, and realized, with that clear-sightedness which men possess who are accustomed to exercising power, that the man was speaking with perfect sincerity. Besides, in looking at his face for a few moments, he could not believe that Aramis would have chosen such a confidant.

''Is it the prisoner,'' said the surintendant to him, ''whom Monsieur d'Herblay carried away the day before yesterday?''

''Yes, monseigneur.''

''And whom he brought back this morning?'' added Fouquet quickly; for he understood immediately the mechanism of Aramis's plan.

''Precisely, monseigneur.''

''And his name is Marchiali, you say?''

''Yes, Marchiali. If monseigneur has come here to remove him, so much the better, for I was going to write about him.''

''What has he done, then?''

''Ever since this morning he has annoyed me extremely. He has had such terrible fits of passion that I thought he would bring down the Bastille.''

"I will soon relieve you of his presence," said Fouquet.

"Ah, so much the better."

"Take me to his prison."

"Will monseigneur give me the order?"

"What order?"

"An order from the king."

"Wait until I sign one for you."

"That will not be sufficient, monseigneur. I must have an order from the king."

Fouquet assumed an irritated expression.

"As you are so scrupulous," he said, "with regard to allowing prisoners to leave, show me the order by which this one was set free."

Baisemeaux showed him the order to release Seldon.

"Very good," said Fouquet; "but Seldon is not Marchiali."

"But Marchiali is not free, monseigneur; he is here."

"But you said that Monsieur d'Herblay carried him away and brought him back again."

"I did not say so."

"You certainly did say so; I can still hear it now."

"It was a slip of my tongue, then, monseigneur."

"Take care, Monsieur de Baisemeaux, take care!"

"I have nothing to fear, monseigneur; I am acting according to strict regulation."

"Do you dare to say so?"

"I would say so in the presence of an apostle himself. Monsieur d'Herblay brought me an order to set Seldon at liberty; and Seldon is free."

"I tell you that Marchiali has left the Bastille."

"You must prove that, monseigneur."

"Let me see him."

"You, monseigneur, who govern this kingdom, know very well that no one can see any of the prisoners without an explicit order from the king."

"Monsieur d'Herblay did enter, however."

"That is to be proved, monseigneur."

"Monsieur de Baisemeaux, once more I warn you to pay particular attention to what you are saying."

"All the documents are there, monseigneur."

"Monsieur d'Herblay is overthrown."

"Overthrown? Monsieur d'Herblay? Impossible!"

"You see that he has certainly influenced you."

"No, monseigneur; what does, in fact, influence me is the king's service. I am doing my duty. Give me an order from him, and you shall enter."

"Wait, Monsieur le Gouverneur, I give you my word that if you allow me to see the prisoner, I will give you an order from the king at once."

"Give it to me now, monseigneur."

"And that, if you refuse, I will have you and all your officers arrested on the spot."

"Before you commit such an act of violence, monseigneur, you will stop and think," said Baisemeaux, who had turned very pale, "that we will only obey an order signed by the king, and that it will be just as easy for you to obtain one to see Marchiali as to obtain one to do me so much injury; me, who am perfectly innocent."

"True, true!" cried Fouquet furiously; "perfectly true. Monsieur de Baisemeaux," he added, in a sonorous voice, drawing the unhappy governor toward him, "do you know why I am so anxious to speak to the prisoner?"

"No, monseigneur; and allow me to say that you are terrifying me out of my senses; I am trembling all over, and feel as if I were going to faint."

"You will stand a better chance of fainting, Monsieur Baisemeaux, when I return here at the head of ten thousand men and thirty cannon."

"Good heavens, monseigneur, you are losing your senses!"

"When I have roused the whole population of Paris against you and your cruel towers, and have battered open the gates of this place, and hanged you from the bars of that tower in the corner there."

"Monseigneur, monseigneur! for pity's sake!"

"I give you ten minutes to make up your mind," added Fouquet, in a calm voice. "I will sit down here, in this armchair, and wait for you; if in ten minutes' time you will persist, I leave this place, and you may think me as mad as you like; but you will see."

Baisemeaux stamped his foot on the ground, like a man in a state of despair, but he did not answer a single syllable; thereupon, Fouquet seized a pen and ink, and wrote:

"Order for Monsieur le Prévot des Marchands to assemble the municipal guard and to march upon the Bastille for the king's service."

Baisemeaux shrugged his shoulders. Fouquet wrote:

"Order for the Duc de Bouillon and Monsieur le Prince de Condé to assume the command of the Swiss guards, of the king's guards, and to march upon the Bastille for the king's service."

Baisemeaux thought quietly. Fouquet still wrote:

"Order for every soldier, citizen, or gentleman to seize and arrest, wherever he may be found, Le Chevalier d'Herblay, Evêque de Vannes, and his accomplices, who are: 1st, Monsieur de Baisemeaux, governor of the Bastille, suspected of the crimes of high treason and rebellion . . ."

"Stop, monseigneur!" cried Baisemeaux; "I do not understand a single thing in this whole matter; but so many misfortunes, even were it madness itself that had set them at work, might happen here in a couple of hours that the king, by whom I shall be judged, will see whether I have been wrong in disobeying the orders before so many imminent catastrophes. Come with me to the dungeon, monseigneur, you shall see Marchiali."

Fouquet darted out of the room, followed by Baisemeaux, as he wiped the perspiration from his face.

"What a terrible morning!" he said, "what a disgrace!"

"Walk faster," replied Fouquet.

Baisemeaux gestured to the jailer to precede them. He was afraid of his companion, which the latter could not fail to notice.

"Let's stop being childish," he said roughly. "Let the man stay here, take the keys yourself, and show me the way. Not a single person, do you understand, must hear what is going to take place here."

"Ah!" said Baisemeaux, undecided.

"Again!" cried Fouquet. "If you say no, I will leave the Bastille and will carry my own orders."

Baisemeaux bowed his head, took the keys, and, un-accompanied, except by the minister, climbed the stair-case. As they went up the spiral staircase, certain smothered murmurs became distinct cries and frightful curses.

"What is that?" asked Fouquet.

"That is your Marchiali," said the governor; "that is the way these madmen howl."

And he accompanied his reply with a glance more in-dicative of injurious allusions, as far as Fouquet was con-cerned, than of politeness. The latter trembled; he had just recognized in one cry more terrible than any that had preceded it, the king's voice. He paused on the stair-case, snatching the bunch of keys from Baisemeaux, who thought this new madman was going to dash out his brains with one of them.

"Ah!" he cried, "Monsieur d'Herblay did not say a word about that."

"Give me the keys at once!" cried Fouquet, tearing them from his hand. "Which is the key of the door I am to open?"

"That one."

A fearful cry, followed by a violent blow against the door, made the whole staircase resound with the echo.

"Leave this place," said Fouquet to Baisemeaux, in a threatening tone.

"I want nothing more," murmured the latter. "There will be a couple of madmen face to face, and the one will kill the other, I am sure."

"Go!" repeated Fouquet. "If you place your foot on this staircase before I call you, remember that you shall take the place of the most wretched prisoner in the Bas-tille."

"This job will kill me, I am sure it will," muttered Baisemeaux, as he withdrew with tottering steps.

The prisoner's cries became louder and louder. When Fouquet had made sure that Baisemeaux had reached the bottom of the staircase, he inserted the key in the first lock. It was then that he heard the hoarse, choking voice of the king, crying out, in a frenzy of rage, "Help! help! I am the king." The key of the second door was not the same as the first, and Fouquet was obliged to look for it on the bunch. The king, however, furious and almost mad with rage and passion, shouted at the top of his voice:

"It was Monsieur Fouquet who brought me here. Help me against Monsieur Fouquet! I am the king! Help the king against Monsieur Fouquet!"

These cries tore the minister's heart. They were followed by a shower of frightening blows against the door with the chair with which the king had armed himself. Fouquet at last succeeded in finding the key. The king was almost exhausted; he could hardly articulate distinctly, as he shouted:

"Death to Fouquet! Death to the traitor Fouquet!"

The door flew open.

CHAPTER XXIII

THE KING'S GRATITUDE

THE two men who were about to dart toward each other suddenly stopped, as a mutual recognition took place, and each uttered a cry of horror.

"Have you come to assassinate me, monsieur?" said the king, when he recognized Fouquet.

"The king in this state!" murmured the minister.

Nothing could be more terrible, indeed, than the appearance of the young prince at the moment Fouquet had surprised him; his clothes were in tatters; his shirt open and torn to rags, was stained with sweat and with the blood which streamed from his cut chest and arms. Haggard, pale, his hair standing on end, Louis XIV was the most complete picture of despair, hunger, and fear that could possibly be united in one figure. Fouquet was so touched and disturbed by it that he ran toward him with his arms stretched out and his eyes filled with tears. Louis held up the massive piece of wood which he had used so furiously.

"Sire," said Fouquet, in a voice trembling with emotion, "do you not recognize the most faithful of your friends?"

"A friend, you!" repeated Louis, gnashing his teeth

in a manner which betrayed his hate and desire for speedy vengeance.

"The most respectful of your servants," added Fouquet, throwing himself on his knees.

The king let the weapon fall. Fouquet approached him, kissed his knees, and took him in his arms with inconceivable tenderness.

"My king, my child," he said, "how you must have suffered!"

Louis, brought to his senses by the change of situation, looked at himself, and ashamed of the disordered state of his clothes, ashamed of his behavior, and ashamed of the air of pity and protection that was shown toward him, drew back. Fouquet did not understand this movement; he did not perceive that the king's feelings of pride would never forgive him for having been a witness of such weakness.

"Come, sire," he said, "you are free."

"Free?" repeated the king. "Oh! you set me free, then, after having dared to lift up your hand against me!"

"You do not believe that!" exclaimed Fouquet indignantly; "you cannot believe me to be guilty of such an act."

And rapidly, warmly even, he told the whole story, the details of which are already known to the reader. While the recital continued Louis suffered the most horrible anguish of mind; and when it was finished the extent of the danger he had been in struck him far more than the importance of the secret of his twin brother.

"Monsieur," he said suddenly, to Fouquet, "this double birth is a falsehood; it is impossible—you cannot have been fooled . . ."

"Sire!"

"It is impossible, I tell you, that the honor, the virtue of my mother can be suspected. And hasn't my prime minister yet done justice to the criminals?"

"Think carefully, sire, before you are carried away by your anger," replied Fouquet. "The birth of your brother—"

"I have only one brother, and that is *Monsieur*. You know it as well as I do. There is a plot, I tell you, that started with the governor of the Bastille."

"Be careful, sire, for this man has been deceived as everyone else by the prince's likeness to yourself."

"Likeness? Absurd!"

"This Marchiali must be very much like your majesty to be able to deceive everyone," Fouquet persisted.

"Ridiculous!"

"Do not say so, sire; those who had prepared everything in order to face and deceive your ministers, your mother, your officers of state, the members of your family, must be quite confident of the resemblance between you."

"But where are these people?" murmured the king.

"At Vaux."

"At Vaux! and do you allow them to stay there?"

"My most pressing duty seemed to be your majesty's release. I have accomplished that duty; and now, whatever your majesty commands shall be done. I am waiting."

Louis thought for a few moments.

"Gather all the troops in Paris," he said.

"All the necessary orders are given for that purpose," replied Fouquet.

"You have given orders?"

"For that purpose, yes, sire; your majesty will be at the head of ten thousand men in less than an hour."

The only reply the king made was to take hold of Fouquet's hand with such an expression of feeling that it was very easy to perceive how strongly he had, until that remark, maintained his suspicion of the minister, in spite of the latter's intervention.

"And with these troops," he said, "we shall go at once and besiege the rebels in your house who by this time will have established and entrenched themselves there."

"I should be surprised if that were the case," replied Fouquet.

"Why?"

"Because their leader—the very soul of the plot, has been unmasked by me, and so the whole plan seems to me to have miscarried."

"Have you unmasked this false prince also?"

"No; I have not seen him."

"Whom have you seen, then?"

"The leader of the plot, not that unhappy young man; the latter is merely an instrument, destined through his whole life to wretchedness, I plainly perceive."

"Most certainly."

"It is Monsieur l'Abbé d'Herblay, Evêque de Vannes."

"Your friend."

"He was my friend, sire," replied Fouquet nobly.

"An unfortunate circumstance for you," said the king, in a less generous tone of voice.

"Such friendships, sire, had nothing dishonorable in them so long as I was ignorant of the crime."

"You should have foreseen it."

"If I am guilty, I place myself in your majesty's hands."

"Ah! Monsieur Fouquet, that was not what I meant," said the king, sorry to have shown the bitterness of his thought in such a manner. "Well, I assure you that, in spite of the mask with which the villain covered his face, I had a vague suspicion that it might be he. But with this leader of the plot there was a man of prodigious strength, the one who threatened me with an almost herculean force—who is he?"

"It must be his friend the Baron du Vallon, formerly one of the musketeers."

"The friend of D'Artagnan? the friend of the Comte de la Fère? Ah!" exclaimed the king, as he paused at the name of the latter, "we must not forget the connection that existed between the conspirators and Monsieur de Bragelonne."

"Sire, sire, do not go too far. Monsieur de la Fère is the most honorable man in France. Be satisfied with those whom I deliver up to you."

"With those whom you deliver up to me, you say? Very good, for you will deliver up those who are guilty to me."

"What does your majesty mean by that?" inquired Fouquet.

"I mean," replied the king, "that we shall soon arrive at Vaux with a large body of troops, that we will lay violent hands upon that nest of vipers, and that not a soul shall escape."

"Your majesty will put these men to death!" cried Fouquet.

"To the last man."

"Oh, sire!"

"Let us understand each other, Monsieur Fouquet," said the king haughtily. "We no longer live in times when assassination was the only and the last resource which kings had in their power. No, thank God! I have parliaments who sit and judge in my name, and I have scaffolds on which my supreme authority is carried out."

Fouquet turned pale.

"I will take the liberty of pointing out to your majesty that any proceedings on these matters would bring down the greatest scandal upon the dignity of the throne. The noble name of Anne of Austria must never be allowed to pass the lips of the people accompanied by a smile."

"Justice must be done, however, monsieur."

"Good, sire; but the royal blood cannot be shed on a scaffold."

"The royal blood! You believe that?" cried the king with fury, stamping his foot on the ground. "This double birth is an invention; and in that invention particularly do I see Monsieur d'Herblay's crime. It is the crime I wish to punish, rather than their violence or their insult."

"And punish it with death, sire?"

"With death, yes, monsieur."

"Sire," said the surintendant, with firmness, as he raised his head proudly, "your majesty will take the life, if you please, of your brother, Philippe of France; that concerns you alone, and you will doubtless consult the queen mother upon the subject. Whatever she may command will be perfectly correct. I do not wish to mix myself up in it, not even for the honor of your crown, but I have a favor to ask of you, and I beg to put it forth to you."

"Speak," said the king, very agitated by his minister's last words. "What do you require?"

"The pardon of Monsieur d'Herblay and of Monsieur du Vallon."

"My assassins?"

"Two rebels, sire, that is all."

"Oh! I understand, then, you ask me to forgive your friends."

"My friends!" said Fouquet, deeply wounded.

"Your friends, certainly; but the safety of the state

requires that an exemplary punishment should be inflicted on the guilty.''

"I will not permit myself to remind your majesty that I have just restored you to liberty, and have saved your life.''

"Monsieur!''

"I will not allow myself to remind your majesty that had Monsieur d'Herblay wished to carry out his role of an assassin, he could very easily have assassinated your majesty this morning in the forest of Sénart, and all would have been over.''

The king trembled.

"A pistol bullet through the head,'' pursued Fouquet, "and the disfigured features of Louis XIV, which no one could have recognized, would be Monsieur d'Herblay's justification.''

The king turned pale with fear at the idea of the danger he had escaped.

"If Monsieur d'Herblay,'' continued Fouquet, "had been an assassin, he would have had no need to inform me of his plan in order to succeed. Freed from the real king, it would have been impossible to guess the false king. And if the usurper had been recognized by Anne of Austria, he would still have been a son for her. The usurper, as far as Monsieur d'Herblay's conscience was concerned, was still a king of the blood of Louis XIII. Moreover, the conspirator, in that course, would have had security, secrecy, and impunity. A pistol bullet would have procured him all that. For your sake, sire, grant me his forgiveness!''

The king, instead of being touched by this true picture of Aramis's generosity, felt cruelly humiliated by it. His unconquerable pride revolted at the idea that a man had held suspended at the end of his finger the thread of his royal life. Every word that fell from Fouquet's lips, and which he thought most effective in getting his friend's pardon, seemed to pour another drop of poison into the already ulcerated heart of Louis XIV. Nothing could soften him. Addressing himself to Fouquet, he said:

"I really don't know, monsieur, why you should solicit the pardon of these men. What good is there in asking what can be obtained without solicitation?''

"I do not understand you, sire.''

"It is not difficult, either. Where am I now?"

"In the Bastille, sire."

"Yes; in a dungeon. I am looked upon as a madman, am I not?"

"Yes, sire."

"And no one is known here but Marchiali?"

"Certainly."

"Well, change nothing in this state of affairs. Let the madman rot in the dungeon of the Bastille, and Monsieur d'Herblay and Monsieur du Vallon will stand in no need of my forgiveness. Their new king will absolve them."

"Your majesty does me a great injustice, sire, and you are wrong," replied Fouquet dryly; "I am not child enough, nor is Monsieur d'Herblay foolish enough to have omitted to make all these reflections; and if I had wished to make a new king, as you say, I had no need to come here to force open all the gates and doors of the Bastille, to free you from this place. That is obvious. Your majesty's mind is disturbed by anger; otherwise you would not offend, groundlessly, the very one of your servants who has rendered you the most important service of all."

Louis perceived that he had gone too far, that the gates of the Bastille were still closed upon him; while, by degrees, the floodgates were gradually being opened behind which the generous Fouquet was controlling his anger.

"I did not say that to humiliate you, God knows, monsieur!" he replied. "Only you are addressing yourself to me, in order to obtain a pardon, and I answer you according to my conscience. And so, judging by my conscience, the criminals we speak of are not worthy of consideration or forgiveness."

Fouquet was silent.

"What I do is as generous," added the king, "as what you have done, for I am in your power. I will even say it is more generous, since you place before me certain conditions upon which my liberty, my life, may depend; and to refuse is to make a sacrifice of them both."

"I was wrong, certainly," replied Fouquet. "Yes—I seemed to extort a favor; I regret it, and ask for your majesty's forgiveness."

"And you are forgiven, my dear Monsieur Fouquet,"

said the king, with a smile, which restored the serene expression of his features, which so many circumstances had altered since the preceding evening.

"I have my own forgiveness," replied the minister, with some degree of persistence; "but Monsieur d'Herblay and Monsieur du Vallon?"

"They will never obtain theirs, as long as I live," replied the inflexible king. "Do me the kindness not to speak of it again."

"Your majesty shall be obeyed."

"And you will bear me no ill will for it?"

"Oh, no, sire; for I anticipated it as being most likely."

"You anticipated that I should refuse to forgive those gentlemen?"

"Certainly; and all my measures were taken in consequence."

"What do you mean to say?" cried the king, surprised.

"Monsieur d'Herblay came, so to speak, to deliver himself into my hands. Monsieur d'Herblay was giving me the happiness of saving my king and my country. I could not condemn Monsieur d'Herblay to death, nor could I, on the other hand, expose him to your majesty's most justifiable wrath; it would have been as if I had killed him myself."

"Well, and what have you done?"

"Sire, I gave Monsieur d'Herblay the best horses in my stable, and four hours' start over all those your majesty might dispatch after him."

"That may be so!" murmured the king. "But still, the world is large enough for my men to make up the four hours' start which you have given Monsieur d'Herblay."

"In giving him those four hours, sire, I knew I was giving him his life, and he will save his life."

"In what way?"

"After having galloped, four hours ahead of your musketeers, he will reach my chateau of Belle-Isle, where I have given him asylum."

"That may be; but you forget that you have given me Belle-Isle."

"But not for you to arrest my friends."

"Are you taking it back, then?"

"As far as that goes—yes, sire."

"My musketeers will capture it, and the affair will be at an end."

"Neither your musketeers nor your whole army could take Belle-Isle," said Fouquet coldly. "Belle-Isle is impregnable."

The king became livid; a light flashed from his eyes. Fouquet felt that he was lost, but he was not one to shrink when the voice of honor spoke loudly within him. He bore the king's wrathful gaze; the latter swallowed his rage, and after a few moments' silence, said:

"Are we going to return to Vaux?"

"I am at your majesty's orders," replied Fouquet, with a low bow; "but I think that your majesty can hardly dispense with changing clothes before appearing before your court."

"We shall go by the Louvre," said the king. "Come."

And they left the prison, passing before Baisemeaux, who looked completely bewildered as he saw Marchiali leave once again, and who tore out the few remaining hairs he had left. It was perfectly true, however, that Fouquet wrote and gave him an authority for the prisoner's release, and that the king wrote beneath it, "Seen and approved, Louis"; a piece of madness that Baisemeaux, incapable of putting two ideas together, welcomed by hitting himself on the jaw.

CHAPTER XXIV

THE FALSE KING

In the meantime, usurped royalty was playing out its part bravely at Vaux. Philippe gave orders that for his *petit lever,* the *grandes entrées,* already prepared to appear before the king, should be introduced. He determined to give this order, in spite of the absence of M. d'Herblay, who was not coming back, and our readers know why. But the prince, not believing this absence would be prolonged, wished, as all rash spirits do, to try his bravery and his fortune when far from all protection and counsel.

Another reason urged him to this—Anne of Austria was about to appear; the guilty mother was about to stand in the presence of her sacrificed son. Philippe did not want, if he had a weakness, to have M. d'Herblay as a witness. Philippe opened his folding doors, and several persons entered silently. Philippe did not stir while his *valets* dressed him. He had watched, the evening before, all the habits of his brother, and played the king in such a manner as to awaken no suspicion. He was then completely dressed in his hunting costume when he received his visitors. His own memory and the notes of Aramis announced everybody to him, first of all Anne of Austria, to whom Monsieur gave his hand, and then Madame with M. de St. Aignan. He smiled at seeing these faces, but trembled on recognizing his mother. That face, so noble, so imposing, ravaged by pain, pleaded in his heart the cause of that famous queen who had sacrificed a child to reasons of state. He found his mother handsome. He knew that Louis XIV loved her, and he promised himself to love her also, and not to prove a cruel punishment for her old age.

He contemplated his brother with a tenderness easily to be understood. The latter had usurped nothing over him, had cast no shadow over his life. A separate branch, he allowed the stem to rise without caring for the elevation or the majesty of his life. Philippe promised himself to be a kind brother to this prince, who required nothing but gold to minister to his pleasures. He bowed with a friendly air to St. Aignan, who was all bows and smiles, and tremblingly held out his hand to Henriette, his sister-in-law, whose beauty struck him; but he saw in the eyes of that princess an expression of coldness which would facilitate, as he thought, her future relations.

"How much easier," he thought, "it will be to be the brother of that woman than her suitor, if she shows toward me a coldness that my brother could not have for her, and which is imposed upon me as a duty."

The only visit he dreaded at this moment was that of the queen; his heart, his mind, had just been shaken by so violent a trial that, in spite of their steadiness, they might not, perhaps, survive another shock. Happily the queen did not come. Then Anne of Austria began a political dissertation on the welcome M. Fouquet had given the house of France. She mixed up hostilities with compliments addressed to the king, and questions as to his health, with little maternal flatteries and diplomatic artifices.

"Well, my son," she said, "are you convinced with regard to Monsieur Fouquet?"

"St. Aignan," said Philippe, "have the goodness to go and inquire after the queen."

At these words, the first Philippe had pronounced aloud, the slight difference that there was between his voice and that of the king was clear to maternal ears, and Anne of Austria looked intently at her son. St. Aignan left the room, and Philippe continued:

"Madame, I do not like to hear Monsieur Fouquet ill spoken of, you know I do not—and you have even spoken well of him yourself."

"That is true; therefore, I only question you on how you feel about him."

"Sire," said Henriette, "I, on my part, have always liked Monsieur Fouquet. He is a man of good taste—he is a superior man."

"A surintendant who is never stingy," added Monsieur; "and who pays in gold all the orders I have on him."

"Everyone is thinking too much of himself, and not of the state," said the old queen. "Monsieur Fouquet, it is a fact, Monsieur Fouquet is ruining the state."

"Well, mother," replied Philippe, in rather a lower key, "do you defend also Monsieur Colbert?"

"How is that?" replied the old queen, rather surprised.

"Why, in truth," replied Philippe, "you speak that just as your old friend, Madame de Chevreuse, would speak."

"Why do you mention Madame de Chevreuse?" she said, "and what do you have against me today?"

Philippe continued:

"Is not Madame de Chevreuse always plotting against somebody? Has not Madame de Chevreuse been to pay you a visit, mother?"

"Monsieur, you are speaking to me now in such a

manner that I can almost imagine I am listening to your father.''

''My father did not like Madame de Chevreuse, and had good reason for not liking her,'' said the prince. ''For my part, I like her no better than he did; and if she thinks it's proper to come here as she formerly did, to sow divisions and hatreds under the pretext of begging money, why . . .''

''Well, what?'' said Anne of Austria proudly, herself provoking the storm.

''Well,'' replied the young man firmly, ''I will expel Madame de Chevreuse out of my kingdom—and with her all who meddle with secrets and mysteries.''

He had not calculated on the effect of this terrible word, or, perhaps, he wished to judge the effect of it, like those who, suffering from a chronic pain, and seeking to break the monotony of that suffering, touch their wound to procure a sharper pang. Anne of Austria was near fainting; her eyes, open but meaningless, ceased to see for several seconds; she stretched out her arms toward her other son, who embraced her without fear of irritating the king.

''Sire,'' she murmured, ''you treat your mother cruelly.''

''How, madame?'' he replied. ''I am only speaking of Madame de Chevreuse; does my mother prefer Madame de Chevreuse to the security of the state and to the security of my person? Well, then, madame, I tell you Madame de Chevreuse came to France to borrow money, and that she went to Monsieur Fouquet to sell him a certain secret.''

''A secret!'' cried Anne of Austria.

''Concerning alleged robberies that Monsieur le Surintendant had committed, which is false,'' added Philippe.

''Monsieur Fouquet rejected her offers with indignation, preferring the esteem of the king to all complicity with schemers. Then Madame de Chevreuse sold the secret to Monsieur Colbert, and as she is insatiable, and was not satisfied with having extorted a hundred thousand crowns from that clerk, she has flown still higher, and has tried to find even deeper springs. Is that true, madame?''

''You know all, sire,'' said the queen, more uneasy than irritated.

"Now," continued Philippe, "I have good reason to dislike this Fury, who comes to my court to plan the dishonor of some and the ruin of others. If God has suffered certain crimes to be committed, and has concealed them in the shade of His clemency, I will not permit Madame de Chevreuse to have the power to counteract the designs of God."

The latter part of this speech so agitated the queen mother that her son had pity on her. He took her hand and kissed it tenderly; she did not realize that in that kiss, given in spite of repulsions and bitterness of the heart, there was a pardon for eight years of horrible suffering. Philippe allowed a moment of silence to swallow the emotions that had just arisen. Then, with a cheerful smile:

"We will not go today," he said, "I have a plan."

And turning toward the door, he hoped to see Aramis, whose absence began to alarm him. The queen mother wished to leave the room.

"Stay where you are, mother," he said; "I want you to make your peace with Monsieur Fouquet."

"I bear no ill will toward Monsieur Fouquet; I only dreaded his lavishness."

"We will put that to rights, and will take nothing of the surintendant but his good qualities."

"What is your majesty looking for?" said Henriette, seeing the king's eyes constantly turned toward the door, and wishing to let fly a little poisoned arrow at his heart, supposing he was anxiously expecting either La Vallière or a letter from her.

"My sister," said the young man, who had guessed her thought, thanks to that marvelous insight which fortune from then on let him use, "my sister, I am expecting a most distinguished man, a most able counselor, whom I wish to present to you all, recommending him to your good graces. Ah! come in, D'Artagnan."

"What does your majesty wish?" said D'Artagnan, appearing.

"Where is Monsieur the Bishop of Vannes, your friend?"

"Why, sire . . ."

"I am waiting for him, and he does not come. Let him be called."

D'Artagnan remained for an instant stupefied; but soon, reflecting that Aramis had left Vaux secretly, with a mission from the king, he concluded that the king wanted to keep it secret.

"Sire," he replied, "does your majesty absolutely require Monsieur d'Herblay to be brought to you?"

"Absolutely is not the word," said Philippe; "I do not want him so particularly as that; but if he can be found . . ."

"I thought so," said D'Artagnan, to himself.

"Is this Monsieur d'Herblay, bishop of Vannes?"

"Yes, madame."

"A friend of Monsieur Fouquet?"

"Yes, madame; an old musketeer."

Anne of Austria blushed.

"One of the four brave men who formerly performed such wonders."

The old queen repented having wanted to bite; she broke off the conversation, in order to preserve the rest of her teeth.

"Whatever may be your choice, sire," she said, "I have no doubt it will be excellent."

All bowed in support of that sentiment.

"You will find in him," continued Philippe, "the depth of Monsieur de Richelieu, without the stinginess of Monsieur de Mazarin."

"A prime minister, sire?" said Monsieur in a fright.

"I will tell you all about that, brother; but it is strange that Monsieur d'Herblay is not here!"

He called out:

"Let Monsieur Fouquet be informed that I wish to speak to him—oh! before you, before you; do not retire."

M. de St. Aignan returned, bringing satisfactory news of the queen, who only stayed in bed out of precaution, and in order to have the strength to carry out all the king's wishes. While everybody was seeking M. Fouquet and Aramis, the new king quietly continued his experiments, and everybody, family, officers, servants, had not the least suspicion, his air, voice, and manners were so like the king's. On his side, Philippe, applying to all faces the faithful description furnished by his accomplice, Aramis, conducted himself so as not to give rise to a doubt in the minds of those who surrounded him.

Nothing from that time could disturb the usurper. With what strange facility had Providence just knocked down the most elevated fortune of the world to substitute the most humble in its stead! Philippe admired the goodness of God with regard to himself, and seconded it with all the resources of his admirable nature. But he felt, at times, something like a shadow gliding between him and the rays of his new glory. Aramis was not coming. The conversation had languished in the royal family; Philippe, preoccupied, was forgetting to dismiss his brother and Mme. Henriette. The latter were astonished, and were losing their patience. Anne of Austria stooped toward her son's ear, and addressed some words to him in Spanish. Philippe was completely ignorant of that language, and grew pale at this unexpected obstacle. But, as if the spirit of the imperturbable Aramis had protected him, instead of being disconcerted, Philippe rose.

"Well, what?" said Anne of Austria.

"What is all that noise?" said Philippe, turning around toward the door of the second staircase.

And a voice was heard, saying:

"This way, this way! A few steps more, sire!"

"The voice of Monsieur Fouquet!" said D'Artagnan, who was standing close to the queen mother.

"Then Monsieur d'Herblay cannot be far off," added Philippe.

But he then saw what he didn't expect to see so near him.

All eyes were turned toward the door where M. Fouquet was expected to enter; but it was not M. Fouquet who entered.

A terrible cry resounded from all corners of the chamber, it was a painful cry uttered by the king and all present.

It is not given to men, even to those whose destiny contains the strangest elements, and the most wonderful accidents, to witness a scene similar to that which was unfolding in the royal chamber at that moment. The half-closed shutters only let in the faintest light that passed through large velvet curtains lined with silk. In this soft shade everyone's eyes were dilated, and everyone saw others somewhat as outlines. However, one cannot escape in these circumstances any of the surrounding details; and the new object which presents itself appears as luminous as if it has been lighted by the sun.

So it happened with Louis XIV, when he appeared, pale and frowning, in the doorway of the secret stairs. The face of Fouquet appeared behind him, marked with sorrow and sternness. The queen mother, who saw Louis XIV, and who was holding the hand of Philippe, uttered the cry of which we have spoken, as if she had beheld a phantom. Monsieur was bewildered, and kept turning his head in astonishment, from one to the other. Madame made a step forward, thinking she saw the form of her brother-in-law reflected in a mirror. And, in fact, the illusion was possible. The two princes, both pale as death—for we give up depicting the fearful state of Philippe—both trembling, and clenching their hands convulsively, were measuring up each other, darting their eyes, like swords, into each other. The unheard-of resemblance of face, gesture, size, even to the resemblance of clothing, produced by chance—for Louis XIV had been to the Louvre and put on a violet-colored outfit—the perfect analogy of the two princes, completed the consternation of Anne of Austria. And yet she did not at once guess the truth. There are misfortunes in life that no one will accept; people would rather believe in the supernatural and the impossible. Louis had not counted on these obstacles. He expected he had only to appear and be acknowledged. A living sun, he could not endure the suspicion of equality with anyone. He did not admit that every torch should not become darkness the instant he shone out with his conquering ray. At the sight of Philippe, then, he was perhaps more terrified than anyone around him, and his silence, his immobility, were, this time, a concentration and a calm which precede violent explosions of passion.

But Fouquet—who could describe his emotion and stupor in the presence of this living portrait of his master? Fouquet thought Aramis was right, that this newly arrived was a king as pure in his race as the other, and that, for having repudiated all participation in this *coup d'état,* so skillfully executed by the general of the Jesuits, he must be a mad enthusiast, unworthy of ever again dipping his hands in political work. And then it was the blood of Louis XIII which Fouquet was sacrificing to the blood of Louis XIII; for a selfish ambition he was sacrificing a noble ambition; for the right of keeping he was sacrificing the right of having. The extent of his fault was revealed to him by the simple sight of the pretender. All that went on in the mind of Fouquet was lost upon the persons present. He had five minutes to concentrate his thoughts on this case of conscience; five minutes, that is to say, five ages, during which the two kings and their family scarcely found time to breathe after so terrible a shock. D'Artagnan, leaning against the wall in front of Fouquet, with his hand to his brow, was wondering the cause of such a wonderful prodigy. He could not have said at once why he doubted, but he knew assuredly that he had reason to doubt, and that in this meeting of the two Louis XIV's lay all the difficulty which, during recent days, had made the behavior of Aramis so suspicious to the musketeer. These ideas were, however, enveloped in thick veils. The actors in this assembly seemed to swim in thick vapors of a confused waking.

Suddenly Louis XIV, more impatient and more accustomed to commanding, ran to one of the shutters, which he opened, tearing the curtain in his eagerness. A flood of bright light entered the chamber, and made Philippe draw back to the alcove. Louis seized upon this movement with eagerness, and addressing himself to the queen:

"My mother," said he, "do you not recognize your son, since everyone here has disowned his king!"

Anne of Austria shuddered, and raised her arms toward heaven, without being able to articulate a single word.

"My mother," said Philippe, with a calm voice, "do you not recognize your son?"

And this time, in his turn, Louis drew back.

As to Anne of Austria, whose head and heart were struck with remorse, she lost her balance. No one aiding her, for all were petrified, she sank back in her armchair, breathing a weak sigh. Louis could not endure this sight and this affront. He bounded toward D'Artagnan, who was beginning to feel dizzy, and who staggered as he caught at the door for support.

"*A moi, mousquetaire!*" he said. "Look us in the face, and say who is the paler, he or I!"

This cry aroused D'Artagnan, and stirred in his heart the fiber of obedience. He shook his head, and without hesitation walked straight up to Philippe, upon whose shoulder he laid his hand, saying:

"Monsieur, you are my prisoner!"

Philippe did not raise his eyes toward heaven, nor stir from the spot where he seemed nailed to the floor, his eye intensely fixed upon the king, his brother. He was reproaching him with a sublime silence for all his misfortunes past, for all his tortures to come. Against this language of the soul the king felt he had no power; he cast down his eyes and left hurriedly with his brother and sister, forgetting his mother, sitting motionless within three paces of the son whom she left a second time to be condemned to death. Philippe approached Anne of Austria, and said to her, in a soft and nobly agitated voice:

"If I were not your son, I should curse you, my mother, for having made me so unhappy!"

D'Artagnan felt a shudder pass through the marrow of his bones. He bowed respectfully to the young prince, and said, as he bent:

"Excuse me, monseigneur, I am but a soldier, and my loyalty is to him who has just left the room."

"Thank you, Monsieur D'Artagnan. But what is become of Monsieur d'Herblay?"

"Monsieur d'Herblay is in safety, monseigneur," said a voice behind them; "and no one, while I live and am free, shall cause a hair to fall from his head."

"Monsieur Fouquet," said the prince, smiling sadly.

"Pardon me, monseigneur," said Fouquet, kneeling, "but he who has just gone out was my guest."

"Here are," murmured Philippe, with a sigh, "brave friends and good hearts. They make me regret the world. On, Monsieur d'Artagnan; I am following you."

Just as the captain of the musketeers was about to leave the room with his prisoner, Colbert appeared, handed an order from the king to D'Artagnan, and retired. D'Artagnan read the paper, and then crushed it in his hand with rage.

"What is it?" asked the prince.

"Read, monseigneur," replied the musketeer.

Philippe read the following words, hastily written by the hand of the king:

"Monsieur d'Artagnan will take the prisoner to the Iles Ste. Marguerite. He will cover his face with an iron mask, which the prisoner cannot raise without peril of his life."

"That is just," said Philippe, with resignation; "I am ready."

"Aramis was right," said Fouquet, in a low voice, to the musketeer, "this one is quite as much of a king as the other."

"More!" replied D'Artagnan. "He only needs you and me."

CHAPTER XXV

IN WHICH PORTHOS THINKS HE IS PURSUING A DUKEDOM

ARAMIS and Porthos, having taken advantage of the time granted them by Fouquet, did honor to the French cavalry by their rapidity. Porthos did not clearly understand for what kind of mission he was being forced to display such velocity; but as he saw Aramis spurring on his horse, he, Porthos, spurred on in the same manner. They had soon, in this manner, placed twelve leagues between them and Vaux; they were then obliged to change horses, and organize a sort of post arrangement. It was during a relay that Porthos ventured to question Aramis discreetly.

"Hush!" replied the latter; "know only that our fortune depends upon our speed."

As if Porthos were still the musketeer without a sou or a *maille* of 1626, he pushed forward. That magic word, "fortune," always means something to the human ear. It means *enough* for those who have nothing; it means *too much* for those who have enough.

"I shall be made a duke!" said Porthos aloud. He was speaking to himself.

"That is possible," replied Aramis, smiling in his own way, as the horse of Porthos passed him. The head of

Aramis was on fire; the activity of the body had not yet
succeeded in subduing that of the mind. All that there is
in raging passions, in severe toothaches, or mortal threats
twisted, gnawed, and grumbled in the thoughts of the
vanquished prelate. His face exhibited very visible traces
of this tough combat. Free upon the highway to abandon
himself to every impression of the moment, Aramis did
not fail to swear at every start of his horse, at every
inequality in the road. Pale, at times drenched in boiling
sweats, then again dry and icy, he beat his horses and
made the blood stream from their sides. Porthos, whose
dominant fault was not sensitivity, groaned at this. Thus
they traveled on for eight long hours, and then arrived in
Orleans. It was four o'clock in the afternoon. Aramis,
on observing this, decided that pursuit was probably impossible. It would be without precedent that a troop capable of overtaking him and Porthos would be furnished
with relays sufficient to perform forty leagues in eight
hours. Thus, admitting pursuit, which was not at all evident, the fugitives were five hours in advance of their
pursuers.

Aramis thought that there might be no imprudence in
taking a little rest, but that to continue would make the
matter more certain. Twenty leagues more covered as
rapidly, twenty more leagues devoured, and no one, not
even D'Artagnan, could overtake the enemies of the king.
Aramis felt obliged, therefore, to inflict again upon Porthos the pain of mounting on horseback. They rode on
till seven o'clock in the evening, and had only one post
more between them and Blois. But here a diabolical accident alarmed Aramis greatly. There were no horses at
the post. The prelate wondered by what infernal machi-
nation his enemies had succeeded in depriving him of the
means of going further—he who never recognized chance
as a deity, he who found a cause for every result, he
preferred believing that the refusal of the postmaster, at
such an hour, in such a country, was the consequence of
an order emanating from above; an order given with a
view of stopping short the kingmaker in the midst of his
flight. But at the moment he was about to fly into a passion, so as to get either a horse or an explanation, he was
struck with the recollection that the Comte de la Fère
lived in the neighborhood.

"I am not traveling," he said; "I do not want horses for a whole stage. Find me two horses to go and pay a visit to a nobleman of my acquaintance who resides near here."

"What nobleman?" asked the postmaster.

"Monsieur le Comte de la Fère."

"Oh!" replied the postmaster, taking off his hat respectfully, "a very worthy nobleman. But even though I would like to make myself agreeable to him, I cannot furnish you with horses, for all mine are engaged by Monsieur le Duc de Beaufort."

"Indeed!" said Aramis, much disappointed.

"Only," continued the postmaster, "if you will put up with a little carriage I have, I will harness an old blind horse, who still has his legs left, and will take you to the house of Monsieur le Comte de la Fère."

"That is worth a louis," said Aramis.

"No, monsieur, that is never worth more than a crown; that is what Monsieur Grimaud, the count's intendant, always pays me when he makes use of that carriage, and I do not want the Comte de la Fère to accuse me with having overcharged one of his friends."

"As you please," said Aramis, "particularly as regards disobliging the Comte de la Fère; only I think I have a right to give you a louis for your idea."

"Oh! of course," replied the postmaster, with delight.

And he himself harnessed the old horse to the creaking carriage. In the meantime, Porthos was strange to behold. He imagined he had discovered the secret, and he felt pleased because a visit to Athos, in the first place, promised him much satisfaction, and, also, gave him the hope of finding a good bed and a good supper. The master, having got the carriage ready, ordered one of his men to drive the strangers to La Fère. Porthos sat in the back with Aramis, and whispered in his ear:

"I understand."

"And what do you understand, my friend?" asked Aramis.

"We are sent by the king to make some great proposal to Athos."

"Pooh!" said Aramis.

"Don't tell me anything," added the worthy Porthos,

trying to place himself so as to avoid the jolting; "don't tell me anything, I shall guess."

"Well, do, my friend; guess away."

They arrived at Athos's about nine o'clock in the evening, favored by a splendid moon. This cheerful light rejoiced Porthos beyond expression; but Aramis appeared annoyed by it in an equal degree. He could not help showing something of this to Porthos, who replied:

"I guess how it is; the mission is a secret one."

These were his last words in the carriage. The driver interrupted him, by saying:

"Gentlemen, you have arrived."

Porthos and his companion got out in front of the gate of the little chateau, where we are about to meet with Athos and Raoul, the latter who had disappeared since the discovery of La Vallière's infidelity. If there is one saying more true than another, it is this: great griefs contain within themselves the germ of their consolation. This painful wound, inflicted upon Raoul, had drawn him nearer to his father; and God knows how sweet were the consolations which were flowing from the eloquent mouth and generous heart of Athos. The wound was not healed, but Athos, by talking with his son and mixing a little more of his life with that of the young man, had brought him to understand that this pang of a first infidelity is necessary to every human existence, and that no one has loved without meeting with it. Raoul would listen, but never understood. Nothing replaces in the deeply afflicted heart the memory of the beloved object. Raoul then would reply to his father:

"Monsieur, all that you tell me is true; I believe that no one has suffered in the affections of the heart so much as you have; but you are a man too intelligent, and too severely tried by misfortunes, not to allow for the weakness of the soldier who suffers for the first time. I am paying a tribute which I shall not pay a second time; permit me to plunge myself so deeply in my grief that I may forget myself in it, that I may drown even my reason in it."

"Raoul! Raoul!"

"Listen, monsieur. Never shall I accustom myself to the idea that Louise, the most chaste and the most innocent of women, has been able so basely to deceive a man so honest and so true a lover as I am. Never can I persuade myself that I see that sweet and good mask change into a hypocritical and lascivious face. Louise lost! Louise infamous! Ah! monseigneur, that idea is much more cruel to me than Raoul abandoned—Raoul unhappy!''

Athos then would use the heroic remedy. He would defend Louise against Raoul, and justify her treachery by her love.

''A woman who yielded to a king because he is a king,'' he said, ''would deserve to be called infamous; but Louise loved Louis. Both young, they have forgotten, he his rank, she her vows. Love absolves everything, Raoul. The two young people love each other with sincerity.''

And when he had dealt this sharp blow, Athos, with a sigh, would see Raoul leap away under the cruel wound, and fly to the thickest recesses of the wood, or the solitude of his chamber, where, an hour later, he would return, pale, trembling, but subdued. Then, coming up to Athos with a smile he would kiss his hand, like the dog who, having been beaten, caresses a good master, to redeem his fault. Raoul would redeem nothing but his weakness, and only confess his grief.

Thus passed the days that followed the scene in which Athos had so violently shaken the indomitable pride of the king. Never, when conversing with his son, did he make any allusion to that scene; never did he give him the details of that vigorous lecture, which might, perhaps, have consoled the young man, by showing him his rival humbled. Athos did not wish that the offended lover should forget the respect due to the king. And when De Bragelonne, ardent, furious, and melancholy, would speak with contempt of royal words, of the equivocal faith which certain madmen draw from promises falling from thrones, when, passing over two centuries, with the rapidity of a bird which crosses a narrow strait, to go from one world to the other, Raoul would venture to predict the time in which kings would become less than other men, Athos would say to him, in his serene, persuasive voice:

''You are right, Raoul; all that you say will happen; kings will lose their privileges, as stars which have com-

pleted their time lose their splendor. But when that moment shall come, Raoul, we shall be dead. And remember well what I say to you. In this world, all—men,
women, and kings—must live for the present. We can
only live for the future, for God.''

This was the manner in which Athos and Raoul were,
as usual, talking, and walking back and forth in the long
alley of linden trees in the park, when the bell which
served to announce to the count either the hour of dinner
or the arrival of a visitor, was rung; and, without attach-
ing any importance to it, he turned toward the house with
his son, and at the end of the alley they found themselves
in the presence of Aramis and Porthos.

CHAPTER XXVI

THE LAST ADIEUS

RAOUL uttered a cry, and affectionately embraced Porthos. Aramis and Athos embraced like old men; and this
embrace itself being a question for Aramis, he immediately said:

"My friend, we do not have a long time with you."

"Ah!" said the count.

"Only time to tell you of my good fortune," interrupted Porthos.

"Ah!" said Raoul.

Athos looked silently at Aramis, whose somber air had
already appeared to him very little in harmony with the
good news Porthos spoke of.

"What is the good fortune that has happened to you?
Let us hear it," said Raoul, with a smile.

"The king has made me a duke," said the worthy Porthos, with an air of mystery, in the ear of the young man,
"a duke by brevet."

But the asides of Porthos were always loud enough to
be heard by everybody. His murmurs were like roars.
Athos heard him, and uttered an exclamation which gave
Aramis a start. The latter took Athos by the arm, and,

after having asked Porthos's permission to say a word to his friend in private:

"My dear Athos," he began, "you see me over-whelmed with grief."

"With grief, my dear friend?" cried the count. "Oh, what?"

"In two words, I have raised a conspiracy against the king; that conspiracy has failed, and at this moment I am, doubtless, pursued."

"You are pursued! A conspiracy? My friend, what are you telling me?"

"A sad truth. I am entirely ruined."

"Well, but Porthos . . . this title of duke—what does all that mean?"

"That is the subject of my greatest pain; that is the deepest of my wounds. I have, believing in an infallible success, drawn Porthos into my conspiracy. He has thrown himself into it, as you know he would, with all his strength, without knowing what he was doing; and now, he is as much compromised as I am—as completely ruined as I am."

"Good God!"

And Athos turned toward Porthos, who was smiling complacently.

"I must tell you the whole story. Listen to me," continued Aramis; and he related the story as we know it.

Athos, as he heard it, felt several times the sweat break from his forehead.

"It was a great idea," he said, "but a great error."

"For which I am punished, Athos."

"Therefore, I will not tell you all my thoughts."

"Tell me, nevertheless."

"It is a crime."

"Capital, I know it is. *Lèse majesté.*"

"Porthos! poor Porthos!"

"What would you advise me to do? Success, as I have told you, was certain."

"Monsieur Fouquet is an honest man."

"And I am a fool for having judged him so badly," said Aramis. "Oh, the wisdom of man! Oh, the vast millstone which grinds a world! and which is one day stopped by a grain of sand which has fallen, no one knows how, in its wheels."

"Say, by a diamond, Aramis. But the thing is done. What are your plans?"

"I am taking Porthos away. The king will never believe that that worthy man has acted innocently. He never can believe that Porthos has thought he was serving the king while acting as he has done. His head would pay for my fault. It shall not be so."

"Where are you taking him?"

"To Belle-Isle, at first. That is an impregnable place of refuge. Then I have the sea, and a vessel to cross to England, where I have many relations."

"You? In England?"

"Yes, or else in Spain, where I have still more."

"But our excellent Porthos? You ruin him, for the king will confiscate all his property."

"All is provided for. I know how, when once in Spain, to reconcile myself with Louis XIV, and restore Porthos to favor."

"You have credit, seemingly, Aramis," said Athos, with a discreet air.

"Much; and at the service of my friends."

These words were accompanied by a warm pressure of the hand.

"Thank you," replied the count.

"And since we have come to that," said Aramis, "you also are a malcontent; you also, Athos, have grievances against the king. Follow our example; cross to Belle-Isle. Then we shall see, I guarantee upon my honor, that in a month there will be war between France and Spain on the subject of this son of Louis XIII, who is also a Spanish prince, and whom France detains inhumanly. Now, as Louis XIV would have no inclination for a war on that subject, I will answer for a transaction, the result of which must bring titles of grandee of Spain to Porthos and to me, and a duchy in France to you, who are already a grandee of Spain. Will you join us?"

"No; for my part, I prefer having something to reproach the king with; it is a pride natural to my race to claim a superiority over royal races. Doing what you propose, I would become obligated to the king: I would certainly gain on this earth, but I would lose in my conscience. No, thank you!"

"Then give me two things, Athos—your absolution."

"I give it to you if you have really wished to avenge the weak and the oppressed against the oppressor."

"That is enough for me," said Aramis, with a blush which was lost in the obscurity of the night. "And now, give me your two best horses to gain the second post, as I have been refused any under the pretext of the Duc de Beaufort traveling in this country."

"You shall have the two best horses, Aramis; and I again recommend Porthos strongly to you."

"Oh! do not be worried. One word more: do you think I am doing the right thing for him?"

"The evil being committed, yes; for the king would not pardon him, and you have, whatever may be said, always a supporter in Monsieur Fouquet, who will not abandon you, he being himself compromised in spite of his heroic action."

"You are right. And that is why, instead of taking to the sea at once, which would proclaim my fear and guilt, I remain on French ground. But Belle-Isle will be for me whatever ground I wish it to be—English, Spanish, or Roman; I will depend on the flag I shall unfurl."

"How so?"

"It was I who fortified Belle-Isle; and, while I defend it, nobody can take Belle-Isle from me. And then, as you have said just now, Monsieur Fouquet is there. Belle-Isle will not be attacked without the signature of Monsieur Fouquet."

"That is true. Nevertheless, be prudent. The king is both cunning and strong."

Aramis smiled.

"I again recommend Porthos to you," repeated the count, with a sort of cold persistence.

"Whatever becomes of me, count," replied Aramis, in the same tone, "our brother, Porthos, will fare as I do."

Athos bowed while pressing the hand of Aramis, and turned to embrace Porthos with much emotion.

"I was born lucky, was I not?" murmured the latter, transported with happiness, as he folded his cloak around him.

"Come, my dear friend," said Aramis.

Raoul had left to give orders for the saddling of the horses. The group was already divided. Athos saw his

two friends about to leave, and something like a mist
passed before his eyes and weighed upon his heart.

"It is strange," he thought, "why do I feel like embracing Porthos once more?"

At that moment Porthos turned around, and he came
toward his old friend with open arms. This last endearment was tender as in youth, as in times when the heart
was warm, and life happy. And then Porthos mounted
his horse. Aramis came back once more to throw his
arms around the neck of Athos. The latter watched them
along the highroad, elongated by the shade, in their white
cloaks. Like two phantoms, they seemed to be enlarged
on departing from the earth, and it was not in the mist,
but in a dip in the ground that they disappeared. Just as
they were almost out of sight, both seemed to have given
a spring with their feet, which made them vanish, as if
evaporated into the clouds.

Then Athos, with an oppressed heart, turned toward
the house, saying to De Bragelonne:

"Raoul, I don't know what it is that has just told me
that I have seen these two men for the last time."

"It does not astonish me, monsieur, that you should
have such a thought," replied the young man, "for I have
at this moment the same, and think also that I shall never
see Messieurs du Vallon and d'Herblay again."

"Oh! you," replied the count, "you speak like a man
saddened by another cause; you see everything in black;
you are young, and if you happen never to see those old
friends again, it will be because they no longer exist in
the world in which you have many years to spend. But
I . . ."

Raoul shook his head sadly, and leaned upon the
shoulder of the count, without either of them finding another word in their hearts, which were ready to overflow.

All at once a noise of horses and voices, from the end
of the road to Blois, attracted their attention. Torchbear-
ers shook their torches merrily on the trees of the road,
and turned around, from time to time, to avoid outdis-
tancing the horsemen who followed them. These flames,
this noise, this dust of a dozen richly-caparisoned horses
formed a strange contrast in the middle of the night with
the melancholy disappearance of the two shadows of Aramis and Porthos. Athos went toward the house; but he

had already reached the parterre when the entrance gate appeared in a blaze; all the torches stopped and lighted up the road. A cry was heard of "Monsieur le Duc de Beaufort!" and Athos sprang toward the door of his house. But the duke had already gotten off his horse, and was looking around him.

"I am here, monseigneur," said Athos.

"Good evening, dear count," said the prince, with that frank cordiality which won him so many hearts. "Is it too late for a friend?"

"My dear prince, come in!" said the count.

And, with M. de Beaufort leaning on the arm of Athos, they entered the house, followed by Raoul, who walked respectfully and modestly among the officers of the prince, with several of whom he was acquainted.

CHAPTER XXVII

M. DE BEAUFORT

THE prince turned around at the moment when Raoul, in order to leave him alone with Athos, was shutting the door, and preparing to go with the other officers into an adjoining apartment.

"Is that the young man I have heard Monsieur le Prince speak so highly of?" asked M. de Beaufort.

"It is, monseigneur."

"He is quite the soldier; let him stay, count; we cannot spare him."

"Stay, Raoul, since monseigneur permits it," said Athos.

"*Ma foi!* he is tall and handsome!" the duke went on. "Will you give him to me, monseigneur, if I ask you?"

"How am I to understand you, monseigneur?" said Athos.

"Why, I call upon you to bid farewell."

"Farewell?"

"Yes, in fact. Don't you have any idea of what I am about to become?"

''Why, I suppose, what you have always been, monseigneur—a valiant prince, and an excellent gentleman.''

''I am going to become an African prince—a Bedouin gentleman. The king is sending me to make conquests among the Arabs.''

''What are you telling me, monseigneur?''

''Strange, is it not? I, the Parisian *par excellence,* I, who have reigned in the faubourgs, and have been called King of the Halles—I am going to move from the Place Maubert to the minarets of Gigelli; I become from a *frondeur*—an adventurer!''

''Oh, monseigneur, if you were not telling me this yourself . . .''

''It would not be believable, would it? Believe me, nevertheless, and let us say farewell. This is what comes of getting into favor again.''

''Into favor?''

''Yes. You are smiling. Ah, my dear count, do you know why I have accepted this venture, can you guess?''

''Because your highness loves glory above everything.''

''Oh! no; there is no glory in firing muskets at savages. I see no glory in that, for my part, and it is more probable that I shall meet there with something else. But I have wished, and still wish earnestly, my dear count, that my life should have that last *facet,* after all the bizarre exhibitions I have seen myself make during fifty years. For, in short, you must admit that it is rather strange to be born the grandson of a king, to have made war against kings, to have been reckoned among the powers of the age, to have maintained my rank, to feel Henry IV within me, to be great admiral of France—and then to go and get killed at Gigelli, among all those Turks, Saracens, and Moors.''

''Monseigneur, you dwell strangely upon that subject,'' said Athos, in a agitated voice. ''How can you suppose that so brilliant a destiny will be extinguished in that remote and miserable scene?''

''And can you believe, just and simple man as you are, that if I go into Africa for this ridiculous motive I will not try to come out of it without ridicule? Will I not give the world reason to speak of me? And to be spoken of nowadays, when there are Monsieur le Prince, Monsieur de Turenne, and many others, my contemporaries, I, admiral of France, grandson of Henry IV, king of Paris, have I anything left but to get myself killed? *Mordieu!* I will be talked of, I tell you; I shall be killed whether or not; if not there, somewhere else.''

''Why, monseigneur, this is only exaggeration; and you have only shown it in bravery.''

''*Peste!* my dear friend, there is bravery in facing scurvy, dysentery, locusts, and poisoned arrows, as my ancestor, St. Louis, did. Do you know those fellows still use poisoned arrows? And then, you know me, I have been thinking about it a long time, and you know that when I once make up my mind to a thing, I do it in earnest.''

''Yes, you made up your mind to escape from Vincennes.''

''But you helped me in that, my master; and, apropos, I turn this way and turn that way, without seeing my old friend, Monsieur Vaugrimaud. How is he?''

''Monsieur Vaugrimaud is still your highness's most respectful servant,'' said Athos, smiling.

''I have a hundred pistoles here for him, which I bring as a legacy. My will is made, count.''

''Ah! monseigneur, monseigneur!''

''And you may understand that if Grimaud's name were to appear in my will . . .'' The duke began to laugh; then, addressing Raoul, who, from the start of this conversation, had sunk into a profound reverie, ''Young man,'' said he, ''I know there is to be found here a certain Vouvray wine and I believe . . .''

Raoul left the room hurriedly to order the wine. In the meantime, M. de Beaufort took the hand of Athos.

''What do you mean to do with him?'' he asked.

''Nothing at present, monseigneur.''

''Ah, yes, I know; since the passion of the king for La Vallière.''

''Yes, monseigneur.''

''That is all true, then, is it? I think I know her, that little La Vallière. She is not particularly handsome, if I remember right.''

''No, monseigneur,'' said Athos.

''Do you know whom she reminds me of?''

''Does she remind your highness of anyone?''

"She reminds me of a very agreeable girl whose mother lived in the Halles."

"Ah! ah!" said Athos, smiling.

"Oh! the good old times," added M. de Beaufort. "Yes, La Vallière reminds me of that girl."

"Who had a son, didn't she?"

"I believe she had," replied the duke, with careless naïveté, and a complaisant forgetfulness of which no words could translate the tone and the vocal expression. "Now, here is poor Raoul, who is your son, I believe?"

"Yes, he is my son, monseigneur."

"And the poor lad has been cut out by the king, and he frets?"

"Better than that, monseigneur, he abstains."

"You are going to let the boy rust in idleness? You are wrong. Come, give him to me."

"My wish is to keep him at home, monseigneur. I no longer have anything in the world but him, and as long as he likes to remain . . ."

"Fine," replied the duke, "I could, nevertheless, have soon put matters to rights again. I assure you, I think he has in him the stuff of which marshals of France are made; I have seen more than one produced from such."

"That is very possible, monseigneur; but it is the king who makes marshals of France, and Raoul will never accept anything from the king."

Raoul interrupted this conversation by his return. He preceded Grimaud, whose still steady hands carried the tray with one glass and a bottle of the duke's favorite wine. On seeing his old *protégé*, the duke uttered an exclamation of pleasure.

"Grimaud! Good evening, Grimaud!" he said. "How goes it?"

The servant bowed deeply, as happy as his noble interlocutor was.

"Two old friends!" said the duke, shaking vigorously honest Grimaud's shoulder, which was followed by another still more profound and delighted bow from Grimaud.

"But what is this, count, only one glass!"

"I do not drink with your highness, unless your highness permits me," replied Athos, with noble humility.

"*Mordieu!* you were right to bring only one glass; we

will both drink out of it, like two brothers in arms. Begin, count.''

"Do me the honor," said Athos, gently pushing back the glass.

"You are a charming friend," replied the Duc de Beaufort, who drank, and passed the goblet to his companion. "But that is not all," he continued. "I am still thirsty, and I wish to do honor to this handsome young man who stands here. I carry good luck with me, viscount," he said to Raoul; "wish for something while drinking out of my glass, and the plague stifle me if your wish does not come to pass!''

He held the goblet to Raoul, who hastily moistened his lips, and replied, with the same promptitude:

"I have wished for something, monseigneur."

His eyes sparkled with a gloomy fire, and the blood mounted to his cheeks; he terrified Athos, if only with his smile.

"And what have you wished for?" replied the duke, sinking back into his armchair, while with one hand he returned the bottle to Grimaud, and with the other gave him a purse.

"Will you promise me, monseigneur, to grant me what I wished for?''

"Pardieu! that is agreed upon.''

"I wished, Monsieur le Duc, to go with you to Gigelli.''

Athos became pale, and was unable to conceal his agitation. The duke looked at his friend, as if to help him to ward off this unexpected blow.

"That is difficult, my dear viscount, very difficult," he added, in a lower tone of voice.

"Pardon me, monseigneur, I have been indiscreet," replied Raoul, in a firm voice; "but as you yourself invited me to wish—"

"To wish to leave me?" said Athos.

"Oh, monsieur—can you imagine—"

"Well, *mordieu!*" cried the duke, "the young viscount is right. What can he do here? He will rot with grief.''

Raoul blushed, and the excitable prince continued:

"War is a distraction; we gain everything by it; we can only lose one thing by it, life; then so much the worse.''

"That is to say, memory," said Raoul eagerly, "and that is to say, so much the better!"

He repented of having spoken so warmly when he saw Athos rise and open the window, which was, doubtless, to conceal his emotion. Raoul sprang toward the count, but the latter had already overcome his emotion, and turned to the lights with a serene and impassible face.

"Well, come," said the duke, "let us see! Shall he go, or shall he not? If he goes, count, he shall be my aide-de-camp, my son."

"Monseigneur!" cried Raoul, bending his knee.

"Monseigneur!" cried Athos, taking the hand of the duke. "Raoul shall do just as he likes."

"Oh, no, monsieur; just as you like!" interrupted the young man.

"By *la Corbleu!*" said the prince, in his turn, "it is neither the count nor the viscount that shall have his way, it is I. I will take him away. The navy offers a superb future, my friend."

Raoul smiled again so sadly that this time Athos felt broken-hearted, and answered him with a severe look. Raoul understood it all; he recovered his calmness, and was so guarded that not another word escaped him. The duke at last rose, on observing the late hour, and said, with much animation:

"I am in a great hurry, but if I am told I have lost time in talking with a friend, I will reply I have gained a good recruit."

"Pardon me, Monsieur le Duc," interrupted Raoul, "do not tell the king so, for it is not the king I will serve."

"My friend, whom, then, will you serve? The times are past when you might have said, 'I belong to Monsieur de Beaufort.' No, nowadays we all belong to the king, great or small. Therefore, if you serve on board my ship, there can be no doubt about it, my dear viscount; it will be the king you will serve."

Athos waited with a kind of impatient joy for the reply about to be made to this embarrassing question by Raoul, the intractable enemy of the king, his rival. The father hoped that the obstacle would overcome the desire. He was thankful to M. de Beaufort, whose lightness or generous reflection had thrown an impediment in the way of the departure of a son now his only joy. But Raoul, still firm and tranquil:

"Monsieur le Duc," he replied, "the objection you make I have already considered in my mind. I will serve on board your ships, because you do me the honor to take me with you; but I shall there serve a more powerful master than the king, I shall serve God!"

"God! how so?" said the duke and Athos together.

"My intention is to take vows, and become a Knight of Malta,"* added De Bragelonne, letting fall, one by one, words more icy than the drops which fall from the bare trees after the storms of winter.

Under this blow Athos staggered, and the prince himself was moved. Grimaud uttered a heavy groan, and dropped the bottle, which was broken without anybody paying attention to it. M. de Beaufort looked the young man in the face, and read plainly, though his eyes were cast down, the fire of resolution before which everything must give way. As to Athos, he was too well acquainted with that tender but inflexible soul; he could not hope to make it deviate from the fatal road it had just chosen. He could only press the hand the duke held out to him.

"Count, I shall set off in two days for Toulon," said M. de Beaufort. "Will you meet me in Paris, in order that I may know your decision?"

"I will have the honor of thanking you there, *mon prince,* for all your kindness," replied the count.

"And be sure to bring the viscount with you, whether he follows me or does not follow me," added the duke; "he has my word, and I only ask for yours."

Having thrown a little balm upon the wound of the paternal heart, he pulled the ear of Grimaud, whose eyes were sparkling more than usual, and joined his escort in the parterre. The horses, rested and refreshed, set off with spirit through this beautiful night, and soon placed a considerable distance between their master and the chateau.

Athos and De Bragelonne were again face to face. Eleven o'clock was striking. The father and son preserved a profound silence toward each other, where an intelligent observer would have expected cries and tears.

* Military and religious order dating back to the Crusades.

But these two men were of such a nature that all emotion sank, lost forever, when they had resolved to confine it to their own hearts. And so they spent silently, almost breathlessly, the hour which preceded midnight. The striking clock reminded them how long the painful journey made by their souls in the immensity of memories of the past and fears of the future, had lasted. Athos rose first, saying:

"It is late. Until tomorrow."

Raoul rose, and in his turn embraced his father. The latter held him clasped to his breast, and said, in a tremulous voice:

"In two days you will have left me, then—left me forever, Raoul!"

"Monsieur," replied the young man, "I had made a plan, that of piercing my heart with my sword; but you would have thought that cowardly. I have renounced that plan, and therefore we must part."

"You leave me by going, Raoul."

"Listen to me again, monsieur, I implore you. If I do not go I shall die here of grief and love. I know how long I have to live. Send me away quickly, monsieur, or you will see me die before your eyes, in your house. This is stronger than my will, stronger than my strength. You may plainly see that within one month I have lived thirty years, and that I approach the end of my life."

"Then," said Athos coolly, "you go with the intention of getting killed in Africa? Oh, tell me, do not lie!"

Raoul grew deathly pale, and remained silent for two seconds, which were to his father two hours of agony. Then all at once:

"Monsieur," he said, "I have promised to devote myself to God. In exchange for this sacrifice which I make of my youth and my liberty, I will only ask of Him one thing, and that is to preserve me for you, because you are the only tie which binds me to this world. God alone can give me the strength not to forget that I owe you everything, and that nothing must count before you."

Athos embraced his son tenderly and said:

"You have just answered me as an honest man; in two days we shall be with Monsieur de Beaufort in Paris, and you will then do what will be right for you to do. You are free, Raoul; adieu."

And he slowly went to his bedroom. Raoul went down into the garden, and spent the night in the alley of linden trees.

CHAPTER XXVIII

PREPARATIONS FOR DEPARTURE

ATHOS did not waste any more time in fighting this immutable resolution. He devoted all his attention to preparing, during the two days the duke had granted him, the proper equipment for Raoul. Grimaud was primarily responsible for this and immediately applied himself with goodwill and intelligence. Athos gave this worthy servant orders to take the road to Paris when the equipments should be ready, and not to expose himself to keeping the duke waiting, or to delay Raoul if the duke should notice his absence; the day after the visit of M. de Beaufort, he set off for Paris with his son.

For the poor young man it was an emotion easily understood, to return to Paris in such a manner among all the people who had known and loved him. Every face reminded him of his suffering, he who had suffered so much, he who had loved so much, some circumstance of his love. Raoul, once in Paris, felt as if he were dying. Once in Paris, he no longer existed. When he reached De Guiche's residence he was informed that De Guiche was with Monsieur. Raoul took the road to the Luxembourg, and when arrived, without suspecting that he was going to the place where La Vallière had lived, he heard so much music and smelled so many perfumes, he heard so much joyous laughter, and saw so many dancing shadows, that, if it had not been for a charitable woman, who noticed him so dejected and pale beneath a doorway, he would have remained there a few minutes, and then would have gone away, never to return. But, as we have said, in the first antechambers he had stopped, solely so as not to mingle with all those happy lives which were moving in the adjacent rooms. And as one of Monsieur's servants, recognizing him, had asked him if he wanted to

see Monsieur or Madame, Raoul had scarcely answered
him, but had sunk down upon a bench near the velvet
doorway, looking at a clock, which had stopped for nearly
an hour. The servant had passed on, and another, better
acquainted with him, had come up, and asked Raoul
whether he should inform M. de Guiche of his presence.
This name did not even rouse the attention of poor Raoul.
The persistent servant went on to tell that De Guiche had
just invented a new game of lottery, and was teaching it
to the ladies. Raoul, opening his large eyes, like the absent man in Theophrastus, had not answered, but his sadness had increased. With his head hanging down, his
limbs relaxed, his mouth half open to let out his sighs,
Raoul remained, thus forgotten, in the antechamber,
when all at once a lady's dress passed, brushing past the
doors of a lateral room which opened upon the gallery.
A lady, young, pretty, and happy, scolding an officer of
the household, entered that way, talking with much vivacity. The officer answered in calm but firm sentences;
it was rather a little love spat than a quarrel of courtiers,
and ended by a kiss on the fingers of the lady. Suddenly,
on noticing Raoul, the lady became silent, and pushing
away the officer:

"Make your escape, Malicorne," she said; "I did not
think there was anyone here. I shall curse you, if they
have either heard or seen us!"

Malicorne hastened away. The young lady came behind Raoul, and bending her joyous face over him:

"Monsieur is a gallant man," she said, "and no
doubt . . ."

She stopped to utter a cry:

"Raoul!" she said, blushing.

"Mademoiselle de Montalais!" said Raoul, paler than
death.

He rose unsteadily, and tried to make his way across
the slippery mosaic of the floor; but she had understood
that savage and cruel grief; she felt that in the flight of
Raoul there was an accusation, or, at least, a suspicion
against herself. A woman, ever vigilant, she did not think
she ought to let the opportunity slip of making a justification; but Raoul, though stopped by her in the middle
of the gallery, did not seem disposed to surrender without a fight. He took it up in a tone so cold and embar-

rassed that if they had been discovered, the whole court would have had no doubt about the intentions of Mlle. de Montalais.

"Ah! monsieur," she said, with disdain, "what you are doing is unworthy of a gentleman. My heart yearns to speak to you; you compromise me by an uncivil reception; you are wrong, monsieur; and you are confusing your friends with your enemies. Farewell!"

Raoul had sworn never to speak of Louise, never even to look at those who might have seen Louise; he was going into another world, that he might never meet with anything Louise had seen, or anything she had touched. But after the first shock of his pride, after having had a glimpse of Montalais, the companion of Louise—Montalais, who reminded him of the turret of Blois and the joys of youth—all his reason faded away.

"Pardon me, mademoiselle; it enters not, it cannot enter into my thoughts to be uncivil."

"Do you wish to speak to me?" she said, with the smile of former days. "Well, come somewhere else; for we may be caught."

"Oh!" he said.

She looked at the clock with indecision, then, having deliberated:

"In my apartment," she said, "we shall have an hour to ourselves."

And running, lighter than a fairy, she went up to her room, followed by Raoul. Shutting the door, and placing in the hands of her maid the mantle she had held upon her arm:

"Are you seeking Monsieur de Guiche?" she said to Raoul.

"Yes, mademoiselle."

"I will go and ask him to come up here in a while, after I have spoken to you."

"Do so, mademoiselle."

"Are you angry with me?"

Raoul looked at her for a moment, then, casting down his eyes:

"Yes," he said.

"Do you believe I was involved in the plot which brought about your break?"

"Break!" he said, with bitterness. "Oh, mademoiselle, there can be no break where there has been no love."

"An error," replied Montalais; "Louise cared for you."

Raoul gave a start.

"Not with love, I know; but she liked you, and you should have married her before you set out for London."

Raoul broke into a sinister laugh, which made Montalais shiver.

"It's easy for you to tell me this, mademoiselle. Do people marry whom they like? Are you forgetting that the king then kept for himself, as his mistress, the one we are speaking of?"

"Listen," said the young woman, pressing the cold hands of Raoul in her own, "you were wrong in every way; a man of your age ought never to leave a woman of hers alone."

"There is no longer any faith in the world, then," said Raoul.

"No, viscount," said Montalais quietly. "Nevertheless, let me tell you that if instead of loving Louise coldly and philosophically, you had tried to awaken her to love—"

"Enough, I beg you, mademoiselle," said Raoul. "I feel that you are all of a different century from me. You can laugh, and you can banter agreeably. I, mademoiselle, I loved Mademoiselle de . . ."

Raoul could not pronounce her name.

"I loved her; well, I put faith in her—now I end up loving her no longer."

"Oh, viscount!" said Montalais, pointing to his reflection in a mirror.

"I know what you mean, mademoiselle; I am greatly changed, am I not? Well, do you know why? Because my face is the mirror of my heart; the inside has changed as you see the outside has."

"You are consoled, then," said Montalais sharply.

"No, I shall never be consoled."

"They will not understand you, Monsieur de Bragelonne."

"I care little for that. I understand myself too well."

"Have you not even tried to speak to Louise?"

"Who, I?" exclaimed the young man, with eyes flashing fire; "I? Why don't you advise me to marry her? Perhaps the king would consent now."

And he rose from his chair, full of anger.

"I see," said Montalais, "that you are not cured, and that Louise has one more enemy."

"One more enemy!"

"Yes; favorites are not well loved at the Court of France."

"Oh! while she has her lover to protect her, is not that enough? She has chosen a man of such quality that her enemies cannot prevail against her." But, stopping all at once, "And then she has you for a friend, mademoiselle," he added, with a shade of irony.

"Who, I? Oh, no; I am no longer one of those whom Mademoiselle de la Vallière deigns to look upon; but . . ."

This *but,* so large with menace and storms; this *but,* which made the heart of Raoul beat, such griefs did it predict for her whom he once loved so dearly; this terrible *but,* so significant in a woman like Montalais, was interrupted by a moderately loud noise heard by the speakers, proceeding from the alcove behind the woodwork. Montalais turned to listen, and Raoul was already rising, when a lady entered the room quietly by the secret door, which she closed after her.

"Madame!" exclaimed Raoul, on recognizing the sister-in-law of the king.

"Stupid wretch!" murmured Montalais, throwing herself, but too late, before the princess, "I got the hour wrong!"

She had, however, time to warn the princess, who was walking toward Raoul.

"Monsieur de Bragelonne, Madame"; and at these words the princess drew back, uttering a cry in her turn.

"Your royal highness," said Montalais, with volubility, "is kind enough to think of this lottery, and . . ."

The princess looked confused. Raoul hastened his departure, without yet guessing everything; but he felt that he was in the way. Madame was preparing a word of transition to recover herself when a closet opened in front of the alcove, and M. de Guiche came out, all radiant, also from that closet. The palest of the four, we must admit, was still Raoul. The princess, however, was near

fainting, and was obliged to lean on the foot of the bed.
No one ventured to support her. This scene occupied
several minutes of terrible silence. But Raoul broke it.
He went up to the count whose inexpressible emotion
made his knees tremble, and taking his hand:

"Dear count," he said, "tell Madame I am too unhappy not to merit my pardon; tell her also that I have
loved in the course of my life, and that the horror of the
treachery that has been practiced on me makes me inflexible for all other treachery that may be committed
around me. This is why, mademoiselle," he said, smiling, to Montalais, "I never would divulge the secret of
the visits of my friend to your apartment. Obtain from
Madame—from Madame, who is so indulgent and so
kind, obtain her pardon for you whom she has just surprised. You are both free, love each other, be happy!"

The princess had a moment of despair which cannot
be described; it was repugnant to her, despite the exquisite delicacy which Raoul had just shown, to feel herself
at the mercy of an indiscretion. It was equally repugnant
to her to accept the evasion offered by this delicate deception. Agitated, nervous, she was struggling with those
two feelings. Raoul understood her, and came once more
to her aid. Bending his knee before her:

"Madame," he said, in a low voice, "in two days I
shall be far from Paris; in a fortnight I shall be far from
France, where I shall never be seen again."

"Are you going away, then?" she said, with great
delight.

"With Monsieur de Beaufort."

"Into Africa?" cried De Guiche. "You, Raoul! Oh,
my friend, into Africa, where everybody dies!"

And, forgetting everything, forgetting that that forgetfulness itself compromised the princess more eloquently
than his presence:

"Ungrateful one," he said, "and you have not even
consulted me!"

And he embraced him. Meanwhile, Montalais led Madame away, and disappeared.

Raoul passed his hand over his brow, and said, with a
smile:

"I have been dreaming!" Then, warmly, to De Guiche,
who, by degrees, was focusing on him, "My friend," he

said, "I conceal nothing from you, who are my best friend. I am going to seek death over there; your secret will not last more than a year."

"Oh, Raoul, a man!"

"Do you know what is my thought, De Guiche? This is it: 'I shall live more, being buried beneath the earth, than I have lived for this past month. We are Christians, my friend, and if such sufferings were to continue, I would not be answerable for my soul.' "

De Guiche wanted to raise objections.

"Not one word more on my account," said Raoul; "but one piece of advice to you, dear friend; what I am going to say to you is of much greater importance."

"What is that?"

"Without doubt, you risk much more than I do, because you love."

"Oh!"

"It is a joy so sweet to me to be able to speak to you thus. Well, then, De Guiche, beware of Montalais."

"What? Of that kind friend?"

"She was the friend of . . . her whom you know. She ruined her by pride."

"You are mistaken."

"And now, when she has ruined her, she wants to rob her of the only thing that renders that woman excusable in my eyes."

"What is that?"

"Her love."

"What do you mean by that?"

"I mean that there is a plot against the mistress of the king, a plot in the very house of Madame."

"Can you believe it?"

"I am certain of it."

"By Montalais?"

"Take her as the least dangerous of the enemies I dread for . . . the other."

"Explain yourself clearly, my friend; and if I can understand you—"

"In two words. Madame has been jealous of the king."

"I know she has."

"Oh, fear nothing—you are loved—you are loved, De Guiche; do you feel the value of these three words? They mean that you can raise your head, that you can sleep peacefully, that you can thank God every minute of your life. You are loved; that means that you may hear everything, even the advice of a friend who wishes to preserve your happiness. You are loved, De Guiche, you are loved! You do not endure those atrocious nights, those nights without end, which, with arid eye and tortured heart, others go through who are destined to die. You will live long, if you act like the miser who, bit by bit, crumb by crumb, collects and heaps up diamonds and gold. You are loved! Allow me to tell you what you must do to be loved forever.''

De Guiche contemplated for some time this unfortunate young man, half-mad with despair; there passed through his heart something like remorse at his own happiness. Raoul was recovering his feverish excitement, to assume the voice and looks of an impassible man.

''They will make her, whose name I would like still to be able to pronounce, they will make her suffer. Swear to me that you will not help them in anything—but that you will defend her, when possible, as I would have done myself.''

''I swear I will!'' replied De Guiche.

''And,'' continued Raoul, ''someday, when you shall have rendered her a great service—someday, when she shall thank you, promise me to say these words to her: 'I have done you this kindness, madame, at the instance of Monsieur de Bragelonne, whom you so deeply injured.' ''

''I swear I will,'' murmured De Guiche.

''That is all. Adieu! I set out tomorrow, or the day after, for Toulon. If you have a few hours to spare, give them to me.''

''All, all!'' cried the young man.

''Thank you.''

''And what are you going to do now?''

''I am going to meet Monsieur le Comte at Planchet's, where we hope to find Monsieur D'Artagnan.''

''Monsieur D'Artagnan?''

''Yes; I want to embrace him before my departure. He is a good man, who loves me dearly. Farewell, my friend; you are expected, no doubt; you will find me, when you wish, at the count's. Farewell!''

The two young men embraced. They who might have

seen them both thus would not have hesitated to say, pointing to Raoul:

"That is the happy man!"

CHAPTER XXIX

PLANCHET'S INVENTORY

ATHOS, during the visit made to the Luxembourg by Raoul, had gone to Planchet's to inquire after D'Artagnan. The gentleman, on arriving at the Rue des Lombards, found the shop of the grocer in great confusion; but it was not the confusion of a lucky sale, or that of an arrival of goods. Planchet was not lording it; as usual, upon sacks and barrels. No. A young man with a pen behind his ear, and another with an account book in his hand, were setting down a number of figures, while a third was counting and weighing. An inventory was being taken. Athos, who had no knowledge of commercial matters, felt a little embarrassed by the material obstacles and the majesty of those who were thus employed. He saw several customers sent away, and wondered whether he, who came to buy nothing, would not be all the more importunate. He therefore asked very politely if he could see M. Planchet. The reply, pretty carelessly given, was that M. Planchet was packing his trunks. These words surprised Athos.

"What! his trunks?" he said; "is Monsieur Planchet going away?"

"Yes, monsieur, directly."

"Then, if you please, inform him that Monsieur le Comte de la Fère wants to speak to him for a moment."

At the mention of the count's name one of the young men, no doubt accustomed to hearing it pronounced with respect, immediately went to inform Planchet. It was at this moment that Raoul, after his painful scene with Montalais and De Guiche, arrived at the grocer's house. Planchet left his job as soon as he received the count's message.

"Ah, Monsieur le Comte!" he exclaimed, "how glad I am to see you! What lucky star brings you here?"

"My dear Planchet," said Athos, pressing the hand of his son, whose sad look he silently observed, "we have come to see how you are. But in what confusion do I find you! You are as white as a miller. Where have you been rummaging?"

"Ah, *diable!* take care, monsieur; don't come near me until I have shaken myself."

"What for? Flour or dust only whiten."

"No; no; what you see on my arms is arsenic."

"Arsenic?"

"Yes; I am making my supplies for the rats."

"I suppose in an establishment like this the rats play a conspicuous part."

"It is not with this establishment I concern myself, Monsieur le Comte. The rats have robbed me of more here than they will ever rob me of again."

"What do you mean?"

"Why, you may have observed, monsieur, my inventory is being taken."

"Are you giving up your business, then?"

"Eh! *mon Dieu!* yes. I have disposed of my business to one of my young men."

"Bah! you are rich, then, I suppose?"

"Monsieur, I have taken a dislike to the city; I don't know whether it is because I am growing old, and as Monsieur d'Artagnan one day said, when we grow old we think more often of the things of our youth, but for some time I have felt myself attracted toward the country and gardening; I was once a peasant."

And Planchet marked this confession with a small but rather pretentious laugh for a man making a profession of humility.

Athos made a gesture of approval, and then added:

"Are you going to buy an estate, then?"

"I have bought one, monsieur."

"Ah! that is still better."

"A little house in Fontainebleau, with something like twenty acres of land around it."

"Very well, Planchet. Accept my compliments on your acquisition."

"But, monsieur, we are not comfortable here; the

cursed dust makes you cough. *Corbleu!* I would not wish
to poison the most worthy gentleman in the kingdom.''

Athos did not smile at this little joke which Planchet
had aimed at him, in order to try his hand at fashionable
bantering.

''Yes,'' he said, ''let us have a little talk by ourselves,
at your home, for example. You have a home, have you
not?''

''Certainly, Monsieur le Comte.''

''Upstairs, perhaps?''

And Athos, seeing Planchet a little embarrassed,
wished to relieve him by going first.

''It is . . .'' said Planchet, hesitating. Athos misunderstood this hesitation, and, attributing it to a fear the
grocer might have of offering humble hospitality:

''Never mind, never mind,'' he said, still going up,
''the house of a tradesman in this quarter is not expected
to be a palace. Come on.''

Raoul nimbly preceded him, and entered first. Two
cries were heard simultaneously—we may say three. One
of these cries dominated over the others; it was uttered
by a woman. The other proceeded from the mouth of
Raoul; it was an exclamation of surprise. He had no
sooner made it than he shut the door sharply. The third
was from fright; Planchet had proffered it.

''I ask your pardon,'' he added; ''madame is dressing.''

Raoul had, no doubt, seen that Planchet was telling
the truth, for he turned around to go downstairs again.

''Madame . . .'' said Athos. ''Oh, pardon me,
Planchet, I did not know that you had upstairs—''

''It is Trüchen,'' added Planchet, blushing a little.

''It is whom you please, my good Planchet; but excuse
my rudeness.''

''No, no; go up now, gentlemen.''

''We will do no such thing,'' said Athos.

''Oh! madame, having notice, has had time—''

''No, Planchet; farewell.''

''Gentlemen, you would not disoblige me by only
standing on the staircase, or by going away without having sat down?''

''If we had known you had a lady upstairs,'' replied

Athos, with his customary coolness, "we would have asked permission to pay our respects to her."

Planchet was so disconcerted by this little bit of insolence that he forced the passage, and opened the door to admit the count and his son. Trüchen was quite dressed: costume of the shopkeeper's wife, rich and stylish; German eyes attacking French eyes. She left the apartment after two curtsies and went down into the shop—but not without having listened at the door to know what Planchet's gentlemen visitors would say of her. Athos suspected that, and, therefore, turned the conversation accordingly. Planchet, on his part, was burning to give explanations, which Athos avoided. But, as certain tenacities are stronger than all others, Athos was forced to hear Planchet recite his idyls of felicity, translated into a language more chaste than that of Longus. So Planchet related how Trüchen had charmed his ripe age, and brought good luck to his business, as Ruth did to Boaz.

"You want nothing now, then, but heirs to your property."

"If I had one, he would have three hundred thousand pounds," said Planchet.

"You must have one, then," said Athos phlegmatically; "if only to prevent your little fortune from being lost."

These words, *little fortune,* put Planchet in his place, like the voice of the sergeant when Planchet was but a *piqueur* in the regiment of Piedmont, in which Rochefort had placed him. Athos understood that the grocer would marry Trüchen, and willy-nilly establish a family. This appeared even more evident to him when he learned that the young man to whom Planchet was selling his business was her cousin. Having heard all that was necessary of the happy prospects of the retiring grocer:

"What is Monsieur d'Artagnan doing?" he said. "He is not at the Louvre."

"Ah! Monsieur le Comte, Monsieur d'Artagnan has disappeared."

"Disappeared?" said Athos, with surprise.

"Oh! monsieur, we know what that means."

"But I do not know."

"Whenever Monsieur d'Artagnan disappears it is always for some mission or some great affair."

"Has he said anything to you about it?"

"Never."

"You knew of his earlier departure for England, did you not?"

"On account of the speculation," said Planchet.

"The speculation!"

"I mean . . ." interrupted Planchet, embarrassed.

"Well, well, neither your affairs nor those of your master* are in question; the interest we take in him alone has induced me to apply to you. Since the captain of the musketeers is not here, and as we cannot learn from you where we are likely to find Monsieur d'Artagnan, we will take our leave. *Au revoir,* Planchet, *au revoir.* Let us leave, Raoul."

"Monsieur le Comte, I wish I were able to tell you . . ."

"Oh, not at all; I am not the man to reproach a servant for being discreet."

This word "servant" hit hard the *demi-millionnaire,* Planchet; but natural respect and *bonhomie* prevailed over pride.

"There is nothing indiscreet in telling you, Monsieur le Comte; Monsieur d'Artagnan came here the other day."

"Ah!"

"And remained several hours consulting a map."

"You are right, then, my friend; say no more about it."

"And the map is there as proof," added Planchet, who went to get from the neighboring wall, where it was suspended by a twist, forming a triangle with the bar of the window to which it was fastened, the map consulted by the captain on his last visit to Planchet. This map, which he brought to the count, was a map of France, upon which the practiced eye of that gentleman discovered an itinerary, marked out with small pins; wherever a pin was missing, a hole denoted its having been there. Athos, by following with his eye the pins and holes, saw that D'Artagnan had taken the direction of the south, and gone as far as the Mediterranean, toward Toulon. It was near Cannes that the marks and the punctured places

* Planchet is D'Artagnan's servant in *The Three Musketeers.*

ceased. The Comte de la Fère puzzled for some time to guess what the musketeer was going to do in Cannes, and what motive could have led him to examine the banks of the Var. The reflections of Athos suggested nothing. His usual insight was at fault. Raoul's researches were not more successful than his father's.

"Never mind," said the young man to the count, who silently, and with his finger, had made him understand the route of D'Artagnan; "we must confess there is a Providence always occupied in connecting our destiny with that of Monsieur d'Artagnan. There he is on the coast of Cannes, and you, monsieur, will, at least, take me as far as Toulon. Be sure that we shall meet with him more easily on our way than on this map."

Then, taking leave of Planchet, who was scolding his shopmen, even the cousin of Trüchen, his successor, the gentlemen set out to pay a visit to M. de Beaufort. On leaving the grocer's shop they saw a coach, the future depository of the charms of Mlle. Trüchen and the bags of crowns of Planchet.

"Everyone journeys toward happiness by the road he chooses," said Raoul, in a melancholy tone.

"The road to Fontainebleau!" cried Planchet, to his coachman.

CHAPTER XXX

THE INVENTORY OF M. DE BEAUFORT

To have talked of D'Artagnan with Planchet, to have seen Planchet leave Paris to bury himself in his country retreat, had been for Athos and his son like a last farewell to the noise of the capital, to their life of former days. What, in fact, were these men leaving behind them—one of whom had exhausted the past age in glory, and the other the present age in misfortune? Evidently neither of them had anything to ask of his contemporaries. They had only to pay a visit to M. de Beaufort and arrange with him the particulars of the departure. The duke was lodged magnificently in Paris. He had one of those superb establishments pertaining to great fortunes, which certain old men remembered to have seen under Henry III's reign. Then, really, several great nobles were richer than the king. They knew it, used it, and never deprived themselves of the pleasure of humiliating his royal majesty. It was this selfish aristocracy which Richelieu had forced to contribute, with its blood, its purse, and its duties, to what was called from then on the king's service. From Louis XI, that terrible mower down of the great, to Richelieu, how many families had raised their heads! How many from Richelieu to Louis XIV had bowed their heads, never to raise them again! But M. de Beaufort was born a prince, and of a blood which is not shed upon scaffolds, unless by the decree of peoples. This prince had kept up a grand style of living. How did he maintain his horses, his people, and his table? Nobody knew; he less than others. Only there were then privileges for the sons of kings; nobody refused to become their creditor, whether from respect, devotion, or persuasion that they would someday be paid.

Athos and Raoul found the mansion of the duke in as much confusion as that of Planchet. The duke was also making his inventory; that is to say, he was distributing to his friends everything of value he had in his house. Owing nearly two million, an enormous amount in those days, M. de Beaufort had calculated that he could not set out for Africa without a good round sum; and, in order to find that sum, he was distributing to his old creditors plate, arms, jewels, and furniture, which was more magnificent than selling it, and brought him back twice as much. In fact, how could a man to whom one owes ten thousand livres refuse to carry away a present of six thousand, enhanced in merit from having belonged to a descendant of Henry IV? And how, after having carried away that present, could he refuse ten thousand livres more to this generous noble?

Therefore this is what had happened. The duke had no longer a house; that had become useless to an admiral whose home is his ship; he had no longer need of superfluous arms, since he had settled amid his cannons; no more jewels, which the sea might rob him of; but he had three or four hundred thousand crowns fresh in his chests. And throughout the house there was a joyous movement of people who believed they were plundering monseigneur. The prince had, in a supreme degree, the art of making happy the creditors the most to be pitied. Every distressed man, every empty purse, found in him patience and understanding. To some he said, "I wish I had what you need, I would give it to you." And to others, "I have but this silver ewer, it is worth at least five hundred livres; take it." As a result, so truly is courtesy a current payment that the prince constantly found means to renew his creditors. This time he used no ceremony, and it might be called a general plunder; he was giving up everything. The Oriental fable of the poor Arab who carried away from the pillage of a palace a kettle at the bottom of which was concealed a bag of gold, and whom everybody allowed to pass without jealousy, this fable had become a truth in the prince's mansion. Many tradesmen paid themselves upon the offices of the duke. Thus, the department, who plundered the clothes presses and the harness rooms, attached very little value to things which tailors and saddlers set great store by. Anxious to carry home to their wives preserves given them by monseigneur, many were seen bounding joyously along, under the weight of earthen jars and bottles gloriously stamped with the arms of the prince. M. de Beaufort ended up giving away his horses and the hay from his lofts. He made more than thirty people happy with kitchen utensils; and thirty more with the contents of his cellar. Still further: all these people went away with the conviction that M. de Beaufort only acted in this manner to prepare for a new fortune concealed beneath the Arab tents. They repeated to each other while looting his hotel that he was sent to Gigelli by the king to rebuild his lost wealth; that the treasures of Africa would be equally divided between the admiral and the King of France; that these treasures consisted in mines of diamonds, or other fabulous stones; the gold and silver mines of Mount Atlas did not even have the honor of being named. In addition to the mines to be worked, which could not begin until after the campaign, there would be the booty made by the army. M. de Beaufort would lay his hands upon all the riches pirates had robbed Christendom of since the battle of Lepanto. The number of millions from these sources defied calculation. Why, then, should someone

who was going in quest of such treasures set any store
by the poor utensils of his past life? And, on the other
hand, why should they spare the property of someone
who spared it so little himself?

Such was the situation. Athos, with his investigating
glance, saw what was going on at once. He found the
admiral of France a little dizzy, for he was rising from a
table laid for fifty, where the guests had drunk long and
deeply to the prosperity of the expedition; where, with
the dessert, the leftovers had been given to the servants,
and the empty dishes and plates to the curious. The prince
was intoxicated with his ruin and his popularity at the
same time. He drank his old wine to the health of his
future wine. When he saw Athos and Raoul:

"There is my aide-de-camp being brought to me!" he
cried. "Come here, count; come here, viscount."

Athos tried to find a passage through the heaps of linen
and plate.

"Step over, step over!" said the duke, offering a full
glass to Athos.

The latter took it; Raoul scarcely moistened his lips.

"Here is your commission," said the prince, to Raoul.
"I had prepared it, expecting you. You will go on before
me as far as Antibes."

"Yes, monseigneur."

"Here is the order." And De Beaufort gave Raoul the
order. "Do you know anything of the sea?"

"Yes, monseigneur; I have traveled with Monsieur le
Prince."

"That is well. All these barges and lighters must be
in attendance to form an escort and carry my supplies.
The army must be prepared to embark in a fortnight at
the latest."

"That shall be done, monseigneur."

"The present order gives you the right to visit and
search all the isles along the coast; there you will make
the enrollments and levies you want for me."

"Yes, Monsieur le Duc."

"And as you are an active man, and will work freely,
you will spend much money."

"I hope not, monseigneur."

"But I hope you will. My intendant has prepared orders of a thousand livres, drawn upon the cities from the

south; he will give you a hundred of them. Now, dear viscount, be gone."

Athos interrupted the prince.

"Keep your money, monseigneur; war is to be made with the Arabs with gold as well as lead."

"I want to try the contrary," replied the duke; "and then you know my ideas on the expedition—plenty of noise, plenty of fire, and, if necessary, I shall disappear in the smoke."

Having spoken thus, M. de Beaufort began to laugh: but his mirth was not reciprocated by Athos and Raoul. He saw this at once.

"Ah!" he said, with the courteous egotism of his rank and his age, "you are the kind of people a man should not see after dinner; you are cold, stiff, and dry, when I am all fire, all suppleness, and all wine. No, devil take me! I shall always see you fasting, viscount; and you, count, if you wear such a face as that, you will see me no more."

He said this, pressing the hand of Athos, who replied:

"Monseigneur, do not talk so grandly because you happen to have plenty of money. I predict that within a month you will be dry, stiff, and cold, in presence of your strongbox, and that then, having Raoul at your side, you will be surprised to see him happy, animated, and generous, because he will have new crowns to offer you."

"God grant it may be so!" cried the delighted duke. "Count, stay with me!"

"No, I shall go with Raoul; the mission you entrust him with is a troublesome and a difficult one. Alone, it would be too much for him to complete. You do not notice, monseigneur, you have given him a command of the first order."

"Bah!"

"And in the navy."

"That may be true. But people like him, don't they do what is required of them?"

"Monseigneur, I don't believe you will find anywhere as much zeal and intelligence, as much real bravery, as in Raoul; but if he failed in your embarkation, you would only meet with what you deserve."

"You are scolding me, then."

"Monseigneur, to supply a fleet, to assemble a flotilla,

to enroll your naval force, would take an admiral a year. Raoul is a cavalry officer, and you give him two weeks!''

"I tell you he will get through.''

"He may; but I will help him.''

"To be sure you will; I am counting on you, and furthermore believe that when we are once in Toulon you will not let him leave alone.''

"Oh!'' said Athos, shaking his head.

"Patience! patience!''

"Monseigneur, permit us to take our leave.''

"Go, then, and may good fortune be with you.''

"Adieu, monseigneur; and may your good fortune attend you too.''

"Here is an expedition admirably started!'' said Athos to his son. "No food—no store flotilla! What can be done?''

"Well!'' whispered Raoul; "if all do as I do, food will not be lacking.''

"Monsieur,'' replied Athos sternly, "do not be unjust and senseless in your egotism, or your grief, whatever you please to call it. If you set out for this war solely with the intention of getting killed, you do not need anybody, and it was scarcely worthwhile to recommend you to Monsieur de Beaufort. But when you have been introduced to the prince commandant, when you have accepted the responsibility of a post in his army, the question is no longer about you, but about all those poor soldiers, who, as well as you, have hearts and bodies, who will weep for their country and endure all the hardships of their human condition. Remember, Raoul, that an officer is a minister as useful as a priest, and that he ought to have more charity than a priest.''

"Monsieur, I know it, and have practiced it; I would have still continued to do so, but . . .''

"You are forgetting also that you come from a country which is proud of its military glory; go and die if you like, but do not die without honor and without advantage to France. Cheer up, Raoul! do not let my words sadden you; I love you, and wish to see you perfect.''

"I love your reproaches, monsieur,'' said the young man gently; "they alone may cure me, because they prove to me that someone still loves me.''

"And now, Raoul, let us be off; the weather is so fine,

the sky is so pure, this sky which we shall always find above our heads, which you will see even purer at Gigelli, and which will speak to you of me there, as they speak to me here of God.''

The two gentlemen, after having agreed on this point, talked over the wild manners of the duke, convinced that France would be served in a very incomplete manner, both in spirit and practice, in the ensuing expedition; and having summed up his policy under the word vanity, they set forward, in obedience to their will, rather than to their destiny. The sacrifice was accomplished.

CHAPTER XXXI

THE SILVER DISH

THE journey went off fairly well. Athos and his son crossed France at the rate of fifteen leagues per day; sometimes more, sometimes less, according to the intensity of Raoul's grief. It took them a fortnight to reach Toulon, and they lost all traces of D'Artagnan in Antibes. They were forced to believe that the captain of the musketeers had wanted to remain incognito on his trip, for Athos derived from his inquiries an assurance that such a horseman as he described had exchanged his horse for a well-closed carriage on leaving Avignon. Raoul was very saddened at not meeting with D'Artagnan. His affectionate heart longed for the farewell and the consolation from that heart of steel. Athos knew from experience that D'Artagnan became impenetrable when engaged in any serious affair, whether on his own account or in the service of the king. He even feared to offend his friend, or harm him by too pressing inquiries. And yet, when Raoul began his labor of organizing the flotilla, and got together the *chalands* and lighters to send them to Toulon, one of the fishermen told the count that his boat had been laid up for repairs since a trip he had made for a gentleman who was in a great hurry. Athos, believing that this man was lying in order to be left alone to fish, and so earn more money when all his companions were gone, insisted upon having details. The fisherman informed him that six days earlier a man had come in the night to hire his boat to visit the island of St. Honorat. The price was agreed upon, but the gentleman had arrived with an immense carriage case, which he insisted upon loading, in spite of all the difficulties faced by that operation. The fisherman had wanted to back out. He had even threatened, but his threats had gotten him only a series of blows from the gentleman's cane, which fell upon his shoulders sharp and long. Swearing and grumbling, he had appealed to the representative of his guild in Antibes, who administer justice among themselves and protect one another; but the gentleman had shown a certain paper, at the sight of which the representative, bowing to the ground, had required obedience from the fisherman, and reproved him for having been rebellious. They then departed with the freight.

"But all this does not tell us," said Athos, "how you have wrecked your boat."

"This is the way. I was steering toward St. Honorat as the gentleman had told me; but he changed his mind, and claimed that I could not pass to the south of the abbey."

"And why not?"

"Because, monsieur, in front of the square tower of the Benedictines, toward the southern point, there is the bank of the Moines."

"A rock?" asked Athos.

"Level with the water, and below the water; a dangerous passage, but one I have cleared a thousand times; the gentleman asked me to land him at Ste. Marguerite's."

"Well?"

"Well, monsieur," cried the fisherman, with his Provençal accent, "a man is a sailor, or he is not; he knows his course, or he is nothing but a freshwater lubber. I was obstinate, and wanted to try the channel. The gentleman took me by the collar, and told me quietly he would strangle me. My mate armed himself with a hatchet, and so did I. We had the affront of the night before to avenge. But the gentleman drew his sword, and used it in such an astonishingly rapid manner that neither of us could get near him. I was about to hurl my hatchet at his head, and I had a right to do so, hadn't I, monsieur? for a sailor aboard is master, as a citizen is in his room; I was about, then, in self-defense, to cut the gentleman in two, when, all at once—believe me or not, monsieur—the carriage case opened by itself, I don't know how, and there came out of it a sort of phantom, his head covered with a black helmet and a black mask, something terrible to look at, which came toward me threatening with its fist.''

"And that was . . . ?" said Athos.

"That was a devil, monsieur; for the gentleman, with great glee, cried out, on seeing him, 'Ah! thank you, monseigneur!' "

"A strange story," murmured the count, looking at Raoul.

"And what did you do?" asked the latter of the fisherman.

"You must know, monsieur, that two poor men, such as we are, could be no match for two gentlemen; but when one of them is the devil, we had no chance. My companion and I did not stop to consult each other; we jumped into the sea, for we were within seven or eight hundred feet of the shore.''

"And then?"

"Why, and then, monsieur, as there was a little wind from the southwest, the boat drifted into the sands of Ste. Marguerite's.''

"But the two travelers?"

"You need not be uneasy about them! It was pretty plain that one was the devil, and protected the other; for when we recovered the boat, after she got afloat again, instead of finding these two creatures injured by the shock, we found nothing, not even the carriage or the case.''

"Very strange! very strange!" repeated the count. "But since then, what have you done, my friend?"

"I made my complaint to the governor of Ste. Marguerite's, who shook his finger at me by telling me if I bothered him with such silly stories he would have me flogged.''

"The governor?"

"Yes, monsieur; and yet my boat was seriously damaged. The prow was left on the point of Ste. Marguerite's, and the carpenter is asking a hundred and twenty livres to repair it."

"Very well," replied Raoul; "you are exempt from service. Go."

"We will go to Ste. Marguerite's, shall we?" said the count to De Bragelonne, as the man walked away.

"Yes, monsieur, for there is something to be cleared up; that man does not seem to me to have told the truth."

"Nor to me either, Raoul. The story of the masked man and the carriage having disappeared may be told to conceal some violence these fellows have committed on their passenger in the open sea, to punish him for his persistence in embarking."

"I formed the same suspicion; the carriage was more likely to contain property than a man."

"We shall see to that, Raoul. This gentleman very much resembles D'Artagnan; I recognize his mode of proceeding. Alas! we are no longer the young invincibles of former days. Who knows whether the hatchet or the iron bar of this miserable sailor has not succeeded in doing that which the best blades of Europe, bullets, and cannonballs have not been able to do in forty years?"

That same day they set out for Ste. Marguerite's, on board a *chasse-marée* under orders from Toulon. The impression they felt on landing was a singularly pleasing one. The isle was full of flowers and fruits. In its cultivated part it served as a garden for the governor. Orange, pomegranate, and fig trees bent under the weight of their golden or purple fruits. All around this garden, in the uncultivated parts, red partridges ran about in coveys among the brambles and tufts of junipers, and at every step of the count and Raoul a terrified rabbit would leave his thyme and heath to scurry away to his burrow. In fact, this fortunate isle was uninhabited. Flat, offering nothing but a tiny bay for the convenience of embarkation, and under the protection of the governor, who shared with them, smugglers made use of it as a provisional warehouse, provided they did not kill the game or devastate the garden. With this agreement, the governor was in a situation to be satisfied with a garrison of eight men to guard his fortress, in which twelve cannons were growing moldy. The governor was a sort of happy farmer, harvesting wines, figs, oil, and oranges, preserving his lemons and oranges in the sun of his casemates. The fortress, encircled by a deep ditch, its only guardian, raised like three heads on its three turrets connected with one another by terraces covered with moss.

Athos and Raoul wandered for some time around the fences of the garden without finding anyone to introduce them to the governor. They ended by making their own way into the garden. It was at the hottest time of the day, when everything seeks shelter beneath grass or stone. Then the sky spreads its fiery veils as if to stifle all noises, to envelop all existences; the rabbit under the broom, the fly under the leaf, sleep as the wave does beneath the sky.

Athos saw nothing living but a soldier, on the terrace beneath the second and third court, who was carrying a basket of food on his head. This man returned almost immediately without his basket, and disappeared in the shade of his sentry box. Athos understood this man was carrying dinner to someone, and, after having done so, was returning to dine himself. All at once he heard someone call him, and raising his head, saw in the frame of the bars of the window something white, like a hand that was waving backward and forward, something shining, like a polished weapon struck by the rays of the sun. And before he realized what it was, he saw a luminous train, accompanied by a hissing sound in the air, which called his attention from the dungeon to the ground. A second dull noise was heard from the ditch, and Raoul ran to pick up a silver plate which was rolling along the dry sand. The hand which had thrown this plate gestured to the two gentlemen, and then disappeared. Athos and Raoul, approaching each other, began an attentive examination of the dusty plate, and they discovered, in letters etched on the bottom of it with the point of a knife, this inscription:

> "I am the brother of the King of France—a prisoner today—a madman tomorrow. French gentlemen and Christians, pray to God for the soul and the reason of the son of your masters."

The plate fell from the hands of Athos, while Raoul was trying to make out the meaning of these dismal words. At the same instant they heard a cry from the top of the dungeon. As quick as lightning, Raoul bent down his head and forced down his father's. A musket barrel glittered from the crest of the wall. A white smoke floated like a plume from the mouth of the musket, and a bullet was flattened against a stone within six inches of the two gentlemen.

"Cordieu!" cried Athos. "What, are people assassinated here? Come down, cowards as you are!"

"Yes, come down!" cried Raoul furiously, shaking his fist at the castle.

One of the assailants—he who was about to fire—replied to these cries by an exclamation of surprise; and as his companion wanted to continue the attack, and was seizing again his loaded musket, he who had cried out raised the weapon, and the bullet flew into the air. Athos and Raoul, seeing them disappear from the platform, expected they would come to them, and waited firmly. Five minutes had not elapsed when a drumbeat called the eight soldiers of the garrison to arms, and they showed themselves on the other side of the ditch with their muskets in hand. At the head of these men was an officer, whom Athos and Raoul recognized as the one who had fired the first musket. The man ordered the soldiers to "make ready."

"We are going to be shot!" cried Raoul; "but, sword in hand, at least, let us leap the ditch. We shall kill at least two of these scoundrels, when their muskets are empty."

And, putting word into action, Raoul was springing forward, followed by Athos, when a well-known voice called out behind them:

"Athos! Raoul!"

"D'Artagnan!" replied the two gentlemen.

"Recover arms! *Mordioux!*" cried the captain, to the soldiers. "I was sure I could not be mistaken!"

"What is the meaning of this?" asked Athos. "What, were we to be shot without warning?"

"It was I who was going to shoot you, and if the governor missed you, I should not have missed you, my dear friends. How fortunate it is that I am accustomed to taking a long aim, instead of firing the instant I raise my weapon. I thought I recognized you. My dear friends, how fortunate!''

And D'Artagnan wiped his brow, for he had run fast, and he was truly moved.

"What!" said Athos. "And is the gentleman who fired at us the governor of the fortress?''

"In person."

"And why did he fire at us? What have we done to him?''

"*Pardieu!* You received what the prisoner threw at you?''

"That is true."

"That plate—the prisoner has written something on the bottom of it, has he not?''

"Yes."

"Good heavens! I was afraid he had."

And D'Artagnan, with all the marks of mortal anguish, seized the plate, to read the inscription. When he had read it a fearful pallor spread over his face.

"Good heavens!" he repeated. "Silence! Here is the governor."

"What will he do to us? Is it our fault?''

"It is true, then?" said Athos, in a subdued voice. "Is it true?''

"Silence! I tell you—silence! If he only believes you can read, if he only suspects you have understood! I love you, my dear friends; I would die for you. But . . .''

" 'But . . .' '' said Athos and Raoul.

"But I could not save you from perpetual imprisonment, if I saved you from death. Silence, then! Silence again!''

The governor was coming up, having crossed the ditch upon a plank bridge.

"Well!" he said, to D'Artagnan, "what is stopping us?''

"You are Spaniards—you do not understand a word of French," said the captain eagerly, to his friends, in a low voice.

"Well!" he replied, addressing the governor. "I was right; these gentlemen are two Spanish captains I knew in Ypres, last year; they don't know a word of French."

"Ah!" said the governor sharply, "and yet they were trying to read the inscription on the plate.''

D'Artagnan took it out of his hands, erasing the characters with the point of his sword.

"What!" cried the governor, "what are you doing? I cannot read them now!"

"It is a state secret," replied D'Artagnan bluntly; "and as you know that, according to the king's orders, anyone who discovers it will be sentenced to death. I will, if you like, allow you to read it, and have you shot immediately afterward."

During this apostrophe—half-serious, half-ironical Athos and Raoul preserved the coolest, most unconcerned silence.

"But is it impossible," said the governor, "that these gentlemen do not understand at least some words?"

"Suppose they do! Even if they do understand a few spoken words, they wouldn't read what is written. They cannot even read Spanish. A noble Spaniard, remember, must never know how to read."

The governor was obliged to be satisfied with these explanations, but he was persistent.

"Invite these gentlemen to come to the fortress," he said.

"That I will do willingly. I was about to propose it to you."

The fact is, the captain had quite another idea, and would have wished his friends a hundred leagues off. But he was obliged to make the best of it. He extended to the two gentlemen an invitation in Spanish, which they accepted. They all turned toward the entrance of the fort, and the incident being over, the eight soldiers returned to their delightful leisure, for a moment disturbed by this unexpected adventure.

CHAPTER XXXII

CAPTIVE AND JAILERS

WHEN they had entered the fort, and while the governor was making some preparations for the reception of his guests:

"Come," said Athos, "let us have a word of explanation while we are alone."

"It is simply this," replied the musketeer. "I have conducted here a prisoner, who the king commands shall not be seen. You came here, he has thrown something at you through the lattice of his window; I was at dinner with the governor, I saw the object thrown, and I saw Raoul pick it up. It does not take long to understand this. I understood it, and I thought you in collusion with my prisoner. And then—"

"And then, you ordered us to be shot."

"Ma foi! I admit it; but if I was the first to seize a musket, fortunately I was the last to take aim at you."

"If you had killed me, D'Artagnan, I should have had the good fortune to die for the royal house of France, and it would be an honor to die by your hand—you, its noblest and most loyal defender."

"What the devil, Athos, do you mean by the royal house?" stammered D'Artagnan. "You don't mean that you, a well-informed and sensible man, can place any faith in the nonsense written by an idiot?"

"I do believe in it."

"With all the more reason, my dear chevalier, that you have orders to kill all those who do believe in it," said Raoul.

"That is because," replied the captain of the musketeers, "every slander, however absurd it may be, has the almost certain chance of becoming popular."

"No, D'Artagnan," replied Athos promptly; "but because the king does not want the secret of his family to be known among the people, and to cover with shame the executioners of the son of Louis XIII."

"Do not talk in such a childish manner, Athos, or I shall begin to think you have lost your senses. Besides, explain to me how it is possible Louis XIII should have a son in the Isle of Ste. Marguerite."

"A son whom you have brought here masked, in a fishing boat," said Athos. "Why not?"

D'Artagnan was brought to a pause.

"Ah!" he said, "how do you know that a fishing boat . . ."

"Brought you to Ste. Marguerite's with the carriage containing the prisoner—with a prisoner whom you called 'monseigneur.' Oh! I know it," the count went on. D'Artagnan bit his mustache.

"If it were true," he said, "that I had brought here in a boat and with a carriage a masked prisoner, nothing proves that this prisoner must be a prince—a prince of the house of France."

"Ask Aramis about that," replied Athos coolly.

"Aramis," cried the musketeer, dumbfounded. "Have you seen Aramis?"

"After his discomfiture at Vaux, yes; I have seen Aramis, a fugitive, pursued, ruined; and Aramis has told me enough to make me believe in the complaints that this unfortunate young man etched upon the bottom of the plate."

D'Artagnan's head sank upon his chest with confusion.

"This is the way," he said, "God toys with what men call their wisdom! A fine secret must that be of which twelve or fifteen people hold the tattered fragments. Athos, cursed be the fate which has brought you face to face with me in this affair! for now . . ."

"Well," said Athos, with his gentle severity, "is your secret lost because I know it? Consult your memory, my friend. Have I not kept secrets as heavy as this?"

"You have never kept one so dangerous," replied D'Artagnan, in a tone of sadness. "I have the sinister impression that all who are concerned with this secret will die, and die unfortunately."

"The will of God be done!" said Athos; "but here is your governor."

D'Artagnan and his friends immediately resumed their parts. The governor, suspicious and hard, behaved toward D'Artagnan with a politeness almost amounting to obsequiousness. With respect to the travelers, he contented himself with welcoming them, and never taking his eye from them. Athos and Raoul observed that he often tried to embarrass them by sudden attacks, or to catch them off their guard; but neither one nor the other gave him the least advantage. What D'Artagnan had said was probable, if the governor did not believe it to be quite true. They rose from the table to rest awhile.

"What is this man's name? I don't like the looks of him," said Athos to D'Artagnan, in Spanish.

"De St. Mars," replied the captain.

"He is, then, I suppose, the prince's jailer?"

"How can I tell? I may be kept at Ste. Marguerite's forever."

"Oh, no, not you!"

"My friend, I am in the situation of a man who finds a treasure in the midst of a desert. He would like to carry it away, but he cannot; he would like to leave it, but he dares not. The king will not recall me, fearing another will not keep watch as well as I; he regrets not having me near him, aware that no one will serve him as I do. But it will happen as it may please God."

"But," observed Raoul, "your not being certain proves that your situation here is temporary, and you will return to Paris."

"Ask these gentlemen," interrupted the governor, "what was their purpose in coming to Ste. Marguerite?"

"They came knowing there was a convent of Benedictines at Ste. Honorat which is considered curious; and from being told there was excellent hunting on the island."

"That is quite at their disposal, as well as yours," replied St. Mars.

D'Artagnan politely thanked him.

"When will they leave?" added the governor.

"Tomorrow," replied D'Artagnan.

M. de St. Mars went to make his rounds, and left D'Artagnan alone with the would-be Spaniards.

"Oh!" exclaimed the musketeer, "here is a life with a society that doesn't suit me. I command this man, and he annoys me, *mordioux!* Come, let us have a shot or two at the rabbits; the walk will be beautiful, and not tiring. The isle is a league and a half in length, and a league in width; a real park. Let us try to amuse ourselves."

"As you please, D'Artagnan; not for the sake of amusing ourselves, but to gain an opportunity for talking freely."

D'Artagnan gestured to a soldier, who brought the gentlemen some guns, and then returned to the fort.

"And now," said the musketeer, "answer me the question asked by that black-looking St. Mars: What did you come to do at the Lerin Isles?"

"To bid you farewell."

"Bid me farewell! What do you mean by that? Is Raoul going anywhere?"

"Yes."

"Then I bet it is with Monsieur de Beaufort."

"With Monsieur de Beaufort it is, my dear friend; you always guess right."

"From habit."

While the two friends were beginning their conversation, Raoul, with his head hanging down and his heart oppressed, had sat on a mossy rock, his gun across his knees, looking at the sea, looking at the sky, and listening to the voice of his soul; he let the sportsmen walk away from him. D'Artagnan noticed his absence.

"He has not recovered from the blow," he said to Athos.

"He is struck to death."

"Oh! you are exaggerating, I hope. Raoul is a fine man. Around all hearts as noble as his there is a second envelope which forms a shield. The first bleeds, the second resists."

"No," replied Athos; "Raoul will die of it."

"Mordioux!" said D'Artagnan, in a melancholy tone. And he did not add a word to this exclamation. Then, a minute after:

"Why do you let him go?"

"Because he insists upon going."

"And why do you not go with him?"

"Because I could not bear to see him die."

D'Artagnan faced his friend.

"You know one thing," the count went on, leaning on the arm of the captain; "you know that in the course of my life I have only been afraid of a few things. Well, I have an incessant, gnawing, insurmountable fear that a day will arrive in which I shall hold the dead body of that boy in my arms."

"Oh!" murmured D'Artagnan, "oh!"

"He will die, I know, I have a perfect conviction of that; but I do not want to see him die."

"How is this, Athos? You come and place yourself in the presence of the bravest man you say you have ever seen, of your own D'Artagnan, of that man without an equal, as you formerly called him, and you come and tell him, with your arms folded, that you are afraid of witnessing the death of your son, you, who have seen all that can be seen in this world! Why do you have this fear, Athos? Man, upon this earth, must expect everything, and ought to face everything.''

"Listen to me, my friend. After having worn myself out upon this earth of which you speak, I have kept but two religions: that of life, my friendships, my duty as a father, and that of eternity, love, and respect for God. Now, I have within me the revelation that if God should decree that my friend or my son should breathe his last sigh in my presence . . . oh! no; I cannot even tell you, D'Artagnan!''

"Speak, speak; tell me!''

"I am strong in the face of everything, except the death of those I love. For that only there is no remedy. He who dies gains; he who sees others die loses. No; you see, to know that I should no more meet upon earth him whom I now behold with joy; to know that there would nowhere be a D'Artagnan anymore, nowhere again be a Raoul . . . I am old, you see, I have no more courage. I pray God to spare me in my weakness; but if He struck me so plainly and in that fashion, I would curse Him. A Christian gentleman ought not to curse his God, D'Artagnan; it is quite enough to have cursed a king!''

"Humph!'' said D'Artagnan, a little upset by this violent tempest of grief. "Let me speak to him, Athos. Who knows?''

"Try, if you please; but I am convinced you will not succeed.''

"I will not attempt to console him, I will serve him.''

"You will?''

"Doubtless, I will. Do you think this would be the first time a woman had repented of an infidelity? I will go to him, I tell you.''

Athos shook his head, and continued his walk alone. D'Artagnan, cutting across the bramble, joined Raoul, and held out his hand to him.

"Well, Raoul! You have something to say to me?''

"I have a kindness to ask of you,'' replied De Bragelonne.

"Ask it, then.''

"You will someday return to France?''

"I hope so."

"Should I write to Mademoiselle de la Vallière?"

"No, you must not."

"But I have so many things to say to her."

"Come and say them to her, then."

"Never!"

"Pray, what virtue do you attribute to a letter, which your speech might not possess?"

"Perhaps you are right."

"She loves the king," said D'Artagnan bluntly, "and she is an honest girl."

Raoul shuddered.

"And you—you, whom she abandons, she, perhaps, loves better than she does the king, but in another fashion."

"D'Artagnan, do you believe she loves the king?"

"To idolatry. Her heart is inaccessible to any other feeling. You might continue to live near her, and would be her best friend."

"Ah!" exclaimed Raoul, with a passionate outburst for such a painful hope.

"Will you do so?"

"It would be cowardly."

"That is a very absurd word, which would lead me to be critical of your mind. Please do understand, Raoul, that it is never cowardly to do that which is imposed by a superior force. If your heart says to you, 'Go there, or die,' why, go there, Raoul. Was she cowardly or brave, she whom you loved, in preferring the king to you, the king whom her heart commanded her imperiously to prefer to you? No, she was the bravest of women. Do, then, as she has done. Obey your heart. Do you know one thing of which I am sure, Raoul?"

"What is that?"

"That by seeing her closely with the eyes of a jealous man . . ."

"Well?"

"Well, you would cease to love her."

"Then you have persuaded me, my dear D'Artagnan."

"To leave to see her again?"

"No; to leave that I may never see her again. I want to love her forever."

"I must confess," replied the musketeer, "that is a conclusion which I was far from expecting."

"Here, my friend. You will see her again, and you will give her a letter which, if you think proper, will explain to her as to yourself, what is taking place in my heart. Read it; I prepared it last night. Something told me I would see you today."

He held the letter out, and D'Artagnan read it:

"MADEMOISELLE: You are not wrong in my eyes in not loving me. You have only been guilty of one fault toward me, that of having led me to believe you loved me. This error will cost me my life. I pardon you, but I cannot pardon myself. It is said that happy lovers are deaf to the complaints of rejected lovers. It will not be so with you, who did not love me, except with anxiety. I am sure that if I had persisted in changing that friendship into love, you would have yielded out of a fear of bringing about my death, or of lessening the esteem I had for you. I am happy to die, knowing you are free and satisfied. How much, then, will you love me, when you will no longer fear either my presence or my reproaches! You will love me, because, however charming a new love may appear to you, God has not made me in anything inferior to him you have chosen, and because my devotion, my sacrifice, and my painful end will assure me, in your eyes, a certain superiority over him. I have allowed to escape, in the candid credulity of my heart, the treasure I possessed. Many people tell me that you loved me enough to eventually love me very much. That idea takes from my mind all bitterness, and leads me only to blame myself. You will accept this last farewell, and you will bless me for having taken refuge in the inviolable asylum where all hatred is extinguished, and where all love endures. Adieu, mademoiselle. If your happiness could be purchased by the last drop of my blood, I would shed that drop. I willingly make the sacrifice of it to my misery!

"RAOUL, VICOMTE DE BRAGELONNE."

"The letter is fine," said the captain. "I have only one fault to find with it."

"Tell me what that is?" said Raoul.

"Why, it is, that it tells everything, except the thing

which exhales, like a mortal poison, from your eyes and from your heart; except the mad love which still consumes you.''

Raoul grew paler, but remained silent.

"Why did you not write simply these words:

" 'MADEMOISELLE: Instead of cursing you, I love you, and I die.' ''

"That is true!" exclaimed Raoul, with a sinister kind of joy.

And tearing the letter he had just taken back, he wrote the following words upon a leaf of his tablets:

"To have the happiness of once more telling you I love you, I commit the baseness of writing to you, and to punish myself for that baseness, I die."

And he signed it.

"You will give her this leaf, captain, will you not?"

"When?" asked the latter.

"On the day," said De Bragelonne, pointing to the last sentence, "on the day when you can place a date under these words."

And he sprung away quickly to join Athos, who was returning with slow steps.

As they reentered the fort the sea rose with that rapid, gusty vehemence that characterizes the Mediterranean; the ill humor of the wind became a tempest. Something shapeless, and tossed about violently by the waves, appeared just off the coast.

"What is that?" said Athos, "a wrecked boat?"

"No, it is not a boat," said D'Artagnan.

"Pardon me," said Raoul, "there is a boat rapidly approaching the port."

"Yes, there is a boat in the creek, which is prudently seeking shelter here; but that which Athos points to in the sand stranded . . ."

"Yes, yes, I see it."

"It is the carriage which I threw into the sea, after landing the prisoner."

"Well!" said Athos, "if you take my advice, D'Artagnan, you will burn that carriage, in order that no ves-

tige of it may remain; otherwise the fishermen of Antibes, who believe they were dealing with the devil, will
try to prove that your prisoner was but a man.''

"Your advice is good, Athos, and tonight I will have
it carried out, or, rather, I will carry it out myself; but
let us go in, for it's going to rain, and the lightning is
terrifying.''

As they were passing over the ramparts to a gallery to
which D'Artagnan had the key, they saw M. de St. Mars
go toward the room inhabited by the prisoner. D'Artagnan gestured to them to hide in an angle of the staircase.

"What is it?'' said Athos.

"You will see. Look. The prisoner is returning from
chapel.''

And they saw, by the red flashes of the lightning against
the violet fog which the wind stamped upon the bank-
ward sky, they saw go by gravely, at six paces behind the
governor, a man clothed in black and masked by a visor
of polished steel, soldered to a helmet of the same nature, which covered his head. The fire of the sky cast red
reflections upon the polished surface, and these reflections, flying off capriciously, seemed to be angry looks
cast by this unfortunate, in the place of curses. In the
middle of the gallery, the prisoner stopped for a moment,
to contemplate the infinite horizon, to breathe the sul-
phurous perfumes of the tempest, to drink in thirstily the
hot rain, and to heave a sigh resembling a roar.

"Come on, monsieur,'' said St. Mars sharply, to the
prisoner, for he already became uneasy at seeing him
look so long beyond the walls. "Monsieur, come on!''

"Say monseigneur!'' cried Athos, from his corner,
with a voice so solemn and terrible that the governor
trembled from head to foot.

Athos insisted upon respect being paid to the fallen
majesty. The prisoner turned around.

"Who spoke?'' asked St. Mars.

"It was I,'' replied D'Artagnan, showing himself
promptly. "You know that is the order.''

"Call me neither monsieur nor monseigneur,'' said
the prisoner, in a voice that penetrated to the very soul
of Raoul; "call me *Accursed!*''

He went on, and the iron door creaked after him.

"That is truly an unfortunate man!'' murmured the

musketeer, in a hollow whisper, pointing out to Raoul the room inhabited by the prince.

CHAPTER XXXIII

PROMISES

SCARCELY had D'Artagnan reentered his apartment with his two friends than one of the soldiers of the fort came to inform him that the governor was looking for him. The boat which Raoul had seen at sea, and which appeared so eager to reach the port, was coming to Ste. Marguerite with an important dispatch for the captain of the musketeers. On opening it D'Artagnan recognized the writing of the king.

"I think," wrote Louis XIV, "you will have executed my orders, Monsieur d'Artagnan; return, then, immediately to Paris, and join me at the Louvre."

"There is the end of my exile," cried the musketeer, with joy. "God be praised! I am no longer a jailer."

And he showed the letter to Athos.

"So then, you must leave us?" replied the latter, in a melancholy tone.

"Yes, but to meet again, dear friend, seeing that Raoul is old enough now to go alone with Monsieur de Beaufort, and will prefer that his father return with Monsieur d'Artagnan rather than forcing him to travel two hundred leagues alone to reach home at La Fère; would you not, Raoul?"

"Certainly," stammered the latter, with an expression of tender regret.

"No, no, my friend," interrupted Athos; "I will never leave Raoul until the day his ship has disappeared on the horizon. As long as he remains in France he shall not be separated from me."

"As you please, dear friend; but we will, at least, leave Ste. Marguerite together; take advantage of the boat which will take me back to Antibes."

"With all my heart; we cannot be too soon away from this fort, and from the sight which saddened us so just now."

The three friends left the little isle, after paying their respects to the governor, and by the last flashes of the departing tempest they saw for the last time the white walls of the fort. D'Artagnan parted from his friends that same night, after having seen set on fire the carriage on the shore by the orders of St. Mars, according to the advice the captain had given him. Before mounting his horse, and after leaving the arms of Athos:

"My friends," he said, "you look too much like two soldiers who are abandoning their post. Something tells me that Raoul will require being supported by you in his rank. Will you allow me to ask permission to go over into Africa with a hundred good muskets? The king will not refuse me, and I will take you with me."

"Monsieur D'Artagnan," replied Raoul, pressing his hand with emotion, "thanks for that offer, which would give us more than we wish, either Monsieur le Comte, or myself. I, who am young, need labor of mind and fatigue of body; Monsieur le Comte needs the deepest rest. You are his best friend. I recommend him to your care. In watching over him, you will hold both our souls in your hands."

"I must go; my horse is getting impatient," said D'Artagnan, with whom the most evident sign of a strong emotion was the change of ideas into a conversation. "Come, count, how many days longer has Raoul to stay here?"

"Three days, at most."

"And how long will it take you to reach home?"

"Oh! a considerable time," replied Athos. "I do not want to be separated too quickly from Raoul. Time will push him fast enough. I shall only travel half stages."

"And why so, my friend? Nothing is duller than traveling slowly; and hostelry life does not become a man like you."

"My friend, I came on post horses, but I wish to purchase two superior horses. Now, to take them home fresh, it would not be prudent to make them travel more than seven or eight leagues a day."

"Where is Grimaud?"

"He arrived yesterday morning, with Raoul's equipment; and I have let him sleep."

"That is, never to come back again," D'Artagnan blurted out. "Good-bye, then, dear Athos—and if you are diligent, well, I shall embrace you the sooner."

So saying, he put his foot in the stirrup, which Raoul held.

"Farewell!" said the young man, embracing him.

"Farewell!" said D'Artagnan, as he mounted into his saddle.

His horse made a move which separated the rider from his friends. This scene had taken place in front of the house chosen by Athos, near the gates of Antibes, where D'Artagnan, after his supper, had ordered the horses to be brought. The road extended from there, white and undulating in the vapors of the night. The horse was breathing eagerly the sharp smell of the marshes. D'Artagnan put him into a trot; and Athos and Raoul turned toward the house. All at once they heard the rapid approach of a horse's steps, and at first believed it to be one of those odd repercussions which deceive the ear at every turn in a road. But it was really the return of the horseman. They uttered a cry of joyous surprise, and the captain, springing to the ground like a young man, seized within his arms the two beloved heads of Athos and Raoul. He held them embraced a long time, without saying a word, without letting out the sigh which was bursting in his chest. Then, as rapidly as he had come back, he set off again, digging his spurs into the sides of his fiery horse.

"Alas!" said the count, in a low voice, "alas! alas!"

"Evil omen!" said D'Artagnan to himself, making up for lost time. "I could not smile on them. An evil omen!"

The next day Grimaud was on foot again. The service ordered by M. de Beaufort had been carried out successfully. The flotilla, sent to Toulon under Raoul's care, had set out, dragging after it in little skiffs, almost invisible, the wives and friends of the fishermen and smugglers requisitioned for the service of the fleet. The time, so short, which remained for the father and son to live together, appeared to have doubled in rapidity, as the speed increases of everything which falls into the gulf of eternity. Athos and Raoul returned to Toulon, which was filling with the noise of carriages, with the noise of arms, with the noise of neighing horses. The trumpeters were sounding their marches; the drums were showing their strength; the streets were overflowing with soldiers, servants, and tradespeople. The Duc de Beaufort was everywhere, hurrying the embarkation with the zeal and interest of a good captain. He encouraged even the most humble of his companions; he scolded his lieutenants, even those of the highest rank. Artillery, supplies, baggage, he insisted upon seeing all himself. He examined the equipment of every soldier; he assured himself of the health and soundness of every horse. It was plain that, light, boastful, egotistical in his mansion, the gentleman became the soldier again, the grand seigneur *capitaine*, in face of the responsibility he had accepted. And yet it must be admitted that, whatever care he took in the preparations for departure, it was easy to see careless haste, and the little caution which make the French soldier the first soldier in the world, because, in that world, he is the one most left to his own physical and moral resources.

All things having satisfied or appearing to satisfy the admiral, he complimented Raoul, and gave the last orders for sailing, which was set for the next morning at daybreak. He invited the count and his son to dine with him; but excusing themselves in the name of the service, they kept to themselves. At their hostelry, situated under the trees of the great square, they ate their meal in haste, and Athos led Raoul to the rocks which dominated the city, vast gray mountains from where the view is infinite, and embraces a liquid horizon which appears, being so remote, to be on a level with the rocks themselves.

The night was fine, as it always is in these happy climates. The moon, rising behind the rocks, unrolled, like a silver sheet, upon the blue carpet of the sea. In the harbor, silently maneuvered the ships which were coming to take their rank to facilitate the embarkation. The sea, loaded with phosphoric light, opened beneath the hulls of the boats which were taking on board the baggage and ammunition; every dip of the prow plowed up a gulf of white flames; and from every oar dropped liquid diamonds. The sailors, rejoicing in the largesses of the admiral, were heard murmuring their slow and artless songs. Sometimes the grinding of the chains was mixed with the dull noise of shot falling into the holds. These harmonies, and this spectacle, oppress the heart like fear, and dilate it like hope. All this life speaks of death.

Athos sat upon the moss and the heather of the promontory. Around their heads flew large bats, carried along in the fearful whirl of their blind chase. Raoul's feet were dangling over the edge of the cliff, and bathed in that void which causes vertigo. When the moon had risen to its full height, creasing with its light the neighboring peaks, when the watery mirror was lighted up in its full extent, and the little red fires had made their openings in the black masses of every ship, Athos collected all his thoughts and all his courage, and said:

"God has made all that we see, Raoul. He has made us also—poor atoms mixed up with this great universe. We shine like those fires and those stars; we sigh like those waves; we suffer like those great ships, which endlessly plow the waves, in obeying the wind which urges them toward a goal, as the breath of God blows us toward a port. Everything likes to live, Raoul; and everything is beautiful in living things."

"Monsieur," said Raoul, "we have before us a beautiful sight."

"How good D'Artagnan is!" interrupted Athos suddenly, "and what a rare good fortune it is to be supported during a lifetime by such a friend as he is! That is what you have missed, Raoul."

"A friend!" cried Raoul. "I have missed a friend!"

"Monsieur de Guiche is an agreeable companion," resumed the count coolly, "but I believe, in the times in which you live, men are more engaged in their own interests and their own pleasures than they were in our times. You have sought a secluded life; that is a great happiness, but you have lost your strength in it. We four, deprived of those refinements which constitute your joy, found in us much more resistance when misfortune appeared."

"I have not interrupted you, monsieur, to tell you that I had a friend, and that that friend is Monsieur de Guiche. Of course, he is good and generous, and moreover he loves me. But I have lived under the protection of another friendship, monsieur, as precious and as strong as the one you are talking about, since it is yours."

"I have not been a friend for you, Raoul," said Athos.

"Monsieur, and why not?"

"Because I have given you reason to think that life has but one face, because, sad and severe, alas! I have always cut off for you, without, God knows, wishing to do so, the joyous buds which incessantly spring from the tree of youth; so that at this moment I repent of not having made you a more expansive, dissipated, animated man."

"I know why you say that, monsieur. No, it is not you who have made me what I am; it was love which took me at the time when children have only inclinations; it is the constancy natural to my character, which, with other creatures, is but a habit. I believed that I would always be as I was; I thought God had cast me on a path quite clear, quite straight, lined with fruits and flowers. I had watching over me your vigilance and your strength. I believed myself to be vigilant and strong. Nothing prepared me; I fell once, and that one time deprived me of courage for the whole of my life. It is quite true that I wrecked myself. Oh, no, monsieur; you are nothing in my past but happiness—you are nothing in my future but hope! No, I have no reproach to make against life, such as you made it for me; I bless you, and I love you ardently."

"My dear Raoul, your words do me good. They prove to me that you will act a little for me in the time to come."

"I shall only act for you, monsieur."

"Raoul, what I have never done for you, I will do from now on. I will be your friend, not your father. We will live in expanding ourselves, instead of living and holding ourselves prisoners, when you come back. And that will be soon, will it not?"

"Certainly, monsieur, for such an expedition cannot be long."

"Soon, then, Raoul, soon, instead of living modestly on my income, I will give you the capital of my estates. It will suffice to launch you into the world until my death; and you will give me, I hope, before that time, the consolation of not seeing my race extinct."

"I will do all you command," said Raoul, much agitated.

"Raoul, your duty as aide-de-camp should not lead you into too hazardous situations. You have proven yourself; you are known to be good under fire. Remember that war with the Arabs is a war of snares, ambushes, and assassinations."

"So they say, monsieur."

"There is never much glory in falling in an ambush. It is a death which always implies a little rashness or want of foresight. Often, indeed, he who falls in it meets with little pity. They who are not pitied, Raoul, have died uselessly. Moreover, the conqueror laughs, and we Frenchmen ought not to allow stupid infidels to triumph over our faults. Do you clearly understand what I am saying to you, Raoul? God forbid I should encourage you to avoid encounters!"

"I am naturally prudent, monsieur, and I am very lucky," said Raoul, with a smile which chilled the heart of his poor father; "for," the young man hastened to add, "in twenty combats in which I have been, I have only received one scratch."

"There is, in addition," said Athos, "the climate to be dreaded; that is an ugly end, that fever. King St. Louis prayed God to send him an arrow or the plague, rather than the fever."

"Oh, monsieur! with sobriety, with reasonable exercise . . ."

"I have already obtained from Monsieur de Beaufort a promise that his dispatches will be sent off every fortnight to France. You, as his aide-de-camp, will be responsible for sending them off, and will be sure not to forget me."

"No, monsieur," said Raoul, almost choked with emotion.

"Besides, Raoul, as you are a good Christian, and I am one also, we must count on a more special protection from God and His guardian angels. Promise me that if anything evil should happen to you, on any occasion, you will think of me at once."

"First, and at once! Oh, yes, monsieur."

"And will call upon me?"

"Instantly."

"You dream of me sometimes, do you not, Raoul?"

"Every night, monsieur. During my early youth I saw you in my dreams, calm and gentle, with one hand stretched out over my head, and that is why I slept so soundly—*formerly.*"

"We love each other too dearly," said the count, "that from this moment when we part, a portion of both our souls should not travel with one and the other of us, and should not dwell wherever we may dwell. When you are sad, Raoul, I feel that my heart will be drowned in sadness; and when you smile thinking of me, be assured you will send me, from over there, a ray of your joy."

"I will not promise you to be joyous," replied the young man; "but you may be certain that I will never spend an hour without thinking of you, not one hour, I swear, unless I am dead."

Athos could contain himself no longer; he threw his arm around the neck of his son, and held him with all the powers of his heart. The moon began to be now eclipsed by twilight; a golden band surrounded the horizon, announcing the approach of day. Athos threw his cloak over the shoulders of Raoul, and led him back to the city, where everything was already in motion, like in a vast anthill. At the extremity of the plateau, which Athos and De Bragelonne were leaving, they saw a dark shadow moving uneasily backward and forward, as if in indecision or ashamed to be seen. It was Grimaud, who, in his anxiety, had tracked his master down, and was waiting for him.

"My good Grimaud," cried Raoul, "what do you want? You come to tell us it is time to leave, have you?"

"Alone?" said Grimaud, addressing Athos and pointing to Raoul in a tone of reproach, which showed to what an extent the old man was troubled.

"You are right!" cried the count. "No, Raoul, do not go alone; no, he shall not be left alone in a strange land, without a friend to support him, and to remind him of all he loved!"

"I?" said Grimaud.

"You—yes, you!" cried Raoul, touched to his inmost heart.

"Alas!" said Athos, "you are very old, my good Grimaud."

"So much the better," replied the latter, with an inexpressible depth of feeling and intelligence.

"But the embarkation has begun," said Raoul, "and you are not prepared."

"Yes, I am," said Grimaud, showing the keys of his trunks, mixed with those of his young master.

"But," again objected Raoul, "you cannot leave Monsieur le Comte alone—Monsieur le Comte, whom you have never left."

Grimaud turned his dimmed eyes upon Athos and Raoul, as if to measure the strength of both. The count uttered not a word.

"Monsieur le Comte will prefer that I go," said Grimaud.

"I will," said Athos, by nodding his head.

At that moment the drums suddenly rolled, and the clarions filled the air with their inspiring notes. The regiments destined for the expedition began to come out from the city. There were five of them, each composed of forty companies. Royals marched first, distinguished by their white uniform, trimmed with blue. The regiments' colors, quartered crosswise, violet and brown, with a sprinkling of golden fleurs-de-lis, let the white flag, with its fleur-de-lis cross, dominate the whole. Musketeers at the wings, with their forked sticks and their muskets on their shoulders; pikemen in the center, with their lances, fourteen feet in length, marched cheerfully toward the transports, which carried them to the ships. The regiments of Picardy, Navarre, Normandy, and Royal Vaisseau followed after. M. de Beaufort had known well how to select his troops. He himself was seen closing the march with his staff—it would take a full hour before he could reach the sea. Raoul, with Athos, turned his steps slowly toward the beach, in order to take his place when the prince went by. Grimaud, boiling with the ardor of a young man, had Raoul's baggage taken into the admiral's vessel. Athos, with his arm passed through that of the son he was about to lose, absorbed in melancholy meditation, was dizzy with the noise around him. An officer came quickly toward them to inform Raoul that M. de Beaufort was anxious to have him by his side.

"Have the kindness to tell the prince," said Raoul,

"that I request he will allow me this hour to enjoy the company of my father."

"No, no," said Athos, "an aide-de-camp ought not thus to leave his general. Please tell the prince, monsieur, that the viscount will join him immediately."

The officer set off at a gallop.

"Whether we part here or part there," added the count, "it is no less a separation."

He carefully brushed the dust from his son's coat, and passed his hand over his hair as they walked along.

"But, Raoul," he said, "you need money. Monsieur de Beaufort lives in great style, and I am certain you'll want to purchase horses and arms, which are very expensive things in Africa. Now, as you are not actually in the service of the king or Monsieur de Beaufort, and are simply a volunteer, you must not count on either pay or largesses. But I do not want you to lack for anything at Gigelli. Here are two hundred pistoles; it would please me, Raoul, if you spent them."

Raoul shook his father's hand and at the turning of a street they saw M. de Beaufort, mounted upon a magnificent white *genet,* which responded with graceful bows to the applause of the women of the city. The duke called Raoul, and held out his hand to the count. He spoke to him for some time, with such a kindly expression that the heart of the poor father even felt a little comforted. It was, however, evident to both father and son that their walk was leading them to utter torment. There was a terrible moment—when, on leaving the sands of the shore, the soldiers and sailors exchanged the last kisses with their families and friends; a supreme moment, in which, in spite of the clearness of the sky, the warmth of the sun, the smells of the air, and the rich life that was circulating in their veins, everything appeared black, everything appeared bitter, everything created doubts of a God, while speaking by the mouth, even, of God. It was customary for the admiral and his suite to embark the last; the cannon waited to announce with its formidable voice, that the leader had placed his foot on board his vessel. Athos, forgetful of both the admiral and the fleet, and of his own dignity as a strong man, opened his arms to his son, and pressed him convulsively to his heart.

"Accompany us on board," said the duke, very much affected; "you will gain a good half hour."

"No," said Athos; "my farewell is spoken. I do not wish to speak a second one."

"Then, viscount, embark—embark quickly!" added the prince, wishing to spare the tears of these two men, whose hearts were bursting. And paternally, tenderly, strong as Porthos might have been, he took Raoul in his arms and placed him in the boat; the oars of which, at a signal, immediately were dipped in the waves. Himself, forgetful of ceremony, he jumped into his boat, and pushed it off vigorously.

"Adieu!" cried Raoul.

Athos replied only by a gesture, but he felt something burning on his hand; it was the respectful kiss of Grimaud—the last farewell of the faithful dog. This kiss given, Grimaud jumped from the step of the mole upon the stem of a two-oared yawl, which had just been taken in tow by a *chaland* served by twelve galley oars. Athos sat on the mole, stunned, deaf, abandoned. Every instant took from him one of the features, one of the shades of the pale face of his son. With his arms hanging down, his eyes fixed, his mouth open, he remained one with Raoul—in one same look, in one same thought, in one same stupor. The sea, by degrees, carried away boats and faces, until men were nothing but dots; loves, nothing but memories. Athos saw his son climb the ladder of the admiral's ship, he saw him lean upon the rail of the deck, and place himself in such a manner as to be always an object in the eye of his father. In vain the cannon thundered, in vain from the ship soared a long and loud tumult, answered by loud cheers from the shore, in vain did the noise deafen the ear of the father, and the smoke obscure the cherished object of all his aspirations: Raoul was in sight up to the last moment; and the imperceptible dot, passing from black to pale, from pale to white, from white to nothing, disappeared for Athos—disappeared very long after for all the eyes of the spectators, had disappeared both gallant ships and swelling sails. Toward midday, when the sun beat down and the tops of the masts hardly rose over the incandescent line of the sea, Athos saw a soft aerial shadow rise, and vanish as soon as seen. This was the smoke of a cannon which M. de Beaufort ordered to be fired as a last salute to the coast of France. The point was buried, in its turn, beneath the sky, and Athos returned painfully to his hostelry.

CHAPTER XXXIV

AMONG WOMEN

D'ARTAGNAN had not been able to hide his feelings from his friends as much as he would have wished. The stoical soldier, the impassible man-at-arms, overcome by fear and foreboding, had yielded, for a few minutes, to human weakness. When, therefore, he had silenced his heart and calmed the agitation of his nerves, turning toward his lackey, a silent servant, always listening in order to obey more promptly:

"Rabaud," he said, "mind, we must travel thirty leagues a day."

"At your pleasure, captain," replied Rabaud.

And from that moment, D'Artagnan, adjusting the pace of his horse, like a true centaur, thought about nothing— that is to say, about everything. He wondered why the king had sent for him; why the Iron Mask had thrown the silver plate at the feet of Raoul.

As to the first subject, the reply was negative; he knew that the king's calling him was from necessity. He knew that Louis XIV must be desperately needing a private talk with one whom the possession of such a secret placed on a level with the highest powers of the kingdom. But as to saying exactly what the king's wish was, D'Artagnan found himself completely at a loss.

The musketeer had no doubts, either, on the reason which had urged the unfortunate Philippe to reveal his character and his birth. Philippe, hidden forever beneath a mask of iron, exiled to a country where the men seemed little more than slaves of the elements; Philippe, deprived even of the company of D'Artagnan, who had loaded him with honors and delicate attentions, had nothing more to see than specters and griefs in this world, and despair beginning to devour him, he was bursting into complaints, in the belief that his revelations would find him an avenger. The manner in which the musketeer had almost killed his two best friends, the destiny which had so strangely brought Athos to participate in the great state secret, the farewell of Raoul, the obscurity of that future which threatened to end in a melancholy death; all this threw D'Artagnan incessantly back to sad predictions, which the rapidity of his pace did not dissipate as it usually did.

D'Artagnan went on to thoughts of the outcasts, Porthos and Aramis. He saw them both, fugitives, tracked, ruined—laborious architects of a fortune they must lose; and, as the king was calling for his man of action in an hour of vengeance, D'Artagnan trembled at the idea of receiving some order that would make his very heart bleed. Sometimes, when ascending hills, when the winded horse breathed heavily and heaved his flanks, the captain, left to more freedom of thought, reflected upon the prodigious genius of Aramis, a genius of shrewdness and intrigue, such as the Fronde and the civil war had produced but two. Soldier, priest, and diplomat; gallant, greedy, and cunning; Aramis took the good things in this life as steppingstones to rise to bad ones. Generous in mind, if not noble in heart, he never did ill but for the sake of shining a little more brilliantly. Toward the end of his career, at the moment of reaching the goal, like the patrician, Fuscus, he had made a false step upon a plank and had fallen into the sea.

But Porthos, the good, harmless Porthos! To see Porthos hungry, to see Mousqueton without gold lace, imprisoned, perhaps; to see Pierrefonds, Bracieux, razed to the very stones, dishonored even to the timber—these were so many poignant griefs for D'Artagnan, and every time that one of these griefs struck him, he bounded like a horse at the sting of the gadfly beneath the vault of leaves where he sought shade and shelter from the burning sun. The man of spirit is never bored if his body is exposed to fatigue; the healthy man never fails to find life light if he has something to engage his mind. D'Artagnan, riding fast, thinking as constantly, arrived in Paris, his muscles fresh and tender as the athlete preparing for the gymnasium.

The king was not expecting him so soon, and had just

gone hunting toward Meudon. D'Artagnan, instead of
riding after the king, as he would formerly have done,
took off his boots, had a bath, and waited till his majesty
returned, dusty and tired. He spent the next five hours in
taking, as people say, the pulse of the house, and in arming himself against all ill luck. He learned that the king,
during the last fortnight, had been gloomy; that the
queen mother was ill and depressed; that Monsieur, the
king's brother, was showing a devotional turn; that Madame had the vapors; and that M. de Guiche had gone
to one of his estates. He learned that M. Colbert was
radiant; that M. Fouquet was consulting a new physician
every day, who still did not cure him, and that his main
illness was one which physicians do not usually cure,
unless they are political physicians. The king, D'Artagnan was told, behaved in the kindest manner to M. Fouquet, and did not allow him to be out of his sight; but
the surintendant, deeply hurt, like one of those fine trees
which a worm has punctured, was declining daily, in spite
of the royal smile, that sun of court trees.

D'Artagnan learned that Mlle. de la Vallière had become indispensable to the king, that the king, if he did
not take her hunting with him, wrote to her frequently, no
longer poetry, but, what was still much worse, prose, and
whole pages at a time.

D'Artagnan then thought of the wishes of poor Raoul,
of that desperate letter destined for a woman who spent
her life hoping, and as D'Artagnan loved to philosophize
occasionally, he resolved to take advantage of the king's
absence to have a minute's talk with Mlle. de la Vallière.
This was a very easy affair; while the king was hunting,
Louise was walking with some other ladies in one of the
galleries of the Palais Royal, exactly where the captain
of the musketeers had to inspect some guards. D'Artagnan did not doubt that if he only could open the conversation on Raoul, Louise might give him grounds for
writing a good letter to the poor exile; and hope, or at
least consolation for Raoul, in the state of heart in which
he had left him, was the sun, was life to two men who
were very dear to our captain. He set out, therefore, to
the spot where he knew he would find Mlle. de la Vallière.

D'Artagnan found La Vallière the center of a circle.

In her apparent solitude, the king's favorite received, like a queen, more perhaps than the queen, an homage of which Madame had been so proud, when the king's eyes were directed to her and commanded the eyes of the courtiers as well. D'Artagnan, although no ladies' man, received, nevertheless, civilities and attentions from the ladies; he was polite, as a brave man always is, and his reputation had won him as much friendship among the men as admiration among the women. On seeing him enter, therefore, they immediately spoke to him; and, as is not unfrequently the case with fair ladies, started with questions.

"Where *had* he been? What *had* become of him so long? Why had they not seen him as usual make his fine horse in such beautiful style, to the delight and astonishment of the curious from the king's balcony?"

He replied that he had just come from the land of oranges. This set all the ladies laughing. Those were times in which everybody traveled, but in which, however, a journey of a hundred leagues was a problem often solved by death.

"From the land of oranges?" cried Mlle. de Tonnay-Charente. "From Spain?"

"Eh! eh!" said the musketeer.

"From Malta?" said Montalais.

"*Ma foi!* You are very close, ladies."

"Is it an island?" asked La Vallière.

"Mademoiselle," said D'Artagnan, "I will not trouble you to seek further; I come from the country where Monsieur de Beaufort is, at this moment, embarking for Algiers."

"Have you seen the army?" asked several warlike fair ones.

"As plainly as I see you," replied D'Artagnan.

"And the fleet?"

"Yes; I saw everything."

"Have we, any of us, any friends there?" said Mlle. de Tonnay-Charente coolly, but in a manner to attract attention to a question that was not without a calculated aim.

"Why," replied D'Artagnan, "yes; there were Monsieur de la Guillotière, Monsieur de Manchy, Monsieur de Bragelonne . . ."

La Vallière became pale.

"Monsieur de Bragelonne!" cried the treacherous Athenaïs. "Eh, what! Has he gone to war?"

Montalais stepped upon her toe, but in vain.

"Do you know what my opinion is?" she continued, addressing D'Artagnan.

"No, mademoiselle; but I should like very much to know it."

"My opinion is, then, that all the men who go to this war are desperate men whom love has treated ill; and who go to try if they cannot find black women less cruel than white ones have been."

Some of the ladies laughed. La Vallière was evidently confused. Montalais was coughing loud enough to waken the dead.

"Mademoiselle," interrupted D'Artagnan, "you are mistaken when you speak of black women at Gigelli; the women there are not black; it is true, they are not white— they are yellow."

"Yellow!" exclaimed the bevy of fair beauties.

"Do not make fun of it. I have never seen a finer color to match with black eyes and a coral mouth."

"So much the better for Monsieur de Bragelonne," said Mlle. de Tonnay-Charente, with persistent malice. "He will be compensated for his loss. Poor fellow!"

A profound silence followed these words; and D'Artagnan had time to observe and reflect that women—those mild doves—treat each other much more cruelly than tigers and bears. But making La Vallière pale did not satisfy Athenaïs; she determined to make her blush. Resuming the conversation without pause:

"Do you know, Louise," she said, "that that is a great sin on your conscience?"

"What sin, mademoiselle?" stammered the unfortunate girl, looking around her for support, without finding it.

"Why?" continued Athenaïs, "the poor young man was engaged to you; he loved you; you cast him off."

"Well, and that is a right every honest woman has," said Montalais, in an affected tone. "When we know we cannot make the happiness of a man, it is much better to cast him off."

"To cast him off is fine," said Athenaïs; "but that is

not the sin Mademoiselle de la Vallière has to reproach
herself with. The actual sin is sending poor De Bragelonne to war; and to a war where death will be met with."
Louise pressed her hand over her icy brow. "And if he
dies," continued her pitiless tormentor, "you will have
killed him. That is the sin."

Louise, half-dead, caught the arm of the captain of the
musketeers, whose face was betraying unusual emotion.

"You wished to speak with me, Monsieur d'Artagnan,"
she said, in a voice broken by anger and pain. "What
did you have to say to me?"

D'Artagnan took several steps along the gallery, holding Louise on his arm; then, when they were far enough
from the others:

"What I had to say to you, mademoiselle," he replied,
"Mademoiselle de Tonnay-Charente has just expressed;
roughly but in its entirety."

She uttered a faint cry, and, broken-hearted by this new
wound, she went on her way, like one of those poor birds
which, struck to death, seek the shade of the thicket to
die. She disappeared at one door, at the moment the king
was entering by another. The first glance of the king was
toward the empty seat of his mistress. Not seeing La
Vallière, a frown came over his brow; but as soon as he
saw D'Artagnan, who bowed to him:

"Ah! monsieur," he cried, "you *have* been diligent.
I am pleased with you."

This was the superlative expression of royal satisfaction. Many men would have been ready to lay down their
lives for such a word from the king. The maids of honor
and the courtiers, who had formed a respectful circle
around the king as he came in, drew back, on observing
he wanted to speak privately with his captain of the musketeers. The king led the way out of the gallery, after
having again looked for La Vallière, whose absence he
could not account for. The moment they were out of the
reach of curious ears:

"Well, Monsieur D'Artagnan," said he, "the prisoner?"

"Is in his prison, sire."

"What did he say on the road?"

"Nothing, sire."

"What did he do?"

"There was a moment when the fisherman who was taking me in his boat to Ste. Marguerite revolted, and did his best to kill me. The . . . prisoner defended me instead of attempting to flee."

The king became pale.

"Enough!" he said; and D'Artagnan bowed.

Louis walked up and down his cabinet.

"Were you at Antibes," he said, "when Monsieur de Beaufort came there?"

"No, sire; I was leaving when Monsieur le Duc arrived."

"Ah!" which was followed by a new silence. "Whom did you see there?"

"A great many people," said D'Artagnan coolly.

The king could tell that he was unwilling to speak.

"I have sent for you, Monsieur le Capitaine, to tell you to go and prepare my lodgings in Nantes."

"In Nantes!" cried D'Artagnan.

"In Bretagne."

"Yes, sire; it is in Bretagne. Will your majesty travel as far as Nantes?"

"The Estates* are assembled there," replied the king. "I have two demands to make of them; I wish to be there."

"When shall I set out?" said the captain.

"This evening—tomorrow—tomorrow evening; for you must need rest."

"I have rested, sire."

"That is well. Then, between this evening and tomorrow, when you please."

D'Artagnan bowed as if to take his leave; but, perceiving the king very much embarrassed:

"Will your majesty," he said, taking two steps forward, "take the court with you?"

"Certainly I shall."

"Then your majesty will, doubtless, want the musketeers?"

And the king lowered his gaze under the penetrating glance of the captain.

"Take a brigade of them," replied Louis.

* Provincial assembly, here of Brittany.

"Is that all? Has your majesty no other orders to give me?"

"No—ah! yes."

"I am all attention, sire."

"At the Castle of Nantes, which I hear is badly laid out, you will adopt the practice of placing musketeers at the door of each of the principal dignitaries I will take with me."

"Of the principal?"

"Yes."

"For instance, at the door of Monsieur de Lyonne?"

"Yes."

"At that of Monsieur Letellier?"

"Yes."

"Of Monsieur de Brienne?"

"Yes."

"And of Monsieur le Surintendant?"

"Without doubt."

"Very well, sire. By tomorrow I will be gone."

"Oh, yes; but one more word, Monsieur D'Artagnan. At Nantes you will meet with Monsieur le Duc de Gesvres, captain of the guards. Be sure that your musketeers are placed before his guards arrive. Precedence always belongs to the first comer."

"Yes, sire."

"And if Monsieur de Gesvres should question you?"

"Question me, sire! Is it likely that Monsieur de Gesvres would question me?"

And the musketeer, turning cavalierly on his heel, disappeared.

"To Nantes!" he said to himself, as he went down the stairs. "Why did he not dare to say afterward to Belle-Isle?"

As he reached the large gates one of M. de Brienne's clerks came running after him, exclaiming:

"Monsieur D'Artagnan! I beg your pardon . . ."

"What is the matter, Monsieur Ariste?"

"The king has ordered me to give you this voucher."

"On your account?" asked the musketeer.

"No, monsieur; upon that of Monsieur Fouquet."

D'Artagnan was surprised, but he took the voucher, which was in the king's own writing, and was for two hundred pistoles.

"What!" he thought, after having politely thanked M. de Brienne's clerk, "Monsieur Fouquet is to pay for the journey, then? *Mordioux!* that is a bit of pure Louis XI! Why was this not drawn on Monsieur Colbert's account? He would have paid it with such joy."

And D'Artagnan, faithful to his principle of never letting a voucher at sight get cold, went straight to the house of M. Fouquet, to receive his two hundred pistoles.

CHAPTER XXXV

THE LAST SUPPER

THE surintendant had no doubt heard of the approaching departure, for he was giving a farewell dinner for his friends. From the bottom to the top of the house, the rush of the servants carrying dishes, and the diligence of the *registres*, denoted an approaching change in both offices and kitchen. D'Artagnan, with his voucher in his hand, presented himself at the office where, he was told, it was too late to pay cash, the cashier's desk was closed. He only replied:

"On the king's service."

The clerk, a little disturbed by the serious air of the captain, replied that "that was a very respectable reason, but that the customs of the house were respectable as well, and that in consequence he begged the bearer to call again the next day." D'Artagnan asked if he could not see M. Fouquet. The clerk replied that M. le Surintendant did not get involved in such details, and rudely closed the outer door in D'Artagnan's face. But the latter had foreseen this stroke, and placed his boot between the door and the door-frame, so that the lock did not catch, and the clerk was still nose to nose with his questioner. This made him change his tone, and say, with terrified politeness:

"If monsieur wishes to speak to Monsieur le Surintendant, he must go to the antechamber; these are the offices, where monseigneur never comes."

"Very well. Where are they?" replied D'Artagnan.

"On the other side of the court," said the clerk, delighted at being free.

D'Artagnan crossed the court, and fell in with a crowd of servants.

"Monseigneur sees nobody at this hour," he was told by a fellow carrying a vermeil dish, in which were three pheasants and twelve quails.

"Tell him," said the captain, stopping the servant by taking hold of the end of his dish, "that I am Monsieur d'Artagnan, captain of his majesty's musketeers."

The fellow uttered a cry of surprise, and disappeared, D'Artagnan following him slowly. He arrived just in time to meet M. Pélisson in the antechamber; the latter, a little pale, was coming hastily out of the dining room to learn what was the matter. D'Artagnan smiled.

"There is nothing unpleasant, Monsieur Pélisson, only a little voucher for cash."

"Ah!" said Fouquet's friend, breathing more freely; and he took the captain by the hand, and, dragging him behind him, led him into the dining room, where a number of friends surrounded the surintendant, placed in the center, and buried in the cushions of an armchair. There were assembled all the Epicureans, who before, at Vaux, had enjoyed the mansion, the wit, and the money of M. Fouquet. Joyous friends, for the most part faithful, they had not fled their protector at the approach of the storm, and, in spite of the threatening sky, in spite of the trembling earth, they remained there, smiling, cheerful, as devoted to misfortune as they had been to prosperity. On the left of the surintendant was Mme. de Bellière; on his right was Mme. Fouquet; as if braving the laws of the world, and putting all vulgar reasons of propriety to silence, the two protecting angels of this man were uniting to offer him, at a moment of crisis, the support of their intertwined arms. Mme. de Bellière was pale, trembling, and full of respectful attentions for Mme. la Surintendante, who with one hand on the hand of her husband, was looking anxiously toward the door by which Pélisson had gone out to bring in D'Artagnan. The captain entered, at first full of courtesy, and afterward of admiration, when, with his infallible glance, he had guessed as well as taken in the expression of every face. Fouquet raised himself up in his chair.

"Pardon me, Monsieur D'Artagnan," said he, "if I did not come to receive you when coming in the king's name."

And he pronounced the last words with a sort of melancholy firmness, which filled the hearts of his friends with terror.

"Monseigneur," replied D'Artagnan, "I only come to you, in the king's name, to demand payment of a voucher for two hundred pistoles."

They all cheered up but Fouquet, who remained somber.

"Ah, then," he said, "perhaps you are also setting out for Nantes?"

"I do not know where I am setting out for, monseigneur."

"But," said Mme. Fouquet, recovered from her fright, "you are not going so soon, Monsieur le Capitaine, as not to do us the honor to take a seat with us?"

"Madame, it would be a great honor for me, but I am so pressed for time that, you see, I had to interrupt your meal to procure payment of my note."

"The reply to which shall be gold," said Fouquet, making a sign to his intendant, who went out with the voucher which D'Artagnan handed to him.

"Oh!" said the latter, "I was not worried about the payment; the house is good."

A painful smile passed over the pale features of Fouquet.

"Are you in pain?" asked Mme. de Bellière.

"Do you feel your attack coming on?" asked Mme. Fouquet.

"Neither, thank you both," said Fouquet.

"Your attack?" said D'Artagnan, in his turn; "are you unwell, monseigneur?"

"I have a certain fever, which seized me after the *fête* at Vaux."

"Caught cold in the grottoes, at night, perhaps?"

"No, no; nothing but nerves, that is all."

"You showed too much heart in your reception of the king," said La Fontaine quietly, without suspicion that he was uttering a sacrilege.

"We cannot show too much heart to the reception of our king," said Fouquet mildly, to his poet.

"Monsieur meant to say too much fervor," interrupted D'Artagnan, with perfect frankness and much amenity. "The fact is, monseigneur, that hospitality was never practiced as at Vaux."

Mme. Fouquet's expression showed clearly that if Fouquet had behaved well toward the king, the king had not reciprocated. But D'Artagnan knew the terrible secret. He alone, with Fouquet, knew it; those two men had not, the one the courage to pity the other, the other the right to accuse. The captain, to whom the two hundred pistoles were brought, was about to leave, when Fouquet, rising, took a glass of wine, and ordered one to be given to D'Artagnan.

"Monsieur," he said, "to the health of the king, 'whatever may happen.' "

"And to your health, monseigneur, 'whatever may happen,' " said D'Artagnan.

He bowed, with these words of evil omen, to all the company, who rose as soon as he had bowed, and they heard the sound of his spurs and boots at the bottom of the stairs.

"I, for a moment, thought it was me, and not my money, he wanted," said Fouquet, trying to laugh.

"You!" cried his friends; "and what for, in the name of Heaven?"

"Do not deceive yourselves, my dear brothers in Epicurus," said the surintendant, "I will not make a comparison between the most humble sinner on earth and the God we adore, but remember, He one day gave His friends a meal which is called the Last Supper, and which was nothing but a farewell dinner, like the one we are having at this moment."

A painful cry of denial arose from all parts of the table.

"Shut the doors," said Fouquet, and the servants disappeared. "My friends," continued Fouquet, lowering his voice, "what was I formerly? What am I now? Consult among yourselves, and reply. A man like me sinks when he does not continue to rise. What shall we say, then, when he really sinks? I have no more money, no more credit; I have no longer anything but powerful enemies, and powerless friends."

"Quick!" cried Pélisson. "Since you explain yourself

with that frankness, it is our duty to be frank, likewise. Yes, you are ruined—yes, you are hastening to your ruin—stop. But first, what money do we have left?''

''Seven hundred thousand pounds,'' said the intendant.

''Bread,'' murmured Mme. Fouquet.

''Relays,'' said Péllison, ''relays, and flee!''

''Where?''

''To Switzerland—to Savoy—but flee!''

''If monseigneur flees,'' said Mme. de Bellière, ''it will be said that he was guilty, and afraid.''

''More than that, it will be said that I have carried away twenty million with me.''

''We will draw up memos to defend you,'' said La Fontaine. ''Flee!''

''I will stay,'' said Fouquet. ''And besides, isn't everything in my favor?''

''You have Belle-Isle,'' cried the Abbé Fouquet.

''And I am naturally going there, when going to Nantes,'' replied the surintendant. ''Patience, then, patience!''

''Before arriving at Nantes, what a distance!'' said Mme. Fouquet.

''Yes, I know that well,'' replied Fouquet. ''But what can I do about it? The king summons me to the Estates. I know well it is for the purpose of ruining me; but to refuse to go would be to show I am worried.''

''Well, I have discovered the means of reconciling everything,'' cried Pélisson. ''You are going to set out for Nantes.''

Fouquet looked at him with an air of surprise.

''But with friends; but in your own carriage as far as Orleans; in your barge as far as Nantes; always ready to defend yourself, if you are attacked; to escape, if you are threatened. In fact, you will carry your money against all chances; and while fleeing you will only have obeyed the king; then, reaching the sea when you like, you will embark for Belle-Isle, and from Belle-Isle you will rush wherever you please, like the eagle which flies into space when it has been driven from its nest.''

A general assent followed Pélisson's words.

''Yes, do so,'' said Mme. Fouquet, to her husband.

''Do so,'' said Mme. de Bellière.

"Do it! do it!" cried all his friends.

"I will do so," replied Fouquet.

"This very evening?"

"In an hour?"

"Immediately."

"With seven hundred thousand pounds you can lay the foundation of another fortune," said the Abbé Fouquet. "What is there to prevent our arming corsairs at Belle-Isle?"

"And, if necessary, we will go and discover a new world," added La Fontaine, intoxicated with projects and enthusiasm.

A knock at the door interrupted this concert of joy and hope. "A courier from the king," said the master of ceremonies.

A profound silence immediately ensued, as if the message brought by this courier was nothing but a reply to all the projects given birth to an instant before. Everyone waited to see what the master would do. His brow was streaming with perspiration, and he was really suffering from his fever at that instant. He passed into his cabinet, to receive the king's message. There prevailed, as we have said, such a silence in the rooms, and throughout the attendance, that from the dining room could be heard the voice of Fouquet, saying, "That is well, monsieur." This voice was, however, broken by fatigue, trembling with emotion. An instant after, Fouquet called Gourville, who crossed the gallery as they all waited breathlessly. At last he reappeared among his guests; but it was no longer the same pale, spiritless face they had seen when he left them; from pale he had become livid, and from spiritless, annihilated. A living specter, he came forward with his arms stretched out, his mouth parched, like a shadow that has just greeted friends of former days. On seeing him thus they all cried out, and they all rushed toward Fouquet. The latter, looking at Pélisson, leaned upon his wife, and pressed the icy hand of the Marquise de Bellière.

"Well!" he said, in a voice which had nothing human in it.

"What has happened, my God?" someone said to him.

Fouquet opened his right hand, which was clinched,

humid, and displayed a paper, upon which Pélisson cast a terrified glance. He read the following lines, written by the king's hand:

" 'DEAR AND WELL-BELOVED MONSIEUR FOUQUET: Give us, upon that which you have left of ours, the sum of seven hundred thousand pounds, which we need to prepare for our departure.

" 'And, as we know your health is not good, we pray God to restore you to health, and to have you in His holy keeping.   LOUIS.

" 'The present letter is to serve as a receipt.' "

A murmur of terror swept through the apartment.

"Well!" cried Pélisson, in his turn, "you have received that letter?"

"I have the receipt—yes."

"What will you do, then?"

"Nothing, since I have the receipt."

"But . . ."

"If I have the receipt, Pélisson, I have paid it," said the surintendant, with a simplicity that tore the heart of all present.

"You have paid it!" cried Mme. Fouquet. "Then we are ruined!"

"Come, no useless words," interrupted Pélisson. "After money, life. Monseigneur, to horse! to horse!"

"What, leave us!" at once cried both the women, with wild grief.

"Monseigneur, in saving yourself you save us all. To horse!"

"But he cannot stand up. Look at him!"

"Oh! if we take time to think . . ." said the intrepid Pélisson.

"He is right," murmured Fouquet.

"Monseigneur! monseigneur!" cried Gourville, rushing up the stairs four steps at once. "Monseigneur!"

"Well, what?"

"I escorted, as you know, the king's courier with the money."

"Yes."

"Well, when I arrived at the Palais Royal, I saw . . ."

"Catch your breath, my poor friend; you are suffocating."

"What did you see?" cried the impatient friends.

"I saw the musketeers on horseback," said Gourville.

"You see!" cried all the voices at once; "you see, there is not a moment to waste." Mme. Fouquet rushed downstairs, calling for her horses; Mme. de Bellière flew after her, catching her in her arms, and saying:

"Madame, in the name of his safety, do not show any alarm."

Pélisson ran to have the horses harnessed to the carriages. And, in the meantime, Gourville gathered in his hat all the gold and silver that the weeping friends were able to throw into it—the last offering, the last charity made to misfortune by poverty. The surintendant, dragged along by some, carried by others, was enclosed in his carriage. Gourville took the reins and mounted the box. Pélisson supported Mme. Fouquet, who had fainted. Mme. de Bellière had more strength, and was well paid for it; she received Fouquet's last kiss. Pélisson easily explained this rushed departure, by saying that an order from the king had summoned the ministers to Nantes.

CHAPTER XXXVI

IN THE CARRIAGE OF M. COLBERT

As Gourville had seen, the king's musketeers were on horseback and following their captain. The latter, who did not like to be limited in his actions, left his brigade under the orders of a lieutenant, and set off, on his own, on post horses, encouraging his men to hurry. However rapidly they might travel, they could not arrive before him. He had time, going down the Rue des Petits Champs, to see something which gave him plenty of food for thought. He saw M. Colbert coming out from his house to get into his carriage, which was stationed before the door. In this carriage D'Artagnan saw the hoods of two women, and being rather curious, he wanted to know the identities of the women concealed beneath these hoods. To get a glimpse at them, for they kept themselves closely covered up, he urged his horse so near the carriage as to shake everything. The terrified women uttered, the one a faint cry, by which D'Artagnan recognized a young woman, the other a curse, by which he recognized the vigor and assurance acquired by half a century of life. The hoods were thrown back; one of the women was Mme. Vanel, the other was the Duchesse de Chevreuse. D'Artagnan's eyes were quicker than those of the ladies; he recognized them, while they did not recognize him; and as they were laughing at their fright, pressing each other's hands:

"Well!" said D'Artagnan, "the old duchess is not as choosy in her friendships as she was before. She is paying court to the mistress of Monsieur Colbert! Poor Monsieur Fouquet! that is a bad omen!"

He rode on. M. Colbert got into his carriage, and this noble trio began a rather slow pilgrimage toward the wood of Vincennes. Mme. de Cherveuse dropped off Mme. Vanel at her husband's house, and, left alone with M. Colbert, she chatted while continuing her ride. She had an inexhaustible fund of conversation, that dear duchess, and as she always talked ill of others, always well of herself, her conversation always amused her interlocutor.

She informed Colbert, who, poor man! was ignorant of it, how great a minister he was, and how Fouquet would soon become nothing. She promised to rally around him, when he became surintendant, all the old nobility of the kingdom, and questioned him as to the role it would be proper to allow La Vallière to take. She praised him, she blamed him, she bewildered him. She showed him the secret of so many secrets that, for a moment, Colbert feared he must have to do with the devil. She proved to him that she was holding in her hand the Colbert of today as she had held the Fouquet of yesterday; and as he asked her very simply the reason for her hatred of the surintendant:

"Why do you hate him?" she said.

"Madame, in politics," he replied, "the differences of system may bring about divisions between men. Monsieur Fouquet always appeared to me to practice a system opposed to the true interests of the king.''

She interrupted him.

''I will say no more to you about Monsieur Fouquet. The journey the king is about to take to Nantes will prove we are right. Monsieur Fouquet, for me, is a finished man—and for you also.''

Colbert made no reply.

''On his return from Nantes,'' continued the duchess, ''the king, who is eager for any reason, will find that the Estates have not behaved well—that they have made too few sacrifices. The Estates will say that the taxes are too heavy, and that the surintendant has ruined them. The king will lay all the blame on M. Fouquet, and then . . .''

''And then?'' said Colbert.

''He will be disgraced. Isn't that your opinion?''

Colbert darted a glance at the duchess, which plainly said, ''If Monsieur Fouquet is only disgraced, you will not be the cause of it.''

''Your place, Monsieur Colbert,'' the duchess hastened to add, ''must be quite a marked place. Do you see anyone between the king and yourself, after the fall of Monsieur Fouquet?''

''I do not understand,'' he said.

''You will understand. To what does your ambition aspire?''

''I have none.''

''It was useless, then, to overthrow the surintendant, Monsieur Colbert. That is idle.''

''I had the honor to tell you, madame . . .''

''Oh, yes, I know, all about the interest of the king; but, if you please, we will speak of your own.''

''Mine! that is to say, the affairs of his majesty.''

''In short, are you, or are you not, ruining Monsieur Fouquet? Answer frankly.''

''Madame, I am ruining nobody.''

''I cannot, then, understand why you have purchased from me the letters of Monsieur Mazarin concerning Monsieur Fouquet. Neither can I conceive why you have shown those letters to the king.''

Colbert, dumbfounded, gave the duchess an uneasy look.

"Madame," he said, "I can conceive even less how you, who received the money, can reproach me for that."

"That is," said the old duchess, "because we must will what we wish for, unless we cannot do what we wish."

"That's it!" said Colbert, quite disconcerted by such coarse logic.

"You can't, can you! Speak."

"I can't, I confess, destroy certain influences near the king."

"Which fight for Monsieur Fouquet? What are they? Stop! let me help you."

"Do, madame."

"La Vallière?"

"Oh, very little influence; no knowledge of business, and small means. Monsieur Fouquet has paid his court to her."

"To defend him would be to accuse herself, would it not?"

"I think it would."

"There is still another influence, what do you say to that?"

"Is it considerable?"

"The queen mother, perhaps?"

"Her majesty, the queen mother, has a weakness toward Monsieur Fouquet which is very harmful to her son."

"Never believe that," said the old duchess, smiling.

"Oh!" said Colbert, with incredulity, "I have often experienced it."

"Formerly?"

"Very recently, madame, at Vaux. It was she who prevented the king from having Monsieur Fouquet arrested."

"People do not always entertain the same opinions, my dear monsieur. What the queen may have wanted recently, she might not want today."

"And why not?" said Colbert, astonished.

"The reason is of very little consequence."

"On the contrary, I think it is of great consequence; for, if I were certain of not displeasing her majesty, the queen mother, all my scruples would be gone."

"Well, have you never heard of a certain secret?"

"A secret?"

"Call it what you like. In short, the queen mother has conceived a horror for all those who have participated, in one fashion or another, in the discovery of this secret, and Monsieur Fouquet I believe to be one of these."

"Then," said Colbert, "we may be sure of the assent of the queen mother?"

"I have just left her majesty, and she assures me so."

"So be it, then, madame."

"But there is something further; do you happen to know a man who was the intimate friend of Monsieur Fouquet, a Monsieur d'Herblay, a bishop, I believe?"

"Bishop of Vannes."

"Well, this Monsieur d'Herblay, who also knew the secret, the queen mother is having him pursued with the utmost rancor."

"Indeed!"

"So hotly pursued that if he were dead, she would not be satisfied with anything less than his head, to be sure he would never speak again."

"And is that the desire of the queen mother?"

"An order is given for it."

"This Monsieur d'Herblay shall be sought for, madame."

"It is well known where he is."

Colbert looked at the duchess.

"Say where, madame."

"He is at Belle-Isle-en-Mer."

"At the residence of Monsieur Fouquet?"

"At the residence of Monsieur Fouquet."

"He shall be captured."

It was now the duchess's turn to smile.

"Do not believe that so easily," said she, "and do not promise it so lightly."

"Why not, madame?"

"Because Monsieur d'Herblay is not one of those people who can be captured just when you please."

"He is a rebel, then."

"Oh, Monsieur Colbert, we folks have spent all our lives being rebels, and yet you see plainly that far from being captured, we capture others."

Colbert fixed the old duchess with one of those fierce looks of which no words can convey the expression, accompanied by a firmness which was not lacking in grandeur.

"The times are gone," he said, "in which subjects gained duchies by making war against the King of France. If Monsieur d'Herblay conspires, he will perish on the scaffold. That will give, or will not give, pleasure to his enemies—that is of very little importance to *us.*"

And this *us,* a strange word in the mouth of Colbert, made the duchess thoughtful for a moment. She caught herself reckoning inwardly with this man.

Colbert had regained his superiority in the conversation, and he was eager to keep it.

"You are asking me, madame," he said, "to have this Monsieur d'Herblay arrested?"

"I? I am asking you nothing of the kind!"

"I thought you did, madame. But as I have been mistaken, we will leave him alone; the king has said nothing about him."

The duchess bit her nails.

"Besides," continued Colbert, "what a poor capture would this bishop be! A bishop game for a king! Oh, no, no; I will not get involved in this."

The hatred of the duchess now was clear.

"Game for a woman!" said she, "and the queen is a woman. If she wishes to have Monsieur d'Herblay arrested, she has her reasons for it. Besides, is not Monsieur d'Herblay the friend of him who is destined to fall?"

"Oh, never mind that," said Colbert. "This man shall be spared, if he is not the enemy of the king. Is that displeasing to you?"

"I say nothing."

"Yes; do you want to see him in prison, in the Bastille, for instance?"

"I believe a secret is better concealed behind the walls of the Bastille than behind those of Belle-Isle."

"I will speak to the king about it; he will clear up the point."

"And while waiting for that enlightenment, Monsieur l'Evêque de Vannes will have escaped. I would do the same."

"Escaped? he—and where would he escape? Europe is ours, in will, if not in fact."

"He will always find an asylum, monsieur. It is evident you know nothing of the man you are dealing with. You do not know D'Herblay; you did not know Aramis. He was one of those four musketeers who, under the late king, made Cardinal de Richelieu tremble, and who, during the regency, gave so much trouble to Monseigneur Mazarin."

"But, madame, what can he do, unless he has a kingdom to back him?"

"He has one, monsieur."

"A kingdom? he? What, Monsieur d'Herblay?"

"I repeat to you, monsieur, that if he wants a kingdom he either has it or will have it."

"Well, as you are so concerned that this rebel should not escape, madame, I promise you he shall not escape."

"Belle-Isle is fortified, Monsieur Colbert, and fortified by him."

"If Belle-Isle were also defended by him, Belle-Isle is not impregnable; and if Monsieur l'Evêque de Vannes is shut up in Belle-Isle, well, madame, the fort will be besieged and he will be captured."

"You may be very certain, monsieur, that the zeal which you show for the interests of the queen mother will touch her majesty, and that you will be magnificently rewarded for it; but what shall I tell her of your projects respecting this man?"

"That once captured, he shall be shut up in a fortress from which her secret shall never escape."

"Very well, Monsieur Colbert, and we may say that, from this moment, we have formed a solid alliance, that is, you and I, and that I am perfectly at your service."

"It is I, madame, who place myself at yours. This Chevalier d'Herblay is a kind of Spanish spy, is he not?"

"More than that."

"A secret ambassador?"

"Higher still."

"Stop—King Philip III of Spain is devout. He is, perhaps, the confessor of Philip III."

"You must go much higher than that."

"*Mordieu!*" cried Colbert, who forgot himself so far

as to swear in the presence of this great lady, of this old friend of the queen mother—of the Duchesse de Chevreuse, in short. "He must, then, be the general of the Jesuits?"

"I believe you have guessed at last," replied the duchess.

"Ah, then, madame, this man will ruin us all if we do not ruin him; and we must make haste to do it, too."

"That was my opinion, monsieur, but I did not dare to give it to you."

"And it is fortunate for us that he has attacked the throne, and not us."

"But, take good note of this, Monsieur Colbert. Monsieur d'Herblay is never discouraged; and if he has failed, he will start again. If he has failed making a king for himself, sooner or later, he will make another, of whom, certainly, you will not be prime minister."

Colbert knitted his brow with a menacing expression.

"I feel assured that a prison will settle this affair for us, madame, in a manner satisfactory for both."

The duchess smiled again.

"If you knew," she said, "how many times Aramis has gotten out of prison!"

"We will take care he shall not get out this time," replied Colbert.

"But haven't you heard what I said to you just now? Don't you remember that Aramis was one of the four invincibles whom Richelieu dreaded? And at that time the four musketeers did not have what they have now—money and experience."

Colbert bit his lips.

"We will give up on the prison," he said, in a lower tone; "we will find a retreat from which the invincible will not possibly escape."

"That is well spoken, our ally!" replied the duchess. "But it is getting late; had we not better return?"

"Willingly, madame, as I have to get ready to leave with the king."

"To Paris!" cried the duchess, to the coachman.

And the carriage returned toward the Faubourg St. Antoine, after the conclusion of the treaty which signed the

death of the last friend of Fouquet, the last defender of
Belle-Isle, the old friend of Marie Michon,* the new enemy of the duchess.

CHAPTER XXXVII

THE TWO LIGHTERS

D'ARTAGNAN had left; Fouquet too had left, and he
with a speed increased by the tender interest of his
friends. The first moments of this journey, or better to
say, of this flight, were troubled by the incessant fear
of all the horses and all the carriages which could be
seen behind the fugitive. It was not natural, in fact, if
Louis XIV was determined to seize this prey, that he
should allow it to escape; the young lion was already
accustomed to hunting, and he had ardent bloodhounds
he could depend upon.

But gradually all the fears were dispersed; the surintendant, by traveling hard, placed such a distance between himself and his persecutors that no one of them
could reasonably be expected to overtake him. As to his
spirit, his friends had made it excellent for him. Was he
not traveling to join the king at Nantes, and what did the
speed prove but his zeal to obey? He arrived, tired, but
reassured, in Orleans, where he found, thanks to the care
of a courier who had preceded him, a handsome eight-
oared lighter. These lighters, in the shape of gondolas,
rather wide and rather heavy, contained a small, covered
chamber, in the shape of a deck, and a chamber in the
poop, formed by a tent, made the trip then from Orleans
to Nantes, by the Loire, and this crossing, a long one in
our days, appeared then easier and more convenient than
the highroad, with its nags or its poor carriages. Fouquet
went on board this lighter, which set out immediately.
The rowers, knowing they had the honor of taking the surintendant of finances, pulled with all their strength, and

* The Duchess of Chevreuse, she figures in *The Three Musketeers* as Marie
Michon.

that magic word, the *finances,* promised them a generous reward of which they wished to prove themselves worthy. The lighter bounded over the tiny waves of the Loire. Magnificent weather, one of those sunrises that make the landscape purple, left the river all its clear serenity. The current and the rowers carried Fouquet along as wings carry a bird, and he arrived before Beaugency without any accident. Fouquet hoped to be the first to arrive in Nantes; there he would see the notables and gain support among the principal members of the Estates; he would make himself necessary, a thing very easy for a man of his merit, and would delay the catastrophe, if he did not succeed in avoiding it entirely.

"Besides," said Gourville to him, "in Nantes you will make out, or we will make out, the intentions of your enemies; we will have horses always ready to take you to the inextricable Poitou, a boat in which to gain the sea, and when once in the open sea, Belle-Isle is the inviolable port. You see, besides, that no one is watching you, no one is following you."

He had scarcely finished, when they discovered at a distance, behind a bend formed by the river, the masts of a large lighter, which was coming down. The rowers of Fouquet's boat uttered a cry of surprise on seeing this galley.

"What is the matter?" asked Fouquet.

"The matter is, monseigneur," replied the captain of the boat, "that it is a truly remarkable thing—that lighter comes along like a hurricane."

Gourville gave a start, and went up on the deck, in order to see better.

Fouquet did not go up with him, but he said to Gourville, with a restrained mistrust:

"See what it is, dear friend."

The lighter had just passed the bend. It came on so fast that one could see the white train of its wake, lit by the sun, quiver behind it.

"How they go!" repeated the captain, "how they go! They must be well paid. I did not think," he added, "that wooden oars could work better than ours, but those over there prove the contrary."

"Well they may," said one of the rowers, "they are twelve, and we are only eight."

"Twelve rowers!" replied Gourville, "twelve—impossible!"

The number of eight rowers for a lighter had never been exceeded, even for the king. This honor had been paid to M. le Surintendant, much more for the sake of haste than of respect.

"What does that mean?" said Gourville, trying to make out beneath the tent, which was already apparent, travelers which the keenest eye could not yet have succeeded in discovering.

"They must be in a hurry, for it is not the king," said the captain.

Fouquet shuddered.

"How do you know that it is not the king?" said Gourville.

"In the first place, because there is no white flag with fleurs-de-lis, which the royal lighter always carries."

"And then," said Fouquet, "because it is impossible it should be the king, Gourville, as the king was still in Paris yesterday."

Gourville answered the surintendant with a look, which said: "You were there yourself yesterday."

"And how do you make out they are in such a hurry?" he added, for the sake of gaining time.

"By this, monsieur," said the captain: "these people must have set out a long while after us, and they have already nearly overtaken us."

"Bah!" said Gourville, "who told you that they do not come from Beaugency or from Niort, even?"

"We have seen no lighter of that shape, except at Orleans. It is coming from Orleans, monsieur, and is hurrying."

Fouquet and Gourville exchanged a glance. The captain noticed their uneasiness, and to mislead him, Gourville immediately said:

"A friend, who has bet he would catch us; let us win the bet, and not allow him to overtake us."

The captain opened his mouth to reply that that was impossible, when Fouquet said, with much hauteur:

"If someone wants to join us, let him come."

"We can try, monseigneur," said the captain timidly. "Come, you fellows, put out your strength; row, row!"

"No," said Fouquet, "stop short, on the contrary."

"Monseigneur! what folly!" interrupted Gourville, leaning toward his ear.

"Quite short!" repeated Fouquet.

The eight oars stopped, and, resisting the water, they created a backward motion in the lighter. It stopped. The twelve rowers in the other did not, at first, see this maneuver, for they continued to urge on their boat so vigorously that it arrived quickly within gunshot. Fouquet was short-sighted, Gourville was troubled by the sun, which was full in his eyes; the captain alone, with that habit and clearness which are acquired by a constant struggle with the elements, saw the travelers distinctly in the neighboring lighter.

"I can see them," he cried; "there are two."

"I can see nothing," said Gourville.

"It will not be long before you make them out; in twenty strokes of their oars they will be within twenty paces of us."

But what the captain announced did not happen; the lighter imitated the movement commanded by Fouquet, and instead of coming to join its supposed friends, it stopped short in the middle of the river.

"I cannot understand this," said the captain.

"Nor I, neither," said Gourville.

"You, who can plainly see the people in that lighter," said Fouquet, "try to describe them to us, captain, before we are too far off."

"I thought I saw two," replied the boatman. "I can only see one now, under the tent."

"What sort of man is he?"

"He is a dark man, large-shouldered, short-necked."

A little cloud at that moment passed across the sky, and darkened the sun. Gourville, who was still looking, with one hand over his eyes, could now see what he was looking for, and all at once, jumping from the deck into the room where Fouquet was waiting for him:

"Colbert!" he said, in a voice broken by emotion.

"Colbert!" repeated Fouquet. "Oh, how strange! But no, it is impossible."

"I tell you I recognized him, and he, at the same time, so plainly recognized me that he has just gone into the chamber on the poop. Perhaps the king has sent him to make us come back."

"In that case he would join us instead of lying by. What is he doing there?"

"He is watching us, without doubt."

"I do not like uncertainty," said Fouquet; "let us go straight up to him."

"Oh, monseigneur, do not do that, the lighter is full of armed men."

"Would he arrest me, then, Gourville? Why does he not come on?"

"Monseigneur, it is not consistent with your dignity to go to meet your ruin."

"But to allow them to watch me like a criminal!"

"Nothing tells us that they are watching you, monseigneur; be patient."

"What is to be done, then?"

"Do not stop; you were only going so fast to appear to obey the king's order with zeal. Go faster. He who lives will see!"

"That's right. Come!" cried Fouquet; "since they remain still over there, let us go on."

The captain gave the signal, and Fouquet's rowers resumed their task with all the success one could expect from rested men. Scarcely had the lighter made a hundred fathoms than the other, that with the twelve rowers, also resumed its course. This position lasted all day, without any increase or diminution of distance between the two vessels. Toward evening Fouquet wished to try the intentions of his persecutor. He ordered his rowers to pull toward the shore, as if to land. Colbert's lighter imitated this maneuver, and steered toward the shore in a slanting direction. By the greatest chance, at the spot where Fouquet pretended to land, a stableman from the Château of Langeais was walking along the flowery banks, leading three horses in halters. Without doubt, the people of the twelve-oared lighter thought that Fouquet was directing his course toward horses prepared for his flight, for four or five men, armed with muskets, jumped from the lighter onto the shore, and walked along the banks, as if to gain ground on the horses and horseman. Fouquet, pleased at having forced the enemy to show his hand, put his boat in motion again. Colbert's people returned to theirs, and the race of the two vessels was resumed with fresh perseverance. Upon seeing this,

Fouquet felt himself closely threatened, and in a prophetic voice:

"Well, Gourville," he said whispering, "what was I saying at our last meal at my house? Am I, or am I not, going to my ruin?"

"Oh, monseigneur!"

"These two boats, which follow each other with so much rivalry, as if we were competing, Monsieur Colbert and I, for a speed prize on the Loire, don't they not aptly represent our two fortunes; and don't you believe, Gourville, that one of the two will be wrecked in Nantes?"

"At least," objected Gourville, "there is still uncertainty; you are about to appear at the Estates; you are about to show what sort of man you are; your eloquence and your genius for business are the shield and sword that will serve to defend you, if not to conquer with. The Bretons do not know you; and when they shall know you, your cause is won! Oh! let Monsieur Colbert watch out, for his lighter is as much in danger of being upset as yours. Both go quickly, his faster than yours, it is true; we shall see which will be wrecked first."

Fouquet, taking Gourville's hand:

"My friend," he said, "everything considered, remember the proverb, 'First come, first served.' Well, Monsieur Colbert takes care not to pass me. He is a prudent man, that Monsieur Colbert."

He was right; the two lighters held their course as far as Nantes, watching each other. When the surintendant landed, Gourville hoped he would be able to seek refuge at once, and have relays prepared. But, at the landing, the second lighter joined the first, and Colbert, approaching Fouquet, saluted him on the quay with marks of the profoundest respect—marks so significant, so public, that their result was the rushing of the whole population upon La Fosse. Fouquet was completely self-possessed; he felt that in his last moments of greatness he had obligations toward himself. He wanted to fall from such a height that his fall should crush one of his enemies. Colbert was there—so much the worse for Colbert. The surintendant, therefore, coming up to him, replied, with that arrogant winking of the eyes peculiar to him:

"Is that you, Monsieur Colbert?"

"To offer you my respects, monseigneur," said the latter.

"Were you in that lighter?" pointing to the one with twelve rowers.

"Yes, monseigneur."

"Of twelve rowers," said Fouquet. "What luxury, Monsieur Colbert! For a moment, I thought it was the queen mother or the king."

"Monseigneur!" and Colbert blushed.

"This is a trip that will be expensive for those who have to pay for it, Monsieur l'Intendant," said Fouquet. "But at last you have arrived. You see, however," he added, a moment after, "that I, who had only eight rowers, arrived before you."

And he turned his back to him, leaving him uncertain whether all the hesitations of the second lighter had escaped the notice of the first. At least, he did not give him the satisfaction of showing that he had been frightened. Colbert, so annoyingly attacked, did not give way.

"I have not been quick, monseigneur," he replied, "because I followed your example whenever you stopped."

"And why did you do that, Monsieur Colbert?" cried Fouquet, irritated by this insolence; "as you had a superior crew to mine, why did you not either join me or pass me?"

"Out of respect," said the intendant, bowing to the ground.

Fouquet got into a carriage which the city sent to him, we know not why or how, and went to la Maison de Nantes, escorted by a vast crowd of people, who for several days had been boiling with the expectation of a convocation of the Estates. Scarcely was he settled, when Gourville went out to go and order horses upon the route to Poitiers and Vannes, and a boat at Paimboeuf. He performed these various operations with so much mystery, activity, and generosity that Fouquet, then suffering from an attack of fever, was never closer to being saved, except for the coöperation of that immense disturber of human plans—chance. A report was spread during the night that the king was coming in a great hurry upon post horses, and that he would arrive within ten or twelve hours at the latest. The people, while waiting for the king, were delighted to see the musketeers, freshly arrived, with M. d'Artagnan, their captain, and quartered in the castle, of which they occupied all the posts, guards of honor. M. d'Artagnan, who was very polite, presented himself about ten o'clock at the surintendant's, to pay his respectful compliments to him; and although the minister suffered from fever, although he was ill and bathed in sweat, he wanted to receive M. d'Artagnan, who was delighted with that honor, as will be seen by the conversation they had together.

CHAPTER XXXVIII

FRIENDLY ADVICE

FOUQUET had gone to bed, like a man who clings to life, and who saves as much as possible that slender fabric of existence, which the shocks and angles of this life so quickly wear out. D'Artagnan appeared at the door of this room, and was greeted by the surintendant with a very affable "good day."

"Good day, monseigneur," replied the musketeer; "how did you get through the journey?"

"Fairly well, thank you."

"And the fever?"

"Not well. I drink, as you see. I have scarcely arrived, and I have already levied a contribution of herb tea on Nantes."

"You should sleep first, monseigneur."

"*Corbleu!* my dear Monseigneur d'Artagnan, I should be very glad to sleep."

"Who keeps you?"

"Why, you, in the first place."

"I? Ah, monseigneur!"

"No doubt you do. Aren't you coming in the king's name in Nantes as it was in Paris?"

"For Heaven's sake, monseigneur," replied the captain, "leave the king alone! The day I shall come in the name of the king, for the purpose you mean, take my word for it, I will not leave you long in doubt. You will see me place my hand on my sword, according to the regulation, and you will hear me say at once, in my ceremonial voice:

" 'Monseigneur, in the name of the king, I arrest you!' "

"You promise me that frankness?" said the surintendant.

"Upon my honor! But we have not to come to that, believe me."

"What makes you think that, Monsieur d'Artagnan? For my part, I think quite the contrary."

"I have heard nothing of the kind," replied D'Artagnan.

"Eh, eh!" said Fouquet.

"Indeed, no. You are an agreeable man, in spite of your fever. The king ought not, cannot help loving you, from the bottom of his heart."

Fouquet's face showed doubt.

"But Monsieur Colbert?" he said, "does Monsieur Colbert love me also as much as you say?"

"I am not speaking of Monsieur Colbert," replied D'Artagnan. "He is an exceptional man, that Monsieur Colbert. He does not love you; that is very possible, but, *mordioux!* the squirrel can guard himself against the adder with very little trouble."

"Do you know that you are speaking to me quite as a friend," replied Fouquet; "and that, upon my life! I have never met with a man of your intelligence and your heart?"

"So you are telling me," replied D'Artagnan. "Why did you wait till today, to pay me such a compliment?"

"Blind as we are!" murmured Fouquet.

"Your voice is getting hoarse," said D'Artagnan; "drink, monseigneur, drink!"

And he offered him a cup of *tisane*, with the most friendly cordiality; Fouquet took it, and thanked him with a smile.

"Such things only happen to me," said the musketeer. "I have spent ten years under your very nose, while you were rolling around tons of gold. You were clearing an annual pension of four million; you never saw me, and you find out there is such a person in the world just at the moment you—"

"When I am about to fall," interrupted Fouquet. "That is true, my dear Monsieur d'Artagnan."

"I did not say so."

"But you think so, and that is the same thing. Well, if I fall, take my word as truth, I will not pass a single day without saying to myself, while striking my brow, 'Fool! fool!—stupid mortal! You had a Monsieur d'Artagnan under your eye and hand, and you did not employ him, you did not enrich him!' "

"You quite overwhelm me," said the captain. "I esteem you greatly."

"There exists another man, then, who does not think as Monsieur Colbert does?" said the surintendant.

"You are obsessed with Monsieur Colbert. He is worse than your fever."

"Oh, I have good cause," said Fouquet. "Judge for yourself."

And he related the details of the lighters' race and the hypocritical persecution of Colbert.

"Isn't this a clear sign of my ruin?"

D'Artagnan became serious.

"That is true," he said. "Yes, that has a bad smell, as Monsieur de Tréville used to say."

And he fixed upon M. Fouquet his intelligent and knowing look.

"Am I not clearly singled out, captain? Is not the king bringing me to Nantes to get me away from Paris, where I have so many friends, and to take possession of Belle-Isle?"

"Where Monsieur d'Herblay is," added D'Artagnan.

Fouquet raised his head.

"As for me, monseigneur," continued D'Artagnan, "I can assure you the king has said nothing to me against you."

"Indeed?"

"The king ordered me to set out for Nantes, it is true, and to say nothing about it to Monsieur de Gesvres."

"My friend."

"To Monsieur de Gesvres, yes, monseigneur," continued the musketeer, whose eyes did not cease to speak a language different from the language of his lips. "The king, moreover, ordered me to take a brigade of musketeers, which is apparently superfluous, as the country is very quiet.''

"A brigade!" said Fouquet, raising himself upon his elbow.

"Ninety-six horsemen, yes, monseigneur. The same number as were taken to arrest Messieurs de Chalais, De Cinq-Mars, and Montmorency.''

Fouquet pricked up his ears at these words, pronounced without apparent meaning.

"And besides?" he said.

"Well, nothing but insignificant orders; such as guard the castle, guard every lodging, allow none of Monsieur de Gesvres's guards to occupy a single post. Monsieur de Gesvres, your friend.''

"And for myself," cried Fouquet, "what orders do you have?''

"For you, monseigneur? Not a single word.''

"Monsieur d'Artagnan, the safety of my honor, and, perhaps, of my life, is at stake. You would not deceive me?''

"I? And to what end? Are you threatened? Only there really is an order with respect to carriages and boats . . .''

" 'An order?' ''

"Yes; but it cannot concern you—a simple police order.''

"What is it, captain—what is it?''

"To forbid all horses or boats to leave Nantes, without a pass, signed by the king.''

"Great God! but . . .''

D'Artagnan began to laugh.

"All that is not to be put into effect before the arrival of the king in Nantes. So you see plainly, monseigneur, the order does not concern you.''

Fouquet became thoughtful, and D'Artagnan pretended not to see his preoccupation.

"Since I am telling you the orders which have been given to me, I must love you, and I must be trying to prove to you that none of them are directed against you.''

"Of course!" said Fouquet, absent-mindedly.

"Let us recapitulate," said the captain, with an earnest look. "A special and strict guard of the castle, in which your lodging is to be—is it not?''

"Do you know that castle?''

"Ah, monseigneur, a true prison. The total absence of Monsieur de Gesvres, who has the honor of being one of your friends. The closing of the gates of the city, and of the river, without a pass; but only when the king shall have arrived. Do you know, Monsieur Fouquet, that if, instead of speaking to a man like you, who are one of the first in the kingdom, I were speaking to a troubled, uneasy conscience, I would compromise myself forever. What a fine opportunity for anyone who wished to be free! No police, no guards, no orders; the water free, the roads free, Monsieur d'Artagnan obliged to lend his horses, if required. All this ought to reassure you, Monsieur Fouquet, for the king would not have left me thus independent, if he had had any evil designs. In truth, Monsieur Fouquet, ask me whatever you like, I am at your service; and, in return, if you will consent to it, do me a favor, say hello to Aramis and Porthos for me, in case you sail for Belle-Isle, as you have a right to do, without changing your dress, immediately, in your robe—just as you are."

Saying these words, and with a profound bow, the musketeer, whose looks had lost none of their intelligent kindness, left the apartment. He had not reached the steps of the vestibule, when Fouquet, quite beside himself, hung on the bell rope, and shouted:

"My horses! my lighter!"

But nobody answered. The surintendant dressed himself with everything that came to hand.

"Gourville! Gourville!" he cried, while slipping his watch into his pocket. And the bell sounded again, while Fouquet repeated, "Gourville! Gourville!"

Gourville at length appeared, breathless and pale.

"Let us leave! Let us leave!" cried Fouquet, as soon as he saw him.

"It is too late!" said the surintendant's poor friend.

"Too late! Why?"

"Listen!"

And they heard the sounds of trumpets and drums in front of the castle.

"What does that mean, Gourville?"

"It is the king coming, monseigneur."

"The king?"

"The king, who has killed horses, and who is eight hours ahead of your calculation."

"We are lost!" whispered Fouquet. "Good D'Artagnan, all is over, you have spoken to me too late!"

The king, in fact, was entering the city, which soon resounded with the cannon from the ramparts, and one from a vessel which answered from the lower parts of the river. Fouquet's brow darkened; he called his servants and dressed in ceremonial costume. From his window, behind the curtains, he could see the eagerness of the people, and the movement of a large troop, which had followed the prince, without anyone's guessing how. The king was led to the castle with great pomp, and Fouquet saw him dismount under the portcullis, and speak something in the ear of D'Artagnan, who was holding his stirrup. D'Artagnan, when the king had passed under the arch, went toward the house Fouquet was in; but so slowly, and stopping so frequently to speak to his musketeers, drawn up as a hedge, that it looked as if he was counting the seconds, or the steps, before accomplishing his message. Fouquet opened the window to speak to him in the court.

"Ah!" cried D'Artagnan, on seeing him, "are you still there, monseigneur?"

And that word *still* proved to Fouquet how much information, and how much useful advice was contained in the first visit the musketeer had paid him. The surintendant sighed deeply.

"Good heavens! yes, monsieur," he replied. "The arrival of the king has interrupted me in the plans I had formed."

"Oh, then, you know that the king has arrived?"

"Yes, monsieur; I have seen him, and this time are you coming from him?"

"To inquire after you, monseigneur, and, if your health is not too bad, to beg you to have the kindness to come to the castle."

"Directly, Monsieur d'Artagnan, directly."

"Ah, well," said the captain, "now the king is here, there is no more walking for anybody—no more freedom; strict orders rule everybody now, you as well as me, me as well as you."

Fouquet heaved a last sigh, got into his carriage, so

great was his weakness, and went to the castle, escorted by D'Artagnan, whose politeness was now as terrifying as it had been before consoling and cheerful.

CHAPTER XXXIX

HOW KING LOUIS XIV PLAYED HIS LITTLE PART

As Fouquet was getting out of his carriage, to enter the Castle of Nantes, a common man went up to him with marks of the greatest respect, and gave him a letter. D'Artagnan tried to prevent this man from speaking to Fouquet, and pushed him away, but the message was given to the surintendant. Fouquet opened the letter and read it, and instantly a vague terror, which D'Artagnan understood easily, appeared on the face of the prime minister. Fouquet put the paper into the portfolio which he had under his arm, and went on toward the king's apartments. D'Artagnan, through the small windows made at every landing of the dungeon stairs, saw, as he went up behind Fouquet, the man who had delivered the note look around him on the square, and signal to several persons, who disappeared in the adjacent streets, after having themselves sent back the signals made by that man. Fouquet was kept waiting for a moment upon the terrace of which we have spoken, a terrace which led to the little corridor, at the end of which the king's cabinet had been set up. Here D'Artagnan passed on before the surintendant, whom, until that time, he had respectfully accompanied, and entered the royal cabinet.

"Well?" asked Louis XIV, who, on seeing him, threw onto the table covered with papers a large green cloth.

"The order is executed, sire."

"And Fouquet?"

"Monsieur le Surintendant is following me," said D'Artagnan.

"In ten minutes bring him in," said the king, dismissing D'Artagnan again with a gesture.

The latter went out, but had scarcely reached the cor-

ridor at the extremity of which Fouquet was waiting for
him, when he was recalled by the king's bell.

"Did he not appear astonished?" asked the king.

"Who, sire?"

"Fouquet," replied the king, without saying monsieur, a detail which confirmed the captain of the musketeer's suspicions.

"No, sire," he replied.

"Good!"

And a second time Louis dismissed D'Artagnan.

Fouquet had not left the terrace where he had been left
by his guide. He was reading over his note, which said:

> "Something is being plotted against you. Perhaps they
> will not dare to carry it out at the castle; it will be on
> your return home. The house is already surrounded by
> musketeers. Do not enter. A white horse is waiting for
> you behind the esplanade."

Fouquet had recognized the writing and the zeal of
Gourville. Not wanting that, if any harm happened to
himself, this paper should compromise a faithful friend,
the surintendant was busy tearing it into a thousand
pieces, spread about by the wind from the balustrade of
the terrace. D'Artagnan found him watching the flight of
the last scraps into space.

"Monsieur," he said, "the king is waiting for you."

Fouquet walked with a deliberate step into the little
corridor, where MM. de Brienne and Rose were at work,
while the Duc de St. Aignan, seated on a chair, also in
the corridor, appeared to be waiting for orders, with feverish impatience, his sword between his legs. It seemed
strange to Fouquet that MM. de Brienne, Rose, and De
St. Aignan, in general so attentive and obsequious,
should scarcely take the least notice, as he, the surintendant, went by. But how could he expect any other behavior from courtiers, he whom the king no longer called
anything but "Fouquet"? He raised his head, determined
to face everything bravely, and entered the king's apartment, where a little bell, which we already know, had
announced him to his majesty.

The king, without rising, nodded to him, and with interest:

"Well, how are you, Monsieur Fouquet?" he said.

"I have a high fever," replied the surintendant; "but I am at the king's service."

"That is well; the Estates assemble tomorrow; do you have a speech ready?"

Fouquet looked at the king with astonishment.

"I have not, sire," he replied; "but I will improvise one. I am too well acquainted with affairs to feel any embarrassment. I have only one question to ask; will your majesty permit me?"

"Certainly, ask it."

"Why has your majesty not done his prime minister the honor of giving him notice of this in Paris?"

"You were ill; I did not want to tire you."

"Never did a labor—never did an explanation tire me, sire; and, since the moment has come for me to ask for an explanation of my king . . ."

"Oh, Monsieur Fouquet! an explanation about what?"

"About your majesty's intentions with respect to me."

The king blushed.

"I have been slandered," continued Fouquet warmly, "and I feel called upon to challenge the justice of the king to make inquiries."

"You say all this to me very uselessly, Monsieur Fouquet; I know what I know."

"Your majesty can only know things as they have been told to you; and, I, on my part, have said nothing to you, while others have spoken many and many times . . ."

"What do you mean?" said the king, impatient to put an end to this embarrassing conversation.

"I will go straight to the fact, sire; and I accuse a man of having injured me in your majesty's opinion."

"Nobody has injured you, Monsieur Fouquet."

"That reply proves to me, sire, that I am right."

"Monsieur Fouquet, I do not like people to accuse."

"Not when one is accused?"

"We have already spoken too much about this affair."

"Doesn't your majesty want me to justify myself?"

"I repeat that I do not accuse you."

Fouquet, with a half-bow, made a step backward.

"It is certain," he thought, "that he has made up his mind. He alone who cannot go back can be so stubborn. Not to see the danger now would be to be blind indeed;

not to shun it would be stupid." He went on, aloud:
"Did your majesty send for me for any business?"

"No, Monsieur Fouquet, but for some advice I have
to give you."

"I am waiting respectfully, sire."

"Rest, Monsieur Fouquet; do not throw away your
strength; the session of the Estates will be short, and
when my secretaries have closed it I do not want business
to be mentioned in France for a fortnight."

"Doesn't the king have anything to say to me about
this assembly of the Estates?"

"No, Monsieur Fouquet."

"Not to me, the surintendant of finances?"

"Rest, I beg you; that is all I have to say to you."

Fouquet bit his lips and hung down his head. He was
obviously worried. The king became worried too.

"Are you angry at having to rest, Monsieur Fouquet?"
he said.

"Yes, sire; I am not used to rest."

"But you are ill; you must take care of yourself."

"Was your majesty speaking just now of a speech to
be given tomorrow?"

His majesty made no reply; this brusque question embarrassed him. Fouquet felt the weight of this hesitation.
He thought he could read a danger in the eyes of the
young prince, which increased his mistrust.

"If I appear frightened, I am lost," he thought.

The king, on his part, was only uneasy at the mistrust
of Fouquet.

"Does he suspect anything?" he murmured.

"If his first word is severe," again thought Fouquet;
"if he becomes angry, or pretends to be angry for the
sake of a pretext, how shall I extricate myself? Let us
smooth matters a little. Gourville was right."

"Sire," he said suddenly, "since the goodness of the
king watches over my health to the point of excusing me
from all work, may I not be allowed to be absent from
tomorrow's council? I could spend the day in bed, and
would ask the king to lend me his physician, that we may
try to find a remedy for this cursed fever."

"So be it, Monsieur Fouquet, as you wish; you shall
have a holiday tomorrow, you shall have the physician,
and shall be restored to health."

"Thanks!" said Fouquet, bowing. Then, "Will I have the happiness of taking your majesty to my residence of Belle-Isle?"

And he looked Louis full in the face, to judge the effect of such a proposal. The king blushed again.

"Do you know," he replied, trying to smile, "that you have just said, 'My residence of Belle-Isle'?"

"Yes, sire."

"Well, don't you remember," continued the king, in the same cheerful tone, "that you gave me Belle-Isle?"

"That is true again, sire. Only as you have not taken it, you will come with me and take possession of it."

"I mean to do so."

"That was, besides, your majesty's intention as well as mine; and I cannot express to your majesty how happy and proud I have been at seeing all the king's military household come from Paris for this event."

The king stammered out that he had not brought the musketeers only for that reason.

"Oh, I am convinced of that," said Fouquet warmly; "your majesty knows very well that you have nothing to do but to come alone with a cane in your hand, to bring to the ground all the fortifications of Belle-Isle."

"*Peste!*" cried the king, "I do not want those fine fortifications, which cost so much to erect, to fall. No; let them stand against the Dutch and English. You would not guess what I want to see at Belle-Isle, Monsieur Fouquet; it is the pretty peasant women, who dance so well, and are so attractive with their scarlet petticoats. Your pretty tenants have been highly praised, Monsieur le Surintendant; well, let me see them."

"Whenever your majesty pleases."

"Have you any means of transport? It would be to-morrow, if you like."

The surintendant felt this blow, which was not clever, and replied:

"No, sire; I was unaware of your majesty's wish; above all, I was unaware of your hurry to see Belle-Isle, and I am not at all ready."

"Do you have a boat of your own, nevertheless?"

"I have five; but they are all in the port, or at Paimboeuf; and to join them, or bring them here, we need at least twenty-four hours. Have I any need to send a courier? Must I do so?''

"Wait a little; put an end to the fever—wait until tomorrow.''

"That is true; who knows if by tomorrow we may not have a hundred other ideas?'' replied Fouquet, now perfectly convinced, and very pale.

The king gave a start, and stretched his hand out toward his little bell, but Fouquet prevented his ringing.

"Sire," said he, "I have a favor—I am trembling with cold. If I remain a moment longer I shall most likely faint. I request your majesty's permission to go and hide beneath the blankets.''

"Indeed, you are all in a shiver; it is painful to see! Come, Monsieur Fouquet, be gone! I will send to inquire after you.''

"Your majesty overwhelms me with kindness. In an hour I shall be better.''

"I will call someone to accompany you,'' said the king.

"As you please, sire; I would gladly take the arm of anyone.''

"Monsieur D'Artagnan!'' cried the king, ringing his little bell.

"Oh, sire," interrupted Fouquet, laughing in such a manner as made the prince feel cold, "are you giving me the captain of your musketeers to take me to my lodgings? A very equivocal kind of honor, that, sire! A simple footman, I beg.''

"And why, Monsieur Fouquet? Monsieur D'Artagnan accompanies me often, and well.''

"Yes, but when he accompanies you, sire, it is to obey you; while me . . .''

"Go on.''

"If I am obliged to return home with the leader of the musketeers, it would be said everywhere you are having me arrested.''

"Arrested!'' replied the king, who became paler than Fouquet himself, "arrested! Oh!''

"And why would they not say so?'' continued Fouquet, still laughing, "and I would bet there would be people wicked enough to laugh at it.''

This sally disconcerted the monarch. Fouquet was

skillful enough, or fortunate enough, to make Louis XIV draw back before the appearance of the fact he contemplated. M. D'Artagnan, when he appeared, received an order to choose a musketeer to accompany the surintendant.

"Quite unnecessary," said the latter; "sword for sword; I prefer Gourville, who is waiting for me below. But that will not prevent me from enjoying the company of Monsieur D'Artagnan. I am glad he will see Belle-Isle, he who is so good a judge of fortifications."

D'Artagnan bowed, not understanding what was going on. Fouquet bowed again, and left the apartment, affecting all the slowness of a man who is taking a walk. Once out of the castle, "I am saved!" he said. "Oh, yes, disloyal king; you shall see Belle-Isle, but it shall be when I am no longer there."

He disappeared, leaving D'Artagnan with the king.

"Captain," said the king, "you will follow Monsieur Fouquet at a distance of a hundred paces."

"Yes, sire."

"He is going home again. You will go with him."

"Yes, sire."

"You will arrest him in my name, and will shut him up in a carriage."

"In a carriage? Fine, sire."

"In such a fashion that he may not, on the road, either converse with anyone or throw notes to people he may meet."

"That will be rather difficult, sire."

"Not at all."

"Pardon me, sire, I cannot stifle Monsieur Fouquet, and if he asks for liberty to breathe, I cannot prevent him by shutting up windows and blinds. He will throw out of the doors all the cries and notes possible."

"We have foreseen this, Monsieur D'Artagnan; a carriage with a trellis will prevent both the difficulties you point out."

"A carriage with an iron trellis!" cried D'Artagnan; "but a carriage with an iron trellis is not made in half an hour, and your majesty is ordering me to go immediately to Monsieur Fouquet's."

"Therefore, the carriage in question is already made."

"That is quite a different thing," said the captain; "if

the carriage is already made, very well, then, we have only to get it going.''

''It is ready, with the horses harnessed to it.''

''Ah!''

''And the coachman, with the outriders, is waiting in the lower court of the castle.''

D'Artagnan bowed.

''I only have to ask your majesty where I shall take Monsieur Fouquet.''

''To the Castle of Angers, first.''

''Very well, sire.''

''Afterward we will see.''

''Yes, sire.''

''Monsieur d'Artagnan, one last word; you have noticed that to arrest Monsieur Fouquet, I am not using my guards, on which account Monsieur de Gesvres will be furious.''

''Your majesty is not using your guards,'' said the captain, a little humiliated, ''because you mistrust Monsieur de Gesvres, that is all.''

''That is to say, monsieur, that I have more confidence in you.''

''I know that very well, sire; and it is of no use to make so much of it.''

''It is only for the sake of arriving at this, monsieur, that if, from this moment, it should happen that by any chance, any chance whatever, Monsieur Fouquet should escape—such things have happened, monsieur . . .''

''Oh! very often, sire; but with others, not with me.''

''And why not with you?''

''Because I, sire, have, for a moment, wished to save Monsieur Fouquet.''

The king gave a start.

''Because,'' continued the captain, ''I had then a right to do so, having guessed your majesty's plan, without your having spoken to me of it, and because I found Monsieur Fouquet interesting. Then, I was free to show my interest in this man.''

''In truth, monsieur, you do not reassure me with regard to your services.''

''If I had saved him, then, I was perfectly innocent. I will say more, I would have done well, for Monsieur Fouquet is not a bad man. But he was not willing; his destiny prevailed; he let the hour of liberty slip by. So much the worse! Now I have orders, I will obey those orders, and you may consider Monsieur Fouquet as good as arrested. Monsieur Fouquet is at the castle of Angers.''

''Oh! you have not got him yet, captain.''

''That concerns me; everyone to his trade, sire; only, once more, do think. Do you seriously give me orders to arrest Monsieur Fouquet, sire?''

''Yes, a thousand times, yes!''

''Write it, then.''

''Here is the letter.''

D'Artagnan read it, bowed to the king, and left the room. From the height of the terrace he saw Gourville, who was going by cheerfully toward the lodgings of M. Fouquet.

CHAPTER XL

THE WHITE HORSE AND THE BLACK HORSE

''THAT is rather surprising,'' said D'Artagnan, ''Gourville running about the streets so happily, when he is almost certain that Monsieur Fouquet is in danger; when it is almost equally certain that it was Gourville who warned Monsieur Fouquet just now by the note which was torn into a thousand pieces upon the terrace, and given to the winds by Monsieur le Surintendant. Gourville is rubbing his hands; that is because he has done something clever. Where is Monsieur Gourville coming from? Gourville is coming from the Rue aux Herbes. Where does the Rue aux Herbes lead?''

And D'Artagnan followed, along the tops of the houses of Nantes dominated by the castle, the line drawn by the streets, as he would have done upon a topographical map; only, instead of the dead, flat paper, the living chart rose in relief with the cries, the movements, and the shadows of men and things. Beyond the city, the great green plains stretched out along the Loire, and appeared to run toward the red horizon, which was streaked by the blue of the

waters and the dark green of the marshes. Immediately
outside the gates of Nantes two white roads branched off
like the separated fingers of a gigantic hand. D'Artagnan, who had taken in all the panorama at a glance by
crossing the terrace, was led by the line of the Rue aux
Herbes to the end of one of those roads which started
under the gates of Nantes. One step more, and he was
about to go down the stairs, take his trellised carriage,
and go toward M. Fouquet's. But chance decreed that at
the moment of descending into the staircase, he was attracted by a moving point which was gaining ground on
that road.

"What is that?" said the musketeer to himself; "a
horse galloping—a runaway horse, no doubt. What a pace
he is going at!"

The moving point came off the road, and entered into
the fields.

"A white horse," the captain went on, who had just
seen the color stand out luminously against the dark
ground, "and he is mounted; it must be some boy whose
horse is thirsty and is taking him to the drinking place."

These reflections, rapid as lightning, simultaneous with
visual perception, D'Artagnan had already forgotten them
when he went down the first steps of the staircase. Some
bits of paper were scattered over the stairs, and shone
out white against the black stones.

"Here are some of the fragments of the note torn by
Monsieur Fouquet," said the captain to himself. "Poor
man! he has given his secret to the wind; the wind doesn't
want it anymore, and brings it back to the king. Fouquet,
you are out of luck! The game is not a fair one, fortune
is against you. The star of Louis XIV obscures yours; the
adder is stronger and more cunning than the squirrel."

D'Artagnan picked up one of these pieces of paper as
he went down.

"Gourville's pretty little hand!" he cried, while examining one of the fragments of the note. "I was not
mistaken." And he read the word "horse." "Stop!" he
said, and he examined another, upon which no letter was
traced. Upon a third he read the word "white"; "White
horse," he repeated, like a child that is spelling. "Ah,
mordioux!" he cried, "a white horse!" And, like that
grain of powder which, burning, expands a hundredfold,

D'Artagnan, full of ideas and suspicions, rapidly climbed back toward the terrace. The white horse was still galloping in the direction of the Loire, at the extremity of which, melted into the vapors of the water, a little sail was appearing, balancing, like an atom.

"Oh!" cried the musketeer, "only a man who is running away would go at that pace across plowed lands; only a Fouquet, a financier, would ride thus in broad daylight upon a white horse; only the lord of Belle-Isle would escape toward the sea while there are such thick forests on land; and only a D'Artagnan in the world would catch Monsieur Fouquet, who has half an hour's start, and who will have reached his boat within an hour."

This being said, the musketeer gave orders that the carriage with the iron trellis should be taken immediately to a thicket situated just outside the city. He selected his best horse, jumped upon his back, galloped along the Rue aux Herbes, taking, not the road Fouquet had taken, but the bank itself of the Loire, certain that he would gain ten minutes, and, at the intersection of the two lines, come up with the fugitive, who would have no suspicion of being pursued in that direction. In the rapidity of the pursuit, and with the impatience of the persecutor getting excited in the hunt as in war, D'Artagnan, so mild, so kind toward Fouquet, was surprised to find himself become ferocious and almost murderous. For a long time he galloped without catching sight of the white horse. His fury changed to rage; he had doubts—he suspected that Fouquet had disappeared in some underground road, or that he had changed the white horse for one of those famous black ones, as swift as the wind, which D'Artagnan, at St. Mandé, had so frequently admired, and envied.

At these moments, when the wind cut his eyes so as to make the tears spring from them, when the saddle had become burning hot, when the galled and spurred horse reared with pain, and threw behind him a shower of dust and stones, D'Artagnan, raising himself in his stirrups, and seeing nothing on the waters—nothing beneath the trees, looked up into the air like a madman. He was losing his mind. In his frenzy he dreamed of aerial ways—the discovery of the following century; he remembered

Daedalus and his vast wings, which had saved him from the prisons of Crete. A hoarse sigh broke from his lips, as he repeated, consumed by the fear of ridicule:

"I, I, duped by a Gourville! I! They will say I am growing old, they will say I have received a million to let Fouquet escape!"

And he again dug his spurs into the sides of his horse; he had ridden astonishingly fast. Suddenly, at the end of some open field, behind the hedges, he saw a white form which showed itself, disappeared, and at last remained distinctly visible upon a rising ground. D'Artagnan's heart leaped with joy. He wiped the streaming sweat from his brow, relaxed the tension of his knees, at which the horse breathed more freely, and, gathering up his reins, curbed the speed of the vigorous animal, his accomplice in this manhunt. He had then time to study the direction of the road, and his position with regard to Fouquet. The surintendant had completely winded his horse by crossing the soft grounds. He felt the necessity of gaining a more firm footing, and turned toward the road by the shortest line. As for D'Artagnan, he had nothing to do but to ride straight beneath the cliff, which concealed him from the eyes of his enemy; so that he would cut him off on the road when he came up with him. Then the real race would begin—then the struggle would be in earnest.

D'Artagnan gave his horse good breathing time. He observed that the surintendant had relaxed into a trot, thus he was also letting his horse get its wind. But both of them were too much pressed for time to allow them to continue long at that pace. The white horse sprang off like an arrow the moment his feet touched firm ground. D'Artagnan dropped his hand, and his black horse broke into a gallop. Both followed the same route; the quadruple echoes of the race were merged. Fouquet had not yet seen D'Artagnan. But on coming out from under the cliff, a single echo struck the air, it was that of the steps of D'Artagnan's horse, which was rumbling like thunder. Fouquet turned around, and saw behind him, within a hundred paces, his enemy bent over the neck of his horse. There could be no doubt—the shining baldrick, the red cassock—it was a musketeer. Fouquet slackened his hand, and the white horse put twenty feet more between his adversary and himself.

"Really," thought D'Artagnan, becoming very anxious, "that is not a common horse Monsieur Fouquet is on, let us see!"

And he attentively examined with his infallible eye the shape and capabilities of the courser. Round, full quarters, a thin, long tail, large hocks, thin legs, as dry as bars of steel, hoofs hard as marble. He spurred his own, but the distance between the two remained the same. D'Artagnan listened attentively; not a breath of the horse reached him, and yet he seemed to cut the air. The black horse, on the contrary, was beginning to gasp.

"I must overtake him, if I kill my horse," thought the musketeer; and he began to saw the mouth of the poor animal, while he buried his spurs in his sides. The maddened horse gained one hundred feet and came up within a pistol shot of Fouquet.

"Courage!" said the musketeer to himself, "courage! The white horse will perhaps grow weaker, and if the horse does not fall, the master will end up falling."

But horse and rider remained upright together and gaining ground by degrees. D'Artagnan uttered a wild cry, which made Fouquet turn around, and added speed to the white horse.

"A great horse! a mad rider!" growled the captain. "*Stop! mordioux!* Monsieur Fouquet, stop, in the king's name!"

Fouquet made no reply.

"Do you hear me?" shouted D'Artagnan, whose horse had just stumbled.

"*Pardieu!*" replied Fouquet laconically, and rode on faster.

D'Artagnan was nearly mad; the blood rushed boiling to his temples and his eyes.

"In the king's name," he cried, again, "stop, or I will bring you down with a pistol shot!"

"Do!" replied Fouquet, without relaxing his speed.

D'Artagnan seized a pistol and cocked it, hoping that the noise of the spring would stop his enemy.

"You have pistols too," he said; "turn and defend yourself."

Fouquet did turn around at the noise, and, looking

D'Artagnan full in the face opened with his right hand the coat which concealed his body, but he did not even touch his holsters. There were not more than twenty paces between the two.

"*Mordioux!*" said D'Artagnan, "I will not murder you; if you will not fire upon me, surrender. What is a prison?"

"I would rather die!" replied Fouquet; "I shall suffer less."

D'Artagnan, drunk with despair, hurled his pistol to the ground.

"I will take you alive!" he said; and by a prodigy of skill, of which this incomparable horseman alone was capable, he threw his horse forward to within ten paces of the white horse; already his hand was stretched out to seize his prey.

"Kill me! kill me!" cried Fouquet; "it is more humane."

"No, alive, alive!" whispered the captain.

At this moment his horse made a false step for the second time, and Fouquet's again took the lead. It was an incredible spectacle, this race between two horses which were only kept alive by the will of their riders. It might be said that D'Artagnan rode, carrying his horse along between his knees. To the furious gallop had succeeded the fast trot, and that had sunk to what might be scarcely called a trot at all. And the chase appeared equally warm in the two exhausted athletes. D'Artagnan, in despair, seized his second pistol, and cocked it.

"At your horse! not at you!" he cried to Fouquet.

And he fired. The animal was hit in the quarters; he sprang furiously, and reared up. At that moment D'Artagnan's horse fell dead.

"I am dishonored!" thought the musketeer; "I am a miserable wretch! For pity's sake, Monsieur Fouquet, throw me one of your pistols, that I may blow out my brains!"

But Fouquet rode on.

"For mercy's sake! for mercy's sake!" cried D'Artagnan, "what you will not do at this moment, I will do within an hour; but here, upon this road, I would die bravely, I would die esteemed; do me that service, Monsieur Fouquet!"

M. Fouquet made no reply, but continued to trot on. D'Artagnan began to run after his enemy. Successively he threw off his hat, his coat, which were hampering him, and then the sheath of his sword, which was getting between his legs as he ran. The sword in his hand even became too heavy, and he threw it after the sheath. The white horse began to rattle in his throat; D'Artagnan was catching up with him. From a trot the exhausted animal sank to a staggering walk, the foam from his mouth was mixed with blood. D'Artagnan made a desperate effort, sprang toward Fouquet, and seized him by the leg, saying, in a broken, breathless voice:

"I arrest you in the king's name! Blow my brains out, if you like; we have both done our duty."

Fouquet hurled far from him, into the river, the two pistols which D'Artagnan might have seized, and dismounting from his horse:

"I am your prisoner, monsieur," he said. "Will you take my arm, for I see you are ready to faint?"

"Thanks!" whispered D'Artagnan, who, in fact, felt the earth moving from under his feet, and the sky melting away over his head; and he rolled upon the sand, without breath or strength. Fouquet hastened to the brink of the river, dipped some water in his hat, with which he bathed the temples of the musketeer, and introduced a few drops between his lips. D'Artagnan raised himself up, looking around with a distraught eye. He saw Fouquet on his knees, with his wet hat in his hand, smiling upon him with ineffable sweetness.

"You are not gone, then?" he cried. "Oh, monsieur, the true king of royalty, in heart, in soul, is not Louis of the Louvre, or Philippe of Ste. Marguerite; it is you, the proscribed, the condemned!"

"I, who this day am ruined by a single error, Monsieur d'Artagnan."

"What, in the name of heaven, is that?"

"I should have had you for a friend. But how shall we return to Nantes? We are very far from it."

"That is true," said D'Artagnan, gloomy and pensive.

"The white horse will recover, perhaps; he is a good horse. Mount it, Monsieur d'Artagnan; I will walk till you have rested a little."

"Poor beast! and wounded, too!" said the musketeer.

"He will go, I tell you; I know him; but we can do better still; let us both ride him."

"We can try," said the captain.

But they had scarcely charged the animal with this double load, than he began to stagger, then, with a great effort, walked a few minutes, then staggered again, and sank down dead by the side of the black horse, which he had just managed to come up to.

"We will go on foot, destiny wills it so, the walk will be pleasant," said Fouquet, passing his arm through that of D'Artagnan.

"*Mordioux!*" cried the latter, with a fixed eye, a contracted brow, and a swelling heart. "A disgraceful day!"

They walked slowly the four leagues which separated them from the wood behind which the carriage with the escort was expecting them. When Fouquet saw that sinister machine he said to D'Artagnan, who was looking down as if ashamed of Louis XIV:

"This idea is not that of a good man, Captain d'Artagnan; it is not yours. What are these gratings for?" said he.

"To prevent you from throwing out letters."

"Clever!"

"But you can speak, if you cannot write," said D'Artagnan.

"Can I speak to you?"

"Why, certainly, if you wish to do so."

Fouquet thought for a moment, then, looking the captain full in the face:

"One single word," he said; "will you remember it?"

"I will not forget it."

"Will you say it to whom I wish?"

"I will."

"St. Mandé," articulated Fouquet, in a low voice.

"Well, and for whom?"

"For Madame de Bellière or Pélisson."

"It shall be done."

The carriage crossed Nantes, and took the road to Angers.

CHAPTER XLI

IN WHICH THE SQUIRREL FALLS—IN WHICH THE ADDER FLIES

IT was two o'clock in the afternoon. The king, full of impatience, went to his cabinet on the terrace, and kept opening the door of the corridor, to see what his secretaries were doing. M. Colbert, seated in the same place M. de St. Aignan had so long occupied in the morning, was chatting, in a low voice, with M. de Brienne. The king opened the door suddenly, and addressing them:

"What are you saying?" he asked.

"We were speaking of the first session of the Estates," said M. de Brienne, rising.

"Very well," replied the king, and returned to his room.

Five minutes later, the bell recalled Rose, whose hour it was.

"Have you finished your copies?" asked the king.

"Not yet, sire."

"See, then, if Monsieur D'Artagnan is back."

"Not yet, sire."

"It is very strange," whispered the king. "Call Monsieur Colbert."

Colbert entered; he had been expecting this moment all morning.

"Monsieur Colbert," said the king, very sharply; "we should really know what has become of Monsieur D'Artagnan."

Colbert, in his calm voice, replied:

"Where would your majesty want him to be sought for?"

"Eh! monsieur, don't you know where I have sent him?" replied Louis harshly.

"Your majesty has not told me."

"Monsieur, there are things that are to be guessed; and you, above all others, do guess them."

"I might have been able to imagine, sire; but I do not presume to guess right."

Colbert had not finished these words when a much rougher voice than that of the king interrupted the interesting conversation thus begun between the monarch and his clerk.

"D'Artagnan!" cried the king, with obvious joy.

D'Artagnan, pale and in evidently bad humor, cried to the king, as he entered:

"Sire, is it your majesty who has given orders to my musketeers?"

"What orders?" said the king.

"About Monsieur Fouquet's house."

"None," replied Louis.

"I was not mistaken then," said D'Artagnan, biting his mustache; "it was monsieur here"; and he pointed to Colbert.

"What orders? Let me know," said the king.

"Orders to turn a house inside out, to beat Monsieur Fouquet's servants, to force the drawers, to sack a peaceful house! *Mordioux!* these are savage orders!"

"Monsieur!" said Colbert, becoming pale.

"Monsieur," interrupted D'Artagnan, "the king alone, understand, the king alone has a right to command my musketeers; but, as to you, I forbid you to do it, and I tell you so before his majesty; gentlemen who wear swords are not fellows with pens behind their ears!"

"D'Artagnan! D'Artagnan!" whispered the king.

"It is humiliating!" continued the musketeer. "My soldiers are disgraced. I do not command *ruffians,* thank you, nor clerks of the intendance, *mordioux!*"

"Well, but what is all this about?" said the king, with authority.

"About this, sire: monsieur—monsieur, who could not guess your majesty's orders, and consequently could not know I was gone to arrest Monsieur Fouquet; monsieur, who had the iron cage built for his patron of yesterday—has sent Monsieur de Roncherat to Monsieur Fouquet's, and, under pretense of taking away the surintendant's papers, they have taken away the furniture. My musketeers have been placed around the house all morning; such were my orders. Why did anyone presume to order them to enter? Why, by forcing them to be present at this looting, have they been made accomplices in it? *Mordioux!* we serve the king, we do, but we do not serve Monsieur Colbert!''

''Monsieur D'Artagnan,'' said the king sternly, ''take care; it is not in my presence that such explanations, and made in this tone, should take place.''

''I have acted for the good of the king,'' said Colbert, in a faltering voice; ''it is hard to be treated by one of your majesty's officers in such a manner, and that without vengeance, on account of the respect I owe the king.''

''The respect you owe the king!'' cried D'Artagnan, whose eyes flashed fire, ''consists, in the first place, in making his authority respected, and making his person beloved. Every agent of a power without control represents that power, and when people curse the hand which strikes them, it is the royal hand that God is blaming, do you hear? Must a soldier, hardened by forty years of wounds and blood, give you this lesson, monsieur? Must mercy be on my side, and ferocity on yours? You had innocents arrested, bound, and imprisoned!''

''The accomplices, perhaps, of Monsieur Fouquet,'' said Colbert.

''Who tells you that Monsieur Fouquet has accomplices, or even that he is guilty? The king alone knows it, his justice is not blind! When he shall say, 'Arrest and imprison such and such people,' then he shall be obeyed. Do not talk to me, then, anymore of the respect you owe the king, and be careful of your words, that they do not contain any menace; for the king will not let those who serve him well be threatened by those who serve him badly; and if in case I should have, which God forbid, a master so ungrateful, I would make myself respected.''

Having said this, D'Artagnan stood haughtily in the king's cabinet, his eye flashing, his hand on his sword, his lips trembling, affecting much more anger than he really felt. Colbert, humiliated and devoured with rage, bowed to the king as if to ask his permission to leave the room. The king, crossed in his pride and in his curiosity, did not know yet what course to take. D'Artagnan saw him hesitate. To remain longer would have been an error; it was necessary to triumph over Colbert, and the only means was to sting the king so near and so strongly to the quick that his majesty would have no other means of extricating himself but choosing between the two antagonists. D'Artagnan then bowed as Colbert had done; but the king, who, in preference to everything else was anxious to have all the exact details of the arrest of the surintendant of finances from him who had made him tremble for a moment—the king, perceiving that the ill humor of D'Artagnan would put off for a quarter of an hour, at least, the details he was burning to know—Louis, we say, forgot Colbert, who had nothing new to tell him, and recalled his captain of the musketeers.

"In the first place," he said, "let me see the result of your errand, monsieur; you may rest afterward."

D'Artagnan, who was just going through the door, stopped at the voice of the king, retraced his steps, and Colbert was forced to leave. His face assumed almost a purple line, his black and threatening eyes shone with a dark fire beneath their thick brows; he stepped out, bowed before the king, half-drew himself up in passing D'Artagnan, and went away with death in his heart. D'Artagnan, being left alone with the king, softened immediately, and adjusting his features:

"Sire," he said, "you are a young king. It is by the dawn that people judge whether the day will be fine or dull. How, sire, will the people, whom the hand of God has placed under your law, foresee your reign, if, between them and you, you allow angry and violent ministers to act? But let us speak of me, sire, let us leave a discussion that may appear idle, and perhaps inconvenient to you. Let us speak of me. I have arrested Monsieur Fouquet."

"You took plenty of time about it," said the king sharply.

D'Artagnan looked at the king.

"I see that I have expressed myself badly. Did I tell your majesty that I had arrested Monsieur Fouquet?"

"You did; and what then?"

"Well, I ought to have told your majesty that Monsieur Fouquet had arrested me; that would have been fairer. I reestablish the truth, then; I have been arrested by Monsieur Fouquet."

It was now Louis XIV's turn to be surprised.

D'Artagnan, with his quick glance, appreciated what was going on in the heart of his master. He did not allow him time to ask any question. He related, with that poetry, that picturesqueness, which perhaps he alone possessed at that period, the escape of Fouquet, the pursuit, the furious race, and, at last the inimitable generosity of the surintendant, who might have fled ten times over, who might have killed the adversary attached to his pursuit, and who had preferred imprisonment, and perhaps worse, to the humiliation of him who wanted to rob him of his freedom. As the tale advanced, the king became agitated, devouring the narrator's words, and knocking his fingernails against one another.

"It results from this, then, sire, in my eyes, at least, that the man who conducts himself thus is a gallant man, and cannot be an enemy to the king. That is my opinion, and I repeat it to your majesty. I know what the king will say to me, and I bow to it: reasons of state. So be it. That, in my eyes, is very respectable. But I am a soldier; I have received my orders, my orders are carried out—very unwillingly on my part, it is true, but they are carried out. I say no more."

"Where is Monsieur Fouquet at this moment?" asked Louis, after a short silence.

"Monsieur Fouquet, sire," replied D'Artagnan, "is in the iron cage that Monsieur Colbert had prepared for him, and is going, as fast as four vigorous horses can take him, toward Angers."

"Why did you leave him on the road?"

"Because your majesty did not tell me to go to Angers. The proof, the best proof of what I advance, is that the king was looking for me just now. And then I have another reason."

"What is that?"

"While I was with him, poor Monsieur Fouquet would never attempt to escape."

"Well!" cried the king, with stupefaction.

"Your majesty ought to understand, and does understand, certainly, that my warmest wish is to know that Monsieur Fouquet is free. I have given him one of my brigadiers, the most stupid I could find among my musketeers, in order that the prisoner might have a chance of escaping."

"Are you mad, Monsieur D'Artagnan?" cried the king, crossing his arms on his chest. "Do people speak such enormities, even when they have the misfortune to think them?''

"Ah! sire, you cannot expect that I should be the enemy of Monsieur Fouquet, after what he has just done for you and me. No, no; if you want him to remain under your locks and bolts, never have me watch him; however closely wired might be the cage, the bird would, in the end, fly away.''

"I am surprised," said the king, in a stern tone, "you have not followed the fortunes of the one Monsieur Fouquet wanted to place upon my throne. You had in him all you want—affection and gratitude. In my service, monsieur, you only find a master.''

"If Monsieur Fouquet had not gone to seek you in the Bastille, sire," replied D'Artagnan, with a deeply impressive manner, "one single man would have gone there, and that man would have been me; you know that, sire.''

The king was brought to a pause. To that speech of his captain of the musketeers, so frankly spoken and so true, the king had nothing to object. On hearing D'Artagnan, Louis remembered the D'Artagnan of former times; him who, at the Palais Royal, held himself concealed behind the curtains of his bed, when the people of Paris, led on by Cardinal de Retz, came to assure themselves of the presence of the king; the D'Artagnan whom he saluted with his hand at the door of his carriage, when going to Notre Dame on his return to Paris; the soldier who had left his service at Blois; the lieutenant whom he had recalled near his person when Mazarin's death restored him his power; the man he had always found loyal, courageous, and devoted. Louis went toward the door and called Colbert. Colbert had not left the corridor where the secretaries were at work. Colbert appeared.

"Colbert, have you made a perquisition at the house of Monsieur Fouquet?"

"Yes, sire.''

"What has it produced?"

"Monsieur de Roncherat, who was sent with your majesty's musketeers, has handed me some papers,'' replied Colbert.

"I will look at them. Give me your hand.''

"My hand, sire!''

"Yes, that I may place it in that of Monsieur D'Artagnan. In fact, Monsieur D'Artagnan,'' he added, with a smile, turning toward the soldier, who, at the sight of the clerk, had resumed his haughty attitude, ''you do not know this man; make his acquaintance.'' And he pointed to Colbert, ''He is a mediocre servant in subaltern positions, but he will be a great man if I raise him to the first rank.''

''Sire!'' stammered Colbert, overwhelmed with pleasure and fear.

''I have understood why,'' whispered D'Artagnan, in the king's ear; ''was he jealous?''

''Precisely, and his jealousy was binding his wings.''

''From now on he will be a winged serpent,'' grumbled the musketeer, with a trace of hatred against his recent adversary.

But Colbert, approaching him, offered to his eyes a face so different from that which he had been accustomed to see; he appeared so good, so mild, so easy; his eyes took the expression of such a noble intelligence that D'Artagnan, a connoisseur of faces, was moved, and almost changed in his convictions. Colbert shook his hand.

''What the king has just told you, monsieur, proves how well his majesty is acquainted with men. The desperate opposition I have displayed, up to this day, against abuses and not against men, proves that I had in mind to prepare for my king a great reign, for my country a great blessing. I have many ideas, Monsieur d'Artagnan; you will see them bloom in the sun of public peace; and if I have not the certainty and good fortune to conquer the friendship of honest men, I am at least certain, monsieur, that I shall obtain their esteem. For their admiration, monsieur, I would give my life.''

This change, this sudden elevation, this mute approbation of the king, gave the musketeer matter for much reflection. He bowed civilly to Colbert, who did not take his eyes off him. The king, when he saw they were reconciled, dismissed them. They left the room together. As soon as they were out of the cabinet the new minister, stopping the captain, said:

''Is it possible, Monsieur D'Artagnan, that with such an eye as yours you have not, at the first glance, at the first inspection, discovered what sort of man I am?''

''Monsieur Colbert,'' replied the musketeer, ''the ray

of the sun which we have in our eyes prevents us from
seeing the most ardent flames. The man in power radi-
ates, you know; and since you are there, why should you
continue to persecute him who has just fallen into disgrace, and fallen from such a height?''

''I, monsieur?'' said Colbert. ''Oh, monsieur, I would
never persecute him! I wanted to administer the finances,
and to administer them alone, because I am ambitious,
and, above all, because I have the most entire confidence
in my own merit; because I know that all the gold of this
country will fall beneath my eyes, and I love to look at
the king's gold; because, if I live thirty years, in thirty
years not a *denier* of it will remain in my hands; because,
with that gold I will build granaries, buildings, cities,
and ports; because I will create a navy, will equip ships
which shall bear the name of France to the most distant
nations; because I will create libraries and academies;
because I will make France the first country in the world,
and the richest. These are the motives for my grudge
against Monsieur Fouquet, who prevented my acting. And
then, when I shall be great and strong, when France is
great and strong, it will be my turn, then, to cry
'Mercy!' ''

''Mercy, did you say? Then ask the king for his freedom. The king is only crushing him on your account.''

Colbert again raised his head.

''Monsieur,'' he said, ''you know that it is not so, and
that the king has his own grudges against Monsieur Fouquet; it is not for me to teach you that.''

''But the king will get tired; he will forget.''

''The king never forgets, Monsieur D'Artagnan. Listen! the king is calling. He is going to issue an order. I
have not influenced him, have I? Listen.''

The king, in fact, was calling his secretaries.

''Monsieur D'Artagnan,'' he said.

''I am here, sire.''

''Give twenty of your musketeers to Monsieur de St.
Aignan, to form a guard for Monsieur Fouquet.''

D'Artagnan and Colbert exchanged looks.

''And from Angers,'' continued the king, ''they will
take the prisoner to the Bastille, in Paris.''

''You were right,'' said the captain to the minister.

''St. Aignan,'' the king went on, ''you will have anyone shot who shall attempt to speak privately with Monsieur Fouquet, during the journey.''

"But myself, sire," said the duke.

"You, monsieur, you will only speak to him in the presence of the musketeers."

The duke bowed, and departed to have the order carried out.

D'Artagnan was also about to leave; but the king stopped him.

"Monsieur," he said, "you will go immediately, and take possession of the isle and fief of Belle-Isle-en-Mer."

"Yes, sire. Alone?"

"You will take a sufficient number of troops to prevent delay, in case the fortress holds out."

A murmur of adulatory incredulity arose from the group of courtiers.

"That has been seen," said D'Artagnan.

"I saw it in my childhood," the king went on, "and I do not wish to see it again. Have you heard me? Go, monsieur, and do not return without the keys of the fort."

Colbert went up to D'Artagnan.

"A mission which, if you carry it out well," said he, "will be worth a marshal's baton to you."

"Why do you use the words, 'if you carry it out well'?"

"Because it is difficult."

"Ah! in what respect?"

"You have friends in Belle-Isle, Monsieur D'Artagnan; and it is not an easy thing for men like you to walk over the bodies of their friends in order to succeed."

D'Artagnan hung down his head, while Colbert returned to the king. A quarter of an hour later, the captain received the written order from the king to blow up the fortress of Belle-Isle, in case of resistance, with the power of life and death over all the inhabitants or refugees, and an injunction not to let a single one escape.

"Colbert was right," thought D'Artagnan; "my marshal's baton would cost the lives of my two friends. Only they seem to forget that my friends are not more stupid than the birds, and that they will not wait for the hand of the fowler to extend their wings. I will show them that hand so plainly that they will have time to see it. Poor

Porthos! Poor Aramis! No; my fortune shall not cost your wings a feather.''

Having reached this conclusion, D'Artagnan assembled the royal army, embarked it at Paimbœuf, and set sail, without wasting a moment.

CHAPTER XLII

BELLE-ISLE-EN-MER

At the end of the mole, which the furious sea beats at evening tide, two men, holding each other by the arm, were conversing in an animated and expansive tone, without the possibility of any other human being hearing their words, swept away, as they were, one by one, by the gusts of wind, with the white foam of the waves. The sun had just gone down in the vast sheet of the reddened ocean, like a gigantic crucible. From time to time one of these men, turning toward the east, would cast an anxious, inquiring look over the sea. The other, studying the features of his companion, seemed to try to guess his thoughts.

Then, both silent, both busied with dismal thoughts, they would resume their walk. Everyone has already realized that those two men were our outcasts, Porthos and Aramis, who had taken refuge in Belle-Isle, since the ruin of their hopes, since the failure of the vast plan of M. d'Herblay.

"It is of no use your saying anything to the contrary, my dear Aramis," repeated Porthos, inhaling vigorously the salt air with which he filled his powerful chest. "It is of no use, Aramis. The disappearance of all the fishing boats that went out two days ago is not an ordinary circumstance. There has been no storm at sea; the weather has been constantly calm, not even the lightest gale; and even if we had had a tempest, all our boats would not have sunk. I repeat, it is strange. This complete disappearance astonishes me, I tell you."

"True," whispered Aramis. "You are right, friend Porthos; it is true, there is something strange in it."

"And, further," added Porthos, whose ideas the assent of the bishop of Vannes seemed to enlarge; "and, further, have you noticed that if the boats have perished, not a single plank has been washed ashore?"

"I have noticed that, as well as you."

"Have you noticed, besides, that the two only boats we had left in the whole island, and which I sent in search of the others . . ."

Aramis here interrupted his companion with a cry, and with so sudden a gesture that Porthos stopped as if he were stupefied.

"What are you saying, Porthos? What! you have sent the two boats . . ."

"In search of the others, yes; to be sure I have," replied Porthos, quite simply.

"Unhappy man! What have you done? Then we are indeed lost!" cried the bishop.

"Lost! What did you say?" exclaimed the terrified Porthos. "How lost, Aramis? How are we lost?"

Aramis bit his lips.

"Nothing! nothing! Excuse me, I meant to say . . ."

"What?"

"That if we had a sudden idea to take an excursion by sea, we could not."

"Very good; and why should that bother you? A fine pleasure, *ma foi!* For my part, I don't miss it at all. What I miss is, certainly not the more or less amusement we can find at Belle-Isle, what I miss, Aramis, is Pierrefonds, is Bracieux, is Le Vallon, is my beautiful France! Here, we are not in France, my dear friend; we are I know not where. Oh, I tell you, in the full sincerity of my soul, and your affection will excuse my frankness, but I declare to you I am not happy at Belle-Isle. No, in good truth, I am not happy!"

Aramis breathed a long but stifled sigh.

"Dear friend," he replied, "that is why it is so sad you have sent the two boats we had left in search of the boats which disappeared two days ago. If you had not sent them away, we would have left."

"Left! And the orders, Aramis?"

"What orders?"

"*Parbleu!* Why, the orders you have been constantly,

and on all occasions, repeating to me: that we were to hold Belle-Isle against the usurper. You know very well."

"That is true!" whispered Aramis again.

"You see, then, plainly, my friend, that we could not leave; and that the sending away of the boats in search of the others is not prejudical to us in any way."

Aramis was silent; and his vague glance, luminous as that of a gull, hovered for a long time over the sea, interrogating space, and seeking to pierce the horizon.

"With all that, Aramis," continued Porthos, who stuck to his idea all the more since the bishop had found it correct, "with all that, you give me no explanation about what can have happened to these unfortunate boats. I am assailed by cries and complaints wherever I go. The children cry at seeing the desolation of the women, as if I could restore the absent husbands and fathers. What are you assuming, my friend, and what ought I to answer them?"

"Let us assume everything, my good Porthos, and let us say nothing."

This reply did not satisfy Porthos at all. He turned away, grumbling some words in a very bad humor. Aramis stopped the valiant soldier.

"Do you remember," he said, in a melancholy tone, pressing the two hands of the giant between his own with an affectionate cordiality, "do you remember, my friend, that in the glorious days of your youth, do you remember, Porthos, when we were all strong and valiant, we, and the other two, if we had felt like returning to France, do you think this sheet of salt water would have stopped us?"

"Oh!" said Porthos, "but six leagues!"

"If you had seen me climb a plank, would you have remained on land, Porthos?"

"No, *pardieu!* No, Aramis. But nowadays what sort of a plank should we want, my friend? I, in particular."

And the Seigneur de Bracieux cast a proud glance over his colossal rotundity with a loud laugh.

"And do you mean seriously to say you are not tired of Belle-Isle also a little, and that you would not prefer the comforts of your home—of your episcopal palace at Vannes? Come, confess."

"No," replied Aramis without daring to look at Porthos.

"Let us stay where we are, then," said his friend, with a sigh which, in spite of the efforts he made to restrain it, escaped loudly from his breast. "Let us stay! let us stay! And yet," he added, "and yet if we were determined to return to France, and there were no boats . . ."

"Have you noticed another thing, my friend—that is, since the disappearance of our boats, during the two days' absence of the fishermen, not a single small boat has landed on the shores of the isle?"

"Yes, certainly, you are right. I have noticed it also, and the observation was the more naturally made, for, before the last two fatal days, we saw fishing boats and launches arrive by dozens."

"I must inquire," said Aramis suddenly, and with great agitation. "And then, if I had a raft constructed . . ."

"But there are some canoes, my friend; shall I go on board one?"

"A canoe! a canoe! Can you think of such a thing, Porthos? A canoe to capsize! No, no," said the bishop of Vannes; "it is not like us to ride upon the waves. We will wait, we will wait."

And Aramis continued walking about with increased agitation. Porthos, who grew tired of following all the feverish movements of his friend—Porthos, who, in his calmness and faith understood nothing of the sort of exasperation which was betrayed by Aramis's continual convulsive starts—Porthos stopped him.

"Let us sit down upon this rock," he said. "Place yourself there, close to me, Aramis, and I conjure you, for the last time, to explain to me in a manner I can understand, explain to me what we are doing here."

"Porthos!" said Aramis, much embarrassed.

"I know that the false king wanted to dethrone the true king. That is a fact that I understand. Well . . ."

"Yes," said Aramis.

"I know that the false king formed the project of selling Belle-Isle to the English. I understand that, too."

"Yes."

"I know that we engineers and captains came and threw ourselves into Belle-Isle to take the direction of the works, and the command of ten companies levied and paid by Monsieur Fouquet, or rather, the ten companies of his son-in-law. All that is plain.''

Aramis arose in a state of great impatience. He looked like a lion pestered by a gnat. Porthos held him by the arm.

''But what I cannot understand, what, in spite of all the efforts of my mind, and all my reflections, I cannot understand, and never shall understand, is, that instead of sending us troops, instead of sending us reinforcements of men, munitions, and supplies, they leave us without boats, they leave Belle-Isle without arrivals, without help; that, instead of establishing with us a correspondence, whether by signals, or written or verbal communications, all relations with us are intercepted. Tell me, Aramis, answer me, or rather, before answering me, will you allow me to tell you what I have thought? Will you hear what my idea is, what I have imagined?''

The bishop raised his head.

''Well, Aramis,'' continued Porthos, ''I have thought, I have had an idea, I have imagined that an event has taken place in France. I dreamed of Monsieur Fouquet all night; I dreamed of dead fish, broken eggs, rooms badly furnished, meanly kept. Bad dreams, my dear D'Herblay; very unlucky, such dreams!''

''Porthos, what is that over there?'' interrupted Aramis, rising suddenly and pointing out to his friend a black spot upon the crimson line of the water.

''A boat!'' said Porthos; ''yes, it is a boat! Ah! we shall have some news at last.''

''There are two!'' cried the bishop, on discovering another mast; ''two! three! four!''

''Five!'' said Porthos, in his turn. ''Six! seven! Ah, *mon Dieu! mon Dieu!* it is a whole fleet.''

''Our boats returning, probably,'' said Aramis very uneasily, in spite of the assurance he affected.

''They are very large for fishing boats,'' observed Porthos, ''and aren't you noticing, my friend, they are coming from the Loire?''

''They are coming from the Loire, yes . . .''

''And look! everybody here sees them as well as ourselves; look! the women and children are beginning to get upon the jetty.''

An old fisherman was going by.

"Are those our boats over there?" asked Aramis.

The old man looked steadily into the horizon.

"No, monseigneur," he replied, "they are lighter boats in the king's service."

"Boats in the king's service?" replied Aramis, giving a start. "How do you know that?" he said.

"By the flag."

"But," said Porthos, "the boat is scarcely visible; how the devil, my friend, can you distinguish the flag?"

"I see there is one," replied the old man; "our boats, or trade lighters, do not carry any. That sort of craft is generally used for the transport of troops."

"Ah!" said Aramis.

"Vivat!" cried Porthos, "they are sending us reinforcements; don't you think they are, Aramis?"

"Probably; unless it is the English coming."

"By the Loire? That would be unfortunate, Aramis; would they have come through Paris?"

"You are right; they are definitely reinforcements, or supplies."

Aramis leaned his head upon his hands, and made no reply. Then, all at once:

"Porthos," he said, "have the alarm sounded."

"The alarm! do you think of such a thing?"

"Yes; and let the cannoneers mount to their batteries, let the artillerymen be at their pieces, and be particularly watchful of the coast batteries."

Porthos opened his eyes wide. He looked attentively at his friend, to convince himself he was in his proper senses.

"I will do it, my dear Porthos," continued Aramis, in his gentlest tone, "I will go and have these orders carried out, if you do not go, my friend."

"Well, I will go instantly," said Porthos, who went to carry out the orders, while looking behind him, to see if the bishop of Vannes had not made a mistake, and if, on returning to more rational ideas, he would not recall him.

The alarm was sounded, the trumpets brayed, and drums rolled; the great bell of the belfry was put in motion. The dikes and moles were quickly filled with the curious and soldiers; the matches sparkled in the hands of the artillerymen, placed behind the large cannon bedded in their stone carriages. When every man was at his post, when all the preparations for the defense were made:

"Permit me, Aramis, to try to understand," whispered Porthos timidly, in Aramis's ear.

"My dear friend, you will understand too soon," whispered M. d'Herblay, in reply to this question of his lieutenant.

"The fleet which is coming over there, with sails unfurled, straight toward the port of Belle-Isle, is a royal fleet, is it not?"

"But as there are two kings in France, Porthos, to which of these two kings does this fleet belong?"

"Oh! you are opening my eyes," replied the giant, stunned by this argument.

And Porthos, for whom the reply of his friend had just opened the eyes, or rather, thickened the bandage which covered his sight, went quickly to the batteries to supervise his people, and exhort everyone to his duty. In the meantime, Aramis, with his eyes fixed on the horizon, saw the ships continue to draw nearer. The people and the soldiers, upon the rocks, could distinguish the masts, then the lower sails, and at last the hulls of the lighters, bearing at the masthead the royal flag of France. It was quite night when one of these vessels which had created such a sensation among the inhabitants of Belle-Isle was moored within cannonshot of the fort. Soon, one saw in spite of the darkness, that a sort of agitation reigned on board this vessel, from the side of which a skiff was lowered, of which the three rowers, bending to their oars, took the direction of the port, and in a few instants landed at the foot of the fort.

The captain of this yawl jumped on shore. He had a letter in his hand, which he waved in the air, and seemed to wish to communicate with somebody. This man was soon recognized by several soldiers as one of the pilots of the island. He was the captain of one of the two boats kept back by Aramis, and which Porthos, in his anxiety with regard to the fate of the fishermen who had disappeared for two days, had sent in search of the missing boats. He asked to be taken to M. d'Herblay. Two soldiers, at a signal from a sergeant, placed him between them, and escorted him. Aramis was upon the quay. The envoy presented himself before the bishop of Vannes.

The darkness was almost complete, in spite of the torches borne at a small distance by the soldiers who were following Aramis in his rounds.

"Well, Jonathan, who is sending you?"

"Monseigneur, those who captured me."

"Who captured you?"

"You know, monseigneur, we set out in search of our comrades?"

"Yes; and afterward?"

"Well, monseigneur, within a short league we were captured by a cutter belonging to the king."

"Ah!" said Aramis.

"Which king?" cried Porthos.

Jonathan opened wide eyes.

"Speak!" the bishop said.

"We were captured, monseigneur, and joined to those who had been taken yesterday morning."

"What was the cause of the mania for capturing you all?" said Porthos.

"Monsieur, to prevent us from telling you," replied Jonathan.

Porthos was again at a loss to understand.

"And they have released you today?" he asked.

"That I might tell you they have captured us, monsieur."

"Trouble upon trouble," thought honest Porthos.

During this time Aramis was thinking.

"Then," he said, "I suppose it is a royal fleet blockading the coasts?"

"Yes, monseigneur."

"Under whose command is it?"

"The captain of the king's musketeers."

"D'Artagnan?"

"D'Artagnan!" exclaimed Porthos.

"I believe that is the name."

"And did he give you this letter?"

"Yes, monseigneur."

"Bring the torches nearer."

"It is his writing," said Porthos.

Aramis eagerly read the following lines:

"Order of the king to take Belle-Isle, or to put the garrison to the sword, if they resist; order to make prisoners of all the men of the garrison; signed, D'ARTAGNAN, who, the day before yesterday, arrested Monsieur Fouquet, to send him to the Bastille.''

Aramis turned pale, and crushed the paper in his hands.

"What is it?" asked Porthos.

"Nothing, my friend, nothing."

"Tell me, Jonathan."

"Monseigneur?"

"Did you speak to Monsieur d'Artagnan?"

"Yes, monseigneur."

"What did he say to you?"

"That for more ample information he would speak with monseigneur."

"Where?"

"On board his own vessel."

"On board his vessel?" and Porthos repeated, "On board his vessel?"

"Monsieur le Mousquetaire," continued Jonathan, "told me to take you both on board my canoe, and bring you to him."

"Let us go at once!" exclaimed Porthos. "Dear D'Artagnan!"

But Aramis stopped him.

"Are you mad?" he cried. "Who knows that it is not a trap?"

"Of the other king?" said Porthos mysteriously.

"A trap, in fact. That's what it is, my friend."

"Very possibly. What is to be done, then? If D'Artagnan is sending for us . . ."

"Who assures you that D'Artagnan is sending for us?"

"Yes, but . . . but his writing . . ."

"Writing is easily forged. This looks forged . . . trembling . . ."

"You are always right; but, in the meantime, we know nothing."

Aramis was silent.

"It is true," said the good Porthos, "we do not need to know anything."

"What shall I do?" asked Jonathan.

"You will return on board this captain's vessel."

"Yes, monseigneur."

"And will tell him that we beg him to come into the island."

"Ah, I understand!" said Porthos.

"Yes, monseigneur," replied Jonathan; "but if the captain should refuse to come to Belle-Isle?"

"If he refuses, as we have canoes, we will make use of them."

"What! against D'Artagnan?"

"If it is D'Artagnan, Porthos, he will come. Go, Jonathan, go!"

"*Ma foi!* I no longer understand anything," whispered Porthos.

"I will make you understand all, my dear friend; the time for it has come. Sit down upon this gun carriage, open your ears, and listen to me."

"Oh! *pardieu!* I shall listen, no fear of that."

"May I leave, monseigneur?" cried Jonathan.

"Yes, leave, and bring back an answer. Let the canoe go by, you men there!"

And the canoe pushed off to join the fleet.

Aramis took Porthos by the hand, and began the explanations.

CHAPTER XLIII

THE EXPLANATIONS OF ARAMIS

"What I have to say to you, friend Porthos, will probably surprise you, but it will instruct you."

"I like to be surprised," said Porthos, in a kindly tone. "Therefore, please do not spare me. I am hardened against emotions; don't fear, speak out."

"It is difficult, Porthos, it is . . . difficult; for, in truth, I warn you a second time, I have very strange things, very extraordinary things, to tell you."

"Oh! you speak so well, my friend, that I could listen to you all day long. Speak, then, I beg, and stop, I have an idea; I will, to make your task easier, I will, to help you in telling me such things, question you."

"Gladly."

"What are we going to fight for, Aramis?"

"If you ask me many such questions as that, if that is how you want to make my task easier by interrupting my revelations, Porthos, you will not help me at all. So far, on the contrary, that is precisely the Gordian knot. But, my friend, with a man like you, good, generous, and devoted, the confession must be made bravely. I have deceived you, my worthy friend."

"Did you deceive me?"

"Good heavens! yes."

"Was it for my good, Aramis?"

"I thought so, Porthos; I thought so sincerely, my friend."

"Then," said the honest seigneur of Bracieux, "you have done me a service, and I thank you for it; for if you had not deceived me, I might have deceived myself. How, then, have you deceived me? Tell me."

"I was serving the usurper against whom Louis XIV at this moment is directing his efforts."

"The usurper!" said Porthos, scratching his head. "That is . . . well, I do not understand too well."

"He is one of the two kings who are contending for the crown of France."

"Very well. Then were you serving the one who is not Louis XIV?"

"You have hit upon the matter in a word."

"It results that . . ."

"It results that we are rebels, my poor friend."

"The devil! the devil!" cried Porthos, much disappointed.

"Oh! but, dear Porthos, be calm; we shall still find means of getting out of the affair, trust me."

"It is not that which makes me uneasy," replied Porthos; "what concerns me is that ugly word *rebels.*"

"Ah! but . . ."

"And so, according to this, the duchy that was promised me . . ."

"It was the usurper who was to give it to you."

"And that is not the same thing, Aramis," said Porthos majestically.

"My friend, if it had only depended upon me, you should have become a prince."

Porthos began to bite his nails, in a melancholy fashion.

"That is where you have been wrong," he continued, "in deceiving me; for I was counting on that promised duchy. Oh! I was counting on it seriously, knowing you to be a man of your word, Aramis."

"Poor Porthos! pardon me, I implore you!"

"So, then," continued Porthos, without replying to the bishop's prayer, "so, then, it seems, I have quite fallen out with Louis XIV?"

"Oh, I will fix all that, my good friend, I will fix all that. I will take it upon myself alone."

"Aramis!"

"No, no, Porthos, I beg you, let me act. No false generosity! No inopportune devotion! You knew nothing of my projects. You have done nothing on your own. With me it is different. I am alone the author of the plot. I stood in need of my inseparable companion; I called upon you, and you came to me, in remembrance of our ancient motto. 'All for one, one for all.' My crime was being selfish."

"Now, that is what I like to hear," said Porthos; "and seeing that you have acted entirely for yourself, it is impossible for me to blame you. It is so natural."

And upon this sublime reflection Porthos shook cordially the hand of his friend.

In presence of this naïve greatness of soul, Aramis felt very small. It was the second time he had been compelled to bend before real superiority of heart, much more powerful than splendor of mind. He replied by a mute and energetic pressure to the kind endearment of his friend.

"Now," said Porthos, "that we have come to an explanation, now that I am perfectly aware of our situation, with respect to Louis XIV, I think, my friend, it is time to make me understand the political intrigue of which we are the victims; for I plainly see there is a political intrigue at the bottom of all this."

"D'Artagnan, my good Porthos, D'Artagnan is coming, and will relate it to you in all its details; but, excuse me, I am deeply grieved, I am overcome with grief, and I need all my presence of mind, all my reflection, to get you out of the difficult situation in which I have so imprudently involved you; but nothing can be clearer, nothing plainer, than your position from now on. The king, Louis XIV, has no longer now but one enemy; that enemy is myself, myself alone. I have made you a prisoner, you have followed me, today I liberate you, you fly back to your prince. You can see, Porthos, there is not a single difficulty in all this."

"Do you think so?" said Porthos.

"I am quite sure of it."

"Then why," said the admirable good sense of Porthos, "then why, if we are in such an easy position, why, my friend, are we preparing cannons, muskets, and engines of all sorts? It seems to me it would be much simpler to say to Captain d'Artagnan: 'My dear friend, we have been mistaken; let us start over; open the door to us, let us go through, and good day!'"

"Ah! that," said Aramis, shaking his head.

"Why do you say 'that'? Don't you approve of my plan, my friend?"

"I see a difficulty in it."

"What is it?"

"The hypothesis that D'Artagnan may come with orders which will oblige us to defend ourselves."

"What! defend ourselves against D'Artagnan? Folly! Against the good D'Artagnan?"

Aramis shook his head once more.

"Porthos," he said at last, "if I have had the fuses lighted and the guns pointed, if I have had the signal of alarm sounded, if I have called every man to his post upon the ramparts, those good ramparts of Belle-Isle which you have so well fortified, it is for something. Wait to judge; or rather, no, do not wait . . ."

"What can I do?"

"If I knew, my friend, I would have told you."

"But there is one thing much simpler than defending ourselves—a boat, and away for France, where . . ."

"My dear friend," said Aramis, smiling sadly, "do not let us reason like children; let us be men in council and execution. But, listen! I hear a hail for landing at the port. Watch out, Porthos!"

"It is D'Artagnan, no doubt," said Porthos, in a thunderous voice, approaching the parapet.

"Yes, it is I," replied the captain of the musketeers,

running lightly up the steps of the mole, and reaching rapidly the little esplanade where his two friends were waiting for him. As soon as he came toward them Porthos and Aramis observed an officer who was following D'Artagnan, treading apparently in his very steps. The captain stopped on the stairs of the mole when halfway up. His companion imitated him.

"Make your men draw back," cried D'Artagnan to Porthos and Aramis; "let them draw back out of hearing."

The order being given by Porthos, was executed immediately. Then D'Artagnan, turning toward the officer who was following him:

"Monsieur," he said, "we are no longer here on board the king's fleet, where, in virtue of your orders, you spoke so arrogantly to me."

"Monsieur," replied the officer, "I did not speak arrogantly to you; I simply but rigorously obeyed what I had been ordered. I have been directed to follow you. I follow you. I am directed not to allow you to communicate with anyone without finding out what you are doing; I am involved, therefore, in your communications."

D'Artagnan trembled with rage, and Porthos and Aramis, who heard this dialogue, trembled also, but with uneasiness and fear. D'Artagnan, biting his mustache with that vivacity which denoted in him an exasperation to be followed by a terrible explosion, approached the officer.

"Monsieur," he said, more quietly and more clearly because an apparent calm was hiding a great rage. "Monsieur, when I sent a canoe here you wanted to know what I wrote to the defenders of Belle-Isle. You produced an order to that effect; and, in turn, I instantly showed you the note I had written. When the captain of the boat sent by me returned, when I received the reply of these two gentlemen" (and he pointed to Aramis and Porthos), "you heard every word of what the messenger said. All that was plainly in your orders, all that was well executed, very punctually, was it not?"

"Yes, monsieur," stammered the officer; "yes, without doubt; but . . ."

"Monsieur," continued D'Artagnan, getting excited— "monsieur, when I showed the intention of leaving my

vessel to cross to Belle-Isle you insisted on accompany-
ing me; I did not hesitate; I brought you with me. You
are now at Belle-Isle, are you not?"

"Yes, monsieur; but . . ."

"But—what matters is no longer Monsieur Colbert,
who has given you that order, or whomever in the world
whose instructions you are following, what matters now
is a man who is in Monsieur d'Artagnan's way, and who
is alone with Monsieur D'Artagnan on steps bathed by
thirty feet of saltwater; a bad position for that man, a bad
position, monsieur! I warn you."

"But, monsieur, if I am in your way," said the officer
timidly, and almost faintly, "it is my duty which . . ."

"Monsieur, you have had the misfortune, you or those
who sent you, to insult me. It is done. I cannot lay the
blame on those who employ you, they are unknown to
me, or are at too great a distance. But you are under my
hand, and I swear that if you take one step behind me
when I start to go up to those gentlemen, I swear to you,
I will split your head in two with my sword, and pitch
you into the water. Oh! it will happen, it will happen! I
have only been angry six times in my life, monsieur,
and, the five times which have preceded this one I have
killed my man."

The officer did not stir; he became pale under this terrible threat, but replied, with simplicity:

"Monsieur, you are wrong in acting against my orders."

Porthos and Aramis, mute and trembling at the top of
the parapet, cried to the musketeer:

"Dear D'Artagnan, watch out!"

D'Artagnan gestured them to keep silent, raised his
foot with a terrifying calmness to go up one step, and
turned around, sword in hand, to see if the officer was
following him. The officer made a sign of the cross and
stepped up. Porthos and Aramis, who knew their D'Artagnan, uttered a cry, and rushed down to prevent the
blow they thought they had already heard. But D'Artagnan took his sword into his left hand:

"Monsieur," he said to the officer, in an agitated
voice, "you are a good man. You ought to understand
better what I am going to say to you now than what I
have said to you a while ago."

"Speak, Monsieur d'Artagnan, speak," replied the good soldier.

"These gentlemen we have just seen, and against whom you have orders, are my friends."

"I know they are, monsieur."

"You can understand if I ought to act toward them as your instructions prescribe."

"I understand your reserve."

"Very well; permit me, then, to talk with them without a witness."

"Monsieur d'Artagnan, if I yielded to your request, if I did what you beg me to do, I would break my word; but if I do not do it, I shall disoblige you. I prefer the one to the other. Talk with your friends, and do not despise me, monsieur, for doing for you, whom I esteem and honor, do not despise me for committing for you, and you alone, an unworthy act."

D'Artagnan, touched, put his arms rapidly around the neck of the young man, and went up to his friends. The officer, wrapped in his cloak, sat down on the damp, weed-covered steps.

"Well," said D'Artagnan to his friends, "such is my position, judge for yourselves."

They all three embraced. All three pressed one another in their arms as in the glorious days of their youth.

"What is the meaning of all these rigors?" said Porthos.

"You ought to have some suspicions of what it is," said D'Artagnan.

"Not much, I assure you, my dear captain; for, in fact, I have done nothing, neither has Aramis," hastened the worthy baron to say.

D'Artagnan cast a reproachful look at the prelate, which pierced that hardened heart.

"Dear Porthos!" cried the bishop of Vannes.

"You see what has been done against you," said D'Artagnan; "interception of all that is coming to or going from Belle-Isle. Your boats are all captured. If you had tried to escape, you would have fallen into the hands of the cruisers which plow the sea in all directions, on the watch for you. The king wants you, and he will capture you."

And D'Artagnan tore several hairs from his gray mustache. Aramis became somber, Porthos angry.

"My idea was this," continued D'Artagnan, "to make you both come on board, to keep you near me, and restore you your liberty. But now, who can say that when I return to my ship I may not find a superior; that I may not find secret orders which will take my command from me to give it to another, who will dispose of me and you without hopes of help?"

"We must remain at Belle-Isle," said Aramis resolutely; "and I assure you, I will not surrender easily."

Porthos said nothing. D'Artagnan noticed the silence of his friend.

"I must test again this officer, this brave fellow who accompanies me, and whose courageous resistance makes me very happy; for it denotes an honest man, who, although an enemy, is a thousand times better than an obliging coward. Let us try to learn from him what he has the right to do, and what his orders permit or forbid."

"Let us try," said Aramis.

D'Artagnan came to the parapet, leaned over toward the steps of the mole, and called the officer, who immediately came up.

"Monsieur," said D'Artagnan, after having exchanged the most cordial courtesies natural between gentlemen who know and appreciate each other, "monsieur, if I wanted to take away these gentlemen from this place, what would you do?"

"I would not oppose it, monsieur; but having direct orders, formal orders, to take them under my guard, I would detain them."

"Ah!" said D'Artagnan.

"It's all over," said Aramis gloomily.

Porthos did not move.

"But take away Porthos," said the bishop of Vannes; "he can prove to the king—I will help him in doing so, and you also, Monsieur d'Artagnan—that he has had nothing to do with this affair."

"Will you come?" said D'Artagnan. "Will you follow me, Porthos? The king is merciful."

"I beg to think," said Porthos nobly.

"Are you staying here, then?"

"Until new orders," said Aramis vivaciously.

"Until we have an idea," went on D'Artagnan; "and I now believe that will not be long, for I have one already."

"Let us say adieu, then," said Aramis; "but, in truth, my good Porthos, you ought to go."

"No," said the latter laconically.

"As you please," replied Aramis, a little wounded in his nervous susceptibility at the morose tone of his companion. "Only I am reassured by the promise of an idea from D'Artagnan, an idea I think I have guessed."

"Let us see," said the musketeer, placing his ear near Aramis's mouth. The latter spoke several words rapidly, to which D'Artagnan replied:

"That is it, precisely."

"Infallible, then!" cried Aramis.

"During the first emotion that this resolution will cause, take care of yourself, Aramis."

"Oh, don't be afraid!"

"Now, monsieur," said D'Artagnan to the officer, "thanks, a thousand thanks! You have made yourself three friends for life."

"Yes," added Aramis.

Porthos alone said nothing, but nodded.

D'Artagnan, having tenderly embraced his two old friends, left Belle-Isle with the inseparable companion M. Colbert had given him. Thus, with the exception of the explanation with which the worthy Porthos had been willing to be satisfied, nothing had changed in appearance in the fate of the one or of the other.

"Only," said Aramis, "there is D'Artagnan's idea."

D'Artagnan did not return on board without examining thoroughly the idea he had discovered. Now, we know that when D'Artagnan did examine, usually, daylight pierced through. As to the officer, become mute again, he left him full measure to meditate. Therefore, on putting his foot on board his vessel, moored within cannon shot of the island, the captain of the musketeers had already got together all his means, offensive and defensive.

He immediately assembled his council, which consisted of the officers serving under his orders. There were eight of them: a chief of the maritime forces, a major directing the artillery, an engineer, the officer we are acquainted with, and four lieutenants. Having assembled them in the chamber of the poop, D'Artagnan arose, took off his hat, and addressed them thus:

"Gentlemen, I have been to reconnoiter Belle-Isle-en-Mer, and I have found in it a good and solid garrison; moreover, preparations are made for a defense that may prove troublesome. I therefore intend to send for two of the main officers of the fort that we may talk with them. Having separated them from their troops and their cannon, we shall be better able to deal with them, particularly with good reasoning. Is this your opinion, gentlemen?"

The major of artillery rose.

"Monsieur," he said, with respect but with firmness, "I have heard you say that the fort is preparing to make a troublesome defense. Is the fort, then, as you know, determined upon rebellion?"

D'Artagnan was visibly put out by this reply; but he was not a man to allow himself to be subdued by so little, and went on:

"Monsieur," he said, "your reply is just. But you do know that Belle-Isle is a fief of Monsieur Fouquet, and the former kings gave the right to the seigneurs of Belle-Isle to arm their people."

The major made a gesture.

"Oh, do not interrupt me," continued D'Artagnan. "You are going to tell me that that right to arm themselves against the English was not a right to arm themselves against their king. But it is not Monsieur Fouquet, I suppose, who is holding Belle-Isle at this moment, since I arrested Monsieur Fouquet the day before yesterday. Now, the inhabitants and defenders of Belle-Isle know nothing of that arrest. You would announce it to them in vain. It is a thing so unheard of and extraordinary, so unexpected, that they would not believe you. A Breton serves his master, and not his masters; he serves his master till he has seen him dead. Now, the Bretons, as far as I know, have not seen the body of Monsieur Fouquet. It is not, then, surprising that they hold out against everything which is not Monsieur Fouquet or his signature."

The major bowed in sign of assent.

"That is why," continued D'Artagnan, "I propose to have two of the main officers of the garrison come on board my vessel. They will see you, gentlemen; they will see the forces we have at our disposal; they will, consequently, know what fate they have to expect, in case of rebellion. We will assure them, upon our honor, that Monsieur Fouquet is a prisoner, and that all resistance can only be prejudicial to them. We will tell them that the first cannon that is fired, there will be no mercy to be expected from the king. Then, I hope at least, they will no longer resist. They will yield without fighting, and we shall have a fort given up to us in a friendly way, which might cost us much trouble to conquer.''

The officer who had followed D'Artagnan to Belle-Isle was about to speak, but D'Artagnan interrupted him.

''Yes, I know what you are going to tell me, monsieur; I know that there is an order of the king's to prevent all secret communications with the defenders of Belle-Isle, and that is exactly why I do not offer to communicate but in the presence of my staff.''

And D'Artagnan nodded to his officers, to point out this compliance.

The officers looked at one another, as if to decipher each other's opinions, with the intention evidently of acting according to the wishes of D'Artagnan after they had agreed. And already the latter saw with joy that the result of their consent would be sending a boat to Porthos and Aramis, when the king's officer drew from his pocket a folded paper, which he placed in the hands of D'Artagnan.

This paper bore upon its address the number 1.

''What, more still!'' whispered the surprised captain.

''Read, monsieur,'' said the officer, with a courtesy that was not free from sadness.

D'Artagnan, full of mistrust, unfolded the paper, and read these words:

> ''Prohibition to Monsieur d'Artagnan to assemble any council whatever, or to deliberate in any way before Belle-Isle has surrendered and the prisoners are shot.
>
> ''(Signed) LOUIS.''

D'Artagnan repressed the movement of impatience that ran through his whole body, and, with a gracious smile:

"That is well, monsieur," he said; "the king's orders shall be complied with."

CHAPTER XLIV

RESULT OF THE IDEAS OF THE KING AND THE IDEAS OF D'ARTAGNAN

THE blow was direct. It was severe, mortal. D'Artagnan, furious at having been anticipated by the king, did not, however, yet despair; and, reflecting upon the idea he had brought back from Belle-Isle, he foresaw from it a new means of safety for his friends.

"Gentlemen," he said suddenly, "since the king has entrusted some other than myself with his secret orders, it must be because I no longer possess his confidence, and I should be really unworthy of it if I had the courage to hold a command subject to so many insulting suspicions. I will go, then, immediately and carry my resignation to the king. I give it before you all, calling upon you all to fall back with me upon the coast of France, in such a way as not to compromise the safety of the forces his majesty has entrusted to me. For this purpose, return all to your posts; within an hour we shall have the ebb of the tide. To your posts, gentlemen! I suppose," he added, on seeing that all prepared to obey him, except the surveillant officer, "you have no orders to object this time?"

And D'Artagnan almost triumphed while speaking these words. This plan was the safety of his friends. The blockade once raised, they might embark immediately, and set sail for England or Spain without fear of being troubled. While they were making their escape D'Artagnan would return to the king, would justify his return by the indignation which Colbert's mistrust had raised in him; he would be sent back with full powers, and he would take Belle-Isle; that is to say, the cage, after the birds had flown. But to this plan the officer opposed a second order of the king's. It was thus conceived:

* * *

"From the moment Monsieur D'Artagnan shall have shown the desire of giving in his resignation, he shall no longer be considered leader of the expedition, and every officer placed under his orders shall be held to no longer obey him. Moreover, the said Monsieur D'Artagnan, having lost that quality of leader of the army sent against Belle-Isle, shall set out immediately for France, in company of the officer who will have handed the message to him, and who will consider him as a prisoner for whom he is answerable."

Brave and carefree as he was, D'Artagnan turned pale. Everything had been calculated with a depth which, for the first time in thirty years, reminded him of the solid foresight and the inflexible logic of the great cardinal. He leaned his head on his hand, thoughtful, scarcely breathing.

"If I were to put this order in my pocket," he thought, "who would know it, or who would prevent my doing it? Before the king had had time to be informed, I would have saved those poor fellows over there. Let us exercise a little daring. My head is not one of those which the executioner strikes off for disobedience. We will disobey!"

But at the moment he was about to adopt this plan, he saw the officers around him reading similar orders which the infernal agent of Colbert's thoughts had just distributed to them. The case of disobedience had been foreseen, as the others had been.

"Monsieur," said the officer, coming up to him, "I am waiting for your good pleasure to leave."

"I am ready, monsieur," replied D'Artagnan, grinding his teeth.

The officer immediately ordered a canoe to receive M. D'Artagnan and himself. At sight of this he became almost mad with rage.

"How," he stammered, "will they carry on the direction of the different corps?"

"When you are gone, monsieur," replied the commander of the fleet, "the king has entrusted his fleet to me."

"Then, monsieur," retorted Colbert's man, addressing the new leader, "this last order that has been handed to me is intended for you. Let us see your powers."

"Here they are," said the sea officer, showing a royal signature.

"Here are your instructions," replied the officer, placing the folded paper in his hands; and, turning toward D'Artagnan, "Come, monsieur," he said, in an agitated voice, such despair did he behold in that man of iron, "do me the favor to leave at once."

"Immediately!" said D'Artagnan feebly, subdued, crushed by implacable impossibility.

And he let himself slide down into the little boat, which started, favored by wind and tide, for the coast of France. The king's guards embarked with him. The musketeer still preserved the hope of reaching Nantes quickly, and of pleading the cause of his friends eloquently enough to move the king to mercy. The boat flew like a swallow. D'Artagnan saw distinctly the land of France profiled in black against the white clouds of night.

"Ah! monsieur," he said, in a low voice, to the officer to whom, for an hour, he had ceased speaking, "what would I give to know the instructions for the new commander! They are all peaceful, are they not? and . . ."

He did not finish; the sound of a distant cannon rolled over the waters, then another, and two or three still louder. D'Artagnan shuddered.

"The fire is opened upon Belle-Isle," replied the officer.

The canoe had just touched the soil of France.

CHAPTER XLV

THE ANCESTORS OF PORTHOS

WHEN D'Artagnan had left Aramis and Porthos, the latter returned to the main fort to converse with greater liberty. Porthos, still brooding, was a constraint upon Aramis, whose mind had never felt itself more free.

"Dear Porthos," he said suddenly, "I will explain D'Artagnan's idea to you."

"What idea, Aramis?"

"An idea to which we will owe our liberty within twelve hours."

"Indeed!" said Porthos, much astonished. "Let us see it."

"Did you notice, in the scene our friend had with the officer, that certain orders restrained him with regard to us?"

"Yes, I did notice that."

"Well, D'Artagnan is going to give his resignation to the king, and during the confusion which will result from his absence, we will get away, or rather, you will get away, Porthos, if there is a possibility of flight only for one."

Here Porthos shook his head, and replied:

"We will escape together, Aramis, or we will remain here together."

"You are a generous heart," said Aramis, "only your anxiety worries me."

"I am not anxious," said Porthos.

"Then you are angry with me."

"I am not angry with you."

"Then why, my friend, this gloomy look?"

"I will tell you: I am drawing up my will."

And, while saying these words, the good Porthos looked sadly in the face of Aramis.

"Your will!" cried the bishop. "What, then, do you think you are lost?"

"I feel tired. It is the first time, and there is a custom in our family."

"What is it, my friend?"

"My grandfather was a man twice as strong as I am."

"Indeed!" said Aramis; "then your grandfather must have been Samson himself."

"No; his name was Antoine. Well, he was about my age, when setting out hunting one day, he felt his legs weak, he who had never known this before."

"What was the meaning of that fatigue, my friend?"

"Nothing good, as you will see; for, having set out, complaining still of the weakness of his legs, he met a wild boar, which threatened him; he missed him with his arquebuse, and was ripped up by the beast, and died outright."

"There is no reason in that why you should alarm yourself, dear Porthos."

"Oh! you will see. My father was as strong again as I am. He was a rough soldier, under Henry III and Henry IV; his name was not Antoine, but Gaspard, the same as Monsieur de Coligny. Always on horseback, he had never known what fatigue was. One evening, as he rose from table, his legs failed him."

"He had eaten heartily, perhaps," said Aramis, "and that was why he staggered."

"Bah! A friend of Monsieur de Bassompierre, nonsense! No, no; he was astonished at feeling this fatigue, and said to my mother, who laughed at him, 'Doesn't it look as if I was going to meet with a wild boar, as the late Monsieur du Vallon, my father, did?' "

"Well?" said Aramis.

"Well, having this weakness, my father insisted upon going down into the garden, instead of going to bed; his foot slipped on the first step; the staircase was steep; my father fell against a stone angle in which an iron hinge was fixed. The hinge opened his temple, and he lay dead on the spot."

Aramis raised his eyes to his friend.

"These are two extraordinary circumstances," he said; "let us not infer that there will be a third. It is not becoming in a man of your strength to be superstitious, my good Porthos. Besides, when were your legs seen to fail? Never have you been so firm, so superb. Why, you could carry a house on your shoulders."

"At this moment," said Porthos, "I feel myself pretty active; but a while ago I was swaying and collapsing; and since then, this phenomenon, as you say, has occurred four times. I will not say that this frightens me, but it annoys me. Life is an agreeable thing. I have money; I have fine estates; I have horses that I love; I have also friends that I love; D'Artagnan, Athos, Raoul, and you."

The admirable Porthos did not even take the trouble to conceal from Aramis the rank he gave him in his friendship. Aramis pressed his hand.

"We will still live many years," he said, "to preserve for the world specimens of rare men. Trust me, my friend; we have no reply from D'Artagnan; that is a good sign. He must have given orders to get the ships together and clear the seas. On my part I have just given directions that a boat should be rolled upon rollers to the mouth of the great cavern of Locmaria, which you know, where we have so often laid in wait for the foxes.''

''Yes, and which ends up at the little creek by a trench which we discovered the day that splendid fox escaped that way.''

''Precisely. In case of misfortunes, a boat is to be concealed for us in that cavern; indeed, it must be there by this time. We will wait for a favorable moment, and, during the night, to sea!''

''That is a good idea; what shall we gain by it?''

''We shall gain by it—that nobody knows that grotto, or rather, its issue, except ourselves and two or three hunters of the island; we shall gain by it—that if the island is occupied, the scouts, seeing no boat upon the shore, will never imagine we can escape, and will stop watching.''

''I understand.''

''Well, the legs?''

''Excellent, just now.''

''You see, then, plainly, that everything conspires to give us peace and hope. D'Artagnan will clear the sea and make us free. No more royal fleet or descent to be dreaded. *Vive Dieu!* Porthos, we still have half a century of good adventures before us, and if I touch Spanish ground, I swear to you,'' added the bishop, with a terrible energy, ''that your title of duke is not so much at risk as it is said to be.''

''We will live in hope,'' said Porthos, a little enlivened by the new warmth of his companion.

All at once a cry resounded in their ears:

''To arms! to arms!''

This cry, repeated by a hundred voices, brought to the room where the two friends were talking, surprise to one, and uneasiness to the other. Aramis opened the window; he saw a crowd of people running with torches. Women were seeking places of safety, the armed population were hastening to their posts.

''The fleet! the fleet!'' cried a soldier, who recognized Aramis.

''The fleet?'' repeated the latter.

''Within a half cannon shot!'' continued the soldier.

"To arms!" cried Aramis.

"To arms!" repeated Porthos formidably.

And both rushed toward the mole, to place themselves within the shelter of the batteries. Boats, laden with soldiers, were seen approaching; they took three directions, in order to land at three points at once.

"What must be done?" said an officer of the guard.

"Stop them; and if they persist, fire!" said Aramis.

Five minutes after, the gunfire started. These were the shots that D'Artagnan had heard as he landed in France. But the boats were too near the mole to allow the cannon to aim correctly. They landed, and the hand-to-hand fighting began.

"What's the matter, Porthos?" said Aramis to his friend.

"Nothing! nothing! only my legs; it is really incomprehensible! they will be better when we charge."

In fact, Porthos and Aramis did charge with such vigor, they so thoroughly roused their men, that the royalists reembarked hurriedly, without gaining anything but the wounds they carried away.

"Porthos," cried Aramis, "we must have a prisoner, quick! quick!"

Porthos bent over the stair of the mole and seized by the nape of the neck one of the officers of the royal army who was waiting to embark until all his people were in the boat. The arm of the giant lifted up his prey, which served him as a shield, and he went back up without a shot being fired at him.

"Here is a prisoner for you," said Porthos coolly, to Aramis.

"Well!" cried the latter, laughing, "have you not maligned your legs?"

"It was not with my legs I took him," said Porthos, "it was with my arms."

CHAPTER XLVI

THE SON OF BISCARRAT

THE Bretons of the isle were very proud of this victory;
Aramis did not encourage them in the feeling.

"What will happen," he said to Porthos, when everybody had gone home, "is that the king's anger will be
roused by the account of the resistance; and the good
people will be decimated or shot when they are taken,
which cannot fail to take place."

"The result, then," said Porthos, "is that what we
have done is of no use."

"For the moment it may be of some," replied the
bishop, "for we have a prisoner from whom we will learn
what our enemies are preparing to do."

"Yes, let us question the prisoner," said Porthos, "and
the means of making him speak are very simple. We are
going to supper; we will invite him to join us; when he
drinks he will talk."

This was done. The officer was at first rather uneasy,
but became reassured on seeing what sort of men he had
to deal with. He gave, without having any fear of compromising himself, all the details imaginable of the resignation and the departure of D'Artagnan. He explained
how, after that departure, the new leader of the expedition had ordered a surprise attack upon Belle-Isle. There
his explanations stopped. Aramis and Porthos exchanged
a glance which showed their despair. They could no more
depend upon the brave imagination of D'Artagnan; consequently they had no more resources in the event of
defeat. Aramis, continuing his interrogations, asked the
prisoner what the leaders of the expedition contemplated
doing with the leaders of Belle-Isle.

"The orders are," he replied, "to kill during the fighting, and to hang afterward."

Porthos and Aramis looked at each other again, and
their faces colored up.

"I am too light for the gallows," replied Aramis; "people like me are not hung."

"And I am too heavy," said Porthos; "people like me break the cord."

"I am sure," said the prisoner gallantly, "that we could have procured you what sort of death you preferred."

"A thousand thanks!" said Aramis seriously.

Porthos bowed.

"One more cup of wine to your health," he said, drinking himself. From one subject to another the chat with the officer was prolonged; he was an intelligent gentleman, and was won by the charm of Aramis's wit and Porthos's cordial *bonhomie*.

"Pardon me," he said, "if I direct a question at you; but men who are in their sixth bottle have a right to forget themselves a little."

"Direct it!" said Porthos, "direct it!"

"Speak!" said Aramis.

"Were you not, gentlemen, both in the musketeers of the late king?"

"Yes, monsieur, and of the best of them, if you please," said Porthos.

"That is true; I should say even the best of all soldiers, messieurs, if I did not fear to offend the memory of my father."

"Of your father?" cried Aramis.

"Do you know what my name is?"

"To be sure, no, monsieur; but you can tell us, and—"

"My name is Georges de Biscarrat."

"Oh!" cried Porthos, in his turn, "Biscarrat! Do you remember that name, Aramis?"

"Biscarrat!" said the bishop, reflecting. "It seems to me . . ."

"Try to remember, monsieur," said the officer.

"*Pardieu!* that won't take me long," said Porthos. "Biscarrat—called Cardinal—one of the four who interrupted us the day on which we formed our friendship with D'Artagnan, sword in hand."

"Precisely, gentlemen."

"The only one," cried Aramis eagerly, "we did not wound."

"Consequently, a good blade," said the prisoner.

"That's true, very true!" exclaimed both friends together. *"Ma foi!* Monsieur Biscarrat, we are delighted to meet such a brave man's son!"

Biscarrat shook the hands held out to him by the two former musketeers. Aramis looked at Porthos as much as to say: "Here is a man who will help us, and without delay."

"Confess, monsieur," he said, "that it is good to have once been a good man."

"My father always said so, monsieur."

"Confess, also, that it is a sad circumstance in which you find yourself, of falling in with men destined to be shot or hung, and to learn that these men are old acquaintances—old hereditary acquaintances."

"Oh! you are not destined for such a frightful fate as that, gentlemen and friends," said the young man warmly.

"Bah! you said so yourself."

"I said so just now, when I did not know you; but now that I know you, I say—you will avoid this dismal fate, if you like."

"How, if we like?" cried Aramis, whose eyes beamed with intelligence as he looked at the prisoner and then at Porthos.

"Provided," continued Porthos, looking fearlessly at M. Biscarrat and at the bishop, "provided nothing disgraceful is required of us."

"Nothing at all will be required of you, gentlemen," replied the officer. "What should they ask of you? If they find you, they will kill you; that is a settled thing. Try, then, gentlemen, to prevent their finding you."

"I don't think I am mistaken," said Porthos, with dignity; "but it appears obvious to me that if they want to find us, they must come and find us here."

"In that you are perfectly right, my worthy friend," replied Aramis, looking questioningly at Biscarrat, who was silent and tense. "You want, Monsieur de Biscarrat, to say something to us, to make us some overture, and you don't dare—isn't it true?"

"Ah! gentlemen and friends, it is because in speaking I betray my duty. But, listen! I hear a voice which liberates mine by dominating over it."

"The cannon!" said Porthos.

"The cannon, and muskets, too!" cried the bishop.

They heard, at a distance, among the rocks, these sinister sounds of a battle which they thought had ceased:

"What can that be?" asked Porthos.

"Eh! *pardieu!*" cried Aramis, "this is just what I expected."

"What is that?"

"The attack you made was nothing but a feint; isn't it true, monsieur? And while your companions let themselves be forced back, you were certain of a landing on the other side of the island."

"Several, monsieur."

"We are lost, then," said the bishop of Vannes quietly.

"Lost! that is possible," replied the Seigneur de Pierrefonds, "but we are not taken or hung."

And so saying, he rose from the table, went to the wall, and coolly took down his sword and pistols, which he examined with the care of an old soldier who is preparing for battle, and who feels that his life, in a great measure, depends upon the excellence and the good condition of his arms.

At the sound of the cannon, at the news of the surprise attack which might give over the isle to the royal troops, the terrified crowd rushed to the fort to demand assistance and advice from their leaders. Aramis, pale and downcast, between two torches, appeared at the window which looked into the main court, full of soldiers waiting for orders and bewildered inhabitants imploring help.

"My friends," said D'Herblay, in a grave and sonorous voice, "Monsieur Fouquet, your protector, your friend, your father, has been arrested by an order of the king, and thrown into the Bastille."

A long cry of fury and menace came floating up to the window at which the bishop stood.

"Avenge Monsieur Fouquet!" cried the most excited of his listeners, "and death to the royalists!"

"No, my friends," replied Aramis solemnly; "no, my friends; no resistance. The king is master in his kingdom. The king is the agent of God. The king and God have struck Monsieur Fouquet. Humble yourselves before the hand of God. Love God and the king who have struck Monsieur Fouquet. But do not avenge your seigneur, do not think of avenging him. You would sacrifice yourselves in vain—you, your wives and children, your property, and your liberty. Lay down your arms, my friends, lay down your arms, since the king commands you to do so; and go back peacefully to your homes. It is I who asks you to do so; it is I who now, in the hour of need, command you to do so, in the name of Monsieur Fouquet.''

The crowd gathered under the window uttered a prolonged growl of anger and terror.

"The soldiers of Louis XIV have landed on the island," continued Aramis. "From this time it would no longer be a battle between them and you—it would be a massacre. Go, then, and forget; this time I command you, in the name of the Lord!''

The mutineers retired slowly, submissive and silent.

"What have you just been saying there, friend?" said Porthos.

"Monsieur," said Biscarrat to the bishop, "you may save all these inhabitants, but you will neither save yourself nor your friend.''

"Monsieur de Biscarrat," said the bishop of Vannes, with a singular accent of nobleness and courtesy, "Monsieur de Biscarrat, be kind enough to resume your liberty.''

"I am very willing to do so, monsieur; but . . .''

"That would help us, for, when announcing to the king's lieutenant the submission of the islanders, you will perhaps obtain some grace for us on informing him of the manner in which that submission has come about.''

"Grace!" replied Porthos, with flashing eyes, "what is the meaning of that word?''

Aramis touched the elbow of his friend roughly, as he had been accustomed to do in the days of their youth, when he wanted to warn Porthos that he had committed, or was about to commit, an error. Porthos understood him, and was immediately silent.

"I will go, messieurs," replied Biscarrat, a little surprised also at the word "grace" pronounced by the haughty musketeer, whose heroic exploits, some instants before, he had related and praised with so much enthusiasm.

"Go, then, Monsieur Biscarrat," said Aramis, bowing to him, "and at parting receive the expression of our entire gratitude."

"But you, messieurs, you whom I take honor to call my friends, since you have been willing to accept that title, what will become of you in the meantime?" replied the officer, deeply moved, at taking leave of the two old adversaries of his father.

"We will wait here."

"But *mon Dieu!* the order is formal."

"I am bishop of Vannes, Monsieur de Biscarrat; and they no more shoot a bishop than they hang a gentleman."

"Ah, yes, monsieur—yes, monseigneur," replied Biscarrat; "it is true, you are right, there is still that chance for you. Then, I will depart; I will repair to the commander of the expedition, the king's lieutenant. Adieu! then, messieurs, or rather, au revoir, I hope."

The worthy officer, then leaping on a horse given him by Aramis, ran in the direction of the sound of the cannon which, by bringing the crowd into the fort, had interrupted the conversation of the two friends with their prisoner. Aramis watched him leave, and when left alone with Porthos:

"Well, do you understand?" he said.

"*Ma foi!* no."

"Didn't Biscarrat bother you here?"

"No; he is a good fellow."

"Yes; but the grotto of Locmaria, must all the world know it?"

"Ah! That is true, that is true; I understand. We are going to escape by the cavern."

"Please," replied Aramis joyously. "Forward, my friend Porthos; our boat is waiting for us, and the king has not caught us yet."

CHAPTER XLVII

THE cavern of Locmaria was far enough from the mole to make it necessary for our friends to save their strength to arrive there. Besides, night was getting on; midnight had struck at the fort. Porthos and Aramis were loaded with money and arms. They walked across the heath, which is between the mole and the cavern, listening to every noise, and trying to avoid ambushes. From time to time, on the road which they had carefully left on their left they passed fugitives coming from the interior at the news of the landing of the royal troops. Aramis and Porthos, hidden behind some projecting mass of rock, overheard the words which escaped from the poor people who were fleeing, trembling, carrying with them their most valuable belongings, and tried, while listening to their complaints, to learn something from them for their own interest. At last, after a quick walk, frequently interrupted by prudent stops, they reached the deep grottoes, into which the prudent bishop of Vannes had taken care to have rolled upon cylinders a good boat capable of handling the sea at this fine season.

"My good friend," said Porthos, after having breathed vigorously, "we have arrived, it seems. But I thought you spoke of three men, three servants, who were to accompany us. I don't see them—where are they?"

"Why should you see them, dear Porthos?" replied Aramis. "They are certainly waiting for us in the cavern, and no doubt are resting for a moment, after having accomplished their rough and difficult task." Aramis stopped Porthos, who was preparing to enter the cavern.

"Will you allow me, my friend," he said to the giant, "to go in first? I know the signal I have given these men, who, not hearing it, would be very likely to fire upon you or throw their knives at us in the dark."

"Go on, then, Aramis, go on—go first; you are all wisdom and prudence; go on. Ah! there is that fatigue again of which I spoke to you. It has just seized me again."

Aramis left Porthos sitting at the entrance of the grotto, and bowing his head, he went inside the cavern, imitating the cry of the owl. A little plaintive cooing, a scarcely distinct cry, replied from the depths of the cave. Aramis made his way cautiously, and soon was stopped by the same kind of cry as he had first uttered, and this cry sounded within ten paces of him.

"Are you there, Yves?" said the bishop.

"Yes, monseigneur; Goenne is here too. His son is with us."

"That is well. Are all things ready?"

"Yes, monseigneur."

"Go to the entrance of the grottoes, my good Yves, where you will find the Seigneur de Pierrefonds, who is resting, tired from the journey. And if he should happen not to be able to walk, lift him up, and bring him to me."

The three men obeyed. But the advice given to his servants was useless. Porthos, refreshed, had already begun the descent, and his heavy step resounded among the cavities, formed and supported by columns of granite. As soon as the Seigneur de Bracieux had joined the bishop, the Bretons lighted a lantern, and Porthos assured his friend that he felt as strong as ever.

"Let us visit the canoe," said Aramis, "and make sure at once what it will hold."

"Do not go too near with the light," said the captain, Yves; "for, as you requested, monseigneur, I have placed under the bench of the poop, in the chest, the barrel of powder and the musket charges that you sent me from the fort."

"Very well," said Aramis; and, taking the lantern himself, he examined minutely all parts of the canoe, with the precautions of a man who is neither timid nor ignorant in the face of danger. The canoe was long, light, drawing little water, thin of keel; in short, one of those which have always been so well constructed at Belle-Isle; a little high in its sides, solid upon the water, very manageable, furnished with planks which, in uncertain weather, form a sort of bridge over which the waves glide and which protect the rowers. In two well-closed chests, placed beneath the benches of the prow and the poop, Aramis found bread, biscuits, dried fruits, a quarter of bacon, a good supply of water in leather bottles; the whole made up rations sufficient for people who did not mean to leave the coast, and would be able to take in fresh supplies if necessary. The arms, eight muskets, and as many horse pistols, were in good condition, and all loaded. There were additional oars, in case of accident, and that little sail called *trinquet*, which helps the speed of the canoe at the same time the boatmen row, which is so useful when the breeze is slack.

When Aramis had seen all these things, and appeared satisfied with the result of his inspection: "Let us consult, Porthos," he said, "to decide if we must try to get the boat out by the unknown extremity of the grotto, following the slope and the darkness of the cavern, or whether it would be better, in the open air, to make it slide upon the rollers through the bushes, leveling the road of the little cliff, which is not even twenty feet high, and has at its foot, in the tide, three or four fathoms of good water on a sound bottom."

"It must be as you please, monseigneur," replied the captain Yves, respectfully; "but I don't believe that by the slope of the cavern, and in the dark, in which we shall be obliged to maneuver our boat, the road will be as convenient as in the open air. I know the cliff well, and can certify that it is as smooth as a grass plot in a garden; the interior of the grotto, on the contrary, is rough; we must also realize, monseigneur, that at the end we shall come to the trench which leads into the sea, and perhaps the canoe will not go through it."

"I have made my calculations," said the bishop, "and I am certain it would go through."

"I hope it will, monseigneur," the captain went on; "but your greatness knows very well that to make it reach the end of the trench, there is an enormous stone to be lifted—under which the fox always passes, and which closes the trench up like a door."

"That can be raised," said Porthos, "that is nothing."

"I know that monseigneur has the strength of ten men," replied Yves; "but that will give monseigneur a great deal of trouble."

"I think the captain may be right," said Aramis; "let us try the open-air passage."

"All the more, monseigneur," continued the fisherman, "that there is so much work that we cannot embark before daybreak, and that as soon as daylight appears a good *vedette* placed outside the grotto will be necessary, indispensable even, to watch the maneuvers of the lighters or the cruisers that are on the lookout for us."

"Yes, yes, Yves, your reasons are good; we will go by the cliff."

And the three robust Bretons went to the boat, and were beginning to place their rollers underneath it to put it in motion, when the distant barking of dogs was heard, from the interior.

Aramis darted out of the grotto, followed by Porthos. Dawn was coloring in purple and white the waves and the plain; through the dim light the young melancholy firs waved their tender branches over the pebbles, and long flights of crows were skimming with their black wings over the thin fields of buckwheat. In a quarter of an hour it would be clear daylight; the birds, awake, were announcing it joyously to all nature. The barking which had been heard, which had stopped the three fishermen engaged in moving the boat, and had brought Aramis and Porthos out of the cavern, echoed along the deep gorge within about a league of the grotto.

"It is a pack of hounds," said Porthos; "the dogs have caught a scent."

"Who can be hunting at such an hour?" said Aramis.

"And particularly around here," continued Porthos, "this way, where they may expect the army of the royalists."

"The noise is coming nearer. Yes, you are right, Porthos, the dogs have caught a scent. But, Yves," cried Aramis, "come here! come here!"

Yves ran toward him, leaving the cylinder which he was about to place under the boat when the bishop's call interrupted him.

"What is the meaning of this hunt, captain?" said Porthos.

"Eh! Monseigneur, I cannot understand it," replied the Breton. "The seigneur de Locmaria would not hunt at such a moment. No, and yet the dogs . . ."

"Unless they have escaped from the kennel."

"No," said Goenne, "they are not the seigneur de Locmaria's hounds."

"Let us go back prudently into the grotto," said Aramis; "the voices evidently are drawing nearer; we shall soon know what to expect."

They reentered, but had scarcely proceeded a hundred steps in the darkness, when a noise like the hoarse sigh of a creature in distress resounded through the cavern, and breathless, rapid, terrified, a fox passed like a flash of lightning before the fugitives, leaped over the boat, and disappeared, leaving behind it its sour scent, which was perceptible for several seconds under the low vaults of the cave.

"The fox!" cried the Bretons, with the joyous surprise of hunters.

"Curses on us!" cried the bishop, "our retreat is discovered."

"How so?" said Porthos, "are we afraid of a fox?"

"My friend, what are you saying? and why are you concerned about the fox? It is not the fox alone, *pardieu!* But don't you know, Porthos, that after the fox come hounds, and after the hounds, men?"

Porthos hung his head. As if to confirm the words of Aramis, they heard the yelping pack come with frightful swiftness upon the trail of the animal. Six foxhounds burst out at once upon the little heath, with a cry resembling the noise of a triumph.

"There are the dogs, plain enough," said Aramis, posted on the lookout behind a chink between two rocks; "now, who are the huntsmen?"

"If it is the seigneur de Locmaria," replied the captain, "he will let the dogs search the grotto, for he knows them, and will not enter it himself, being quite sure that the fox will come out at the other side; he will go there and wait for him."

"It is not the seigneur de Locmaria who is hunting," replied Aramis, turning pale in spite of his efforts.

"Who is it, then?" said Porthos.

"Look!"

Porthos put his eye to the slit, and saw, at the summit of a hillock, a dozen horsemen, urging on their horses in the track of the dogs, shouting:

"Taïaut! taïaut!"

"The guards!" said he. "Yes, my friend, the king's guards."

"The king's guards! do you say, monseigneur?" cried the Bretons, now turning pale in their turn.

"And Biscarrat at their head, on my gray horse," Aramis went on.

The hounds at the same moment rushed into the grotto like an avalanche, and the depths of the cavern were filled with their deafening cries.

"The devil!" said Aramis, resuming all his coolness at the sight of this certain, inevitable danger. "I know that we are lost, but we have, at least, one chance left. If the guards who follow their hounds happen to discover there is an outlet to the grotto, there is no more help for us, for on entering they must see both us and our boat. The dogs must not go out of the cavern. The masters must not enter."

"That is clear," said Porthos.

"You understand," added Aramis, with the rapid precision of command: "there are six dogs, which will be forced to stop at the great stone under which the fox has slipped—but at the too narrow opening of which they shall be themselves stopped and killed."

The Bretons sprung forward, knife in hand. In a few minutes there was a pathetic concert of growls and mortal howlings—and then, nothing.

"Good!" said Aramis coolly; "now for the masters!"

"What is to be done with them?" said Porthos.

"Wait for their arrival, conceal ourselves, and kill them."

"Kill them?" replied Porthos.

"There are sixteen," said Aramis, "at least, at present."

"And well armed," added Porthos, with a smile of consolation.

"It will last about ten minutes," said Aramis. "To work!"

And with a determined air, he took up a musket and placed his hunting knife between his teeth.

"Yves, Goenne, and his son," continued Aramis, "will pass the muskets to us. You, Porthos, will fire when they are close. We shall have killed eight before the others are aware of anything—that is certain; then all, there are five of us, we will do away with the other eight, knife in hand.''

''And poor Biscarrat?'' said Porthos.

Aramis thought a moment.

''Biscarrat the first,'' he replied coolly. ''He knows us.''

CHAPTER XLVIII

THE GROTTO

In spite of the sort of intuition which was the remarkable side of the character of Aramis, the event, subject to the chances of things over which uncertainty presides, did not take place exactly as the bishop of Vannes had foreseen. Biscarrat, better mounted than his companions, arrived first at the opening of the grotto, and understood that the fox and the dogs were all engulfed in it. But struck by that superstitious terror which every dark and underground path naturally impresses upon the mind of man, he stopped at the outside of the grotto, and waited for his companions to gather around him.

''Well,'' asked the young men, coming up out of breath, and unable to understand the meaning of his inaction.

''Well, I cannot hear the dogs; they and the fox must be engulfed in this cavern.''

''They were too close up,'' said one of the guards, ''to have lost scent all at once. Besides, we should hear them from one side or another. They must be, as Biscarrat says, in this grotto.''

''But, then,'' said one of the young men, ''why don't they bark?''

''It is strange!'' said another.

''Well,'' said a fourth, ''let us go into this grotto. Are we forbidden to enter it?''

''No,'' replied Biscarrat. ''But, as it looks as dark as a wolf's mouth, we might break our necks in it.''

''Witness the dogs,'' said a guard, ''who seem to have broken theirs.''

''What the devil could have become of them?'' asked the young men, in chorus.

And every master called his dog by name, whistled to him in his favorite note, without a single one replying to either the call or the whistle.

"It is, perhaps, an enchanted grotto," said Biscarrat; "let us see."

And, jumping from his horse, he took a step into the grotto.

"Stop! stop! I will accompany you," said one of the guards, on seeing Biscarrat disappear in the darkness of the cavern's entrance.

"No," replied Biscarrat, "there must be something extraordinary in the place—let us not risk ourselves all at once. If in ten minutes you have not heard from me, you can come in, but not all at once."

"Fine," said the young men, who, besides, did not think that Biscarrat ran much risk in the undertaking; "we will wait for you."

And, without getting off their horses, they formed a circle around the grotto.

Biscarrat entered then alone, and advanced through the darkness until he came in contact with the muzzle of Porthos's musket. The resistance which his chest met with astonished him; he naturally raised his hand and got hold of the icy barrel. At the same instant Yves lifted a knife against the young man, which was about to fall upon him with all the force of a Breton's arm when the iron wrist of Porthos stopped it halfway. Then, like low, muttering thunder his voice growled in the darkness:

"I will not have him killed!"

Biscarrat found himself between a protection and a threat, the one almost as terrible as the other. However brave the young man might be, he could not prevent a cry from escaping him, which Aramis immediately suppressed by placing a handkerchief over his mouth.

"Monsieur de Biscarrat," he said, in a low voice, "we mean you no harm, and you must know that, if you have recognized us; but at the first word, the first sigh, or the first breath, we will be forced to kill you as we have killed your dogs."

"Yes, I recognize you, gentlemen," said the officer, in a low voice. "But why are you here—what are you doing here? Unfortunate men, I thought you were in the fort!"

''And you, monsieur, you were to obtain conditions for us, I think?''

''I did all I was able, messieurs, but . . .''

''But what?''

''But there are positive orders.''

''To kill us?''

Biscarrat made no reply. It was too painful to speak of the rope to gentlemen. Aramis understood the silence of the prisoner.

''Monsieur de Biscarrat,'' he said, ''you would be already dead if we did not respect your youth and our long-time association with your father; but you may yet escape from here by swearing that you will not tell your companions what you have seen.''

''I will not only swear that I will not speak of it,'' said Biscarrat, ''but I still further swear that I will do everything in the world to prevent my companions from setting foot in the grotto.''

''Biscarrat! Biscarrat!'' cried several voices from the outside, coming like a whirlwind into the cave.

''Reply,'' said Aramis.

''Here I am!'' cried Biscarrat.

''Now, go; we depend upon your loyalty.''

And he let go of the young man, who hastily returned toward the light.

''Biscarrat! Biscarrat!'' cried the voices, still nearer.

And the shadows of several human forms were seen projected inside the grotto.

Biscarrat rushed to meet his friends in order to stop them, and met them just as they were venturing into the cave. Aramis and Porthos listened with the intense attention of men whose lives depend upon a breath of air.

''Oh!'' exclaimed one of the guards, as he came to the light, ''how pale you are!''

''Pale!'' cried another; ''you ought to say livid.''

''I?'' said the young man, trying to collect his wits.

''In the name of Heaven! what has happened to you?'' exclaimed all voices.

''You don't have a drop of blood in your veins, my poor friend,'' said one of them, laughing.

''Messieurs, it is serious,'' said another; ''he is going to faint; does any one of you happen to have any salts?''

And they all laughed.

All these queries, all these jokes crossed one another around Biscarrat as the bullets cross one another in the fire of a fight. He recovered himself amid a deluge of questions.

"What do you suppose I have seen?" he asked. "I was too hot when I entered the grotto, and I have been struck with the cold; that is all."

"But the dogs, the dogs, have you seen them again—did you see anything of them—do you know anything about them?"

"I suppose they have gone out another way."

"Messieurs," said one of the young men, "there is in what is happening, in the paleness and silence of our friend, a mystery which Biscarrat will not, or cannot reveal. Only, and that is a certainty, Biscarrat has seen something in the grotto. Well, for my part, I am very curious to see what it is, even if it were the devil. To the grotto, messieurs, to the grotto!"

"To the grotto!" repeated all the voices. And the echo of the cavern carried like a menace to Porthos and Aramis, "To the grotto! to the grotto!"

Biscarrat threw himself before his companions.

"Messieurs, messieurs!" he cried, "in the name of Heaven! do not go in!"

"Why, what is there so terrifying in the cavern?" asked several at once. "Come, speak, Biscarrat."

"It is surely the devil he has seen," repeated the one who had before advanced that hypothesis.

"Well," said another, "if he has seen him, he need not be selfish; it's our turn to have a look at him."

"Messieurs! messieurs! I beg you," urged Biscarrat.

"Nonsense! let us pass!"

"Messieurs, I implore you not to enter!"

"Why, you went in yourself."

Then, one of the officers who—of a riper age than the others—had until this time remained behind, and had said nothing, came forward.

"Messieurs," he said, with a calmness which contrasted with the animation of the young men, "there is in there some person, or something, that is not the devil; but, which, whatever it may be, has had sufficient power to silence our dogs. We must know who this someone is, or what this something is."

Biscarrat made a last effort to stop his friends, but it was useless. In vain he threw himself in front of the most rash; in vain he clung to the rocks to bar the passage, the crowd of young men rushed into the cave, in the steps of the officer who had spoken last, but who had sprung in first, sword in hand, to face the unknown danger. Biscarrat, pushed back by his friends, not able to accompany them without passing in the eyes of Porthos and Aramis for a traitor and a perjurer, with painfully attentive ear and still supplicating hands leaned against the rough side of a rock, which he thought must be exposed to the fire of the musketeers. As to the guards, they went in further and further, with cries that grew weaker as they advanced. All at once a discharge of musket, growling like thunder, exploded beneath the vault. Two or three bullets were flattened against the rock where Biscarrat was leaning. At the same instant, cries, howlings, and imprecations burst forth, and the little troop of gentlemen reappeared—some pale, some bleeding—all enveloped in a cloud of smoke, which the outward air seemed to draw from the depths of the cavern.

"Biscarrat! Biscarrat!" cried the fugitives, "you knew there was an ambush in that cavern, and you did not warn us! Biscarrat, you are the reason that four of us have been killed! Woe to you, Biscarrat!"

"You are the cause of my being wounded to death," said one of the young men, gathering his blood in his hand, and casting it into the face of Biscarrat. "My blood be upon your head!"

And he rolled in agony at the feet of the young man.

"But, at least, tell us who is there?" cried several furious voices.

Biscarrat remained silent.

"Tell us, or die!" cried the wounded man, raising himself upon one knee, and lifting toward his companion an arm bearing a useless sword.

Biscarrat rushed toward him, opening his breast for the blow, but the wounded man fell back not to rise again, with a sigh which was his last. Biscarrat, with hair on end, haggard eyes, and bewildered head, advanced toward the interior of the cavern, saying:

"You are right. Death to me, who have let my companions be assassinated. I am a coward!"

And, throwing away his sword, for he wished to die without defending himself, he rushed head first into the cavern. The others followed him. The eleven who remained out of sixteen followed his example; but they did not go further than the first. A second volley laid five upon the icy sand; and as it was impossible to see where this murderous thunder was coming from, the others fell back with a terror that can be better imagined than expressed. But, far from fleeing, as the others had done, Biscarrat remained safe and sound, seated on a fragment of rock, and waited. There were only six gentlemen left.

"Seriously," said one of the survivors, "is it the devil?"

"Ma foi! it is much worse," said another.

"Ask Biscarrat, he knows."

"Where is Biscarrat?"

The young men looked around them, and saw that Biscarrat did not answer.

"He is dead!" said two or three voices.

"Oh, no!" replied another; "I saw him through the smoke, sitting quietly on a rock. He is in the cavern; he is waiting for us."

"He must know those who are there."

"And how should he know them?"

"He was taken prisoner by the rebels."

"That is true. Well, let us call him, and learn from him whom we have to deal with."

And all voices shouted: "Biscarrat! Biscarrat!" But Biscarrat did not answer.

"Good!" said the officer who had shown so much coolness in the affair. "We don't need him anymore; here are reinforcements coming."

In fact, a company of guards, left in the rear by their officers, whom the excitement of the chase had carried away—from seventy-five to eighty men—arrived in good order, led by their captain and the first lieutenant. The five officers hastened to meet their soldiers; and, in a language the eloquence of which may be easily imagined, they related the adventure, and asked for help. The captain interrupted them.

"Where are your companions?" he asked.

"Dead!"

"But there were sixteen of you."

"Ten are dead. Biscarrat is in the cavern, and we are five."

"Is Biscarrat, then, a prisoner?"

"Probably."

"No, for here he is—look!"

In fact, Biscarrat appeared at the opening of the grotto.

"He is beckoning us to come on," said the officer. "Come on!"

"Come on!" cried all the troop.

And they advanced to meet Biscarrat.

"Monsieur," said the captain, addressing Biscarrat, "they assure me that you know who the men in that grotto are, who are making such a desperate defense. In the king's name, I command you to declare what you know!"

"Captain," said Biscarrat, "you have no need to command me; my word has been restored to me this very instant, and I am coming in the name of these men."

"To tell me who they are?"

"To tell you they are determined to defend themselves to the death, unless you grant them good terms."

"How many are there of them, then?"

"There are two," said Biscarrat.

"There are two—and want to impose conditions upon us?"

"There are two, and they have already killed ten of our men."

"What sort of people are they—giants?"

"Better than that. Do you remember the story of the bastion St. Gervais, captain?"

"Yes; where four musketeers held out against an army."

"Well, these two men were of those musketeers."

"And their names?"

"At that time they were called Porthos and Aramis. Now, they are called Monsieur d'Herblay and Monsieur du Vallon."

"And what interest have they in all this?"

"It is they who held Belle-Isle for Monsieur Fouquet."

A murmur ran through the ranks of the soldiers on hearing the two words, "Porthos and Aramis."

"The musketeers! the musketeers!" they repeated.

And among all these brave men, the idea that they were going to fight against two of the oldest glories of the French army made a shiver, half enthusiasm, half terror, run through them. In fact, those four names—D'Artagnan,

Athos, Porthos, and Aramis—were venerated among all who wore a sword; as, in antiquity, the names of Hercules, Theseus, Castor, and Pollux were venerated.

"Two men—and they have killed ten in two volleys! That is impossible, Monsieur Biscarrat!"

"Eh! captain," replied the latter, "I do not tell you that they have not with them two or three men, as the musketeers of the bastion St. Gervais had two or three lackeys; but, believe me, captain, I have seen these men, I have been taken prisoner by them—I know they alone would be enough to destroy an army."

"That we shall see," said the captain, "and that in a moment, too. Gentlemen, attention!"

At this reply no one moved, and all prepared to obey. Biscarrat alone risked a last attempt.

"Monsieur," he said in a low voice, "believe me, let us pass on our way. Those two men, those two lions you are going to attack, will defend themselves to the death. They have already killed ten of our men: they will kill twice as many, and end by killing themselves, rather than surrender. What shall we gain by fighting them?"

"We shall gain the honor, monsieur, of not having eighty of the king's guards retreat before two rebels. If I listened to your advice, monsieur, I should be a dishonored man, and by dishonoring myself I would dishonor the army. Forward, men!"

And he marched first as far as the opening of the grotto. There he halted. The object of this halt was to give to Biscarrat and his companions time to describe to him the interior of the grotto. Then, when he believed he had enough knowledge of the places, he divided his company into three bodies, which were to enter successively, keeping up a sustained fire in all directions. No doubt, in this attack they would lose five more men, perhaps ten; but, certainly, they must end by taking the rebels, since there was no opening: and, at any rate, two men could not kill eighty.

"Captain," said Biscarrat, "I beg to be allowed to march at the head of the first platoon."

"Fine," replied the captain; "you have all the honor of it. That is a present I am giving you."

"Thank you!" replied the young man, with all the firmness of his race.

"Take your sword, then."

"I shall go as I am, captain," said Biscarrat, "for I do not go to kill, I go to be killed."

And, placing himself at the head of the first platoon, with his head uncovered and his arms crossed:

"Let us march, gentlemen!" he said.

CHAPTER XLIX

A HOMERIC SONG

It is time to pass into the other camp, and to describe at once the combatants and the field of battle. Aramis and Porthos had gone to the grotto of Locmaria to find there their canoe ready armed, as well as the three Bretons, their assistants; and at first they hoped to have the boat go through the little opening of the cavern, concealing, in that fashion, both their labors and their flight. The arrival of the fox and the dogs had obliged them to remain concealed. The grotto extended the space of about six hundred feet, to that little slope dominating a creek. Formerly a temple of the Celtic divinities, when Belle-Isle was still called Colonese, this grotto had seen more than one human sacrifice accomplished in its mysterious depths. The first entrance to the cavern was by a moderate descent, above which heaped-up rocks formed a low arcade; the interior, very uneven as to the ground, dangerous from the rocky inequalities of the vault, was subdivided into several compartments which commanded one another and joined one another by means of several rough, broken steps, fixed right and left, in enormous natural pillars. At the third compartment the vault was so low, the passage so narrow, that the boat would scarcely have gone through without touching the two sides; nevertheless, in a moment of despair, wood softens and stone becomes compliant under the breath of human will.

Such was the thought of Aramis, when, after having fought the fight he decided upon flight—a flight certainly dangerous, since all the assailants were not dead; and that, admitting the possibility of putting the boat to sea, they would have to flee in broad daylight before the conquered, so eager, on recognizing their small number, in pursuing their conquerors. When the two volleys had killed ten men, Aramis, used to the windings of the cavern, went to reconnoiter them one by one—counted them, for the smoke prevented seeing outside; and he immediately ordered that the canoe should be rolled as far as the big stone, the closure of the liberating opening. Porthos collected all his strength, took the canoe up in his arms, and raised it up, while the Bretons made it run rapidly along the rollers. They had gone down into the third compartment; they had arrived at the stone which walled up the outlet. Porthos seized this gigantic stone at its base, applied to it his robust shoulder, and gave a heave which made the wall crack. A cloud of dust fell from the vault with the ashes of ten thousand generations of sea birds, whose nests stuck like cement to the rock. At the third shock the stone gave way; it oscillated for a minute. Porthos, placing his back against the neighboring rock, made an arch with his foot, which drove the block out of the calcareous masses which served for hinges and cramps. The stone fell, and daylight was visible, brilliant, radiant, which rushed into the cavern by the opening, and the blue sea appeared to the delighted Bretons.

They then began to lift the boat over the barricade. One hundred more feet, and it might glide into the ocean. It was during this time that the company arrived, was drawn up by the captain, and disposed for either a climb or an assault. Aramis was watching everything, to help the labors of his friends. He saw the reinforcements, he counted the men, he convinced himself at a single glance of the insurmountable peril to which a new fight would expose them. To escape by sea, at the moment the cavern was about to be invaded, was impossible. In fact, daylight which had just reached the two last compartments would have shown the soldiers the boat being rolled toward the sea, the two rebels within musket shot, and one of their discharges would riddle the boat, if it did not kill the five navigators. Besides, supposing everything—if the boat escaped with the men on board, how could the alarm be suppressed—how could notice to the royal lighters be prevented? What could hinder the poor canoe, followed by sea and watched from the shore, from succumbing before the end of the day? Aramis, digging his hands into his gray hair with rage, called on God and called on the Devil. Calling to Porthos, who was working alone more than all the rollers—whether of flesh or wood:

"My friend," he said, "our adversaries have just received a reinforcement."

"Ah!" said Porthos quietly, "what is to be done, then?"

"To start fighting again," said Aramis, "is hazardous."

"Yes," said Porthos, "for it is difficult to suppose that out of two one should not be killed, and certainly, if one of us were killed, the other would get himself killed also."

Porthos spoke these words with that heroic nature which, with him, grew greater in proportion to his size.

Aramis felt it like a spur to his heart.

"We shall neither of us be killed, if you do what I tell you, my friend Porthos."

"Tell me what."

"Are these people coming down into the grotto?"

"Yes."

"We could kill about fifteen of them, but no more."

"How many are there in all?" asked Porthos.

"They have gotten a reinforcement of seventy-five men."

"Seventy-five and five, eighty!" said Porthos.

"If they fire all at once they will riddle us with bullets."

"Certainly they will."

"Without taking account," added Aramis, "that the detonations might cause the cavern to collapse."

"A piece of falling rock just grazed my shoulder a little," said Porthos.

"You see, then!"

"Oh, it is nothing!"

"We must decide something quickly. Our Bretons are going to continue to roll the canoe toward the sea."

"Very well."

"We two will keep the powder, the bullets, and the muskets here."

"But the two of us, my dear Aramis, we shall never fire three shots together," said Porthos innocently, "the defense with muskets is difficult."

"Find a better way, then."

"I have found one," said the giant eagerly; "I will place myself in ambush behind the pillar with this iron bar, and invisible, unattackable, if they come in in floods, I can let my bar fall upon their skulls, thirty times in a minute. Hey! what do you think of the plan? Do you like it?"

"Excellent, dear friend, perfect! I approve of it greatly; only you will frighten them, and half of them will remain outside to starve us out. What we want, my good friend, is the entire destruction of the troop; a single man left standing ruins us."

"You are right, my friend; but how can we attract them?"

"By not stirring, my good Porthos."

"Well, we won't stir, then; but when they will be all together . . ."

"Then leave it to me, I have an idea."

"If it is so, and your idea is a good one—and your idea is likely to be good—I am satisfied."

"Lie in wait, Porthos, and count how many enter."

"But you, what will you do?"

"Don't worry about me; I have a task to perform."

"I think I can hear cries."

"It is they! To your post. Keep within reach of my voice and hand."

Porthos took refuge in the second compartment, which was absolutely black with darkness. Aramis slipped into the third; the giant was holding in his hand a fifty-pound iron bar. Porthos handled this lever, which had been used in rolling the boat, with marvelous facility. During this time the Bretons had pushed the boat to the beach. In the lighted compartment, Aramis, stooping and concealed, was busy in some mysterious maneuver. A command was given in a loud voice. It was the last order of the captain commandant. Twenty-five men jumped from the upper rocks into the first compartment of the grotto, and having landed, began to fire. The echoes growled, the hissing of the bullets cut the air, an opaque smoke filled the vault.

"To the left! to the left!" cried Biscarrat, who, in his first assault, had seen the passage to the second chamber, and who, excited by the smell of powder, wished to guide his soldiers in that direction. The troop accordingly rushed to the left—the passage gradually growing narrower. Biscarrat, with his hands stretched forward, devoted to death, was walking toward the muskets.

"Come on! come on!" he cried; "I see daylight!"

"Strike, Porthos!" cried the sepulchral voice of Aramis.

Porthos breathed a heavy sigh—but he obeyed. The iron bar fell full and direct upon the head of Biscarrat, who was dead before he had ended his cry. Then the formidable lever rose ten times in ten seconds, and made ten corpses. The soldiers could see nothing; they heard sighs and groans; they stumbled over dead bodies, but as they had no idea of the cause of all this, they came forward, jostling one another. The implacable bar, still falling, annihilated the first platoon, without a single sound having warned the second, which was quietly advancing, only this second, commanded by the captain, had broken a thin fir, growing on the shore, and, with its resinous branches twisted together, the captain had made a torch. On arriving at the compartment where Porthos, like the exterminating angel, had destroyed all he touched, the first rank drew back in terror. No firing had replied to that of the guards, and yet their way was stopped by a heap of dead bodies—they were literally walking in blood. Porthos was still behind his pillar. The captain, on lighting with the trembling flame of the fir this frightful carnage, of which he in vain sought the cause, drew back toward the pillar behind which Porthos was concealed. Then a gigantic hand came out from the shadow, and fastened on the throat of the captain, who uttered a stifled rattle; his stretched-out arms beating the air, the torch fell and was extinguished in blood. A second later, the corpse of the captain fell close to the extinguished torch, and added another body to the heap of dead which blocked up the passage. All this was done as mysteriously as if by magic. On hearing the rattling in the throat of the captain, the soldiers who accompanied him had turned around; they had caught a glimpse of his extended arms, his eyes starting from their sockets, and then the torch fell and they were left in darkness. From an unreflective, instinctive, mechanical feeling, the lieutenant cried:

"Fire!"

Immediately a volley of musketry flamed, thundered, roared in the cavern, bringing down enormous fragments from the vaults. The cavern was lighted for an instant by this volley, and then immediately returned to a darkness rendered still thicker by the smoke. After this there was a profound silence, broken only by the steps of the third brigade, now entering the cavern.

CHAPTER L

THE DEATH OF A TITAN

JUST as Porthos, more accustomed to the darkness than all these men coming from open daylight, was looking around him to see if in this night Aramis were not giving him some signal, he felt his arm gently touched, and a voice low as a breath murmured in his ear:

"Come!"

"Oh!" said Porthos.

"Hush!" said Aramis, if possible, still more softly.

And amid the noise of the third brigade, which continued to advance, amid the imprecations of the guards left alive, of the dying, rattling their last sigh, Aramis and Porthos slipped imperceptibly along the granite walls of the cavern. Aramis led Porthos into the next to the last compartment, and showed him, in a hollow of the rocky wall, a barrel of powder weighing from seventy to eighty pounds, to which he had just attached a fuse.

"My friend," he said to Porthos, "you will take this barrel, the fuse of which I am going to light, and throw it amid our enemies; can you do so?"

"Parbleu!" replied Porthos, and he lifted the barrel with one hand. "Light it!"

"Wait," said Aramis, "until they are all together, and then, my Jupiter, hurl your thunderbolt among them!"

"Light it," repeated Porthos.

"On my part," continued Aramis, "I will join our Bretons, and help them to get the canoe to the sea. I will wait for you on the shore; launch it strongly, and run back to us."

"Light it," said Porthos a third time.

"But do you understand me?"

"Parbleu!" said Porthos again, with a laugh that he did not even attempt to restrain; "when a thing is explained to me, I understand it; be gone, and give me the light."

Aramis gave the burning match to Porthos, who held

out his arm to him, his hands being engaged. Aramis
pressed the arm of Porthos with both his hands, and fell
back to the outlet of the cavern where the three rowers
were waiting for him.

Porthos, left alone, applied the spark bravely to the
fuse. The spark—a feeble spark, first principle of an immense fire shone in the darkness like a firefly and then,
as Porthos blew on it, reached the fuse. The smoke was
a little dispersed, and by the light of the sparkling fuse
objects might, for two seconds, be distinguished. It
was a short but a splendid spectacle, that of this giant,
pale, bloody, his face lighted by the fire of the fuse burning in surrounding darkness. The soldiers saw him—they
saw the barrel he held in his hand—they at once understood what was going to happen. Then, these men, already filled with terror at the sight of what had been
accomplished—filled with terror at thinking of what was
going to be accomplished—shrieked with horror. Some
tried to flee, but they encountered the third brigade which
blocked their passage; others mechanically took aim and
attempted to fire their discharged muskets; others fell
upon their knees. Two or three officers cried out to Porthos to promise him his liberty if he would spare their
lives. The lieutenant of the third brigade was ordering
his men to fire; but the guards had before them their
terrified companions, who served as a living rampart for
Porthos. We have said that the light produced by the spark
and the fuse did not last more than two seconds; but
during these two seconds this is what it lit up—in the first
place, the giant enlarged in the darkness; then at ten paces
from him, a heap of bleeding bodies, crushed, mutilated,
in the midst of whom still lived some last struggle of
agony, which lifted the mass as a last gasp raises the
sides of a shapeless monster expiring in the night. Every
breath of Porthos, blowing on the fuse, sent toward this
heap of bodies a sulphureous hue, mingled with streaks
of purple. In addition to this principal group, scattered
about the grotto, as the chance of death or the surprise
of the blow had stretched them, some isolated bodies
seemed to threaten with their gaping wounds. Above the
ground, soaked by pools of blood, rose, heavy and sparkling, the short, thick pillars of the cavern, of which the
strongly marked shades threw out the luminous particles.

And all this was seen by the tremulous light of a match attached to a barrel of powder, that is to say, a torch which, while throwing a light upon the dead past, showed the death to come.

As I have said, this spectacle did not last more than two seconds. During this short space of time an officer of the third brigade got together eight men armed with muskets, and, through an opening, ordered them to fire upon Porthos. But they who received the order to fire trembled so that three guards fell by the shots, and the five other bullets went hissing to splinter the vault, plow the ground, or indent the sides of the cavern.

A burst of laughter answered this volley; then the arm of the giant swung around; then was seen to pass through the air, like a falling star, the train of fire. The barrel, hurled a distance of thirty feet, cleared the barricade of the dead bodies, and fell amid a group of shrieking soldiers, who threw themselves on their faces. The officer had followed the brilliant train in the air; he endeavored to hurl himself upon the barrel and tear out the fuse before it reached the powder it contained. Useless courage! The air had made the flame attached to the conductor more active; the fuse, which at rest might have burned five minutes, was consumed in thirty seconds, and the infernal work exploded. Furious whirls, hissings of sulphur and niter, devouring ravages of the fire, the terrible thunder of the explosion, this is what the second which followed the two seconds we have described disclosed in that cavern, equal in horrors to a cavern of demons. The rock split like planks of pine trees under the ax. A jet of fire, smoke, and debris sprang up from the middle of the grotto, enlarging as it rose. The large walls of silex tottered and fell upon the sand, and the sand itself, an instrument of pain when launched from its hardened bed, riddled the faces with its myriads of cutting atoms. Cries, howling, curses, and existences—all were extinguished in one immense crash.

The three first compartments became a gulf into which fell back again, according to its weight, every vegetable, mineral, or human fragment. Then the lighter sand and ashes fell in their turns, stretching like a gray winding sheet and smoking over those dismal funerals.

And now, seek in this burning tomb, in this subterraneous volcano, seek for the king's guards with their blue coats laced with silver. Seek for the officers shining with gold; seek for the arms upon which they depended for their defense; seek for the stones that have killed them, the ground that has borne them. One single man has made of all this a chaos more confused, more shapeless, more terrible than the chaos which existed an hour before God had created the world. There remained nothing of the three compartments—nothing by which God could have known His own work.

As to Porthos, after having hurled the barrel of powder amid his enemies, he had fled, as Aramis had directed him to do, and had gained the last compartment, into which air, light, and sunshine penetrated through the opening. Therefore, scarcely had he turned the angle which separated the third compartment from the fourth, than he saw, at a hundred paces from him, the boat dancing on the waves; there were his friends, there was liberty, there was life after victory. Six more of his formidable strides, and he would be out of the vault; out of the vault! two or three vigorous springs, and he would reach the canoe. Suddenly he felt his knees give way; his knees appeared powerless, his legs were yielding under him.

"There is my fatigue seizing me again!" he murmured. "I can walk no further! What is this?"

Aramis saw him through the opening, and unable to conceive what could induce him to stop:

"Come on, Porthos! come on," he cried; "come quickly!"

"Oh!" replied the giant, making an effort which acted upon every muscle of his body, "oh! but I cannot."

While saying these words, he fell upon his knees; but with his robust hands he clung to the rocks, and raised himself up again.

"Quick, quick!" repeated Aramis, bending forward toward the shore, as if to draw Porthos toward him with his arms.

"Here I am," stammered Porthos, collecting all his strength to take one more step.

"In the name of Heaven! Porthos, make haste! the barrel will blow up!"

"Make haste, monseigneur!" shouted the Bretons to Porthos, who was floundering as in a dream.

But there was no longer time; the explosion resounded,

the earth gaped, the smoke which rushed through the large fissures obscured the sky; the sea flowed back, as if driven by the blast of fire which darted from the grotto as if from the jaws of a gigantic chimera; the reflux carried the boat out one hundred feet; the rocks cracked to their base, and separated like blocks beneath the operation of wedges; a portion of the vault was carried up toward heaven, as if by rapid currents; the rose-colored and green fire of the sulphur, the black lava of the argillaceous liquefactions clashed and fought for an instant beneath a majestic dome of smoke; then, one saw at first oscillate, then lean, then fall successively the long ridges of rock which the violence of the explosion had not been able to uproot from their bed of ages; they bowed to one another like grave and slow old men, then prostrated themselves, lying forever in their dusty tomb.

This frightful shock seemed to restore to Porthos the strength he had lost; he arose, himself a giant among these giants. But just as he was escaping between the double hedge of granite phantoms, the latter, which were no longer supported by the corresponding links, began to roll with a crash around this Titan, who looked as if hurled from heaven amid the rocks which he had just been launching at it. Porthos felt the earth beneath his feet shaken by this long rending. He stretched his vast hands to the right and left to push back the falling rocks. A gigantic block was held back by each of his extended hands; he bent his head and a third granite mass sank between his two shoulders. For a moment, the arms of Porthos gave way, but the Hercules gathered all his forces, and the two walls of the prison in which he was buried fell back slowly and gave him some room. For a moment he appeared in this frame of granite like the ancient angel of chaos, but in pushing back the lateral rocks, he lost his point of support for the monolith which weighed upon his strong shoulders, and the monolith, lying upon him with all its weight, brought the giant down upon his knees. The lateral rocks, first pushed back, then drew together again, and added their weight to the original weight which would have been sufficient to crush ten men.

The giant fell without crying for help; he fell while answering Aramis with words of encouragement and hope, for, thanks to the powerful arch of his hands, for a moment, he might believe that, like Enceladus, he would shake off the triple load. But by degrees Aramis saw the block sink; the hands clenched for an instant, the arms, stiffened for a last effort, gave way, the extended shoulders sank, wounded and torn, and the rocks continued to lower gradually.

"Porthos! Porthos!" cried Aramis, tearing his hair. "Porthos! where are you? Speak!"

"There, there!" murmured Porthos, with a voice growing evidently weaker, "patience, patience!"

Scarcely had he said these words, when the momentum of the fall increased the weight; the enormous rock sank down, pressed by the two others which sank in from the sides, and swallowed up Porthos in a grave of broken stones. On hearing the dying voice of his friend, Aramis had jumped to shore. Two of the Bretons followed him, each with a lever in his hand—one man being enough to take care of the boat. The last rattles of the valiant struggler guided them amid the ruins. Aramis, dazzling, active, and young as at twenty, sprang toward the triple mass, and with his hands, delicate as those of a woman, raised by a miracle of vigor a corner of the immense grave of granite. Then he caught a glimpse, in the darkness of that grave, of the still-bright eye of his friend, to whom the momentary lifting of the mass restored his breathing. The two men came rushing up, grasped their iron levers, united their triple strength, not merely to raise it, but hold it. All was useless. The three men slowly gave way with cries of grief, and the rough voice of Porthos, seeing them exhaust themselves in a useless struggle, murmured, in a jeering tone, those supreme words which came to his lips with his last breath: "Too heavy!"

After which his eye darkened and closed, his face became pale, his hand whitened, and the Titan sank down, breathing his last sigh. With him sank the rock, which, even in his agony, he had still held. The three men dropped the levers, which rolled upon the tombstone. Then, breathless, his brow covered with sweat, Aramis listened, his chest oppressed, his heart ready to break.

Nothing more! The giant slept the eternal sleep, in the grave which God had made to his measure.

CHAPTER LI

ARAMIS, silent, icy, trembling like a timid child, arose shivering from the stone. A Christian does not walk on tombs. But though capable of standing, he was not capable of walking. It might be said that with Porthos's death something had died within him. His Bretons surrounded him; Aramis yielded to their kind exertions, and the three sailors, lifting him up, carried him into the canoe. Then, having laid him down upon the bench near the rudder, they took to their oars, preferring to get off by rowing to hoisting a sail, which might betray them.

Of all that leveled surface of the ancient grotto of Locmaria, of all that flattened shore, one single little hillock attracted their eyes. Aramis never took his eyes off it; and, at a distance out in the sea, as the shore receded, the menacing and proud mass of rock seemed to draw itself up, as before Porthos used to draw himself up, and raise a smiling and invincible head toward heaven, like that of the honest and valiant friend, the strongest of the four, and yet the first dead. Strange destiny for these men of brass! The most simple of heart allied to the most crafty; strength of body guided by subtlety of mind; and in the decisive moment, when vigor alone could save mind and body, a stone, a rock, a vile and material weight, triumphed over vigor, and, falling upon the body, drove out the mind.

Worthy Porthos! born to help other men, always ready to sacrifice himself for the safety of the weak, as if God had only given him strength for that purpose; when dying he only thought he was carrying out the conditions of his pact with Aramis, a pact, however, which Aramis alone had drawn up, and which Porthos had only known to suffer by its terrible solidarity. Noble Porthos! of what good are the chateaus overflowing with sumptuous furniture, the forests overflowing with game, the lakes overflowing with fish, the cellars overflowing with wealth! Of what good are the servants in brilliant liveries, and in the midst of them Mousqueton, proud of the power delegated by you! Oh, noble Porthos! careful gatherer of treasures, did you have to work so hard to sweeten and gild life, in order to come upon a desert shore, to the cries of sea birds, and lay yourself, with broken bones, beneath a cold stone? Did you have, in short, noble Porthos, to heap so much gold, and not even have the couplet of a poor poet upon your tombstone? Valiant Porthos! He still, without doubt, sleeps, lost, forgotten, beneath the rock which the shepherds of the heath take for the gigantic abode of a *dolmen*. And so many twining branches, so many mosses, caressed by the bitter wind of the ocean, so many vivacious lichens have soldered the grave to the earth, that the passerby will never imagine that such a block of granite can ever have been supported by the shoulders of one man.

Aramis, still pale, still icy, his heart upon his lips, Aramis looked, until the last ray of daylight at the shore faded on the horizon. Not a word escaped his lips, not a sigh rose from his deep breast. The superstitious Bretons looked at him, trembling. The silence was not of a man, it was of a statue. In the meantime, with the first gray lines that came from the sky, the canoe had hoisted its little sail, which, swelling with the kisses of the breeze, and carrying them rapidly from the coast, headed bravely toward Spain, across the terrible Gulf of Gascony, so rife with tempests. But scarcely half an hour after the sail had been hoisted the rowers became inactive, reclining upon their benches, and making an eye shade with their hands, pointed out to each other a white spot which was appearing on the horizon as motionless as a gull rocked by the waves. But what might have appeared motionless to ordinary eyes was moving at a quick rate to the experienced eye of the sailor; what appeared stationary on the ocean was cutting a rapid way through it. For some time, seeing the profound torpor in which their master was plunged, they did not dare to rouse him, and merely exchanged their conjectures in a low, disturbed voice. Aramis, in fact, so vigilant, so active, Aramis, whose eye, like that of the lynx, was forever watching, and saw better by night than by day, Aramis had fallen asleep in the despair of his soul. An hour went by, during which daylight gradually disappeared but during which also the sail in view gained so swiftly on the boat that Goenne, one of the three sailors, ventured to say aloud:

"Monseigneur, we are being chased!"

Aramis made no reply; the ship was still gaining on them. Then, of their own accord, two of the sailors, by the direction of the captain, Yves, lowered the sail, in order that that single point which appeared above the surface of the waters would no longer be a guide to the eye of the enemy who was pursuing them. As for the ship in sight, on the contrary, two more small sails were run up at the top of the masts. Unfortunately, it was the time of the finest and longest days of the year, and the moon, in all her brilliancy, followed this inauspicious daylight. The *balancelle,* which was pursuing the little boat before the wind, still had half an hour of twilight, and a whole night almost as light as day.

"Monseigneur, monseigneur! we are lost!" said the captain. "Look! they see us although we have lowered our sail."

"That is not surprising," murmured one of the sailors, "since they say that, with the devil's help, the people of the cities have fabricated instruments with which they see as well far as near, by night as well as by day."

Aramis took a telescope from the bottom of the boat, arranged it silently, and passing it to the sailor:

"Here!" he said, "look."

The sailor hesitated.

"Don't be alarmed," said the bishop, "there is no sin in it; and if there is any sin, I will take it upon myself."

The sailor lifted the telescope to his eye, and uttered a cry. He had believed that the vessel, which appeared to be at a cannonshot distance, had suddenly cleared the distance. But, on withdrawing the instrument from his eye, he saw that, except the distance which the *balancelle* had been able to cover during that short instant, it was still as far away.

"So," murmured the sailor, "they can see us as we see them."

"They see us," said Aramis, and sank again into his calm.

"What—they see us!" said Yves. "Impossible!"

"Well, captain, look for yourself," said the sailor. And he passed him the telescope.

"Does monseigneur assure me that the devil has nothing to do with this?" asked the captain.

Aramis shrugged his shoulders.

The captain lifted the telescope to his eyes.

"Oh, monseigneur," he said, "it is a miracle; they are there; it seems as if I were going to touch them. Twenty-five men, at least! I see the captain forward. He is holding a telescope like this one, and is looking at us. He turns around, and gives an order; they are rolling a piece of cannon forward—they are charging it—they are pointing it. Mercy! they are firing at us!"

And, by a mechanical movement, the captain took the telescope off, and the objects, sent back to the horizon, appeared again in their true aspect. The vessel was still at the distance of nearly a league, but the maneuver announced by the captain was not less real. A light cloud of smoke appeared under the sails, more blue than they, and spreading like a flower opening; then, at about a mile from the little canoe, they saw the cannon ball take the crown of two or three waves, dig a white furrow in the sea, and disappear at the end of that furrow, as inoffensive as the stone which a boy skips in water. That was at the same time a menace and a warning.

"What is to be done?" asked the captain.

"They will sink us!" said Goenne; "give us absolution, monseigneur."

And the sailors fell on their knees before him.

"You forget that they can see you," he said.

"That is true," said the sailors, ashamed of their weakness. "Give us your orders, monseigneur; we are ready to die for you."

"Let us wait," said Aramis.

"What—let us wait?"

"Yes; don't you see, as you were just saying, that if we try to escape, they will sink us?"

"But, perhaps," the captain ventured to say, "perhaps, by the favor of the night, we could escape them."

"Oh!" said Aramis, "they surely have some Greek fire to light their own course and ours likewise."

At the same moment, as if the little vessel wished to reply to the appeal of Aramis, a second cloud of smoke went up slowly to the sky, and from the bosom of that cloud sparkled an arrow of flame, which followed its arc like a rainbow, and fell into the sea, where it continued to burn, illuminating a space of a quarter of a league in diameter.

The Bretons looked at one another in terror.

"You see plainly," said Aramis, "it will be better to wait for them."

The oars dropped from the hands of the sailors, and the little boat, stopping, rocked motionless on top of the waves. Night came on, but the vessel still approached nearer. It might be said it increased its speed with the darkness. From time to time, as a bloody-necked vulture rears its head out of its nest, the formidable Greek fire darted from its sides, and cast its flame into the ocean like an incandescent snow. At last it came within gunshot. All the men were on deck, arms in hand; the cannoneers were at their guns, the matches were burning. It might be thought they were about to board a frigate and to combat a crew superior in number to their own, and not to take a canoe manned by four people.

"Surrender!" cried the commander of the *balancelle,* with the aid of his bullhorn.

The sailors looked at Aramis. Aramis nodded. Yves waved a white cloth at the end of a stick. This was like striking their flag. The vessel came on like a racehorse. It launched a fresh Greek fire, which fell within twenty paces of the little canoe, and threw a stronger light upon them than the most ardent ray of the sun could have done.

"At the first sign of resistance," cried the commander of the *balancelle,* "fire!"

And the soldiers lowered their muskets.

"Did not we say we surrender?" said Yves.

"Alive! alive! captain!" cried some highly excited soldiers; "they must be taken alive!"

"Well, yes, alive," said the captain.

Then, turning toward the Bretons:

"Your lives are all safe, my friends!" he cried, "except the Chevalier d'Herblay."

Aramis quivered imperceptibly. For an instant his eye was fixed upon the depths of the ocean, lighted by the last flashes of the Greek fire—flashes which ran along the sides of the waves, played upon their crests like plumes, and rendered still more dark, more mysterious, and more terrible the abysses they covered.

"Do you hear, monseigneur?" said the sailors.

"Yes."

"What are your orders?"

"Accept."

"But you, monseigneur?"

Aramis leaned further forward, and with the tips of his long, white fingers played with the green water of the sea, smiling at it as at a friend.

"Accept," he repeated.

"We accept," repeated the sailors; "but what security shall we have?"

"The word of a gentleman," said the officer. "By my rank and by my name, I swear that all but Monsieur le Chevalier d'Herblay shall have their lives spared. I am lieutenant of the king's frigate, the *Pomona,* and my name is Louis Constant de Pressigny."

With a rapid gesture, Aramis—already bent over the side of the bark toward the sea—with a rapid gesture, Aramis raised his head, drew himself up, and with a flashing eye, and a smile upon his lips:

"Throw out the ladder, messieurs!" he said, as if the command belonged to him. He was obeyed.

Then Aramis, seizing the rope ladder, climbed up first, but instead of the terror which was expected on his face, the surprise of the sailors of the *balancelle* was great when they saw him walk straight up to the commander, with a firm step, look at him earnestly, make a sign to him with his hand, a mysterious and unknown sign, at the sight of which the officer turned pale, trembled, and bowed his head. Without saying a word, Aramis then raised his hand close to the eyes of the commander, and showed him the setting of a ring which he wore on the ring finger of his left hand. And while making this sign, Aramis, draped in cold, silent, and haughty majesty, had the air of an emperor giving his hand to be kissed. The commandant, who for a moment had raised his head, bowed a second time with marks of the most profound respect. Then, stretching his hand out, in his turn, toward the poop, that is to say, toward his own cabin, he drew back to let Aramis go first. The three Bretons, who had come on board after the bishop, looked at one another, stupefied. The crew were struck with silence. Five minutes later, the commander called the second lieutenant, who returned immediately, ordering to head toward Corunna. While the given order was being carried out, Aramis reappeared upon the deck, and took a seat near the rails. The night had fallen, the moon had not yet risen, and yet Aramis looked incessantly toward Belle-Isle. Yves then approached the captain, who had returned to take his post in the stern, and said, in a low and humble voice:

"What course are we to follow, captain?"

"We take what course monseigneur pleases," replied the officer.

Aramis spent the night leaning upon the rails. Yves, on approaching him the next morning, remarked that "the night must have been very humid, for the wood upon which the bishop's head had rested was soaked with dew."

Who knows? that dew was, perhaps, the first tears that had ever fallen from the eyes of Aramis!

What epitaph would have been worth that, good Porthos?

CHAPTER LII

THE ROUND OF M. DE GESVRES

D'Artagnan was not accustomed to resistance like that he had just experienced. He returned, profoundly irritated, to Nantes. Irritation with this vigorous man expressed itself in an impetuous attack, which few people, until then, were they king, were they giants, had been able to resist. D'Artagnan, trembling with rage, went straight to the castle, and asked to speak to the king. It was about seven o'clock in the morning, and, since his arrival in Nantes, the king had been an early riser. But on arriving at the little corridor with which we are acquainted, D'Artagnan found M. de Gesvres, who stopped him very politely, telling him not to speak too loudly and disturb the king.

"Is the king asleep?" said D'Artagnan. "Well, I will let him sleep. But at what time do you suppose he will rise?"

"In about two hours; the king has been up all night."

D'Artagnan took his hat again, bowed to M. de Gesvres, and returned to his own apartments. He came back at half-past nine, and was told that the king was at breakfast.

"That will just suit me," said D'Artagnan; "I will talk to the king while he is eating."

M. de Brienne reminded D'Artagnan that the king did not receive anyone during his meals.

"But," said D'Artagnan, looking askance at Brienne, "you do not know, perhaps, monsieur, that I have *entrée* anywhere, and at any hour."

Brienne took the hand of the captain kindly, and said:

"Not in Nantes, dear Monsieur D'Artagnan. The king on this journey has changed everything."

D'Artagnan, a little softened, asked about what time the king would have finished his breakfast.

"We don't know."

"Don't know? What does that mean? Don't you know how much time the king devotes to eating? It is generally an hour; and, if we allow that the air of the Loire gives an additional appetite, we will extend it to an hour and a half; that is enough, I think. I will wait where I am."

"Oh, dear Monsieur D'Artagnan, the order is not to allow any person to remain in this corridor; I am on guard for that purpose."

D'Artagnan felt his anger rise a second time to his brain. He went out quickly, for fear of complicating the affair with a display of ill humor. As soon as he was out he began to think.

"The king," he said, "will not receive me, that is clear. The young man is angry; he is afraid of the words I may speak to him. Yes; but in the meantime Belle-Isle is besieged, and my two friends are taken or killed. Poor Porthos! As to Master Aramis, he is always full of re-sources, and I rest easy on his account. But, no, no; Porthos is not yet an invalid, and Aramis is not yet in his dotage. The one with his arm, the other with his imagination, will find work for his majesty's soldiers. Who knows if these brave men may not get up for the edification of his most Christian majesty a little bastion of St. Gervais! I don't despair. They have cannon and a garrison. And yet," continued D'Artagnan, "I don't know whether it would not be better to stop the fighting. For myself I would not put up with surly looks or treason from the king; but for my friends, I must bear rebuffs and insults. Shall I go to Monsieur Colbert? Now, there is a man whom I must acquire the habit of terrifying. I will go to Monsieur Colbert."

And D'Artagnan set forward bravely to find M. Col-bert; but he was told he was working with the king, at the Castle of Nantes.

"Good!" he cried, "the times are returned in which I paced from De Tréville to the cardinal, from the cardinal to the queen, from the queen to Louis XIII. Truly is it said that men, in growing old, become children again. To the castle then!"

He returned there. M. de Lyonne was coming out. He gave D'Artagnan both hands, but told him that the king had been busy the preceding evening and night, and that orders had been given that no one should be admitted.

"Not even the captain who takes the order?" cried D'Artagnan. "I think that is rather too much."

"Not even he," said M. de Lyonne.

"Since that is the case," replied D'Artagnan, wounded to the heart, "since the captain of the musketeers, who has always entered the king's chamber, is no longer allowed to enter it, his cabinet, or his dining room, either the king is dead, or his captain is in disgrace. In either case, he can no longer want him. Do me the favor, then, Monsieur de Lyonne, you who are in favor, to return and tell the king plainly, I am sending him my resignation."

"D'Artagnan, beware of what you are doing!"

"For friendship's sake, go!" and he pushed him gently toward the cabinet.

"I will go," said Lyonne.

D'Artagnan waited, walking about the corridor. Lyonne returned.

"Well, what did the king say?" exclaimed D'Artagnan.

"He simply answered, 'That is well,' " replied Lyonne.

"That that is well!" said the captain, with an explosion. "That is to say, that he accepts it? Good! Now, then, I am free. I am only a plain citizen, Monsieur de Lyonne. I have the pleasure of bidding you good-bye. Farewell, castle, corridor, antechamber! a bourgeois, about to breathe at liberty, bids his farewell of you."

And without waiting longer, the captain sprang from the terrace down the staircase where he had picked up the fragments of Gourville's letter. Five minutes after, he was at the hostelry, where, according to the custom of all great officers who have lodgings at the castle, he had taken what was called his city chamber. But when there, instead of throwing off his sword and cloak, he took his pistols, put his money into a large leather purse, sent for his horses from the castle stables, and gave orders for reaching Vannes during the night. Everything went according to his wishes. At eight o'clock in the evening he was putting his foot in the stirrup, when M. de Gesvres appeared at the head of twelve guards, in front of the hostelry. D'Artagnan saw everything from the corner of his eye; he could not fail seeing thirteen men and thirteen horses. But he pretended not to notice anything, and was about to put his horse in motion. Gesvres rode up to him.

"Monsieur D'Artagnan!" he said, aloud.

"Monsieur de Gesvres! Good evening!"

"One would say you were getting on horseback."

"More than that—I am on horseback, as you see."

"It is fortunate I have met you."

"Were you looking for me, then?"

"Mon Dieu! yes."

"In the name of the king, I guess?"

"Yes."

"As I, three days ago, was looking for Monsieur Fouquet?"

"Oh!"

"Nonsense! It is of no use being delicate with me; you are wasting your time. Tell me you have come to arrest me."

"To arrest you? Good heavens, no!"

"Why do you come to meet me with twelve horsemen at your heels, then?"

"I am making my round."

"Pretty good. And are you picking me up on your round?"

"I am not picking you up; I meet with you, and I beg you to come with me."

"Where?"

"To the king."

"Good!" said D'Artagnan, with a bantering air; "the king has nothing to do!"

"For heaven's sake, captain," said M. de Gesvres, in a low voice, to the musketeer, "do not compromise yourself. These men are hearing you."

D'Artagnan laughed aloud, and replied:

"Walk! People who are arrested are placed between the six first guards and the six last."

"But as I am not arresting you," said M. de Gesvres, "you will walk behind, with me, if you please."

"Well," said D'Artagnan, "that is very polite, duke, and you are right in being so; for if ever I had had to make my rounds near your *chambre-de-ville*, I would have been courteous to you, I assure you, by the oath of a gentleman. Now, one favor more: what does the king want with me?"

"The king is furious!"

"Very well; the king, who has taken the trouble to be furious, may take the trouble of calming down; that is all. I won't die of that, I swear."

"No, but—"

"But—I will be sent to keep company with poor Monsieur Fouquet. *Mordioux!* There is a gallant man, a worthy man. We shall live very agreeably together, I swear."

"Here we are at our destination," said the duke. "Captain, for heaven's sake, be calm with the king!"

"How kind you are with me, duke," said D'Artagnan, looking defiantly at De Gesvres. "I have been told that you are hoping to unite your guards with my musketeers. This strikes me as a perfect opportunity."

"I will not take it, God help me, captain."

"And why not?"

"Oh, for many reasons—in the first place, for this: if I were to succeed you in the musketeers, after I have arrested you—"

"Then you admit you have arrested me?"

"No, I don't."

"Say met me, then. So, you were saying, *if* you were to succeed me, after having arrested me?"

"Your musketeers, at the first drill, would all fire toward me, by mistake."

"As to that, I won't say, for the fellows do love me."

Gesvres made D'Artagnan go in first, and took him straight to the cabinet, where the king was waiting for his captain of the musketeers, and placed himself behind his colleague in the antechamber. The king could be heard distinctly, speaking aloud to Colbert in the same cabinet where Colbert might have heard, a few days before, the king speaking aloud with M. D'Artagnan. The guards remained as a mounted picket before the main gate; and the report was quickly spread through the city that M. le Capitaine of the Musketeers had just been arrested by order of the king. Then these men were seen to be in motion, as in the good old times of Louis XIII and M. de Tréville; groups were formed, the staircases were filled; vague whispers from the court below came rolling up to the upper stories, like the hoarse moaning of the tide waves. M. de Gesvres became very anxious. He looked at his guards, who, after being questioned by the musketeers who had just joined them, were beginning to draw away from them, also showing anxiety. D'Artagnan was certainly less anxious than M. de Gesvres, the captain of the guards, was. As soon as he entered he sat on the ledge of a window, from where he saw with his eagle glance all that was going on, and didn't show the least emotion. None of the progress of the excitement which had manifested itself at the report of his arrest had escaped him. He foresaw the moment when the explosion would take place; and we know that his previsions were pretty correct.

"It would be very odd," he thought, "if, this evening, my men should make me King of France. How I would laugh!"

But, everything suddenly stopped. Guards, musketeers, officers, soldiers, whispers, and worries, all dispersed, vanished, died away; no more tempest, no more menace, no more sedition. One word had calmed all the waves. The king had just asked Brienne to say:

"Hush, messieurs! you are disturbing the king."

D'Artagnan sighed.

"All is over," he said; "the musketeers of the present day are not those of His Majesty Louis XIII. All is over!"

"Monsieur D'Artagnan, to the king's apartment!" cried an usher.

CHAPTER LIII

KING LOUIS XIV

THE king was seated in his cabinet, with his back turned toward the entrance door. In front of him was a mirror, in which, while turning over his papers, he could see with a glance those who came in. He did not take any notice of the entrance of D'Artagnan, but laid over his letters and plans the large silk cloth which he made use of to conceal his secrets from the curious. D'Artagnan understood his play, and kept in the background; so that, at the end of a minute, the king, who heard nothing, and saw nothing but with the corner of his eye, was obliged to cry:

"Is not Monsieur D'Artagnan there?"

"I am here, sire," replied the musketeer, coming forward.

"Well, monsieur," said the king, fixing his clear eye upon D'Artagnan, "what have you to say to me?"

"I, sire!" replied the latter, who was waiting the first blow of his adversary in order to make a good reply; "I have nothing to say to your majesty, unless it be that you have had me arrested, and here I am."

The king was going to reply that he had not had D'Artagnan arrested, but the sentence appeared too much like an excuse, and he was silent. D'Artagnan kept an obstinate silence as well.

"Monsieur," the king took up at last, "what did I entrust you to go and do at Belle-Isle? Tell me, if you please."

The king, while speaking these words, looked fixedly at his captain. Here D'Artagnan was too fortunate; the king seemed to place the game in his hands.

"I believe," he replied, "that your majesty does me the honor of asking what I went to Belle-Isle to do?"

"Yes, monsieur."

"Well, sire, I know nothing about it; you should not ask *me,* but that infinite number of officers of all kinds, to whom have been given an infinite number of orders of all kinds, while, I, head of the expedition, was ordered nothing precise."

The king was wounded; he showed it by his reply.

"Monsieur," he said, "orders have only been given to those who were judged faithful."

"And, therefore, I have been astonished, sire," retorted the musketeer, "that a captain like myself, who ranks with a marshal of France, should have found himself under the orders of five or six lieutenants or majors, good to make spies of, possibly, but not at all fit to lead warlike expeditions. I was coming to ask an explanation of your majesty, when I found the door closed on me, which, the last insult made to a brave man, has led me to quit your majesty's service."

"Monsieur," replied the king, "you still believe you are living in an age when kings were, as you are complaining of having been, under the orders and at the discretion of their inferiors. You seem to forget that a king owes an account of his actions to none but God."

"I am forgetting nothing at all, sire," said the musketeer, wounded by this lesson. "Besides, I do not see how an honest man offends his king when he asks him how he has ill-served him."

"You have ill-served me, monsieur, by taking sides with my enemies against me."

"Who are your enemies, sire?"

"The men I sent you to fight."

"Two men! enemies of your majesty's army? That is incredible!"

"You have no right to judge my decisions."

"But I do have the right to judge my own friendships, sire."

"He who serves his friends does not serve his master."

"I have so well understood that, sire, that I have respectfully offered your majesty my resignation."

"And I have accepted it, monsieur," said the king. "Before being separated from you, I was willing to prove to you that I know how to keep my word."

"Your majesty has kept more than your word, for your majesty has had me arrested," said D'Artagnan, with his cold, bantering air; "you did not promise me that, sire."

The king ignored this joke, and continued seriously:

"You see, monsieur," he said, "what your disobedience has forced me to do?"

"My disobedience!" cried D'Artagnan, red with anger.

"That is the mildest name I can find," pursued the king. "My idea was to take and punish rebels; was I supposed to inquire whether these rebels were your friends or not?"

"But I was," replied D'Artagnan. "It was a cruelty on your majesty's part to send me to capture my friends and lead them to your gallows."

"It was a test I had to make, monsieur, of my so-called servants, who eat my bread and ought to defend my person. The test has failed, Monsieur D'Artagnan."

"For one bad servant your majesty loses," said the musketeer, with bitterness, "there are ten who have, on that same day, gone through their ordeal. Listen to me, sire; I rebel when I am required to do wrong. It was wrong to send me to pursue two men whose lives Monsieur Fouquet, your majesty's savior, had implored you to save. Still further, these men were my friends. They were not attacking your majesty, they succumbed to a blind anger. Besides, why were they not allowed to escape? What crime had they committed? I admit that you may question my right to judge their conduct. But why suspect me before the action? Why surround me with spies? Why disgrace me before the army? Why me, in whom you have up to this time showed the most complete confidence—me who for thirty years have been attached to your person, and have given you a thousand proofs of devotion—for it must be said, now that I am accused— why reduce me to see three thousand of the king's soldiers march in battle against two men?"

"You seem to have forgotten what these men have done to me," said the king, in a hollow voice, "and that it was no merit of theirs that I was not lost."

"Sire, you seem to forget I was there."

"Enough, Monsieur D'Artagnan, enough of these dominating interests which arise to keep the sun from my interests. I am founding a state in which there shall be but one master, as I promised you before; the moment has come to keep my promise. Do you want to be, according to your taste or your friendships, free to destroy my plans and save my enemies? I will thwart you, or will leave you. Seek a more compliant master. I know full well that another king would not conduct himself as I do, and would let himself be dominated by you, at the risk of sending you someday to keep company with Monsieur Fouquet and the others; but I have a good memory, and for me, services are sacred titles to gratitude, to impunity. You shall only have this lesson, Monsieur D'Artagnan, as punishment for your lack of discipline, and I will not imitate my predecessors in their anger, not having imitated them in their favor. And then other reasons make me act gently toward you; in the first place, because you are a man of sense, a man of great sense, a man of heart, and that you will be a good servant for him who shall have mastered you; secondly, because you will cease to have any motives for insubordination. Your friends are destroyed or ruined by me. These supports, upon which your capricious mind instinctively relied, I have made disappear. At this moment my soldiers have captured or killed the rebels of Belle-Isle.''

D'Artagnan became pale.

''Captured or killed!'' he cried. ''Oh, sire, if you meant what you tell me, if you were sure you were telling me the truth, I would forget all that is just, all that is magnanimous in your words, to call you a barbarous king and an unnatural man. But I pardon you these words,'' said he, smiling with pride; ''I pardon them to a young prince who does not know, who cannot understand what such men as Monsieur d'Herblay, Monsieur du Vallon, and myself are. Captured or killed! Ah! sire, tell me, if the news is true, how much it has cost you in men and money. We will then decide if the game has been worth the stakes.''

As he spoke, the king went up to him in great anger, and said:

''Monsieur D'Artagnan, your replies are those of a rebel. Tell me, if you please, who is King of France? Do you know any other?''

''Sire,'' replied the captain of the musketeers coldly, ''I remember very well that one morning at Vaux you asked that question to many people who did not answer it, while *I* did answer it. If I recognized my king on that day, when the thing was not easy, I think it is useless to ask me now, when your majesty is alone with me.''

At these words Louis cast down his eyes. It seemed to him that the shadow of the unfortunate Philippe passed between D'Artagnan and himself, to bring back that terrible adventure. Almost at the same moment an officer entered and placed a dispatch in the hands of the king, who, in his turn, changed color while reading it.

''Monsieur,'' he said, ''what I learn here you would know later; it is better I tell you, and that you learn it from the mouth of your king. A battle has taken place at Belle-Isle.''

''Oh!'' said D'Artagnan, calmly, though his heart beat enough to break through his chest. ''Well, sire?''

''Well, monsieur—and I have lost a hundred and ten men.''

A beam of joy and pride shone in the eyes of D'Artagnan.
"And the rebels?" he said.

"The rebels have fled," said the king.

D'Artagnan could not restrain a cry of triumph.

"Only," added the king, "I have a fleet which closely blockades Belle-Isle, and I am certain no boat can escape."

"So that," said the musketeer, brought back to his dismal idea, "if these two gentlemen are captured . . ."

"They will be hanged," said the king quietly.

"And do they know it?" replied D'Artagnan, repressing his trembling.

"They know it, because you must have told them yourself; and all the country knows it."

"Then, sire, they will never be taken alive; I will answer for that."

"Very well," said the king negligently, taking up his letter again. "They will be dead then, Monsieur D'Artagnan, and that will come to the same thing, since I was only capturing them to have them hanged."

D'Artagnan wiped the sweat flowing from his brow.

"I have told you," pursued Louis XIV, "that I would one day be an affectionate, generous, and constant master. You are now the only man of former times worthy of my anger or my friendship. I will not be sparing of either to you, according to your conduct. Could you serve a king, Monsieur D'Artagnan, who would have a hundred kings his equals in the kingdom? Could I, tell me, do with this weakness the great things I meditate? Have you ever seen an artist build solid works with a rebellious instrument? Far from us, monsieur, those old turmoils of feudal abuses! The Fronde, which threatened to ruin the monarchy, has emancipated it. I am master at home, Captain D'Artagnan, and I shall have servants who, wanting, perhaps, your genius, will carry devotion and obedience up to heroism. Of what consequence, I ask you, of what consequence is it that God has given no genius to arms and legs? It is to the head He has given it, and the head, you know, all the rest obey. *I* am the head."

D'Artagnan gave a start. Louis XIV continued as if he had seen nothing, although this emotion had not at all escaped him.

"Now let us conclude between us two that bargain which I promised to make with you one day when you found me very small in Blois. Do me justice, monsieur, when you think that I do not make anyone pay for the tears of shame that I then shed. Look around you; lofty heads have bowed. Bow yours, or choose the exile that will best suit you. Perhaps, when reflecting upon it, you will find that this king is a generous heart, who is counting sufficiently upon your loyalty to allow you to leave him dissatisfied, when you possess a great state secret. You are a good man; I know you to be so. Why have you judged me before term? Judge me from this day forward, D'Artagnan, and be as severe as you please.''

D'Artagnan remained bewildered, mute, undecided for the first time in his life. He had just found an adversary worthy of him. This was not longer cunning, it was calculation; it was no longer violence, it was strength; it was no longer passion, it was will; it was no longer boasting, it was advice. This young man who had brought down Fouquet, and could do without D'Artagnan, upset all the headstrong calculations of the musketeer.

''Come, let us see what is stopping you?'' said the king kindly. ''You have given in your resignation; shall I refuse to accept it? I admit that it may be hard for an old captain to recover his good humor.''

''Oh!'' replied D'Artagnan, in a melancholy tone, ''that is not my most serious care. I hesitate to take back my resignation because I am old in comparison with you, and I have habits difficult to abandon. From now on, you must have courtiers who know how to amuse you—madmen who will get themselves killed to carry out what you call your great works. Great they will be, I feel—but if by chance I should not think them so? I have seen war, sire, I have seen peace; I have served Richelieu and Mazarin; I have been scorched with your father, at the fire of La Rochelle; riddled with shots like a sieve, having made a new skin ten times, as serpents do. After affronts and injustices, I had a command which was formerly something, because it gave the bearer the right of speaking as he liked to his king. But your captain of the musketeers will be now an officer guarding the lower doors. Truly, sire, if my position must be such, seize the opportunity of our being on good terms to take it from me. Do not imagine that I bear malice; no, you have tamed me, as you say; but it must be confessed that in taming me you

have lessened me; by bending me you have convicted me
of weakness. If you knew how well it suits me to carry
my head high, and what a poor figure I shall cut smelling
the dust of your carpets! Oh, sire, I miss sincerely, and
you will miss as I do, those times when the King of France
saw in his vestibules all those insolent gentlemen, thin,
always swearing—dogs, who could bite mortally in days
of battle. Those men were the best of courtiers for the
hand which fed them—they would lick it; but for the hand
that struck them, oh! the bite that followed. A little gold
on the lace of their cloaks, a paunch in their *hauts-de-
chausses,* a little sprinkling of gray in their dry hair, and
you will behold the handsome dukes and peers, the
haughty marshals of France. But why should I tell you all
this? The king is my master; he wants me to write poetry,
he wants me to polish the mosaics of his antechambers
with satin shoes. *Mordioux!* that is difficult, but I have
gotten over greater difficulties than that. I will do it. Why
should I do it? Because I love money? I have enough.
Because I am ambitious? I have gone as far as I can in my
career. Because I love the court? No. I will remain because I have been accustomed for thirty years to go and
take the orderly word of the king, and to have said to me,
'Good evening, D'Artagnan,' with a smile I did not beg
for. That smile I will beg for. Are you content, sire?''

"Thank you, my old servant, my faithful friend," he
said. "Since, from this day, I have no longer any enemies
in France, it remains for me to send you to a foreign field
to gather your marshal's baton. Depend on me to find
you an opportunity. In the meanwhile, eat my best bread,
and sleep peacefully."

"That is all kind and well," said D'Artagnan, much
agitated. "But those poor men at Belle-Isle? One of them,
in particular—so good, so brave, so true!"

"Do you ask their pardon of me?"

"Upon my knees, sire!"

"Well, then, go and take it to them, if there is still
time. But do you answer for them?"

"With my life, sire."

"Go, then. Tomorrow I set out for Paris, Return by that
time, for I do not wish you to leave me in the future."

"Be assured of that, sire," said D'Artagnan, kissing
the royal hand.

And with a heart swelling with joy, he rushed out of the castle on his way to Belle-Isle.

CHAPTER LIV

THE FRIENDS OF M. FOUQUET

THE king had returned to Paris, and with him D'Artagnan, who, in twenty-four hours, having made with the greatest care all possible inquiries at Belle-Isle, had learned nothing of the secret so well kept by the heavy rock of Locmaria, which had fallen on the heroic Porthos. The captain of the musketeers only knew what those two valiant men—what those two friends, whose defense he had so nobly taken up, whose lives he had so earnestly tried to save—helped by three faithful Bretons, had accomplished against a whole army. He had been able to see, launched onto the neighboring heath, the human remains which had stained with blood the stones scattered among the flowering heather. He learned also that a boat had been seen far out at sea, and that, like a bird of prey, a royal vessel had pursued, overtaken, and devoured this poor little bird which was flying with rapid wings. But there D'Artagnan's certainties ended. The whole issue was thrown open to speculation at this point. The vessel had not returned. It is true that a brisk wind had prevailed for three days; but the corvette was known to be a good sailer and solid in its timbers; it did not fear gales of wind, and it ought, according to the calculation of D'Artagnan, to have either returned to Brest or come back to the mouth of the Loire. Such was the news, ambiguous it is true, but in some degree reassuring to him personally, which D'Artagnan brought to Louis XIV, when the king, followed by all the court, returned to Paris.

Louis, satisfied with his success, Louis—gentler and more affable since he felt himself more powerful—had not ceased for an instant to ride close to the carriage door of Mlle. de la Vallière. Everybody had been anxious to amuse the two queens, so as to make them forget this abandonment of the son and the husband. Everything breathed of the future; the past was forgotten. Only that past came like a painful and bleeding wound to the hearts of some tender and devoted spirits. Scarcely was the king settled in Paris when he received a touching proof of this. Louis XIV had just risen and taken his first meal, when his captain of the musketeers presented himself before him. D'Artagnan was pale and looked unhappy.

"What is the matter, D'Artagnan?" asked Louis.

"Sire, a great misfortune has happened to me."

"Good heavens, what is that?"

"Sire, I have lost one of my friends, Monsieur du Vallon, in the affair at Belle-Isle."

And, while speaking these words D'Artagnan was staring at Louis XIV with his falcon eye, to catch the first feeling that would show itself.

"I knew it," replied the king quietly.

"You knew it and did not tell me!" cried the musketeer.

"To what good? Your grief, my friend, is so respectable! It was my duty to treat it kindly. To have informed you of this misfortune, which I knew would pain you so greatly, D'Artagnan, would have been, in your eyes, to have triumphed over you. Yes, I knew that Monsieur du Vallon was buried beneath the rock of Locmaria; I knew that Monsieur d'Herblay had taken one of my ships with its crew, and had compelled it to take him to Bayonne. But I wanted you to learn these matters in a direct manner, in order that you might be convinced my friends are respected and sacred for me; that always in me the man will sacrifice himself to men, while the king is so often bound to sacrifice men to his majesty and power."

"But, sire, how could you know?"

"How do you know, D'Artagnan?"

"By this letter, sire, which Monsieur d'Herblay, free and out of danger, writes me from Bayonne."

"Look here," said the king, drawing from a box placed upon the table close to the seat on which D'Artagnan was leaning, "here is a letter copied exactly from that of Monsieur d'Herblay. Here is the very letter, which Colbert placed in my hands eight hours before you received yours. I am well served, you see."

"Yes, sire," whispered the musketeer, "you were the only man whose fortune was capable of dominating the fortunes and strength of my two friends. You have used it, sire, but you will not abuse it, will you?"

"D'Artagnan," said the king, with a smile full of kindness, "I could have Monsieur d'Herblay carried off from the territories of the King of Spain, and brought here alive to inflict justice upon him. But, D'Artagnan, be assured, I will not yield to this first and natural impulse. He is free, let him be free."

"Oh, sire! you will not always remain so clement, so noble, so generous as you have shown yourself with respect to me and Monsieur d'Herblay; you will have about you counselors who will cure you of that weakness."

"No, D'Artagnan; you are mistaken when you accuse my council of urging me to pursue rigorous measures. The advice to spare Monsieur d'Herblay comes from Colbert himself."

"Oh, sire!" said D'Artagnan, extremely surprised.

"As for you," continued the king, with a kindness very uncommon with him, "I have several pieces of good news to announce to you; but you shall know them, my dear captain, the moment I have straightened my accounts. I have said that I wanted to make, and would make, your fortune; that promise will soon be a reality."

"A thousand times thanks, sire; I can wait. But I implore you, while I go and practice patience, that your majesty will deign to notice those poor people who have for so long a time besieged your antechamber, and come humbly to lay a petition at your feet."

"Who are they?"

"Enemies of your majesty."

The king raised his head.

"Friends of Monsieur Fouquet," added D'Artagnan.

"Their names?"

"Monsieur Gourville, Monsieur Pélisson, and a poet, Monsieur Jean de la Fontaine."

The king took a moment to think.

"What do they want?"

"I do not know."

"How do they appear?"

"In mourning."

"What do they say?"

"Nothing."

"What do they do?"

"They weep."

"Let them come in," said the king, with a serious brow.

D'Artagnan turned rapidly on his heel, raised the curtain which closed the entrance to the royal chamber, and, directing his voice to the adjoining room, cried:

"Bring them in!"

The three men D'Artagnan had named soon appeared at the door of the cabinet in which were the king and his captain. A profound silence prevailed as they went by. The courtiers, at the approach of the friends of the unfortunate surintendant of the finances, the courtiers, we say, drew back, as if fearful of being infected with disgrace and misfortune. D'Artagnan, with a quick step, came forward to take by the hand the unhappy men who stood trembling at the door of the cabinet; he led them to the front of the armchair of the king, who, having placed himself in the embrasure of a window, was waiting the moment of presentation, and was preparing himself to give the supplicants a rigorously diplomatic reception.

The first of the friends of Fouquet that came forward was Pélisson. He was not weeping anymore, but his tears were only restrained that the king might hear better his voice and his prayer. Gourville bit his lips to check his tears, out of respect for the king. La Fontaine buried his face in his handkerchief, and the only signs of life he gave were the convulsive motions of his shoulders, raised by his sobs.

The king had preserved all his dignity. His face was expressionless. He had even maintained the frown which had appeared when D'Artagnan had announced his enemies. He remained standing, looking deeply at these despondent men. Pélisson bowed down to the ground, and La Fontaine knelt as people do in churches. This obstinate silence, disturbed only by such dismal sighs and groans, began to elicit in the king, not compassion, but impatience.

"Monsieur Pélisson," he said, in a sharp, dry tone. "Monsieur Gourville, and you, Monsieur—" and he did not name La Fontaine—"I cannot, without real displeasure, see you come to plead for one of the greatest criminals that it is the duty of my justice to punish. A king allows himself to be softened only by tears and remorse; the tears of the innocent, the remorse of the guilty. I have no faith either in the remorse of Monsieur Fouquet or the tears of his friends, because the one is tainted to the very heart, and the others ought to dread coming to offend me in my own palace. For these reasons, I beg you, Monsieur Pélisson, Monsieur Gourville, and you, Monsieur——, to say nothing that will not proclaim the respect you have for my wishes."

"Sire," replied Pélisson, trembling at these terrible words, "we have come to say nothing to your majesty that is not the deepest expression of the most sincere respect and love which are due to a king from all his subjects. Your majesty's justice is formidable; everyone must yield to the sentences it pronounces. We respectfully bow before it. Far from us be the idea of coming to defend him who has had the misfortune to offend your majesty. He who has incurred your displeasure may be a friend of ours, but he is an enemy to the state. We abandon him with tears to the severity of the king."

"Besides," interrupted the king, calmed by that supplicating voice and those persuasive words, "my parliament will decide. I do not strike without having weighed a crime; my justice does not use the sword without having used the scales."

"Therefore we have every confidence in that impartiality of the king, and hope to make our feeble voices heard, with the consent of your majesty, when the hour for defending an accused friend shall strike for us."

"In that case, messieurs, what do you ask of me?" said the king, with his most imposing air.

"Sire," continue Pélisson, "the accused is leaving a wife and a family. The little property he had was scarcely sufficient to pay his debts, and Madame Fouquet, since the captivity of her husband, is abandoned by everybody. The hand of your majesty strikes like the hand of God. When the Lord sends the curse of leprosy or pestilence into a family, everyone flies and shuns the home of the leper or the plague-stricken people. Sometimes, but very rarely, a generous physician dares to approach alone the cursed threshold, crosses it with courage, and exposes his life to fight death. He is the last resource of the dying, he is the instrument of heavenly mercy. Sire, we beg you, with clasped hands and bended knees, as one begs God! Madame Fouquet has no longer any friends, or any support; she weeps in her poor deserted house, abandoned by all those who besieged its doors in the hour of prosperity; she has neither credit nor hope left. At least, the unhappy wretch upon whom your anger falls receives from you, however culpable he may be, the daily bread which is moistened by his tears. As afflicted as her husband, and more destitute, Madame Fouquet—she who had the honor to receive your majesty at her table—Madame Fouquet, the wife of the former surintendant of your majesty's finances, Madame Fouquet has no longer bread.''

Here the mortal silence which was restraining the breath of Pélisson's two friends was broken by an outburst of sobs: and D'Artagnan, whose heart was breaking at hearing this humble prayer, turned around toward the angle of the cabinet to bite his mustache and conceal his sighs.

The king had preserved his eye dry and his face severe; but color had risen to his cheeks, and his confidence was weakening.

''What do you wish?'' he said, in an agitated voice.

''We come humbly to ask your majesty,'' replied Pélisson, upon whom emotion was fast gaining, ''to permit us, without incurring the displeasure of your majesty, to lend to Madame Fouquet two thousand pistoles collected among the old friends of her husband, in order that the widow may not stand in need of the necessities of life.''

At the word *widow,* pronounced by Pélisson while Fouquet was still alive, the king turned very pale; his pride fell; pity rose from his heart to his lips; he cast a softened look upon the men who knelt, sobbing, at his feet.

''God forbid,'' he said, ''that I should confound the innocent with the guilty. They know me but ill who doubt my mercy toward the weak. I will never strike but the arrogant. Do, messieurs, do all that your hearts counsel you to relieve the grief of Madame Fouquet. Go, messieurs—go!''

The three men arose in silence with dried eyes. The tears had been dried up by contact with their burning cheeks and eyelids. They had not the strength to address their thanks to the king, who himself cut short their solemn reverences by taking refuge suddenly behind the armchair.

D'Artagnan remained alone with the king.

"Well," he said, approaching the young prince, who was looking at him questioningly. "Well, my master! If you had not the motto which belongs to your sun, I would recommend you one which Monsieur Convart should translate into Latin, 'Mild with the lowly; rough with the strong.' "

The king smiled, and went into the next apartment, after having said to D'Artagnan:

"I give you the leave of absence you must need to put in order the affairs of your friend, the late Monsieur du Vallon."

CHAPTER LV

PORTHOS'S WILL

At Pierrefonds everything was in mourning. The courts were deserted—the stables closed—the flowerbeds neglected. In the basins, the fountains, formerly so noisy and sparkling, had stopped on their own. Along the roads around the chateau came a few serious persons on mules or farm nags. These were country neighbors, curés, the bailiffs of adjacent estates. All these people would enter the chateau silently, give their nags to a melancholy-looking groom, and direct their steps, led by a huntsman in black, to the great hall where Mousqueton would receive them at the door. Mousqueton had become so thin in two days that his clothes hung upon him like sheaths which are too large, and in which the blades of swords dance about at each motion. His face, blotchy like the Madonna of Vandyke's, was furrowed by two silver rivulets which had dug their beds in his cheeks, as full formerly as they had become flabby since his grief began. At each fresh arrival Mousqueton found fresh tears, and it was pitiful to see him press his throat with his fat hand to keep from bursting into sobs and lamentations. They had all come to hear Porthos's will, announced for that day, and whether out of lust or friendship they were all anxious to be present, as he had left behind no relative.

The visitors took their places as they arrived, and the great hall had just been closed when the clock struck twelve, the hour set for the reading of the important document. Porthos's procureur began by slowly unfolding the vast parchment upon which the powerful hand of Porthos had traced his last will. The seal broken—the glasses put on—the preliminary cough having sounded—everyone was all ears. Mousqueton had huddled in a corner, to weep better and to hear better. All at once the folding doors of the great hall, which had been shut, were thrown open as if by a prodigy, and a manly figure appeared upon the threshold, resplendent in the full light of the sun. This was D'Artagnan, who had come alone to the gate, and finding nobody to hold his stirrup, he had tied his horse to a knocker and announced himself. The splendor of the daylight invading the room, the murmur of all present and, more than all that, the instinct of the faithful dog, drew Mousqueton from his reverie; he raised his head, recognized the old friend of his master, and, howling with grief, he embraced his knees, watering the floor with his tears. D'Artagnan raised up the poor intendant, embraced him as if he had been a brother, and, having nobly saluted the assembly, who all bowed as they whispered his name to one another, he went and took his seat at the end of the great carved oak hall, still holding by the hand poor Mousqueton, who was suffocating, and sank down upon the steps. Then the procureur, who was as moved as the others, began the reading.

Porthos, after a profession of faith of the most Christian character, asked pardon of his enemies for the wrong he might have done them. At this paragraph a ray of inexpressible pride beamed from the eyes of D'Artagnan. He remembered the old soldier and tried to count all those enemies of Porthos brought down by his valiant hand, and said to himself that Porthos had acted wisely not to detail his enemies or the wrongs done to them, or the task would have been too much for the reader. Then came the following enumeration:

"I possess at this present time, by the grace of God:
"1. The domain of Pierrefonds, lands, woods, meadows, waters, and forests, surrounded by good walls.
"2. The domain of Bracieux, chateau, forests, plowed lands, forming three farms.
"3. The little estate Du Vallon, so named because it is in the valley." (Good Porthos!)
"4. Fifty farms in Touraine, amounting to five hundred acres.

"5. Three mills upon the Cher, bringing in six hundred
pounds each.

"6. Three fish pools in Berry, producing two hundred
pounds a year.

"As to my personal or movable property, so called because
it can be moved, as is so well explained by my learned friend,
the bishop of Vannes"—(D'Artagnan shuddered at the
gloomy memory attached to that name: the procureur continued imperturbably)—"they consist of:

"1. Goods which I cannot detail here for want of room,
and which furnish all my chateaux or houses, but of
which the list is drawn up by my intendant."

Everyone turned his eyes toward Mousqueton, who was
absorbed in his grief.

"2. Twenty horses for saddle and draught, which I have
particularly at my chateau of Pierrefonds, and which
are called—Bayard, Roland, Charlemagne, Pépin,
Dunois, La Hire, Ogier, Samson, Milo, Nimrod,
Urganda, Armida, Falstrade, Delilah, Rebecca, Yo-
lands, Finette, Grisette, Lisette, and Musette.

"3. Sixty dogs, forming six packs, divided as follows:
the first, for the stag; the second, for the wolf; the
third, for the wild boar; the fourth, for the hare;
and the two others, for setters and protection.

"4. War and hunting weapons contained in my gallery
of weapons.

"5. My wines of Anjou, selected for Athos, who liked
them formerly; my wines of Burgundy, Champagne,
Bordeaux, and Spain, stocking eight cellars and
twelve vaults, in my various houses.

"6. My pictures and statues, which are said to be of
great value, and which are sufficiently numerous to
bore anyone.

"7. My library, consisting of six thousand volumes,
quite new, and have never been opened.

"8. My silver dishes, which are, perhaps, a little worn,
but which ought to weigh from a thousand to twelve
hundred pounds, for I had great trouble in lifting
the chest which holds them, and could not carry it
more than six times around my room.

"9. All these objects, in addition to the table and house
linen, are divided in the residences I liked the best."

Here the reader stopped to catch his breath. Everyone
sighed, coughed, and was more attentive than ever. The
procureur went on:

"I have lived without having any children, and it is probable I never shall have any, which to me is a bitter grief.
And yet I am mistaken, for I have a son, in common with
my other friends; that is Monsieur Raoul Auguste Jules de
Bragelonne, the true son of Monsieur le Comte de la Fère.

"This young nobleman has appeared to me worthy to
succeed to the three valiant gentlemen, of whom I am
the friend and the very humble servant."

Here a sharp sound interrupted the reader. It was
D'Artagnan's sword, which, slipping from his belt, had
fallen on the resonant floor. Everyone turned his eyes
that way, and saw that a large tear had rolled from the
thick lid of D'Artagnan onto his aquiline nose, the luminous edge of which was shining like a crescent.

"This is why"—(continued the procureur)—"I have
left all my property, movable or immovable, included in
the above enumerations, to Monsieur le Vicomte Raoul
Auguste Jules de Bragelonne, son of Monsieur le Comte
de la Fère, to console him for the grief he seems to suffer, and enable him to bear his name gloriously."

A long murmur ran through the audience. The procureur
continued, seconded by the flashing eye of D'Artagnan,
which, glancing over the assembly, quickly restored silence:

"On condition that Monsieur le Vicomte de Bragelonne
do give to Monsieur le Chevalier d'Artagnan, captain of
the king's musketeers, whatever the said Chevalier d'Artagnan may ask of my property. On condition that Monsieur le Vicomte de Bragelonne do pay a good pension
to Monsieur le Chevalier d'Herblay, my friend, if he
should need it in exile. I leave to my intendant, Mousqueton, all my city, war, or hunting clothes, to the number of forty-seven suits, with the assurance that he will

wear them until they are worn out for the love of and
memory of his master. Moreover, I will to Monsieur le
Vicomte de Bragelonne my old servant and faithful
friend, Mousqueton, already named, providing that the
said viscount shall so act that Mousqueton shall declare,
when dying, he had never ceased to be happy.''

On hearing these words, Mousqueton bowed, pale and
trembling; his large shoulders shook convulsively; his
face, marked with frightful grief, appeared from between
his icy hands, and the spectators saw him stagger and
hesitate, as if, though wishing to leave the hall, he did
not know the way.

"Mousqueton, my good friend," said D'Artagnan,
"prepare yourself. I will take you with me to Athos's
house, where I shall go on leaving Pierrefonds."

Mousqueton made no reply. He was scarcely breathing, as if everything in that hall would from then on be
foreign. He opened the door, and disappeared slowly.

The procureur finished his reading, after which the
greater part of those who had come to hear the last will
of Porthos dispersed by degrees, many disappointed, but
all full of respect. At to D'Artagnan, left alone, after
having received the formal compliments of the procureur, he was lost in admiration of the wisdom of the testator, who had so judiciously left his wealth to the
neediest and the most worthy, with a delicacy that none
among the most refined courtiers and the most noble
hearts could have displayed more becomingly. When Porthos asked Raoul de Bragelonne to give to D'Artagnan
all he would ask, he knew well, that worthy Porthos, that
D'Artagnan would ask or take nothing; and, in case he
did ask for anything, none but himself could say what.
Porthos left a pension to Aramis, who, if he should be
inclined to ask too much, was checked by the example
of D'Artagnan; and that word *exile*, thrown out by the
testator, without apparent intention, was it not the most
mild, the most exquisite criticism of Aramis's conduct
which had brought about the death of Porthos. But there
was no mention of Athos in the testament of the dead.
Could the latter, for a moment, suppose that the son
would not offer the best part to the father? The rough
mind of Porthos had judged all these causes, seized all

these shades, better than the law, better than custom, better than taste.

"Porthos had a heart," said D'Artagnan to himself, with a sigh.

And he thought he heard a groan in the room above him; and he thought immediately of poor Mousqueton, whom he felt he had to divert from his grief. For this purpose he left the hall hastily to seek the worthy intendant, as he had not returned. He went up the stairs leading to the first floor, and saw, in Porthos's own chamber, a heap of clothes of all colors and materials, upon which Mousqueton had laid himself down after heaping them together. It was the legacy of the faithful friend. Those clothes were truly his own; they had been given to him; the hand of Mousqueton was stretched over these relics, which he was kissing with all his lips, with all his face, which he was covering with his whole body. D'Artagnan stepped forward to console the poor fellow.

"My God!" he said, "he is not moving—he has fainted!"

But D'Artagnan was mistaken—Mousqueton was dead. Dead, like the dog who, having lost his master, comes back to die upon his cloak.

CHAPTER LVI

THE OLD AGE OF ATHOS

WHILE all these affairs were separating forever the four musketeers, formerly bound together in a manner that seemed indissoluble, Athos, left alone after the departure of Raoul, began to pay his tribute to that anticipated death which is called the absence of those we love. Back at his house in Blois, no longer having even Grimaud to receive a poor smile when he went through the flowerbeds, Athos daily felt the decline of the vigor of a nature which for so long a time had appeared infallible. Age, which had been kept back by the presence of the beloved object, was coming, with its procession of pains and inconveniences. Athos had no longer his son to induce him to walk firmly, with his head erect, as a good example; he had no longer, in those bright eyes of the young man, an ever-ardent focus that could regenerate the fire of his looks. And then, must it be said, that nature, exquisite in its tenderness and its reserve, no longer finding anything that held his enthusiasm, gave itself up to grief with all the warmth of vulgar natures when they give themselves up to joy. The Comte de la Fère, who had remained a young man up to his sixty-second year; the warrior who had preserved his strength in spite of fatigues, his freshness of mind in spite of misfortunes, his gentle serenity of soul and body in spite of Milady, in spite of Mazarin, in spite of La Vallière; Athos had become an old man in a week, from the moment he had lost the support of his latter youth. Still handsome, though bent; noble, but sad; gently, and tottering under his gray hair, he sought, since his solitude, the glades where the rays of the sun penetrate through the foliage. He discontinued all the strong exercises he had enjoyed through life, now that Raoul was no longer with him. The servants, accustomed to see him stirring at dawn in all seasons, were astonished to hear seven o'clock strike before their master had left his bed. Athos remained in bed with a book under his pillow, but he did not sleep, neither did he read. Remaining in bed so that he might no longer have to carry his body, he was letting his soul and spirit fly out of their body, and return to his son, or to God.

His people were sometimes terrified to see him for hours absorbed in a silent reverie, mute and insensitive; he no longer heard the timid step of the servant who came to the door of his room to watch the sleeping or the waking of his master. He often forgot that half the day had passed away, that the hours for the first two meals had passed. Then he was awakened. He would rise, go down to his shaded walk, then come out a little into the sun, as if to share its warmth for a minute with his absent child. And then the dismal, monotonous walk would start again, until, quite exhausted, he would go back to his room and his bed, his favorite place. For several days the count did not speak a single word. He refused to receive his visitors, and, during the night, he was seen to light his lamp again and pass long hours writing or examining parchments.

Athos wrote one of these letters to Vannes, another to Fontainebleau; they remained without answer. We know why; Aramis had left France, and D'Artagnan was traveling from Nantes to Paris, from Paris to Pierrefonds. His valet observed that he shortened his walk every day.

The great alley of linden trees soon became too long for feet that used to cross it formerly a hundred times in a day. The count would walk feebly as far as the middle trees, sit on a mossy bank which sloped toward a lateral walk, and there wait for the return of his strength, or, rather, the return of night. Very soon a hundred steps exhausted him. At last Athos refused to rise at all; he refused all nourishment, and his terrified people, although he did not complain, although he had a smile on his lips, although he continued to speak with his sweet voice—his people went to Blois in search of the former physician of the late Monsieur, and brought him to the Comte de la Fère in such a fashion that he could see the count without being seen. For this purpose they placed him in a closet adjoining the room of the patient, and implored him not to show himself, in the fear of displeasing their master, who had not asked for a physician. The doctor obeyed; Athos was a model for the gentlemen of the country; the Blaisois boasted of possessing this sacred relic of the old French glories. Athos was a great lord compared with such nobles as the king improvised by touching with his young, fertile scepter the dried trunks of the heraldic trees of the province.

People respected, we say, and loved Athos. The physician could not bear to see his people weep, and to see flock around him the poor of the district, to whom Athos gave life and consolation by his kind words and his charities. He examined, therefore, from his hiding place, the nature of that mysterious illness which bent down and devoured more mortally every day a man who was not long ago so full of life and a desire to live. He noticed upon the cheeks of Athos the fever, which fires itself and feeds itself; slow fever, pitiless, born in a fold of the heart, sheltering itself behind that rampart, growing from the suffering it engenders, at once cause and effect of a perilous situation. The count spoke to nobody; he did not even talk to himself. His mind feared noise; it approached that degree of overexcitement which borders upon ecstasy. Man thus absorbed, though he does not yet belong to God, already belongs no longer to earth. The doctor remained for several hours studying this painful struggle of the will against superior power; he was terrified at seeing those eyes always fixed, always directed toward an invisible object; he was terrified at seeing beat in the same even manner that heart from which never a sigh arose; sometimes the acuteness of pain is the hope of the physician. Half a day passed away in such a manner. The doctor made up his mind like a brave man, like a firm mind; he came out suddenly from his place of retreat, and went straight up to Athos, who saw him without showing more surprise than if he had understood nothing of the apparition.

"Monsieur le Comte, I beg your pardon," said the doctor, coming up to the patient with open arms; "but I have a reproach to make—you shall hear me."

And he sat by the pillow of Athos, who had great trouble in rousing himself from his preoccupation.

"What is the matter, doctor?" asked the count, after a silence.

"Why, the matter is, you are ill, monsieur, and have had no advice."

"I! ill!" said Athos, smiling.

"Fever, consumption, weakness, wasting away, Monsieur le Comte."

"Weakness!" replied Athos; "is that possible? I do not get up."

"Come, come, Monsieur le Comte, no subterfuges; you are a good Christian?"

"I hope so," said Athos.

"Would you kill yourself?"

"Never, doctor."

"Well, monsieur, you are close to doing so; to remain as you are is suicide; get well, Monsieur le Comte, get well."

"Of what? Find the disease first. For my part, I was never better; never did the sky appear more blue to me; never did I take more care of my flowers."

"You have a hidden grief."

"Hidden? not at all; I have the absence of my son, doctor; that is my illness, and I do not hide it."

"Monsieur le Comte, your son is living, he is strong, he has all the future before him of men of his merit, and of his race; live for him—"

"But I do live, doctor, don't worry," he added, with a melancholy smile; "as long as Raoul lives, it will be plainly known, for as long as he lives, I shall live."

"What do you say?"

"A very simple thing. At this moment, doctor, my life is at a standstill. A forgetful, dissipated, indifferent life would be above my strength, now that I no longer have Raoul with me. You do not ask the lamp to burn when the spark has not lit the flame; do not ask me to live amid noise and light. I vegetate, I prepare myself, I wait. Look, doctor; remember those soldiers we have so often seen together at the ports, where they were waiting to embark; lying down, indifferent, half upon one element, half upon the other; they were neither where the sea was going to carry them nor where the earth was going to lose them; baggage prepared, minds tense, looks fixed— they waited. I repeat, that word is the one which paints my present life. Lying down, like the soldiers, my ear pricked up for the reports that may reach me, I wish to be ready to leave at the first call. Who will make me that leave? life or death? God or Raoul? My baggage is packed, my soul is prepared, I am waiting for the signal—I am waiting, doctor, I am waiting!"

The doctor knew the quality of that mind; he appreciated the strength of that body; he reflected for a moment, told himself that words were useless, remedies absurd, and he left the chateau, exhorting Athos's servants not to leave him for a moment.

The doctor being gone, Athos showed neither anger nor resentment at having been disturbed. He did not even ask that all letters that came should be brought to him directly. He knew very well that every distraction which should arise would be a joy, a hope, which his servants would have paid with their blood, to get for him. Sleep had become rare; by intense thinking, Athos forgot himself, for a few hours at most, in a reverie more profound, more obscure, which others would have called a dream. This momentary rest would bring forgetfulness to the body, for Athos lived a double life during these wanderings of his mind. One night he dreamed that Raoul was dressing himself in a tent, to go on an expedition led by M. de Beaufort in person. The young man was sad; he fastened his cuirass slowly, and slowly he girded on his sword.

"What is the matter?" asked his father tenderly.

"What afflicts me is the death of Porthos, our dear friend," replied Raoul. "I suffer here of the grief you will feel at home."

And the vision disappeared with Athos's sleep. At day-break one of his servants entered his master's apartment, and gave him a letter from Spain.

"The writing of Aramis," thought the count; and he read.

"Porthos is dead!" he cried, after the first lines. "Oh, Raoul, Raoul, thank you; you kept your promise, you warned me!"

And Athos, seized with a mortal sweat, fainted in his bed without any other cause than his weakness.

CHAPTER LVII

THE VISION OF ATHOS

WHEN Athos's fainting was over, the count, almost ashamed of having given way before this supernatural event, got dressed and ordered his horse, determined to ride to Blois, to open more definite correspondence with either Africa, D'Artagnan, or Aramis. In fact, this letter from Aramis informed the Comte de la Fère of the failure of the expedition of Belle-Isle. It gave him sufficient de-tails of the death of Porthos to move the tender and de-voted heart of Athos to its last fibers. Athos wished to go and pay his friend Porthos a last visit. To render this honor to his companion in arms, he meant to get in touch with D'Artagnan, to prevail upon him to take again the painful trip to Belle-Isle, to accomplish in his company that sad pilgrimage to the tomb of the giant he had so much loved, then to return to his home to obey that secret influence which was leading him to eternity by a myste-rious road.

But scarcely had his servants cheerfully dressed their master, whom they saw with pleasure preparing himself for a journey which might dissipate his melancholy; scarcely had the count's gentlest horse been saddled and brought to the door, than the father of Raoul felt his head become confused, his legs give way, and he clearly un-derstood the impossibility of going one step further. He ordered himself to be carried into the sun; they laid him upon his bed of moss, where he spent a full hour before he could recover his spirits. Nothing could be more nat-ural than his weakness after the inertia of the latter days. Athos drank a cup of bouillon, to give him strength, and

bathed his dried lips in a glassful of the wine he loved
the best—that old Anjou wine mentioned by Porthos in
his admirable will. Then, refreshed, free in mind, he had
his horse brought again; but he needed his servants' help
to mount painfully into the saddle. He did not go a hundred paces; he started shivering at the turn of the road.

"This is very strange!" he said to his servant, who
accompanied him.

"Let us stop, monsieur—I beg you!" replied the faithful servant. "How pale you are becoming!"

"That will not prevent my pursuing my route, now I
have started," replied the count.

And he gave his horse his head again. But suddenly the animal stopped, instead of obeying the thought of his master. A
gesture, which Athos was not aware of, had checked the bit.

"Something," said Athos, "wills that I should go no
further. Help me," he added, stretching out his arms.
"Quick! come closer. I feel all my muscles relaxing, and
I shall fall from my horse."

The servant had seen the gesture made by his master
at the moment he received the order. He went up to him
quickly, received the count in his arms, and as they were
still close enough to the house that the servants, who had
remained at the door to watch their master's departure,
could perceive the disorder in the usually regular walk of
the count, the valet called his comrades, and all rushed
to help. Athos had gone but a few steps toward the house
when he felt himself better again. His strength seemed
to revive, and with it the desire to go to Blois. He made
his horse turn around; but, at the animal's first steps, he
sank again into a state of torpor and anguish.

"Well," he said, "it is *willed* that I should stay at home."

His people flocked around him; they lifted him from
his horse, and carried him as quickly as possible into the
house. Everything was soon prepared in his room, and
they put him to bed.

"You will be sure to remember," he said, getting ready
to sleep, "that I am expecting letters from Africa today."

"Monsieur will, no doubt, hear with pleasure that
Blaisois's son has gone on horseback, to gain an hour
over the courier of Blois," replied his valet.

"Thank you," replied Athos, with his kind smile.

The count fell asleep, but his disturbed sleep looked

like pain. The servant who was watching him several times saw the expression of an inner torture on his features. Athos was perhaps dreaming. The day passed away. Blaisois's son returned; the courier had brought no news. The count was counting the minutes with despair; he would shudder when those minutes had formed an hour. The idea that he was forgotten seized him once, and brought on a fearful pain to his heart. Everybody in the house had given up all hopes of the courier—his hour had long passed. Four times the express sent to Blois had made his journey, and there was nothing for the count. Athos knew that the courier only arrived once a week. Here, then, was a delay of eight mortal days to be endured. He began the night with this painful belief. All that a sick man, irritated by suffering, can add of melancholy suppositions to probabilities always sad, Athos heaped up during the early hours of this dismal night. The fever rose; it invaded his chest, where soon the fire caught, according to the expression of the physician, who had been brought back from Blois by Blaisois at his last journey. It soon reached his head. The physician made two successive bleedings, which relieved it, but left the patient very weak, and without power of action in anything but his brain. And yet this terrible fever had ceased. It attacked with throbbings his stiffened extremities; it dropped as midnight struck.

The physician, seeing the unquestionable improvement, returned to Blois, after having ordered some prescriptions, and declared that the count was saved. Then began for Athos a strange, undefinable state. Free to think, his mind turned toward Raoul, that beloved son. His imagination painted the fields of Africa around Gigelli, where M. de Beaufort must have landed his army. There were gray rocks, made green in certain parts by the sea, when it lashed the shore in storms and tempest. Beyond, the shore, strewed over with these rocks like tombs, ascended in form of an amphitheater among mastick trees and cactus, a sort of small town, full of smoke, confused noises, and terrified movements. All on a sudden, from the heart of this smoke arose a flame, which succeeded, by creeping along the houses, in covering the whole surface of this town, and which increased by degrees, uniting in its red whirls tears, cries, arms extended toward heaven.

There was, for a moment, a frightful jumble of *madriers* falling to pieces, of swords broken, of stones charred, of trees burned and disappearing. It was a strange thing that in this chaos, in which Athos distinguished raised arms, in which he heard cries, sobs, and groans, he did not see one human figure. The cannon thundered at a distance, musketry cracked, the sea moaned, flocks made their escape, bounding over the green slopes. But not a soldier to apply the match to the batteries of cannon, not a sailor to assist in working the fleet, not a shepherd for the flocks. After the ruin of the village, and the destruction of the forts which towered over it, a ruin and a destruction brought about magically without the cooperation of a single human being, the flame was extinguished, the smoke began to ascend, then grew dim, and disappeared entirely. Night then came over the scene; a night dark upon the earth, brilliant in the sky. The large, blazing stars which sparkled in the African sky shone without lighting anything even around them.

A long silence followed, which for a moment gave rest to the troubled imagination of Athos; and, as he felt there was still much to see, he concentrated on the strange spectacle which his imagination was presenting him. This spectacle soon went on. A mild and pale moon rose behind the slopes of the coast, and streaking at first the undulating ripples of the sea, which had calmed down after the roarings it had sent forth during the vision of Athos— the moon shed its diamonds and opals on the briers and the bushes of the hills. The gray rocks, like so many silent and attentive phantoms, appeared to raise their green heads to examine also the field of battle by the light of the moon, and Athos saw that the field, entirely void during the combat, was now strewed over with fallen bodies.

An inexpressible shudder of fear and horror seized his soul when he recognized the white and blue uniform of the soldiers of Picardy, with their long pikes and blue handles, and their muskets marked with the fleur-de-lis on the butts. When he saw all the gaping, cold wounds, looking up to the blue sky as if to ask for the souls for which they had opened a passage—when he saw the slaughtered horses, stiff, with their tongues hanging out at one side of their mouths, sleeping in the icy blood around them, staining their saddle clothes and their manes—when he saw the white horse of M. de Beaufort, with his head beaten to pieces, in the first ranks of the dead, Athos passed a cold hand over his brow, which he was astonished not to find burning. He was convinced by this touch that he was present, as a spectator without fever, at the day after a battle fought upon the shores of Gigelli by the army of the expedition, which he had seen leave the coast of France and disappear in the horizon, and of which he had saluted with thought and gesture the last cannonshot fired by the duke as a signal of farewell to his country.

Who can describe the mortal agony with which his soul followed, like a vigilant eye, the traces of these dead bodies, and examined them, one after the other, to see if Raoul slept among them? Who can express the mad joy with which Athos bowed before God, and thanked Him for not having seen among the dead him he was frightened to find? In fact, fallen dead in their ranks, stiff, icy, all these dead, easy to be recognized, seemed to turn obligingly toward the Comte de la Fère, to be the better seen by him during his funereal inspection. But yet he was astonished, while viewing all these bodies, not to see the survivors. His illusion was such that this vision was for him a real voyage made by the father into Africa, to obtain more exact information about his son.

Tired, therefore, from having crossed seas and continents, he sought repose under one of the tents sheltered behind a rock, on the top of which was floating the white fleur-de-lised pennon. He looked for a soldier to take him to the tent of M. de Beaufort. Then, while his eye was wandering over the plain, he saw a white form appear behind the resinous myrtles. This figure was dressed as an officer; it held in its hand a broken sword; it came slowly toward Athos, who, stopping short and fixing his eyes upon it, neither spoke nor moved, but wished to open his arms, because in this silent and pale officer he had just recognized Raoul. The count tried to utter a cry, but it remained stifled in his throat. Raoul, with a gesture, directed him to be silent, placing his finger on his lips and drawing back by degrees, without Athos being able to see his legs move. The count, paler than Raoul, more trembling, followed his son, painfully crossing briers and bushes, stones and ditches, Raoul not appearing to touch the earth, and no obstacle impeding the lightness of his walk. The count, tired by his walk along the rugged path, soon stopped, exhausted. Raoul still beckoned him to follow him. The tender father, to whom love restored strength, made a last effort, and climbed the mountain after the young man, who was calling him with a gesture and a smile.

At last he reached the top of the hill, and saw, thrown out in black upon the horizon whitened by the moon, the elongated aerial form of Raoul. Athos stretched out his hand to get closer to his beloved son on the plateau, and the latter also stretched out his; but suddenly, as if the young man had been drawn away in spite of himself, still retreating, he left the earth, and Athos saw the clear blue sky shine between the feet of his child and the ground of the hill. Raoul was rising gradually into the void, smiling, still calling with a gesture; he was going up toward heaven. Athos uttered a cry of terrified tenderness. He looked below again. He saw a camp destroyed, and all those white bodies of the royal army, like so many motionless atoms. And then, when raising his head, he saw his son beckoning him to ascend with him.

CHAPTER LVIII

THE ANGEL OF DEATH

ATHOS was at this part of his marvelous vision when the spell was suddenly broken by a great noise rising from outside the gates of the house. A horse was heard galloping over the hard gravel of the great alley and the sound of most noisy and animated conversations came up to the room in which the count was dreaming. Athos did not move; he scarcely turned his head toward the door to learn sooner what these noises could be. A heavy step came up the stairs; the horse which had recently galloped departed slowly toward the stables. Great hesitation appeared in the steps, which were approaching Athos's room. A door then was opened, and Athos, turn-

ing a little toward the part ᴏ the room the noise came
from, cried, in a weak voice:

"It is a courier from Africa, is it not?"

"No, Monsieur le Comte," replied a voice which made
the father of Raoul start upright in his bed.

"Grimaud!" he whispered.

And the sweat began to pour down his cheeks. Grimaud appeared in the doorway. It was no longer the Grimaud we have seen, still young with courage and
devotion, when he jumped first into the boat destined to
take Raoul de Bragelonne to the ship of the royal fleet.
He was a stern and pale old man, his clothes covered
with dust, with a few scattered hairs white with old age.
He was trembling while leaning against the door frame,
and almost fell on seeing, by the light of the lamps, his
master's face. These two men, who had lived so long
together in a community of intelligence, and whose eyes
were accustomed to saying so many things silently—these
old friends, one as noble as the other in heart, if they
were unequal in fortune and birth, remained silent while
looking at each other. By the exchange of a single glance
they had just read to the bottom of each other's hearts.
Grimaud bore upon his face the impression of a grief
already old, of a dismal familiarity with it. He appeared
to have in use but one single version of his thoughts. As
formerly he was accustomed not to speak much, he was
now accustomed not to smile at all. Athos read at a glance
all these shades upon the face of his faithful servant, and
in the same tone he would have employed to speak to
Raoul in his dream:

"Grimaud," he said, "Raoul is dead, isn't he?"

Behind Grimaud, the other servants were listening
breathlessly, with their eyes fixed upon the bed of their
sick master. They heard the terrible question, and an aw-
ful silence followed.

"Yes," replied the old man, tearing up the monosyllable
from his chest with a hoarse, broken sigh.

Then arose voices of lamentation, which groaned un-
controllably, and filled with regrets and prayers the room
where the dying father searched with his eyes the portrait
of his son. For Athos this was like the transition which had
led to his dream. Without uttering a cry, without shed-
ding a tear, patient, mild, resigned as a martyr, he raised

his eyes toward heaven, in order to see there again, rising
above the mountain of Gigelli, the beloved shadow which
was leaving him at the moment of Grimaud's arrival.
Without doubt, while looking toward heaven, when resuming his marvelous dream, he went through the same
road by which the vision, at once so terrible and so sweet,
had led him before, for, after having gently closed his
eyes, he reopened them and began to smile; he had just
seen Raoul, who had smiled upon him. With his hands
clasped upon his breast, his face turned toward the window, bathed by the fresh night air, which brought to his
pillow the smell of the flowers and the woods, Athos
entered, never again to come out of it, into the contemplation of that paradise which the living never see. God
willed, no doubt, to open to this elect the treasures of
eternal bliss at the hour when other men tremble with the
idea of being severely received by the Lord, and cling to
this life they know, in the dread of the other life of which
they get a glimpse by the dismal, murky torches of death.
Athos was guided by the pure and serene soul of his son,
which was carrying away the paternal soul. Everything
for this just man was melody and perfume on the rough
road which souls take to return to the celestial country.
After an hour of this ecstasy Athos softly raised his hands
as white as wax; the smile did not leave his lips, and he
whispered low, so low as scarcely to be audible, these
three words addressed to God or to Raoul:

"Here I am!"

And his hand fell down slowly, as if he himself had
placed them on the bed.

Death had been kind and mild to this noble man. It
had spared him the tortures of agony, the convulsions of
the last departure; it had opened with an indulgent finger
the gates of eternity to that noble soul worthy of every
respect. God had no doubt ordained that the pious memory of this death would remain in the hearts of those
present, and in the memory of other men, and so would
it be for those other good men who have nothing to fear
at the last judgment. Even in eternal sleep, Athos preserved that calm and sincere smile—an ornament which
was to accompany him to the tomb. The calm of his features made his servants doubt for a long time whether
he had really died. The count's people wanted to remove

Grimaud, who, from a distance, was looking intensely at the face growing so pale, and was not coming near, from the pious fear of bringing to him the breath of death. But Grimaud, tired as he was, refused to leave the room. He sat upon the threshold, watching his master with the vigilance of a sentinel, and jealous to receive either his first waking look or his last dying sigh. The noises were all quieted in the house, and everyone was respecting the slumber of their lord. But Grimaud, by anxiously listening, could tell that the count was no longer breathing. He raised himself with his hands leaning on the ground, and looked to see if there did not appear some motion in the body of his master. Nothing! Fear seized him; he rose up completely, and, at that very moment, heard someone coming up the stairs. A noise of spurs knocking against a sword—a warlike sound, familiar to his ears—stopped him as he was going toward Athos's bed. A voice still louder than brass or steel resounded within three paces of him.

"Athos! Athos, my friend!" cried this voice, moved to tears.

"Monsieur le Chevalier D'Artagnan!" stammered Grimaud.

"Where is he? where is he?" continued the musketeer. With his bony fingers, Grimaud seized his arm and pointed to the bed, where on the sheets already showed the pale tints of the dead.

A choked breath, the opposite to a sharp cry, swelled the throat of D'Artagnan. He advanced on tiptoe, trembling, frightened at the noise his feet were making on the floor, and his heart torn by a nameless agony. He placed his ear on Athos's chest, his face to the count's mouth. Neither noise nor breath! D'Artagnan drew back. Grimaud, who had followed him with his eyes, and for whom each of his movements had been a revelation, came timidly, and sat at the foot of the bed, and glued his lips to the sheet which was raised by the stiffened feet of his master. Then large drops began to flow from his red eyes. This old man in despair, who was weeping, bent double without uttering a word, was the most moving sight that D'Artagnan, in a life so filled with emotion, had ever met with.

The captain remained standing in contemplation before that smiling dead man, who seemed to have kept his last thought to make to his best friend, to the man he had loved next to Raoul, a gracious welcome even beyond life; and as if to answer to that supreme flattery of hospitality, D'Artagnan went and kissed Athos fervently on the brow, and with his trembling fingers closed his eyes. Then he sat by the pillow without dread of that dead man, who had been so kind and affectionate to him for thirty-five years; he fed himself greedily with the memories which the noble face of the count brought to his mind in crowds—some blooming and charming as that smile—some dark, dismal, and icy as that face with its eyes closed for eternity.

All at once, the bitter flood which was rising from minute to minute invaded his heart, and swelled his chest almost to bursting. Incapable of mastering his emotions, he got up, and tore himself violently from the room where he had just found dead the man to whom he was coming to report the news of the death of Porthos. He uttered sobs so heartrending that the servants, who seemed to have been waiting for an explosion of grief, answered it by their lugubrious clamors, and the dogs of the late count by their lamentable howlings. Grimaud was the only one who did not raise his voice. Even in the paroxysm of his grief he would not have dared to profane death, or for the first time disturb his master's sleep. Athos had accustomed him never to speak.

At daybreak D'Artagnan, who had wandered about the lower hall, biting his fingers to stifle his sighs—D'Artagnan went up once more, and watching for the moment when Grimaud would turn his head toward him, he gestured to come to him, which the faithful servant obeyed without making more noise than a shadow. D'Artagnan went down again, followed by Grimaud; and when he had reached the vestibule, taking the old man's hands:

"Grimaud," he said, "I have seen how the father died; now let me know how the son died."

Grimaud drew from his chest a large letter, upon the envelope of which was traced the address of Athos. He recognized the writing of M. de Beaufort, broke the seal, and began to read, walking about in the first blue rays of day, in the dark alley of old linden trees, marked by the still visible footsteps of the count who had just died.

CHAPTER LIX

THE BULLETIN

THE Duc de Beaufort wrote to Athos. The letter destined for the living only reached the dead. God had changed the address.

The prince wrote in his large, bad schoolboy's hand:

> "My Dear Count,
> A great misfortune has struck us amid a great triumph. The king loses one of the bravest of soldiers. I lose a friend. You lose Monsieur de Bragelonne. He has died gloriously, and so gloriously that I have not the strength to weep as I would wish. Receive my sad compliments, my dear count. Heaven distributes trials according to the greatness of our hearts. This is an immense one, but not above your courage. Your good friend,
> LE DUC DE BEAUFORT."

The letter contained an account written by one of the prince's secretaries. It was the most touching report, and the truest, of that dismal episode which undid two existences. D'Artagnan, accustomed to battle emotions, and with a heart armed against tenderness, could not help trembling on reading the name of Raoul, the name of that beloved boy who had become a shadow as his father had.

"In the morning"—said the prince's secretary—"monseigneur ordered the attack. Normandy and Picardy had taken position in the gray rocks dominated by the heights of the mountain, on the side of which rise the bastions of Gigelli.

"The cannon beginning to fire, opened the action; the regiments marched full of resolution; the pikemen had their pikes up, the bearers of muskets had their weapons ready. The prince followed attentively the march and movements of the troops, so as to be able to sustain them with a strong reserve. With monseigneur were the oldest captains and his aide-de-camp. Monsieur le Vicomte de Bragelonne had received orders not to leave his highness. In the meantime, the enemy's cannon, which at first had thundered with little success against the masses, had regulated its fire, and the bullets, better directed, had killed several men near the prince. The regiments which were advancing against the ramparts, were rather roughly handled. There was a sort of hesitation in our troops, who found themselves ill-seconded by the artillery. In fact, the batteries which had been established the evening before had but a weak and uncertain aim, on account of their position. The direction from low to high lessened the precision of the shots as well as their range.

"Monseigneur, understanding the bad effect of this position of the siege artillery, ordered the frigates moored in the little road to begin a regular fire against the fort. Monsieur de Bragelonne offered at once to carry this order. But monseigneur refused the viscount's request. Monseigneur was right, for he loved and wished to spare the young nobleman. He was quite right, and the event justified his foresight and refusal; for scarcely had the sergeant entrusted with the message reached the seashore, when two shots from long carbines went off from the enemy's ranks and laid him low. The sergeant fell, dyeing the sand with his blood; observing this, Monsieur de Bragelonne smiled at monseigneur, who said to him, 'You see, viscount, I have saved your life. Report that, someday, to Monsieur le Comte de la Fère, in order that, learning it from you, he may thank me.' The young nobleman smiled sadly, and replied to the duke, 'It is true, monseigneur, that but for your kindness I would have been killed where the poor sergeant has fallen, and would be at rest.' Monsieur de Bragelonne made this reply in such a tone that monseigneur answered him warmly, 'Good god! young man, one would say that you long for death; but, by the soul of Henri IV! I have promised your father to bring you back alive, and, please the Lord, I will keep my word.' Monsieur de Bragelonne blushed, and replied, in a lower voice, 'Monseigneur, pardon me, please; I have always had the desire to take advantage of opportunities; and it is sweet to distinguish oneself before one's general, particularly when that general is Monsieur le Duc de Beaufort.'

"Monseigneur was a little softened by this; and, turning to the officers who surrounded him, gave various orders. The grenadiers of the two regiments got near enough to the ditches and the entrenchments to launch their grenades, which had little effect. In the meanwhile, Monsieur d'Estrées, who was in command of the fleet, having seen the attempt of the sergeant to approach the ship, understood that he must act without orders, and opened fire. Then the Arabs finding themselves hit by the bullets from the fleet, and beholding the ruins of their bad walls, uttered the most fearful cries. Their horsemen went down the mountain galloping, bent over their saddles, and rushed full tilt upon the columns of infantry, which, crossing their pikes, stopped this mad assault. Pushed back firmly by the battalion, the Arabs threw themselves with great fury toward the état-major, which was not on its guard at that moment.

"The danger was great! monseigneur drew his sword; his secretaries and people imitated him; the officers of the corps engaged in combat with the furious Arabs. Then Monsieur de Bragelonne was able to satisfy the inclination he had shown from the beginning of the action. He fought near the prince with the valor of a Roman, and killed three Arabs with his small sword. But it was evident that his bravery did not arise from one of those sentiments of pride natural to all who fight. It was impetuous, affected, even forced; he was trying to intoxicate himself with the noise and carnage. He got so excited that monseigneur called out to him to stop. He must have heard the voice of monseigneur, because we who were close to him heard it. He did not, however, stop, but kept on running toward the entrenchments. As Monsieur de Bragelonne was a well-disciplined officer, this disobedience to the orders of monseigneur surprised everybody, and Monsieur de Beaufort redoubled his earnestness, crying, 'Stop, Bragelonne! Where are you going? Stop! I command you!'

"Imitating the gesture of Monsieur le Duc, we all raised our hands. We were expecting the cavalier to turn bridle; but Monsieur de Bragelonne kept on riding toward the palisades.

" 'Stop, Bragelonne!' repeated the prince, in a very loud voice; 'stop! in the name of your father!'

"At these words Monsieur de Bragelonne turned around, his face expressed a violent grief, but he did not stop; we then concluded that his horse must have run away with him. When Monsieur le Duc had imagined the viscount was not master of the horse, and had seen him precede the first grenadiers, his highness cried, 'Musketeers, kill his horse! A hundred pistoles for him who shall kill his horse!' But who could expect to hit the beast without at least wounding his rider? No one dared. At last one presented himself; he was a sharpshooter of the regiment of Picardy, named Luzerne, who took aim at the animal, fired, and hit him in the quarters, for we saw the blood redden the white coat of the horse. Instead of falling, the cursed horse was irritated, and carried him on more furiously than ever. Every Picard who saw this unfortunate young man rushing on to meet death, shouted in the loudest manner, 'Throw yourself off, Monsieur le Vicomte!—off!—throw yourself off!' Monsieur de Bragelonne was an officer much beloved in the army. The viscount had already arrived within pistolshot of the ramparts; a volley went off, and enveloped him in its fire and smoke. We lost sight of him; the smoke dispersed; he was seen on foot, standing; his horse was just killed.

"The viscount was summoned to surrender by the Arabs, but he shook his head, and continued to walk toward the palisades. This was a mortal imprudence. Nevertheless, the whole army was pleased that he would not retreat, since misfortune had led him so near. He walked a few paces further, and the two regiments clapped their hands. At this moment the second volley shook the walls, and the Vicomte de Bragelonne again disappeared in the smoke; but this time the smoke was dispersed in vain; we no longer saw him standing. He was down, with his head lower than his legs, among the bushes, and the Arabs began to think of leaving their entrenchments to come and cut off his head, or take his body, as is the custom with the infidels. But Monseigneur le Duc de Beaufort had followed all this, and the sad spectacle drew from him many painful sighs. He then cried aloud, seeing the Arabs running like white phantoms among the mastick trees, 'Grenadiers, piquers! will you let them take that noble body?'

"Saying these words and waving his sword, he himself rode toward the enemy. The regiments, rushing in his steps, ran also, uttering cries as terrible as those of the Arabs were wild.

"The fighting started over the body of Monsieur de Bragelonne, and with such fury was it fought that a hundred and sixty Arabs were left upon the field, by the side of at least fifty of our troops. It was a lieutenant from Normandy who took the body of the viscount on his shoulders and carried it back to the lines. The gain was, however, carried on, the regiments took the reserve with them, and the enemy's palisades were destroyed. At three o'clock the Arabs ceased fire; the hand-to-hand combat lasted two hours; that was a massacre. At five o'clock we were victorious on all sides; the enemy had abandoned his positions, and Monsieur le Duc had ordered the white flag to be planted upon the culminating point of the little mountain. Then we had time to think of Monsieur de Bragelonne, who had eight large wounds through his body, and who had lost almost all his blood. He was, however, still breathing, which afforded inexpressible joy to monseigneur, who insisted upon being present at the first dressing of the wounds and at the consultation of the surgeons. There were two among them who declared Monsieur de Bragelonne would live. Monseigneur threw his arms around their necks and promised them a thousand louis each if they could save him.

''The viscount heard these cries of joy, and whether he was in despair, or whether he suffered much from his wounds, he looked annoyed, which made one wonder, particularly one of the secretaries, when he heard what follows. The third surgeon was the brother of Sylvain de St. Cosme, the most learned of ours. He probed also the wounds, and said nothing. Monsieur de Bragelonne fixed his eyes steadily upon the skillful surgeon, and seemed to question his every movement. The latter, upon being questioned by monseigneur, replied that he saw plainly three mortal wounds out of eight, but so strong was the constitution of the wounded, so rich was he in youth, and so merciful was the goodness of God, that perhaps Monsieur de Bragelonne might recover, particularly if he did not move at all. Frère Sylvain added, turning toward his assistants, 'Above all, do not allow him to move even a finger, or you will kill him'; and we all left the tent in very low spirits. That secretary I have mentioned, on leaving the tent, thought he perceived a faint and sad smile glide over the lips of Monsieur de Bragelonne when the duke said to him, in a cheerful, kind voice, 'We shall save you, viscount, we shall save you!'

"In the evening, when it was believed the wounded young man had taken some rest, one of the assistants entered his tent, but rushed immediately out again, uttering loud cries. We all ran up in confusion, Monsieur le Duc with us, and the assistant pointed to the body of Monsieur de Bragelonne on the ground, at the foot of his bed, bathed in the remainder of his blood. It appeared that he had some convulsion, some febrile movement, and that he had fallen, that the fall had accelerated his end, according to the prognostic of Frère Sylvain. We picked up the viscount; he was cold and dead. He held a lock of fair hair in his right hand, and that hand was pressed tightly upon his heart."

Then followed the details of the expedition, and of the victory obtained over the Arabs. D'Artagnan stopped at the account of the death of poor Raoul.

"Oh!" he whispered, "unhappy boy! a suicide!"

And turning his eyes toward the room of the chateau in which Athos slept in eternal sleep:

"They kept their words with each other," he said, in a low voice; "now I believe them to be happy; they must be reunited."

And he returned through the flowerbeds with slow and melancholy steps. All the village, all the neighborhood, were filled with grieving neighbors relating to each other the double catastrophe, and making preparations for the funeral.

CHAPTER LX

THE LAST CANTO OF THE POEM

THE next day, all the nobility of the vicinity, and wherever messengers had carried the news, were seen to arrive. D'Artagnan had shut himself up, without being willing to speak to anybody. The two tragedies, occurring so soon after the death of Porthos, oppressed his once invulnerable spirit. Except Grimaud, who entered his room once, the musketeer saw neither servants nor guests. He supposed, from the noises in the house, and the continual coming and going, that preparations were being made for the count's funeral. He wrote to the king to ask for an extension of his leave of absence. Grimaud, as we have said, had entered D'Artagnan's apartment, had sat on a stool near the door, like a man who meditates profoundly; then, rising, he gestured to D'Artagnan to follow him. The latter obeyed in silence. Grimaud went down to the count's bedroom, pointed out to the captain the empty bed, and raised his eyes eloquently toward heaven.

"Yes," replied D'Artagnan, "yes, good Grimaud— now with the son he loved so much!"

Grimaud left the room, and led the way to the hall, where, according to the custom of the province, the body was laid out before its being buried forever. D'Artagnan was struck at seeing two open coffins in the hall. In reply to the mute invitation of Grimaud he came forward, and saw in one of them Athos, still handsome in death, and in the other, Raoul, with his eyes closed, his cheeks pearly as those of the Pallas of Virgil, with a smile on his purple lips. He shuddered at seeing the father and son, those two departed souls represented on earth by two silent, melancholy bodies, incapable of touching each other, however close they might be.

"Raoul here!" he whispered. "Oh, Grimaud, why did you not tell me this?"

Grimaud shook his head, and made no reply; but, taking D'Artagnan by the hand, he led him to the coffin, and showed him, under the thin shroud, the black wounds by which life had escaped. The captain turned away his eyes, and, judging it useless to question Grimaud, who would not answer, he remembered that M. de Beaufort's secretary had written more than he, D'Artagnan, had had the courage to read. Taking up the account of the affair which had cost Raoul his life, he found these words, which made up the last paragraph of the letter:

"Monsieur le Duc has ordered that the body of Monsieur le Vicomte should be embalmed, after the manner practiced by the Arabs when they wish their bodies to be carried to their native land; and Monsieur le Duc has appointed relays, so that a confidential servant who brought up the young man might take back his remains to Monsieur le Comte de la Fère."

* * *

"And so," thought D'Artagnan, "I shall follow thy funeral, my dear boy—I, already old—I, who am of no value on earth—and I shall scatter the dust upon that brow which I was still kissing two months ago. God has willed it to be so. Thou hast willed it to be so. I have no longer the right even to weep. Thou hast chosen death; it hath seemed to thee preferable to life."

At last the moment came when the cold remains of these two gentlemen were to be returned to the earth. There was such an affluence of military and other people that up to the burial place, which was a chapel in the plain, the road from the city was filled with horsemen and pedestrians in mourning clothes. Athos had chosen for his resting place the little enclosure of a chapel he had erected near the boundary of his estates. He had had the stones, cut in 1550, brought from an old Gothic manorhouse in Berri, which had sheltered his early youth. The chapel, thus rebuilt, thus transported, was pleasant under a clump of poplars and sycamores. Mass was said there every Sunday by the curé of the neighboring village, to whom Athos paid an allowance of two hundred francs for this service; and all the vassals of his domain, to the number of about forty, the laborers, and the farmers, with their families, would come there to hear mass, without having to go to the city.

Behind the chapel lay, surrounded by two high hedges of nut trees, elders, white thorns, and a deep ditch the little enclosure—uncultivated, it is true, but cheerful in its sterility; because the mosses there were high, because the wild heliotropes and ravenelles there mixed their perfumes, because beneath the tall chestnuts gushed a large spring, a prisoner in a cistern of marble, and that upon the thyme all around tumbled down thousands of bees from the neighboring plants, while chaffinches and redthroats sang cheerfully among the flowers of the hedge. The two coffins were brought there, in the midst of a silent and respectful crowd. The office of the dead being celebrated, the last adieus paid to the noble dead, the assembly dispersed along the roads, talking of the virtues and gentle death of the father, of the hopes the son had given, and of his melancholy end upon the coast of Africa. Little by little all noises died out, like the lamps in the humble nave. The priest bowed for a last time to the altar and the still fresh graves; then, followed by his

assistant, who rang a hoarse bell, he slowly took the road
back to the rectory. D'Artagnan, left alone, noticed that
night was coming on. He had forgotten the hour while
thinking of the dead. He rose from the oak bench on
which he was seated in the chapel, and wanted, as the
priest had done, to go and bid a last adieu to the double
grave which contained his two lost friends.

A woman was praying, kneeling on the moist earth.
D'Artagnan stopped at the door of the chapel, to avoid
disturbing this woman; and also to try to see who was
the pious friend who performed this sacred duty with so
much zeal and perseverance. The unknown woman was
hiding her face in her hands, which were white as ala-
baster. From the noble simplicity of her dress one
guessed she was a woman of distinction. Outside the enclosure were several horses mounted by servants, and a
traveling carriage waiting for this lady. D'Artagnan in
vain sought to make out what caused her delay. She continued praying, she frequently passed her handkerchief
over her face. D'Artagnan understood she was weeping.
He saw her strike her breast with the solemnity of a
Christian woman. He heard her several times exclaim, as
if from a wounded heart, ''Forgive me! forgive me!''
And as she appeared to abandon herself entirely to her
grief, as she threw herself down, almost fainting, amid
moans and prayers, D'Artagnan, touched by this love for
his so much regretted friends, took a few steps toward
the grave, in order to interrupt the melancholy colloquy
of the penitent with the dead. But as soon as his step
sounded on the gravel the unknown woman raised her
head, revealing to D'Artagnan a tear-stained, but well-
known face. It was Mlle. de la Vallière!

''Monsieur D'Artagnan,'' she whispered.

''You!'' replied the captain, in a stern voice—''you
here! Oh, madame, I'd rather have seen you decked with
flowers in the mansion of the Comte de la Fère. You
would have wept less—they, too—I, too!''

''Monsieur!'' she said, sobbing.

''For it is you,'' added this pitiless friend of the dead,
''it is you who have put these two men in the grave.''

''Oh, spare me!''

''God forbid, madame, that I should offend a woman, or

that I should make her weep in vain; but I must say that the place of the murderer is not upon the grave of her victims."

She tried to answer.

"What I now tell you," he added coldly, "I told the king."

She clasped her hands.

"I know," she said, "I have caused the death of the Vicomte de Bragelonne."

"Ah! you know it?"

"The news arrived at court yesterday. I have traveled forty leagues during the night to come and ask for the count's forgiveness, whom I supposed to be still living, and to beg God, upon the tomb of Raoul, that He would send me all the misfortunes I have deserved, except a single one. Now, monsieur, I know that the death of the son has killed the father; I have two crimes to reproach myself with; I have two punishments to look for from God."

"I will repeat to you, mademoiselle," said D'Artagnan, "what Monsieur de Bragelonne said of you in Antibes, when he was already contemplating death: 'If pride and flirtation have misled her, I pardon her while despising her. If love has produced her error, I pardon her, swearing that no one could have loved her as I have.'"

"You know," interrupted Louise, "that for my love I was about to sacrifice myself; you know I suffered when you met me lost, dying, abandoned. Well, never have I suffered so much as now; because then I had hope—now I have nothing to wish for; because this death drags away all my joy into his tomb; because I can no longer dare to love without remorse, and I feel that he whom I love—oh! that is the law—will repay me with the tortures I have inflicted on others."

D'Artagnan made no reply; he knew too well she was not mistaken.

"Well, then," she added, "dear Monsieur D'Artagnan, do not condemn me today, I again implore you. I am like the branch torn from the trunk, I no longer hold to anything in this world, and a current drags me on, I cannot say where. I love madly, I love to the point of coming to tell it, impious as I am, over the ashes of the dead, and I do not blush for it—I have no remorse on account of it. This love is a religion. However, since later on you will see me alone, forgotten, disdained; since you will see me punished, spare me in my ephemeral happi-

ness, leave it to me for a few days, for a few minutes.
At the moment I am speaking to you, perhaps it no longer
exists. My God! this double murder is perhaps already
expiated!''

While she was speaking thus the sound of voices and
the steps of horses drew the attention of the captain.
M. de St. Aignan was coming for La Vallière.

''The king,'' he said, ''is prey to jealousy and anxiety.''

St. Aignan did not see D'Artagnan, half-concealed by
the trunk of a chestnut tree which shaded the two graves.
Louise thanked St. Aignan, and dismissed him with a
gesture. He rejoined the party outside the enclosure.

''You see, madame,'' said the captain bitterly to the
young woman, ''you see that your happiness still exists.''

The young woman raised her head solemnly.

''A day will come,'' she said, ''when you will repent
of having so ill-judged me. On that day, it is I who will
pray God to forgive you for having been unjust toward
me. Besides, I shall suffer so much that you will be the
first to pity my sufferings. Do not reproach me with that
happiness, Monsieur D'Artagnan; it costs me much, and
I have not paid all my debt.''

Saying these words, she again knelt down, softly and
affectionately.

''Pardon me, one last time, my fiancé, Raoul!'' she
said. ''I have broken our chain; we are both destined to
die of grief. It is thou who departest the first; fear nothing, I shall follow thee. Do see that I have not been
cowardly, and that I have come to bid thee this last adieu.
The Lord is my witness, Raoul, that if with my life I
could have redeemed thine, I would have given that life
without hesitation. I could not give my love. Once more,
forgive me!''

She gathered a branch, and struck it into the ground;
then, wiping the tears from her eyes, she bowed to D'Artagnan, and disappeared.

The captain watched the departure of the horses,
horsemen, and carriage, then, crossing his arms upon his
swelling chest:

''When will it be my turn to depart?'' he said, in a sad
voice. ''What is there left for man after youth, after love,
after glory, after friendship, after strength, after riches?

That rock, under which sleeps Porthos, who possessed all I have named; this moss, under which rest Athos and Raoul, who possessed still much more!''

He hesitated a moment, with a dull eye; then, drawing himself up:

"Forward! still forward!'' he said. "When it shall be time God will tell me, as He has told others!''

He touched the earth, moistened with the evening dew, with the tips of his fingers, crossed himself, as if he had been at the font of a church, and rode back alone—ever alone—on the road to Paris.

EPILOGUE

FOUR years after the scene we have just described, two horsemen, well mounted, crossed Blois early in the morning, in order to plan a bird hunt which the king intended to hold in that uneven plain which the Loire divides in two, and which borders on the one side on Meung, on the other on Amboise. These were the captain of the king's greyhounds and the governor of the falcons, greatly respected in the time of Louis XIII, but rather neglected by his successor. These two horsemen, having reconnoitered the ground, were returning, their observations made, when they saw a few little groups of soldiers, here and there, whom the sergeants were placing at distances at the openings of the enclosures. These were the king's musketeers. Behind them came, on a good horse, the captain, known by his richly embroidered uniform. His hair was gray, his beard graying. He appeared a little bent, although sitting and handling his horse with ease. He was looking about him watchfully.

"Monsieur d'Artagnan does not get any older,'' said the captain of the greyhounds to his colleague, the falconer; "with ten years more than either of us, he has the seat of a young man on horseback.''

"That is true,'' replied the falconer. "I haven't seen any change in him over the last twenty years.''

But this officer was mistaken. D'Artagnan in the last four years had lived twelve years. Age had put its pitiless claws at each angle of his eyes; his brow was bald; his hands, formerly brown and nervous, were getting white as if the blood was beginning to chill there.

D'Artagnan met the officers with the courtesy which distinguishes superior men, and received in return two most respectful bows.

"Ah! how lucky to see you here, Monsieur D'Artagnan!" cried the falconer.

"It is rather I who should say that, messieurs," replied the captain, "for nowadays the king makes more frequent use of his musketeers than of his falcons."

"Ah! it is not as it was in the good old times," sighed the falconer. "Do you remember, Monsieur D'Artagnan, when the late king flew the magpie in the vineyards beyond Beaugency? Ah! *dame!* you were not captain of the musketeers at that time, Monsieur D'Artagnan."

"And you were nothing but undercorporal of the tiercelets," replied D'Artagnan, laughing. "Never mind that, those were good times—the times always are when we are young. Bonjour, Monsieur le Capitaine des Leverettes."

"You do me honor, *Monsieur le Comte,*" said the latter.

D'Artagnan made no reply. The title of count had not struck him; D'Artagnan had become a count four years ago.

"Are you not very tired with the long journey you just took, *Monsieur le Capitaine?*" continued the falconer. "It must be two hundred leagues from here to Pignerol."

"Two hundred and sixty there, and as many to come back," said D'Artagnan quietly.

"And," said the falconer, "is *he* well?"

"Who?" asked D'Artagnan.

"Why, poor Monsieur Fouquet," continued the falconer, still in a low voice.

The captain of the greyhounds had prudently withdrawn.

"No," replied D'Artagnan, "the poor man frets terribly; he cannot understand how imprisonment can be a favor; he says that the parliament had absolved him by banishing him, and that banishment is liberty. He doesn't see that they had sworn his death, and that to save his life from the claws of the parliament was to have too much obligation to God."

"Ah! yes; the poor man came close to the scaffold," replied the falconer; "they say that Monsieur Colbert had given orders to the governor of the Bastille, and that the execution was ordered.''

''Enough!'' said D'Artagnan pensively, cutting short the conversation.

''Yes,'' said the captain of the greyhounds, drawing toward them, ''Monsieur Fouquet is now at Pignerol; he has richly deserved it. He has had the good fortune to be led there by you; he had robbed the king enough.''

D'Artagnan launched at the master of the dogs one of his mean looks, and said to him:

''Monsieur, if anyone told me you had eaten your dogs' meat, not only would I refuse to believe it; but, still more, if you were condemned to jail for it, I would pity you, and would not allow people to speak ill of you. And yet, monsieur, honest man as you may be, I assure you that you are not more so than poor Monsieur Fouquet was.''

After having received this sharp rebuke, the captain of the greyhounds hung his head, and let the falconer get two steps ahead of him nearer to D'Artagnan.

''He is happy,'' said the falconer, in a low voice, to the musketeer; ''we all know that greyhounds are in fashion nowadays; if he were a falconer he would not talk in that way.''

D'Artagnan smiled in a melancholy manner at seeing this great political question resolved by the discontent of such humble interests. For a moment he ran over in his mind the glorious existence of the surintendant, the crumbling away of his fortunes, and the melancholy death that awaited him; and, to conclude:

''Did Monsieur Fouquet love falconry?'' he said.

''Oh, passionately, monsieur!'' replied the falconer, with an accent of bitter regret, and a sigh that was the funeral oration of Fouquet.

D'Artagnan allowed the ill humor of the one and the regrets of the other to pass, and continued to advance into the plain. They could already catch glimpses of the huntsmen at the entrance to the wood, the feathers of the outriders, passing like shooting stars across the clearings, and the white horses cutting like luminous apparitions the dark thickets of the copses.

''But,'' resumed D'Artagnan, ''will the sport be long?

Pray, give us a good swift bird, for I am very tired. Is it a heron or a swan?''

"Both, Monsieur d'Artagnan," said the falconer; "but you need not worry, the king is not much of a sportsman; he does not sport on his own account, he only wishes to amuse the ladies.''

The words "the ladies" were so strongly accented that it set D'Artagnan listening.

"Ah!" he said, looking at the falconer with surprise.

The captain of the greyhounds was smiling, no doubt to make it up with the musketeer.

"Oh! you may safely laugh," said D'Artagnan; "I know nothing of current news; I only arrived yesterday, after a month's absence. I left the court mourning the death of the queen mother. The king was not willing to take any amusement after receiving the last sigh of Anne of Austria; but everything has an end in this world. Well, then he is no longer sad, so much the better.''

"And everything begins as well as ends," said the captain of the dogs, with a coarse laugh.

"Ah!" said D'Artagnan, a second time—he burned to know, but dignity would not allow him to interrogate people below him—"is there something beginning?"

The captain gave him a significant wink; but D'Artagnan was unwilling to learn anything from this man.

"Shall we see the king early?" he asked the falconer.

"At seven o'clock, monsieur, I shall fly the birds.''

"Who is coming with the king? How is madame? How is the queen?''

"Better, monsieur.''

"Has she been ill, then?''

"Monsieur, since the last sorrow he had, her majesty had been unwell.''

"What sorrow? Don't think your news is old. I am just back.''

"It appears that the queen, a little neglected since the death of her mother-in-law, complained to the king, who replied to her: 'Do I not sleep with you every night, madame? What more do you want?' ''

"Ah!" said D'Artagnan, "poor woman! She must hate Mademoiselle de la Vallière.''

"Oh, no! not Mademoiselle de la Vallière," replied the falconer.

"Who then?"

The horn interrupted this conversation. It summoned the dogs and the hawks. The falconer and his companion set off immediately, leaving D'Artagnan alone in the midst of a sentence. The king appeared at a distance, surrounded by ladies and horsemen. All the troop advanced in beautiful order, at a walking pace, the horns of various sorts exciting the dogs and the horses. It was a movement, a noise, a mirage of light, of which nothing now can give an idea, unless it be the fictitious splendor or false majesty of the theater. D'Artagnan, with an eye a little weakened, distinguished behind the group three carriages. The first was intended for the queen; it was empty. D'Artagnan, who did not see Mlle. de la Vallière by the king's side, looked about for her and saw her in the second carriage. She was alone with two women, who seemed to be bored like their mistress. On the left hand of the king, upon a high-spirited horse, restrained by a bold and skillful hand, shone a lady of the most dazzling beauty. The king was smiling at her, and she was smiling at the king. Loud laughter followed every word she spoke.

"I must know that woman," thought the musketeer; "who can she be?"

And he leaned toward his friend, the falconer, to whom he addressed this question. The falconer was about to reply, when the king, seeing D'Artagnan:

"Ah, count!" he said, "you are back, then! Why have I not seen you?"

"Sire," replied the captain, "because your majesty was asleep when I arrived, and not awake when I resumed my duties this morning."

"Still the same," said Louis, in a loud voice, denoting satisfaction. "Take some rest, count; I command you to do so. You will dine with me today."

A murmur of admiration surrounded D'Artagnan like an immense caress. Everyone was eager to salute him. Dining with the king was an honor his majesty was not as generous with as Henry IV had been. The king took a few steps, and D'Artagnan found himself in the midst of a new group, among whom Colbert was shining.

"Good day, Monsieur D'Artagnan," said the minister,

with affable politeness; "did you have a pleasant journey?"

"Yes, monsieur," said D'Artagnan, bowing to the neck of his horse.

"I heard the king invite you to his table for this evening," continued the minister; "you will meet an old friend there."

"An old friend of mine?" asked D'Artagnan, plunging painfully into the dark waves of the past, which had swallowed up for him so many friendships and so many hatreds.

"Monsieur le Duc d'Alméda, who arrived this morning from Spain."

"The Duc d'Alméda?" said D'Artagnan, wondering.

"I!" said an old man, white as snow, sitting bent in his carriage, which he had opened to go and meet the musketeer.

"Aramis!" cried D'Artagnan, struck with perfect stupor.

And he let, inert as it was, the thin arm of the old nobleman hang around his neck.

Colbert, after having observed them in silence for a minute, put his horse forward, and left the two old friends together.

"And so," said the musketeer, taking the arm of Aramis, "you, the exile, the rebel, are again in France?"

"Ah! and I shall dine with you at the king's table," said Aramis, smiling. "Yes, are you wondering what is the use of fidelity in this world? Stop! let us let poor Vallière's carriage go. Look, how uneasy she is! How her eye, dimmed with tears, follows the king, who is riding on horseback over there!"

"With whom?"

"With Mademoiselle de Tonnay-Charente, now Madame de Montespan," replied Aramis.

"She is jealous; is she, then, deserted?"

"Not quite yet, but it will not be long."

They chatted together, while following the hunt, and Aramis's coachman drove them so cleverly that they arrived just when the falcon, attacking the bird, was forcing him down, and falling upon him. The king dismounted; Mme. de Montespan followed his example. They were in front of an isolated chapel, concealed by large trees,

which had lost their leaves in the first winds of autumn.
Behind this chapel was an enclosure with a latticed gate.
The falcon had beat down his prey in the enclosure belonging to this little chapel, and the king wanted to go
in to take the first feather, according to custom. The cortège formed a circle around the building and the hedges,
too small to receive so many. D'Artagnan held back Aramis by the arm, as he was about to get out of his carriage, and in a hoarse, broken voice he said:

"Do you realize, Aramis, where chance has led us?"

"No," replied the duke.

"Here lie people I have known," said D'Artagnan,
moved.

Aramis, without guessing anything, and with a trembling step, entered the chapel by a little door which
D'Artagnan opened for him.

"Where are they buried?" he said.

"There, in the enclosure. There is a cross, you see,
under that little cypress. The little cypress is planted over
their tomb; don't go to it; the king is going that way; the
heron has fallen there."

Aramis stopped and concealed himself in the shade.
They then saw, without being seen, the pale face of La
Vallière, who, neglected in her carriage, had at first
looked on, with a melancholy heart, from the door, and
then, carried away by jealousy, had entered the chapel,
where, leaning against a pillar, she contemplated in the
enclosure the king smiling and gesturing to Mme. de
Montespan to come near, as there was nothing to be afraid
of. Mme. de Montespan complied; she took the hand the
king held out to her, and he, plucking out the first feather
from the heron, which the falconer had strangled, placed
it in the hat of his beautiful companion. She, smiling
back, kissed tenderly the hand which gave her this present. The king blushed with pleasure; he looked at Mme.
de Montespan with all the fire of love.

"What will you give me in exchange?" he said.

She broke off a little branch of cypress and offered it
to the king, who looked intoxicated with hope.

"The present is a sad one," said Aramis to D'Artagnan, "for that cypress is shading a tomb."

"Yes, and the tomb is that of Raoul de Bragelonne,"

said D'Artagnan, aloud, "of Raoul, who sleeps under that cross with his father."

A moan resounded behind them. They saw a woman fall fainting to the ground. Mlle. de la Vallière had seen all, and heard all.

"Poor woman!" muttered D'Artagnan, as he helped the attendants to carry her back to her carriage; "it's her turn to suffer."

That evening D'Artagnan was seated at the king's table, near M. Colbert and M. le Duc d'Alméda. The king was very cheerful. He paid a thousand little attentions to the queen, a thousand kindnesses to Madame, seated at his left hand, and very sad. It might have been that calm time when the king used to watch the eyes of his mother for the approval or disapproval of what he had just done.

Of mistresses there was no question at this dinner. The king addressed Aramis two or three times, calling him M. l'Ambassadeur, which increased the surprise already felt by D'Artagnan at seeing his friend the rebel so marvelously well received at court.

The king, getting up from the table, gave his hand to the queen, and nodded to Colbert, whose eye was watching his master's. Colbert took D'Artagnan and Aramis aside. The king began to chat with his sister, while Monsieur, very uneasy, was talking to the queen with a preoccupied air, without ceasing to watch his wife and brother from the corner of his eye. The conversation between Aramis, D'Artagnan, and Colbert turned upon indifferent subjects. They spoke of preceding ministers; Colbert related the feats of Mazarin, and required those of Richelieu to be related to him. D'Artagnan could not overcome his surprise at finding this man, with the heavy eyebrows and the low forehead, with so much sound knowledge and cheerful spirits. Aramis was astonished at that lightness of character which permitted a serious man to delay with advantage the moment for a more important conversation, to which nobody made any allusion, although all three interlocutors felt the imminence of it. It was very plain from the embarrassed appearance of Monsieur, how much the conversation of the king and Madame was bothering him. The eyes of Madame were almost red; was she going to complain? Was she going to commit a little scandal in open court? The king took her aside, and in a tone so tender that it must have reminded the princess of the time when she was loved for herself:

"Sister," he said, "why do I see tears in those beautiful eyes?"

"Why . . . sire . . ." she said.

"Monsieur is jealous, is he not, sister?"

She looked toward Monsieur, an infallible sign that they were talking about him.

"Yes," she said.

"Listen to me," said the king; "if your friends are compromising you, it is not Monsieur's fault."

He spoke these words with so much kindness that Madame, encouraged, she who had so many sorrows for so long a time, almost burst into tears, so full was her heart.

"Come, come, dear little sister," said the king, "tell me your sorrows; in the name of a brother, I sympathize with them; in the name of a king, I will put an end to them."

She raised her fine eyes, and, in a melancholy tone:

"It is not my friends who compromise me," she said; "they are either absent or hidden; they have been brought into disgrace with your majesty; they, so devoted, so good, so loyal!"

"Do you say this on account of De Guiche, whom I have exiled, at Monsieur's request?"

"And who, since that unjust exile, has tried to get himself killed once every day!"

"Unfair, do you say, sister!"

"So unfair, that if I had not had the respect mixed with friendship that I have always entertained for your majesty . . ."

"Well?"

"Well, I would have asked my brother Charles, upon whom I can always . . ."

The king gave a start.

"What then?"

"I would have asked him to point out to you that Monsieur and his favorite, Monsieur le Chevalier de Lorraine, ought not destroy with impunity my honor and my happiness."

"The Chevalier de Lorraine," said the king; "that somber man?"

"Is my mortal enemy. While that man lives in my

household, where Monsieur keeps him and delegates his powers to him, I shall be the most miserable woman in this kingdom.''

"So," said the king slowly, "you call your brother of England a better friend than I am?"

"Actions speak for themselves, sire."

"And you would prefer going to ask for help there . . ."

"To my own country!" she said, with pride; "yes, sire."

"You are the grandchild of Henry IV as I am, my friend. Cousin and brother-in-law, does not that amount to the title of first cousin?"

"Then," said Henriette, "act."

"Let us form an alliance."

"Begin."

"I have, you say, unjustly exiled De Guiche."

"Oh, yes!" she said, blushing.

"De Guiche shall return."

"Good."

"And now you say that I am wrong in having in your household the Chevalier de Lorraine, who gives Monsieur ill advice about you?"

"Remember well what I tell you, sire; the Chevalier de Lorraine some day . . . Observe, if ever I come to an ill end, I beforehand accuse the Chevalier de Lorraine; he has a soul capable of any crime."

"The Chevalier de Lorraine shall no longer annoy you, I promise you that."

"Then that will be a true preliminary of alliance, sire—I sign it; but since you have done your part, tell me what shall be mine."

"Instead of getting me in trouble with your brother Charles, you must make him my more intimate friend than ever."

"That is very easy."

"Oh! not quite so much so as you may think, for in ordinary friendship people embrace or exercise hospitality, and that only costs a kiss or a reception, easy expenses; but in political friendship . . ."

"Ah! it's a political friendship, is it?"

"Yes, my sister; and then, instead of embraces and feasts, it is soldiers, it is soldiers alive and well equipped, that we must serve up to our friend; ships we must offer,

all armed with cannons and supplies. The result is that
we have not always our coffers in a fit state to form such
friendships.''

"Ah! you are quite right," said Madame; "the coffers
of the King of England have been sounding empty for
some time."

"But you, my sister, who have so much influence over
your brother, you can obtain more than an ambassador
could ever obtain."

"Then I must go to London, my dear brother."

"I have thought so," replied the king eagerly; "and I
have thought that such a trip would do your spirits good."

"However," interrupted Madame, "I may fail. The
King of England has dangerous counselors."

"Counselors, do you say?"

"Precisely. If, by chance, your majesty had any intention—I am only supposing so—of asking Charles II his
alliance for a war . . ."

"For a war?"

"Yes, well, then the lady counselors of the king—there
are seven of them: Mademoiselle Stewart, Mademoiselle
Wells, Mademoiselle Gwynn, Miss Orchay, Mademoiselle Zunga, Miss Davies, and the proud Countess of
Castlemaine—will represent to the king that war costs a
great deal of money; that it is better to give balls and
suppers at Hampton Court than to equip vessels of the
line at Portsmouth and Greenwich."

"And then your negotiations will fail?"

"Oh! those ladies have all negotiations fail that they
don't make themselves."

"Do you know the idea that has struck me, sister?"

"No; tell me what it is."

"It is that searching well around you, you might perhaps find a female counselor to take with you to your
brother, whose eloquence might paralyze the ill will of
the seven others."

"That is really an idea, sire, and I will search."

"You will find what you want."

"I hope so."

"A pretty person is necessary; an agreeable face is
better than an ugly one, is it not?"

"Surely."

"An animated, lively, daring character."

"Certainly."

"Nobility; that is, enough to enable her to approach the king without awkwardness—little enough, so as not to trouble herself about the dignity of her race."

"Quite right."

"And who knows a little English."

"*Mon Dieu!* why, someone," cried Madame, "like Mademoiselle de Kéroualle, for instance!"

"Of course!" said Louis XIV, "you have found . . . it is you who have found her, my sister."

"I will take her; she will have no cause to complain, I suppose."

"Oh, no; I will name her *séductrice plénipotentiaire* at once, and will add the dowry to the title."

"That is . . . well."

"I fancy you already on your road, my dear little sister, and consoled for all your sorrows."

"I will go, on two conditions. The first is, that I shall know what I am negotiating."

"This is it. The Dutch, you know, insult me daily in their newspapers, and by their republican attitude. I don't like republics."

"That may easily be conceived, sire."

"I see with pain that these kings of the sea—they call themselves so—keep trade from France in the Indies, and that their boats will soon occupy all the ports of Europe. Such a power is too near me, sister."

"They are your allies, nevertheless."

"That is why they were wrong in having the medal you have heard of struck—a medal which represents Holland stopping the sun, as Joshua did, with this legend: 'The sun has stopped before me.' There is not much fraternity in that, is there?"

"I thought you had forgotten that miserable affair."

"I never forget anything, my sister. And if my true friends, such as your brother Charles, are willing to help me . . ."

The princess remained pensively silent.

"Listen to me; there is the empire of the seas to be divided," said Louis XIV. "For this division, which England submitted to, could I not represent the second half as well as the Dutch?"

"We have Mademoiselle de Kéroualle to handle that matter," replied Madame.

"Your second condition for going, if you please, sister?"

"The consent of Monsieur, my husband."

"You shall have it."

"Then consider me gone, my brother."

On hearing these words, Louis XIV turned around toward the corner of the room in which D'Artagnan, Colbert, and Aramis stood, and made an affirmative sign to his minister. Colbert then broke the conversation at that point, and said to Aramis:

"Monsieur l'Ambassadeur, shall we talk business?"

D'Artagnan immediately withdrew discreetly. He went toward the fireplace, within hearing of what the king was going to say to Monsieur, who, evidently uneasy, had gone to him. The face of the king was animated. Upon his brow was stamped a will, whose formidable expression already met with no more opposition in France, and was soon to meet none in Europe.

"Monsieur," said the king to his brother, "I am not pleased with Monsieur le Chevalier de Lorraine. You who do him the honor to protect him, must advise him to travel for a few months."

These words fell with the crush of an avalanche upon Monsieur, who adored this favorite, and concentrated all his affections on him.

"In what has the chevalier been able to displease your majesty?" he cried, looking furiously at Madame.

"I will tell you that when he is gone," replied the impassive king. "And also when Madame, here, shall have crossed over into England."

"Madame! into England!" whispered Monsieur, in a perfect state of stupor.

"In a week, my brother," continued the king, "while we two will go where I will tell you."

And the king turned upon his heel, after having smiled at his brother, to sweeten a little the bitterness of that news.

During this time Colbert was talking with the Duc d'Alméda.

"Monsieur," said Colbert to Aramis, "this is the moment for us to come to an understanding. I have reconciled you with the king, and I owed that clearly to a man of your merit; but as you have often expressed friendship for me, an opportunity presents itself for giving me a proof of it. You are, besides, more a Frenchman than a Spaniard. Shall we have, answer me frankly, the neutrality of Spain, if we undertake anything against the United Provinces?''

''Monsieur,'' replied Aramis, ''the interest of Spain is very clear. To sow discord between Europe and the United Provinces, against whom subsists the old resentment of their conquered liberty, is our policy, but the King of France is allied with the United Provinces. You are aware, besides, that it would be a maritime war, and that France is not in a state to wage such a war with profit.''

Colbert, turning around at this moment, saw D'Artagnan, who was seeking an interlocutor during the ''aside'' of the king and Monsieur. He called him, at the same time saying, in a low voice, to Aramis:

''We may talk with D'Artagnan, I suppose?''

''Oh! certainly,'' replied the ambassador.

''We were saying, Monsieur d'Alméda and I,'' said Colbert, ''that war with the United Provinces would be a maritime war.''

''That's obvious enough,'' replied the musketeer.

''And what do you think of it, Monsieur D'Artagnan?''

''I think that to carry that war on successfully you must have a very large land army.''

''What did you say?'' said Colbert, thinking he had misunderstood him.

''Why such a land army?'' said Aramis.

''Because the king will be beaten by sea if he does not have the English with him, and that when beaten by sea he will be soon invaded, either by the Dutch in his ports, or by the Spaniards by land.''

''The neutral Spaniards?'' asked Aramis.

''Neutral as long as the king shall be the stronger,'' answered D'Artagnan.

Colbert admired that sharpness which never touched a question without enlightening it thoroughly. Aramis smiled, as he had long known that in diplomacy D'Artagnan acknowledged no master. Colbert, who, like all proud men, dwelt upon his fantasy with a certainty of success, resumed the subject:

"Who told you, Monsieur D'Artagnan, that the king had no navy?"

"Oh! I have paid no attention to these details," replied the captain. "I am but a middling sailor. Like all nervous people, I hate the sea; and yet I have an idea that with ships, France being a seaport with two hundred heads, we might have sailors."

Colbert drew from his pocket a little oblong book divided into two columns. On the first were the names of vessels, on the other the figures recapitulating the number of cannon and men needed to equip these ships.

"I have had the same idea as you," he said to D'Artagnan, "and I have an account drawn up of the vessels we have altogether—thirty-five ships."

"Thirty-five ships! that is impossible!" cried D'Artagnan.

"Something like two thousand pieces of cannon," said Colbert. "That is what the king possesses at this moment. With thirty-five vessels we can make three squadrons, but I must have five."

"Five!" cried Aramis.

"They will be afloat before the end of the year, gentlemen; the king will have fifty ships of the line. We can fight with that, can't we?"

"To built vessels," said D'Artagnan, "is difficult, but possible. As to arming them, how is that to be done? In France there are neither foundries nor military docks."

"Bah!" replied Colbert, beaming. "I have instituted all that a year and a half ago; did you not know it? Don't you know Monsieur d'Imfreville?"

"D'Imfreville?" replied D'Artagnan. "No."

"He is a man I have discovered; he has a specialty; he is a man of genius—he knows how to set men to work. It is he who has cast cannon and cut the woods of Bourgogne. And then, Monsieur l'Ambassadeur, you may not believe what I am going to tell you, but I have a further idea."

"Oh, monsieur!" said Aramis civilly, "I always believe you."

"Imagine that, counting upon the character of the Dutch, our allies, I said to myself, 'They are merchants, they are friends with the king; they will be happy to sell to the king what they fabricate for themselves; then the more we buy . . .' Ah! I must add this: I have Forant—do you know Forant, D'Artagnan?''

Colbert, in his warmth, forgot himself; he called the captain simply D'Artagnan, as the king did. But the captain only smiled at it.

''No,'' he replied; ''I don't know him.''

''He is another man I have discovered, with a genius for buying. This Forant has purchased for me three hundred and fifty thousand pounds of iron in cannonballs, two hundred thousand pounds of powder, twelve cargoes of northern timber, matches, grenades, pitch, tar—I know not what—with a saving of seven percent upon what all those articles would cost me made in France.''

''That is a good idea,'' replied D'Artagnan, ''to cast Dutch cannonballs, which will return to the Dutch.''

''Isn't it? with loss, too.''

And Colbert laughed aloud. He was delighted with his own joke.

''Still further,'' he added, ''these same Dutch are building for the king, at this moment, six vessels after the model of the best of their marine. Destouches . . . Ah! perhaps you don't know Destouches?''

''No, monsieur.''

''He is a man who has an unfailing eye to discern, when a ship is launched, what are the defects and qualities of that ship—that is valuable, you know. Nature is truly odd. Well, this Destouches appeared to me to be a man likely to be useful in a port, and he is supervising the construction of six vessels of seventy-eight, which the Provinces are building for his majesty. It results from all this, my dear Monsieur D'Artagnan, that the king, if he wished to quarrel with the Provinces, would have a very pretty fleet. Now, you know better than anybody else if the land army is good.''

D'Artagnan and Aramis looked at each other, admiring the mysterious labors this man had accomplished in a few years. Colbert understood them, and was touched by this best of flattery.

''If we, in France, didn't know it,'' said D'Artagnan, ''out of France they know it even less.''

''That is why I told Monsieur l'Ambassadeur,'' said

Colbert, "that Spain promising its neutrality, England helping us—"

"If England is helping you," said Aramis, "I pledge the neutrality of Spain."

"I take you at your word," Colbert hastened to reply, with his blunt *bonhomie*. "And speaking of Spain, you do not have the 'Golden Fleece,' Monsieur d'Alméda. I heard the king say the other day that he would like to see you wear the *grand cordon* of St. Michael."

Aramis bowed.

"Oh!" thought D'Artagnan, "and Porthos is no longer here! What ells of ribbon would there be for him in these largesses! Good Porthos!"

"Monsieur D'Artagnan," went on Colbert, "between us two, you will have, I would guess, an inclination to lead your musketeers into Holland. Can you swim?"

And he laughed like a man in a very good humor.

"Like a fish," replied D'Artagnan.

"Ah! but there are some rough passages of canals and marshes over there, Monsieur D'Artagnan, and the best swimmers are sometimes drowned."

"It is my profession to die for his majesty," said the musketeer. "Only as it is seldom that in war one meets much water without a little fire, I declare to you beforehand that I will do my best to choose fire. I am getting old; water freezes me, fire warms, Monsieur Colbert."

And D'Artagnan looked so handsome in juvenile vigor and pride, as he pronounced these words, that it was Colbert's turn to admire him. D'Artagnan noticed the effect he had produced. He remembered that the best tradesman is he who fixes a high price upon his goods when they are valuable. He prepared, then, his price in advance.

"So, then," said Colbert, "we are going into Holland?"

"Yes," replied D'Artagnan; "only . . ."

"Only?" said M. Colbert.

"Only," repeated D'Artagnan, "there is in everything the question of interest and the question of self-love. The captain of the musketeers gets a fine pay; but, observe this: we have now the king's guards and the military household of the king. A captain of musketeers ought either to have the command of all that, and then he would need a hundred thousand pounds a year for expenses of representation and table . . . ''

"Well, but do you suppose, by chance, that the king would haggle with you?'' said Colbert.

"Eh! monsieur, you have not understood me,'' replied D'Artagnan, sure of having won the question of interest; "I was telling you that I, an old captain, formerly chief of the king's guard, having precedence over the marshals of France—I saw myself one day in the trenches with two other equals, the captain of the guards and the colonel commanding the Swiss. Now, at no price will I suffer that. I have old habits, and I will stand by them.''

Colbert felt this blow, but he was prepared for it.

"I have been thinking of what you said just now,'' he replied.

"About what, monsieur?''

"We were speaking of canals and marshes in which people are drowned.''

"Well?''

"Well, if they are drowned, it is for want of a boat, a plank, or a stick.''

"Of a stick, however short it may be,'' said D'Artagnan.

"Exactly,'' said Colbert. "And, therefore, I never heard of an instance of a marshal of France being drowned.''

D'Artagnan became pale with joy, and in a not very firm voice:

"People would be very proud of me in my country,'' he said, "if I were a marshal of France; but a man must have led an expedition to receive the baton.''

"Monsieur,'' said Colbert, "here is in this notebook, which you will study, a plan of a campaign for a body of troops which the king is putting under your command next spring.''

D'Artagnan took the book tremblingly, and his fingers meeting with those of Colbert, the minister shook the hand of the musketeer loyally.

"Monsieur,'' he said, "we had both been seeking revenge, one over the other. I have begun; it is now your turn.''

"I will do you justice, monsieur,'' replied D'Artagnan, "and implore you to tell the king that at the first opportunity, he may depend upon a victory, or seeing me dead.''

"Then I will have the fleur-de-lis for your marshal's baton prepared immediately," said Colbert.

The next day, Aramis, who was setting out for Madrid to negotiate the neutrality of Spain, came to embrace D'Artagnan at his hotel.

"Let us love each other for four," said D'Artagnan, "we are now but two."

"And you will, perhaps, never see me again, dear D'Artagnan," said Aramis; "if you knew how I have loved you! I am old, I am worn, I am dead."

"My friend," said D'Artagnan, "you will live longer than I shall; diplomacy commands you to live; but, for my part, honor condemns me to die."

"Bah! such men as we are, Monsieur de Maréchal," said Aramis, "die only satiated with joy or glory."

"I assure you, Monsieur le Duc," replied D'Artagnan with a melancholy smile, "I feel very little appetite for either."

They embraced once more, and, two hours after, they were separated.

THE DEATH OF D'ARTAGNAN

CONTRARY to what always happens, whether in politics or morals, each kept his promise, and did honor to his engagements.

The king recalled M. de Guiche, and banished M. le Chevalier de Lorraine; as a result, Monsieur became ill. Madame set out for London, where she applied herself so earnestly to make her brother, Charles II, have a taste for the political advice of Mlle. de Kéroualle, that the alliance between England and France was signed, and the English vessels, bolstered by a few millions of French gold, made a terrible campaign against the fleets of the United Provinces. Charles II had promised Mlle. de Kéroualle a little gratitude for her good advice; he made her Duchess of Portsmouth. Colbert had promised the king vessels, munitions, and victories. He kept his word, as is well known. At last Aramis, upon whose promises there was least dependence to be placed, wrote Colbert

the following letter, on the subject of the negotiations
which he had undertaken at Madrid:

> "Monsieur Colbert: I have the honor to send to you the
> R. P. d'Oliva, general *ad interim* of the Society of Jesus,
> my temporary successor. The reverend father will ex-
> plain to you, Monsieur Colbert, that I am keeping the
> direction of all the affairs of the order which concern
> France and Spain; but that I am not willing to retain the
> title of general, which would throw too much light upon
> the march of the negotiations with which his Catholic
> majesty wishes to entrust me. I shall resume that title by
> the command of his majesty, when the labors I have un-
> dertaken in concert with you, for the great glory of God
> and His Church, shall be brought to a good end. The
> R. P. d'Oliva will also inform you, monsieur, of the
> consent which his Catholic majesty gives to the signature
> of a treaty which assures the neutrality of Spain, in the
> event of a war between France and the United Provinces.
> This consent will be valid, even if England, instead of
> being active, should remain neutral. As to Portugal, of
> which you and I have spoken, monsieur, I can assure you
> it will contribute with all its resources to help the most
> Christian king in his war. I beg you, Monsieur Colbert,
> to stay my friend, as also to believe in my profound at-
> tachment, and to lay my respect at the feet of his most
> Christian majesty.
>
> > "(Signed) Le Duc d'Alméda."

Aramis had then performed more than he had promised;
it remained to be known how the king, M. Colbert, and
D'Artagnan would be faithful to one another. In the spring,
as Colbert had predicted, the land army took the field. It
preceded, in magnificent order, the court of Louis XIV,
who, setting out on horseback, surrounded by carriages
filled with ladies, and courtiers, was taking the *élite* of his
kingdom to this bloody *fête*. The officers of the army, it is
true, had no other music but the artillery of the Dutch
forts; but it was enough for a great number, who found in
this war honors, advancement, fortune, or death.

M. d'Artagnan set out commanding a body of twelve thousand men, cavalry and infantry, with which he was ordered

to take the different fortresses which form the knots of that strategic network which is called La Frise. Never was an army led more gallantly to an expedition. The officers knew that their leader, prudent and skillful as he was brave, would not sacrifice a single man, nor yield an inch of ground without necessity. He had the old habits of war, to live upon the country, keep his soldiers singing and the enemy weeping. The captain of the king's musketeers placed his coquetry in showing that he knew his business. Never were opportunities better chosen, *coups de main* better supported, errors of the besieged taken better advantage of.

The army commanded by D'Artagnan took twelve small fortresses within a month. He was engaged in besieging the thirteenth, which had held out five days. D'Artagnan had the trenches opened without appearing to suppose that these people would ever allow themselves to be captured. The pioneers and laborers were, in the army of this man, a body full of emulation, ideas, and zeal, because he treated them like soldiers, knew how to render their work glorious, and never let them get killed if he could prevent it. It should have been seen then with what eagerness the marshy soils of Holland were turned over. Those turf heaps, those mounds of potter's clay, were melting, according to the soldiers, like butter in the vast frying pans of the Friesland housewives.

M. D'Artagnan dispatched a courier to the king to give him an account of the last successes, which increased the good humor of his majesty and his inclination to amuse the ladies. These victories of M. D'Artagnan gave so much majesty to the prince that Mme. de Montespan no longer called him anything but Louis the Invincible. So that Mlle. de la Vallière, who only called the king Louis the Victorious, lost much of his majesty's favor. Besides, her eyes were frequently red, and for an Invincible nothing is more disagreeable than a mistress who is weeping while everything is smiling around her. The star of Mlle. de la Vallière was being drowned in the horizon in clouds of tears. But the gayety of Mme. de Montespan increased with the successes of the king, and consoled him for other unpleasant circumstances. The king owed this to D'Artagnan; and his majesty was anxious to acknowledge those services; he wrote to M. Colbert:

"Monsieur Colbert: We have a promise to fulfill with
Monsieur D'Artagnan, who is keeping his so well. This
is to inform you that the time has come for performing
it. All details of the matter shall be furnished in due
time.

"Louis."

In consequence of this, Colbert, who detained the envoy of D'Artagnan, placed in the hands of that messenger
a letter from himself for D'Artagnan, and a small ebony
chest inlaid with gold, which was not very voluminous
in appearance, but which, without doubt, was very heavy,
as a guard of five men was given to the messenger, to
help him carry it. These people arrived before the fortress which D'Artagnan was besieging toward daybreak,
and presented themselves at the lodgings of the general.
They were told that D'Artagnan, annoyed by a sortie
which the governor, an artful man, had made the evening
before, and in which the works had been destroyed,
seventy-seven men killed, and the reparation of the
breaches begun, had just gone with half a score companies of grenadiers to reconstruct the works.

M. Colbert's envoy had orders to go and seek M. D'Artagnan, wherever he might be, or at whatever hour of the
day or night. He directed his course, therefore, toward
the trenches, followed by his escort, all on horseback.
They saw M. D'Artagnan in the open plain, with his gold-
laced hat, his long cane, and his large gilded cuffs. He
was biting his white mustache, and wiping off, with his
left hand, the dust which the passing cannonballs threw
up from the ground they plowed near him. They also saw,
amid this terrible fire, which filled the air with its hissing
whistle, officers handling the shovel, soldiers rolling bar-
rows, and vast fascines, rising by being either carried or
dragged by from ten to twenty men, cover the front of
the trench reopened to the center by this extraordinary
effort of the general animating his soldiers. In three hours
all had been reinstated. D'Artagnan began to speak more
mildly, and he became quite calm when the captain of
the pioneers approached him, hat in hand, to tell him
that the trench was again lodgeable. This man had
scarcely finished speaking, when a cannonball took off
one of his legs, and he fell into the arms of D'Artagnan.

The latter lifted up his soldier, and quietly, with soothing words, carried him into the trench, amid the enthusiastic applause of the regiments. From that time, it was no longer ardor—it was delirium; two companies stole away up to the advance posts, which they destroyed instantly.

When their comrades, restrained with great difficulty by D'Artagnan, saw them lodged upon the bastions, they also rushed forward; and soon a furious assault was made upon the counterscarp, upon which depended the safety of the place. D'Artagnan perceived there was only one means left of stopping his army, and that was to lodge it in the fortress. He directed all his force to two breaches, which the besieged were busy in repairing. The shock was terrible; eighteen companies took part in it, and D'Artagnan went with the rest, within half cannonshot of the fortress, to support the attack by échelons. The cries of the Dutch, who were being stabbed upon their guns by D'Artagnan's grenadiers, were distinctly audible. The struggle grew fiercer with the despair of the governor, who was fighting his position foot by foot. D'Artagnan, to put an end to the affair, and silence the fire, which was unceasing, sent a fresh column, which penetrated like a wimble through the posts that remained solid; and he soon perceived upon the ramparts, through the fire, the terrified flight of the besieged pursued by the besiegers.

It was at this moment the general, breathing freely and full of joy, heard a voice behind him, saying:

"Monsieur, if you please, from Monsieur Colbert."

He broke the seal of a letter which contained these words:

"Monsieur D'Artagnan: The king wants me to inform you that he has made you Marshal of France, as a reward of your good services, and the honor you do to his arms. The king is highly pleased, monsieur, with the captures you have made; he commands you, in particular, to finish the siege you have begun, with good fortune to you, and success for him."

D'Artagnan was standing with a heated face and a sparkling eye. He looked up to watch the progress of his troops upon the walls, still enveloped in red and black volumes of smoke.

"I have finished," he replied to the messenger; "the city will have surrendered in a quarter of an hour."

He then resumed his reading:

"The chest, Monsieur D'Artagnan, is my own present. You will not be sorry to see that while your warriors are drawing the sword to defend the king, I am encouraging the peaceful arts to create rewards worthy of you. I commend myself to your friendship, Monsieur le Maréchal, and beg you to believe in all mine.

"COLBERT."

D'Artagnan, intoxicated with joy, beckoned the messenger, who approached, with his chest in his hands. But just as the marshal was going to look at it, a loud explosion resounded from the ramparts, and called his attention toward the city.

"It is strange," said D'Artagnan, "that I don't see yet the king's flag upon the walls, or hear the drums beat the *chamade.*"

He launched three hundred fresh men, under a high-spirited officer, and ordered another breach to be beaten. Then, being more tranquil, he turned toward the chest, which Colbert's envoy was holding out to him. It was his treasure—he had won it.

D'Artagnan was holding out his hand to open the chest when a cannonball from the city crushed the chest in the arms of the officer, struck D'Artagnan full in the chest, and knocked him down upon a sloping heap of earth, while the fleur-de-lised baton, escaping from the broken sides of the box, came rolling under the powerless hand of the marshal. D'Artagnan tried to raise himself up. It was thought he had been knocked down without being wounded. A terrible cry broke from the group of his terrified officers; the marshal was covered with blood; the paleness of death ascended slowly to his noble face. Leaning upon the arms which were held out on all sides to receive him, he was able once more to turn his eyes toward the fort, and to distinguish the white flag at the crest of the principal bastion; his ears, already deaf to the sounds of life, caught feebly the rolling of the drum which announced victory. Then, clasping in his nerveless hand the baton, ornamented with its fleur-de-lis, he cast down upon it his eyes, which had no longer the power of looking upward toward heaven, and fell back, murmuring those strange words, which appeared to the soldiers cabalistic words—words which had formerly represented so many things upon earth, and which none but the dying man understood:

"Athos—Porthos, farewell till we meet again! Aramis, adieu forever!"

Of the four valiant men whose history we have told, only one body was left. God had taken back three souls.

T H E   E N D

Afterword

Actually, the title of this book should be *The Last of the Musketeers*, for the man in the iron mask is nothing but an incidental figure in this remarkable romance of intrigue, adventure, love, honor, and politics that depicts the final years of those gallant musketeers first made famous in *The Three Musketeers* (1844). When Dumas published *The Man in the Iron Mask* in 1848–50 as *Le Vicomte de Bragelonne*, he intended to portray the end of an era of romantic chivalry, and he sought to use the novel form as an epic drama, much in the same manner that cinematists today employ the film to adapt historical novels to actualize the significance of the past for his present time. Consequently, each chapter of his novel is like a scene from an endless drama that stretches from the middle of the seventeenth century to the middle of the nineteenth. The triumph of King Louis XIV in *Le Vicomte de Bragelonne* marked both the death of chivalry in 1661 and in Dumas's own day and age, and it announced the full flowering of realpolitik in the nineteenth century. In this regard, Dumas's "romance" has tragic undertones that can clearly be heard in his nostalgic yearning for a code of honor and decency which he believed could only be maintained in fiction.

But did this code ever exist? Was Dumas in effect longing for something that was missing all the time? Was he actually projecting into the future a code that he wanted to realize against the uncivilized behavior of his contemporaries? Dumas's historical depiction of the reign of King Louis XIV needs to be compared with a more documentary account of the times, not because he drew a "false" picture of the seventeenth century, but because such a comparison will enable us to grasp the utopian projections in his romance. There is a fine line between "real" history and historical fiction. In Dumas's case his romantic interpretation of the ancien régime may reveal more about the machinations of King Louis XIV and absolutism than scholarly factual accounts of this period, and at the same time it is an interesting historical record of his concerns about reactionary trends in his own times.

The Man in the Iron Mask focuses on a crucial, if not pivotal, period of French history, 1661–62, that would determine the future of France. Generally speaking, the French monarchy of the seventeenth century is associated with absolutism, but neither Louis XIII nor Louis XIV had absolute control over the provinces, nor did they care much about what happened there unless events affected their rule in Paris or at court. There were constant revolts throughout the seventeenth century, primarily due to unfair taxation, oppression, and religious intolerance. Soon after Louis XIII died in 1643, his wife, Queen Anne of Austria, was appointed regent with her lover, the Cardinal Mazarin, as prime minister. Louis XIV was only five at the time. Since there was a great deal of corruption at the court and numerous disputes with regard to unfair taxation, and since the king was only a child, the aristocracy and members of Parlement eventually joined forces in what was termed a Fronde or movement of rebellion against the king by 1648. However, the Fronde was formed by groups that kept shifting their alliances, and eventually, by 1653 Mazarin and Anne of Austria were able to defeat the opposition and save the throne for Louis XIV.

From 1653 on, the cunning Cardinal Mazarin was virtually in charge of the government, and the corrupt Nicolas Fouquet, Superintendant of Finance, was in complete command of budgetary matters. Therefore, it was not by chance that these two men became the richest and most powerful in the kingdom. Fouquet used his wealth to build a glorious chateau at Vaux and an island fortress on Belle-Isle off the coast of Nantes, while Mazarin also had marvelous estates and treasures. Louis XIV ruled in name only, and he was obliged to honor the wishes and policies of his mother and Mazarin. In keeping with Mazarin's political ambition and political diplomacy of that time, Louis was compelled to marry Maria Theresa of Spain, even though he was more in love with Mazarin's niece, Marie Mancini. Neither Mazarin nor

France would have profited much if his niece had married Louis, for royalty was expected to marry royalty and form mutually beneficial alliances. In this instance, Mazarin realized that France could rise to supremacy in Europe only by establishing peaceful relations with Spain, placing England in France's debt, and rigorously training Louis XIV in handling the affairs of the state in a cold and calculating manner. By the time Mazarin died on March 10, 1661, he had done his job: France was on the verge of becoming the dominant force in Europe, and Louis was ready to take personal charge of France's destiny.

Louis XIV was a bon vivant. He enjoyed dancing and hunting and had expert training in fighting and military tactics. His love affairs were numerous, and he paid more attention to his luxurious court than he did to the people of France and their difficulties due to war, famine, and taxation. Until he moved permanently to Versailles in 1683, he spent much of his time at his chateau in St. Germain and visited his other residences at Vincennes and Fontainebleau mainly for pleasure and hunting. Gradually, even before he assumed complete control of power in 1661, he established a set routine of etiquette and pleasure at court that eventually set a standard throughout Europe. After official business was conducted during the morning, there were huge meals followed by hunting, fetes, plays, operas, music, or fireworks. Though Louis did not have much of a literary or artistic education, he had good taste and also knew how to listen and administer. Most important, Louis learned to cover his feelings and intentions behind an austere presence, and he became a master of secrecy and deception. Once he assumed total power, the major crime in the kingdom was anything that his majesty considered an offense, ranging from breach of etiquette to high treason. Louis demanded total loyalty to the throne and discretion in public and private behavior. Furthermore, he expected everyone at court or associated with the government to comply with royal edicts and decorum, and distinguished himself by practicing what he preached. In fact, he exercised great self-control by working six to eight hours a day and establishing a code and timetable for work and play that eventually seemed to be natural law.

In 1661, Louis's first major act was to abolish the position of prime minister, the post held by Mazarin, and to appoint a council composed of three men whom he could trust. Fouquet was not one of them. In fact, since Fouquet had become the richest man in France and the government was actually in debt to him, Louis had been planning to depose him. His most trusted servant in this case was Jean-Baptiste Colbert, who had already proven to be completely loyal to Louis in personal matters and who hated Fouquet. Once he was appointed Intendant of Finances, Colbert began an investigation into Fouquet's shady dealings (all of which had been previously approved by Mazarin) and was able to procure enough information by May 1661 to convict Fouquet of illegal acts. However, it was not just Fouquet's wealth and power that irritated Louis XIV, but his interference in the king's private life.

Louis had begun an affair with Henrietta, his brother's wife, who was from the royal family of England, in April, but by May his fickleness began to show, and he had fallen in love with one of Henrietta's ladies-in-waiting, Louise de la Vallière. This affair created turmoil in the royal household, but Louis was able to maintain control over the unleashed fury of Henrietta, who began having an affair with the Comte de Guiche, one of her husband's favorites. When Fouquet heard about the king's relationship with Louise, he decided to ingratiate himself by offering her twenty thousand gold pistoles and his protection, thinking that he would also win Louis's favor by doing this. However, Louis was incensed by Fouquet's audacity and interference in his private life. In addition, Fouquet made a second enormous mistake at this time. He sold his judicial office of Procureur Général to the Parlement, a position which had granted him indemnity in all legal trials, and he decided to invite Louis to his chateau at Vaux so that the king would be impressed by his wealth and grandeur and perhaps include him as one of his majesty's favorites. However, since Louis was not as wealthy as Fouquet and had not begun his project of building a magnificent chateau at Versailles, he was actually humiliated by Fouquet's show of splendor and would have arrested him at Vaux if his mother, Anne of Austria, had not restrained him.

However, the queen could not prevent him from completing plans with Colbert in August 1661 to crush Fouquet for his insolence and ambition. Louis arranged to have the court transferred to Nantes, Fouquet's stronghold, to deceive him into believing that he was still in the king's favor. But after Louis presided over a meeting of the Council on September 5, he had M. D'Artagnan, Captain of a brigade of musketeers, arrest Fouquet in a show of power that was to signal to the entire nation that Louis XIV was in control of France.

1661 was indeed the year of the rising Sun King. After arresting Fouquet, Louis reconstituted the government with men like Colbert who were absolutely dedicated to him. He humiliated the King of Spain in an incident in England. His wife gave birth to a son, the Grand Dauphin, on November 1. And, much to the chagrin of various members of the royal family, he continued his liaison with Louise de la Vallière, with whom he soon had a child. In many respects, by the end of 1661 Louis had consolidated his power within his immediate household and in the nation, and it could be said that the destiny of France became inextricably linked to his own destiny in this year.

It could also be said that Alexandre Dumas had always felt his own destiny was somehow tied to the historical reign of kings in France, for his father, like D'Artagnan, had been a loyal servant to king and country. His extraordinary career, however, was marked by a complex relationship with his sovereign that ultimately led to his downfall and perhaps to his son Alexandre's writing the Musketeer cycle of novels.

Born in Haiti in 1762, Thomas-Alexandre Dumas was an illegitimate child of the plantation owner Alexandre-Antoine Davy de la Pailleterie and a black slave named Marie-Cessette Dumas. After his father brought him to France, there was a quarrel about whether the son, a mulatto, would be considered the true heir to his father's estate. Consequently, Thomas-Alexandre broke with his father and enlisted in the army in 1786. During this time he met and fell in love with Marie-Louise Labouret when he was stationed in Villers-Cotteret, a small village near Paris. Since he was such an imposing and noble individual, her father agreed to allow her to marry him once he rose above the rank of private. Indeed, his advance in

the military ranks occurred sooner than they had expected due to the Revolution in 1789, which favored the
promotion of common soldiers. Based on his merits as a
soldier and his achievements in battle, he became a lieutenant colonel by 1792, when he married Marie-Louise.
The very next year he was promoted to general of the
army in the western Pyrenees. Later, he joined Napoleon
Bonaparte in Italy and helped the French gain important
victories in the Mediterranean and also in Egypt. However, at one point he offended Napoleon by questioning
his policies in Egypt, where the French were suffering
tremendous losses. At that point Thomas-Alexandre decided to return to France and was captured by forces
loyal to the King of Naples, who was hostile toward
France. Since Napoleon refused to help him, Thomas-
Alexandre was held for ransom by the Neapolitans and
spent two hard years in a fortress prison. When he eventually returned to his wife in Villers-Cotterets in 1801,
he was a broken man in health and spirit. Though a general, he was not granted much of a pension, and he lived
in humble circumstances until his death in 1806. His only
son, Alexandre, was born in 1802, and though he formed
a close attachment to the distinguished gentleman, he
knew more about his father from the stories told about
his heroic deeds than from personal experience. In fact,
Thomas-Alexandre had been an extraordinary soldier,
and in some cases, he had single-handedly put enemy
forces to rout. But he had also had this complex relationship to Napoleon Bonaparte, the Emperor of France.

Since Dumas grew up during Napoleon's reign, and
since he also met the heroic symbol of France moving
through Villers-Cotterets with his troops in 1815, it was
always difficult for Dumas to reconcile his father's noble
image with an incalcitrant sovereign who did not have
the humanity or decency to recognize his father's service. In other words, history in the form of his father and
Napoleon struck the imagination of young Dumas, and
there are strong signs in his youth that he felt compelled
to explore and rewrite history, perhaps to exculpate his
father and celebrate a code of life that was never given
the recognition that it deserved.

As is well known, when Dumas arrived in Paris as a
young man in 1823 and began writing plays, he chose

historical topics for his subject matter. His very first play, *Henri et sa cour* (*Henry and his Court*, 1829), based on court memoirs of the sixteenth century, was a drama of love and intrigue rewritten by Dumas with great poetic license. After the success of this play, Dumas wrote many other historical dramas with the theme of loyalty and deceit as the major leit motif throughout his works. By the time he turned to writing historical novels in the 1840s, he had developed a romantic technique of glamorizing history in the tradition of Sir Walter Scott. However, there are major differences between the two that distinguished Dumas as the French ''champion'' of a chivalric code that honored his father's memory. Moreover, Dumas's ''romance'' with history was also based on a profit motive and teamwork, not unlike the motto first proclaimed in *The Three Musketeers*—''All for one and one for all.''

Dumas rarely worked alone. The tradition of collaboration was a given in the theater, and it became his trademark as a novelist. In 1841, he met Auguste Maquet, a teacher of history at a Paris lycée, and with the young man's permission, he reworked one of Maquet's stories, *Le chevalier d'Harmental,* into a novel for publication in a newspaper in 1842. From this point on, Dumas hired Maquet and other writers to do historical research and to provide him with basic plot outlines for his novels. Though he, too, did a great deal of historical research, Dumas depended on a ''factory'' of writers for collaboration. Generally speaking, however, he conceived the plot and discussed the ideas of the novel with his collaborators in advance. In addition, the final shape and ideas of each novel were distinctly marked by Dumas's style and concerns, which were tied to his desire to make a great deal of money and maintain a luxurious life-style.

Money can be considered a second factor in Dumas's production of historical novels. Generous to a fault, Dumas liked to hold great dinners and live as comfortably as he could. Moreover, he had numerous mistresses, to whom he gave gifts, and he also tried to support his children, one of whom, Alexandre, turned out to achieve fame as the author of *Camille*. The money he earned from his numerous theater productions had never been sufficient enough to keep him in style. The novel attracted him as another possible remunerative source that could keep his imagination and body alive at the same time. Indeed, his works were conceived more as chapter/ scenes for Parisian newspapers than as traditional novels to be read in one sitting. By the 1840s the daily press in France had begun publishing novels in serial form known as *roman-feuilleton,* and authors were paid extremely well for their daily contributions. Given Dumas's remarkable talent as a dramatist, this new form of the serialized novel enabled him to earn great amounts of money and to continue his project of rewriting history in a romantic light and reaching an even greater public than he did with his plays.

From 1842 to 1852, Dumas wrote some of the best-loved popular novels in French history. Among them are *The Count of Monte Cristo* (1844–46) and *The Black Tulip* (1850). By far the most famous of his works is the Musketeer cycle consisting of *The Three Musketeers* (1844), *Twenty Years After* (1845), and *The Man in the Iron Mask* (1848–50), which simultaneously depict the maturation of Louis XIV and the formation and dissolution of perhaps the greatest friendship ever created in fiction. Dumas never had to invent Louis XIV and his court, nor did he ever have to invent D'Artagnan, but he did invent the friendship between D'Artagnan, Aramis, Porthos, and Athos, symbolic figures of human virtues that constitute a chivalric code which really never existed but which Dumas created as a means to comment on its lack in historical France and in the France of his own times. This is why the death of three of the Musketeers is so striking in *The Man in the Iron Mask:* Dumas is concerned neither about Louis XIV nor his alleged twin brother locked in the Bastille. (He was said to have cried while writing the death scene of Porthos.) His focus throughout the novel is on the behavior and conduct of the four musketeers plus Raoul, the son of Athos, who also dies fighting for his honor (and by consequence, the honor of the musketeers) in Algeria.

As in all his novels, Dumas takes actual historical events and transforms them to make an ideological statement about France as a nation and a philosophical statement about mores, customs, values, and behavior. Dumas had always been a supporter of democratic causes in France, and sided with both the revolutions of 1830 and

1848. *The Man in the Iron Mask* was written during the
Revolution of 1848 and its aftermath that included the
counter-revolution. He himself was bankrupt and went
into exile in Belgium, where other leading writers such
as Victor Hugo had sought refuge. Though far less polit-
ically committed than Hugo, Dumas was always critical
and distrustful of the French monarchy. In fact, he was
intrigued by the cruel and deceitful ways in which French
aristocrats dealt with each other, and this is why he always linked the personal with the political in the Musketeer cycle.

In the case of *The Man in the Iron Mask,* he adapts
the memoirs of Madame de La Fayette, concerning the
intrigues at court, and the history of a mysterious person
obliged to wear a black velvet mask, who was imprisoned
on the island of Sainte-Marguerite and later in the Bastille between 1679 and 1703 to speculate about what might
have happened if Louis XIV had been replaced by a man
who was indebted to Spain and the pope. The cast of
characters and scenes is great. The original novel of *Le
Vicomte de Bragelonne* consists of six volumes, and our
present translation, *The Man in the Iron Mask,* forms the
latter part of the narrative that focuses on the measures
taken by D'Artagnan, ironically with the help of Fouquet, to enable Louis XIV to avoid a catastrophe. In contrast to historical documentation, it is, in Dumas's eyes,
the lesson of humiliation, not the training that Louis received from Cardinal Mazarin, that wakens Louis to his
senses so that he takes full control of the government. At
the same time, Louis's rise to greatness demands cold
calculation and total administration that will not and does
not have any use for the strength (Porthos), dignity
(Athos/Raoul), and loyalty (D'Artagnan) of the Musketeers. Only Aramis survives at the end because he is un-
scrupulous and cunning and embodies a modern spirit
that is on the rise in France of 1848–50, similar in a sense
to the spirit of Louis XIV and Colbert, a mixture of cold
aristocratic autocracy and bourgeois calculation. Aramis's saving grace is his friendship to his Musketeer
friends, but once they are gone, once the moral fiber of
the society is gone, he will be free to act for his own
aggrandizement just as Louis the Sun King will.

However, by no means can Dumas's novel be read as

a critique of absolute monarchy. Dumas legitimizes Louis XIV's realpolitik and behavior through the devotion of D'Artagnan, who is reconciled with him at the end and rewarded in royal fashion. Dumas had a double purpose in writing his final novel about Louis XIV and the Musketeers. First, he wanted to show how the court functioned on a private and public level and invented characters and scenes to give a fuller picture of the costumes, etiquette, intrigues, and machinations of Louis and the people who surrounded him. Second, he added the unusual characters of the Musketeers to show what qualities were lacking in the court and in France at large. By inducing readers to recognize this lack, Dumas raises our utopian hopes that such virtues represented by the Musketeers can still be recaptured as Dumas has done in his work, or at least, they can be read as ideals that we can recognize.

Dumas's relationship to French history can thus be seen as ambivalent. Given the manner in which his father had been treated by Napoleon, and given Dumas's admiration for Napoleon, representative of France's glory, it is possible to speculate that the creation of the Musketeers, especially D'Artagnan, was his means of reconciling his lost father to France or providing him with the recognition that the son thought he deserved. The valiant D'Artagnan dies fighting for his country and king. When he dies and bids adieu to his great friends, his words are not understood by those who surround him. How can they understand? The world has changed. It is no longer a world in which "all for one, one for all" is revered. Louis XIV's words were "L'etat, c'est moi," or "When you speak of the state, you speak of me." Dumas's novel, then, ends in a secret pact with his readers, who know what D'Artagnan's words truly mean and who are thus encouraged to keep the spirit of the musketeers alive.

—*Jack Zipes*

Selected Bibliography

Bassan, Ferdinand. "Le Cycle des *Trois Mousquetaires—du Roman au Théatre*." *Studia Neophilogica* 57 (1985): pp. 243–49.

Bell, A. Craig. *Alexandre Dumas: A Biography and Study.* Folcroft, PA., 1979.

Bouvier-Ajam, Maurice. *Alexandre Dumas ou cent ans après.* Paris: Editeurs Français Réunis, 1972.

Charpentier, John. *Alexandre Dumas.* Paris, 1947.

Clouard, Henri. *Alexandre Dumas.* Paris, 1955.

Coward, David. "Introduction to *The Man in the Iron Mask*". New York: Oxford University Press, 1988.

Eckert-Goodman, ed. *The Road to Monte Cristo: The Memoirs of Alexandre Dumas.* New York: Charles Scribners' Sons, 1956.

Erlanger, Philippe. *Louis XIV.* Trans. Stephen Cox. New York, 1970.

Furneaux, Rupert. *The Man Behind the Mask: The Real Story of the "Ancient Prison".* London, 1954.

Gaillard, Robert. *Alexandre Dumas.* Paris, 1953.

Hemmings, F.W.J. *Alexandre Dumas: The King of Romance.* New York, 1979.

——. "Alexandre Dumas Pére" in *European Writers : The Romantic Century.* Eds. Jacques Barzun and George Stade, vol. 6. New York, 1985. pp. 719–43.

Jan, Isabelle. *Alexandre Dumas, romancier.* Paris, 1973.

Jongué, Serge. *"Histoire et Fiction chez Alexandre Dumas".* *Europe* 542 (June 1974): pp. 94–101.

Maurois, Andre. *The Titans: A Three-Generation Biography of the Dumas.* Trans. Gerard Hopkins. New York, 1957.

Molino, Jean. *"Alexandre Dumas et le Roman Mythique".* *L'Arc* 71 (1977): pp. 56–59.

Ross, Michael. *Alexandre Dumas.* Newton Abbot, 1981.

Schopp, *Alexandre Dumas, Genius of Life*. Trans. A. J. Koch. New York, 1988.

Stowe, Richard S. *Dumas*. Boston, 1976.

Tadie, Jean-Yves. *Le roman d'aventures*. Paris, 1982.

Tranouez, Pierre. *"Cave filium! Étude du Cycle des 'Mousquetaires'"*. *Poétique* 71 (September 1987): pp. 321–31.